OF LOVE AND LIFE

OF LOVE AND LIFE

Three novels selected and condensed by Reader's Digest

CONDENSED BOOKS DIVISION

The Reader's Digest Association Limited, London

The Reader's Digest Association Limited
11 Westferry Circus, Canary Wharf, London E14 4HE

www.readersdigest.co.uk

ISBN 0-276-42735-1

For information as to ownership of copyright in the material of this book, and acknowledgments, see last page.

CONTENTS

Facing the Light

ADÈLE GERAS

As Leonora's seventy-fifth birthday approaches, her mind constantly wanders to the past. One memory is of being frightened down by the lake near her home, just before her eighth birthday, just before her mother died. And, strangely, she remembers her Nanny's constant mantra at the time: 'What you don't know can't hurt you.' Ironically, in the course of the birthday celebrations, Leonora is to discover that what you don't know *can* hurt you—and it can hurt others.

WHAT YOU DON'T KNOW can't hurt you but she does know and she must forget what she knows. It is secret secret secret. She must pretend she doesn't know or it will hurt her. The house . . . that's where the secret lives and all she wants is not to know, somewhere far away.

She is standing at the window. There's not a breath of wind to move the white curtains and the grass outside lies dry and flat under the last of the summer sun. She's nearly eight and it's too soon for sleeping. Everyone is somewhere else and no one is looking. The shadows of trees are black on the lawn and silvery water is glittering through the weeping willow leaves. That's the lake. Swans swim on the lake and she could go down to the water to see the white birds. No one would know and what you don't know can't hurt you.

She has to go across the carpet woven with flowers and twisted trees, and the door opens and she's in the dark corridor and a thick stillness takes up all the space and spreads down the staircase and she moves from step to step on tiptoe so as not to disturb it. Paintings on the walls stare at her as she passes. Still lifes and landscapes spill strange colours and their own light into the silence and the portraits scream after her and she can't hear them. The marble floor in the hall is like a chequer-board of black and white and she makes sure to jump the black squares because if you don't something bad is sure to happen and maybe she just touched one black square but that wouldn't count, would it?

Then she's in the garden and the air is soft, and she runs as fast as she can down the steps of the terrace and over the lawn and between high clipped hedges until she reaches the Wild Garden where the plants brush her skirt, and she's running to where the swans always are and they've gone. They have floated over to the far bank. She can see them. It's not too far away so she starts walking.

Something catches her eye. It's in the reeds and it's like a dark stain in the water and when she gets a little nearer it looks like a cloth and there are water plants and willow leaves hiding some of it. If only she can get nearer to where the water meets the bank she can reach in and pull it and see what it is. The water is cool on her hand and there's something that looks like a foot poking out from under the material.

Suddenly there's cold all round her and what she doesn't know won't hurt her but she knows this is wrong. This is bad. She should run and fetch someone but she can't stop her hand from reaching out. She pulls at the dark cloth and something heavy comes towards her and the time is stretched so the moment goes on for ever and there's a face with glassy open eyes and pale greenish skin, and hair all loose and spreading like a terrible billowing weed that drifts across the water and moves in and out of the open mouth and she feels herself screaming but no sound comes out and she turns and runs back to the house. Someone must come, and she runs to call them and she's screaming and no one can hear her. Wet drowned fingers rise up from the lake and stretch out over the grass and up into the house to touch her and she will always feel them, even when she's very old, and she knows the fingers and she knows the unseeing eyes streaming with silver water and the hair undone. Now she knows them all and she can't ever ever stop knowing them.

Wednesday, August 21, 2002

I'M ALLERGIC TO MY MOTHER, Rilla thought. She leaned back in the bath and closed her eyes. It happened every time. The white snake had come back. She could feel it, uncoiling from deep inside her head, winding itself round the separate parts of her brain. Tension headaches, the doctor had said. She knew exactly what caused them. It was Leonora, her mother, and not just her. I'm allergic to the whole package, she told herself: Willow Court, Gwen, the entire set-up. Every time I have to visit the place, it's the same: the white snake tightens his scaly loops round bits of my head, and my heart beats strangely too. Usually, after a few hours in her mother's presence Rilla recovered sufficiently to function in a more or less normal manner, but there was no getting away from it: the prospect of visiting Leonora filled her with something approaching dread.

She looked round her bathroom, her haven. It was the room she loved best in the whole world. Her small Chelsea home was in need of redecoration, but Rilla thought that she and the house went well together. We're past our best, she thought, but we've still got what it takes, oh yes. Gwen, her elder sister, had never lived anywhere but at Willow Court, under Leonora's gaze. She seemed happy enough, though you could never tell with Gwen; maybe she'd been dying to get away for years. But if anyone had asked her why she and her husband spent their days in the depths of Wiltshire, she'd doubtless have murmured something about what a privilege it was to be entrusted with the care of the paintings of their grandfather, Ethan Walsh. She wouldn't mention that her constant attendance on Leonora and her lifelong devotion to the house made it the most natural thing in the world for her to inherit Willow Court when Leonora died. Well, Gwen was welcome to it. Rilla would have regarded having to stay there for ever as a kind of prison sentence.

So why did she keep visiting? Love, as usual, was the answer. All that nonsense about blood being thicker than water was, it appeared, the truth. Also, there were things she remembered from her childhood that still shone, after everything, and you didn't throw such memories away in a hurry. You kept hold of them as a kind of talisman to guard against the others, the things you couldn't bear to think about.

Rilla sat up and squeezed a spongeful of water onto her shoulder. Gwen and Mother love me too, she thought, even though they disapprove of me. Rilla got out of the bath and found one of the enormous soft towels that covered her from head to toe and made her way into the bedroom. Ivan was awake, humming tunelessly as he looked at the paper. She had to get ready. She wanted to be at Willow Court as early as possible and definitely before dinner.

Sitting in front of her dressing table, Rilla peered into the triple mirror and saw far too many reflecting images of her lover, lying already fully dressed on the bed behind her. She couldn't decide which was more depressing—looking at him, or contemplating the wreck that she'd suddenly turned into. Back in the bathroom, it was easy to pretend that she was still the creamy-skinned, gorgeous creature in the photograph that mocked her from behind the perfume bottles. More fool me, she thought, keeping a movie still from over twenty years ago.

Rilla had been madly in love with Jon then, just about to marry him, happy and full of passion. Jon Frederick was a pop star, and while he was never at the very top, even at the height of his fame, they'd been one of London's bright young couples in those days. *Night Creatures* was a silly sort of movie but at least it paid well. And she'd been allowed to keep the rings she was wearing in the photograph: ornate silver set with moonstones and opals. They were still around somewhere.

Half the photograph was white roses, spilling off the bed like an avalanche. I must be a masochist, she thought. That hair, rippling over a lace-trimmed pillow, those perfect shoulders in the satin nightie . . . no wonder the monster, or whatever it was in *Night Creatures*, was tempted. I should take it away. It's ridiculous to keep it there as a reminder.

She stared at her reflection and sighed. She smiled. That was a mistake. Could all these wrinkles and dark circles and sagginess of neck and chin have sprung up overnight? I'm only forty-eight, she thought. And there's Gwen, two years older and all milk and roses with never more than a spot of powder and a dab of lipstick on special occasions. No bloody justice in the world. She could hear her mother's voice saying, as she always did, *Fairness has nothing to do with it, Cyrilla darling. Your sister is one person and you are another and you are both precious to me.* Only Leonora was allowed to use the really too silly name she'd saddled her younger daughter with. Her sister had to contend with Gwendolen, which wasn't brilliant, but at least people had heard of it. When Rilla first went to school, everyone asked, Is Cyrilla a family name? But they could barely suppress their laughter whenever it was spoken, so she had quickly shortened it, and short was how it had mostly stayed.

If her father had lived, he might have suggested something more sensible, but her mother would have carried the day, as she usually did. Peter Simmonds, Rilla's father, had died in a car accident six months before she was born. Rilla knew it was irrational, but she'd always felt faintly guilty, as though she herself were to blame for the crash which, according to Leonora, had been the indirect result of telling Peter she was pregnant again. The subject wasn't one Rilla discussed with Leonora, but she and Gwen had grown up with stories about the relationship that had existed between their parents. By all accounts, this love was like something out of a fairy tale: transcendent, immutable and deeper by far than the ordinary passions of other people.

'What for do you look so sour, beloved Rilla?' came Ivan's lazy tones, husky from last night's cigarettes and well-rehearsed affectation.

'Nothing,' said Rilla, keeping her voice light, 'only it's going to take a hell of a lot of slap to reconstruct something resembling my face.'

'You are beautiful, my darling,' said Ivan. 'You have a twilight beauty.'

'And you are full of shit,' said Rilla sharply, and instantly regretted it. 'I'm sorry, Ivan. It's just that I'm a bundle of nerves about going back to my mother's house. I can't help it.'

'What will I do without you? How will I bear it? How will I live?'

'There's no need to be melodramatic, darling! It's only a few days.'

'You do not love me. You could not speak so if you did.'

She couldn't deny it. She didn't love him, of course she didn't, but it was sharp of him to have spotted it. Rilla thought she put on a reasonable show of affection, and certainly she was always whole-hearted about the sex, but her heart, well, that had been out of bounds for years.

'It's nothing to do with love,' she explained patiently. 'I've told you, Mother's seventy-fifth birthday party is strictly a family affair, otherwise I'd take you.'

That wasn't quite true. Partners, husbands, boyfriends, girlfriends were all invited, but Rilla never considered taking Ivan. She knew exactly how her mother would react to him. She'd be oh so polite, but her blue eyes would strip away all his pretences, and it would be made entirely clear to him, without so much as a word being spoken, that he was not, to use one of Leonora's phrases, *one of us*.

'Do get up, Ivan, please,' said Rilla. 'I have to decide what to take. I really want to get to Willow Court as soon as I can.'

She began to throw garments from the wardrobe onto the bed. Why was almost everything she owned either silky or satiny or feathered or beaded? Whenever she visited Willow Court, she felt the need to find a disguise, a costume that wouldn't instantly make Leonora wrinkle her mouth. Why couldn't she manage neat skirts and crisp blouses?

She closed her eyes. What did it matter, really, when it came down to it? However she was dressed, the visit was going to be excruciating. The one thing she tried every minute of her life not to think about, to thrust into the most secret corners of her heart, was known to everyone who was coming. What if they spoke of it? How would she bear that? She drew a deep breath. Willow Court. So many ghosts, so much pain, and her mother, Leonora Simmonds, monarch of all she surveyed.

Rilla didn't even glance at the landscape streaming past the window. She'd seen it too many times before, on her way back to Willow Court. Gwen will be walking from room to room, she thought, checking that everyone has the right towels. I'll be in the Blue Room, where Mother always puts me because it faces the back. No view of the lake. Rilla shivered in spite of the heat. She hadn't been down there for years but in her worst dreams she still saw the water shimmering with a sort of fluorescence. Rilla turned on the cassette player and let the sound of Billie Holiday's voice fill the car, blue and velvety and freighted with pain.

And then she was there, at Willow Court. The wrought-iron gates were standing open. The leaves of the scarlet oaks leading up to the house were still green. Rilla's mouth suddenly felt dry. She slowed the car right down. She knew that Leonora and Gwen would have been looking out for her, and sure enough, there they were, waiting on the front steps like figures in a tableau. Leonora upright and self-possessed, standing one step above Gwen, slim as a young girl, wearing well-cut trousers and a cream shirt that Rilla knew cost a small fortune.

Rilla stopped the car and got out as elegantly as she could, conscious of her mother's eyes on her. She ran up the steps. 'Darling,' she said, and threw her arms round her sister, suddenly filled with affection. 'How super to see you!' She went up to the next level to embrace her mother.

'Rilla!' Leonora was smiling, but she stood quite still as her younger daughter kissed her. Soft skin, Rilla thought, but somewhere in her core something that doesn't want to bend, to relax. Something frozen.

'Mother, you look wonderful. As usual.' And it was true. Leonora's skin was hardly wrinkled, and her blue eyes seemed undimmed. As for the bone structure, well, as Ivan was forever telling her, there was no better basis for beauty than good bones. Rilla knew that her own bones were rather too well covered, and waited for her mother to make some allusion to the weight she had put on.

On this occasion Leonora said only, 'You look lovely, too, Rilla darling. It's been such a long time. I've missed you.' Leonora paused, and scrutinised her daughter more carefully. 'But you do look a little tired. Never mind. You can have a nice long rest now that you're here.'

Rilla stopped herself from saying, *Fat chance!* She mumbled something about getting her bags out of the boot and taking them upstairs.

'You're in the Blue Room, darling,' said Leonora. 'I know you feel comfortable in there. Gwen will help you settle down, and then you've got plenty of time to change for dinner. Come down when you're ready. I shall be in the conservatory. I'm longing to have a chat, if you're not too tired after such a long drive.' She smiled at Rilla, then turned and went inside, walking as she always did—slowly, and as though people were looking at her. Which, Rilla reflected, they very often were.

She walked to the back of the car with Gwen. Together they took out the luggage and went into the house carrying one bag each. Tangles of television cable snaked over the black and white tiles of the hall.

'They're here already, then, are they? The TV people?' Rilla said as she followed Gwen upstairs.

'Sean Everard, the director, he's coming tomorrow,' said Gwen, turning her head to talk over her shoulder, 'but the rest of the crew's here, doing what they call "establishing shots". They're very good, really. We hardly know they're around most of the time. They're staying down at the Fox and Goose, and they have all their meals there too.'

She turned left at the top of the staircase. As they passed the old nursery, Rilla asked, 'The doll's house is still in there, isn't it?'

'Oh, yes. But Mother's absolutely adamant that they mustn't film that.'

She strode along the corridor to the Blue Room with Rilla close behind her. Nothing in it had changed since her last visit, but Gwen had put buff-coloured roses in a vase on the table by the window.

'Lovely Buff Beauty, Gwennie. Thank you so much.'

Gwen blushed at the childish nickname. 'You like the ones that go on flowering all through the summer, I know . . .' she murmured and put down the bag she was carrying. She turned to go, started saying something like 'I'll see you later', but Rilla interrupted her.

'I'm going to have a look at it. At the doll's house. Come with me, Gwen. You don't have anything to do exactly now this minute, do you?'

Gwen hesitated, then said, 'Oh, all right. But only for a moment.'

'Good.' Rilla stepped out of the Blue Room and looked along the corridor. 'I'll make sure no one catches us.'

'Stop teasing, Rilla.' Gwen laughed. '*We're* allowed in the nursery. It's just the TV people Mother wants to keep out.'

'Can't imagine why . . . has she said? The doll's house was Ethan Walsh's crowning achievement if you ask me.'

'She likes to keep it to herself for some reason,' Gwen said. 'She's always adored it, and of course it brings back memories for her.'

Rilla had always loved the nursery, too. In the old days, it had been Nanny Mouse's domain, but for the last few years the old lady had been living in a cottage down at the end of the drive by the gates, looked after by a nurse-companion. She would have been sad to see it all quiet and echoey, stripped of its toys, its bookshelves empty. Gwen's grandson, Douggie, Efe and Fiona's son, could have slept there whenever they visited, but Fiona liked to keep him near her. He was only two and a half. Perhaps when he was older, he'd bring the room to life again.

Gwen opened the door and there was the doll's house in its usual place against the wall. Rilla smiled. Mother was not a sentimental person, but when it came to this, which she often referred to as *almost my only link with my mother*, she behaved somewhat eccentrically. Only older children were allowed to play with it. Leonora would never permit toddlers to smear their grubby fingers over the wallpaper, or mistreat the tiny pieces of furniture. OK, Gwen was right, and it had been made for Leonora by her father, and her mother had decorated every room. Perhaps she didn't want everyone in the world peering and poking at it, but still, not allowing the film crew to see it was taking matters a bit far.

Rilla found it hard to imagine her artistic grandfather, who'd been a bit of a Tartar by all accounts, getting down to child level to create this beautiful residence. Grandmother Maude had decorated it with the same care she had lavished on Willow Court. She had also made three little rag dolls to live in it, recognisable as herself and her husband and daughter. Ethan was the biggest of the dolls, with a dark moustache and heavy eyebrows over piercing blue eyes. Maude had nut-brown hair drawn into a bun, and wore a blouse with a high lace collar. The smallest doll was in a dress cut from the same lilac fabric Leonora wore in one of the portraits. Each doll had a smile embroidered onto its face in pink silk. When she was a little girl, Rilla used to say that you could see they were a happy family.

'Do you remember the dolls that Grandmother Maude made?' she asked her sister.

Gwen nodded. 'Yes, Mother used to let us look at them at Christmas time. I don't even know where she keeps them these days.'

'She didn't let us play with them, though, did she?' Rilla said. 'I suppose she gave us our own dolls as a sort of distraction, and we did love them, didn't we?'

'Of course we did,' said Gwen. 'I can't remember it bothering us at all that we couldn't play with the ones Grandmother Maude made.'

Rilla stared at the shape of the house under its white dustsheet. The roof was at the level of her waist.

Gwen smiled at her sister. 'Go on then,' she said.

Rilla folded back the sheet, so that the doll's house was revealed. 'I used to call it Paradise Mansions,' she said. 'Do you remember?'

'That really annoyed me,' Gwen laughed. 'I played with it first when you were no more than a baby. I called it Delacourt House. And the family were the Delacourt family. That was their proper name.'

Rilla crouched down to look at everything more carefully. There were three floors, with kitchen and dining room on the ground floor, drawing room and study on the first floor, and two bedrooms and a bathroom on the second floor. Ethan had made all the furniture—beds and chests of drawers, sideboards, tables and chairs—and each was an intricate masterpiece of carpentry. Every wall was covered with some of the paper that Maude Walsh had chosen to hang in Willow Court. The roof, surprisingly, was Maude's own work. She had painted sheets of thick paper with an intricate pattern of roof tiles in watercolours and these had been glued to the plain wood. Leonora had often told them the story of how the new roof had been a birthday surprise from her mother, just before her eighth birthday, just before Maude's tragic death.

Rilla suddenly thought what a sensation it would cause among art critics if they could see it. It must be worth a small fortune. How come her own stepdaughter, Beth, never spoke about it these days? Why didn't Gwen's children, particularly Efe (who was very mercenary, it seemed to Rilla), realise what a treasure was stashed away up here?

The dolls were all present and correct. Queen Margarita (whom Gwen called Mrs Delacourt) and her husband, and the children, Lucinda and Lucas (Dora and Dominic for Gwen). They were peg dolls with painted faces and unmoving bodies, but what life they'd breathed into them!

'We did have fun with them, didn't we?' Rilla said to her sister.

'Yes, of course we did,' Gwen replied. 'Even though I seem to remember I always thought you got things wrong all the time. I suppose I wanted it all to myself. Aren't children horrible a lot of the time?'

'Not me! I was totally lovable!'

'That's what you think!' Gwen was laughing. 'You could be a real pest. But I suppose I was a bit bossy, wasn't I?'

'A confession! Wonders never cease, Gwen.' Rilla stood up and lifted the sheet to cover everything again.

'Come down when you've unpacked,' Gwen said, 'and I'll go and see to the drinks. It's going to be such fun, Rilla, isn't it? This party?'

'It'll be great,' Rilla answered, and felt that she was telling no more than the truth.

'**A**nd where,' said Leonora, turning to Gwen, 'are you putting Chloë and her young man? What's his name? Philip something. Smart, that's it. Doesn't he do something rather fascinating for a living?' She took a sip of wine from her glass and applied herself to buttering a Bath Oliver.

'He's a picture restorer,' said Gwen. 'He works at the V and A. I'm putting them in my old room. Chloë's always liked it.'

Rilla concentrated on peeling an apple. It had been only her and Gwen and Leonora at dinner. There was no sign of Gwen's husband, James.

As though she were reading Rilla's mind, Leonora said, 'James, I take it, is still in town?'

Gwen nodded. 'Yes, he phoned me just before dinner. He's chatting with wine merchants and seeing about the marquee. Liaising, he calls it. In any case, he said he'd pick up a sandwich on his way home.'

Rilla helped herself to another cup of coffee. James might be liaising, she thought, but on the other hand he might not. She glanced at her sister. Gwen must have worked out a way of coming to terms with her husband's past infidelities. Nowadays, she was a little tense when he came home late and somewhat the worse for wear, but why did she put up with it at all? She must love him, Rilla supposed. She knew that she couldn't have stood life with James. She wouldn't have been able to overlook the women, right at the start of the marriage. As far as she was concerned, it would take only one tiny slip, one kiss even, and she'd send him packing. Fidelity wasn't too much to ask for. Or was it? Did people nowadays even care? She had no idea, and on her present form, she wasn't likely to find out. Who the hell found true love at her age?

She bit into her apple and turned her attention to what Leonora was saying. Something about her work. Rilla sighed inwardly, opened her mouth and prepared to make two cameos on afternoon soap operas sound like star parts for the Royal Shakespeare Company. Talking yourself up, it was called, and she'd grown rather good at it over the years.

In some cupboards, wire hangers made a sound like wind chimes when you hung your clothes up, but not at Willow Court. Leonora didn't believe in wire hangers. You might just as well take your best dresses and shred them at the shoulders, she used to say, with typical exaggeration. Still, Rilla had to admit that padded hangers covered in satiny material were oddly comforting. At least my garments will be in good shape, she thought. Even if I'm not.

She'd been here for some hours and everything was all right. She had managed to look out of the window, earlier on, and there was the kitchen garden in the afternoon sunshine, looking restful and pretty and not a bit threatening. She had to be careful of some places, of course, even in the house. If she wasn't on her guard all the time, he'd appear in front of her eyes and the pain of that was too much to bear.

If there was one thing in the whole world you never forgot, not ever, it was a dead child, and Mark was always with her, in every atom of her body. But it was only here, at Willow Court, that she sometimes heard his voice, and even actually *saw* him, behind the curtain in the drawing room where he loved to hide, or sitting on the bench in the Quiet Garden. This, she thought sleepily, is a haunted house. I should be used to it by now, but I dread it. I dread the sight of him, the impossibility of it actually *being* him. And of course she couldn't sleep in her old room.

Rilla wondered who *would* be sleeping there. She'd ask Gwen. Dinner had been quiet and peaceful tonight, but from tomorrow everything was going to be different. Gwen's younger son, Alex, was getting a lift down with Beth. Efe, her eldest, would arrive in the afternoon with his family, and Sean Everard, the TV director, was expected before dinner. There would hardly be time to turn round, and no time at all for heart-to-hearts of any kind. Not too much time for Leonora to interrogate her even further about work or the current state of her love life or ask her in a roundabout way what she intended to do about her weight.

Rilla reached into her enormous carpetbag to find her secret supply of chocolate bars. It was going to be a long time till breakfast.

Thursday, August 22, 2002

IT WAS NEARLY TIME TO GO. Beth Frederick looked around her flat and thought of the layers of tissue paper between every garment in her suitcase and how impossible she found it not to line up the shirts in her drawer and the sheets in her linen cupboard. It was probably a good thing that she lived by herself. She would have hated to share the space with anyone. Anyone except Efe.

She found her breath catching in her throat at the thought of seeing him again. Efe. Pronounced 'Eefee'. She was the one who'd named him, when they were both two years old, and she couldn't say 'Ethan'. Yesterday, before leaving work, she'd printed out his latest email. It was folded up and hidden away in her handbag, in a pocket in the lining.

> Hey, Beth! What a fantastic few days coming up, eh? But I do have something of utmost urgency to put to you. Can't say anything now, but we'll talk more at Willow Court. The whole matter is rather important and may have quite serious repercussions. Look forward to seeing you there, kiddo. Love and kisses, Efe.

It was the longest message she'd ever had from him, the Efe equivalent of a thesis. And *Love and kisses* was unprecedented. *Kiddo* was a bit depressing, though, with its older-brother overtones. And what did he mean by 'repercussions'? What did he have up his sleeve? She was curious to know, of course, but mainly she wanted to see his face again.

All through their childhood Efe had led, and Beth followed him slavishly. *Even though they're only step-cousins, and not related by blood in any way, Beth and Efe are devoted to one another*, Leonora told everyone, and that was the family wisdom. He confided in her still. Whenever he had a problem, she was the one he came to, in spite of being twenty-eight, married now and head of his little family.

Usually, Beth kept her feelings for Efe locked away inside herself, and tried to ignore them. The day he told her he was marrying Fiona McVie was the first time she'd admitted to herself that she loved Efe in an altogether uncousinly way. At first she felt guilt, as though the emotion might have been in some way incestuous, but it wasn't. She was unrelated to him. She was allowed to love him. For one wild moment, she'd nearly blurted out the words that would have spoilt everything: *Don't marry Fiona. Look at me. Look at how much I love you. Look at how well we get on.*

'Getting on' was not what love was about, though, was it? Beth knew that. Efe didn't fancy her and that was that. Fiona was so pretty, like a blonde doll, with long legs and long eyelashes. There was nothing about her that one could dislike, except perhaps the way she always did exactly what she thought Efe would like, almost obliterating her own desires and opinions. Still, Beth felt a sour emotion not far removed from hatred whenever she saw her. Even thinking about Fiona with Efe was enough to fill her with anguish. In her wallet, she kept a photograph of herself and Efe that his brother, Alex, had taken at the wedding reception. It comforted her and tortured her in equal measure.

Efe looked glorious. He was almost too good-looking: tall, dark, blue-eyed. In this photograph he could have been advertising Ralph Lauren, and she looked ridiculous in all that frilly nonsense she'd had to wear as a bridesmaid. Her hair had been pulled away from her forehead and fastened in a complicated arrangement at the nape of her neck. She was standing against a wall, and Efe was looking down at her with something like love in his eyes. That was what she liked to think, anyway. Whenever she examined the photo carefully, though, she could see the truth. He was looking affectionate and friendly, but no more. All the love was in *her* eyes, turned to look up at him. Love, and something like desperation. There were times when she felt like tearing up the photo, but something always stopped her, a vain hope that the next time she looked, magically, Efe's expression would be different.

Sometimes she chided herself for her ridiculous fantasies. There was no reason on earth why Efe should leave Fiona for her. He liked beautiful women and Beth knew that no one could call her that.

She was slim, and her dark hair fell almost to her shoulders in a well-cut bob. She wore little make-up and her clothes were understated, safe.

She worked as personal assistant to the senior partner in a firm of architects, where dark trouser-suits were something like a uniform. No one would have guessed she was the offspring of a rock star. *You're a good-looking girl but you don't make enough of yourself*, Rilla said all the time.

Beth smiled, as she often did when she thought of Rilla. She's batty, she said to herself, but fun, which is more than most people can say for their parents. Beth realised she'd been lucky, ending up with Rilla out of all her father's girlfriends. She was warm and affectionate and funny and forever flinging together unexpected ingredients and making wonderful smells—and a dreadful mess—in the kitchen. She was self-absorbed, but Beth never minded that, because it meant that she herself had been allowed to do more or less what she'd wanted to all her life.

Beth looked at her watch. She really ought to go and pick up Alex. Efe's younger brother had no car and she always gave him lifts when she could. He would, she knew, be waiting for her outside his flat with his rucksack and assorted carrier bags on the ground beside him, looking like a student. His wavy dark hair would be flopping over his forehead, and he'd have flung his clothes on anyhow with no thought to his appearance. Efe called his style shambolic, but Beth found it rather touching. She smiled as she locked the flat and made her way down to the street.

As she drove to Alex's flat, she reflected on family secrets. No one knew about her feelings for Efe. But she knew that certain members of her family felt sorry for her. *Twenty-eight and still living alone*. I bet they've decided I'm a virgin, Beth thought. She smiled to think of their reaction if they knew. Just because you were suffering from unrequited love didn't mean you had to do without sex. It was just that you never committed. Never let yourself get involved.

These days in Efe's company would be a test. She was longing to see him, to talk to him, to be near him, to smell his smell when they kissed 'hello', and at the same time she dreaded it. It would be an ordeal.

'You drive, Alex, go on,' said Beth. 'You know you're longing to.'

They'd piled his belongings onto the back seat, with Beth taking great care to see that everything was tidily stacked.

Alex grinned at her. 'Sure you don't mind?'

'No, go on. I'm exhausted. I'll be rotten company. I might even fall asleep.'

'I'm used to you being rotten company,' said Alex. 'Go to sleep and see if I care. I'd rather listen to whatever crap you've got in the tape deck.'

'It's the Buena Vista Social Club. Take it or leave it.'

'No, that's OK. Quite civilised for you. Branching out, are you?'

'Shut up and drive, Alex. I'm going to sleep.'

'Right,' Alex said, and pressed some buttons. The music filled the car, and he saw Beth relaxing into her seat and closing her eyes.

There were very few people in the world Alex felt comfortable with and Beth was one of them. He was two years younger than she was, and he'd always known how much she liked looking after him. She had a gift for making him speak, and he confessed things to her that he wouldn't have dreamed of telling anyone else, not even Efe. Worries he had, like, why didn't he feel what he was supposed to feel for all the various women he'd had short and unsatisfactory relationships with? Beth had patience and never minded listening to him mumbling and muttering. She often did it while feeding him delicious meals because she believed he never ate properly.

Alex was on the staff of a good newspaper and often photographed beautiful women. He got sent all over the place to take shots of this starlet and that pop singer and the other society person, and sometimes he even got lucky and pulled somebody, but one-night stands was what they always turned out to be. Love never seemed even to be a possibility.

It wasn't just he who made confessions. Alex was willing to bet he was the only person who knew that Beth was in love with someone. She'd made him swear not to tell a soul, and he never had. She'd told him about it at Efe's wedding, and fair enough, she'd had a bit to drink, but she knew what she was saying. He remembered the conversation well.

I'm brokenhearted, Alex. Have I told you?

No, but you can, Beth. You know you can tell me anything.

I do know that. Yes, I do. But I can't speak about this. It's secret.

Even from me?

From everyone. It's secret and it's hopeless and I'm going to grow up and forget all about him.

Alex had wanted to ask every sort of question. Who is this person and why can't he love you and are you quite sure he doesn't, but in the end, as usual, he'd said nothing. Later he decided that Beth's secret love was probably married. Nothing more secret and terrible than that. Married and not going to leave his wife. One day, he thought, I'll ask her about it again.

He changed gear, and turned his mind to Willow Court. It would be great to see Efe again. They didn't meet nearly enough in London. This morning there'd been a brief text message on his mobile that mentioned needing to discuss something urgently. Everything for Efe was urgent. Alex had always idolised his elder brother. There was only a two-year age difference, but when they were kids, he'd followed Efe around and Efe put up with it because a brother who didn't say much and never told tales was useful.

Alex's inability to speak was something that hadn't changed. Ridiculous to find yourself tongue-tied at his age, but words often struck him as causing nothing but trouble and misunderstanding. He saw how his mother flinched when his sister Chloë was being particularly nasty to her; he noticed how Leonora never managed to speak properly to Rilla, as though her love had somehow got bottled up on the journey between her heart and her mouth; he knew his father thought it was a joke, calling his mother silly, or a fool, or some such, but it wasn't really. It was meant. Words were always meant in some way, and Alex wasn't going to risk saying too many in case they hurt someone when he spoke them.

He was looking forward to seeing his grandmother. And Ethan Walsh's paintings. They all talked about them a lot, and spent ages setting up visits for this or that art expert to come and look at them. Every summer, people came trooping past them dutifully, but Alex wondered whether anyone apart from him and Leonora actually looked at them. That was a bond between them. They understood what was going on in the pictures. They realised that there was much more to them than just paint on canvas, or pastels on thick paper, or watercolours.

For one thing, they were uncharacteristically modern. Most of them had been painted in the early years of the twentieth century, and you could see the influences on them of Impressionism and Surrealism, but there were tricks of perspective there that were much more modern than that. And then there was the matter of light. Certain of the paintings seemed to shed light outside the frame. And the colours were always strangely luminous. The painting of a blue teapot, for example, was one of Alex's favourites. The blue paint sang and vibrated and flooded your heart with joy. The real thing was still used by Mary, the housekeeper at Willow Court, and was nothing to write home about. Just a teapot. That was Ethan Walsh's gift, Alex thought. He made things more than they were in life. Better. Brighter and filled with light. That's what I want as well. That's what I want my photos to do.

'Wake up, Beth,' he said. 'We're here.'

He looked down at her. She opened her eyes and smiled at him.

'I'd like to photograph you looking like that,' he found himself saying.

'You're mad!' Beth answered. 'I must look all crumpled and sleepy. You should have woken me earlier, Alex. I could have driven for a bit.'

'No, that's OK. I love your car.' He smiled at Beth. 'And you can't be a back-seat driver if you're sound asleep, can you?'

Beth stood in the corridor. She could hear Fiona and Douggie giggling in their room. She listened for a while, but couldn't hear Efe's voice. They must have just got here too, she thought. I should go and say hello at least. She sighed. I can't face them, not just yet, but they'll know where Efe is. She stood listening to Douggie's childish words, gathering herself as though for a battle, and then knocked lightly on the door.

'It's me, Fiona,' she said. 'Hello.'

'Oh, Beth, how lovely! Douggie and I were just having a little game of Lego before lunch. Come and play with us.' Fiona was perfectly dressed in designer jeans and an expensive-looking white blouse. Beth's gaze was drawn, as always, to Fiona's wedding ring.

'I can't really,' she said, and crouched down to kiss the little boy. 'I've got to go and find my mother and say hello to Chloë. Is she here yet?'

'Yes, we're all here now, I think. It's going to be a wonderful party, and I'm dying to meet the television director, aren't you? Efe says he's famous.'

'Where is Efe, by the way?'

'He's gone out with James. To the village, I think. You know what he's like when he gets here . . .'

Beth nodded. She did know. He liked to walk around everywhere to make sure that nothing had changed. She knew how he felt, because she, too, liked everything to be as it always was.

'I'll see you later, Fiona,' she said, edging towards the door. 'I'll just go and say hi to Chloë.'

'Right,' said Fiona. 'Super to see you.'

Beth hadn't really meant to go and find Chloë. That was just the first thing she'd thought of to say to Fiona, but now that she was safely out of there, she might as well just say hello. She walked back to Chloë's room, which was next door to her own, and knocked at the door.

'Come!' said her voice, an unmistakable mixture of brash and girlish.

Beth stepped into a room that was already so Chloë-esque that she had to laugh. 'Chloë, honestly! This room's a tip!'

'Fuck off if you're going to be like my mum, Beth!' Chloë said, but she was grinning. Her black lipstick, white skin and spiky fair hair were supposed, Beth knew, to make her look dangerous, but only succeeded in making her look vulnerable. She was wearing a floral dress, with a Rugby shirt over the top. She didn't stir from her place on the bed. The duvet had vanished under piles of underwear and make-up and crumpled bits of paper, and her clothes were scattered on the floor, together with the clumpy-looking shoes she always wore.

'I'm an art student,' Chloë said, lighting a cigarette. 'This is what art students do, didn't you know? This isn't a mess. It's an installation.'

'Leonora will have a fit if she catches you smoking.'

'I don't care. I'll spray some of my perfume about. Have you seen Efe and Fiona? They're around somewhere. Oh God, it's going to be gruesome, this party, days and days of Fiona. I can't bear it, Beth.'

Beth went over to the open window and looked down into the garden at the front of the house, and there was Efe. She waved, but he was too far away. He was walking with James, coming nearer and nearer. Even at this distance, Beth thought, you can tell how elegant he is. She swallowed hard.

'I must go and find Rilla,' she said. 'And where, by the way, is Philip?'

'Gone to the village for something or other. He'll be back later.'

Beth almost ran down the stairs to the hall. Efe was walking about outside. She'd see him soon. She was going to ignore Fiona and just concentrate on Efe. Days and days of being with him. A triangle-shaped wedge of sunshine lay across the bottom step, flooding it with light.

The sky outside Leonora's window looked like four o'clock. She'd been asleep for a while. Lunch had been rather tiring, with Douggie needing attention and Fiona making a fuss about everything. It was time to get up. Mr Everard . . . Sean . . . would be here soon, and she'd promised to talk to him. And before that, she had to go and visit Nanny Mouse.

Leonora put her feet to the floor and felt around for her slippers. She stood up slowly, checking that her limbs were in working order. It had been a busy day already. Gwen—darling, reliable, kind Gwen—had been rushing about for weeks, organising everything.

The party would, she told herself, be wonderful. An occasion for rejoicing. And like a reflex, she felt the pain that was always there, somewhere inside her, whenever she was really happy. It was a mixture of regret that Peter couldn't be with her, sharing the pleasure, and the ache she could still feel when she remembered him. She could still summon up Peter's smile, the touch of his hands, his mouth on hers. She sighed. Also, in a place she couldn't exactly reach with her mind, there was something like a shadow. Why was that? A kind of sick dread? True, when the girls were together, there were quite often fireworks, always had been. She knew they loved one another, but there was always some kind of competition between them. They were both, she knew, seeking her love and approval, and she tried, she really *did* try, to be fair with them. She recognised, though, that Rilla just sometimes rubbed her up the wrong way, irritated her in ways that Gwen never did.

She opened a drawer in her dressing table and took out from under a pile of scarves a square purse made of thick cotton. The letters clumsily embroidered there *(MUMMY)* made her eyes fill with tears. Rilla had stitched the purse at school, as a present for her. Leonora kept her precious dolls in it. No one else knew where they were hidden. She opened the purse now and took out the little doll that looked as she herself had once looked: pretty, very young, in a lovely dress. How I wish I could be her again, Leonora thought. Not an old woman with too many sorrows.

She replaced the doll and soothed herself by looking at the photograph that stood on her dressing table. Alex had taken it a couple of years ago. She smiled to think of her younger grandson. From the very first time he'd held a camera when he was six years old, he'd almost never put it down. Whatever the occasion, there he'd be, snapping away instead of talking to people. There was, she felt, a special bond between her and the quiet little boy. Even as an adult, he was still her darling, and she didn't think anyone quite appreciated how talented he was.

He has a gift, Leonora thought, for seizing the right moment. There they were, she and Gwen and Rilla, fixed for ever as they were that day, sitting on the bench under the magnolia tree in the Quiet Garden. Rilla looked happy in this picture, which made a change. She wasn't often seen to smile in photographs and Leonora knew that was because Rilla felt they made her look fat. She had on a long, gold-coloured dress, quite unsuitable for the country, and Leonora felt a momentary irritation. Willow Court wasn't a long-dress sort of place, Rilla knew that. Also, she was wearing too many necklaces, which was typical of her. Leonora sighed, and turned her attentions to her face in the mirror.

It was quite passable for nearly seventy-five, she thought, but that white hair. Where had it come from? When she wasn't confronted by her own image in the glass, it was easy for her to think of herself as Leonora Simmonds the beauty, the young mother whose two little daughters were her pride and joy. Concentrate on the good things. Keep problems in their place. That was always her style. It was what made her *a force to be reckoned with*. She smiled. Sean had called her that. She'd liked his words and summoned them up now to help sustain her till she saw him. A force to be reckoned with.

Nanny Mouse was so old that everyone had lost count. She'd been Leonora's nanny, then Gwen's and Rilla's, and she'd always been called that. Anyone who met her asked, of course, how she had acquired her name and had to be told, rather boringly, that Leonora had called her that when she was tiny and unable to say Miss Mussington. Mouse she had become, and Mouse she remained, and the name suited her. Even in her young days there was something rodent-like about her small hands and neat waist, and the way her teeth protruded ever so slightly.

She lived in Lodge Cottage, the pale, square little house at the bottom of the drive beside the main gate. Leonora had decided ten years ago that she was too old to live alone and, for all that time, Miss Lardner had been Nanny Mouse's companion. Miss Lardner was at least sixty-five herself, but was tall and well built. She talked to Nanny, cooked for her, and made sure she didn't slip in the bath. And was well paid. Nanny resented the waning of her powers and spent many happy hours grumbling at poor Miss Lardner, who seemed to take it all with equanimity.

Miss Lardner was waiting when Leonora arrived. 'She's in a good mood today, Mrs Simmonds,' she said, opening the door.

The front room of the cottage was golden with sunshine, and Leonora smiled. There was Nanny Mouse, asleep in the chair by the unlit fire. The table under the window had been polished and a vase stood ready.

'I knew you'd bring flowers,' said Miss Lardner. 'If you give them to me, I'll put them in the vase and bring them in with the tea.'

'Thank you,' said Leonora, handing over the roses Gwen had picked. The old lady was sitting quite upright in the chair with her eyes closed.

'I'm not sleeping, Maude dear,' Nanny Mouse said quietly. 'You can come and sit down and tell me things.'

'You startled me, Nanny!' Leonora said, kissing the cheek that smelt of lavender talcum powder. 'And I'm not Maude. I'm Leonora.' She sat down in the chair on the other side of the fireplace and began to talk. Nanny Mouse liked to keep up with what was going on at Willow Court. She was particularly interested in the filming.

'The television people. Are they coming to see me?'

'Of course, Nanny. You'll be in the film. You're the only person in the family apart from me who actually knew Ethan Walsh.'

Nanny Mouse nodded. 'I did. He was good to me. In his way, you understand. He wasn't much of a one for women. Poor Maude!' The old woman fell silent. She was twisting the corner of her handkerchief.

Leonora spoke to disperse the silence. 'The children are here, Nanny. I'll bring little Douggie to see you. You remember him, don't you? Efe's son? My great-grandson. Of course you do. He's such a lovely little boy.'

'But he mustn't wander,' Nanny said, looking up and leaning forward and plucking at Leonora's knee. 'Terrible when they wander. Were you here when he wandered away?'

'Douggie's never wandered away,' Leonora said, and she could feel her heart beating in her throat. Nanny wasn't talking about Douggie. Change the subject. She said, 'You should see the food up at the house, Nanny. We've got pounds and pounds of strawberries. Enough for an army. I'll send some down to you tomorrow if you like.'

'Strawberries,' Nanny Mouse repeated. 'Oh, yes, I do like them! We had them for the wedding, didn't we?'

'My wedding, yes,' Leonora said, trying to keep up.

'He was dead by then, of course, or maybe he died just after that.'

'Daddy? Yes, he died just before my wedding.'

'And good riddance!' Nanny Mouse said firmly.

Miss Lardner came into the room just then with the vase of roses. 'Look, Nanny!' she said. 'Leonora has brought us some lovely roses.'

Nanny Mouse stared at the flowers, not seeing them. 'No one knows anything,' she said to Leonora, her hands trembling in her lap. 'No one hears what I say any more, and I say good riddance. I'm glad he's dead.' She leaned back in her chair, tired from the emotion she'd expended.

Leonora sighed. She knew that Ethan Walsh was a subject best avoided. Poor old Nanny is irrational when it comes to Daddy, Leonora thought. A little soft in the head, I expect. Well, she is frightfully old. It was time to change the subject again.

'Alex will come and see you, Nanny. Everyone's here for my birthday.'

'Is it Leonora's birthday come round again? Will she have a magician?' Nanny Mouse's eyes sparkled. Leonora shivered. Please God don't let me become like this, she thought. How ghastly to have a kind of wilderness in your head, and be forever wandering around in it. How unbearable to be so lost! She closed her eyes. I pray it never happens to me. I couldn't bear to be lost in my own head.

Sean Everard was bowling along the M4 to Wiltshire with the top down, smiling to himself. Ethan Walsh, Willow Court, those pictures. Sean had been obsessed with them for more than thirty years.

As an eighteen-year-old, in 1970, he'd been taken to the house by an aunt with an interest in other people's gardens. The avenue of scarlet oaks leading up to the front door was impressive, but as for the rest of the garden, well, houses were more his thing, and so he'd made his way inside. Hadn't asked anyone, just strolled up the steps and the French windows had been open and he'd found himself in an empty room.

All the usual things that are always in rooms must have been there—chairs, tables, sofas—but Sean didn't see them. On the wall above the fireplace were three paintings. He gazed and stared and his mouth may have fallen open. It was the first time he'd seen real paintings. One picture was a still life of apricots in a white china bowl. Soft-bloomed apricots, pink-gold against the crockery and the blue-and-white-checked tablecloth, and Sean looked at it and felt that if he could only sit there, in the painting, those apricots would be all he ever needed. Next to the still life was a landscape, and Sean recognised it as the view up the drive to the house, painted in autumn to show off the disconcerting scarlet of the trees. The house looked mysterious and full of secrets, with every window like a closed eye. The third picture showed a young girl of about six, sitting on a bed. She was dressed in some pale purplish colour, and the light was probably coming through a window, and the sheets and pillowcases behind her looked like a mountain range: white peaks and dark valleys of cloth all the way up to the top of the canvas. A brass plate under this picture announced *Leonora Walsh. 1934*. He had no idea then, but this was the woman he now thought of as his Leonora.

When he'd gone to pitch the programme, Sean had told himself not to hope. OK, so Ethan Walsh was well known and his reputation was riding high these days, but there wasn't much crowd appeal in an English painter who lived all his life in one place. Sean hadn't been able to believe his luck when the powers that be had OK'd the project and when the artist's daughter, Leonora Simmonds, had agreed to see him.

And now he was going to Willow Court for her seventy-fifth birthday party. It had been *her* idea to include these festivities in the programme about her father. She might be delicate-looking and old-fashioned, but she was a shrewd cookie when it came to public relations.

'I'm an asset, aren't I?' she'd said to him, and she was flirting. There wasn't any question about it.

He arrived at Willow Court at exactly the right time and there it was, the vista that had made him catch his breath all those years ago: a long line of trees crowned with leaves that held, deep within their greenness, the promise of scarlet. It was strange and beautiful and somehow fitting.

Leonora herself had been standing at the front door when Sean drove up and he felt privileged. He looked round at the beautiful room he'd been given and checked that his tie was straight. Then he picked up his portable tape recorder and made his way to the conservatory.

'Come in, Sean. Sit down,' Leonora said, indicating the chair next to her. 'I am treating this as a conversation between friends. You can put that machine on this table. Is that all right?'

'Perfect! This is such a lovely room.'

It wasn't a formal conservatory, but more like a sitting room with glass walls. The plants were amassed against the glass and some of them had spread right up to the high ceiling. The table was covered with seed catalogues, books, and Leonora's correspondence.

'Shall we start then?' Sean asked.

'Yes, I'm ready.' Leonora folded her hands in her lap.

'Let's begin with your early childhood. Tell me about that.'

'My mother died when I was eight.' Leonora gave a small nervous cough. 'My father was always busy painting. I was mainly brought up by Nanny Mouse. She was very young in those days, but they promoted her when I was born, to look after me. I think my mother was rather delicate. You'll meet Nanny Mouse. She's over ninety, and very frail now, of course. She lives in the cottage at the bottom of the drive.'

'Has the estate been in the Walsh family for many generations?'

'Oh, no!' Leonora laughed. 'My grandfather bought the land after making a fortune in some boring bit of industry—parts of engines, I think. Frightfully important without being at all *visible*, if you know what I mean. And in fact when Daddy told his father that he wanted to go to London and study to be an artist, there was the most enormous row. In those days young men were expected to follow in their fathers' footsteps, not go and fritter their time away on what were called "daubs". It must be quite hard for you young people to understand.'

Sean smiled. 'I think quite a lot of parents even today might consider art a rather uncertain career path.' God, he thought, how pompous I sound! I must watch that. 'May I turn to the subject of your mother?'

'She was very quiet. Unassuming. She never seemed to be there, that's what I remember. Whenever I asked Nanny Mouse where she was, I was told she was resting or writing letters. I'm rather vague about her death, because I was quite ill round that time. I remember that. But everything changed after she'd gone. Daddy was terribly affected by her death. It was ghastly. I can't recall him as particularly affectionate to her while she was alive, but of course children don't see everything, do they?'

'Where did he meet her?'

'In London, at art school.'

'So she gave up her art to be with him?'

'Yes. Nanny Mouse told me that they quite scandalised everyone by eloping to Paris and marrying there. Maude Cotteridge was a penniless orphan and my grandfather wouldn't have been best pleased at the match. The gossip was'—Leonora bent forward and lowered her voice—'that they lived together before they were married. Their affair was the talk of artistic London, apparently. You'd have thought she'd be miserable here in the country, wouldn't you, after being used to London up till her marriage, but she loved the garden. In those days, Willow Court had four gardeners. We have to manage with two these days, but of course I have very green fingers.'

He smiled at her. 'That's great,' he said. 'We've made a good start, but we'd better stop for now. I must go and change for dinner.'

'I've enjoyed it. Tomorrow I'll take you up to my father's studio.'

'Yes, I'm looking forward to seeing that. And I'm most grateful to you for being so helpful. I hope this film lives up to your expectations.'

Leonora looked up at him. 'I'm sure it'll all be wonderful,' she said. 'If you don't mind, I'm going to sit here for a while. Drinks on the terrace at six o'clock.'

'Lovely. I'll see you later,' said Sean, and left the room, shutting the door quietly behind him.

Leonora closed her eyes. For a moment, she had the impression that she wasn't alone in the conservatory. Perhaps Gwen had come in to see where she was. She breathed in, and her nostrils were filled with a fragrance she recognised: lily of the valley. Who used it? Where did she know it from? Maybe James had brought it back for Gwen from one of his trips abroad. Or perhaps it was Rilla, or even Chloë, but why was it so familiar? She opened her eyes to see which of the women now at Willow Court had crept in here while she was sitting with her eyes closed, but she was quite alone. The fragrance hung in the air and there was no one at all. I imagined it, Leonora thought. It's in my head. She shivered slightly and shut her eyes again. I'll go up soon, she told herself. I'll just sit here for a moment.

September 1935

Leonora half opened her eyes. There was someone standing at the window, looking out at the garden. Rain beat against the panes, and the piece of sky she could see from the bed was horrid and grey. The dark shape between her curtains wasn't Nanny. It was too tall and sort of thick. Nanny was small and skinny. Could it be Daddy? She felt a sudden chill and pulled the quilt up round her shoulders. Then she sat up on one elbow and her head hurt. She tried to speak, but only a faint noise came out of her mouth. She coughed to clear her throat.

At once, the shadow at the window turned round and it *was* Daddy. He strode over to the bed and sat down next to her and took her hand. Leonora was so surprised that she fell back against the pillows. He was wearing a black suit and his eyes were rimmed with red. Leonora fixed her gaze on the gold watch chain that crossed his waistcoat.

'My darling child,' he said, 'I didn't mean to wake you. You need your sleep, do you not? You've been rather ill. Do you remember?'

'Have I had my birthday yet?' Leonora asked. 'Was it measles?'

'No, no, nothing like that. A fever, the doctor said, but we have been a little concerned. And yes, you are eight years old. Happy birthday, sweetheart. We shall have to celebrate when you're feeling better.'

Leonora wanted to cry. How could she have missed her birthday and not even known? There were so many things she didn't understand. Why was he here? Where was Mummy? And Nanny? Why were all his clothes black? She asked, 'Where's Mummy?' thinking that if she knew the answer to that, everything else would be much clearer.

'Don't you remember, darling, how ill she was?'

'Is she better now?' Leonora said. 'I don't remember.'

Her mother often kept to her room. She liked lying on the chaise longue in the drawing room for hours at a time. Sometimes she disappeared altogether and Nanny said she was 'indisposed'.

Suddenly, Daddy spoke. 'Are you a brave girl, Leonora?'

She nodded. Now that she was really eight, she had to be brave.

'I'm so sorry to tell you this, Leonora.' Daddy took his handkerchief out and wiped his eyes. 'She's dead. My beloved Maude . . .'

And then he was crying. Leonora stared at him, too shocked by his grief to take in what he was saying. Daddy never cried. He was the strongest, tallest, strictest person in the whole world and not this sobbing, wretched creature, whose voice was breaking as he went on.

'I had no idea. No idea that she'd been so . . . so ill. So ill. She kept it from me, not wanting to worry me. She was without a doubt the most unselfish person. And then she was gone, and now I've buried her, and we must be brave, Leonora. We must take care of one another, mustn't we? Such a cruel loss for you, my poor child. I will . . . do my best, but it will not be the same. Nothing will be the same. How will I bear it?'

He stood up and squared his shoulders. Leonora looked up at him and said nothing, because she didn't know what to say. Then he spoke again and sounded more like himself.

'Nanny will be here shortly, to see if you want to get up today. Perhaps we'll have tea together later. Would you like that?'

Leonora nodded. What would she find to say to him as they helped themselves to sandwiches and scones from the cake stand?

Daddy made his way over to the door and turned to smile at her. 'We'll survive, Leonora, won't we?' he said.

'Yes, Daddy,' said Leonora, wondering what he could mean. Was he, too, in danger of falling ill and dying?

As soon as he'd gone, she pushed back the covers and got out of bed. She felt wobbly. She remembered Nanny saying, *Only two more days to your birthday, dear*. So she'd been ill for days. How could that happen without her knowing about it? Tears filled her eyes. Mummy's dead, she said to herself. Under the ground, and stiff and cold. She shivered, and tried hard to remember the last time she'd seen her mother. Was it saying good night? Or maybe they were in the garden. Mummy must have died in her bed because that was where people *did* die. She imagined the body lying among the pillows wearing one of her mother's lace-trimmed nighties and it was her and not her at the same time.

On the wall behind Leonora's bed there was a portrait of her, painted by Daddy, and she turned to look at it. She was a little girl in this picture, and she was sitting on the floor beside the doll's house, the one in the nursery that she played with every day. Leonora could see every detail on the wallpaper; all the little lamps and pieces of furniture and even the tiny dolls that Mummy had made. The light in the picture seemed to be pouring out of the doll's house and it lit up the edge of the child's, Leonora's, cheek. I'll go and look at it, she thought. My doll's house. The one my Daddy and Mummy made for me.

She went into the nursery and there it was, standing against the wall. She looked down at the roof, painted with a pattern of overlapping roof tiles. A memory, like the wing of a butterfly, fluttered briefly at the edge of her thoughts. For the tiniest part of a second, she saw her mother standing beside the doll's house in a long, white nightgown and then she was gone. Leonora blinked and tried to bring the memory back, but it wouldn't return and it felt to her as though a light had been extinguished somewhere inside her. She began to weep.

Leonora was growing fretful. Nanny Mouse had made her lie in bed for days. Sometimes the words *My mummy is dead* came into her mind and then her eyes filled with tears and her head started aching, but she couldn't think of Mummy all the time, and she started wanting ordinary things. I wish Nanny Mouse had taken me into the village with her, she thought. I could have bought some sweets from the shop. Liquorice allsorts, or a sherbet fountain. Nanny Mouse always chose barley sugar twists, and Leonora had had too many of those to think them exciting.

Where was Daddy? He came in every afternoon and sat with her for a while, but he was still sad and didn't want to talk very much. Perhaps he was in the studio, painting. The studio was out of bounds. It was an attic really, the big attic next to the maids' rooms. The door of the studio was always kept shut when Daddy was in there working, but he wouldn't be working now. She'd heard Nanny Mouse and Mrs Page, the cook, talking about it when Mrs Page brought up her supper tray.

'The poor man,' Mrs Page said. 'He isn't eating properly. And all he does is pace around the house like a caged beast.'

'He's not working, I know that,' Nanny Mouse said. 'He stands at the studio window and stares out of it. I saw him when I set out for church yesterday and he was still there when I came back. I swear he hadn't moved an inch.'

Perhaps he's up there now, Leonora thought. I'll go and find him. I'll talk to him and cheer him up. He won't mind. He's not working. She pushed back the bedclothes and put on her dressing gown and slippers.

She tiptoed up the stairs, and made her way along the corridor to the studio door. She turned the brass doorknob. The studio was long and thin. Canvases were propped up facing the wall so that you couldn't see the pictures. The easel had nothing on it. Paint had dried to crusty flowers of colour on the palette. Leonora walked the length of the room and went to stand at the window that looked down on the garden and the lake. She stared out, wondering if she could catch a glimpse of the swans. Her headache had come back, and she leaned her forehead against the glass. Nanny said I was getting better, she thought, but now I feel bad again. Maybe if I go and sit down . . .

She stumbled to the chaise longue that stood in the middle of the room and lay down on it. She closed her eyes and the pain in her head grew weaker. She put her hand in the narrow gap between the seat of the chaise longue and its wooden frame, and something soft caught in her fingers. She sat up to investigate. A small piece of cloth. She could see a corner of it sticking out, a white triangle of lace. She pulled on it and recognised it at once. It was one of Mummy's hankies. Leonora sniffed it and tears sprang up in her eyes. Mummy's smell. Lily of the valley, it was called, and all of Mummy's clothes smelt like that. Used to smell like that. Tears ran down Leonora's cheeks but she wouldn't use the hankie to wipe them away. She tucked the precious square into her pocket and used the sleeve of her dressing gown to dry her eyes.

'What are you doing up here, Leonora?' said a voice, and there he was, Daddy, filling the doorway with his body.

Leonora wanted to melt into the floorboards. 'I was looking for you, Daddy,' she whispered. 'I only came here to look for you.'

Ethan Walsh strode to the chaise longue and Leonora felt his hard fingers on her flesh, pulling her to her feet, leading her to the door, pinching her hard on the upper arm. 'You are never to come up here again,' he muttered. 'Do you understand, Leonora? Never. You are quite forbidden to come into this room. Am I making myself clear?'

He knelt beside her, put his hands on her shoulders and brought his face closer to hers. The love Leonora usually saw in his eyes when he looked at her had disappeared and this person, pinching her shoulders with bony fingers, didn't like her a bit. Hated her, perhaps, and there was something else in his face. Daddy looked scared.

'Yes, Daddy,' she said, 'I understand. I won't come up here again. Not ever. Never. I promise. Cross my heart and hope to die.'

'Don't say that!' he almost shouted. 'Just go back to your room and stay there, please. Wait for Nanny to come back. I have to think.'

He turned away from her and blundered back into the studio, slamming the door behind him. It sounded like thunder in the empty house. Leonora ran back to her room and flung herself face down on the bed. She never would go there again. It was a horrid room, cold and unwelcoming and filled with a light that was too bright.

The hanky in her pocket. As soon as Leonora remembered it, she knew she must hide it. If Daddy found she had it, he'd be angry all over again. Where could she put it? Nanny Mouse went through her drawers to make sure they were tidy, and if she left it in her pocket it would be found when her clothes were washed, and the scent would be gone for ever. Then suddenly Leonora smiled. She knew where it would be safe.

She got off the bed and went into the nursery. There, she crouched down in front of the doll's house. She took her mother's hanky and folded it over twice. She tucked the fine cotton neatly over the body of the doll that her mother had made to look like the real Leonora, then sat back on her heels and looked at the doll's bed. They'll never see it there, she thought, because grown-ups don't look properly. I shall know about it, though, and I can come and sniff it whenever I want to.

Evening, Thursday, August 22, 2002

Fiona was feeling queasy. She wondered whether she would get through dinner without throwing up. It wasn't fair. Some people only got morning sickness, but she had it at different times of day, and it ought to have been getting better by now.

Douggie was busy on the floor at her feet, constructing a fort out of Lego bricks. Efe emerged from the bathroom with his mobile clamped to his ear. Fiona tried to guess who he was speaking to and what exactly was going on. He'd been in a funny mood for the last few days, and, anyway, he was always a bit strange down here at Willow Court. It was something to do with the Collection, she realised, but was a bit hazy about the details. All she knew was that her husband was preoccupied with those bloody paintings. *They're my responsibility ultimately*, he'd often say. *Leonora won't last for ever, and then they're in my hands.*

Fiona had more than once pointed out to Efe that when his grandmother died, Willow Court would actually pass to Gwen, his mother. And Efe always laughed and said, 'Well, yes, of course, but that means me, doesn't it? Ma will do exactly as I say, because she knows I'm right.'

Fiona thought the terms of Leonora's will rather unfair, and had once dared to say, 'What about your aunt Rilla? Doesn't she get anything?'

Efe had smiled and said, 'She'll get a fair old dollop of money, don't you fret. And she'd hate to be saddled with dealing with the paintings. Willow Court is not her favourite place in the world.'

Efe was still on the phone, discussing some boring thing about money. She knew, because he moaned about it so much, that things were hard for him at work, as far as money went. That was one reason he was so keen that Leonora should agree to his plan; he stood to earn a huge commission if the deal went through. Fiona would have been happy to give him as much money as he needed, but when she'd dared to suggest it, Efe had been enraged. 'Fine kind of a husband I'd be if I came running to my wife every time I had cash-flow problems,' he'd almost spat at her. She never suggested it again.

Now Efe caught Fiona looking at him as he spoke and signalled that he'd be finished soon. And he smiled at her. Her heart melted. There were times when he went for ages without smiling at her and she felt as though the sun had gone behind a cloud. He spoke unkindly to her, too, sometimes, when he was fed up with her, and Fiona resolved each time that happened to try hard not to annoy him. When he frowned or showed his disapproval at something she did or said, she made a note of what it was, and determined to try to be more the sort of person he wanted her to be. She loved him too much, that was the problem. She knew his faults and still loved him. Sometimes she wondered what it was about her that had attracted him in the first place. She knew she was pretty, but feared that prettiness on its own wasn't enough to keep him interested in her for ever. There'd be many women here on Sunday for the party. What if one of them caught Efe's eye?

Cold dread rose in her as she began to think about it. She found it hard not to worry about all those hours when he was at the office, away from her. Wasn't there a good chance that he'd meet someone else, someone cleverer than she? But Fiona was determined to stay married to Efe. She would do exactly what he wanted. He must never have anything to complain about, ever. If being pregnant was what was required, she would bear one child after another, just as long as he never left her.

'Come on, Fiona,' said Efe, putting the mobile away. 'Let's get down there. Come on, Douggie. We're going to the garden to see the others.'

'Piggyback!' the little boy said.

'Tomorrow, old chap, OK?' Efe replied.

Fiona knew he was anxious not to crease his shirt. Well, so what? she thought, as she followed her husband and child out of their room. There was nothing wrong with wanting to look nice.

Sean came into the drawing room and looked around tentatively.

Leonora was waiting for him. 'Ah, Sean,' she said. 'Perfect timing! We've all started on the drinks, but you'll soon catch up.'

Gwen stood just inside the room, and smiled at him. 'Hello, Sean. Shall I introduce you to everyone?'

'I'll do that, darling,' said Leonora. She tucked her arm in his and led him towards the French windows, which stood open, letting the warm scent of summer flowers drift indoors.

James Rivera, whom he'd met briefly on his last visit, stood beside the drinks trolley looking debonair. 'Sean, what are you drinking?' James called out, gesturing to the bottles ranged before him.

'Dry sherry, please.'

Leonora directed Sean's attention to the sofa. 'You haven't met my younger daughter, Cyrilla,' she said. 'Cyrilla, this is Sean Everard.'

'It's exciting, isn't it? The film I mean. Only please call me Rilla,' said the rather plump, red-headed woman dressed in a long, purple silky blouse and black silk trousers. She indicated the younger woman sitting beside her and said, 'This is my daughter, Beth Frederick.'

'Stepdaughter,' said Gwen, coming to sit down on Beth's other side. 'Her father is Jon Frederick, do you know him?'

'The singer? Are you really his daughter? Gosh, yes, I remember him well. He was quite big in the seventies. Well!'

Sean was saying the first thing that came into his head. He had noticed the furious look that Rilla shot at her sister when Gwen had pointed out that Beth was not a blood relation. Even now, after he'd moved the subject to the music of the seventies, Rilla's mouth was still set in a line, and she was eating one pistachio nut after another from the small dish on the table beside her, discarding the shells into an ashtray.

'Darling, do leave some of those for other people,' said Leonora. 'And, Sean, we can't let you be monopolised, can we? You haven't met my grandchildren and you really must! Come out onto the terrace. I won't allow smoking in the house, so they all puff away out there.'

Sean followed Leonora outside. A young man and a very pretty woman were sitting on white chairs at a white table. A boy of about three, who was surely their son, was rolling down the grassy slope beyond the terrace, then running to the top and rolling all over again.

The young man leapt to his feet and said, 'Darling Leonora, how super you're looking. As usual. Sit down for a moment.'

'Thank you, Efe dear.' Leonora sat down, saying to Sean, 'You've spoken to Efe on the telephone, I believe? Efe, this is Sean Everard. Do sit down, Sean.'

'It's good to meet you face to face,' said Efe. 'We're all very excited about the film. This is my wife, Fiona. And that's Douggie, my son.'

'My son', Sean noticed. Not 'our son'. He wondered whether Fiona minded that excluding possessive pronoun.

'How d'you do?' said the young woman and stretched out a hand for Sean to shake. Her clasp was rather limp. She was like a doll, with long fair hair, and blue eyes fringed with ridiculously long lashes.

'Where's Chloë?' Leonora asked. 'Shouldn't she be down by now?'

'Oh, you know Chloë!' said Efe. 'She's never been on time in her life.' He explained to Sean. 'Chloë's my younger sister. She's a bit of a law unto herself. Anything she can do to cause trouble, she'll do.'

'Efe!' Fiona breathed. 'You are mean! Oh, here's Chloë!'

A strangely dressed figure was striding round the side of the house. She began shouting out while still approaching them. 'What's the betting you're already tearing me to shreds, Efe? How's it going, Gran? You're looking dead pretty as usual, Fiona. And vice versa.'

Fiona's brow wrinkled as she tried to work out what Chloë was saying, but Sean got it at once. Dead pretty and pretty dead. Clever but cruel. Had Efe understood? Just to make sure that a fight wasn't about to break out between the siblings, Sean stepped into the silence.

'I'm Sean Everard,' he said. 'I'm directing a programme about Ethan Walsh and we're filming your grandmother's birthday celebrations.'

'Right,' said Chloë. 'They did say, only I didn't quite take it in. I'm Chloë, by the way.' She flung herself into the chair next to Leonora and grinned at her. 'Your face, Gran! Honestly! You should see it.'

'My face, dear, doubtless reflects my feelings about the clothes you're wearing. And I dislike being called Gran, as you know very well.'

'Sorry!' Chloë said. 'And my personal appearance is out of bounds, don't you remember? You promised.' She turned to Sean. 'My mother and grandmother disapprove of the way I dress. They always have ever since I was a kid. Only they don't seem to realise that I'm grown up now, and to be frank with you, it's none of their fucking business.'

'Chloë!' Efe and Fiona said in unison.

'I will not stand for such language!' Leonora stood up and swept away into the drawing room. Sean was unsure whether to follow her or stay.

'Take no notice,' Chloë said. 'She's in a huff. I don't care.'

'That's always been your trouble,' Efe said, frowning. 'You're selfish.'

'Me? You're calling me selfish? King Selfish himself? Bloody nerve!' She leaned forward, scooped some peanuts out of a china dish, and tipped them into her mouth.

Sean sat awkwardly for a moment, noticing how Chloë's arrival had disturbed the gathering. Fiona had moved to the grassy slope to play with her son, Efe had followed Leonora into the house. And now Rilla had stepped out onto the terrace and was making her way to the table.

'Oh God, pass me a cigarette, Chloë darling!' she said, sinking into the chair beside her niece.

Sean thought she seemed familiar in some way. Could he have met her? 'I hope you won't think I'm being rude,' he said, 'but I'm sure I've seen your face before, and I can't quite remember where.'

'In the movies. My auntie Rilla is a movie star,' said Chloë. 'You must have seen *Night Creatures*?'

'Oh, Chloë, do you have to? I'm not exactly proud of my work in films, Mr Everard. Schlock, really, all of it. Hammer Horror, that sort of thing. I'm sure you can't—'

'Yes! Yes, that's it! And please call me Sean. I adore *Night Creatures*. It's a cult classic. You were marvellous.'

Rilla held her hand out for Sean to kiss. 'You've made my day,' she said. 'No one around here feels it's any sort of achievement.'

'My mum's jealous, that's all,' Chloë said.

Sean glanced towards the French windows. Efe was there, leaning against the frame and talking to Beth. Sean couldn't hear what they were saying, but Efe was gesturing earnestly with one hand, and Beth's eyes never left his face. She was gazing up at him with a glance of such naked adoration that he felt embarrassed. He looked to see where Fiona and Douggie had got to, and there they were, coming up the slope of the lawn. It was impossible to tell if she'd noticed anything. She was carrying the child on her hip but she waved at her husband and he waved back. Instantly, Beth stepped away from Efe and walked along the terrace to where Chloë, Rilla and Sean were sitting.

'Hello again,' she said, and Chloë smiled.

'Hi, Beth!' she said. 'Beth and I see eye to eye about a lot of things,' she explained to Sean. 'Specially things about the family. Only she's got a bit of a blind spot where Efe's concerned. She can't see that my beloved brother doesn't give a damn about anyone but himself.'

Beth blushed. 'Leonora wants us all to go in now,' she said. 'That's the main reason I came out . . . to fetch you. Dinner will be ready soon,

Philip's in there, too. Hadn't you better rescue him from your dad?'

Chloë stood up. 'Oh God, yes, I'd better. Poor old Philip. Well, Sean, see you at dinner, I'm sure.' She followed Beth over the flagstones.

The sun was low now, shadows stretched black over the grass and the last of the light filled the sky with a glow of blue and rose.

'We should go in,' Rilla said. 'Mother hates being kept waiting.'

She stood up and they walked together to the drawing room. The lights hadn't been turned on yet in the room and, for a moment, Sean had the feeling that he was stepping into darkness.

Rilla sipped at her coffee and resisted the urge to reach out for another chocolate. She was sitting next to James, far away from Leonora, but you could bet your bottom dollar that, even with all the conversation and the to-ing and fro-ing of platters and glasses and wine, her mother would have been keeping tabs on Rilla's consumption of bittermints.

Leonora, at the top of the table, had Sean on her right and Efe on her left. Efe looked divine as usual. Fiona, sitting opposite him, didn't take her eyes from his face. Darling Beth was next to Efe, not saying much. Not eating much either. She'd left almost all her pudding. Could she be ill? She had dark rings under her eyes. Tomorrow we'll have a proper talk, Rilla thought. We haven't had a heart-to-heart for ages. She sighed. Beth was so striking. Why on earth did she practically erase herself in public? She was wearing a white shirt and black trousers and might just as well have picked up some plates and taken over as a waitress!

Rilla noticed Sean looking at her. He smiled. He wasn't a bit smooth, which was what she'd feared when the dreaded words 'TV director' were spoken. He was a craggy sort of man, with dark, grey-streaked hair and a nice nose. Not a lot of people had nice noses in Rilla's opinion, so you paid attention when you came across one. Gwen was talking to Leonora, so she risked it and put her hand out for one more chocolate.

Efe tapped his wineglass with a fork. Silence fell in the room.

'Thanks, everyone,' he said. 'I don't mean to stop the chatting or anything, but there is something I want to say.'

A murmur went round the table. Much later, when she was staring at the ceiling and trying to sleep, Rilla thought back to that second, when everyone thought that Efe was about to make a toast or say how lovely the food had been. When everything had been untroubled.

'I wouldn't normally bring up matters like this at a party,' he continued, when everyone was quiet, 'but time is important here and we don't have too much of it.' He looked directly at his grandmother. 'It's about the Collection, Leonora. I know what it means to you. They're your pictures, in every way. But they're not being seen at their best, and so many people out there would like to look at them, to understand them better, and they can't. Now, I know you've turned down all sorts of offers, but I have been in touch with Reuben Stronsky.'

No one said a word. They sat quite still, as though a spell had been cast, freezing them in their chairs. Rilla knew Stronsky was a millionaire financier from the States with a great interest in the arts.

Efe went on. 'Stronsky is offering to buy the Collection and build a museum especially to house it. It goes without saying that he is offering a very large amount of money indeed.' He picked up his wineglass and drank from it. 'That's it. We can talk through all the details tomorrow, but that's what I want you to consider, Leonora darling.'

No one spoke. Rilla looked at her mother, who had gone as white as a sheet and hadn't moved. Oh, please God, don't let her have a heart attack or anything. Not now. Not just before her party!

Leonora stood up and, with her hands resting on the table, smiled at everyone. 'Well now,' she said quietly. 'You've given us something to think about, Efe. It's been a wonderful day, and I don't intend to spoil it. We'll speak further about this, as you say, but I should warn you that my father's paintings leave Willow Court over my dead body.' She smiled again. 'I'm very tired now, so you'll forgive me, I'm sure, if I retire to my bedroom. I wish you all a very good night.'

She turned and left the room, and, as always, every eye followed her. The silence in the dining room grew as, one by one, everyone stood up from the table and melted away. Some of them would go to their bedrooms, others would probably slope off to the village pub. Rilla sighed. That's it, she thought. No more peaceful family party from now on. And no after-dinner coffee and liqueurs in the drawing room, either. She walked into the hall, dreading another early night. Bloody Efe! Couldn't he have waited one more day? Hours stretched before her, dark time, in which she would try to sleep and fail. Should she phone Ivan? No, damn it, she thought. I'll leave it and I won't go up to my bedroom and vegetate either. I'll make myself a coffee, even if it's only instant decaff.

Gwen was in the kitchen bending over the sink and Rilla could see, from a single glance at her back, that she was making a superhuman effort not to cry.

'Gwen,' she said, going over to her sister. 'What's the matter?'

'Oh, Rilla, as if you need to ask!' Gwen turned round, her eyes full of unshed tears. 'I could strangle Efe. How could he . . .?' Her voice faded away. 'I told Mary I'd wash up. I'll go mad if I don't do something.'

Rilla spooned some coffee into a mug and switched the kettle on. 'It'll be all right,' she said. 'We'll talk to Mother tomorrow. Persuade her that this whole thing with the paintings is nothing we can't discuss next week.'

'But Efe insists that it's all got to be done now!' Gwen wiped her hands on a tea towel and sat down at the kitchen table. 'Something to do with cash flow in his firm. And all the work that I've put in for this weekend will be wasted if everyone's squabbling and people are closeted in corners and Mother's sulking.' She sniffed. 'You cannot believe how much work I've put in, organising everything, and now Efe's little bombshell just crashes onto the table and threatens it all.'

'It'll be fine,' Rilla said. 'The filming will take Mother's mind off things. She'll have a chat with Efe tomorrow and put him straight. It's much more likely that he's going to be the one left sulking, because he hasn't got his way. Mother never does anything she doesn't want. And you know she's longing for this party. She won't let anything spoil it.'

'I hope you're right. Efe in a sulk won't be much fun either, but I suppose he'll behave himself. I'll speak to him in the morning. God, I'm exhausted, Rilla. I haven't slept properly for days.'

'If there's anything I can do to help you, Gwen, just say. You ought to be able to relax a bit and enjoy the weekend, too, you know. Have a brandy or something. Have a cigarette. I've got one here.'

Gwen sighed. 'No, no, I mustn't. It's nearly ten years since I gave up. I'm not going to wreck all that just for a whim.'

'Well, I need one. Have you got an ashtray?'

'You can't smoke here,' Gwen said. 'Mother would have a fit. She's got a kind of X-ray nose when it comes to cigarettes.'

Rilla sighed. 'OK, OK, I'll go and sit on the terrace. You get a good night's sleep, Gwen. Everything will look better tomorrow morning.'

Gwen squeezed Rilla's arm on her way out of the kitchen, and smiled. 'I'm really glad you're here, Rilla,' she said. 'Sleep well.'

Rilla stared after her, pleased and moved by her sister's unaccustomed gesture of affection. She picked up her handbag and left the room.

Rilla sat down on a bench that stood in an alcove on the terrace. The silhouette of the marquee, down on the lawn, looked like an illustration from a fairy tale. The moon kept appearing and disappearing behind clouds that were drifting slowly across the sky. There was a trellis nailed to the wall on her right, and the roses growing all over it were almost fragrant enough to mask the smell of her cigarette smoke.

A noise on the path, someone walking along the terrace, made her catch her breath. Damn and blast! Rilla wanted to think, to unravel the implications of Efe's announcement at dinner.

'Oh,' she said as she caught sight of Sean. 'I thought it might be one of the kids.' She shook her head. 'I must stop calling them that. They're all grown up now, and Beth hates it when I say "kids", but it's hard to break bad habits.' I'm babbling, she thought. She put her cigarette to her lips, and sucked so hard that the tip glowed brightly. She exhaled slowly and said, 'Do sit down, Sean. I didn't mean to blast you with conversation. I expect you came out here for a bit of peace and quiet too.'

'No, really, it's OK,' he said, and sat down beside her. 'I came to find you, actually. Everyone else seems to have disappeared.' He laughed. 'That hasn't come out quite as I intended. I didn't mean that I wanted to talk to anyone else. I was just stating a fact. I came to find you.'

'Really? Why?' (Oh my God, is that too direct? Why the hell, Rilla thought, can't I *think* before I blurt out what's going through my mind?)

Sean was looking, she noticed, straight ahead and not at her. Had she embarrassed him? She was just about to speak again when he said, 'I think I'd like to get to know you better.' He laughed. 'God, doesn't that sound awful? Like something from a magazine. Only what I said before is true. I am an admirer. I really did love you in *Night Creatures*.'

'Thank you,' Rilla said, very gratified. She stubbed her cigarette out under her shoe, then picked the stub up and pushed it into the earth around the roses. 'Leonora would kill me if she found a fag end out here.' She turned to face him and smiled. 'It's kind of you to say all that. I don't do enough work these days to be blasé about meeting a fan.'

'I can't imagine why not. Those casting directors must all be mad.'

'Let's change the subject, OK?' Rilla made sure to smile. 'How's the filming going?'

Sean sighed. 'I've got no idea how I'm going to fit everything I want to show into an hour. Your mother's amazing, isn't she?'

'Amazing is only the half of it,' Rilla said, and then regretted it. 'I truly don't mean to sound catty, but she's hard work sometimes, that's all. She's got very high standards, and I sometimes fail to meet them. That's what I feel anyway. But every family has its things, hasn't it? It's not that we're not devoted to one another. But there's always some sort of friction around when we all get together. It's only to be expected, I suppose.'

'Of course it is,' Sean said. 'There isn't a family in the land that doesn't have its share of troubles. You all seem to get on rather well, actually.'

'Oh, we do. We really do. Only I suppose I'm not the best person to talk to about Willow Court and what goes on here. I haven't been a regular visitor for, oh, more than twenty years.'

Sean didn't say a word. He's waiting, Rilla thought, for me to explain. She opened her handbag, looking for another cigarette. She said, 'D'you mind if I have another? Only it's so firmly banned indoors that I feel I have to puff away like a chimney the minute I step over the threshold.'

'Go ahead,' he said. 'I only ever smoke about twice a year, but I'll have one now, if you can spare one.'

Rilla shook two cigarettes out of the packet and held one out to Sean. She struck a match and he took hold of her wrist as the flame came close. He breathed in, then released her hand, which he'd held on to for a heartbeat longer than was strictly necessary. She lit her own cigarette, thinking, how many years has it been since I felt that small thrill? And am I entitled to be feeling any sort of thrill? It's the night, and the roses and the moonlight and all the bloody clichés getting to me, that's all. She said, 'I ought to explain, oughtn't I? Why I don't usually come here?'

'You mustn't feel you have to.'

'No, I don't mind.' She looked at him again. 'You're easy to talk to. You listen.' She paused and looked at her shoes. 'My son, Mark, drowned in the lake down there. Twenty years ago. He was four when he died. So little. It was an accident, of course, but it's hard to live with, still. I manage to put it to the back of my mind when I'm in London. Most of the time, anyway, but when I'm here . . . well. The place is haunted, that's all.'

'I'm so sorry, Rilla,' Sean said quietly. 'I think you're very brave to come back for an occasion like this. Very brave.'

'Not really,' Rilla said, blinking back the tears that had suddenly filled her eyes. Oh, no, she thought. Surely I must be all cried out by now. 'I'm sorry,' she said, fumbling in her bag for a tissue. 'I can't help it. You'd think that after all these years I'd have found some self-control—'

Sean interrupted. 'You've nothing to reproach yourself with, Rilla.'

Rilla smiled and dabbed at her eyes. 'It's your doing really. I'm not used to having such a sympathetic listener. I'm all right now. Honestly.'

'Any time. Even if it might mean you bursting into tears.'

Rilla laughed. 'Thank you. It's been lovely talking to you, but I should go in now. Don't feel you have to come in if you want to stay out here.'

'No, that's all right. I'll call it a night as well. But, before we go in, I wanted to ask you whether you'd come with me to Nanny Mouse's tomorrow afternoon? Are you busy?'

'No, of course not. I'd love to. It's ages since I've seen her.'

They walked together to the door of the drawing room and went in. This is the second time he's come into the house with me, Rilla thought. She was surprised to realise that she found his presence at her elbow comforting. They walked into the hall, and made their way upstairs, just like an elderly married couple going slowly up to bed together. Oh, grow up, Rilla Frederick, she said to herself. What planet are you on?

He should have done as Rilla suggested and stayed outdoors. Here he was in his bedroom and it wasn't even midnight yet. Sean sat on the edge of the bed and sighed. He'd never felt less like sleep in his life, and wondered why Rilla should have had this effect on him. In his job, beautiful women were part of the landscape. But Rilla was different. He hadn't been flattering her when he'd told her of his admiration for her work. She was a good actor, with a screen presence that was both sexy and unthreatening, almost cosy. He wondered why she hadn't been doing much lately. He knew that for women no longer in their first youth, there were fewer and fewer parts on screen and in the live theatre, but still. Rilla was not like other people. She had something.

It had been so long since he'd made a play for anyone. Tanya, his ex-wife, once accused him of being emotionally illiterate, though how she managed to find out anything about him when she was busy in so many extramarital beds, he had no idea. But all that was in the distant past, and if anyone had asked him, Sean would have said his life was full and rewarding. Now he realised how lonely he'd been, and for how long.

He lay back on the bed and sighed. You're here to do a job, he told himself. Fancying one of the daughters of the house isn't part of your brief. Apart from anything else, time is so short. You'll be away from here on Monday. Do some work. That'll get your mind off her.

He went to the table where he'd spread his papers, to find the shooting schedule for tomorrow. Above the table was a very small Walsh, a pastel drawing of Leonora aged about five, he supposed. She was facing directly out of the frame, peeping from behind the skirts of . . . who could it be? Nanny Mouse? No, she'd never have worn a skirt in such a delicate fabric. You couldn't tell much, really, from seeing only the lower half of the body. Perhaps it was her mother, Maude Walsh.

Sean sat down and stared at the picture. Something occurred to him and he shuffled the papers on his desk till he found what he was looking for—an inventory of all the pictures hanging at Willow Court. He turned to the list of portraits and ran his finger down the column of titles. It couldn't be true, but it was. Among the fifteen portraits there were only two depicting Maude, and she was hidden in both. He knew all the paintings so well that their titles brought them into his mind complete in every detail. One was a domestic interior in which Maude's figure was bent over some needlework, her face turned away, the lamp on the table being the focus of the artist's attention. In the other, she was walking down a path bordered with lavender bushes which echoed the colour of her parasol. This accessory made a most beautiful composition, but it hid the face from view. All the artist's skill had been devoted to depicting the lace of the glove on Maude's one visible hand.

What sort of relationship did the artist have with his wife which prevented him from ever attempting a likeness? Ethan's portraits of his child were delicate and skilful and his self-portraits astonishing. There were several of these, in which Ethan could be seen glaring out of the picture. Sean thought there was something chilly about the eyes, something off-putting. Young Efe had inherited the same look, and both he and Leonora had Ethan Walsh's clear blue eyes.

Maude, Sean supposed, was the one who'd passed down to Rilla her creamy skin, reddish hair and those hazel eyes with flecks of gold in them. I'll ask Leonora about her mother's looks tomorrow, he decided, and started to undress.

Friday, August 23, 2002

ALEX SLUNG HIS CAMERA over his shoulder and made his way back to the house. He'd gone out at seven o'clock, to photograph the men moving along the scaffolding, carrying stage lights to fix to the steel skeleton inside the marquee. Then he'd wandered down to the lake. He was working on Leonora's present: a photograph album. On her birthday, the leather album would be empty, but as soon as she opened it, he'd tell her about his surprise. A history of the whole celebration in pictures.

The swans were right over on the far bank and he didn't have the energy to go all the way round there without so much as a cup of coffee. I'll get some breakfast, he thought, and go back later. As he approached the French windows of the drawing room, he heard Efe's voice coming from the conservatory. Tearing a strip off someone, by the sound of it. Alex stood still for a moment, then looked in at the window.

Fiona was cowering near the door, holding Douggie close to her. Her arm was hugging the little boy into her skirt, shielding him from the full force of his father's anger, though the poor kid was obviously terrified.

'I *can't*. Don't you understand how impossible this is? Jesus, the house is full to the rafters with doting relatives. How come it's today I have to be the perfect new man? You're a fool, Fiona. You can't help it, but, honestly . . . How *could* you? When you know how much hinges on this and how Leonora, by being so bloody obstinate, can wreck my career?'

He'd run out of steam. It took all Alex's self-control to stop from rushing in there and hitting Efe. Fat lot of good that would do. But poor Fiona looked as though she were about to burst into tears and it occurred to Alex that he could create a diversion. He knocked on the window and smiled, as though he'd only just glanced in.

'What do you want?' Efe mouthed at him.

'Thought Douggie might like to go and look at the men putting up the lights in the marquee.'

Fiona ran to open the door from the conservatory to the terrace. 'Oh, Alex, would you? That would be super, wouldn't it, Douggie? Go with Alex to see the men working in the big tent?'

Douggie nodded gravely and put his hand in Alex's.

'Thanks, Alex,' said Fiona. 'That's so nice of you.'

She was wearing a long-sleeved blouse but the cuff fell back as she pushed a lock of hair away from her forehead and Alex noticed bruises on the lower part of her arm, dark, purple stains in a pattern like fingers. Was Efe capable of that? Suddenly, Alex felt chilly, even though the sun was rising in the sky and it was going to be a hot day.

'Come on, Douggie. Got to grab some food from the kitchen and then we'll go. Bet you'd like a biscuit, right?'

Beth turned to walk up to the house. She'd been hanging round the marquee now for ages and Efe hadn't appeared. Alex and Douggie arrived just as she'd decided she'd had enough of pretending to be interested in the problems of where to put the spotlights, and although she could see that Alex would have been only too glad of a bit of help with child care, her need simply to lay eyes on Efe was too strong.

'I'm off back to the house, Alex,' she'd said as kindly as she could, and could sense his disappointment as she walked away. She hadn't dared to ask him where Efe was. She wanted to preserve her dignity.

As she stepped inside, the shade of the hall felt cool and silent after the light and the bustle of so many people around the marquee. Efe might be using his laptop in the conservatory, she thought, probably emailing Reuben Stronsky to tell him about Leonora's reaction. Beth felt rather sorry for him. He didn't realise quite how stubborn his grandmother was, and how adamant she was about her father's paintings.

She could hear his voice. Was someone in the conservatory with him? She stood in the dark corridor and looked into the room. She saw Efe talking on his mobile phone. She couldn't quite hear what he was saying but she caught the tone. It was seductive, and occasionally he'd laugh in the way you only laughed at something a lover said to you. Beth found herself unable to move, and strained to catch a word, or a name. Who was it who'd turned Efe, on this morning of all mornings, into this loving, almost purring creature? His voice was a little louder now.

'Not long, my darling . . .' she heard. 'Me too.' Then a long silence, then, 'Not now, for God's sake, Melanie. Stop. Please stop.'

The only Melanie Beth knew was a friend of Gwen's, who kept an antique shop in the next village. Melanie Havering, she was called. Efe couldn't possibly be talking to *her*. She found herself as jealous of this Melanie as she was of Fiona. More surprisingly, she felt sorry for Fiona. The most surprising feeling, though, was disappointment. She'd never thought Efe was particularly well behaved, but something about this whispered conversation going on in a place where his wife and child might walk in at any moment struck her as tawdry.

Beth waited till he'd put the mobile phone back into his briefcase and then she went into the conservatory.

'Hello, Beth,' he said. 'You're up early.'

'It's ten o'clock, Efe. I've been up for hours. What have you been doing? I'd have thought you'd be in there ordering workmen around.'

'Other fish to fry, haven't I? I spoke to Reuben last night and he's getting on a plane. He's coming over here to talk some sense into Leonora. Don't say a word to anyone. I don't want to spoil the party.'

Beth sat down in a cane armchair. 'Did I hear right? You don't want to spoil the party but you're getting this Stronsky chap to come and put pressure on Leonora?'

'Reuben Stronsky isn't the sort of man to put any pressure on anyone. In any case, I thought you'd be on my side,' Efe said, frowning.

'Well, I'm not. I think the paintings look very nice here. And haven't you thought that maybe the very fact that one has to make a bit of an effort to get here adds to their desirability? Makes them fashionable?'

Efe said, 'I can't stay here chatting to you, Beth. I'm a bit disappointed, if you must know. I thought I could rely on you.'

Part of her longed to say, *Please smile again, Efe, and I'll agree with anything you want*. But then she remembered the conversation with Melanie. 'Oh dear,' she said. 'Sorry to disappoint you. I expect you'll get over it.'

He swept out of the room scowling and Beth blinked back tears. She'd always hated crossing Efe.

Alex was finding it difficult to concentrate. He was crouched down in the shrubbery, taking close-up shots of the parasol mushrooms growing around the roots of the rhododendrons. He had to talk to Beth, that was becoming obvious. Part of him had always known she loved Efe, but it was only yesterday that he got an inkling that this feeling might be more than sisterly affection. At dinner last night, for instance, she'd looked at Efe all the time, not even bothering to turn and face whoever was talking to her. Today, he could have sworn she was looking for Efe, ready to trail round after him just as she used to do when they were all kids.

Would it do any good to tell her about Efe's behaviour where women were concerned? Warn her off? If he did that, she'd probably deny she felt anything at all. He reasoned that Beth must feel some sort of embarrassment about her devotion to Efe. They were cousins, for God's sake. A small voice in the back of Alex's head said, *She isn't really. She's not related to you and Efe at all. There's nothing to stop her loving Efe. Nor Efe loving her, if he felt like it.* The next thought he had was unexpected: *Beth isn't your cousin either. She's no relation of yours.*

He stood up, put his camera back into its case and walked slowly towards the house. He was wondering why that thought, that revelation about Beth, which he'd known all his life and which hadn't affected him in any way at all, should suddenly, just today, burst in on him.

Beth sat at one end of the table and listened to the conversation between Leonora, Gwen and Rilla. Everyone else had decided to be somewhere else this lunchtime. Efe and James had driven into town to talk to Bridget, the caterer. Beth privately thought they wanted to be as far as possible from whatever flak Leonora decided to dish out today. Fiona had nibbled at something and then excused herself because she had to settle Douggie for his nap. Alex never ate lunch and was probably taking photos in the garden. Sean had joined his crew, who were setting up equipment in the studio, ready for an interview with Leonora.

'I'm rather glad it's just us,' Leonora said. 'I'm interested to hear what everyone has to say, but in the end it's my decision.'

'Yes, Mother.' Gwen took a sip of mineral water and looked for support from Rilla, whose attention seemed to be fixed on her asparagus quiche. 'I do think,' Gwen continued bravely, 'that you should listen to Efe. It was naughty of him to take you by surprise last night, but you might find it's not such a terrible offer. And think of the money!'

Leonora sniffed. 'This has nothing to do with money,' she said. 'We all have quite sufficient money for our needs. The house, these pictures, are a separate world. Visitors like coming here. They enjoy seeing the place where the pictures were painted at the same time as the pictures themselves. That's far, far preferable to some concrete monstrosity somewhere in America.' Leonora looked at Rilla, who was still concentrating on her food, and spoke with some irritation. 'Darling, do lift your head from your plate for one second and tell us what you think.'

Rilla swallowed quickly, and patted her mouth with a napkin. 'I think you're probably right, Mother, but I see Gwen's point of view as well. Maybe it would be good for the paintings to be seen by more people. Somehow everyone seems to be more willing to visit museums in the States than a country house in Wiltshire.'

'Ethan Walsh was an English painter and his work is intimately bound up with this place,' said Leonora, standing up. 'There can't be more than a dozen or so things by him in other collections, and those are very early works. All the rest is here, and here is where they should stay. I'm expected up in the studio but when Efe gets back, please tell him I want to speak to him at once.'

The moment Leonora left the room, Rilla helped herself to another slice of quiche. 'Phew!' she said. 'We can all come out of our foxholes now. That wasn't nearly as hairy as it might have been, was it, Gwennie?'

'Efe's the one,' Gwen said. 'He'll get it in the neck, I'm sure. And I don't quite know what you're looking so bloody happy about, Rilla.'

Gwen's right, thought Beth. She *does* look a lot happier than she's done for ages. Something good has happened to her. She waited until Gwen had finished her lunch and gone off on some errand and then she said, 'Come on, Rilla, you can tell me. What's happened? You look like the cat who's swallowed the cream.'

'I'm not saying a word at this stage,' Rilla blushed. She got up from her chair and smiled down at her daughter. 'There may be nothing in it.'

'It doesn't suit you to be enigmatic, Rilla. Tell me what's going on.'

'The minute something goes on, you'll be the first to know, my love.'

'**M**y father used to spend hours and hours up here,' Leonora said over her shoulder to Sean. 'I was never allowed across the threshold, of course. He hated anyone to see him working.'

'But what about all the portraits of you? You must have sat for him?'

Leonora looked out of the window for a long time. She wasn't going to admit it to Sean, but the studio gave her the creeps and always had. 'No,' she answered at last. 'I never did sit for him that I can remember. I suppose he painted those portraits from sketches.'

'Do you remember him sketching you?' Sean asked.

'No, not really. My mother did, sometimes. She never showed the sketches to anyone, though, and just stuck them into a kind of writing case she had. I have no idea what happened to them.'

'Could your father have used your mother's sketches?'

'I suppose he could, but I think it most unlikely. He . . . he didn't have a very high opinion of her, I don't think.'

'As an artist, do you mean?'

Again, Leonora thought for a few seconds before answering. 'Neither as an artist nor as a woman. I never'—she looked down at the floor—'had the impression that he loved her very much. Although, naturally, I didn't know about their life together. Everything was different in those days. I didn't know my parents in the way young people do today. Life was full of rules. It was all very formal. I do recall, though, how heart-broken Daddy was after Mummy's death.'

The crew was gathered near the door, talking about technical matters. The lights were on already, shining too brightly.

'Right, Leonora, just turn to me a little. I'm going to ask you about your mother. Take no notice of the camera or the microphone.' Sean nodded at the crew and then said, 'Tell me a little about your mother. Did you have a good relationship with her?'

'I was rather irritated by her, to tell you the truth.' Leonora smiled at him. 'You know how uncharitable children are. I think I felt that her constant indisposition was designed to avoid having anything to do with me. Though, as her early death proved, she was properly ill all along.'

'Do you remember her funeral?' Sean asked.

'That whole time is very hazy. I didn't go to the funeral because I was ill too, at that time. She was buried in the graveyard of the village church. I visit her grave when I go and . . .' Leonora closed her eyes. 'I go and see Peter's memorial, of course, and so I make sure that everyone else has a tidy grave as well.' She turned the wedding ring round and round on her finger, lost in her memories. Then she squared her shoulders and turned her full attention to Sean again.

'I'm sorry, Sean. We were talking about my childhood. When I think of it now, it's like peering through a misty curtain. I can make out some shadows and flickering things in corners but nothing's clear. Nothing at all. I do remember that it was shortly after my mother's death that I came up here for the very first time.'

'And what sort of life did you have after that?'

'I didn't notice much difference, day to day. Nanny Mouse looked after me, just as she always had. I went to school and my friends were particularly kind to me for a while because of my bereavement. So were the teachers. And my father, well, he became like the person in the story about the Snow Queen. Chilly, as though a splinter of ice had entered his heart.'

'Cut!' Sean called out and to Leonora he said, 'That was wonderful,

Leonora. Thank you so much. I think we've got enough now, from up here. May I escort you downstairs again?'

'No, no, thank you. I'll stay up here for a moment, if you don't mind.'

She couldn't have said why she wanted to do that. The words simply came out of her mouth before she'd thought about them. She watched the crew pack up the equipment and leave the room and then Sean was gone as well and she was alone.

It had been quite warm here while the interview was going on but now, as she sat down on the chaise longue, she felt chilly. This room is cold because it's empty, she told herself. White walls, no curtains at the window, high ceiling. The empty easel standing in the corner. Visitors to the house liked that. And the palette, Ethan Walsh's palette with the colours dried onto it, beside the jar of paintbrushes on the table.

Leonora closed her eyes and listened to the silence. No one would miss her if she stayed here for a while. If only it weren't so cold.

January 1947

The fire in the drawing room was making no difference at all. Flames leapt and blazed and struggled to heat more than the space around the hearth, but it was so cold that Leonora could see her breath rising like white ribbons and drifting in front of her face.

She was sitting at the window, looking out at the snowy garden. She was wearing two cardigans and some woolly socks over her stockings, which made her feel like a child again. The knitted gloves she wore had their fingers cut off, but drawing was still difficult.

The terrace steps, the stone urns, and the icy lawn in the background looked inadequate on the page, not what she wanted them to be like at all. Crosshatching. Perhaps that would help to make shadows appear in the right places, make everything seem more solid. She began to stroke the pencil again and again over the paper.

Leonora's father sat very near the fire, wrapped in a shawl. She could feel his presence behind her, even though he wasn't saying anything. He spoke very little at the best of times and these times were certainly not the best. He stared at her sometimes as though he didn't quite remember who she was. His eyes were as blue as they'd ever been, but his hair was white now. Leonora still thought of her father as dark and handsome, and catching sight of him these days shocked and saddened her.

We must be the only people in the country, she thought, who miss the war. Willow Court had been a convalescent home for officers, and for five years the drawing room was a dormitory and the corridors had been full of soldiers, laughing, shouting, groaning sometimes because of their wounds, but in any case bringing some life to the house.

Leonora was fourteen in 1941 when the iron bedsteads were brought in. The servants had rolled up the carpets, and taken all the pictures off the walls and moved them upstairs to the studio. The carpets were in place now, and the chairs and sofa, but no one had put back the paintings. The drawing room looked strangely bare and chilly with only picture-shaped spaces on every wall. When Leonora asked for them to be rehung, Ethan Walsh was having none of it.

'Nothing but dust-traps,' he'd said. 'Much better off where they are.'

'But, Daddy, aren't you proud of them? Don't you want everyone to see them? To admire them?'

He'd looked at her most strangely then, and said, 'I'm better off without them. And so are you.'

Leonora knew that her father was no longer painting. He'd never *had* to paint for a living, because he had an income from the money left to him by his father, in stocks and shares. But the sad truth was that his wife's death and the coming of war had combined to end Ethan Walsh's career.

The war had been in the background for all the years that Leonora was growing up. The fighting, the bombs, fires and ruined buildings were all so far away that it had been hard for her to imagine them.

At first, when the wounded soldiers arrived, she couldn't bear to look at their injuries. Missing legs and arms in particular brought horror to her dreams, and she was ashamed of being so squeamish when the soldiers were so brave. They laughed and chatted to her whenever she came into the ward. That was what the nursing staff called the drawing room, and where the men were while they needed most care. When they were on the mend, they moved up into some of the bedrooms.

Leonora had loved the house when it was full of soldiers. They'd all liked her and made a fuss of her. And she'd liked the admiration she saw in their eyes. She had gone to a girls' grammar school where she didn't have very many close friends, because of the shyness that her contemporaries thought of as stand-offishness, but she did have two friends who lived nearby, Bunny Forster and Grace Wendell. They were forever grumbling about their looks, and Leonora quickly realised that it was the done thing to pretend you weren't pretty even if you were.

And I was, she thought. A robin had appeared on the terrace and Leonora sketched it in. I *was* pretty and I still am. I have good skin and Daddy's blue eyes and my hair is as dark and shiny as his used to be. Perhaps pretty's the wrong word. *Gorgeous*. Peter used to say that. Quite ridiculous. Leonora blinked. I mustn't think about Peter, she said to herself. Not any more. He's not coming back. It's more than three years since I had a letter from him and five years since I last saw him. He could have decided he wants nothing more to do with me because he's found someone else. Someone he loves better than he loves me.

Leonora felt dreadfully guilty, but secretly she preferred the hideous option of Peter's death in action, and whenever that idea crossed her mind, she prayed, *Oh, God, I don't mean it. Please don't let him be dead.*

She kept the letters he'd written to her, dozens of them, in an old biscuit tin, and every night she opened it and took one out to read to herself before she fell asleep. The letters were a secret from Daddy, of course. They would arrive in envelopes addressed to Nanny Mouse, who pretended to disapprove, but Leonora knew she thought the correspondence romantic. Perhaps Daddy wouldn't have minded, but she hadn't felt she could take the risk of arousing his anger. What if he'd forbidden her to write back? She would never have been able to defy him.

Three of Peter's letters were different from the others. Leonora thought sometimes that Peter had been drunk when he'd written them; it was as though something had been loosened inside him. She'd hidden these messages in the doll's house, under the carpet that her father had laid in every room. No one would think to look there. Leonora had to work at the tiny carpet tacks with a nail file to lift a corner and pull out the tightly folded paper.

I want to kiss you all over your white skin. I think of touching you, your breasts, your neck, and your mouth open under mine. I think of this until I'm nearly mad with wanting you . . . There are other women here, my darling, and I can't bear to look at them. It's you. Wait for me, Leonora. We will do nothing but make love all day long when I come back. All day long.

Stop it, she said to herself, shivering. Don't think of that now. Think of something else. She closed her eyes and allowed herself the luxury of hearing Peter's voice in her head. The first time he'd ever spoken to her she was in the scullery all by herself, peeling potatoes.

'I say, frightfully sorry, but I'm lost. I'm looking for Sister Coleridge.'

'I'll take you, shall I?' Leonora could see that the young man at the door was struggling with his kitbag. His left arm was in a sling and his head was bandaged. 'I can carry the bag, too, if you can't manage it.'

He'd smiled and his eyes that were somewhere between blue and green looked straight into Leonora's and she felt something moving in her chest, a kind of fluttering under her rib cage. He was tall and slim and his smile made his eyes light up and his teeth really did shine, white in a suntanned face. He had red hair and looked, Leonora thought, like a handsome fox turned by some enchantment into a human being.

'No, I'll manage, thanks. Not such a crock that I have to have gorgeous young ladies carrying my kit. What's your name?'

'I'm Leonora Walsh.'

'And I'm Peter Simmonds. Delighted to meet you. Walsh. Isn't that the name of the chap who owns the house? Jolly decent of him to turn it over to the army. Don't know if I'd relish having the military running wild over my ancestral acres.'

'The men don't run wild at all, really. They play the gramophone rather loudly, it's true, but I love the music. And sometimes they make a lot of noise at mealtimes, but I don't mind. Ethan Walsh is my father.'

'Then he's a lucky man,' Peter said. He'd smiled at her as Sister Coleridge came out of the drawing room and walked towards them.

'I hope you get better very quickly,' Leonora said, and went back to peeling the potatoes.

'Cheerio!' said Peter. 'Thank you for your help.'

Leonora knew from that moment that she loved him. It wasn't quite love at first sight. She'd taken about two minutes to decide. I shan't tell anyone, she thought, not even Bunny and Grace, because they won't believe me. They'll say I've got a crush on him, or something. She longed for Peter Simmonds to stay at Willow Court for months and months, and immediately felt guilty at wanting such a dreadful thing. Fancy wishing someone wouldn't get better! How selfish she was!

I can't help it, she decided, and wondered what she had to do to make Peter Simmonds fall in love with her.

She'd made herself indispensable: reading to Peter when he was feeling low; playing card games with him and his chums, Georgie, Freddy and Mike; listening to him talk about terrible things that he'd seen. They'd walked for hours in the Quiet Garden, and sat on the bench built round the magnolia tree, breathing in the peace while he told her the hideous details of everything he'd seen happening all round him.

'I shouldn't speak of it to you, Leonora. It's not fair. You're only a kid.'

'I'm not a kid!' Leonora said, and nearly contradicted herself by bursting into tears because that was how he still thought of her, after all these weeks. She'd wanted to tell him how she felt a hundred times and then funked it. Instead, she lay in her bed every night, too hot under the bedclothes, and daydreamed about kissing him.

Then one day, while they were alone in the conservatory, Peter said, 'I'll miss these times with you, Leonora. When I go. You've saved my life.'

She looked at him and wanted to say so many things but the words dried and shrivelled in her mouth. She couldn't speak. All she could think was, *Don't go. Stay with me. What if you're sent back to the war and killed? What'll become of me then? Oh, stay . . . please stay!*

At last she managed, 'When? When will you have to go?'

'This evening. My mother's sending a car to fetch me. I really ought to convalesce at home. I'm all she's got left since Dad died, and she's not well. I . . . I'll miss you so much, Leonora . . .' He turned to her.

They were sitting on the ancient sofa that had been moved into the conservatory from the drawing room. Silence filled the space all around them. Someone looking into the room from the hall wouldn't see them, Leonora knew. The plants were in the way. If she didn't do it now, he'd be gone and she'd never see him again.

She put out both hands and pulled his face close to hers. 'I wish you could stay,' she said, and then, 'Please kiss me, Peter. Please.'

His eyes widened. His face was so close to hers that she could almost count his eyelashes. He kissed her, and she tasted his mouth and felt the hardness of his arms on her back, pulling her into the heat of his body. She wanted it never to stop, but it did and she found she was crying. She felt him breathing; felt his arms encircling her and they clung to one another until her crying subsided a little.

'I'm sorry,' Leonora whispered at last. 'I know you have to go back to your regiment. Only I love you so much. I couldn't bear it if you never came back.' She looked down at the floor. 'I shouldn't have said that, I expect. You'll think I'm very forward.'

'Oh, Leonora, if only you knew!' He turned her face up to his. 'If you knew how much *I* loved *you*. How hard it's been not to tell you.'

'You should have told me. Oh, Peter, why didn't you?'

'I thought that if I told you, it would be like lighting a fuse. You're so young, Leonora. Not even fifteen, and I'm seven years older.' He laughed ruefully. 'I had to behave myself, don't you see? You're a child.'

'I'm not. I'm not a child and even if I am, I shan't always be one. I'll grow up soon. I'll wait for you, Peter.'

'Will you? Really? Oh, my darling, I'll come through anything this bloody war can throw at me if I can believe that. I'll write to you every day. I'll write from home and from wherever they're going to send me when I'm a hundred per cent fit. Oh, Leonora, kiss me again.'

They stayed in the conservatory until it was time for Peter to collect his bags and wait for the car. Leonora's mouth was swollen from their kissing and she went straight to her bedroom. When Nanny Mouse came to call her for dinner, she said she didn't feel well, and stayed in bed until she was sure Peter had gone. She jumped out of bed every time she heard a car, and she watched him leave. Then she buried her face in her pillow and wept. When at last she ventured downstairs,

Georgie gave her a letter Peter had left for her. *No one knows what will happen, Leonora, my darling. If I survive this war, I'll come back and we will love one another for ever and ever. I promise.*

She could bear time passing. She could face every day because of the letters. Then, three years ago they had stopped arriving. Leonora refused to think of why he might not have been able to write, and went through the motions of her life. She met other young men, but they all seemed dull. She went to dances and found herself dreaming of Peter even while she was talking to other people. It was no good at all. There would never be another man ever again whom she could love. If Peter never came back, she would grow into a wrinkled old maid.

She was so absorbed in her memories that she jumped when she heard Ethan speaking just behind her.

'What's that you're doing?' he said.

'It's dreadfully hard, Daddy,' she answered. 'I was just trying to make everything solid and rounded. Maybe if you showed me . . .'

He turned away. 'There's no point, Leonora. You don't have the talent and that's all there is to it. The world is overflowing with amateurs. No point adding to them. You'd be better off learning how to cook and mend socks. Perhaps I ought to write to that young man of yours and tell him to come and take you off my hands. If he's still keen, that is.'

'What young man?' Leonora asked. He never knew about Peter, did he?

'Peter Simmonds. Don't pretend you don't know what I'm talking about, Leonora. I wrote to him. I told him he was to have nothing to do with you till you were of age.'

Leonora felt heat filling her, in spite of the cold. 'When did you write to him, Daddy?'

'More than three years ago, it must be.'

'Why did you feel you had to do that?'

'Why? Oh, don't pretend innocence, Leonora. I intercepted one of his letters. Nanny Mouse left it lying about. It wasn't the sort of letter a chap should have been writing to a young girl who wasn't of age, so I forbade any further communication. Any good father would have done the same.'

'You didn't say a word to me!' Leonora shouted. 'How could you do such a dreadful cruel thing! If you read one of his letters, you must have known how much we loved one another.'

'You were too young to know about love,' Ethan said dismissively.

'I hate you!' Leonora screamed. 'I'll never forgive you. Peter may be dead. How could you have done such a thing to your own daughter?'

'I was looking after your interests, Leonora. Just as I'm looking after your interests when I discourage you from a life devoted to art.'

'It's nothing to do with you. You can't tell me what I can and can't do.'

She turned and looked at the page on which she'd been drawing. Maybe he was right about that. She was a fool, setting herself up as some kind of artist when her father was Ethan Walsh.

She picked the picture up and tore it across once, and then again. 'There,' she said. 'I hope you're satisfied. Now that you've ruined my life in every possible way.' She went on tearing till her picture was reduced to confetti. She wanted to grind the white flakes under her feet, but gestures like that didn't go down well with Daddy. She went over to the waste basket and let the paper drop into it like so many flower petals.

'I'm going out. I have to be by myself to think.'

'In this weather? You'll freeze. There's nothing to do out there.'

'There is. I'm going skating.' Mentally, she added, *And just you try to stop me!* She almost wanted him to try to prevent her so that she could scream at him again; tell him that she was nearly of age and it was none of his business what she did and if he didn't treat her better she'd leave Willow Court and see how he managed without her. He didn't say a word.

When I have children, Leonora thought, I shall love them more than anything. And I shall never, never, interfere with them when they're in love. I shall never meddle in their lives. Tears of rage sprang to her eyes once more as she walked into the hall.

She put on her coat and Wellington boots, her gloves, a knitted hat and a scarf and, holding her ice skates, she made her way out of the front door. The cold was so sharp that breathing hurt her chest. When she thought of what Ethan had done, fury boiled up in her. Then she grew calmer and wondered whether it would be possible for her to find out where Peter was. She could write to the colonel of the regiment.

Every blade of grass under her feet was iced white and the pale sun was sinking towards the horizon. She could see the lake now, silver in the remaining daylight, with the swans huddled together on the far bank. The gardener's lads had to break up the ice near their nest each day so that the birds had a little open water. I must be the only person in the world who likes the lake like this, when it isn't like itself at all, Leonora reflected. She hardly ever came down to walk round it in the summer, and she couldn't really think why that was.

Leonora sat down on a tree stump to put on her skates. She didn't dare remove her gloves, but at last she managed to do up the laces. She went out onto the ice, sliding and skimming across the surface. The only sounds were the *ssshing* noise of steel blades on ice, and the occasional cry of a bird.

I won't think about Daddy, she thought, and the cold was so intense that it was easy to put all other thoughts out of her mind except, keep moving. If she kept going round and round on the ice long enough, her anger and disappointment would dissolve. That was her hope.

Something caught her eye, a figure coming towards her over the lawn, through the Wild Garden, bundled up in a heavy coat and scarf and hat. It was a man, that was certain, but no one from the house. Perhaps it was Daddy, coming to apologise. She dismissed that idea at once. As far as she knew, he hadn't left the house for weeks, and she'd never heard him saying he was sorry for anything.

'Leonora!' The figure was calling to her. 'Leonora . . . it's me!'

She slid to the nearest tree and stopped moving. There was a time between hearing the voice and knowing who it was that seemed to go on for so long that she had the sensation of falling into somewhere white and quiet and empty. A sound that had been trapped between the willow branches, trying to reach her, came to her now, flying through the cold, waking memories, filling her with hope and love and warmth: Peter's voice. She looked intently and recognised the set of the shoulders, the way Peter walked, his head held high. It was him. *He's come back, he's not dead, he's come back.* Every other thought in her head disappeared, and she skated over to where he was now standing, beside another tree almost on the very edge of the ice.

'Peter? Is it you? Really?' Her breath, as she spoke, rose up in front of her face and she moved her hands to brush it away, so that she could see more clearly. Yes, it *was* Peter, older, his skin paler now in winter and the freckles more visible, his blue-green gaze and long straight nose, above lips a little chapped from the cold.

'I said I'd come, didn't I?'

'It's you. It's really you, Peter,' she whispered.

He put out his gloved hand and Leonora took it. 'I can't believe that after everything I'm with you again,' he said. 'And you're so beautiful.'

'Oh, Peter . . . Peter . . ' Leonora wanted to say so many things, but all she could manage was his name over and over again. 'Peter . . . I thought you were dead.'

'No, I couldn't have died without seeing you again. I've been waiting, that's all. Waiting for you to be nearly of age. Your father wrote to me and told me to keep away till then. Not to write. I expect he told you.'

'No. I've only just found out about that. I was so angry I couldn't even look at him. But it doesn't matter. Nothing matters now you're here.'

He hugged her to him and they kissed for a long moment. Then Peter stepped away from her.

'You waited for me. And you're grown-up now, aren't you?'

Leonora nodded. 'Quite grown-up. I've been dreaming about you coming back for five years. I'm so happy.'

He gave her his hand, and as she sat on the tree stump, he helped her take off her skates and put on her Wellington boots again. He was kneeling in front of her, so that all she could see was the top of his hat.

He raised his head and looked at her and said, 'Now that you are grown-up, and now that I seem to be kneeling at your feet, I can ask you what I've wanted to ask you for so long. Will you marry me, Leonora?'

'Yes!' she cried. 'Of course I will. As soon as possible. Oh, Peter, I love you so much. Will you love me for ever and ever?'

'Absolutely!' He laughed and stood up. 'Even longer.'

A thought occurred to Leonora. 'My father doesn't know you're here, does he? You didn't go up to Willow Court first?'

'No, I saw someone skating on the lake as I walked up the drive and I knew it was you. We'll go and find him now and I shall ask him formally for your hand in marriage. Sort of thing he'd like, I suppose.'

'I suppose it is,' said Leonora, 'But I'll marry you whether he gives us his blessing or not. I'm nearly twenty-one now.'

As they made their way together through the Wild Garden towards Willow Court, Leonora could feel herself thawing out, could feel the years of waiting falling away. I haven't been breathing, she thought. For five years, I've not been living at all. Not properly. I'm going to be happy now. For ever. I'm going to be warm and happy for ever and ever.

Afternoon, Friday, August 23, 2002

You're an old fool, Leonora said to herself on her way down from the studio. It's all long ago, and gone for ever. Somewhere far away she could hear someone whistling 'I Can't Give You Anything But Love', which had been their tune, hers and Peter's. Leonora shivered. Who would be whistling it today? She shook her head, to clear it. I'm thinking too much about those days. No one's whistling. It's just that the tune is suddenly in my head, because I've been remembering Peter. Melodies did sometimes take up residence in the brain. His face was there, too. It was always there, whenever she closed her eyes. Whenever she allowed herself to remember everything she had lost.

Leonora watched Efe coming across the grass towards her. She was sitting on her favourite seat under the magnolia tree in the Quiet Garden.

'I knew you'd be here, Leonora,' he said, standing in front of her.

Leonora smiled. 'You like this bit of the garden too, don't you? Aren't you going to sit down beside me? You always used to when you were in some kind of trouble as a boy.'

'I'm not in trouble now, though,' he said. 'I've come to do a bit of persuading. I shouldn't have sprung it on you last night in front of everyone like that, and I apologise. But I do think you haven't thought the whole thing through. You'd be the main person to profit from this plan.'

'Financially, I dare say I would. But Willow Court is my home. How can you imagine that at my time of life I'd be willing to see it stripped of the paintings that remind me of all that was best about my father?'

'But you'd be able to keep some of the paintings, and lend them to the new museum in some kind of rotation. And you know there's no room at Willow Court to hang all the pictures, and some real treasures are packed away in the studio. We'd fix everything to suit you, you know. Reuben Stronsky is a very reasonable sort of man. Really.'

Leonora shook her head. 'I know this means a lot to you, Efe, but I can't do it. My father made me promise to keep the pictures at Willow Court. Please tell Reuben Stronsky that I'm sorry to disappoint him.'

Efe took Leonora's hand and squeezed it. 'Will you wait and give me your final answer after the party? It's your special day and I want it to be a day you'll always remember, but will you just do this one thing for me? Wait till after the party? Please?'

'Very well, if it's going to make you any happier, I'll tell you again on Sunday night. But my mind won't have been changed.'

'You don't know, Leonora. Anything could happen.'

'Anything but that, really. And if you're harbouring any thoughts along the lines of *Maybe we can do all this when the old lady's dead*, then put it right out of your mind. The terms of my will are as clear as those of my father's. The paintings stay at Willow Court.'

Leonora looked at Efe and saw that his mood was darkening. 'Efe, you're not to sulk,' she said. 'Forget about the whole matter till after the party. Try to enjoy yourself a little. You know, don't you, that I've always done everything I can to help you. Once, as you know, I helped you when perhaps I shouldn't have done, and I've had more than a few sleepless nights about that, believe me, but I forgave myself because whatever happened, I could say, *Efe'll be all right. I did it for him.*'

That day came back to her now. She could almost taste the horror and the pain. She could remember how she'd wiped Efe's tears and told him over and over that everything would be all right and that she'd look after him. She'd promised him then that she'd never mention what he'd done ever again, to him or anyone else, and now she'd broken that promise. She should have been more careful. He wasn't saying anything but she could see that he was hurt and angry. He was also, it occurred to her, reliving his version of the same scene. She said, 'I'm sorry, Efe. I know I shouldn't have mentioned it. I didn't mean to . . . remind you.'

Efe stood up. 'Well you bloody well have reminded me, haven't you?'

'Efe! Don't swear at me, please.' Leonora's voice was uncharacteristically shaky. 'I know . . . I know you're right to be furious with me—'

Efe interrupted her. 'I can't stay here any longer. I don't know how to speak about that. And I don't want to. I don't ever want to.'

'I'm sorry, Efe. I really am.' Leonora spoke as gently as she could.

A vein was throbbing in Efe's forehead. 'Don't you realise how hard I try not to think about all that?' He sank down onto the bench next to Leonora and put his head in his hands. 'I used to want to thank you, you know. I used to lie awake and think of things I could do for you in return.' His voice was full of suppressed tears.

Leonora put her arm round him, and he turned to her and buried his head in her shoulder, just as he used to do when he was a small boy. He used to come and find her whenever he had bad dreams, and she could remember him weeping, and saying, Don't tell anyone I was crying.

Now she said, 'You don't need to do anything in return, Efe. I did it for myself as much as for you. Let's say no more about it, shall we? Look, here comes your mother and she's got Douggie with her.'

As soon as the little boy caught sight of his father, he pulled his hand out of Gwen's and began a wobbly run across the grass towards Efe.

'Dada!' he called. 'Dada!'

Efe stood up and caught him and swung him up to his face and gave him a big kiss on the cheek.

Douggie immediately settled into Efe's arms and began talking. 'Want to see doll house, Dada. Want doll house. Dada take Douggie. Now.'

'We need to ask Leonora, Douggie,' Efe said. 'It's her doll's house.'

Douggie began to squirm and Efe lowered him to the ground. The boy went straight to where Leonora was sitting and began to pull at her skirt. 'Doll house! Please take me to doll house! Now!'

'Your son has inherited your demanding nature,' Leonora said. 'Come on, Douggie. We'll go and visit the doll's house, if it'll make you happy.'

'Happy!' Douggie agreed, putting his small, pink hand into Leonora's.

She stood up and Douggie began to pull her across the grass towards the house. She said, 'I'm much, much older than you are, Douggie. I walk more slowly than you do, too, so you must wait for me. And when we get to the doll's house, you must be a good boy and touch everything gently. The doll's house is special. We have to look after it.'

Douggie nodded solemnly and slowed down to Leonora's pace.

'Here we are, darling,' Leonora said, as they reached the closed door of the nursery. 'Let's go in.'

The curtains had been partly drawn across the window and the afternoon sunshine was no more than a dim glow. The doll's house loomed against one wall and for a second Leonora thought she saw someone leaning over it, touching the place where the roof lay hidden under its protective covering. A woman, wearing something long and white.

Leonora blinked and looked again and there was nothing there. Her heart was beating fast and she took two deep breaths to calm herself. A shadow, that's all. I'm getting old and my eyes are not what they were.

Douggie was pulling at her. 'Doll house? Where's it? Where?'

'Here.' Leonora was surprised to find her voice trembling. 'We'll draw the curtains, then take the cloth off and see if the dolls are at home.'

As she spoke she pulled the curtains back and light spread to every corner of the room. Then she went over to the doll's house and lifted the sheet right off it, laying it on one of the shrouded armchairs. Douggie knelt on the floor and put his face up close to the miniature rooms.

'This is the mother doll,' said Leonora, bending down to show him. 'And that's father, and those are the children. Play gently with them now.'

Douggie hardly played with the peg dolls at all. He just stared. From time to time, his plump little hand would snake into one of the rooms and he'd move a chair or stroke the face of one of the dolls.

'We should go now, Douggie,' Leonora said gently after a while, preparing herself for an argument. 'It's nearly time for your supper.'

To her surprise, Douggie nodded and stood up. He leaned over the doll's house roof and said, 'Woof.'

'That's right, it's the roof. Clever boy!'

He ran his hand over the paper painted to look like tiles. 'Paper woof,' he said, and smiled up at Leonora. He had Efe's enchanting smile. How strange it was, this passing down of pieces of oneself, through the years. The smile wasn't only Efe's. It had been her father's as well and here it was now, on this small child's face. Just the same.

Leonora picked up the sheet and arranged it over the doll's house again. 'I'm covering it up so that it stays nice and clean,' she explained.

'Night-night, house,' she heard Douggie whisper as the white cloth fell over the roof. 'Night-night.'

The refreshments provided by Miss Lardner for Sean and Rilla were more suited to a teddy bears' picnic, Rilla decided. Fondant fancies and Earl Grey tea that should have been called Pale Grey, for that was its colour. I don't care, she thought, biting into an achingly sweet square of iced sponge. She was happy simply to sit here while Sean spoke gently to Nanny Mouse, happy that he'd asked her to join him. She was reluctant to admit, even to herself, how attracted she was to him, but all the evidence was there.

When he wasn't anywhere to be seen, she looked for him. When she was alone, she indulged in fantasies she'd thought were the exclusive province of the under-twenties. When she was with other people, her mind wandered. When she was near him, she felt as though parts of her were at melting point, and when she walked beside him she forgot all about her feet and could have walked for hours.

Oh, I've got it bad, Rilla thought. And what if nothing comes of it? Can I take the hurt? This sobering thought made her put down her teacup. She helped herself to another fondant fancy while she considered the ghastly possibility that the signals that she'd been reading last night were just Sean being charming and nothing to do with liking her in particular. The truth is, she told herself, you hardly know him and you're behaving like a teenager. And what about Ivan? Trying to imagine him back in London, was like peering at something far away. I'll deal with all that stuff when I have to, she thought, and I may never have to.

Sean smiled at her from across the room and something in her leapt and glowed. Oh, act your age, she told herself. She turned her attention to what Nanny Mouse was saying.

'I remember the wedding. They let me go. I was only a parlour maid then but Mr Walsh said I could be her lady's maid. Miss Maude's. I called her that before she was married and couldn't get out of the habit. She was a pretty thing, but quiet. I'm as much of a mouse as you are, she said to me once. She was, too. Hardly opened her mouth.'

Nanny Mouse was muddling her weddings, Rilla thought. Ethan and Maude had eloped. She must have been thinking of Leonora's wedding.

'And Ethan Walsh loved her very much,' Sean said, his voice making the words a statement rather than a question.

'Funny way he had of showing it!' Nanny Mouse said firmly. She began to stare at a point in the middle distance. When she next spoke, her voice was quite different, wavering and uncertain, and her memory had gone sliding through the years from one wedding to another. Rilla listened for clues. *Mr Peter*. So she must be thinking of Leonora. Sean gently reminded her of Maude, and her early days at Willow Court.

'Maude? Yes, you'll find her in the garden most likely. She's planting a border. No yellow, she hates yellow flowers.'

Rilla felt tears pricking in her eyes. Poor old Nanny! God, I hope I don't live to be as confused as that!

'Leonora was very ill, you know,' Nanny Mouse said, leaning towards him and lowering her voice. 'She got soaked through, you see, and took a dreadful chill which turned into pneumonia. Such a high fever, for days and days. And when they had the funeral, I didn't know who to be with. It was so hard to choose, but I chose my baby, because she was still alive, and the living come before the dead. Oh dear, but I didn't like to think of my Maude all closed up in that coffin.' Tears fell from Nanny Mouse's eyes and she blinked.

Sean handed her his clean handkerchief and muttered something about not distressing herself. Then he changed the subject. 'What did Maude do while Ethan was painting? Did she help him at all? Give him advice? She was an artist, too, wasn't she? Before they married?'

Nanny Mouse shrank back into her armchair and began to mumble to herself under her breath.

'Don't distress yourself, Nanny,' he said quickly. 'We won't talk about that if you don't want to. You can tell me whatever you like about Maude. You choose. Tell me about the garden again.'

Nanny Mouse sat up straighter. 'He has to have her with him while he works. Don't you think that's odd? Cook says she hears him throwing things. I'm not one to gossip, you know. I never speak ill of anyone without good reason. Only the way he goes into those long silences and doesn't even pass the time of day with her . . . well, is it any wonder she's got so thin and pale? She sits there with that book of hers and scribbles and scribbles and I know what goes on. I don't dare say, though. He's warned me. He took me aside in the scullery last night and I've got his fingermarks on my arm, see . . .' Nanny Mouse pulled back the sleeve of her dress and showed Sean her wrinkled forearm, marked with nothing more sinister than age spots. Then, tired by this outburst, she dropped her head to her chest.

'That's splendid, thank you very much,' Sean said. 'Don't worry, I'll leave you to rest now. We'll come and see you tomorrow and bring a camera so that you can be on the television.'

Even the magic word television failed to rouse Nanny Mouse. Her eyes were closed and Miss Lardner, who'd been sitting quietly in a corner listening, stood up and said, 'Miss Mussington needs to rest now, I'm afraid. It's all been a little too much for her.'

'I understand,' Sean said. 'Don't worry, we'll see ourselves out.'

'Thank you for the tea, Miss Lardner. Everything was delicious.' Rilla bent down to kiss Nanny Mouse. 'Goodbye, Nanny,' she said.

The old lady's eyes opened. For a second she struggled to understand who was crouched in front of her, then she smiled. 'Rilla! How lovely to see you! You're quite the lady now, aren't you? Not a little girl any more.'

'No, not a girl any longer. I'll come and see you again soon.'

Nanny Mouse plucked at Rilla's sleeve. 'She'd never have agreed to it if she hadn't been frightened to death. D'you understand. She lived in fear. All the time. Fear of him. Yes.'

Outside Lodge Cottage, Sean exhaled as though he'd been holding his breath for a long time. 'Well . . .' he said. 'Who do you think she meant? Maude? Or Leonora?'

'Maude. It has to be. Leonora isn't frightened of anything. Besides, my father died young and she's been a widow for most of her life. What Nanny Mouse was describing sounded like a really brutal man.'

'You're probably right. Ethan Walsh is beginning to emerge as something of a domestic tyrant.' Sean shook his head. 'Of course you can't learn very much about a person's character from the art they produce.'

They began walking together up the drive to the house, and the works of Ethan Walsh and his relationship with his wife were the last thing on her mind. She wished the avenue of scarlet oaks could stretch for miles. 'I think . . .' she began, just as Sean said, 'I won't . . .' They laughed and Rilla said, 'You start.'

'Right. I won't be at supper tonight,' he said. 'I've promised the crew I'd go and eat down at the pub with them. I wish I didn't have to.'

'No, that's all right. I understand.' Rilla smiled, feeling foolish at being so disappointed. 'It'll be another family circus, I'm sure. I don't think you'll be missing much.'

'I expect you'll need a cigarette, though, won't you? Like last night?' Sean took her hand, and she found it hard to speak in a level voice.

'Oh, yes, I always do. This time, though, I might have my cigarette in the gazebo. Do you know where that is?'

'I do.' He grinned at her. 'I'll be there. At about midnight, say? Can you bear to wait up till then? It's awfully late.'

Rilla nodded, not trusting herself to speak. She could scarcely believe her own daring. How was she going to keep her excitement under control? They'd begun walking up to the house again, but he hadn't let go of her hand. He kept hold of it until they were almost at the front steps.

This was the best part of the day in summer: the hour or two before dusk, when the sun was low in the sky but not quite setting. Beth was on her way to the lake, and wondered why the pearly light and the warmth and the sight of butterflies hovering above the poppies, which normally lifted her spirits, were not having their usual effect.

Efe hadn't been in a holiday mood today either. He looked sulky and cross whenever she caught sight of him. And when he wasn't looking like a thundercloud, he was being a sort of businesslike, superficially charming Efe and not the friend of her childhood. Beth hated admitting it to herself, but the man who'd been on display over the last twenty-four hours wasn't the sort of person she liked at all.

She looked over to the marquee and there he was, deep in talk with his father. She stood for a moment, wondering whether Efe might catch sight of her, realise that she was on her way down to the lake and run over to join her. Fat chance! He didn't even notice her standing there.

She set off down the slope. Once she reached the Wild Garden, she knew no one up by the marquee could see her. She was safe to take out her anger and frustration by swishing through the long grass as fast as she could, almost running, crushing flowers under her feet, wanting to get out of breath, to shut all thoughts of Efe out of her mind.

'Watch where you're going!' said a voice at her feet and Beth jumped.

'Alex! What on earth are you doing down there?'

He was lying on his stomach in the grass with his camera held up to his face, and for a few moments he said nothing as he pointed the lens in one direction after another before clicking off a few quick shots.

Beth sighed and sat down beside him. 'Taking photos of the ground, are you? Or some amazingly beautiful blades of grass?'

'As a matter of fact, yes,' Alex answered, rolling over on his back. 'I've got some good shots of the lake through a frame of grass and flowers.'

'Sounds very artistic,' Beth said, and pulled a blue flower out of the ground by its stalk.

'Don't take it out on me,' Alex said.

'Take what?'

'You know very well. You're not pleased with the way the weekend is going, and it shows. I don't know what you thought was going to happen.'

'I didn't think anything in particular was going to happen,' Beth said, and wondered how much Alex had guessed. For a mad second, she considered telling him everything and then decided that life would be easier, at least for now, if she changed the subject. 'I love the lake,' she said. 'Doesn't it look great in this light? You should take some pictures of it. Come down there with me. The swans are over on this side, look.'

Alex stared at the sky. 'I've taken entire films of the bloody place,' he said. 'Because Leonora would expect it but . . .' His words were left hanging in the air.

Beth shivered. The afternoon of Mark's death was still clear in her head and came into her mind often. It had been a blustery day, and the wind had blown sharp and chilly over the water and she could see, as though it were yesterday, Efe bending down into the black lake to pick up Markie's body, and how every part of her baby brother had been dripping and streaming as he was carried back to the riverbank. Alex was at the edge of the water, silently weeping, as Efe kept trying to bring some life back into her little brother's body, shaking it and turning it upside-down. An icy dread had crept over her as she realised that Mark wasn't ever going to breathe again.

'It was a long time ago, Alex,' she said gently, shaking her head to clear it of those images. 'My mother hasn't looked at the lake since then.'

'I don't blame her,' Alex murmured. 'Beth . . .'

'Yes?'

'May I tell you something? Nobody else knows I know this. I'm not sure I should be saying anything, but . . .' His voice died away.

Beth nodded. She knew that Alex in a confessional mood was like a bird poised on a branch. One loud noise and he'd be gone.

'That day, the day Mark died, we were playing a special kind of game. Trappers. We used to play it a lot. Do you remember it?'

Beth closed her eyes. She could see herself as she was then, racing down through the Wild Garden towards the edge of the lake and then going further along the path. The boys were already in the water. They weren't supposed to be. Mark was sitting under a willow tree.

'You were on the far side of the trees,' Alex continued. 'Efe was shouting at Markie.'

Beth shivered and Efe's clear voice came to her as though he was speaking now. *Shut up, Markie! I'm busy. I've got to get to my trap.*

'Bloody hell, you two!' Chloë was all of a sudden there in front of her, her arms full of willow branches. 'What are you doing skulking about in the grass ready to trip up unsuspecting people?'

Beth could have strangled Chloë. Why did she have to spring out of the grass just at that very moment? Alex was already sitting up and pushing his photographic equipment into a bag. He was frowning.

Beth touched him on the shoulder. 'Don't go, Alex,' she said, then turned to Chloë. 'We could say the same thing. What are you doing?'

'I'm going to make a tree. Like a Christmas tree but of willow branches. A birthday tree. I'm going to decorate it and display all Leonora's presents under it. Good idea, eh?'

'Super!' said Beth trying to sound enthusiastic. 'It'll be great.'

'You coming up to the house?' Chloë asked.

'In a sec,' Beth said. 'We'll follow you.' Once Chloë was out of earshot, she turned to Alex. 'Go on with what you were saying,' she said.

'Never mind, it was nothing really,' he said, getting to his feet. Beth stood up too and he went on, 'Just forget about it, OK?'

'Not OK! You can't do that, Alex, it's cruel. You've left it all dangling and unresolved. I hate it when people do that.'

'It wasn't anything,' he insisted. 'I was just teasing you. I'm sorry.'

Beth was sure that Alex had been going to tell her something important about that day. But now he needed to backtrack, to pretend that he was kidding. He was looking worried about it, too. Practically sweating.

'Fine,' she said. 'Let's leave it and go up to the house.'

'I'll see you up there, Beth,' he said. 'I've got a couple more places to shoot before the light goes.' She could see how relieved he was. His shoulders relaxed and the whole set of his body altered visibly.

She watched him as he strode over the grass, tall and thin, his blue denim shirt flapping loose over his trousers. Poor Alex! He never could articulate his thoughts very well. If he'd been nearer, if he'd stayed still for a while beside her, she'd have hugged him. Hugged him, and wanted to hit him too, for being so vulnerable and so impossible at the same time. He knew something about that day, the day Markie had drowned, and Beth was willing to wait until he told her. He would tell her one day.

Alex walked as quickly as he could, wanting to exhaust himself, wanting to take back every word he'd said to Beth. What had possessed him? he thought. What good would it do to dredge up all that old stuff?

He found himself by the gates, outside Nanny Mouse's cottage. I don't want to be here, he thought. I want to be out of Willow Court and its grounds, and away from everyone who lives here. He walked through the gates and strode down the road towards the village, oblivious to the world around him. He saw nothing but Beth's face as he'd begun to talk about that day. He should never have done it. It would be perfectly natural now for her to want to know exactly what he'd been about to say.

The tumult in Alex's head subsided a little as he walked. Perhaps Beth wouldn't bring it up again. She must have noticed how distressed he was just before Chloë popped up. Thank God she did! He had no idea what he would have said if she hadn't. He could never tell Beth the truth.

Alex had never spoken to anyone about what had really happened to Mark. He was quite sure of one thing: his brother was convinced that Alex had seen nothing. He knew this because he'd lied from the very first. Even at six years old, some instinct told Alex that he had to do this.

It wasn't my fault, Alex. Was it? He shouldn't have come. He shouldn't have shouted.

I didn't notice. I was over there. What's the matter, Efe? What's the matter with Markie?

Nothing. Shut up. I've got to think. Where's Beth?
Gone to get Mummy.

That was the last time Alex could remember seeing his brother weeping. He'd been down on the ground next to Markie, cradling the little boy's head on his lap. Efe's face had been red and wet and his eyes swollen almost shut from all the tears.

Alex hadn't known what to do at the time and, even all these years later, thinking about how useless he'd been made him feel ashamed. Maybe if I'd told him then exactly what I'd seen, he thought, and then comforted him in some way, everything would be different. It occurred to Alex that perhaps it was *because* Efe had suppressed the events of that day that he had become the sort of person he was, someone who was comfortable with deception, someone who didn't allow himself to show too much affection, even to the people he loved.

As he walked, Alex decided that if Beth asked him what he'd meant to say, he'd make something up, anything really, as long as it wasn't the truth. There was also the possibility that Beth would never ask him. If she suspected that the story he was about to tell her reflected badly on her beloved Efe, maybe she simply wouldn't want to know it.

He came to a sudden stop. That's it, he thought. I started telling Beth about that day because I wanted her to think less of Efe. She loves him too much. I've always known that, really.

He turned and started walking back to Willow Court, not exactly sure why he was so worried for Beth. Perhaps it was because he knew that nothing good could come of her love for Efe that Alex wondered whether to warn her or to do what he generally did and keep quiet. Whatever he did, it would probably turn out to be wrong. Oh, bloody hell, he thought. This isn't going to be easy at all.

Beth could hear splashing noises coming from the bathroom as she made her way to her room to change for dinner. It was Douggie's bathtime and the house rang with his shouts. As she approached the bathroom, she became aware of another noise. Someone was crying. It was Fiona. She was trying to be quiet, but the door stood open, and Beth could hear suppressed sobs and sniffs beneath Douggie's splashing and babbling. For a split second she considered walking silently past and closing her bedroom door, pretending she hadn't heard, but then curiosity mixed with some sort of impulse to be kind made her go in.

Fiona was sitting on the low stool beside the bath, dabbing at her eyes and nose with a wodge of tissues. Douggie was moving a little toy boat through imaginary waves. Fiona's face was pale and blotchy and her eyes were red-rimmed and filled with tears.

'Fiona . . . sorry. Only I heard a noise and thought I'd better come in and see . . .' Beth's voice faded away. She coughed and said more firmly, 'Would you like me to dry Douggie?'

Fiona nodded. 'Would you? I feel so awful. I'd better wash my face. Here's his towel. Thanks, Beth. I don't know what's the matter with me.'

'Come on, darling,' Beth said to Douggie. 'Time to go and put your pyjamas on now.' She picked the little boy up, wrapped him up in a towel and hugged him to her. She looked over at Fiona, who was calmer now and making an effort to smile.

'Thanks so much, Beth,' she said. 'Take no notice, really. It all just got too much for me. Let's go to my room.'

Fiona led the way down the corridor and held the door open. 'It's a bit of a mess, I'm afraid,' she said. 'I haven't felt like tidying it.'

'When I've dressed Douggie,' Beth said, 'I'll give you a hand.'

She prevented Fiona from saying any more by talking to Douggie in a constant stream of childish chatter. It was hard not to feel sorry for Fiona, but still she couldn't bear to imagine her with Efe, just over there in the double bed, without a sharp pang of jealousy. Think about something else, she told herself. Talk to Fiona.

'D'you want to talk about it? Whatever's wrong, I mean?' Beth pulled up Douggie's pyjama bottoms. I'm not saying the right thing, she thought. She'd be much better off talking to almost anyone else.

'I don't know what to say, especially not to you,' Fiona answered. 'I mean, you and Efe are so close. I feel quite jealous sometimes when you're chatting.' Beth looked so amazed at this revelation that Fiona smiled. 'You didn't know that, did you? I'm sorry. It's not your fault, but I *am* stupid where Efe's concerned. I know that. I expect he'd like me to be a different sort of person, but I can't be.'

'No, I'm sure he wouldn't,' Beth said. 'He's devoted to you.'

'Has he said?' Fiona asked, desperation in her voice.

Beth found herself lying without any hesitation. 'Oh, yes,' she said.

Fiona seemed visibly to brighten. 'I do try, you know. To do what he wants me to do. I try all the time.'

'Maybe you shouldn't,' Beth said, taking Douggie onto her lap and cuddling him. 'Maybe you should assert yourself more.'

Fiona's eyes widened. 'I daren't,' she said. 'He gets so angry if anyone disagrees with him. Look.' She pushed her sleeve back, up above her elbow, and held out her arm for Beth to examine. There were bruises on the white skin, blue marks of fingers digging into flesh.

Beth was shocked and revolted by this evidence of Efe's brutality. She swallowed and said to Fiona, 'He shouldn't be allowed to do this to you.'

'He lost his temper. He apologised straight away, really. He was terribly, terribly sorry. Really. I'm only showing you because you suggested I should stand up to him. It's just easier to agree, that's all.'

Beth stroked Douggie's hair. 'Has he ever hurt you before?'

Fiona nodded. 'Once or twice. It's always my fault. And he's always sorry. It doesn't mean he doesn't love me.'

Beth stood up, feeling nauseous. What could she say? You mustn't put up with it? You must leave him? Suddenly, she wanted to be alone to think. I must be stupid, she told herself, if knowing that Efe is capable of such behaviour doesn't make me think of him differently.

'I've got to go and get ready for dinner now, Fiona,' she said. 'Will you be OK?'

'Yes, of course I will, Beth. Thanks so much for helping with Douggie. Everything just gets too much, all of a sudden, you know.'

'Of course I do,' Beth said. She went over to Fiona and kissed her on the cheek. 'You look after yourself.'

She glanced at the dressing table as she spoke. What caught her eye was a photograph in a leather frame that Fiona must have brought with her and put up next to her make-up. It showed them being a family, her and Efe and Douggie. The little boy was on his father's shoulders and grabbing at his hair. Fiona was looking up at them both, with her hair blowing across her face. She looked radiant. They were walking down a beach somewhere with nothing but blue skies behind them.

Late afternoon sunlight made golden diamond shapes on the raspberry-pink carpet in Leonora's bedroom. Leonora lay on the bed with her eyes closed, ticking off a mental checklist of things that should have been done for Sunday's party. Every one of them had been. The marquee had been erected successfully and without fuss. It looked wonderful already, with the lights in place and the lining falling smooth and pale green from the central point, like a circus tent. They'd started putting up the decorations, and tomorrow the chairs and tables were arriving and the final touches would be added, flowers and pale green tablecloths.

Leonora suspected that perhaps when you were seventy-five you ought not to be feeling this rising thrill at the idea of a party, but she couldn't help it. She thought of all the guests who would be coming to Willow Court on Sunday. The only person who won't be here, she thought sadly, is my beloved Peter. Rage at the unfairness of this swept over her suddenly and she closed her eyes. Peter. She tried not to think about him too often, but now she allowed herself to remember everything.

June 1948

Leonora woke up very early on the day after her wedding, and she was a different person from the one who'd gone to bed last night. She turned to look at Peter's head on the pillow next to her own and wondered how it was possible to be so close to another human being and still find them mysterious. Peter awake, Peter talking to her or kissing her she could say she knew, but this sleeping man was altogether strange and wonderful. She wanted to put a hand out and stroke his face. She wanted him to wake up and fold her body in his arms again.

She smiled to remember how Nanny Mouse had tried to tell her about what would happen when her new husband took her into bed. 'I have to mention these matters,' she'd said a few days before the wedding. 'I wish your poor mother had lived and been able to talk to you about the duties of a wife.' Her head was turned to examine a piece of darning and she was careful not to meet Leonora's gaze.

'I love Peter, Nanny,' Leonora tried to help, to suggest that this conversation was quite unnecessary, but Nanny Mouse went doggedly on.

'Men have certain needs, dear. It's a wife's duty to submit to those needs, and I believe at first the act itself can be quite painful. Though they do say you get used to it.'

Leonora stifled a giggle. 'It's all right, Nanny,' she said. 'I do know all about that. Really.'

This wasn't altogether true, but Nanny Mouse relaxed visibly and even managed to look at Leonora and smile at her.

'Good, dear. I just wanted to make sure you wouldn't be frightened.'

'No, I could never be frightened of Peter. I love him.'

Everything had happened both too quickly for her to be aware of any conscious thought, and also so slowly that she thought the world must have stopped turning. Perhaps she had a special talent for love because she'd felt no pain, or perhaps the blinding flood of feeling was what other people thought of as hurting. I didn't, Leonora thought. I don't.

For what seemed like hours, Peter had kissed her all over, touched her, spoken words into her ear that warmed and melted her. She'd never realised how close two bodies could be. One flesh. That was what they had become. And Leonora longed for those feelings all over again.

She turned her head to see whether Peter was awake yet, but he wasn't. His eyelids were pale blue and she could see veins in his forehead she'd never noticed before. She closed her eyes.

The words from yesterday's ceremony sounded in her head, weirdly entwined with those of the funeral service: *Who gives this woman . . . to love and to cherish . . . ashes to ashes . . . in sure and certain hope of the resurrection . . . let no man put asunder.*

It was now three full weeks since her father's death, and still Leonora expected to see him every day. When she woke up each morning, the fact of his no longer being at Willow Court came to her like a blow.

He died on the afternoon before Leonora's wedding was to take place. The housekeeper found him slumped in his favourite armchair. The doctor said it must have been a heart attack.

Leonora couldn't help feeling cheated of a farewell from her father. She felt ashamed that her grief was mingled with anger at Ethan Walsh for spoiling her wedding. Now everything would have to be rearranged.

'Never mind, darling,' Peter said. 'We'll have the wedding in a few weeks. You will be just as beautiful then. I'm happy to wait for you.'

And here she was, exactly three weeks later, and she was married. The wedding had been a quieter affair than she'd planned, but she had worn the dress—white satin, ankle-length, the bodice embroidered with tiny seed pearls—and her friends had been there to celebrate.

As soon as her father was buried, things began to change at Willow Court. Peter helped her to understand matters she'd previously dismissed as boring, like investments and income. She was surprised to find that she was wealthy, even though, as Peter said, 'You must have known that you'd be inheriting all your parents' money and property.'

She *had* known, but the knowledge had never meant anything until now, when the money could be used to make Willow Court beautiful. They'd talked about how they would take down the dowdy old curtains and put up new ones, and paint the rooms in pastel colours and have new parquet laid on some of the floors, and replace some of the black and white tiles in the hall that had cracked over the years.

For the first time since it had stopped being a convalescent home for wounded soldiers, music was being played. As soon as Peter came into the house, he put a record on the gramophone in the drawing room. Glen Miller, Duke Ellington, Billie Holiday and Louis Armstrong—they were the ones she loved best. The melodies were lodged in Leonora's heart. 'String of Pearls', 'Mood Indigo' and 'I Can't Give You Anything But Love', the song that Peter used to sing to her, imitating Armstrong's gravelly voice very badly and making her laugh.

'Wake up, my love,' said a voice in Leonora's ear. 'Wake up, Mrs Simmonds.'

'I've been awake for ages,' Leonora whispered. 'I've been thinking about all sorts of things and waiting for you to wake up.'

'What were you thinking about? Tell me.'

He started to kiss her then, and she wanted to say, *I can't remember. I can't remember anything. You're the only thing I can think of. Just you.* But the words were starting to slip and slide about in her head and soon she had no thoughts that could properly be called thoughts at all.

Gwendolen Elizabeth Simmonds was born in her parents' bedroom at Willow Court on February 7, 1952. King George VI had died the day before, and the papers carried photographs of the new Queen, who used to be Princess Elizabeth, wearing black and heavily veiled at the King's funeral. Leonora's labour had lasted only six hours and, even though she'd been in agony and shrieking like a banshee, the midwife told her she'd had an easy time of it. It was true that within minutes of the birth, every bit of pain seemed to have been forgotten in the joy of meeting the daughter that she and Peter together had made.

The whole country was feeling sad, but Leonora and Peter were happier than they'd ever been. Calling their baby after the new Queen, even only as a second name, was their way of showing how sorry they were to lose the King, who'd been much too young to die. Gwendolen's first name honoured Peter's late grandmother. Leonora had thought that perhaps she would name the baby after her own mother, but then they'd agreed that Maude sounded too old-fashioned and Victorian.

Towards the end of her pregnancy, Leonora had worried about being able to love the child when it was born. She and Peter were so bound up in one another that it seemed to her anyone else coming into their lives was sure to receive short rations.

They'd had three years together, and they still found it hard to restrain their desire. A transformation overcame them when they were alone. They turned from ordinary people who went to work in a firm of insurance brokers, or managed the house and estate, or had dinner and tea with their friends, into panting, heedless creatures who bit and sucked and kissed every part of each other's bodies for hours and yet ended up wanting only more of one another. Their bed was a separate universe where even speech was unrecognisable; where words and sentences splintered into a private, intimate language of their own.

Now here was this tiny creature with her waving pink fingers and her tightly shut eyes and Leonora looked down at her and realised that the love she felt for this baby was different from anything she had ever felt before, but, miraculously, no less strong. Peter, she could see, was enchanted by his daughter and sat beside the bed staring at her.

'She's the most beautiful baby in the whole world,' he said. 'I bet every father says that, but it's true in this case. She looks just like you.'

'She looks like a baby,' Leonora said, gazing at her daughter, and feeling love flow into every part of her in exactly the same way as the milk was coming into her breasts.

'I'm so happy, my darling,' Peter said. 'I love you both so much.' He leaned over the baby and kissed Leonora on the mouth. 'I couldn't possibly love you more than I do, and now Gwendolen's going to be the most adored baby in the world.'

Leonora couldn't find any words to express what she wanted to say. She closed her eyes and leaned back against the heaped-up pillows.

Gwendolen Elizabeth soon became Gwen. She was a most untroublesome baby. She loved sleeping; she never stopped smiling; she didn't mind Nanny Mouse looking after her when her mother was otherwise occupied; she burbled at her father whenever he picked her up, and everyone agreed that she was the best-tempered child they'd ever seen.

The work on Willow Court went on, and neither Leonora nor Peter ever tired of making things more beautiful. One day in May, just before the Coronation, Peter said, 'It's time now, darling. Let's go up to the studio and bring all the paintings down. Let's hang them everywhere.'

At first, Leonora didn't know what she felt about seeing her father's pictures all over the house, but after thinking about it for a while, she knew she would be happy to have them around her again. 'It's taken me a bit of time to realise it,' she said to Peter at dinner, 'but Willow Court didn't feel right without them. And they deserve to be seen, don't they?'

Peter picked up his glass and took a sip of wine. 'Actually,' he said, 'I think it's a pity we can't sell just a few. There was that chap, don't you remember? The one who came to see you after Ethan died? He wanted to pay you a great deal of money, as I recall, for that portrait of you in the lilac dress.'

'I'm not allowed to, Peter. You know that. Daddy's will made that quite clear. The paintings are to stay at Willow Court.'

Peter understood better than she did the complicated legal clauses which meant that her children would have no claim on the estate if the paintings were sold. It was all too confusing, but she'd never made the effort to understand the detail for the simple reason that she had no intention whatsoever of selling the pictures her father had created. They were part of him, the very best part, and now that she could see them again, she realised how much she loved them.

'Anyway,' she added, 'I gave him my word.'

She thought about her father while Peter poured the coffee. Being a widower hadn't suited him. He'd stopped painting altogether, and nothing Leonora said or did made any difference. Walking in the Quiet Garden one day, sitting under the magnolia tree, Leonora had dared to ask gently, 'Wouldn't this make a painting, Daddy? Isn't it beautiful?'

'Sentimental nonsense, flowers,' he answered. 'Not my sort of thing.'

'But the water lily pictures, Daddy! And the one with the roses on the table. You paint flowers so beautifully. And everyone loves them. We could make a lot of money, you know, if you sold some of them.'

Her father frowned. 'Over my dead body,' he said. 'The pictures stay here, at Willow Court.' Suddenly he leaned forward and stared into Leonora's eyes. 'Promise me, Leonora,' he said. 'Promise me they'll never be sold. Not even when I'm dead. Promise.'

And I did promise, Leonora thought. I had to. Daddy always got his way and he's still getting it, more than four years after his death. She said to Peter, 'I kept that man's card. The man from the gallery. His name's Jeremy Bland. I shall telephone him and ask him down to have a look and tell me what he thinks of the paintings. We can make money from them, don't you think? We can let people into Willow Court to see them. If they're as good as all that, everyone will be longing to come.'

'Would you want every Tom, Dick and Harry traipsing around the house? I don't know if I think it's such a good idea, darling.'

'But we'd become famous, Peter. You'd like that, wouldn't you? Imagine, there might be photographs of us in a magazine. We don't have to open the house every day, either. We can choose when we let people in.'

'Oh, well,' said Peter, 'if it means that much to you, I won't object.'

'You're a darling.' Leonora smiled at him. 'I hadn't realised how much I've missed those pictures. Daddy would be pleased, wouldn't he? He'd have loved the idea of people walking round, admiring his handiwork.'

'Look! Look, Gwen, darling!' Leonora pointed at the tiny screen of the television where a grainy greyish picture of the coach carrying the new queen back from Westminster Abbey was partly visible through what looked like a snowstorm. It wasn't really a snowstorm, just a rather unclear picture, but still, everyone had gathered in the drawing room to watch the royal progress.

Gwen was on Leonora's lap. 'Ween!' she lisped, and everyone laughed.

'Yes, it's the new Queen, sweetiepie,' Leonora whispered into her baby's ear. 'Can you see her crown?'

Gwen nodded gravely.

'It's been quite a day,' said Peter, who had come in from the office specially to watch the ceremony on the television. Leonora's friend, Bunny Forster, and her husband Nigel were there, too, and the occasion had turned into a party of sorts. It wasn't every day that a monarch was crowned, after all. In the end, though, when the tea things had been cleared away, Bunny and Nigel went home, and Nanny Mouse took Gwen upstairs to have her bath.

'I know what you're going to say,' Leonora said to Peter, leaning back against the cushions of the sofa.

'No, you don't.'

'I do. You're going to say *Peace at last.* Or something along those lines.'

'A good guess, but not quite. I was actually going to say *Alone at last!*'

'You sound surprised. We're often alone.'

'Not often enough for me.' He came over to the sofa and sat down next to Leonora and put his arms round her.

'Oh, darling! We're an old married couple. Much too old to canoodle on a sofa. There's a proper place for such things, you know.'

She didn't mean a word of it. They would be undisturbed for a while, and they were both aware of that, and aware of the special festive atmosphere that had coloured the whole day. They'd had rather a lot of champagne at lunch and Leonora's head was swimming a little.

All at once, everything was happening very quickly. Her skirt and the silk slip she wore under it pushed up, and her knickers somehow on the carpet and Peter making love to her and the delicious terror that maybe someone would overhear them or see them so they had to be quick and it was easy to be quick because they couldn't stop and all the sounds rising in their throats and being stifled, and then nothing but silence broken by panting as though they'd been running for a long time.

Afterwards, they arranged their clothes and lay back against the cushions. 'Time to go and kiss Gwen good night, I think,' Peter said at last.

'You go first,' Leonora murmured. 'I'll be there in a minute.'

She could have gone with him, but she didn't want to. She wanted to sit on the sofa and remember this time. Remember how full of love she was for him. How heavy her limbs were. How very little she felt like ever getting up and moving again.

'**D**arling? Darling, can you hear me?' Leonora was speaking clearly into the telephone, which still struck her as a rather magical invention.

'I can hear you, Leonora,' said Peter. He sounded amused but she was aware that he probably wanted to get on with his work. Never mind, she thought. He'll forget all about that when I tell him the news.

'I wanted you to know at once. I was going to wait till you came home, only Dr Benyon's just been and I want to tell Nanny Mouse but I can't tell her before I tell you and so I thought I'd telephone.'

'Can I guess?' Peter sounded different now.

'I expect you can. We're going to have another baby. Oh, Peter, I wish you could be here.'

'Oh, darling, that's the most wonderful news. The very best news. Oh God, I can't stay here now. I shall come home.I'll be as quick as I can.'

Leonora replaced the telephone in its cradle and wondered what she should do until Peter arrived. Nanny Mouse had taken Gwen upstairs for her afternoon nap. The September afternoon was warm and sunny. I'll go for a walk round the lake, she decided, and by the time I come back to the house, Peter might be here to greet me.

As she walked slowly round the lake, smiling at the swans, Leonora focused all her attention on the person growing in her womb. She put her hand on her still-flat stomach and wondered briefly whether the child she was carrying was a boy or a girl. She could never understand why anyone would care about such things. If the child was healthy and happy, that was quite enough.

What time was it? Leonora looked at her watch and began to walk more quickly. She'd been out daydreaming for over an hour. Even if Peter isn't home yet, she thought, Gwen must have woken up by now.

She made her way through the Wild Garden and then over the lawn to the terrace. There were two police cars parked near the front door and at first Leonora wondered what they could possibly want at Willow Court. She stepped into the hall and saw them, two male police officers and a woman constable, holding their hats in their hands. She would have found some explanation that didn't affect her, if it hadn't been for Nanny Mouse, who ran towards Leonora, her face wet with tears.

'Oh, Leonora,' she said, folding her in her arms. 'Be brave, my love. Oh, it's so dreadful, my poor darling. Never mind, never mind.'

Leonora felt herself becoming ice cold all over. She pushed Nanny Mouse away roughly and part of her wanted to turn round and say sorry but her mouth was dry and she could only make sounds, like a baby.

'Mrs Simmonds,' said the woman constable. 'Please come and sit down.' She took hold of Leonora's elbow and guided her to a chair.

Leonora didn't want to sit down. 'I don't know why you're here, but if you are prepared to wait a little while, my husband will come home and I'm sure he'll be happy to answer any questions you may wish to ask.'

Behind her, Nanny Mouse stifled a cry.

The most senior of the police officers—you could tell, because he was grey-haired and looked like someone's strict uncle—came to her and gently indicated that she should sit down. 'I'm afraid we have some very bad news, Mrs Simmonds. Very bad news indeed.'

Grief shrouded Leonora like a thick fog, and for days after that terrible afternoon when she'd listened with every appearance of calm to what the police had told her *(driving too fast . . . a tree . . . instantaneous death)* and then fainted away, she had wept until she felt there was not a bit of moisture left in her body. When the tears stopped, everything she laid eyes on filled her with rage. She hid the records he loved in a box in a corner of the studio. She took the love letters she'd hidden in the doll's house years before and put them with all the others in the biscuit tin in her bottom drawer. Maybe she would burn them. She couldn't even glance at his handwriting without wanting to burst into tears. Looking at Gwen filled her with pain. It wasn't that she resembled him at all, only that her very presence in the world was a result of their love, their passion, and thinking about that was unbearable. She felt a howl of anguish rising in her throat, and the small moans she found herself uttering seemed ridiculous, no reflection of how much she was hurting.

Sleep had disappeared from her life. Every night she lay in their bed in a half-doze, her mind alive with memories, her body aching for Peter's touch, her whole being raw and sore as though someone had taken a knife to her skin and removed it.

Nanny Mouse tried to help her. She cajoled and soothed and stroked Leonora's brow with a cool damp cloth after hours of tears had turned her into a red-eyed, swollen-faced creature who bore little resemblance to the elegant Mrs Simmonds. In the end, that was how Nanny Mouse made her pull herself together sufficiently to attend the funeral.

'Leonora dear, it's Peter's funeral tomorrow morning. I've taken out your black suit and brushed it, and the hat with the veil. But now, you know, you will have to take yourself in hand a little.'

'How can you speak of such things, Nanny? Don't you realise what I've lost? My whole life, my whole happiness, everything.'

'Nonsense,' said Nanny Mouse. 'You are a mother. Gwen needs you. She will need you even more now she is fatherless, poor little thing.'

Leonora wanted to shout obscenities at this stupid woman who was telling her to pull herself together when she knew she would never be able to face the world again. I don't have to, she suddenly thought. I can die. I can take pills and never wake up again. She closed her eyes and considered this for a moment, but that voice, that Nanny voice that had been in her ears since the day she was born, went on speaking.

'I know you'd never do anything foolish. You know, after all, what it is for a girl to grow up without a mother. Think of little Gwen, and think of what Peter would say if he knew you'd abandoned his daughter.'

It was that possessive pronoun that brought her to her senses. Gwen was indeed Peter's daughter. Leonora opened her eyes and sniffed and said, 'Thank you, Nanny. I will have a bath now. And, yes, I will be perfectly all right for the funeral. I shan't disgrace you. Or Peter.'

Saying his name aloud was torture, but she gritted her teeth and continued, 'I wish I'd never told him. I wish I'd waited. Oh God, it's too late to wish anything, but I do because if it hadn't been for me telling him . . .'

'Telling him what, dear?' Nanny Mouse looked puzzled.

Leonora smiled. 'I thought you might have guessed. I'm pregnant again. I'm going to have a baby next March. I'd phoned Peter to tell him. That was why he was hurrying home. I think he died because of that. Oh, Nanny, Nanny, what will I do without him? How will I manage?'

'You will manage by getting through one day at a time. You mustn't think of the future. And you must try not to think of the past either. Not yet. There'll be time for that later.'

The small village church was full for Peter's funeral. All their friends, all his colleagues from work and from his days in the army crowded into the pews. Nanny Mouse stood beside Leonora, ready to catch her if she should faint. She was, after all, nearly three months pregnant.

Leonora had helped herself to some Dutch courage before the ceremony. A quick swig from the whisky decanter and she felt a little better. A little less shaky. If Nanny Mouse finds out, she thought, she'll be cross. It's not good for you in your condition, she'd say. But I don't mind what happens to me. I don't want this baby. This baby made Peter die. I don't want to have it. I wish it would go away and never be born. Maybe it won't. Maybe I'll have a miscarriage. I'll pray for one while I'm in the church. Oh God, no. What am I saying? Oh, Peter, don't listen to me. I'm not myself. I'm not. I'm mad with grief, thinking things no one should ever think. But how I wish I'd waited to tell you. You would have driven home slowly. You'd still be alive, and so would I.

The words of the funeral service went past her ears like blown leaves. She followed the coffin out to the place under the yew trees where a hole was waiting. The black veil on her hat covered her face a little but she knew that they were all watching her to see how brave she was. I'm not brave, she wanted to shout. I want to die too. I want to jump in and have earth filling my mouth and covering me up and then I'd never have to suffer ever again . . . Gwen, she thought. Think of Gwen. Think of how much Peter loved her and how angry he'd be if he knew you'd left her. She closed her eyes. Let it be finished, she said to herself, as the vicar's voice blew away in the wind . . . *all flesh is as grass* . . . *dust to dust.* Oh, Peter, my darling. Where have you gone?

Leonora gave birth to her second daughter on a wild day in March 1954. The labour was long and painful, and by the time it was over and her baby was placed in her arms, she was exhausted. She looked down at a red-faced, crumpled creature wrapped up in a blanket, and began to cry, bitter tears of grief and complete weariness.

'What a bonny baby,' said the midwife. 'Have you thought of a name for her?'

'Not really,' said Leonora. 'I'm sure I'll think of something.'

She closed her eyes and wished she never had to open them again. It was seven months since Peter's death. She'd fallen in with what was required of her by her friends and Nanny Mouse. She'd looked after Gwen and read her stories and given her a little patch of earth to dig in the garden and she'd waited for the arrival of her second child, all the while filled with a resentment that she wasn't allowed to express.

Nanny Mouse brought Gwen to see her sister. 'Babba!' said Gwen, and put out a finger to stroke the fine reddish hairs on the baby's head.

Now Leonora considered the baby and wondered what to name it. The doctor she'd consulted to help her with her grief had been a kindly man called Cyril Rotherspoon, with a practice in Swindon, and now he came into her mind. Why not? she thought. It'll do. *Cyrilla.* It sounds like the heroine of a romance. The baby started to rootle around for the breast, and Leonora sighed, and allowed the greedy mouth to fasten on her nipple. There was nothing to be done about it. She was weeping all over again. She felt as though her sorrow would go on for ever.

Evening, Friday, August 23, 2002

The conversation at dinner was more tentative than usual. It seemed to Leonora that everyone was guarding their tongues.

She turned to her elder daughter. 'You look a little preoccupied, Gwen dear. Is something the matter?'

'No, Mummy, I'm just going over my checklist in my head. I'm so sorry. Did I miss part of the conversation?'

'No, not at all. I don't think we've had much conversation tonight.' Leonora noticed that every face was suddenly turned towards her and she smiled to show she wasn't blaming anyone. She said, 'Rilla, I believe you and Sean went down to see Nanny Mouse. How is she?'

'She was rather well, actually,' Rilla said. 'She knew who we were for most of the time. But . . .' She paused. 'There was one rather interesting thing. She seemed to be saying that Ethan Walsh was cruel to Maude.'

'I don't think you ought to put too much faith in Nanny Mouse, even at her clearest. I don't remember anything like that at all,' Leonora said quickly, but she found that her heart had started to beat rather fast and her mouth was suddenly dry. She took a sip of water.

Rilla's remarks had certainly got some conversation going, and that had been what she wanted. She let the talk flow over her, and fixed her eyes on the shadows behind Rilla's chair at the far end of the table. The lights in this room were deliberately kept low because Leonora couldn't bear dazzle. She'd never really thought of herself as old before, but lately the physical world was behaving so strangely that she'd begun to think this was how things were when you were about to turn seventy-five.

Look at what was happening, for instance, at the other end of the table. Rilla was dissolving. She was shimmering and shifting and when Leonora tried to make her out properly, she wasn't there. She'd disappeared and someone else was sitting in her chair. Leonora blinked. It's Maude, she thought. She opened her mouth to say 'Mummy' and realised suddenly that she must be the only person in the room who could see what she supposed she ought to call a ghost.

'Are you all right, Leonora?' James was speaking to her, leaning towards her looking anxious.

'Yes, yes, of course. Nothing to fuss about. I just felt a little faint for a moment. Too much apple pie, I expect.'

'Let's go through to the drawing room for coffee, Mother,' said Gwen.

'Yes, a cup of coffee would be most welcome. Thank you, darling.' Leonora stood up, and as they walked out into the hall she said, 'I've never really liked the dining room, you know. It's such a cold place.'

'It used to be,' Gwen agreed. 'But you've made it look lovely now. Not a bit cold any more.' She hurried on to the kitchen to organise the coffee.

Leonora went into the drawing room and sat down in her favourite armchair. I'd almost forgotten, she thought, why I hate that room. Seeing Maude there reminded me. They'd let me come in sometimes as a special treat and I couldn't bear it. It was full of icy silences and I remember feeling that at any moment Mummy might break into pieces and Daddy might shout, or be very cross. With me or with her.

Leonora sat up all at once, listening out for Gwen, and thought she heard someone sighing, and stifling a sob. Over there by the sofa. The room was in near darkness. 'Fiona? Is that you?' she whispered. Fiona had been crying before dinner, she was almost sure of that.

No one answered her question, and there was a rustling of something in the dimness near her and a fragrance of lily of the valley.

'Here we are, Mother!' Gwen put the tray down and switched on the lamp. Magical electric light scattered the phantoms.

'Can you smell something?' said Leonora. 'Scent . . . lily of the valley.'

'No, I can't, I'm afraid. Actually, it's not a perfume I like at all,' Gwen said, as she arranged the cups and saucers. 'Maybe Fiona? She does lay it on a bit thick sometimes, but I hadn't noticed it being lily of the valley.'

'It doesn't matter, darling. I expect I was imagining it.'

Could you imagine a fragrance, Leonora wondered. Could a perfume linger in the air for more than sixty years? She closed her eyes. There was something like a door in her mind which she felt she was desperately trying to keep closed while something, or someone, was pushing at it from the other side. Nonsense, she said to herself. I'm becoming silly and fanciful in my old age. A cup of coffee will pull me together.

Saturday, August 24, 2002

I'M CINDERELLA IN REVERSE, Rilla thought, and giggled. Going out after midnight instead of coming home. It's Saturday already, and I've had too much wine. I'm unsteady on my feet, or maybe it's these shoes. She kicked them off and left them on the path. I'll collect them on my way back, she thought. I don't need them now. The night was stiflingly hot and the moon, coming and going behind puffs of cloud, diluted the darkness and washed the whole garden in a sort of grey, shadowy light.

She set off again over the lawn towards the gazebo, wondering how many years it was since she'd felt the cool grass under her bare feet. This was the very path she followed on days when Hugh came to stay. Rilla smiled. It was a miracle, really, the ways they'd found to outwit Leonora, who always had her eyes peeled for any hint of amorous behaviour. The gazebo was one of their favourite trysting places. Hugh had called it that, a trysting place. Rilla was surprised to find that she could say his name to herself and not feel overwhelmed by a rising tide of regret and fury.

She had reached the gazebo. It was quite beautiful, a hexagon of wrought iron and glass, with a white-painted bench running all round the walls. Ethan Walsh had it built for his wife on their second wedding anniversary. So Leonora said. She also said she remembered her mother sitting there for hours, reading or just staring into space.

We found different things to do here, Rilla thought, Hugh and I. She opened the door and let herself in. The moon was hidden for the moment behind thick cloud, but Rilla didn't want to risk glancing up to see a flash of silvery water somewhere beyond the trees. She sat down facing away from the lake and closed her eyes. Where was Sean?

All through dinner she had been longing to leave the table and get out—out here where he'd be arriving, he said, as soon as he could. But where was he? Maybe he'd changed his mind. Rilla shivered and firmly pushed this thought away. He *will* come, she told herself. He must. I'm not going back to the house. Not yet.

She leaned her head against the back of the chair and made herself think about something else. Hugh. They'd come here once after swimming naked in the lake. It was about three in the morning and the weather was hot and airless. They'd sunk into one of the chairs, oblivious to everything but the demands of skin and flesh and open, gasping mouths. Rilla smiled. When you were young you didn't care about anything. Not comfort, not shame, nothing. The fire in the blood just burned through whatever was in its path. Hugh. She could practically taste him, even after all these years.

July / August 1971

I hate her. I absolutely hate her. I wish I didn't have to live in this horrible place with horrible people who don't understand anything, not any of them. Not Mummy, not Nanny Mouse, and not Gwen, who's never here anyway but in bloody Switzerland most of the time, learning how to fold napkins, and only coming home for a couple of weekends over the summer with James in tow because she's two years older and she can do what she wants and not have anyone criticise her.

Rilla's thoughts went round and round in her head and she could hardly see through her tears. Nevertheless, she was marching down the avenue of scarlet oaks towards the gate and freedom. Everything would be all right once she'd got away from Willow Court.

'You are not,' her mother had said, just as she was about to open the front door, 'leaving this house looking like that.'

'Looking like what?' Rilla had answered. 'I don't know what you mean.'

'Well, then, I shall tell you.' Leonora looked Rilla up and down. 'Your skirt is too short. Your blouse is too tight. You have too much eye make-up on and high-heeled shoes are inappropriate for a trip to the village. Go back to your room and put on something more suitable.'

'It's none of your business how I look,' Rilla said. Unfortunately, the front door was so heavy that slamming it shut was never an option, but she did her best to leave in a way that would convey her fury.

As soon as she had run down the steps to the drive, the tumult in her head began. Now that she was nearly at the gate, it had subsided somewhat and she was thinking more normally.

She slowed down a little on the road to the village and part of her had to confess that her shoes were killing her. I don't care, she said to herself. They're beautiful. And Hugh will love the way I look in them. Her heart began to thump. I shan't think about Mummy or anyone else. I'm going to meet him. Hugh. I'm going to meet Hugh.

Rilla was in love. She'd fallen in love at eleven o'clock on a Tuesday morning, three weeks ago. She remembered this because while she was in the shop and speaking to him for the first time the church clock was chiming. He'd been behind her in the queue and as she turned to go she'd bumped into him and stumbled over his feet. He'd had to grab her by the arms so that she didn't fall over. 'Terribly sorry!' he said, and he had a voice like someone you heard on the radio.

'That's OK,' she said, her whole body trembling. 'It was my fault. I wasn't looking where I was going.'

He held out his hand. 'Hello. I'm Hugh Kenworthy. Just moved into that cottage over there. For a bit of peace and quiet.'

'I'm Rilla Simmonds,' she said. 'I live at Willow Court.'

'Then you're very lucky,' he said. 'I went round Willow Court a few years back. Those pictures are quite amazing.' He smiled. 'I didn't see you though. I'm sure I'd have remembered.'

'I must have been at school,' Rilla said, making a face. 'But Ethan Walsh was my grandfather.'

Hugh's eyes widened. 'How astonishing! Really delighted to meet you, Rilla . . . and what an unusual name.'

'It's short for Cyrilla,' she said. She never told anyone that, but all she could think was, I wish we could stay talking like this for ever.

The other people in the queue were getting restless. He took her arm, and before she knew what was happening they were outside the shop, walking together towards his cottage.

He wasn't a bit like the men she met usually, but more like someone who might be on the cover of a magazine. His brown hair was long, falling almost to his shoulders, and his eyes were such a pale blue that they looked almost silver. He wore a denim shirt, jeans and cowboy boots. Rilla had no idea how old he was, but he was not a boy.

She knew all about boys. In fact, she was a bit of an expert. She'd kissed more of them than most girls in her class had done, and more than once she'd nearly gone all the way . . . but something had stopped her. Now, walking beside Hugh, she was glad she'd waited. His skin would feel rougher. His body would be hard. Rilla breathed in and out slowly, so that he shouldn't see what she was feeling.

'Here we are,' he said, opening the front door of a cottage at the end of the street. 'Come in and have a cup of coffee. Or are you expected at home? Maybe you'd better phone your mum or something.'

'No, that's OK,' she said, angry with him for a second before gratitude for his invitation flooded through her. 'I'm seventeen. Old enough to be out on my own.' She said it flirtatiously. Rilla was good at flirting.

He pointed to the sofa and smiled. 'Right. Fine. Sit down, then, and I'll see if I can find a couple of mugs that aren't dirty.'

Rilla had never seen a living room that was at the same time such a mess and so enchanting. There were books stacked on the floor, clothes heaped on chairs, records on the table next to an open jar of strawberry jam and, in the sink, used plates and cups and saucers in tottering piles that overflowed out onto the draining board. On the mantelpiece there were postcards, a clock and a vase of peacock feathers. On one wall was a huge mirror, its gilt frame decorated with fat cherubs.

'I like that!' she said.

'My grandmother's,' said Hugh. 'D'you take sugar in your coffee?'

'Yes, please. Two.'

He handed her the drink, then sat down on a chair opposite the sofa.

Rilla took a sip and said, 'I like your cottage. It's unusual, isn't it?'

'A mess, you mean. I'm sorry. I didn't know I was going to be entertaining. I'd have made more effort, truly.'

'That's OK,' said Rilla. 'I like it. Are you an actor?'

He shook his head. 'No, I'm a potter. I've got a kiln in a shed out in the garden. I used to work full-time in an advertising agency in London, but it all got too much . . . the rat race, and so on. So I've gone part-time, and this cottage is a sort of bolt hole. Somewhere to escape to, where I can be myself. And see whether I can make a go of the pots.'

'I'd love to live in London,' Rilla said. 'I think I'd enjoy the rat race. After the holidays, all I have is weeks of school to look forward to. But I'm leaving next year and then I'm going to drama school. My mother didn't want me to at first, but now she's given in. Well, Gwen, that's my sister, she's doing a domestic science course in Switzerland, so Mummy couldn't really say no. I'm dying to get there. It's so dead around here. There's nothing to do and no one to talk to.'

Hugh made a sad face, and Rilla laughed. 'I mean, till I met you.'

'I hope you feel you can talk to me,' he said. 'Or I shall be lonely, and I'd hate that. Will you come and visit me sometimes?'

'Yes,' said Rilla. 'I'd love to.' She put her cup down and stood up. 'I ought to get home now. My mother will wonder where I am if I stay any longer. I'm sorry I haven't finished my coffee. It was lovely, really.'

'My pleasure,' said Hugh. 'Do come again soon.'

He'd waved from the doorway as she walked to the gate. Mrs Pritchard, who lived next to the pub and was one of her mother's bridge ladies, was passing by on the other side of the road as she left. She can stare all she likes, Rilla thought. I don't care if it's not the done thing to go drinking cups of coffee with men who live on their own. I don't care about anything. For two pins, she'd have turned round and hammered on his door and cried, Let me in! I want to stay with you.

That was how it began. Now she was a totally different being and walked through her life in a daze, longing for Hugh every second they were apart. She'd fallen into the habit of going to see him in the afternoons when he wasn't in London. To her mother she said she was visiting this or that friend from her primary school days . . . a few of them still lived near the village. On her third visit, they went upstairs to the surprisingly tidy bedroom, and Rilla lost her virginity willingly, happily, and with considerably less pain than she'd been expecting.

'I've never spoken to anyone like this before,' Rilla said, turning to look at Hugh's profile on the pillow next to her. 'I didn't realise you could. I love you. I love this: just lying here like this with the sun coming in and everything.' She giggled. What would Mummy say, or Gwen, if they knew that she was here, in bed with a man? 'I think I must have been born into the wrong family,' she said.

He traced a line with his finger from where her hair ended, down her forehead and her nose. 'Little kids think they're in the wrong family, don't they?' he said. 'They've been kidnapped away from a king's house, or something like that. Is that what you mean?'

When she felt him touching her lips, she kissed him, and put out her tongue and licked the finger, tasting his skin. 'No, nothing like that. It's just that in my family everyone's so stiff, so formal. My mother is always properly dressed. I've never seen her in a dressing gown, for instance. She gets dressed as soon as she gets up. No chatting over cups of tea at the kitchen table for her. And my sister's nearly as bad.'

'She's older, right?'

'Yes. She's the good one in the family. She's very quiet and not at all like me. She's one of those people, you know, reliable and kind and good with animals. And she and Mummy get on much better than we do. Me and my mother, I mean. I annoy Mummy sometimes. She does her best to hide it, but it comes out every so often.'

'I can't imagine anyone not adoring you,' Hugh said, lying back on the pillows. 'Just can't imagine it.'

'Oh, she adores me, I expect,' Rilla said. 'But she gets annoyed all the same. It's what I told you. I'm not in the right family. Maybe I'm a whatsit. A changeling. The fairies came and stole her real baby away and left me instead. They're often redheads, aren't they? Changelings?'

Hugh was snoring slightly. He was always doing that, Rilla reflected. Men just naturally fell asleep quickly after sex. She'd read about it in books. I'm good at it, she said to herself. I'm good at sex. The thought made her happy. She became a different person when she was with Hugh, and it wasn't just the sex which, OK, was brilliant, and which she liked better than any other thing she'd ever done. But they talked, too, about everything: books, music, his work. He told her things. He asked her opinion and often agreed with her. He thought she was clever. She loved to watch him as he made his pots. He would throw the clay onto the wheel and stroke it into beautiful shapes. And when he kissed her, there in the shed behind the cottage where the wheel was, his hands—greyish and chalky from the drying clay—on her hair or her back, she sank into her own pleasure, maddened by wanting him so much.

She mooched around at Willow Court on the days when Hugh was up in London. He came down for only two or three nights a week and occasionally for a weekend. Soon the holidays would be over, and then she'd hardly ever see him at all. How was she going to concentrate on her A levels knowing he was just a few miles away?

Rilla got out of bed and went to the window. She drew back at once behind the curtain, because there was that Mrs Pritchard again. It was almost as though she came past the cottage deliberately when Rilla was there. Is she spying on me? she wondered. Nosy old woman. She was actually looking up at Hugh's bedroom window. What a cheek! There wasn't anything wrong with what she was doing. Some people would say that Hugh was too old for her, but ten years wasn't much at all. Her father had been seven years older than her mother, so Mummy couldn't object. So why didn't she take Hugh up to Willow Court and introduce him to Leonora? She didn't really know, but there was something wonderful about the fact that Hugh was her secret and she wanted to keep him to herself for a little longer. She slipped back into bed and began kissing Hugh's shoulder. His skin was golden and smooth.

He opened his eyes and smiled. 'Know something?' he murmured. 'You're a very greedy little girl.'

'You've no idea how greedy I am.' She could hardly speak.

'Show me, then,' he said, covering her body with his.

Hugh stopped being Rilla's secret on the day of the church summer fête. She walked slightly behind Leonora as they trailed round in the hot sun from one stall to the next, saying hello to everyone they met. Mummy knows everyone in the village, she thought, and just *has* to chat and let them bore us all silly. Who gives a shit about the size of Bill's marrows, or how *inspired* the white elephant stall is this year?

And, wouldn't you know it, Mrs Pritchard was running the cake stall, which was Rilla's favourite. She was just about to pay for a scrumptious-looking meringue when everything happened at once. Her mother came up on her left, Hugh came up on her right and Mrs Pritchard just had to say, 'Oh, Leonora dear, what an amazing coincidence! Here he is! The young man I was telling you about? The one who's taken the Albertons' cottage. You know Mr Kenworthy, Rilla, don't you?'

Then there were clumsy introductions, with Leonora saying how pleased she was to meet him and Hugh muttering about having meant to ask Rilla to take him up to Willow Court because he was such an admirer of Ethan Walsh. Then Hugh went off in one direction and Leonora and Rilla in another and she hadn't even had her meringue.

Typically, Leonora said nothing about Hugh till suppertime. Rilla had hardly taken a bite of her cold salmon salad when Leonora said, 'He's rather good-looking, isn't he, the chap who's taken the Albertons' cottage? I've forgotten his name.'

'Hugh Kenworthy,' said Rilla, thinking, *Liar! You've just done that to hear how I say his name.*

'D'you know him well? You've not mentioned him, have you?'

'No,' said Rilla. 'I don't know him terribly well. He's a potter. He chatted to me about the pictures in the shop, and I've had coffee with him a couple of times, that's all.'

Leonora looked at her daughter searchingly for a moment. 'You ought to ask him to come up here some time,' she said. 'Why don't you invite him for lunch next Sunday? Gwen and James might be coming up.'

'Right,' said Rilla. 'I will. That's a good idea.'

'It was vile! You were vile! I've never hated a day more in my life. Why did you have to . . .?' Rilla was screaming at Hugh. Part of her mind registered that this was their first row, but that didn't matter. She was so angry that even her love couldn't stop her.

'Stop it, Rilla!' Hugh was trying to be soothing. 'You're blowing this up out of all proportion. What actually are you so het up about?'

'You don't know? You're seriously telling me you don't know?' They were still in the lounge of the cottage. Normally, the moment she came through the door, they started kissing and were halfway upstairs before a word had been said, but not this time. 'I can't see straight. I don't know what to think. I can't believe you didn't realise.'

'Didn't realise *what* exactly?' said Hugh. He was sounding bored. How dare he sound bored?

'You didn't realise when you were swarming all around my mother and sister that you were hurting me? You didn't even look at me the entire day. We could have been strangers, people who mean nothing to one another. You kept talking to Mummy as though she was the most fascinating person in the world. You even disappeared with her for hours. What were you doing? How d'you think I felt? You didn't say a word to me the whole day . . .' Words failed Rilla and she burst into tears.

'You are a silly thing, Rilla darling,' Hugh said, gathering her into his arms. 'Did you really want everyone to know what I feel for you? Don't you think your mother might be a bit . . . upset to discover what her little girl has been up to? Your mother very kindly took me up to see Ethan Walsh's studio because I'd expressed an interest. That's all.'

'I wouldn't care if people knew about us!' Rilla said. 'I'm not ashamed.'

'I know, I know,' he murmured, kissing her on the lips, on the neck, touching her breasts, distracting her from her anger. 'Still, it's better not to rock the boat, don't you think? Aren't things good? Isn't this good?'

Rilla said nothing. She felt the fury slide away from her. Her body wouldn't let her keep it any longer. Never mind, she thought. He was pretending to be nice to them. He loves me. I can feel that he does, oh he does, he does, and I'm going to faint because I love him so much.

'**R**illa dear,' said Leonora. 'I think we should talk.'

Rilla was was going to see Hugh, but she was so surprised to hear her mother *ask* to speak to her that she stopped on her way to the door.

'Of course, Mummy, is anything wrong?'

'Just come to the conservatory for a few minutes.'

Rilla felt a little frightened as she sat down. What did Leonora want from her? It couldn't be something to do with Hugh, could it? No, surely not. Hugh fitted so well into life at Willow Court.

Since his first visit, he'd come up often. Partly Rilla was pleased, because it meant that she, just like Gwen, had a boyfriend, even though hers wasn't officially recognised as one. The disadvantage of having him constantly at Willow Court was that they had less time alone together. Less time for sex, Rilla said to herself, although there was the night they went to the gazebo after swimming in the lake. Hugh hadn't said anything about marriage. In fact, he hadn't even said he loved her, which worried her sometimes, although she'd heard that some men just didn't like saying the words, whatever their feelings might be.

'It's about Hugh, I'm afraid,' Leonora said.

Rilla jumped out of her seat. 'What's wrong? Has he had an accident?'

'No, no, darling. Nothing like that at all. Please sit down again.'

'What's the matter with Hugh?' she said, sitting down.

'I'm going to ask you something, Rilla, which I wouldn't normally ask, but I have to, in the circumstances. Have you slept with him?'

Rilla blushed and knew that the blush had given her away. I'm not ashamed, she told herself. There's nothing to be ashamed of. She looked up at Leonora and said, as bravely as she could, 'Yes. Yes, I have.'

Leonora sighed. 'I thought so,' she said. 'This is going to be hard for you to understand, darling, but I'm afraid all that's over now.'

'I don't understand. How can it be over? I was on my way to see him.'

'He won't be there. He's gone back to London. He won't be coming down here again.'

A pounding started behind Rilla's eyes. *Don't lose control. Keep calm*, she told herself. When she spoke, her voice came out in a strangled squeak, it was such an effort not to cry. 'Mummy, if you're going to say hurtful things, you have to explain. You can't just sit there and announce that he's not coming back. He wouldn't leave me. He loves me.'

Leonora shook her head. 'He's been taking advantage of you, Rilla. There's no easy way to say this, but he's . . . he's dishonest. He's not what he appears to be. For one thing, how old did he tell you he was?'

'I know how old he is. He's twenty-seven.'

'Hugh is thirty-four. He looks younger, but he really is.'

'That's not true. How do you know? Did he tell you? Not that it matters. I'd love him anyway.'

'It was a remark he made about remembering a street party at the end of the war. I realised at once that he must be over thirty. And then I made a few enquiries, from friends in London. He's thirty-four, Rilla—but that's not all. Are you ready for this?'

'Ready for what? I don't care what you've dug up. Is he a white slaver? A drug dealer?'

'Nothing so dramatic. Just the banal fact that he's already married. He has two children, one of them a girl only three years younger than you.'

Rilla felt as though all the breath had left her body. She opened her mouth to speak, and couldn't. She tried again. 'Is . . .? Do they . . .? I mean, maybe they're separated. That must be it. That must be why he comes to the cottage. To get away from her. They must be thinking of divorce. I'll talk to him. I'll ask him what's happening. He'll tell me the truth. He won't need to hide anything from me any more. He loves me.'

'That may be true, Rilla, but it makes no difference. And of course he didn't tell you. He was having a wonderful time with you, why should he spoil it? But he spoke to me, when I asked him to tell me the truth.'

'What did he say? When did you speak to him? Where?'

'Here. The day before yesterday when he came for lunch. While you were out in the Quiet Garden talking to Gwen and James, I think.'

Rilla closed her eyes. All the time she was lying on the grass, looking up into the magnolia leaves, he had been telling Leonora these hideous things. It was unbearable. Rilla felt as though someone had beaten her all over. It's never going to end, she thought. I'm going to hurt for ever.

She breathed deeply and looked at her mother. 'Please tell me everything he said. Every single word.'

'He confessed to me that he was older, as I'd suspected. He admitted that he should have had more sense than to fall under the spell of a young girl, but he said he was susceptible. Susceptible to the charms of young girls. He seemed to know that this was not something to be proud of. I asked him about his wife. They have one of those—what do you call them? Open marriages. But she knows nothing about what he gets up to when he's not with her. He told her his cottage here was for his pottery. He begged me to say nothing to her about you. Not because you were his mistress, but simply because you are so much younger than—and these are his words—*his usual lovers*. He assured me you wouldn't become pregnant, because he's had a vasectomy. I told him that he must leave the cottage and he agreed. He left yesterday, I believe. He undertook never to get in touch with you, and you must never contact him again, Rilla. It's best that way.'

Rilla didn't say a word. She got up from her chair and left the conservatory. A whiteness filled her field of vision and her heart felt as though someone was squeezing it. She stumbled upstairs and went straight to the nursery. She sat down in front of the doll's house and looked into the rooms where the small figures of Lucinda and Lucas still lived, even though she'd stopped playing with them years ago. Their lives were lovely. They lived in Paradise Mansions and no one came to hurt them and tear them apart. I'll never see him again, she thought. Bastard. He was a bastard and she ought to hate him. How was it then that she still loved him with every single cell in her body? I will never forgive her, she thought, as she picked up Queen Margarita, and felt the first tears running down her cheeks. She shouldn't have asked him all that. It wasn't any of her business. He'd have left his wife for me in the end. I know he would have. She meddled in my life and ruined it for ever.

Early morning, Saturday, August 24, 2002
'Rilla? Rilla, are you asleep?'

Sean. Sean's voice. Rilla struggled to her feet, smoothing her hair with one hand. 'No. No, honestly,' she said. 'I was just thinking with my eyes closed. I was on the point of giving up on you. Isn't it very late?'

'About one o'clock,' Sean said. 'I can't tell you how sorry I am. I've been like a cat on hot bricks. One round of drinks after another and I was longing to escape, but I didn't want it to look obvious. Got to work with everyone tomorrow.' He laughed. 'Well, today actually.'

'It doesn't matter,' Rilla said. 'I'm not a bit tired. Are you?'

Sean shook his head. 'Not at all. And I've brought some wine.' He held it out to show her. 'I got the cork out before I came down here, but I forgot the glasses.'

'Never mind. We'll just swig.'

Sean sat down on the bench and leaned against the glass wall of the gazebo. 'What have you been thinking about?' he asked. 'You said you'd been thinking. Don't say if you don't want to. If it's private.'

She sat down beside him and held up the bottle. 'May I?'

'Sure.'

She took a gulp of the icy, dry wine and handed the bottle to Sean. 'It's not a bit private. I was thinking about a man I used to know. My first lover, actually. His name was Hugh.'

'What happened to him?'

'Oh God, it's very run-of-the-mill stuff, I'm afraid. I fell for him and it turned out he was married. Mother found out and sent him packing.'

'And I expect you never forgave her for that.'

Rilla laughed. 'How did you guess? No, of course she did the right thing, but it didn't feel like that at the time. I sometimes think she still looks on me as the naughty little girl she thought I was then. I don't feel approved of, much of the time. Again, boring stuff. I'm sorry.'

'Nothing to do with you is boring, Rilla,' Sean said.

She found that his hand was stroking her wrist, gently, slowly and a shiver of pleasure went through her.

'You're sad, though,' he went on. 'That's obvious. And I know why because you told me. I've been thinking of you suffering like that, when your son died. Where was Jon Frederick when it happened?'

Rilla looked at the floor. 'He came at once. He did the best he could, but of course he was as hurt as I was. And he was angry with me.'

'That's unforgivable!' Sean said. 'It wasn't your fault. It was an accident, surely. A tragic accident. Did he blame you? How could he?'

Rilla didn't answer for a while. She was struggling with a sorrow that seemed to have become lodged in her throat. Tears trickled down her cheeks as she spoke. 'He was right to be angry. It *was* my fault. I should have been here. I shouldn't have left other people to take care of my baby. I shouldn't have taken my eyes off him for a second.'

Sean put his arm round Rilla's shoulders and she buried her face in his neck and cried as though she never intended to stop. At last, the sobs subsided and she lifted her head and looked at Sean and smiled.

'Oh, Sean, I didn't mean tonight to be like this! Look at us. I'm bedraggled and red-eyed and you're soaked to the skin. I'm so sorry.'

Sean removed his arm from Rilla's shoulder, took a hanky out of his pocket and handed it to her. 'Have a good blow,' he said, and she did as he suggested. 'Then we'll have another sip of wine and begin again. I'll have my turn. I'll tell you about my failed marriage. How my ex-wife said I was a complete failure who'd never amount to anything—'

'How could she?' Rilla was indignant. 'You're a well-known director. What did she want you to be?'

'I don't know. Prize-winning. Visible. Glitzy. All the things I'm not. I just like making the programmes I want to make. I have to be passionate about my subjects, as I am about Ethan. I've always loved his paintings, you know. I fell in love with them the first time I saw them.'

Silence fell between them again. Then Sean said, 'You know what follows, Rilla. You know what I want to say, only I'm not sure I can say it well. It'll sound contrived.'

'What did you want to say, Sean? Tell me. I won't laugh, I promise.'

'I was going to say that I fell in love with the paintings the first time I saw them and the same thing exactly happened when I saw you. There you are. That's the sort of sentiment that shouldn't really be expressed outside the confines of a valentine card, don't you think?'

'I would think that,' Rilla said, and she was smiling as she spoke, 'only I felt just the same. Like a kid. Silly and giggly, watching out for your tiniest action. Did it mean anything? Were you really looking at me like that or was I imagining it? That sort of silliness. And then I'd think, hang on a minute, you're going too fast. It's undignified in a woman of your age.'

'What I think,' Sean said, taking Rilla's face in his hands and turning it gently so that she was facing him, 'is that we haven't been going nearly fast enough. We've been wasting time. We shouldn't waste any more.'

He bent his head. She closed her eyes and waited and then his mouth was on hers and it felt to her as though something golden and warm was racing through every vein in her body, flooding her with happiness.

The kitchen was cool and quiet. Five o'clock in the morning was the perfect time, Rilla thought, for baking. She knew she wouldn't sleep if she went to bed now, so this was the most sensible thing to do.

They had talked all night, nearly, and walked hand in hand over the dewy lawn to the house as the dawn was coming up.

Rilla had stopped to pick up her shoes, and said, 'I've decided to make a strawberry shortcake for my mother. I might do it now, before I go to sleep. Although I doubt I'll ever sleep again. I shall just lie on my bed and long for you. What have you done to me?'

'Nothing,' Sean said. 'Nothing compared to what I'm going to do.'

As they kissed good night, kissed as though they never meant to stop, Rilla had closed her eyes and allowed herself to imagine it all.

Now she put on Mary's apron, which she found hanging on the back of the kitchen door, and opened cupboards silently, conscious that the whole household was still fast asleep. All the ingredients—sugar, icing sugar, cornflour, butter—were present and correct. Rilla mixed, kneaded, rolled out the pastry and put the tins into the oven. Then she stepped out of the back door and sat down on a bench in the kitchen garden while she waited for the shortcake to be ready.

She tried to put the night's events out of her mind, but her thoughts returned to Sean again and again. When she was with him, everything seemed possible, but doubts had already crept into her mind. Perhaps it was just Willow Court working a sort of magic. Maybe real life, London life, would dissolve the enchantment.

The buzzer on the cooker sounded and put such ideas out of her mind. She went into the kitchen and removed the tins from the oven, then put the shortcake to cool in the larder and made her way upstairs.

She was on the landing when a noise she couldn't identify made her start. She looked along the corridor and saw that the door to the nursery was open. That wasn't right. No one should be there at this hour of the morning. She tiptoed up to it, her heart beating fast.

'Douggie darling!' Rilla saw that the little boy was standing by the doll's house. He'd pulled the white sheet away and was holding something like a ribbon in his hand. It fell to the floor when he caught sight of her. 'You shouldn't be here, sweetheart. It isn't time to wake up yet. Not nearly. Come with me, and I'll take you back to bed.'

She went over to him and picked him up. How sweet he smelt! Markie used to smell just like this, she thought, blinking back tears. 'Come on, Douggie. Let's get you back to your room.'

'Want Mama!' Douggie began to cry.

'We'll go and find her, shall we? Don't cry! Sssh! Everyone's asleep.'

Fiona was already up. She was almost running down the corridor as they left the nursery, wearing only her nightie. 'Oh, Rilla, I'm so sorry. Did he wake you? Come on, Douggie. Come with me.'

Rilla transferred the child to his mother's arms. 'It's quite all right,' she told Fiona. 'No harm done.'

As mother and child returned to their room, Rilla went back to the nursery to cover the doll's house again. She saw at once what Douggie had done. 'Oh, no . . . ' she whispered. 'Oh God.'

He'd stripped off a piece of the paper that Maude had painted to look like roof tiles. The strip lay curled on the carpet like skin peeled from a huge apple. Rilla bent down, rolled it up and put it in her trouser pocket. Then she spread the sheet over the house and left the room, closing the door behind her. She went into her bedroom filled with foreboding. What would Leonora say? Could the roof be repaired? The strip of paper stuck back? I can't think about this now, she thought. I must sleep.

'You're up early,' Beth said.

'So are you,' Efe replied. 'Douggie woke me.' He poured himself another coffee. Black with no sugar. Macho coffee, Beth called it. He raised the coffeepot in the air and smiled at her. 'Want a cup?'

'Yes, please,' Beth answered. She cut herself two slices of bread and put them into the toaster. Then she pulled out a chair and sat down opposite Efe. 'Where are all the others?'

'Mum's out and about with Dad. They're waiting for the chairs and tables people. Haven't a clue where Alex and Rilla are. Chloë won't get cracking till about noon, probably.'

The toast popped up and Beth went to fetch it. This opportunity for a private talk with Efe had presented itself quite unexpectedly, and there were questions she had to ask, even though she wasn't sure she wanted to know all the answers. OK, she said to herself. No hesitations.

'Who's Melanie?' she asked.

'Why? What do you mean? I don't know a Melanie.'

'Yes, you do. I overheard you talking to one yesterday.'

'You were eavesdropping!' A typical Efe answer, Beth thought. Throw the blame on someone else.

'I wasn't,' she replied. 'You weren't exactly hiding yourself away. Anyone could have walked in. What if Fiona had overheard you instead of me?'

'I'd have pretended there was nothing in it. She always believes me.'

'You'd have *pretended*. That means there *is* something in it.'

Efe held his hands up, in a gesture of surrender. 'Got me there!'

'OK. So who is she?'

He leaned across the table, took hold of her hand and gazed into her eyes. 'I can't tell you, Bethie darling, unless you swear not to tell a soul.'

I don't need to know details, Beth said to herself. He's admitted he's being unfaithful to Fiona. That should be enough . . . but I want to know everything. She said, 'OK, go on. I shan't say a word.'

'It's Melanie Havering. You've met her, surely?'

'From the antique shop? But . . .'

'I know, I know. Don't say it. She's old!'

'I wasn't going to say that. Only she's a good friend of Gwen's.'

'So? Gwen's friends are allowed to be sexy, you know. And Melanie isn't that old, actually. She's only forty-five.'

'That's fine, then,' Beth said. 'That makes it all all right. God, Efe, your mum's friend! Isn't it embarrassing? What happens when she comes here to see Gwen and James? And hasn't Melanie got a husband?'

Efe smiled. 'She's divorced. And when she does come while I'm here, it all gets fantastically exciting. We have to take chances sometimes.'

'I don't want to hear about it, thanks very much. It's revolting.'

'Oh, grow up, Beth! You know what goes on. My dad used to be a bit of a lad in the early days, apparently, and got up to all sorts of stuff.'

'I don't suppose Gwen was exactly ecstatic when she found out.'

'She stayed with him.' Efe picked up Beth's second piece of toast and started to butter it. 'She'd have left him if she had any strong objections.'

There was no point, Beth could see, in explaining to Efe about the other reasons his mother might have had for turning a blind eye. Like the fact that she had three children to consider. And that she loved him in spite of his infidelities. In any case, he was a reformed character now. Men were such fools sometimes, and Efe was beginning to irritate her.

'Right then,' she said, pushing back her chair and standing up. 'I'm going out to see what's going on in the marquee. See you.'

She knew she should have asked Efe about his violence towards his wife, but she hadn't felt brave enough.

The chairs and tables had been unloaded from the truck that brought them and several men were going into the marquee, setting them down, and coming out again in a kind of procession.

'Hello, there, Beth!' said James, who was enjoying overseeing this work. He looked rather like an army officer in his khaki trousers and shirt. 'Very efficient, these chaps, aren't they?'

Alex was beside the truck photographing the whole operation. He came across the grass towards Beth as soon as he caught sight of her.

'Hi, Alex!' she said, and smiled at him. James had disappeared into the marquee to make sure all the furniture was properly distributed. 'Your dad's enjoying himself, isn't he?'

'Thinks he's General Montgomery. Sleep well?'

Beth nodded. 'You're up early, aren't you?'

'Didn't want to miss this light. I'm finished now. Come for a walk?'

'OK.' Beth fell in beside him and they made their way towards the drive. 'Where are we going? And do we really have to go so fast?'

'Sorry.' Alex slowed down at once. 'Let's drop in and see Nanny Mouse, shall we? I haven't been down there yet.'

'Nor me. I always mean to go and see her, but I hate going on my own. I'm not sure if she knows who I am and I can't think what to say.'

'I find her quite restful, really. Doesn't matter what you say, she'll have forgotten it before you've left the room.'

The sun shone through the leaves of the trees along the drive and made shadows flicker over Alex's face. For a moment, Beth considered asking him again about that day by the lake, the day when Mark died, but thought better of it. He might know about Efe, though, and Fiona.

'Alex, may I ask you something?' she said.

'Go on, then. What is it?'

'I caught Fiona crying in the bathroom yesterday. She showed me her arm and it was covered in bruises. She told me Efe sometimes loses his temper with her. Did you know that?'

'I saw them too. The bruises.' Alex paused. 'He's capable of it, Beth. He does get kind of out of control sometimes.'

Beth sighed. 'I know. I've seen him, only I never thought . . . ' Her voice faded away. 'Oh, Alex, what can we do? Shouldn't we say something? Maybe we ought to tell your mum and dad. What do you think?'

'I could speak to him, I suppose,' Alex said. 'But he'd probably deny it. Fiona's the one who has to deal with it. You could maybe talk to her.'

'I hardly know her and . . .'

'I know. You don't think much of her, either.'

Beth looked searchingly at Alex. 'You don't miss much, do you? I feel sorry for her now, though.' She stopped walking and leaned against a tree. 'I don't feel the same today as I did yesterday about anything. What's happening, Alex? Why is Efe so different from how he usually is?'

'He's not different at all,' Alex said gently. 'It's just that this is the first time for ages that we've all been together and so you've seen other sides to him. He's always managed to charm people when he wants something out of them. He's been charming you for years, hasn't he?'

'Alex! You sound as though you're jealous!' Beth started to laugh, but she stopped at once when she saw Alex's face.

'Of course I'm not jealous,' he said, 'but I notice certain things. The way you look at him, for instance. I'm surprised no one else has seen it.'

'He makes me angry, most of the time. And anyway, you're just as bad. We've both of us worshipped him since we were kids, haven't we?'

Alex nodded and changed the subject. 'When we last went down to see Nanny Mouse, she thought I was Efe at first. Then she got confused all over again and called me Peter. I hope we can get her to recognise us.'

'It'll be OK. She drifts in and out of real life, doesn't she? You have to catch those moments when she's making sense as they go past you.'

Alex smiled at her and Beth was surprised how comforted he made her feel. He hadn't changed. Unlike Efe. For years Efe had been the focus of all her dreams. It was only in the last few hours that she'd begun to realise that he was not who she'd thought he was, but someone quite different. Someone who was capable of violence, and who thought nothing of being unfaithful to his wife. I still love him, Beth thought, but was immediately aware of a tiny doubt creeping over her, some inkling that she would never again feel quite the same about him.

'We're here, Beth,' Alex said.

'Sorry, Alex, I was miles away.'

Alex knocked at the door of Lodge Cottage and Miss Lardner opened it at once. 'I saw you coming down the drive,' she said. 'How very good it is to see you both! You're just in time for elevenses.'

Beth smiled. This was the only place in the world where everyone still believed in elevenses. 'That'll be lovely, Miss Lardner,' she said, catching Alex's eye. 'We'd love some elevenses, wouldn't we, Alex?'

'Can't think of anything I'd like better,' Alex answered. He sounded dangerously close to laughter. He followed Beth into the tiny drawing room where Nanny Mouse was nodding in her favourite armchair.

Whenever he sat in one of Nanny Mouse's armchairs, Alex felt like Alice after she'd taken the magic potion and grown too big for the White Rabbit's house. He put his feet together and pulled them as close as he possibly could to his chair. The cups and saucers at Lodge Cottage were so dainty it made him feel clumsy just to look at them. He hurried to finish his coffee and put the cup and saucer down on the tiny table that Miss Lardner had placed beside him.

Beth was doing a grand job. He looked at her, chatting and smiling with Nanny Mouse, and wondered whether she'd realised what he felt. I'm an idiot, he thought. It's taken me all these years to recognise it. To acknowledge that I love her and there's nothing to stop her from loving me. Nothing but the fact that she's besotted with Efe. Alex sighed. Nanny

Mouse was talking to him now and he made a big effort to concentrate.

'She was very ill, you know,' Nanny Mouse confided. 'She should never have run out of doors like that. It wasn't allowed.'

'Wasn't it?' Alex said.

Beth smiled at him and came to his rescue. 'Who was ill, Nanny? Do you mean Leonora?'

'Yes, of course. She caught a dreadful chill which turned to pneumonia. I nursed her through it. Oh, she was burning up with the fever! She missed her birthday, you know. We had to give her all her presents later. There was a little boy who drowned too. Did you know that?'

Beth nodded and changed the subject. 'What lovely flowers, Nanny! You like roses best, don't you?'

'If you keep them for a very long time, they turn into beautiful dried roses. Did you know that? I used to make potpourri.'

Alex raised his eyebrows. Life was too short to discuss potpourri.

Beth winked at him and said, 'We must go now, Nanny. It'll be lunchtime soon. We'll come again.' She stood up and kissed the old lady, who suddenly turned and clung to her hand.

'She was wearing her best dress,' she said, her voice wobbling. 'Lilac lace, it was. She looked beautiful. But it was ruined, of course. Soaked and torn and quite, quite spoilt. I gave it to Tyler to burn with the garden rubbish. The master wasn't in a state to do anything.'

'Goodbye, Nanny,' Alex said, leading Beth over to the door. 'Thanks for elevenses.'

As Alex and Beth left Lodge Cottage, a car came to a screeching halt on the drive beside them. It was Efe's Audi, with Fiona and Douggie in it, too, and although Alex guessed that they'd gone into the village on some errand for Gwen, they looked as though they'd all been out for a delightful jaunt. Douggie waved at them from his child seat. Fiona seemed prettier and more relaxed, and after she'd wound down her window, Efe leaned right over her to speak to them.

'Bloody hell. You're a bit early with the duty visits, aren't you?'

'Not duty at all. We've had elevenses,' Beth said, smiling. 'Remember those? We used to have them when we were kids.'

'Rich Tea biscuits and cocoa,' Efe said. 'Want a lift up to the house?'

'Love one, thanks,' Beth said and turned to Alex. 'Coming, Alex?'

Alex shook his head. 'No, that's OK. I'm going into the village myself now, I think.' He didn't really need to go there, but nothing would have made him get into the same car with Beth and Efe. A shadow had fallen over the day, and he realised as he saw her stepping into the car exactly how much he'd been waiting to talk to her again once they'd left Nanny

Mouse. Now he had no idea when he'd be able to get her alone.

Alex stood by the gate wondering whether he had the energy to walk into the village. Perhaps he was imagining it, but Beth seemed relieved to be getting into Efe's car. Relieved to be getting away from me, Alex thought. She hadn't even waved at him as they left, much less actually said goodbye. You've got no chance, Alex, he said to himself, and set off down the road, staring at the tarmac, seeing nothing.

Rilla lay in bed and wished she hadn't drunk quite so much the night before. I'm getting too old for it, she thought. She hadn't been so drunk, though, that she had forgotten what had happened. It was coming back to her in every delicious detail and she stretched out under the duvet, wondering why it was that she wasn't completely, totally happy.

A dream. She'd had a dream, and fragments of it came drifting back now to trouble her. Mark was somewhere in it, as he always was. Running out of the gazebo with his hands outstretched and there was a mirror behind him. There wasn't any logic to dreams, Rilla knew, and she should put this one out of her mind on a day like today.

There were things she should be doing. She ought to go and tell Mary about the strawberry shortcake. She ought to make a huge effort to look beautiful for Sean. She ought to check that Gwen didn't need any help, even at the risk of being rebuffed. She ought to phone Ivan. He must think she'd vanished off the face of the earth. What she certainly ought not to do was lie in bed and cry and that was what she was doing. She could feel the tears trickling down her cheeks and gathering in the crease of her neck. I did it, she thought miserably. That's why I can never be happy, whatever good things happen. Mark's death was my fault. I never should have left him and I'll never forgive myself.

March 1982

Rilla tucked the phone under her chin, held her lighter as far as possible from the mouthpiece, and clicked it into flame as quietly as she could to light the cigarette that was already in her mouth.

'Rilla? Rilla darling, is that you lighting another cigarette?'

'Cigarette? Of course not. Must be something you heard on the line.'

Was that convincing? In normal circumstances Rilla could lie to her mother with the best of them. She'd been doing it for years. Just lately, though, Leonora had been particularly sharp about tuning in to what her daughter was really feeling. Rilla's marriage was over. She and Jon had come to that conclusion weeks ago, but now it was going to be public property, and even though they were determined to have what was known as a 'civilised divorce', the fact that Jon was a pop star meant that the whole world seemed to be interested in such gory details as there were. Trust Leonora to be the first to find out that the Fredericks' split had made the front pages.

'Listen to this, Rilla!' she said. 'It's from the *Sun*, the front page. I thought I should warn you. I knew you wouldn't be up yet.'

Rilla wondered how the hell her mother had managed to get hold of a copy of the *Sun* at Willow Court first thing in the morning. One of the gardening lads must have brought it into the house. She pulled her silk kimono more closely round herself and said, 'Go ahead. I'm listening.'

'"Jon Frederick and his wife, the luscious Rilla Frederick, star of *Night Creatures*, have enjoyed a lavish party-giving lifestyle since they tied the knot five years ago. But all good things are coming to a sticky end with the couple's upcoming divorce. Their four-year-old son will continue to live with his mother, along with Jon's daughter by his first wife (the late Carol Edmonds). 'That's fine by me,' Jon says, 'because Rilla is a perfect mother, and I'm a bit of a rover. Footloose and fancy free, that's me. And what children need is security.' Our showbiz reporter adds that Jon's fancy-free status is under attack from gorgeous starlet Chansonne Dubois." What do you think about all that, Rilla?'

'Actually, I think it's rather good. Accurate, in any case.'

Leonora's sigh travelled down the line, and Rilla said quickly, 'Don't sigh, Mother. I'm OK. I'll manage.'

'I'm sure you will, darling, but I worry about you. Why don't you come down to Willow Court for a bit?'

'It's kind of you to ask us, Mother, but it's the middle of the week and there's school. And anyway, haven't you got your hands full with Chloë?'

Leonora laughed. 'Yes, she *is* quite a handful, that child. But a couple more children here will hardly be noticed, I promise you. And I wouldn't worry about Beth's school. She's such an intelligent child.'

'It's getting late, Mother. Markie'll be waking up in a minute and I must go and get breakfast for Beth and take her to school. I'll phone you tonight and tell you what I've decided. Thanks for ringing. Bye!'

'Goodbye, darling. Kiss Beth and that sweet baby of yours for me.'

When Rilla put the phone down, there was Beth, standing quietly by the door. She was already dressed for school and had plaited her own long, dark hair. At eight years old, she was self-possessed and self-sufficient, but shy. She was looking at Rilla now with a smile that lit up her serious, pale face and made her eyes shine. That smile was Jon's. Mark had it too, even though he was much more like Rilla. The love she felt for her son seemed to Rilla like an ocean deep inside her, washing over her all the time. As for Beth, she'd been Rilla's child even before Mark was born, and Mark's birth hadn't changed that. She loved Beth as much as she would have loved a daughter of her own and no longer thought of herself as a stepmother. Beth was hers, and that was that. Now that she'd given birth, she realised the truth of what her mother and Gwen and countless friends had all told her. The feelings you have for each child are different, but the intensity of the love is just the same. She adored Beth and, strangely, this feeling grew stronger once Mark was born. She was constantly amazed and delighted that her heart could contain so many different strands of love, all at the same time.

'Hello, chicken!' said Rilla. 'I was just coming to get you. How long have you been standing there? Leonora's been chewing my ear off.'

'Did she say we could go to Willow Court? Please, please say we can, Rilla! I love going there.'

'I know you do,' she said. 'Yes, I expect we will, tomorrow. I dare say it won't hurt you to miss a couple of days of school.' Rilla went up to dress Mark, whom she could hear wandering around in the bathroom.

Beth followed her up the stairs, skipping with happiness. 'I can play with Efe and Alex. We've got a den in those bushes by the lake. Efe said he's going to get a boat in the summer, so we can go out on the water.'

Rilla wasn't really listening. She was thinking about what Leonora had read out to her. The truth, which Rilla had told no one, was that getting a 'civilised divorce' was not as easy as it looked. She'd loved her husband well enough, and they'd had a good enough life together while it lasted, for her to feel let-down and miserable and angry. She'd cried so much that her eyes seemed permanently red and there were shadows under them that on bad days looked like two black eyes. She slathered on the make-up, knowing she was doing no more than putting on a mask to disguise the fact that she wasn't coping.

I'm good at disguises, she thought. Nobody knows I'm kept afloat by pills. The tranquillisers didn't exactly make her tranquil, but dulled the pain a little and made it possible to go through the motions of her life. Beth, though, was sharper than everyone else, always looking anxiously at Rilla to make sure she was all right. One evening, as they sat down to their supper after Mark was asleep, she'd asked, 'We'll be all right, won't we, Rilla? Now that Dad's gone, I mean.'

'Course we will, honeybunch!' Rilla had answered.

Now that they were outside the bathroom, Rilla tried to focus on what needed to be done. Dress Mark. Take Beth to school.

'Come on, sweetiepie,' she said to her son, who was busy floating a family of four yellow plastic ducks in the basin. 'Put the ducks on the shelf and brush your teeth and then we have to get dressed. Beth's going to be late for school if we don't hurry up.' Before Mark had time to object, Rilla wet a flannel and began to wash his face.

'No!' he shouted. 'I want ducks! I don't want dressing.'

'We're going to Willow Court, Markie,' Beth said from the door.

He grinned. 'Willow Court! Now. Now today?'

'Tomorrow. If you're good,' said Rilla, 'and stand still while I dress you, then we'll be able to pack everything up ready while Beth's at school and as soon as we wake up tomorrow, we'll be off.'

'Will Efe be there? And Alex?' Her son's eyes were bright.

'Of course. And the baby. Remember Chloë? Their new baby sister?'

'Babies don't play,' Mark said firmly, dismissing his little cousin with a shrug that reminded Rilla of Jon. 'Will I see Nanny Mouse?'

'Oh, yes, Nanny Mouse is longing to see you. She always says so on the phone when I speak to her. She says, "When's my little Markie coming to see me?" And you, Beth. She's always asking after you, too.'

Rilla pushed Mark's socks onto his feet, just a little way, so that he could pull them up all by himself, and while he was absorbed in this, Beth asked, 'Does Nanny Mouse really ask about me?'

Rilla put both hands on Beth's shoulders. 'Of course she does! Honestly, Beth, it's about time you got it into your head that they're all mad about you down there. Everyone. Leonora, Gwen, James. They all love you to pieces. They're dying to see you. All of them.'

'What about Efe?' Beth said.

Rilla grinned. 'You love him best of all, don't you?'

'He thinks up good games,' said Beth. 'He's fun, that's all.'

Beth's blushing, Rilla noticed with some amusement. It'll do us all good to get to the country for a bit. Forget our troubles. Have some fun. Be cosseted by Nanny Mouse. Heavenly bliss!

The adults sat in the drawing room having tea while Efe, Alex and Beth played outside, with Mark trying his best to join in. Chloë was sleeping in a carry-cot at Gwen's feet.

'There you are, Gwen,' said James. 'Good as gold, my little princess.' He smiled at Rilla. 'Gwen always tells me Chloë's a difficult baby. Not like either of the boys. I don't find her a problem at all, I must say.'

'All very well for you, darling,' Gwen said. 'You don't ever have to deal with her yourself.'

'And neither do you, really, do you?' said James. 'You'd be lost without Nanny Mouse. Admit it!'

'I know, I know,' said Gwen. 'You're right, but there's always quite enough work for both of us, I promise you. And of course we have to keep an eye on Efe and Alex and Mark and Beth as well.'

Rilla looked out of the window. At least the kids seemed happy enough at the moment, running up and down the grassy slope. Markie, bless him, was chasing after Efe and Alex, screaming with laughter, but Beth was now sitting on the terrace, looking at the others; grave, pretty, with her best blue hair ribbon on in honour of Efe who wouldn't notice it, or if he did, wouldn't think of saying how pretty it was. I'm a bloody fool, Rilla said to herself. No eight-year-old boy would dream of complimenting a girl on her hair ribbon. The pills are making me stupid.

Rilla woke up suddenly and for a moment couldn't think what it was, that unending wail that set every nerve on edge. That was the trouble with sleeping pills. You fell into darkness the minute you got into bed, but if you woke for any reason, it was like struggling up from the bottom of a pond with weeds and scum filling your mouth and nose.

The wailing was, of course, a baby crying. Rilla sat up and thought, It's Mark. I must get up and feed him. Then she remembered that the baby wasn't Mark but Chloë, who was notorious for making nights a misery for everyone. Rilla sank back on her pillows. Nanny Mouse would be taking care of it. There was no need to get out of bed.

Nanny Mouse came into her own with new babies. She knew how to make the right noises and do all the things that seemed miraculously to soothe them. When Mark was born, she'd travelled up to London to help Rilla 'establish a routine' for the child, and Rilla was endlessly grateful to her. Nanny Mouse was the best baby-tamer in the world.

Rilla stared into the darkness. The wails had stopped now but she was wide awake. She got out of bed, pulled on her silk robe and went out into the corridor. There was a line of light under the nursery door. Probably the silence meant that Chloë was being given a bottle. Nanny Mouse wouldn't mind if she came and chatted for a while. Rilla tiptoed along the carpet and opened the nursery door.

There was Nanny Mouse with Chloë in her arms, on the nursing chair by the window. 'Rilla my dear, come in!' she whispered, smiling. The baby was sucking gently from a bottle. 'I shan't be long dealing with this little one and then I'll make us a nice milky drink.'

'Lovely!' said Rilla, sitting down at the nursery table.

'How are you, dear?' Nanny Mouse said. 'You don't have to put on a brave face with me, you know. Are you managing?'

'Oh, yes, I'm managing,' Rilla said. 'But I do get lonely sometimes.'

'You'll get used to that, dear, don't you worry. It's bound to be difficult at first. After a while,' she looked up at Rilla and smiled in a way you could only describe as knowing, 'it'll seem quite natural to be on your own and you'll be relieved not to have to consider the needs of a man. You'll be able to please yourself, Rilla, and that's always nice, isn't it?'

She had a point, Rilla thought. It *was* nice, that part of it. What wasn't so nice was having no one to share with; no one to chat to about everything that came into your head, no one in the bed with you when you woke up every day, no one to see how lovely the children were and how they changed every day. There was also the small matter of sex.

'I'm fine, actually,' she said to Nanny Mouse. 'Just from time to time, I get a bit weepy. Nothing that won't get better, honestly.'

'That's my brave Rilla,' said Nanny Mouse, and stood up to lower the sleeping Chloë gently into her cot. 'Now come downstairs with me, and we'll have a real treat. Hot chocolate tonight, I think.'

Suddenly, Rilla felt ridiculously happy. She followed Nanny Mouse down the stairs to the kitchen. Everything would be better after a mug of hot chocolate. Everything was going to be all right. She'd work again. There had to be a part out there for her, somewhere. It was just a question of searching it out. She'd manage, all on her own. And before she got back into bed, she'd look in on Markie and Beth, asleep in the next room. Her children. Her reasons for being happy.

'What's going on? Nanny Mouse, what's happening?' Rilla stood on the bottom step of the staircase and the grandfather clock on the landing struck nine as she spoke. Nanny Mouse was dressed in her travelling suit and blue felt hat, holding a small suitcase in one hand and her handbag in the other. She looked as though she were about to burst into tears.

Leonora had an arm round her. Gwen and James were by the door. James said, 'Come along, Nanny, or you'll miss that train . . .'

'But I haven't said goodbye to the children,' Nanny Mouse cried. 'Nor to Rilla. I haven't explained . . .'

'Here I am, Nanny,' said Rilla. 'And I'll say goodbye to the children for you. You go and get your train. Mother'll explain everything, I'm sure.'

'I'm so sorry, dear, truly,' said Nanny Mouse as James guided her towards the door. 'I shan't be gone longer than a few days. I may come back tomorrow if all's well. If I can arrange for someone else to be with Gladys. Goodbye! . . . Thank you, James dear. I'm just coming.'

When the car had finally driven off, Leonora said, 'Well, it can't be helped. Poor Nanny Mouse!' She led the way to the dining room.

The children were already up and about in the garden. Whatever emergency had caused Nanny Mouse to leave Willow Court, she'd managed to get the children washed and dressed and fed first.

Rilla helped herself to cereal and a bowl of fruit and sat down next to Gwen. 'So,' she said. 'How come all of you haven't eaten yet? I thought I'd missed breakfast altogether, it's so late.'

'We've been at sixes and sevens,' said Leonora. 'Nanny Mouse had a telephone call early this morning. Her cousin Gladys has fallen and sprained her ankle. She can't walk, and Nanny Mouse is going to help her for a couple of days, and see if she can arrange nursing care.'

'Poor thing!' Gwen cut her toast into two neat triangles and spread one of them with butter and marmalade. 'She hates leaving the children. I don't think she trusts us to look after them properly.'

'We'll manage splendidly,' said Leonora. 'There are, after all, three of us to share the work.'

Rilla said nothing. Damn, she thought. Damn and blast. This is all I need. We'll have to be on duty the whole time, watching the kids, making sure they're bathed and fed and amused. I came here to have a rest from that. She blinked tears away, knowing how selfish she was. Of course Nanny Mouse had to go and look after her cousin. And she wasn't one of those mothers who was always dumping her kids on someone else. I'm not like that, she thought. I love playing with them, reading to them, being with them, but just this once I felt like some time to myself.

By Saturday morning, Rilla was determined to escape Willow Court and play truant. She dressed in a pair of black wool trousers, a white silk shirt, and a moss-green velvet jacket—a costume, she hoped, that would reflect the new Rilla, the one who wasn't going to ask permission to go down to the village for a while, but was simply going to announce her intentions at breakfast and go.

The door to her bedroom opened and Mark came running in. 'What you doing, Ma? You're pretty!'

Rilla gathered him into her arms and put her face into the crook of his neck, smelling his warm skin, and kissing him in the tickly way he loved, batting her eyelashes against his cheek. 'A fluttie kiss' they called it, because that was Mark's word for butterfly.

'Not as pretty as you,' Rilla said.

'No! I'm not pretty!' Mark was indignant.

'All right, not pretty, but my best, loveliest wonderboy.'

That met with Mark's approval and he beamed at Rilla and began pulling her hands. 'Come to breakfast. Breakfast time. Come on.'

'I'm going out after breakfast, Markie,' Rilla said, following him out of the room and wondering whether her determination would stand up to objections from her son. But there were none.

'Efe and Alex got a den. I seed it,' he said.

'I *saw* it, Markie.'

'No, you didn't seed it. I seed it.'

Rilla gave up. This wasn't the time to correct Mark's speech. Everything was going to work out splendidly. He'd be fine without her and she would be much better off away from Willow Court for a bit.

At breakfast, she spoke clearly and firmly. 'I'm off down to the village this morning. I'll be back before lunch.' She looked at Leonora and tried not to see Gwen tightening her lips. 'I'm sure you'll all manage for a while without me, won't you?' An extra bright smile was evenly distributed round the table. 'I noticed that new antique shop, what's it called?'

'The Treasure Chest,' Leonora said.

'That's the one! I need to buy a birthday present for a friend who's just mad about such things. You don't mind, do you, Gwen?'

'No, of course not. Have a good time.'

Rilla bounded out of her chair and made for the door. 'I'll see all of you later,' she said as brightly as she knew how. 'Goodbye, Markie darling, and you too, Beth. Be good for Gwen and Leonora now.'

'**M**ay I help you?' said a rather angular woman from behind a till that could have come from the TV version of some Dickens novel.

'I'm just browsing, thanks,' said Rilla, peering around the small, shadowy room. The stock was so closely packed together that if you wanted something specific you'd have had a hard time finding it. Something caught her eye. Light from the door bounced off a mirror, half hidden behind a rocking horse. As she approached it, she noticed that the corner of the frame that she could see looked exactly like . . . She pulled it out and propped it against the edge of the table. It was. It was Hugh's mirror, the one that had hung in the cottage, the one that had belonged to his grandmother. What was it doing here? Why didn't he take it with him? Rilla thought she knew the answer. The tale of the grandmother was probably another of his lies. But here it was. She peered into the glass and saw her face younger, happier, reflected more kindly.

'How much is this mirror?' she said, holding it up with difficulty.

'A hundred pounds,' said the angular woman.

'I'll take it,' Rilla said. 'Only I'll have to collect and pay for it later. I came out without my chequebook. I live up at Willow Court.'

'I know,' said the woman. 'You're Rilla Frederick. I read about your divorce. I *am* so sorry. I loved *Night Creatures*.'

'How kind of you to say so! Thank you!' Rilla smiled. No one remembers me in anything else, she thought. She made her way to the antique till, glancing out of the window and saw . . . no, it couldn't be. Could it? Yes, it was Mrs Pritchard. The old busybody! Rilla took a step towards the window and caught her foot in something, and in a split second that seemed to go on for ever, the mirror slipped out of her hand and fell to the floor. She cried out, 'Oh, oh my God! Oh, it's cracked. The mirror's cracked. I'm so sorry. Of course, I'll pay for the damage. I don't know what happened.' She burst into tears. 'Do forgive me.'

'That's all right, dear,' said the woman, coming to comfort her. 'You can replace the glass. The frame isn't broken. And it's beautiful, isn't it?'

'Yes, yes, it is.' Rilla sniffed, and wiped her nose with a tissue. 'And yes, I *will* replace the glass. It'll be almost as good as new, won't it?'

'It will,' said the woman.

Rilla 's gaze was drawn to the broken glass and she was filled with foreboding. *Bad luck. Bad luck for ever.* The mirror had shattered into an almost perfect spiderweb pattern. She looked into it and saw her own face broken into a thousand separate pieces.

Rilla, walking up the avenue of scarlet oaks towards the house, knew at once that something unspeakably dreadful was about to engulf her. Beth was running full tilt down the avenue towards her, screaming and screaming. Beth was hurt. Who had hurt her?

'Rilla! Oh, Rilla, please, please . . . I can't . . . I can't . . .'

'What's wrong, chicken?' Rilla's voice came out a squeak, her words tumbling into nonsense as Beth threw both arms round her waist and howled like a wounded animal. 'Are you hurt, Beth? Has someone hurt you? Tell me. Tell me what's wrong!'

'Markie,' Beth cried. 'It's Markie.'

Rilla heard the name and it was all she needed to hear. She knew. She began to run towards the house, stumbling in her haste. She could see two cars, one of them a police car and the other Dr Benyon's black Daimler. As she came closer, she saw her mother standing on the front steps. Why was her mouth twisted out of shape from pain?

'Oh, my darling child, oh, Rilla,' Leonora said, and came to hold her daughter. 'There's been an accident. A terrible accident. Markie . . .'

'He's dead, isn't he?' Rilla said. She heard herself shrieking, 'Markie, Markie, oh my God, my baby, Markie, oh God . . .' over and over again. Making no sense. Keening. Howling. She fell to the ground and tore at the stone steps with her bare nails. Shrieking, 'No, oh God, no. Not this. Please no. Please. Oh, Mummy, Mummy, I can't bear it.'

In the darkness that fell over her vision, she sensed someone lifting her to her feet, taking her into the house.

'Where is he? Where's Mark? I want to see him, Mummy. Take me to see my baby. I want to. Please. Take me now. Please. Let's hurry.'

'Yes, my darling,' said Leonora, and each word was thickened with tears.

A voice in Rilla's head said, *If I get there quickly, maybe I can save him. Breathe life into him . . .* She started to run upstairs. *Where is he?* she wanted to say, but the words wouldn't come. *Where have you put him?* Hands took hold of her and led her to one of the spare rooms.

Mark was laid out on the bed. He was pale. His hair was wet. His body was covered with a sheet. Rilla thought that the pain she felt must split her in two. She bent down to kiss her boy, her baby, and his skin was cold. She whispered in his ear. She kissed him. Real kisses, and the fluttie kisses that used to make him laugh with pleasure.

'Come away now, Rilla,' said Gwen, who was weeping as she held her sister up, carrying almost all her weight. 'Come and lie down.'

'What happened, Gwen? Tell me what happened.'

'An accident. Mark wandered away and fell into the lake. He drowned. Oh, Rilla . . .' Gwen was weeping as though she would never stop.

Rilla, frozen into silence, walked slowly along the corridor to her own room, leaning on her sister. It was too late and she couldn't bring him back and he was dead and it was her fault. *I wasn't here.*

She lay down on her bed and there was Dr Benyon, suddenly leaning over her. 'Take this pill, my dear. To calm you a little. To ease the pain.'

Rilla swallowed the pill and thought what a fool Dr Benyon was. Nothing could ease the pain. Nothing. Not ever.

'Thank you,' she said, acting calm because that was what they all wanted. There was a bitter taste in her mouth and a rage that frightened her, somewhere under the pain. Where were her mother and her sister when her son went into the water? What were they doing? How could they take their eyes away from such a small child? How could they? As soon as this thought came into her mind, her agony hissed back. *But where were you? You were the mother. You left him. You didn't think. You should have been there. Not Gwen. Not Leonora. You, his mother.*

Morning, Saturday, August 24, 2002

Rilla sat at the dressing table and peered at herself in the glass. She wondered whether the fact that she'd been crying was obvious.

'Not too bad, old thing,' she said aloud to her reflection, which, she noticed somewhat to her surprise, was actually smiling a rather smug smile. 'What have you got to be so smug about? As if I didn't know.'

Grow up, woman, she told herself sternly. You're middle-aged. You need to lose weight. Your hair would be grey if left to its own devices. There's nothing for you to feel happy about. *Oh, yes, there is*, said another voice in her head, a singsong pantomime voice. *There certainly is.*

Suddenly Rilla felt hungry. She picked up the trousers she'd worn yesterday and went to hang them up. Her hand felt something through the thin cloth. She felt in the pocket and brought out the rolled-up strip of wallpaper. I must be losing my mind, she thought. How could I have forgotten? The doll's house. The roof, stripped of some of its paper. Douggie. Oh my God, what is Leonora going to say?

I must dress quickly, she thought suddenly, and go and find Gwen. She'll know what we should tell Mother. Oh, please, don't let anyone go into the nursery till I've told Gwen.

Gwen looked at her watch and felt a stab of irritation. It was a quarter to twelve and where was Rilla? She was hardly ever about. Had she even got up this morning? Typical of her, she thought, not to offer to help.

No sooner had she thought of her sister than Rilla came round the side of the house, almost running. Gwen felt a chill come over her.

'What's wrong?' she asked.

'Something's happened, Gwen, which I have to ask you about.'

'Oh God, don't tell me. Is it Mother? Is she OK?'

'Don't worry. No one's ill. Can we go somewhere a bit private?'

Gwen opened the door to the conservatory and sat down at the table. 'What is it? You're being very mysterious, Rilla.'

Rilla took something out of her trouser pocket. 'Here you are. It's a piece of the wallpaper from the doll's house roof.'

Gwen watched as she unrolled a long strip of the familiar paper onto the table, and as soon as she let it go, it curled up again.

'Where did that come from? How could it possibly . . .?'

'Douggie got into the nursery. I found him there early this morning.'

'What were you doing up early in the morning?'

'Doesn't matter now. I'll tell you later. We've got a crisis here. If Mother finds out that the doll's house has been wrecked, she'll be livid.'

Gwen wasn't listening. 'Have you seen?' she asked. 'There's something written on the back of this. It's very faint but you can read bits of it.'

Rilla picked up the strip of wallpaper and peered at it. 'You're right,' she said, 'but the main thing is, what are we going to tell Mother?'

'It'll wait till after lunch. At least we can have one meal in peace.'

'Fine, but I want you there when I tell her, Gwennie. I can't face her alone. I wouldn't know what to say.'

'All right. We'll get her on her own somehow. She'll be going upstairs for her rest anyway and to get changed for this afternoon's filming. Sean's taking her down to talk to Nanny Mouse.'

Rilla was holding the strip of paper near her face. 'The things that are written here are rather strange,' she said. 'The way it's been torn off makes it look as though there's more.'

'Of course there's more. It's part of a letter or something. Can you actually read any of the words?'

Rilla nodded. 'Yes. There's *glow and shine and leap out* and *fragile* and what's this? Can you read these words?'

Gwen frowned and tried to decipher the faded sepia ink. '*Paint never lies.* That's what it looks like, anyway. Who do you think wrote it?'

'I've no idea,' said Rilla. 'But we've got to see what the rest of the letter, or whatever it is, says, or I'll die of curiosity. This little strip is just mystifying.' She rolled the wallpaper up again and put it back into her pocket. 'I wonder whether it'd be possible to peel off the rest of the paper from the roof, and then we could read whatever else is there.'

'We can't do that before we've told Mother, though,' said Gwen.

'But what if she just wants to patch the roof up again without reading any more? If we got it off before she saw it, then—'

'No.' Gwen shook her head. 'We can't do that. We'll have to leave it to her, but she always wants to know everything about everything, so I doubt she'd be able to resist reading the rest.'

'Yes, you're right,' Rilla said. 'Are you coming in to lunch now?'

'I might as well. This has rather driven other things from my mind. I don't know, nothing ever does seem to go smoothly, does it? You deal with one problem and another three crop up in its place.'

'Food helps,' Rilla said. 'Come and have some lunch.'

'My appetite's left me,' Gwen said. 'I'm dreading telling her.'

'Me too,' said Rilla, 'but it doesn't affect my appetite. I'm starving!' She gave Gwen a hand to pull her out of her chair and linked arms with her as they walked along the corridor to the dining room. 'United we stand!'

Gwen smiled gallantly. They'd always said that when they were girls. It was comforting that Rilla hadn't forgotten.

'**M**other, would you mind coming up to the nursery with Gwen and me, just for a minute?' Rilla said, taking her mother's arm.

'Now?' Leonora looked put out. 'I have to rest, you know. Sean is coming to fetch me at three. Can't it wait, dear?'

'No, Mother,' said Gwen. 'There's something you ought to see.'

When they reached the nursery, Rilla went straight to the doll's house and took off the sheet that was covering it. Leonora crossed the room quickly, and ran her hands over the roof.

'Who did this?'

'It was Douggie. He got in here early this morning. He dropped the strip he tore off . . .' She held out the roll of paper.

Leonora took it from her without looking at it. Her gaze was fixed on the white space on the roof. She was breathing rather loudly.

'Maybe you should sit down, Mother,' Rilla said.

Leonora ignored her and went on staring at the doll's house. When she spoke at last, her voice was falsely bright. 'Matters could be even worse,' she said. 'Perhaps we could stick it on again, if it's not ruined.'

'Someone's written on the back of it,' Rilla said. 'Look.'

Leonora sat down on one of the covered chairs and began to unroll the paper. Rilla, looking at her, couldn't believe what she was seeing. Her mother was shrinking, becoming smaller and weaker by the second as she stared at the writing. Her mouth was trembling and there were tears in her eyes. 'Mummy.' Leonora's voice sent shivers up Rilla's spine. 'My mummy's writing . . .'

'Are you all right?' Gwen said, kneeling beside her mother.

Leonora's breathing had become ragged. She blinked and Rilla could see that she was making an enormous effort to regain control. 'I'll be all right in a minute,' she said, sounding tearful. She wiped her eyes with the back of her hand, like a small child.

Rilla was shocked. Leonora never wiped her eyes with anything less than a handkerchief. Even tissues were only for dire emergencies.

Now she was holding the strip of paper up to her eyes.

'Shall I get your reading glasses, Mother?' Gwen asked.

'No,' said Leonora. 'I can see enough.' She was sounding more normal. She looked in the pocket of her trousers, found her handkerchief and patted at her eyes. She said, 'My mother wrote this. Can you make out what it says, one of you? It's such faint handwriting.'

'I think so,' said Gwen, taking the strip. 'I think I can.'

'Read it to me,' Leonora said. She had her eyes closed now, listening.

'It won't make much sense, Mother. There are only a few whole words on each line. But I'll have a go. It says: *was coming to life/the window, brushing/getting that highlight/object (or subject)/mories of what it was. /nished, wanted it to be like a/ glow and shine and leap out/to do that and they didn't /than saw that. Even while/than his. Also, he/is clever. Didn't/for years. He said doesn't/Paint never lies. You/and not ask for fame/said you're fragile.*

You'll/away from my door, and he/to say this to him, but it is . . . That's it. That's all. I'm afraid it doesn't really make much sense.'

Rilla looked at her mother, who was stiff and upright in her chair. Tears came from her eyes and ran down her cheeks unchecked.

'Mother?' she said, feeling suddenly afraid. 'Mother, please. Don't be sad. What is it? Tell us. We're here. Aren't we, Gwen?'

'I'm sorry, darling,' Leonora answered, visibly pulling herself together. 'It's just that it's been many years since I saw my mother's handwriting. It brings back memories. I'm perfectly all right, really, but of course I shall need to see the rest. What Gwen's just read is only a part of something. My mother must have written it just before her death, because the doll's house roof was a present for my birthday . . . and . . .' Her voice faltered. Rilla knew about that terrible time, though Leonora rarely referred to it.

'Can we get it off, though?' Gwen said. 'Without damaging it, I mean.'

'Didn't you tell me that young man of Chloë's is a picture restorer? He'll know what to do.'

Gwen looked relieved. 'Philip. Of course. How clever of you to remember, Mother! I'll go and find him. I'm sure he'll be able to help.' She left the room and Rilla could hear her going downstairs, calling for Chloë.

Leonora stood up and made her way to the door. 'Will you find Sean, please, Rilla? Tell him I'll see him at four o'clock if he'd be good enough to delay the filming.' She left the room before Rilla could answer.

Rilla picked up the sheet again and spread it out over the doll's house. She looked at the sharp edge of the roof outlined against the wall, and felt a small shiver of apprehension at what might be hidden under the fall of white material.

A noise was coming from her own mouth that Leonora didn't recognise. It sounded like a wounded animal, not like a person. Not like me, she thought. She was lying on her bed, seeing suns and stars and purple streaks exploding behind her closed eyelids. She couldn't stop herself from trembling, and she was aware of a dark heaviness lodged within her. She had carried that weight inside her all her life, she realised, and had always thought of it as the pain that any child who loses a parent at an early age has to bear. But now . . . She opened her eyes. There's something, she thought. Something my mother's words may tell me. If only I could know, this lump of darkness in my heart might dissolve. I should think of ordinary things. The party. Leonora tried to fix her thoughts on tomorrow's celebration but what came into her mind was another day, long ago. I have been like something buried underground for a long time, she told herself. Something struggling to wake after a long sleep.

August 1935

Leonora hesitated as she came into the drawing room. It was the grandest room in the house and usually she only went in there if Mummy or Daddy invited her to. Mummy didn't look round when she came in, though she must have heard her walking across the floor. She was standing at the window looking out at the garden and you could tell, just from her back, that she felt sad. Maude . . . that's my mother's name, she thought, staring at the small figure. It fits her. It's a gentle sort of name. If I wasn't looking for her, it would be easy not to see her, because she's so still and small.

Leonora crossed the carpet and made her way towards the window. 'Mummy! Tyler's making a bonfire in the garden. May I go and look?'

Maude moved her mouth into a smile. 'I was just thinking about the bonfire myself. I can see Tyler out of the window, look.'

There was their gardener, piling up wood and logs. Near him in a wheelbarrow was a heap of assorted papers, small sheets like letters and bigger sheets with drawings all over them. Those were Daddy's sketches. Every so often, Daddy had told her, the paper all got too much and had to be burned. Leonora was used to this, and she loved the bonfires; loved the leap and the gold and the scorching heat of the flames and the way the paper shrank into curling grey ash, and how sometimes a glowing fragment went up and up, carried by the wind, like a fiery butterfly. Sometimes, too, there were showers of sparks, like tiny fireworks.

She wanted to ask her mother something but had to make sure that the question wasn't too upsetting. She knew that lots of things upset Mummy. Nanny Mouse said she was sensitive, which meant that she felt everything more than other people. It also meant that she was often ill, and kept to her room. Sometimes, Leonora didn't see her for days, because when she wasn't ill she spent hours keeping Daddy company in the studio, where Leonora wasn't allowed to go.

'Why can't I?' she'd asked Nanny Mouse once. 'Why can Mummy go up there and not me? I wouldn't disturb him. I'd be very quiet, really.'

Nanny Mouse had shaken her head. 'It's not the noise. It's just that your father likes to be alone when he's painting, apart from your mother, who's a sort of muse to him.'

'What's that? What's a muse?'

'A muse is a person who inspires a painter or a poet to do good work.'

'I could do that,' Leonora had said. 'I could be a muse. Couldn't I?'

'I expect you could, dear, but your daddy has chosen your mummy and there's nothing to be done about that.'

Now Leonora took a deep breath. 'You don't like bonfires, Mummy, do you?' she asked.

'No. No, I don't. They're so . . . so final. Once a thing has been burned, there's really no getting it back at all, is there?'

'But if you make sure that you don't want the things that are going on the fire, then you don't mind, do you? Not getting them back, I mean.'

Maude smiled at her daughter and briefly stroked her hair. 'I never know, you see. Whether I really want something or not. I change my mind. You can *think* you don't want something and then wake up in the middle of the night and want it most desperately.'

Leonora looked sideways at her mother, and saw that she had tears in her eyes. 'Is it all right if I go and watch Tyler?' she said. 'Watch the bonfire? Nanny Mouse said I was to ask you or Daddy.'

'Yes, darling, of course it is,' Maude said.

'You could come with me if you like. We could watch it together.'

'That's very kind of you, sweetheart, but I think I must go and lie down. I have a headache this afternoon. Run along, now.'

Tyler had lit the bonfire by the time she reached the kitchen garden. Everything that had been put out for burning had been fed into it, and fire had already crisped every sheet of paper into glowing red and gold.

'How do, missie.' Tyler was shouting a bit. The noise of the flames always surprised Leonora. They really did crackle and spit and roar.

'It's a lovely fire!' she cried. 'It's bigger than ever.'

'Months' worth of rubbish, that's what Mr Ethan said, but it didn't rightly look like rubbish to me. Proper lovely, some of it was.'

A small triangle of paper blew off the bonfire and leapt towards the sky. Leonora followed it with her eyes. It was being carried away across the lines of growing vegetables. Leonora ran after it as it blew into the Quiet Garden. She found it where it had drifted down to the earth, near some delphiniums, and picked it up. The paper had scratchy pencil marks on it and some of the marks were words. She could just make out 'light' and 'window' and 'ora'. Maybe that was a bit of a word but the rest had been torn away. She knew her father's spiky handwriting well from staring at letters he'd put out for the post. These words, these parts of words, were in her mother's sloping, tiny script. Surely Daddy wouldn't let Mummy write words on the corners of his paper? Leonora tucked the piece of paper into the pocket of her cotton dress. Later, she would take it out and put it with the collection of secret objects that she kept in a biscuit tin. She knew she shouldn't say anything about having this scrap of paper, though she couldn't have said exactly why not.

Leonora was a good reader, but she loved those nights when her father read aloud to her. He would sit on her bed and pick up whatever book she had started and just go on from where she'd got to for a few pages. Tonight, she leaned back against her pillows with her teddy bear tucked under her arm, and listened while Daddy read from *Little Women*, her favourite book. They'd got to the part where Beth was most awfully ill. Daddy was sitting up and leaning forward, about halfway up the bed. Suddenly he stopped reading and put the book down on the eiderdown.

'What's this, Leonora? Where did you get this?'

The scrap of paper! She'd left it on her bedside table and forgotten to put it away. Now Daddy had seen it and he looked very angry.

She said, 'It flew off the bonfire this afternoon and I picked it up, that's all. May I keep it, Daddy? It doesn't look very important.'

Ethan Walsh stood up with the scrap of paper still in his hand. His head was just in front of the light where it hung down from the ceiling, so she couldn't see his features properly. He said, 'No, I'm afraid you can't keep it, Leonora. It was wrong of you to take something that didn't belong to you. I must go now, I'm afraid, dear. Good night.'

He left the room before she could say a word in her defence and the injustice of the whole thing brought tears to her eyes. She hadn't done anything wrong. No one wanted those papers or they wouldn't be burning them. They were rubbish, and rubbish didn't belong to anyone, did it? Leonora closed her eyes and hugged her teddy bear closely.

Suddenly, she was quite wide awake again, and for a moment didn't know whether she'd been asleep or not. She crept out of bed and opened her door quietly. She couldn't see any light coming from Nanny Mouse's room. It must be terribly late, which meant she must have slept. The house was quiet, but Daddy was working still, because a faint glow filtered down the corridor from the studio. He must have not quite shut the door, which was most extraordinary.

Leonora tiptoed downstairs to look at the grandfather clock in the hall. It was nearly two o'clock, which was the latest she'd ever been up in the night. She wasn't afraid of the dark, only everything looked different, even Daddy's pictures on the walls. There were no colours at night, but every frame held shadows and gleaming spaces and shapes that seemed to move as she passed them. She fled up to the safety of the night nursery, closing her door tight.

There was a noise, like something heavy had crashed to the ground. She opened the door again and put her head out into the corridor. She heard some more bumps from upstairs. What was Daddy doing there? Leonora listened, stiffening in terror as his angry voice came to her. You could hear that he was trying to be quiet, but some of his words reached her: 'Bloody careless . . . what we agreed . . . You can't do this now. I shan't allow it . . . Stop that snivelling . . . I won't tolerate it, Maude . . . if I hurt you, of course, but . . . Get out of my sight . . . tomorrow . . .'

Was it possible? Was he shouting at Mummy? She'd definitely heard him say her name. Leonora heard footsteps and ran back into the night nursery. She stood, trembling, just inside the door and kept it open a crack. Someone was coming down the stairs and she'd see who it was. Did she want to? Too late. She could see clearly now. There was Mummy, in her nightgown. She was sobbing, making noises that sent shivers through the whole of Leonora's body. She knew she ought to close the door and not see this, but her fingers wouldn't move and she *did* see. There was only a split second when Mummy was exactly level with where she was and in that moment she saw it: a cut under Mummy's eye, which was bleeding so that two thin lines of blood that looked black were scribbled on her white cheek. She must have fallen over. That must be why she was crying.

Mummy had gone now, into her bedroom. Leonora stood for a few minutes, waiting for Daddy to come down from the studio, but he didn't. Perhaps she was in a nightmare, and if she pinched herself, she'd wake up safe in her own bed. She nipped hard at her arm and almost cried out with the pain. No, she was definitely not dreaming.

She tiptoed to Nanny Mouse's door and opened it. Nanny Mouse was sleeping tidily, as she always did, on her back with her hands folded on her chest. Leonora went over to her and touched her arm.

'Wake up, Nanny. I'm scared. Please wake up.'

Nanny Mouse opened her eyes at once. 'What is it, my love? Have you had a bad dream?' She pushed back the sheets and got up. Her hair, normally carefully done up in a neat bun, hung down her back in a long plait and her nightdress was blue. She put a soothing arm round Leonora's shoulders. 'Come, I'll tuck you back into bed and bring you a warm drink. Then you can tell me all about your dream.'

She put her dressing gown and slippers on and took Leonora by the hand. They walked into the night nursery and Nanny Mouse made sure that Leonora's night light was on. 'I'll be back before you can blink,' she said. 'With a nice mug of warm milk and a biscuit as a special treat.'

As she waited, Leonora wondered again whether she'd dreamed it all. Maybe she'd imagined her mother with a bloodstained face. She slipped into a doze for a while, but woke up when Nanny Mouse returned.

'Now then, Leonora, I'll sit down here and you drink this and tell me all about your nightmare.'

Leonora felt a little silly. Everything was safe and comfortable now, and it was hard to recollect the terror she'd felt earlier. She said, 'I heard something banging about. I thought it was coming from upstairs, and I went out into the corridor to listen and then I saw Mummy. She was sort of sobbing and whimpering and she ran right past me and there was blood on her cheek. I felt so frightened that I came to get you.'

'Poor little pet!' Nanny Mouse took the mug out of Leonora's hands and put it on the bedside table. 'Never you mind about things that the grown-ups do, my love. It's not for us to wonder what goes on between a man and his wife. Best to forget all about it. What I always say is what you don't know can't hurt you. It'll be all right, Leonora. You'll see. In the morning, it'll just be like a bad dream. And look at you now, child. Your eyes are closing. I'll wait here till you're asleep.'

Leonora felt herself falling into darkness and silence and as she fell she could hear Nanny Mouse's voice, saying the words, saying them over and over: *what you don't know can't hurt you what you don't know can't hurt you.*

And then all at once she was wide awake, and it was morning, and there was Nanny Mouse drawing the curtains open.

'Wake up, sleepyhead! It's a lovely day. Rise and shine. It's nearly time for breakfast. I've put out your yellow skirt today.'

Leonora sat up and rubbed her eyes. 'I went to sleep quickly last night, didn't I? After you'd brought me a drink.'

'I didn't bring you a drink, dear. You've been dreaming again.'

Leonora frowned. 'You did, Nanny! I know you did. I saw Mummy, don't you remember? With blood on her face? And I came and woke you up and you brought me a drink and then I fell asleep.'

Nanny Mouse sat on the bed and took Leonora's hand. 'Now you know you have a vivid imagination, dear, and that brings on very vivid dreams. I slept like a log all through the night. What's all this about your mummy? I shouldn't tell her about it if I were you; she wouldn't like to think of herself there in your nightmares with blood on her face. Now go and brush your teeth, dear. It's quite late already.'

Nanny Mouse left the room and Leonora stared after her, amazed. It *wasn't* a dream, she thought. I saw her. I heard her. I even pinched myself to make sure I wasn't dreaming. I can't have been, but Nanny Mouse would never say I didn't wake her up if I did. Would she?

Leonora dressed slowly, thinking hard all the time. She could remember everything that happened, and every word that Nanny Mouse had said. *What you don't know can't hurt you.* That's what she'd told her, but dreams were funny things and sometimes they were as real as anything.

Never mind, she thought, I'll know when I go down to breakfast. I'll see whether Mummy's hurt her cheek. I'll see her and then I'll know.

She almost ran into the dining room and when she saw that her mother's place was empty, tears of disappointment came to her eyes. She blinked them away before Daddy could look up from his newspaper. She said, 'Good morning, Daddy,' and sat down at her place.

'Ah, Leonora! Good morning,' Daddy said, lowering his newspaper for only a second.

'Where's Mummy?' Leonora asked, pouring milk over her cornflakes. 'Is she still asleep?'

Leonora thought perhaps Daddy hadn't heard her. She wondered if she ought to repeat it, and decided to wait a little longer. Maybe he was reading something important. She gazed at the black lines of type on the back page with the spoon halfway to her lips, and then with a rustle he lowered the newspaper again and stared straight at her.

'Finish that spoonful, Leonora, before we continue our conversation.'

The crunching of the cornflakes sounded loud in her ears. She put her spoon down when she'd finished and looked at her father. He was very pale this morning and there were purple shadows under his eyes.

'I'm afraid your mother is not well today,' he said. 'She'll be keeping to her bed for the next couple of days and you must try not to disturb her.'

'But can I see her? Just for a second. I won't be noisy, I promise.'

Leonora watched her father pushing his chair away from the table. He stood up, and when he spoke to her she heard that coldness in his voice, a tone that froze the air all round her head. He said, 'Your mother is unwell, Leonora. That means she does *not* wish to be disturbed. Not by anyone. You will see her all the sooner if you allow her to return to health. You are not to visit her, is that clear, child?'

'Yes, Daddy,' said Leonora. 'I'm sorry.'

I'm not sorry, she thought, as she ate another spoonful of cornflakes. I'm only saying I am, because you have to say you're sorry with Daddy and then he's cheerful again. Sometimes. Today, though, the magic word didn't work and he swept crossly out of the room.

Leonora felt that her whole head was in a muddle, and her eyes felt sore and itchy, as though she'd been crying. Now she'd have to wait till Mummy was better before she could see if her cheek was all right, and every time she thought about what she'd seen in the night it got less clear in her mind. Maybe I did dream it, she thought. *What you don't know can't hurt you*, Nanny Mouse said in the dream. What did that mean? And why were those words still there in her head, as loud as could be?

Her birthday was a week and a half away now. Leonora had been longing for it for ages. Time had slowed down. Mummy had been in her room for three days, and surely, Leonora thought, today she'd have to get up. The doctor hadn't come, and Daddy had gone off to London this morning in the car. He wouldn't be back till tomorrow, so she could go and see Mummy without worrying about him catching her. It'll be all right, I'm sure, Leonora thought, if I just creep in and say hello to her. Nanny Mouse was busy in the kitchen, chatting to Mrs Page, the cook, and Leonora hoped they were discussing her birthday cake.

She walked down the corridor to Mummy's bedroom. Mummy wasn't there. Leonora knew she should have left at once, but instead she crossed the carpet and looked out of the window and then she saw her, down in the gazebo. Leonora ran out of the room and down the stairs.

Nanny Mouse was just coming out of the kitchen. 'Where are you off to, dear?' she asked.

'To the gazebo, to see Mummy,' Leonora said over her shoulder, and she could hear Nanny Mouse telling her not to disturb her mother if she wanted to be by herself. She took no notice, but ran down over the lawn till she reached the small glass and wrought-iron house.

Maude looked up as she came in and smiled and held out her hands. 'Hello, darling. Have you come to talk to me?'

'Oh, yes, Mummy! I've been longing to see you. Are you feeling better?'

Maude didn't answer the question but said, 'Come and sit by me and tell me what you've been up to. It's so hot, isn't it?'

Leonora sat in the chair on her mother's right. That was the side that had been bleeding. She began to talk, telling stories of seeing the new cygnets on the lake and playing croquet with Bunny, and all the time she kept glancing up at her mother's face. She saw it at last, even though there was a lot of foundation cream and powder over it. Mummy must have tried to hide it, but it *was* there, underneath—a small bruise with a thin, long scab right in the middle of it. That meant that Nanny Mouse *had* been lying to her, and only pretending that she'd been dreaming.

'You've hurt your cheek, Mummy,' Leonora said after a pause.

'Oh, that was silly of me,' Maude answered. 'I walked into your father's easel, up in the studio. Can you imagine how foolish I felt?'

'Was it in the middle of the night? I heard noises. They woke me up.'

'No, no,' Maude shook her head. 'In the morning. I remember distinctly. It happened on Wednesday. Quite early in the morning.'

Leonora looked up at the blue sky through the glass. Today was Friday. Monday night was when she'd had her dream (but it wasn't a dream: there was the scar, on her cheek). Mummy was still in her room on Wednesday. Could she have gone upstairs to see Daddy and bumped into his easel? Leonora felt confused and a little frightened, too. Should she tell Mummy about the dream? Should she say she'd seen her? She was just opening her mouth to speak when Maude said, 'I'm busy making a little surprise for you, in time for your birthday.'

'Tell me about it, Mummy! Do tell me.'

Maude smiled. 'If I told you it wouldn't be a surprise, would it?'

Leonora saw tears in Maude's eyes. 'You're sad, Mummy!' she burst out, and put her arms round Maude's thin body. 'Don't be sad. Please be happy.' She kept clinging to her mother, till Maude gently disentangled herself from Leonora's arms and lifted her face up and kissed it.

'Oh, my darling child,' she said. 'You must forgive me. I'm so sorry. Please say you forgive me, Leonora. Please say it.'

Leonora didn't know what the words meant. What should she forgive? Had Mummy done something bad? She saw the tear-streaked face looking down at her and wanted more than anything to be gone, to be safe with Nanny Mouse and away from Mummy whom she didn't understand, and whose crying made her feel embarrassed and nervous. She said, 'I forgive you, Mummy. Please stop crying. Please be happy.'

'I will, darling.' Maude had let go of Leonora and was dabbing at her eyes with a white lace handkerchief that smelt of lily of the valley. 'You can go and play if you like. I'll be perfectly all right, I promise.'

'Will you? Will you really?'

'Yes, I'm going to the Quiet Garden for a little walk—I want to have a look at all my plants and flowers. You run along now, Leonora.'

Leonora made her way towards the house, feeling guilty. Should she be so relieved to leave her mother's company? There must be something wrong with me, she thought. I'm a bad daughter, and maybe that's why Mummy's sad. Maybe if I loved her better, she'd be happy. Leonora was just about to run back to her mother and swear she loved her best of anyone in the whole world, when Nanny Mouse came across the lawn.

'Come along, dear,' Nanny Mouse said. 'It's nearly time for lunch.'

'Yes, Nanny,' Leonora said. I'll make sure to tell Mummy how much I love her later, she thought. There'll be time later on.

'I had such a funny dream last night, Nanny,' Leonora said as she was getting dressed the following morning. 'I was lying in my bed and I saw a person in a long white dress with long hair hanging down at the back coming into the nursery. She stood by the doll's house and I could smell wallpaper paste and she was sticking something on the doll's house roof. Then she went away and I can't remember anything after that.'

Nanny Mouse went on plaiting Leonora's hair. 'That wasn't a dream, dear,' she said. 'Your mummy came in last night and did some work on the doll's house. That's part of your birthday present. She did tell me she was going to make it a surprise, but she must have changed her mind.'

'May I go and see? Please, Nanny! Let me go and see.'

'Sit still and let me finish your hair, Leonora, and then you can.'

Leonora looked over to the doll's house. There was nothing different about it that she could see. As soon as her hair was plaited to Nanny Mouse's satisfaction, she raced to see what her mother had done.

'Oh, it's the roof, Nanny! Look!'

Where before there was plain wood stained a reddish colour, now the roof was covered in pale grey and yellowish tiles, painted on two large sheets of paper. Every one seemed different from the ones next to it.

'It looks just like a real roof, doesn't it, Nanny? It must have taken her hours and hours, mustn't it?'

'It's most beautiful,' Nanny Mouse said. 'You make sure to thank her.'

'Yes, I will,' Leonora said. She knew Mummy must have taken enormous trouble over painting the roof tiles, and they *were* exactly like real tiles and very beautiful, but she couldn't help feeling disappointed. It wasn't what *she* would have called a birthday surprise. A new doll for the house would have been more exciting. You couldn't *play* with a roof. All you could do was look at it, and she'd scarcely paid any attention at all to the old one, so why did Mummy think she'd like a new one?

As she went down to breakfast, she tried to cheer herself up by thinking that maybe this wasn't the whole surprise, but only part of it. After all, it wasn't even her birthday yet and she was being allowed to see it. By the time she reached the dining room, she'd persuaded herself that there was something much better to come. But, she said to herself, if Mummy is there I shall thank her very much and give her a kiss as well.

Mummy and Daddy were both sitting at their places when Leonora came into the dining room, but she could see from the way they were sitting that something was wrong. They didn't even look at her and Nanny Mouse as they came into the room and took their places at the other end of the table. Silence fell over everything, so that the noise of spoons on cereal bowls and cups being put down on saucers sounded really loud. Daddy was frowning and his lips were pressed together, as if he wanted to shout but was holding himself back. Mummy's gaze was on her plate, but she hadn't touched her toast.

'Nanny,' Daddy said, not looking at Nanny Mouse. 'I'd be grateful if you kept Leonora occupied outside today. It's a fine morning. Mrs Walsh and I have matters to discuss, and wouldn't want to be interrupted.'

'Of course, sir,' said Nanny Mouse. 'We'll go for a walk in the fields behind the church. We can take a picnic, Leonora. Would you like that?'

Leonora nodded. She didn't trust herself to speak. How *could* Daddy be so beastly? She never interrupted them when they were busy. She never went up to the studio because she knew she wasn't allowed to. She bit into her toast and glared at her father, but he was looking out of the window and didn't see how cross she was. I'll say something to Mummy, Leonora thought. I'll thank her for repapering the doll's house roof. She took a deep breath and said, 'Mummy, I love the new paper for the doll's house roof. Thank you for making it for me.'

To her astonishment, Mummy turned so pale that Leonora thought she might be going to faint. She looked across the table at her daughter with something like terror in her face. She was trembling too. Leonora wished fervently that she'd never opened her mouth.

'Maude, my dear,' said Daddy, in a voice that was icy and soft at the same time, 'what paper is this? Have you shown it to me?'

'No, dear,' her mother answered. 'I painted some paper to decorate the doll's house roof. It's of no consequence, really.'

'A waste of your time, I'd have thought.'

'It was a special treat for Leonora's birthday.'

'It's beautiful, Daddy,' Leonora cried, hoping to divert her father's displeasure away from Mummy. 'The doll's house looks so much nicer now. Thank you, Mummy!' She left her place and ran round the table to her mother's chair. She flung both arms round her neck and hugged her.

Daddy stood up. 'Nanny, please take Leonora away now. This scene has gone on long enough.' He left the room, and Leonora could hear his footsteps on the marble floor of the hall and then going up the stairs.

'I love you, Mummy!' Leonora cried, not sure what was happening.

'And I love you, my baby,' said Maude and burst into tears.

'Go to your room, dear, and wait for me,' Nanny Mouse said. 'Your mummy will be quite all right. I shall look after her. Don't worry.'

Leonora made her way slowly to the nursery, wanting to scream with rage and weep with anguish at the same time. Stupid Nanny Mouse, she thought, kicking against every step of the staircase. How can she tell me not to worry? My mummy's sad and I don't know why. She slammed the nursery door behind her and flung herself onto the bed. Why, she wondered, does Daddy want me out of the house? What is he going to do?

Leonora came in from outside and stood in the hall. Nanny Mouse had stopped in the drive to talk to Mrs Page, who was on her way to the village, and she'd told Leonora to run on ahead. Daddy and Mummy were quarrelling. She could hear loud, angry voices. Mummy usually spoke quietly, and to think she could shriek like that made Leonora feel sick and frightened. She knew that they wouldn't want her to hear them, so she shrank against the wall, but she didn't run away. A longing to *know*, a desire to understand exactly what was troubling her mother, kept her standing there, with her mouth half-open and her eyes wide. They were in the drawing room and she could hear almost every word.

'No more. I utterly refuse. And if you lay one more finger on me, I swear I'll tell.' Then there came a laugh from Maude that chilled Leonora's blood: shrill, horrible, not really laughter at all. '. . . Well, I've had enough, that's all. The worm is turning. I'm warning you, Ethan. I'm tired of being the one you take everything out on. Tired of it.'

Her mother's voice faded to a whisper and Leonora didn't catch the next murmured remarks. She could hear her father's voice, too, but not what he was saying. Could it be that he was calming Mummy down?

Leonora was just beginning to feel more normal, when she heard her father say, 'I don't want to hear any of this again, d'you understand? If I ever discover that you've told anyone, anyone at all, then you'll be very sorry indeed. And remember. I, too, can speak. I can have Dr Mannering up here in twenty minutes and tell him that my poor dear wife has gone insane. It's well known that your health is what they call "delicate". You'd be in the asylum within the hour.'

Tears started from Leonora's eyes, and she tiptoed as quietly as she could to hide behind the curtain near the hall window before her parents came out of the drawing room. Too late! There was Daddy, striding towards her across the marble tiles.

'What are you doing, Leonora?' he said, gripping her arms. 'How long have you been in the hall?'

'I've only just come in. We've been in the village, and then we went for ever such a nice walk . . .' Leonora knew that she had to keep talking, as though she'd really just come in and hadn't overhead anything. She went on babbling, the words spilling out of her mouth and, gradually, her father's hold on her arms relaxed.

'Go to the nursery, Leonora. I have work to do now.'

He went up the stairs two at a time. Leonora listened hard and heard the door of the studio slam shut. She let out a breath that she felt she'd been holding for ages. She wanted to run to Mummy and make sure she was all right, but just then Nanny Mouse came into the hall.

'What's the matter, child?' asked Nanny Mouse. 'You look as though you've seen a ghost.'

'Mummy and Daddy were quarrelling. It was horrid. He said—'

'Don't say a word, dear. Remember what I told you? What you don't know can't hurt you. All this grown-up arguing is none of our business.'

They were walking up the stairs. 'When did you tell me? When did you say that what I don't know can't hurt me?'

'Why, the night you came and woke me with stories of blood on your poor mother's face.'

'But you said it was a dream! You did, you did.'

Nanny Mouse sighed, and took her hat off and turned it round and round in her hand. She looked down at the carpet outside the nursery and blushed. 'Yes, I'm so sorry, dear. I did say that, and it was very naughty of me, but I was only trying to make you feel less frightened. I shouldn't have done it, but it's difficult to know what to do for the best sometimes. Never mind, you just stay in the nursery for now, till bedtime. I'll bring your supper up for you tonight. Just keep out of the way for now. It'll be all right, you'll see.'

Nanny Mouse made her way downstairs again. Leonora went into the nursery and stood by the window for a long time, not moving. What I don't know can't hurt me, she thought. I *do* know some things, but I must pretend I don't. I must pretend that my daddy is a good daddy, who loves my mummy, and not someone who shouts at her and makes her cheek bleed and tells her she's mad. I must pretend that what I saw was a dream, but I know it wasn't.

Afternoon, Saturday, August 24, 2002

Gwen's tea had gone cold and she didn't have the energy to get up and make more. Rilla was busy whipping cream for the strawberry shortcakes. The housekeeper, Mary, wasn't due back in the kitchen for another couple of hours and had reacted rather better than Gwen had expected to the news that Rilla wanted to be in charge of dessert for tonight.

Gwen had hulled the strawberries and was cutting them into neat slices. She felt herself relaxing more than she had for a long time.

'I wonder what Philip and Chloë might be uncovering,' she said. 'Up there in the nursery.'

Rilla was absorbed in spreading the shortbread with cream. 'It might be nothing at all,' she said. 'A shopping list or something.'

'It didn't look remotely like any list I've ever seen. You don't seem to be in the least worried.'

'I don't know what to be worried about. Your problem is, Gwen, that you go searching out the difficulties instead of waiting for them to happen.' She was now arranging strawberry slices in concentric circles on lustrous white.

'Well, one of us has to be prepared,' said Gwen. 'And you seem to be in cloud-cuckoo-land.'

Rilla smiled enigmatically. 'I'd forget all about it until you have to deal with it. It would have to be quite something to ruin the party, surely?'

Gwen frowned. 'I give up, I do really. You don't even admit to the possibility of a catastrophe.'

Rilla looked at her sister. 'My idea of what constitutes a catastrophe is a bit different from yours. The cancellation of a party doesn't come anywhere near it, I promise you.'

'Oh God, Rilla, I'm sorry!' Gwen was near tears. 'I don't know what I'm saying any more. Of course I didn't mean. Don't think—'

'It's OK, Gwen. Don't start crying, please. That's all we need.'

Gwen was silent, remembering the funeral. A grey March day, and the wind like a knife and she and Leonora holding Rilla up, one on each side of her, their arms linked through hers as the tiny coffin was lowered into the earth and Rilla, pale and trembling with grief. Gwen wiped a tear away while Rilla was moving the plates into the larder.

'Now come on,' Rilla said as she came back into the kitchen. 'Let's go and find James and see how the marquee's coming on. It's going to be the best party, whatever they're finding up in the nursery.'

Gwen followed Rilla out of the back door, and shut it carefully behind her. I wish I shared her optimism, she thought.

Leonora picked up the rose-patterned teapot and said, 'No sugar for you, Sean, is that right?' She hoped that she was sounding normal. She felt as though an earthquake had taken place inside her, and it surprised her that no one could see it. She felt confused, mystified, and uncertain of what she remembered. Something—she was not sure what it was—hovered at the edge of her memory, just out of reach.

'Yes, thank you,' Sean said. 'Now, Nanny Mouse, shall we get started?'

They were sitting in the front room of Lodge Cottage. Miss Lardner had set tea, on a table that had been polished to such a dazzling shine that the lighting man had asked for a cloth to cover it up.

'Do you remember whether Ethan Walsh ever came into the nursery when Leonora was a little girl?' Sean asked the old lady.

Nanny Mouse was silent for a while, and Leonora wondered whether it would be necessary to prompt her, but then, like a bottle suddenly uncorked, she started talking. 'The Master loved the nursery. That's what he told me. And he liked to read to Miss Leonora at bedtime. Of course she could read perfectly well herself, but it's not the same is it? Not the same as having your daddy reading to you.'

'What about her mother?' Sean asked. 'What about Maude?'

'Oh, no, she never read to her. She wasn't that sort of mother really. She was always very shy. She had one layer of skin missing, that's what I told her. Thin-skinned. She wasn't very strong, and she bruised easily. I knew about the bruises, though she thought I didn't see them. I did. I saw everything. It was my job to see things. I had Miss Leonora to think about and the Master was most particular that she shouldn't know.'

'What?' Leonora asked, hearing her own heart beating. 'What was it that Daddy didn't want me to know?'

'Oh, he didn't want you to know anything, dear,' said Nanny Mouse sunnily. 'Not about the bruises. Certainly not about how Miss Maude died, but you don't remember that at all, do you? The Master told me you couldn't possibly remember, and you've never said a word so I suppose he's right, though I've always thought it strange that you could put such a thing out of your mind. Still, it's a mercy.'

The air in the room seemed to thicken and darken round Leonora's head. What was Nanny Mouse saying? She closed her eyes and saw an image on the inside of her eyelids, as clear as any photograph: the lake and something dark in it, spreading on the surface of the water, under the willows. A skirt, that was what it was. Leonora opened her eyes and spoke to Nanny Mouse in a voice that sounded to her like the voice of a small child. 'Mummy drowned in the lake, didn't she, Nanny?'

'Leonora found her,' Nanny Mouse said confidentially, shifting focus again. 'Poor little mite. She'd run down to the lake because everything in the house was out of sorts. Dreadful atmosphere for a child, and they never paid her the least mind, you know. Quarrelling all around her and worse. Much worse. I don't hold with children seeing all that.'

Somewhere so distant that it might have been in another universe, Leonora was aware that the camera was still turning, but she could feel the tears starting up again. She could hear Sean saying something. She pulled her attention over to where he was sitting and tried to listen.

'Leonora, I've stopped filming. Are you all right?'

She nodded, not caring. She was somewhere else. She was down by the lake and there was her mother, floating on the water, her face all white and her eyes staring. I found her, she thought. I found her and she was dead and I ran back to the house to get everyone and then I fainted, and I was wet and cold, and after I went to bed there was nothing but fever and bad dreams and pain in my chest, and when I woke up, they told me a lie. They told me my mother had been very ill and had died from her illness and I believed them. Nanny told me and Daddy told me and I believed them because I didn't want to know that I'd found my own mother with water filling her mouth and dragging at her skirt and making her skin all pruney and white. I didn't want to know that, so I forgot it. Pretended I never ever knew it at all. Pretended that she'd died neatly in her bed and I'd never seen her floating in the lake with willow leaves caught up in her fingers. But I remember now.

'I'm so sorry, Sean,' Leonora said, putting her glass down on the place mat beside her. 'I think I'm quite recovered now.'

They were back at Willow Court, in the conservatory, where leaves formed a dark green canopy over their heads. Sean had fetched a drink for Leonora and now they sat facing one another in the two cane armchairs. He could see that Leonora's hands were still trembling and that, although she was doing her best to appear in control, she was obviously still trying to come to terms with what Nanny Mouse had been saying.

'I think you're being very brave,' he said. 'There's no need for any apology. That kind of discovery would knock anyone sideways.'

'I've always tried not to let things get the better of me.' Leonora attempted a smile. 'With every single thing that's happened to me—my father's death, my husband's death, other things—I've always felt that if I could keep my head, everything would be all right.'

'You don't mention your mother's death,' Sean remarked. 'That must have been the most traumatic thing of all, for such a young child.'

Tears sprang into Leonora's eyes. 'But it wasn't. That's why I feel so terrible now. I wasn't close to my mother. I loved her, of course, but I always felt that I could never really get near her. Nanny Mouse was more of a parent to me than she was, and what I most remembered from those days was being ill and missing my birthday. The fact that my mother was gone when I came to myself was sad, of course it was, and it troubled me, but not in a way I could understand. And after a while I seemed to recover. But all my life it's as though I've been stifling something. Covering it up. And now I feel as though I've opened a door into some dark space in my mind. It's as though I've walked into this blackness carrying a candle. I feel as though I'm holding it out in front of me and different things are catching the light.'

'What do you see,' Sean asked her gently, 'in the light of the candle?'

'Almost the worst thing of all is what I've come to realise about my father. The person I thought he was is nothing but a childish illusion. He was a bully, Sean. I see now that my love for him blinded me to all sorts of cruel things he said and did. My father deceived me. And yet it is him I'm weeping for as much as my poor mother. More even. I feel I've lost more where he's concerned. I feel guilty about that, and also guilty about something I've discovered about my own behaviour. I think I've kept things covered up all my life. Protecting people, including myself. I always thought that was for the best, but it isn't. You have to know the truth of things, even though sometimes it's painful.'

'Has it all come back to you, Leonora? Do you remember everything?'

'I think so. I can remember running down to the lake. I can see the dark thing on the water very clearly. I can remember seeing my mother's face, but everything else is still very hazy. I can't bring it back into my mind properly, but it doesn't matter. I can imagine. From when little Mark drowned. I did see him. I don't need anyone to remind me of that.' She placed one hand over her eyes.

Sean spoke into the silence that grew between them. 'Rilla feels responsible, you know. Because she wasn't there when Mark drowned.'

Leonora took her hand away from her face and Sean could see how white she was. 'Does she? Does she still? After all this time? Oh, no. How terrible. Oh God!' Leonora's voice shook. 'How stupid of me not to see my own daughter's pain. Maybe because of my own. There's nothing worse than the death of a child. I blamed myself. And thought Rilla blamed me too, because after all she'd left her child in my care. Mine and her sister's. And you'd think a grandmother and an aunt would be responsible enough to take care of one small child, wouldn't you? I've never forgiven myself, but Rilla always said that she didn't blame us. I didn't realise that was because she still felt herself to be at fault.'

'Perhaps Rilla hid her pain from you.'

Leonora nodded. 'Yes, there's been a great deal of hiding of things, one way and another.' She sighed. 'I'll have to do something about it if it's not too late. I should have spoken to Rilla more frankly. About many things. I always criticise her, but we don't really talk. I will, though. I'll talk to her.' She leaned against the back of the chair and closed her eyes. Sean was aware of her gathering her strength. He could almost see the struggle that was going on in Leonora's mind in the reactions of her body: the twitching of the muscles round her mouth, the way she kept turning one of her rings round and round on her finger, and a trembling that came over her from time to time, as though a sorrowful memory was washing over her body like a wave.

'**R**illa? Rilla, wake up!' Beth touched the shoulder that stuck up out of the sheet covering the sleeping body on the bed.

Rilla turned over and opened an eye, groaning slightly. 'God, Beth, must I? I was having such a lovely nap. What's wrong?'

Beth grinned. 'You only just got up before lunch, Rilla. Honestly! This is what comes of burning the candle at both ends.'

Rilla swung her feet to the floor and pushed her fingers through her hair. 'I'd have you know that it was well worth losing a night's sleep.'

'Spare me the gory details and get dressed,' Beth said. 'You've been summoned. Leonora says would you mind coming to the conservatory.'

Rilla washed her face and hurried to brush her hair and get back into her clothes. 'Have I got time to put my make-up on?'

'No, you haven't. You look fine.'

'I look,' said Rilla, 'like a rather plump ghost. And why on earth does she need to see me now, anyway? Do you have any idea?'

Beth shook her head. 'Not a clue. She just told me she wants to see you and Efe and me for what she called "a quiet chat".'

'Right, let's get it over with then. Whatever it is.'

Downstairs, the door to the conservatory stood open.

'Is that you, Rilla?' Leonora called out. 'Come in, darling.'

Rilla went in and Beth followed her. Efe was there, taking up most of the sofa. Beth hesitated.

Leonora said, 'Beth, shut the door behind you, please. You can sit by the window. Rilla, why don't you take the other cane chair?'

Beth sat down. This is bizarre, she thought. Why on earth does she want to talk to us? And why does the door have to be shut? She looked at Efe, but he was staring down at his shoes.

'You must all be wondering why I've asked you to come in here like this,' said Leonora. 'It's all rather cloak and dagger and I don't mean it to be, only the house is upside-down what with the cleaners and the film crew and I wanted a quiet word.'

'Has anything happened?' asked Rilla. 'Is something wrong?'

'I suppose,' Leonora said slowly, 'that something has happened. And something *is* wrong, but I'm going to try to put it right. Yes, that's it.' She smiled, almost triumphantly. 'I'm going to put it right. I've felt for some time that I owe both you, Rilla, and you, Efe, an apology.'

Rilla looked anxious and Beth knew she would have loved to light a cigarette. Leonora was twisting the rings round on her fingers.

She said, 'When I was a little girl, there was something Nanny Mouse used to say to me. I was brought up on it really. *What you don't know can't hurt you.* It was a—what do you call it nowadays?—a mantra. I believed it. I really did. Now I see that what you don't know *can* hurt you almost more than any other single thing.'

Efe was getting bored. Beth could almost hear him thinking, Cut to the chase. Leonora obviously sensed his discomfiture as well. She looked directly at him and said, 'Efe, my darling, the reason I wanted to see you is because we've been keeping something hidden, you and I, for many years. It's time to talk about it now, Efe. Don't you think?'

Efe clenched his hands into fists. 'I don't believe this,' he spat out. 'After all this time? You're going to make me tell Rilla?'

'Tell Rilla what?' said Rilla. 'What do you want to tell me, Efe?'

'I don't want to tell you anything. Nothing.'

'If you don't,' Leonora said, 'then I will. I want you to know about Mark's death. I want Efe to tell you exactly what happened that day.'

'I know what happened. You told me, Mother. I don't think we should . . .' Rilla's voice was shaking.

'I think we must, my dear. This is all my fault, I know, but I'm trying to put it right. Because I was protecting you, Efe, I hurt my own daughter, and I'll never forgive myself for that. But you were so very young, Efe. I thought, he's a child and his whole life might be ruined, but can't you see how Rilla has suffered? How she still blames herself?'

Beth could feel her heart thumping in her chest. Rilla was sitting quite motionless, very upright, with her mouth tightly closed.

'And it's not just Rilla, Efe,' Leonora went on. 'It's you, too. I think that living with this weight on your conscience has altered you. I should have encouraged you to tell the truth instead of helping you to bury it.'

All the time that Leonora was speaking, Efe had his head in his hands. When he lifted his face, his whole demeanour had changed. He seemed younger, somehow. More vulnerable. Different.

'I tried to,' Efe said, and Beth had never heard him sound so tentative. 'I tried to that night. I went to Rilla's room. I wanted to tell her, but she was . . . well, she was sort of asleep and not asleep and I didn't know what to do so I came to you, Leonora, and you said it would be all right. I believed you. You said no one ever needed to know and that it was a hideous accident. Not my fault.' He covered his face again.

Rilla coughed, breaking the silence. 'Tell me what happened, Efe. I'm not going to blame you for anything. I promise,' she said gently.

'We were playing down there. By the lake.' Efe directed his words straight to the floor, so that Beth had to lean forward to catch what he was saying. 'Alex and Beth and I. We were playing trappers. I didn't want Markie to come, but he did anyway, and I thought it wouldn't matter. He was OK, for a little kid. We didn't mind him tagging along.'

Efe looked up suddenly, and Beth saw that his cheeks were wet with tears. He said, 'Rilla, I could have saved him. That's what I came to tell you. I could have. I didn't take any notice when he called out to me over and over again. I thought he was messing. Alex was about to find the secret trap and I had to stop him. It was the most important thing in the world that my trap shouldn't be found.'

He started crying quietly again. 'It wasn't even a real trap. It didn't exist. I was more caught up in a pretend game than in a real little boy shouting something behind me. I didn't even ask myself what he was doing in the water. Alex was in the water and so was I, so I didn't think anything of it. It wasn't very deep, the lake. He must have lost his footing. Alex was down by the willows and Beth was even further away. She was being a trapper's wife, getting the dinner ready.' He laughed without mirth. 'You always did what I told you to, didn't you, Beth?'

Beth nodded. 'I heard the shouting,' she whispered, 'and when I got back to where Efe and Alex were, there was Markie, all wet and lying at the side of the lake. I went to fetch someone. Efe sent me. I couldn't see because I was crying so much. I could see that Markie was dead. I never asked what happened. I didn't want to know, I think.'

'I turned round and saw him,' Efe said. 'I saw his arms waving and I didn't go back to help him and then I couldn't hear him any more and Alex was screaming and it wasn't till I heard Alex that I went to look for Markie. It was too late, though. I didn't go when I should have. I killed him. I thought I'd killed him till you told me I hadn't, Leonora. You said it was an accident and I should never say anything about it to anyone. And I never have. Rilla, I'm sorry. It's a pathetic thing to say, and I don't know if you'll ever speak to me again, but I'm sorry. I shouldn't have listened to you, Leonora. When I was a kid, there was a reason for it, but lately, well, I knew you blamed yourself, Rilla, and I still never dared to say anything. I wish I could go back and do it differently.' Efe went and half knelt down next to Rilla. 'Will you ever be able to talk to me again?'

'Oh, Efe.' Rilla put both arms round him and drew him to her. 'I still blame myself. I always will, because it was *my* business to look after Markie, not yours or Mother's or Gwen's. But I'm glad you've spoken about it now, if you can feel less bad. I suppose we all ought to have spoken about it straight away and comforted one another, but we didn't. I couldn't have at the time, and once you've started not saying things, it's so easy to carry on. It was brave of you to speak now, Efe, and of course I forgive you. You were only a child. I'd never have blamed you.'

Efe sat up and took a handkerchief from his trouser pocket. He said, 'I'd better go and wash my face, hadn't I? Leonora, will you excuse me?'

'Yes, Efe. I'll see you at dinner.' She turned to Rilla as he left the room. 'You've said you forgive Efe, but I want to know whether you can forgive me. I should have told you, Rilla. I see that now. I protected Efe at the expense of your happiness. I think I felt that you could cope with tragedy better than he could. I'm so sorry, Rilla. So dreadfully sorry.'

Beth could see that Leonora wanted to touch her daughter, gather her up in her arms, and didn't know how to. The struggle was visible in her face. Oh God, Beth thought, please let Rilla reach out to her. Please.

'No need, Mother,' Rilla said, and she put her arms round her mother. Leonora made a sound that was something between a groan and a sigh.

Thank heavens, Beth thought. Everything will be easier now.

'Beth dear,' Leonora said, sounding almost like herself again. 'See that your mother rests before dinner. That's why I asked you to come with her. So that you could look after her. I'm going to my room now.'

She left the conservatory and Beth could hear her slow footsteps as she made her way to the hall.

'Are you all right, Rilla? Would you like a drink or something?'

'I don't know. I don't know what I want. Oh, Beth, it's so hard to forget things, isn't it? I've been so good at pushing bad things away all my life, but now here's Leonora bringing it all back. Am I ready for this?'

'Of course you are, Rilla.' Beth knelt down beside her and took her hand. 'You're so brave. I've always thought you were . . . Please say something. Please smile. Oh, Rilla, I hate it when you're sad.'

'I'm not sad, my love. Just a bit shaken up. That's all. And the heat doesn't help.' Rilla smiled as though she were trying out something new. 'Have you ever seen a run of hot weather like this? I feel as though I'm about to melt. I'm going to have a long, cool bath.' The smile had grown stronger: wider and more normal. 'And that's the first time I've heard Leonora call me your mother. Ever.' Rilla was looking much happier now, Beth was glad to see. 'I'll be OK now. Go and get me a stiff gin and tonic and bring it to the bathroom.'

Beth made her way to the kitchen, feeling relieved, as though a crisis had been averted.

Philip stood on one side of the doll's house, which he'd moved carefully away from the wall. A bath towel was spread out under the window for the wallpaper to lie on when it came off the roof.

'Right,' he said to Chloë. 'We've got to make it just wet enough to peel it away, without going through and wrecking the writing on the other side. A bit tricky, but we'll do it, I think. I'll do the watery stuff.'

He smoothed a moist sponge over the paper. Chloë had brought a knife from the kitchen and was busy inserting the long, thin blade under the damp paper on her side.

She said, 'Look, it's coming away, I think.'

'OK, if you're sure. Take care.' Philip looked on anxiously.

Chloë pushed the knife a little further under one edge of the paper. 'It's coming off beautifully, look,' she said and lifted one corner. The paper peeled away cleanly in a single piece.

'Brilliant,' said Philip. 'Now you can get the sheet from this side.' As Chloë got to work with her knife again, he added, 'This is a really beautiful piece of work. If we can dry it out properly, I might be able to put it back, you know. Almost as good as new.'

'You're a gem and a treasure,' said Chloë. 'But what if Leonora wants to keep what's on the back?'

'She could make a copy, surely?'

'I don't know.' Chloë sounded as though she wasn't paying attention. She placed the second piece she'd managed to peel off beside the first, which lay with its painted side face down on the towel. She knelt down and peered closely at the writing. 'It's hard to make out, this writing,' she said. 'But I think . . . Oh my God! It can't be . . . Philip, come over here. If this means what I think it does, it's unbelievable.'

Philip went over and crouched down beside Chloë to read. After a minute or two, he pushed his hand through his hair and grimaced. 'Bloody hell, Chloë,' he said. 'You'd better tell Leonora.'

'I think my mother must have been the most camera-shy person ever,' Leonora said to Alex.

They were sitting close together on the bench in the gazebo, looking through the photograph album open on Alex's lap. During her conversation with Sean in the conservatory, it occurred to Leonora that there wasn't a single photograph of Maude on display in Willow Court. She'd racked her brains for several minutes before she remembered the ancient album in the bottom drawer of her chest of drawers. Alex had been coming in at the front door as she was on her way upstairs to find it, and she'd sent him for it, to spare, as she put it, 'my ancient legs'.

She peered now at the page Alex was holding up for her. There was her mother in the distance, but if you didn't know what she looked like, this photo wouldn't have told you. The tiny, tiny, figure of a thin woman far away down a garden path. A bank of flowers in the foreground. Quite a lot of sky filled with puffs of cloud. A second snapshot showed Maude beside an espaliered fruit tree in full bloom. She'd evidently wanted to show off the blossom, spread like a fan all over the wall, and her face was turned away from the camera.

'I wonder who took them,' said Alex. 'Ethan Walsh, I suppose.'

Leonora shook her head. She could not imagine her father snapping pictures in the garden. 'It was probably Nanny Mouse,' she said. 'Or Tyler, the gardener.'

'This one by the piano is better. Bigger, too. It was taken by a photographer, I'm sure.' Alex passed the album to Leonora and she brought it up to her face to look at it more carefully.

She took a deep breath and let it out again. 'She's pretty, isn't she? In a rather faded, quiet sort of way. She reminds me of a startled deer.'

'Yes, she's very pretty. But she doesn't look like you at all, Leonora. You take after Ethan, don't you?'

At that moment, the door of the gazebo burst open and Chloë came in, holding a folded sheet of paper in her hand. 'I'm sorry to interrupt, Leonora, but I'd like to speak to you, if that's OK.'

'Of course, darling. Alex and I were only looking at an old album. Come and sit down here by me.'

'D'you mind if I speak to you alone, Leonora? I'm sorry, Alex.'

Alex looked puzzled. 'No problem,' he said. He closed the album and stood up. 'Shall I take this back to the house with me.'

'That would be very kind,' said Leonora. 'We won't be long, I'm sure.'

Chloë closed the door of the gazebo behind Alex and went to sit next to her grandmother. 'I'm sorry to send him off like that, but I thought it ought to be just us. I've typed out the message that we found on the doll's house roof. This is it.'

Leonora squeezed Chloë's hand. 'You're a kind child, aren't you? I'm so glad it's you who's deciphered it all.'

'And Philip. He got it off the roof without damaging it. He's brilliant.'

'What does it say? I'd better know what it says.' Leonora took the sheet of paper from Chloë. Then she unfolded it and began to read.

Beth had spent much of the afternoon dealing with Leonora's presents. When Gwen had asked her to be in charge of those that had come by post she'd said yes at once. Everyone, it seemed, was running around getting things ready, and it would be good to be occupied with something.

She hadn't realised that Leonora had so many friends and aquaintances. Nearly seventy people were coming to the party and on top of that there were all these things from those who couldn't make it. Some of the gifts were worth displaying. There was an antique bonbon dish, luxurious soaps, handmade chocolates and fur-lined slippers.

Beth stood up to take the first batch of gifts into the hall. They were to be placed under the tree that Chloë had created there. It was like something out of a fairy tale. Bows of tinfoil and thin gold ribbons were tied among the willow leaves, catching the light and twinkling as they moved in the air. Beth found Douggie and Fiona looking at the tree, entranced. As she approached them, the front door opened and Gwen came in from the garden, carrying a bucket full of flowers.

'You're going to catch flies in your mouth, Douggie darling,' Gwen said, 'if you keep it open like that.'

The little boy took no notice at all, and Fiona laughed. 'You can't really blame him,' she said. 'It's the most beautiful tree I've ever seen.'

'It *is* lovely, isn't it?' Gwen said. 'I'm so pleased Chloë thought of it. It'll be quite a talking point, I'm sure. I see you're busy arranging the presents. It's going to look amazing.' She set off towards the scullery. 'I'd better get on with my flower arrangements.'

Beth started to take the gifts one by one off the tray and caught sight of Douggie out of the corner of her eye, staring longingly at her. 'Would you like to help, Douggie? With putting the presents under the tree?'

Douggie nodded solemnly and Fiona said, 'That'll be fun, won't it? Only you'll have to be extra careful. Here, I'll help you give them to Beth and she'll put them all in their proper places . . . Carefully, Douggie. It would be so awful if anything got broken. That's right.'

'Hello, ladies!' said a voice, and Efe crossed the hall, picked Douggie up and kissed him. 'What are you doing and can anyone join in?'

'Of course, darling,' said Fiona. 'We'd love you to join in, wouldn't we, Beth?'

Beth nodded.

Efe was wearing a khaki T-shirt and trousers with rather more pockets than were strictly necessary. He looked amazingly nonchalant considering the state he'd been in while they were in the conservatory, and she marvelled at his ability to hide his true feelings.

'I've been helping Dad in the marquee. It looks great. Really excellent. Have you seen it, Beth?'

'No, not yet. Douggie, bring that bottle you're holding back here right this minute, please. I need it to go on this little pile.'

Douggie trotted obediently over to her and Beth took it from him and put it down before any harm could come to it.

'I see you're being about as useful as a chocolate teapot, beloved,' Efe said, smiling at his wife. Then he turned to Beth. 'My wife is very silly, Beth. I'm married to a moron. That sounds like a movie title, doesn't it?'

Fiona had tears in her eyes. Beth glared at Efe and opened her mouth to say something when she saw that Alex had come in and was standing silently beside the door.

'Apologise, Efe,' he said. 'That's an insult to your wife and if you weren't my brother I'd hit you. I might hit you anyway.'

Efe smiled. 'Oh, right. You've become some kind of knight errant have you, Alex? A bit late in the day, isn't it? Having kept your mouth shut your whole life, don't you think this is none of your business?'

'It *is* my business. You think you can get away with everything.'

'Oh, shut up, Alex. You're boring, d'you know that?'

Fiona said, 'Douggie, come on now.' She picked up her son and almost ran from the hall, frantic in her haste to get away.

Beth hesitated. She wanted to see what Alex would do next, but knew that someone had to look after Fiona. By the time she'd left the hall, though, there was no sign of her. Beth sighed. She was standing in a dark part of the corridor that wasn't visible from where Efe and Alex were, though she could see them both perfectly well.

'You are an arrogant bastard,' Alex shouted, and before Beth knew what was happening he had gone right up to his brother and punched him in the face.

Efe was caught by surprise, and stumbled back against the banisters, but he recovered quickly and hit out at Alex almost reflexively. His fist connected with the corner of Alex's mouth. Efe was pale with fury. 'Shit, man, what's got into you?' he shouted. 'Lay off, will you?'

'Apologise, then. Go on. Go and find Fiona and say you're sorry.'

Efe scowled. 'What I say to my wife is none of your damn business.'

'I don't care. Say you'll apologise or I'll hit you again. Harder this time.'

'Ooh, I'm scared,' Efe said, in the voice he'd always used to tease Alex when they were children. 'OK, I'll apologise, OK? I will. When I see her.' He stalked away towards the staircase and took the steps two at a time.

When Beth saw that he was safely upstairs, she came out of her hiding place and went over to Alex, who was leaning against the door frame, touching his bottom lip, which was already swollen.

'You're hurt, Alex,' Beth said. 'You're going to have a huge lip and a bruise. Come into the kitchen and I'll fix you up.'

'Do I need fixing?' Alex said, but he followed her willingly enough and sat down at the kitchen table.

'You do a bit.' Beth went to find a clean tea towel. She turned on the cold tap and wet a corner, then wrung it out as hard as she could. 'OK, don't move,' she said, leaning over Alex, who turned his face to her.

His eyes were shut and he looked suddenly vulnerable. She noticed the blue veins in his eyelids. She could smell his hair and his skin. The sore lip was swollen and cut and one side of Alex's lower face was already showing bruising. There was something turning over in her stomach, a kind of fluttering, a thrilled nervousness she hadn't felt in Alex's company before. What was wrong with her? She was meant to be in love with Efe, wasn't she? So why was being so close to Alex having this effect on her. She felt hot and cold at once and closed her eyes because she thought that if she didn't she might faint.

'Beth?' Alex whispered.

'Mmm,' she said. She was overcome by a fierce desire to kiss him, to comfort him by wrapping her arms round his shoulders. Everything she had previously felt, everything she'd believed for so long, all her emotions and desires, were like pieces in a kaleidoscope, and feeling Alex so close to her was shaking and rearranging them into shapes she didn't recognise. She lost all sense of who she was, where she was. There was nothing in her whole world but this mouth, which was on hers before she could find a word to say that might stop it, and her own lips were opening and she closed her eyes against the light and the heat that was running through her veins. 'Alex,' she murmured. 'Oh, Alex.'

'Don't say anything,' he whispered. 'Kiss me again.'

Alex stood up then, and put his arms round her. Beth could feel everything changing. Nothing would be the same again. And she knew that what she was feeling now was true. It had nothing to do with fantasy or imagination or dreams.

'What's happened?' she said. 'What's happened to us?'

'It's me,' Alex said. 'Something's happened to me. I've been stupid and slow and haven't admitted it to myself.'

'What? What haven't you admitted?'

'That I love you. I think I always have, only there was Efe and I could see how you felt about him, and I couldn't . . . Oh, Beth, I didn't think you'd ever be able to feel the way I want you to feel.'

'I didn't think I could either.' Beth smiled. 'But that was because Efe was dazzling me. I wasn't seeing or feeling anything properly.'

Alex stroked her hair. 'And you were right, I *was* jealous. You noticed it, remember? On the way to see Nanny Mouse.'

'You don't have to be any longer, Alex.' She stood on tiptoe to kiss him and then drew back, breathless from the force of what she had begun to feel. 'We can't,' she said. 'Not here. Anyone could come in.'

He sat down shakily on the kitchen chair again and grinned at her, and at that moment the kitchen door opened and there was Rilla.

'What's going on, darlings?' she said, coming in and sitting down immediately next to Alex. 'I just saw Efe looking like a thundercloud. Have you two been fighting? Whatever about? Tell all, go on. Alex, sweetiepie, what *has* happened to your lip?'

'It wasn't anything, Rilla, honestly,' Alex said weakly.

'Of course it was.' She turned to Beth and gave her a smile. 'I wouldn't say no to a biscuit, darling, if you'd pass that tin from the dresser.'

Beth put the biscuit tin in front of Rilla. 'I'll leave you two to it,' she said. 'I'm going out for a bit of fresh air.'

She knew as she stepped out into the kitchen garden that Alex would have given anything to come with her, to be rescued from Rilla's interrogation, but she wanted to be on her own. She needed to think.

She needed to think about what had just happened. It was as though by kissing her like that Alex had made her aware of him for the first time. Oh God, what a lot of time I've wasted, Beth thought. I could have saved myself so much anguish. I could have been spared loving Efe altogether if I'd had any sense. I never noticed Alex before because I was dazzled. She sat down on the bench near the shed, which was out of sight of the house, and let the late-afternoon sun fall on her face.

Fiona managed to put Douggie down in his cot. She sang him a song and he stuck his thumb in his mouth and closed his eyes. He's exhausted, she thought, but he'll never want to go to bed at his proper time if he has a sleep now. She found that she didn't care. She didn't care about anything but getting Efe back into a good mood.

What had got into him? Why had he been so horrible to her? She was finding it hard to understand him these days and even harder to make up with him after quarrels. In the first months of their marriage, she had only to press her body against his and he would turn to her and make a moaning noise and they'd sink down onto the bed or the floor and once or twice they'd even done it standing up, in the kitchen against the sink.

They'd made love this morning, while Gwen was looking after Douggie. Fiona's body was still humming with pleasure, even though Efe hadn't said a word to her from beginning to end. Before that, though, the last time they'd made love was more than three weeks ago.

She had never managed to work out what to do to bring Efe out of his black moods when lovemaking was out of the question. She could never find the right words. Maybe I *am* stupid, she thought.

Efe came into the room now, and Fiona didn't dare to ask him where he'd been. He went and stood at the window while she hovered tentatively before moving across to the dressing table. Sitting in front of the mirror, she was able to do her hair and keep an eye on Efe at the same time. She could see him reflected in the glass. She was about to say something neutral about Douggie being exhausted when Efe spoke. He didn't look in her direction, but went on staring out of the window.

'Alex has got a bloody cheek interfering in my marriage,' he said.

Fiona had been full of gratitude for Alex's uncharacteristically macho behaviour, and she was still hurting from her husband's unkind words, but it didn't do to disagree with Efe when he was in this mood.

'I know,' she said. 'I don't expect he meant any harm.'

Efe didn't answer for a while. Then, still not looking at her, he said, 'I'm sorry, Fi. I shouldn't have been so foul. It's all the uncertainty about the pictures. I'll be myself again when Leonora's made her decision.'

'That's OK,' said Fiona, amazed to get any apology at all. He found it almost impossible to say sorry. 'I knew you were joking.'

'Course I was,' said Efe, and Fiona knew he was lying but didn't care because his mood, she could see, was lifting. 'I'm going down now, Fiona. I could do with a drink, I can tell you, after all that. See you.'

He blew her a kiss as he left the room. Tears welled up in Fiona's eyes. He never includes me, she thought, feeling sorry for herself again. He doesn't care whether I'm around or not, most of the time. That's what hurts. Her tears spilled onto her cheeks and she brushed them away. I'll have a nice cool bath, she thought, and then get ready for dinner.

She was on her way to the bathroom when she noticed that Efe had left his mobile phone on the bedside table. It wasn't like him to put it down and forget about it, especially not today when she knew he was expecting a call from Reuben Stronsky. She picked up the phone and saw at once that there was a text message. She hesitated—she'd been brought up never to read other people's letters, but this was different. It might be an urgent message from Mr Stronsky. She was ready for her bath and didn't fancy traipsing around Willow Court in her kimono looking for him, but if the call was important, she could dress again and go and find him and have a bath later on.

Fiona sat on the bed, pressed the tiny silver button and saw that Efe was being asked whether he'd received some call or other. I'll listen to it, she thought, and only go and find him if it's urgent. It turned out to be a call from someone in Efe's office who actually said he'd be happy to wait till Monday. Before she'd had time to switch the message off, another recording of an old call began. She should have turned it off there and then, but it was a woman's voice and once she'd heard the first few words, she had to go on listening.

For some moments after the voice stopped speaking, she didn't move. She was aware of her whole body trembling. Her mouth was dry and she was suddenly freezing cold in spite of the heat of the day. It isn't true, she said to herself. It can't be. This isn't happening. Not to me.

She forced herself to breathe. Breathe in, breathe out and calm down. The hope flashed into her mind that maybe the call was a wrong number. Did the person actually mention Efe's name? She had to know.

She pressed the button again and the voice, distorted by distance and thickened by lust, spoke into her ear again.

Efe darling. There they were, the words she was dreading. *Efe darling. It's me. Can you guess what I'm doing? I wish it was you doing it, sweetheart, exactly as you did last time but maybe it won't be too long. I can't bear the waiting, I want you so much. Tomorrow. Will there be a chance for us to go somewhere for a bit in the afternoon? Otherwise I might disgrace myself . . . Oh God, Efe, I need you. Can you hear how much I need you?*

Fiona went on listening through several seconds of groaning and sighing. Oh God, how revolting! She deleted the message and flung the phone away from her and it fell on the floor. I don't care. I don't care if it's broken. Oh God. She closed her eyes and fell back on the bed, hurting too much even to cry. She stood up again and put a hand over her mouth, certain that she was going to throw up, but the feeling passed.

She walked over to the window in a daze, and looked down at her husband's car, parked near the top of the drive. The keys were still on the bedside table. I don't have to stay here, she thought suddenly. I don't have to be anywhere near him ever again. I can pack up and leave. Her mind raced. They'll all be busy somewhere, making arrangements for the party. I don't want to go to the bloody party.

She went to the wardrobe and took out the larger of the two suitcases they'd brought with them and started to throw her clothes into it. She wouldn't write a note. She didn't feel like saying another word to him ever again, though she'd probably have to, one day. Just not now. It was a good thing Douggie was having a nap. She wouldn't wake him until she was ready to go. Efe would go ballistic when he discovered she'd taken the car. He'd have to come home by train, and serve him right, only she wouldn't be there. She'd get to her parents' house before it was time for them to leave for Willow Court. Mummy would be cross to miss the party. Leonora would be cross that three people who said they'd come wouldn't be there. It would spoil the table plans. Well, to hell with the table plans. On Monday morning, her father would make her an appointment with his lawyer. Daddy would look after her.

Tears sprang into Fiona's eyes at the thought of how little Efe would probably miss her. He'd miss Douggie all right, and what would become of the new baby? That thought was the final straw, and Fiona covered her face with her hands and sobbed.

'I'm not sure I get it,' said Alex. He was in Efe's room, sitting on Douggie's bed. Efe was staring out of the window, not saying much.

Alex was still light-headed from what had happened in the kitchen with Beth, and kept going over and over it in his mind. As soon as she'd gone into the garden, he'd started worrying. She was only making do with him because she was angry with Efe. She'd come to her senses and realise she didn't really mean it. That kiss. But he knew she did. He'd felt it in every part of her body, held close to his. He shook his head to dispel this memory. No more daydreams, he said to himself.

He could see that his brother was in a terrible state. Alex had been on his way to shower before dinner when Efe suddenly came out of his room and nabbed him.

'It's perfectly simple,' Efe said now. 'Fiona's buggered off. She's taken Douggie with her. She won't answer her mobile. On the way to her parents, I bet. What am I meant to do? She knows something like this could wreck Leonora's party. What she's done is a kind of sabotage.'

'Are you quite sure you apologised?'

'Of course I bloody did. I told you I did.'

'I know.' Alex tried not to sound impatient. 'But did Fiona realise?'

Efe nodded. 'She was fine when I left the room. I'd swear she was. We'd been getting on OK. I don't know what's got into her.'

Alex said nothing. This wasn't the time to go over the things Efe had done that would have driven another woman away long ago.

Efe came to sit on the edge of the bed and put his head in his hands. 'I *do* know, actually,' he said. 'She opened a text message of mine she might have thought was urgent. That led her to a missed call and then I suppose she just kept on listening and picked up an old message. I went to listen to it again and it's been deleted. I assume it was her. In any case, it's not there and neither is she, so I'm putting two and two together.'

Alex groaned. 'The message was from a woman, right?'

'Right. And it wasn't the sort of message I'd have wanted her to hear.'

Alex was silent. He could guess why Efe hadn't deleted the offending words. He said, 'What are you going to do, then? D'you want her back? You could persuade her if you do.'

'Dunno what I want. That's the truth. But Fiona's leaving isn't exactly going to help the celebratory mood, is it?'

Alex thought of tonight's dinner. 'I reckon you shouldn't tell anyone. Not tonight anyway, and by tomorrow everything will be in full swing and no one'll mind so much.' He looked at Efe. A thought had suddenly struck him. 'Did you say you went to listen to the message again?'

'Yes. Why?'

'No special reason,' Alex answered. How heartbroken could Efe have been if, in the midst of discovering his wife had left him, he'd wanted to listen again to what was probably an obscene message from his mistress?

Not very heartbroken at all, but just annoyed because this was something he hadn't planned and over which he had no control.

'Right, then.' Efe sat up suddenly and got off the bed. He ran his hands through his hair and said, 'I'll tell them she's not feeling too good. Headache or something. Tired. Don't you breathe a word, OK?'

Alex nodded. Not breathing a word was second nature to him.

Rilla looked into the dressing-table mirror but saw nothing. Her mind was still crowded with images of the lake as it must have been that day, and her child calling out to a heedless Efe who could have turned, could have looked behind him, instead of plunging further into his game. She let out a breath she didn't even know she was holding and thought, Poor Efe! How terrible for a child to have that always in his history.

She wondered whether this confession that Leonora had dragged out of him would make him feel worse, and decided that it wouldn't. It might even make life easier for him. But Leonora hadn't done it for Efe but to make her, Rilla, feel better. She felt a lump forming in her throat. Oh, stop, she told herself. No need to feel that sorry for her. She would feel better too. One always did after a confession. It was true, though, that over the last few days her mother had been far less acerbic than she normally was. Could she be mellowing in her old age? Rilla tried to recall any critical remarks or exasperated looks, and only two or three came to mind. It's also me, she thought. I'm distracted by love.

Her mobile phone began to sing its ridiculous tune. I must change the tone, Rilla thought. It drives me mad. As she picked it up, her heart sank. It could only possibly be Ivan. She'd never got round to phoning him after all. She would stall him for now and arrange a meeting next week. She pressed the button and held the phone to her ear.

'Ivan! How lovely to hear from you . . . Yes, I'm so sorry. You cannot imagine what it's like round here. Military campaigns are sloppy in comparison. Tell me what you've been doing.'

She listened with half an ear while Ivan droned on about a party he'd attended. When he got to the slushy stuff about how much he was missing her, she took a deep breath.

'Ivan, I can't talk now, but we have to meet early next week. Could we? There are some things I really do have to talk over with you.'

'I think,' said the disembodied voice in her ear, 'you are making this arrangement so that you can . . . how do you say? . . . finish with me. Am I right? You have perhaps met someone else. Am I right?'

A silence developed. Rilla wondered frantically what to say next.

'You cannot answer because it is the truth.' Ivan sounded triumphant.

'Well, yes, there is someone, but I didn't want . . .'

'I know. You wanted to do the proper thing. To tell me to my face. This is very good of you, but I will release you from such obligations. You are free, Rilla. I will not tie you down.' His voice rang with emotion.

Rilla couldn't help smiling. What an old drama queen he was! She said, 'It's very kind of you, Ivan. I don't deserve it, and I didn't—don't—mean to hurt you, but I've fallen in love. Does that sound ridiculous?'

'No,' said Ivan. 'I fell in love with you the very first time I saw you.'

Rilla couldn't help feeling that his love wasn't the real thing. He didn't exactly sound as though he was suffering. 'I've got to go now, Ivan,' she said. 'We'll talk properly when I get back to London, OK?'

When Rilla put the phone back on the bedside table she felt suddenly light-headed. It was going to be all right. Ivan had been much more understanding than she'd had any right to hope for. Some femme fatale you are, she told herself, and began to consider her options for this evening. Black satin trousers again, and perhaps the pink silk top?

A gentle knock at the bedroom door surprised her in the midst of these thoughts. Who can that be? she wondered, hoping that it wasn't anyone wanting her actually to *do* anything. She said, 'Come in.'

'I'm sorry to disturb you, darling . . .' Leonora's voice faded away.

'Mother!' Rilla supposed that Leonora was checking she was OK after the revelations about Efe. She said, 'Sit down here, Mother. Are you all right? You look rather tired.'

'I'm fine, darling,' said Leonora, her voice as strong and vibrant as ever. 'I came because there was still something I wanted to say to you. First, though, I have to ask you a question. Do you mind?'

'Not at all,' Rilla said. 'Fire away.'

'Do you ever think of Hugh Kenworthy?' Leonora turned her head towards the window as she spoke, allowing Rilla to collect her thoughts.

What kind of a question was that? Rilla would have bet good money that the whole episode had faded from Leonora's mind years ago. In the end she said, 'Yes, of course. From time to time.' I will not, she thought, remind you how much I hated you for what you did.

'I hesitated about coming to see you, Rilla, but I thought about it and decided that, in the end, it was better that you should know everything.'

'About Hugh?'

'About why I sent him away.'

'I remember it all perfectly, Mother. He was married. He was unreliable and unsuitable in every way. I know all this. I was very young then—now I understand that you had to do what you did. I expect I'd have done the same thing if Beth had been in such a situation.'

Leonora said, 'There was something else, though, that I didn't tell you. It would have hurt you too much, and I was deeply ashamed.'

She's blushing, Rilla thought. How astonishing! What is all this?

'Hugh made a pass at me,' Leonora said. 'Up in the studio one afternoon while I was showing him round. I was sitting on the chaise longue and we'd been chatting. I'd let myself get far friendlier than I should have, I suppose. He was terribly charming and handsome, wasn't he?'

Rilla nodded, but Leonora was already going on with her confession as though she had to get to the end of it, or she might lose her nerve.

'He came to sit beside me. I don't know when I noticed that his arm was round my shoulders, but there it was and then somehow I had turned to him and he was kissing me and it was minutes . . . whole minutes . . . before I came to my senses and pushed him away and told him to leave.' Leonora stared down at her hands. 'The worst thing was, I wanted him, Rilla. My love for your father was not like other kinds of love, you know. I've never, ever loved another man, and yet Hugh managed to get under my skin a little. I confess that.'

She shook her head. 'It's not something a child wants to hear about her mother, is it? But I did think you should know. That all the anger you felt towards me was . . . a little justified. I was jealous of you, Rilla. Of what you and Hugh had together. That's a dreadful thing for a mother to feel. I'm so, so sorry, darling. Can you forgive me?'

It occurred to Rilla that this was the first time in her life that she'd heard Leonora allude to her own sexual feelings. They were not something Rilla ever thought about. But Leonora was younger then than I am now, she thought. And what had Rilla been thinking about since she'd met Sean, to the exclusion of almost everything else, but sex?

She said, 'Mother, there's nothing to forgive. Hugh *was* handsome and charming. Only a log would have been immune to that. And you were a very beautiful woman, you know.'

Leonora smiled. 'Thank you, Rilla darling. I couldn't have done things differently but I *am* sorry you were hurt. And I regret not talking to you about it before.' She sighed. 'I haven't ever talked to you properly. It has never occurred to me before and I'm ashamed to admit it, but I think the fact that your father died while I was expecting you coloured everything. Even after all these years I blush when I think of how terribly unfair it was. But I was half mad with grief. And I blamed you, my poor little baby. Blamed you for his death, although of course you had nothing to do with it.' Tears stood in Leonora's eyes. 'I've never said anything like this to anyone before, but I was *too* much in love with Peter. And it's made me unfair to you, all your life, really. But you *do* know that I love you, Rilla darling, don't you?'

'Yes, Mother, of course I do.' She could see the physical signs of relief in Leonora: her shoulders straighter, her head higher, her eyes brighter.

'I'm glad, because you've been on my conscience so much lately, and I find it hard to apologise for anything, as you know.' She smiled to show that this last remark was not meant entirely seriously. 'But I *am* sorry, darling. I hope you can forgive me.'

Rilla bit her lip to stop herself from crying. 'Of course, Mother,' she answered somewhat shakily. 'But there's nothing to forgive, honestly. It must have been so ghastly to lose a husband you loved so much. I can't begin to imagine it. Don't feel bad about it any more. Promise me?'

'You're being kind to me, darling, and I'm so grateful. I'll go now, and let you get dressed for dinner. But I did just want to warn you about something. You won't think I'm an interfering old busybody, will you?'

Rilla laughed. It was a relief to hear Leonora sounding like herself again. 'Go on, Mother,' she said. 'What have I done wrong now?'

'Nothing, Rilla. It's just that I couldn't help noticing that you and Sean were . . . getting a little close. Don't you think you're rushing things?'

This is not the time, Rilla thought, to tell her roughly to butt out.

'Now, Mother,' she said as mildly as she could, 'what have you always told me about meeting Daddy and knowing within a few seconds that he was the one you would always love? And you were only a child. I'm nearly fifty. I do know my own mind, you know, and actually, I agree with you. It *is* quick, and at first I worried about that but now I've decided I don't care. I don't want to waste any more time. That's the truth, Mother, and I hope you don't mind me speaking so frankly.'

Leonora laughed. 'You're quite right. Of course you are, and none of this is my business at all. But I don't want you to be hurt, darling.'

'I'm sure I won't be,' Rilla said. 'But you couldn't prevent it, I'm afraid, whatever you do.'

'I know. I know that, Rilla, but I've learned some things about my own mother today that have made me reconsider everything.' She smiled. 'I'm being enigmatic, I know, and I will tell you everything at dinner, but I just wanted to say it. I worry about you and I haven't always been the best of mothers.' Leonora walked over to the dressing table, and before Rilla could say anything, she felt her mother's hands on her shoulders and a kiss on the crown of her head. 'I'm a silly old woman,' Leonora murmured. 'Bless you, darling.'

Rilla blinked back tears. 'You too, Mummy,' she managed to say, before Leonora turned and went to the door. She hasn't kissed me like that, Rilla thought, since I was about five years old.

Sean looked round the table. It struck him how different the atmosphere was now from what it had been for his first meal at Willow Court. There was the sort of excitement in the air that he generally associated with Christmas. The seating plan was different, too. He was next to Rilla, who looked perfect and smelt of something so delicious that he had to restrain himself from burying his face in her neck. Fiona was indisposed. Sean remembered seeing a car speeding down the drive earlier and he thought he'd seen Fiona at the wheel. But Efe told them she was going to get an early night in order to be ready for tomorrow. She was sorry, he said, to have to miss Leonora opening her presents.

Leonora had chosen to wear black. She looked pale and rather fragile, and the pearls of her necklace were lustrous against the chiffon lapels of her blouse. She had been quieter than usual, even though he'd tried to engage her in conversation several times. She'd eaten very little of the avocado and hardly any salmon at all. Sean was just on the point of asking her, tactfully, whether anything was wrong, when she tapped gently on the side of her wineglass with her fork. Everyone fell silent.

'Thank you,' she said. 'I have something extremely important to tell all of you, and I thought it would be best to do it now, before dessert is served. This is going to be an ordeal for me, so I hope you'll bear with me and let me finish what I have to say before you ask any questions.'

Sean looked round the table at the family, nodding and murmuring their agreement. Leonora opened her sequinned handbag and took out a sheet of paper, which she carefully unfolded and laid on the tablecloth. Then she opened her spectacle case and put on her reading glasses.

'This,' she said, tapping the sheet of paper with one finger, 'is a suicide note written by my mother.'

For a moment, Leonora thought she would faint. The faces round the table seemed to be blurring: white circles against the dark walls of the dining room. She could feel the silence stretching and knew she had to speak again. It had taken all her strength to keep the contents of this letter to herself from the time Chloë had brought it to her until now.

While she and Chloë were still in the gazebo, she'd wept and sobbed in an undignified way, as much from rage as sorrow, and the poor child hadn't known what to do to comfort her. But she'd pulled herself together and had even managed to be her normal self when she'd spoken to Rilla. I'm used to it, she said to herself. I'm used to putting a brave face on things. It's what I've been brought up to do.

Now, she looked round at her family, who were all staring up at her. Ought she to explain the background before she started? No, she would plunge straight in and let her mother's voice be heard at last. She coughed and began to read, trying to think neither of her audience nor of the writer, but only of the words themselves.

Went up to the studio where your voice didn't reach and painted every hour of the day. Solace. Comfort. Consolation, in those days. Didn't care if the pictures went out under another name. Didn't care at all. Unimportant, all that was. Paint mattered. What was coming to life under my fingers, that was the important thing. Light shone in from the window, brushing the side of a teapot and for hours nothing mattered but getting that highlight exactly right. Not precisely as it was in life, but more than it was; object (or subject) had to be what it was and also be all the possibilities, dreams, memories of what it was. Hard to explain, all this, but when a painting was finished, wanted it to be like a source of light to whoever looked at it. Wanted everything to glow and shine and leap out of the frame. Wanted to make beautiful things, and knew how to do that and they didn't cry and didn't bruise under my hands.

I was the better artist, that was all it was. Ethan saw that. Even while we were still both at art school, my paintings were more praised than his. Also, he realised that there was a fortune and a reputation to be made. He is clever. Didn't question his words for years. He said doesn't matter whose name it is on the canvas. He said the work abides. Paint never lies. You should be satisfied, he said, with being able to make such things, and not ask for fame and glory on top of that. He said you're delicate, Maude. You're fragile. You'll crack under the attention. He swore he'd keep the world away from my door, and he succeeded and now I bitterly regret it. Have tried to say this to him, but it is too late and he doesn't listen to me. Deception is too deep, and has gone on for too long to change now, he says. If you say anything (he says this all the time, many times) I'll tell them you're mad, and point to my signature. I'll say you're deluded. They would believe him. No one doubts him.

There is a way out. Will take it. Very soon. Am not braver than I used to be, only tired of everything, weary in my very bones. Nothing pleases me any longer. Want to punish him, but not brave enough to speak of what he has made me do, because he would destroy me if I did. Know he would. He is a cruel man, however he may charm people with his smile and clever talk. Have lost count of times he has hit me, but for days and days have kept to my room so that world shouldn't see the bruises and red eyes from the crying. Eyes always red now, but shall stop it all soon. No more pictures, ever, from my hand, and that will hurt him more than anything else. That may make him cry. Not losing me, but losing the paintings he has almost persuaded himself are his own. He has swallowed me up so that everything of mine is part of him. My fault. My weakness. Am such a coward. Cannot forgive myself for that, for locking myself away from my darling baby when she was so tiny. For not speaking. For not packing a suitcase and walking down the drive. But how? How to leave my child and my garden and my house that I love? Am a coward, a dreadful weakling and hate myself beyond anything else. Cannot look at myself in the mirror without feeling disgust and horror. Will end it. But have made a surprise for Leonora's birthday. It's very soon and so will try to wait till after that is over before stopping my painting for ever. There is one thing he doesn't know. No one knows. Have signed my own paintings. Somewhere in each one have made an arrangement of lines or colours in the shape of a lion. Very tiny lion, for Leonora, who is fierce and unafraid like her father, and beautiful, and for whom only wish is that she may face the light always and never turn away to cry into the darkness, like me. Darling child, forgive me. Have loved you from the moment you were born and think of you every moment of every day.

Your mother, Maude Walsh.

Leonora looked up from the page. The familiar faces round the table had been transformed into creatures from a nightmare. Beth gasped, her eyes wide. Gwen had her hand clamped over her mouth, and Rilla was openly weeping. Alex had both hands over his face, covering his eyes. Chloë and Philip were sitting very upright, and James was reaching for the wine bottle. Darkness had gathered in the corners of the dining room while she'd been speaking. Leonora broke the silence.

'It's rather a long letter, I'm afraid, but I felt I should read all of it, so that you would understand. It was written on the back of the wallpaper used to cover the doll's house roof, and I'm very grateful to Philip and Chloë for removing it so carefully that not a word has been lost, and for making me the typed copy I've just read. Thank you, both of you.'

Still no one spoke. She continued, 'I hope that my mother's somewhat disjointed style wasn't too difficult to follow. What this letter does not make clear—how could it?—is that I found her. I found her dead, floating in the lake, just before my eighth birthday.'

Gwen and Rilla cried out almost in unison, 'Oh, Mother . . . how . . . how . . .' and both started to get up from their chairs. Leonora put out a hand to stop them, and they sank back. Gwen was as white as the tablecloth and Rilla's tears were running unchecked down her face. Sean whispered something to her and put an arm round her shoulders.

'I will find it easier in my mind if everyone is aware of the truth,' said Leonora. 'When I say it out loud like this, I still find it hard to believe, but it's true. Maude Walsh, my mother, is the person who painted the pictures hanging all over the house. My father took her work and passed it off as his. Oh, it's a monstrous thing to have done. Monstrous.'

She took her reading glasses off and leaned forward. 'My father acted in a way that I find unforgivable. He stole from my mother the one thing, the *best* thing, she had and made it his own. And the very worst thing of all is . . .' Leonora felt tears come to her eyes. She blinked fiercely to stop them from falling and took two deep breaths. 'The worst thing is that I've helped him. I believed his hideous lies and helped him in his deception. I've guarded the canvases from the world in exactly the way he wanted. And I've loved him. I've loved him and his memory all my life and I can't any longer. The person I thought I loved didn't exist. He dressed himself in my mother's talent and helped himself to the honour that should have been hers. And to all my love. I didn't have any left over for her. I've overlooked her, not only since she died but also while she was alive. I'm sorry to be crying, but I can't help it.'

Gwen and Rilla both stood up and went to comfort Leonora.

'Please don't say sorry,' Gwen murmured, her arms round her mother.

'You should cry if you want to,' Rilla added. 'As much as you like.'

'I'm all right, darlings, honestly. Do sit down. Some of these tears are simply rage. I feel murderous when I think about him. He wanted the paintings kept at Willow Court not only because he didn't want to be found out, but because he wanted to make sure that my mother was never acknowledged as the artist. He made me promise to carry out his instructions, as he'd written them down in his will. That promise was unfairly extracted from me. As you know, there are instructions in my will, too, but on Monday morning I shall see to it that they're altered.'

She took a sip of wine. I must pull myself together, she thought, and dabbed at her eyes with a lace-edged handkerchief.

'There's a prayer I used to recite when I was a girl: *If I should die before I wake*. I have no intention of dying before I wake and missing my birthday party, but just in case I do . . .' She smiled. 'I'd like to say in front of all of you, and you're my witnesses, that I intend to spread the story of Maude Walsh's paintings throughout the art world, and, Efe dear . . .'

'Yes, Leonora?'

'Please get in touch with Mr Stronsky and tell him that nothing would give me greater pleasure than a purpose-built gallery to display my mother's work.'

Those words broke the spell and everyone began to applaud. Sean said, 'I'm going to have to add some things to my film, Leonora. Maybe we could get together next week?'

'You're welcome to come back whenever it suits you, Sean,' Leonora said. 'I hadn't given any thought to the programme, I'm sorry to say. And I should warn everyone that I am going to tell my guests about this at the party tomorrow. I want everyone to know the truth.'

'I must get onto various people at once,' Efe said. 'D'you think we should tell the press? They could all be down here by tomorrow.'

'Efe, please behave yourself.' Leonora spoke sharply. 'Tomorrow is my seventy-fifth birthday party and I would like to enjoy it with my family and friends. My mother's story has been unknown since 1935. I shall tell my guests but the world can wait another couple of days.'

Efe had the grace to blush. 'I'm sorry, Leonora. Of course I don't want to spoil your day, but I just thought . . . I don't know. You and your birthday are a part of the story. You found her, after all. It's very dramatic. A human-interest angle, the suicide and everything.'

'It will be just as humanly interesting next week,' Leonora said in a tone that managed to bring the discussion to a full stop. She noticed that Rilla was looking towards the door and asked, 'What's the matter, Rilla? What are you waiting for?'

'Are you ready to ring for dessert?' Rilla asked.

'You can always be depended upon to bring the conversation back to earth, darling. But you're quite right. We must get on with the meal otherwise we'll be here for ages and we should all get an early night.'

Sean leaned closer to Rilla as everyone began to talk about the party. 'Not us, please, Rilla,' he whispered. 'We're going for a walk, aren't we?'

Rilla nodded. 'We certainly are,' she said.

Mary came into the room then and put the strawberry shortcake in front of Leonora.

'What's this, Mary? I thought we were having fruit salad tonight.'

'Rilla had other ideas,' Mary said, with a smile.

'I made it, Mother,' Rilla said. 'Last night when everyone was asleep.'

'It looks wonderful,' Leonora said. 'Thank you, darling. I hope I can manage to cut it neatly. It looks too beautiful to spoil, doesn't it?'

'No, it doesn't,' said James. 'It looks far too good to leave on the plate.' He grinned. 'Get cracking with the knife, Leonora! I can't wait.'

Alex was alone on the terrace in the soft darkness waiting for Beth. She was helping Leonora carry all the presents she'd opened up to her bedroom but she'd said she wouldn't be long.

He wished he'd taken his camera into dinner. The faces round the table when Leonora was reading her mother's words should have been caught on film. Gwen and Rilla with tears in their eyes; Efe looking as though someone had dealt him a knockout blow, then slowly realising how he could turn the situation to his advantage, especially his financial advantage. He could scarcely sit still through the strawberry shortcake.

'Alex?' Beth's voice broke into his thoughts. He stood up and said, 'I'm over here. In the alcove.'

She sat down next to him, and leaned back against the wall. 'I'm exhausted,' she said. 'Too much has happened today.'

'More than you know, actually,' said Alex. 'Have you spoken to Efe?'

Beth snorted. 'Don't talk to me about Efe. Honestly. You could practically see the dollar signs flashing in his eyes when he heard Maude's letter. He's so greedy and selfish.'

'Haven't you always known that?'

Beth thought for a moment. 'Yes, I suppose I have. Only I never really saw the effect his behaviour had on people. But look at poor Fiona!'

'She's left him,' Alex said.

'What? Fiona's left Efe? I don't believe it! She wouldn't dare. She'd be afraid of what he'd do to her when he found her again.'

'He may not go looking for her. That's the impression I got, anyway. Don't say a word, Beth. Efe doesn't want the party to be wrecked.'

'She's put up with so much. Something drastic must have happened. Tell me, Alex, go on. I shan't say a word.'

'She listened to a message on his mobile. By accident.'

Beth was quiet for a moment. She said, 'From a woman, I suppose.'

'Telephone sex, from what I can gather.'

Beth sat without speaking for a few moments. 'Efe has had quite a lot happening to him today. I feel rather sorry for him.'

'He seems OK to me,' Alex said, feeling a stab of jealous anger.

'Leonora spoke to Efe and Rilla in the conservatory this afternoon—don't tell anyone about this, Alex—she made Efe tell Rilla about the day Mark died. Was that what you were trying to tell me earlier? About Efe not saving him? Being too involved in the game to bother?'

Alex nodded. 'I should have said something, I suppose. And I've felt bad too, sometimes, wondering whether I could have done something.'

'You weren't that much older than Markie. You mustn't blame yourself, Alex. It was an accident. Maybe it could have been prevented, but that's what it was. I think we should try and put that day behind us.'

Alex listened to the night sounds all around them. The scent of evening filled the air. This was a chance. He sensed that if he didn't speak, Beth would stand up soon and go to bed. He said, 'Beth?'

'Mmm?'

Alex looked at her. She had her eyes closed. She hadn't mentioned what had happened earlier, in the kitchen. Did that mean she regretted it? Could he have imagined her reaction to his kiss? Should he say something? If so, what? *I love you* was out of the question. Not those words, out of the blue. Nor could he ask what he really needed to know: *What about Efe? Do you still love him? Am I a sort of second best?* Maybe he shouldn't speak at all, but just kiss her. He bent over her and touched his lips to hers as lightly as he could.

'Nothing,' he said. 'I don't know what to say.'

Beth opened her eyes. 'You're wondering, aren't you, about this afternoon? If I really meant it. Well, I did. I don't know why it's taken me so long to realise.'

Before he knew what was happening, she'd wound her arms around him and her mouth was on his, open, eager, sweet. Alex closed his eyes and returned her kiss. They clung together for a long moment.

'Never mind,' Alex said breathlessly. 'As long as you realise now . . .'

'You're talking too much,' Beth said. 'Shut up and kiss me again.'

'That's where we're going, isn't it?' said Rilla. 'To the lake.' They had been walking through the Wild Garden. They both knew where they were heading, but neither of them had mentioned it until now.

'If you can,' Sean said. 'I don't want to force you but I thought we might exorcise some of the bad memories if we went together.'

Rilla nodded. She said, 'It'll be all right. If I'm there with you. I shan't feel so scared.' There was hope in her voice, a rising inflection.

'Here we are,' Sean said gently. 'This is it.'

The lake glittered where the moonlight touched it, and the willow branches were black against the sky.

'It must have been here,' Rilla whispered. 'I shouldn't cry, I'm sorry.'

Sean took a handkerchief from his pocket and wiped away Rilla's tears. 'Take it,' he said. 'Cry as much as you like.'

'No, no, I'm fine. It's better here, in the place where it really happened. Perhaps I should have come a long time ago, only I didn't dare.' Shadows moved across the surface of the water. 'Isn't it strange,' she said. 'I can't get the thought out of my mind of my mother as a little girl, finding the body. It's sort of mixed up with Mark and what happened to him. Let's walk to the other side. I might feel more comfortable there.'

'And you get a really fine view of the house from over there.'

They walked without speaking until they were opposite Willow Court. The building was a black shape at the top of a slope. Light showed at some of the windows.

'You can't see much at night,' Sean said. 'It's better during the day.'

Rilla laughed. 'You're a fraud. Promise me a decent view and all I get is a few lights against a black background.'

'I didn't bring you here to show you the view.'

'I know you didn't,' Rilla said, and she closed her eyes as she stepped into the circle of his arms.

Leonora sat on the armchair in her bedroom with her eyes closed. It was not even eleven o'clock and she was determined to have an early night. She wanted to wake up fresh on her birthday, not slide into it at the end of the most exhausting few hours she had experienced for years.

I'm not the same person I was when I woke up, she thought. There had been a few other days in her life when she'd also felt altered. Her wedding day. The days when she'd given birth to Gwen and Rilla. The day Mark died. Every death was sad but some were out of the natural order of things, and you were never the same after that.

She thought about her mother's death, and tried to imagine the misery and desperation that had led her to do such a thing. She took a deep breath and resolved to spend all her energy and time in promoting Maude's genius. She looked up at the painting above her bed. White swans on the lake, always on the point of moving. Feathers that seemed about to ruffle in the breeze.

Her eyes were not up to searching for the hidden signature, the little lion, among the green and the white and the dark blue brush strokes. It struck her as astonishing that no one had noticed it all through the years, but tomorrow . . . no, not tomorrow, that was going to be busy enough . . . on Monday she would ask Alex to find it for her.

She turned to the presents her family had given her. Chloë's gift was a little chest of drawers, painted in a shade between blue and green. Its tiny drawers were full of items that brought back her past. There was a wedding ring and one dried pink rose from her wedding, baby boots for Gwen and Rilla, all sorts of lovely things. Clever, talented Chloë!

Efe and Fiona had given her a beautiful cameo brooch, set in gold, and matching earrings. They would look perfect with her dress tomorrow. Leonora hoped that Fiona would be feeling better by then. Douggie had slept well tonight. She couldn't remember when she'd last seen him, which puzzled her a little. Efe generally brought him in to say good night to her before he went to bed, but today was so unsettled that all the routines of Willow Court had been thrown into confusion.

Gwen and James's gift was in an envelope: two tickets for a long weekend in a very good hotel in Venice, in October. All expenses paid. Who should she take with her? There would be time to decide that when the party was over, but what a glorious thing to look forward to.

Sean's present was a white television set and video recorder. It stood on the table at the end of her bed. She smiled. She'd held out for so long against television in the bedroom, yet she was longing for the winter evenings when she'd be able to lie on her bed under a soft blanket and watch her own set all by herself. It would be bliss. Sean had also promised her a tape of the Ethan Walsh—no, the Maude Walsh—programme. It was, she considered, a very thoughtful present.

Beth had bought her an antique cheval glass, which she'd put near the window. I can take down the old full-length mirror on the inside of the wardrobe door now, which Beth said was dreadfully unflattering. Leonora smiled to read what Beth had written on the card attached to the mirror. *For someone beautiful who deserves a proper reflection*.

She leaned forward to touch Rilla's present. When the packet fell open, she wasn't a bit sure that what she could see would be her sort of thing. How typical of Rilla to buy me something *she'd* like to wear, she'd thought. She didn't even know what to call it. 'Dressing gown' signalled cosy, comfortable, fleecy. *Peignoir* brought into mind something flimsy and probably transparent. This garment was probably a *robe*, with all its associations of grandeur and splendour. Leonora picked it up from the bed and put it on over her clothes, and it fell to the ground in a glitter of brocade, gold thread in a rose pattern on a darker gold background.

She looked in the cheval mirror and smiled. I look resplendent, she thought, like an empress. She was surprised at how satisfying the fabric felt on her body. The robe fell open to reveal its secret beauty: the whole thing was lined with pink velvet, silky, opulent, and exactly the sort of dusty pink she adored, like a rose that had started to fade. She stared at her reflection and thought, I love it. I don't ever want to take it off.

Still in the robe, she sat down at the dressing table to look at Alex's gift. The album which he had promised to fill with images of Willow Court and of her birthday was almost empty, but there were a couple of photographs already in place. One was an exact copy of the painting of the vista up the drive, with the oak trees scarlet and the house grey and small at the top of the avenue. Alex must have taken this last October. On the next page, there was a portrait of her in the nursery, sitting next to the doll's house. I look as though I'm talking to someone, she thought. Talking to Alex, it must be, because he took the photograph.

She examined the picture more closely. Why had she never had the doll's house photographed before? It looked magnificent, perfect, with all the dolls visible and seeming to be almost on the point of moving. She closed the album. There was still one more thing she had to do.

She opened the drawer where she kept her scarves and took out Rilla's home-stitched purse. The dolls that had lain in it for most of the last half-century were exactly as they were when Leonora had stopped playing with them. The lilac dress of the little-girl doll was unfaded, her embroidered smile unchanged. The mother and father dolls reminded her of Ethan and Maude, and yet of course they were nothing like the real people. Dolls did what you wanted them to. Dolls were actors in the dramas that children created. She ought to have let these three be played with. It wasn't too late.

Leonora went to the bedroom door and opened it. There was no one in the corridor and she walked along to the nursery and switched on the lights. The strips of wallpaper from the roof had been put away safely in her desk until she could think about what should be done with them.

She took off the dust sheet that covered the doll's house. It oughtn't to be hidden, she thought. I will keep it open for everyone to look at from now on. She stroked the roof. What would she be doing now, thinking now, if Douggie hadn't started tearing at the paper? Maude's sorrow, Ethan's secret, would still be lying there, undiscovered. All our lives, she thought, hinge on the tiniest of events.

She took all the Delacourts out of the house and put them on the windowsill. Then she knelt down carefully and placed her own precious dolls round the table in the miniature dining room. She put a tiny roast chicken in front of them, and a red jelly made of *papier-mâché*. It's going to be a lovely meal, she decided. Everyone will have the most wonderful time. There will be no quarrels. Never again. They are going to live happily ever after. Leonora gathered the folds of her rose-and-gold robe around her and left the nursery, closing the door quietly behind her.

Sunday, August 25, 2002

Leonora's Birthday

EVEN IN THE MIDST of her nightmare, Leonora was aware that she was dreaming. A man was standing next to her bed and singing. His voice was not a human voice but something between a bird's cry and the grinding of gears. His face was turned away, and Leonora knew that this was the right time to wake up because, if she didn't, the man would turn round and his face would be unspeakable. She opened her eyes and settled into the comfort of finding her own bedroom all around her.

Her bedside clock told her that it was just after half past four, far too early to get up, but Leonora knew she wouldn't fall asleep again. She sat up against her pillows and thought of her birthday guests, all over the county, getting up and choosing their best clothes and making their way towards Willow Court. She felt like the conductor of an orchestra, waiting to raise her baton. Whatever could have been done to make sure that the day went well had been done. She'd even remembered to ask Sean to go down to Lodge Cottage in good time and fetch Nanny Mouse and Miss Lardner up to the house in his car. He didn't mind. In fact, he appeared delighted. It was perhaps rather impulsive of Rilla to attach herself to him so quickly, but he was, as far as Leonora could see, a good man, a kind man, and he appeared to be fond of Rilla. Leonora smiled. Her daughter had been right to remind her of that moment, all those years ago, when a young soldier had walked into the kitchen and she'd known she loved him before he'd even opened his mouth to speak. She's not a child, Leonora thought. She can look after herself.

Reuben Stronsky spent the first part of his drive to Willow Court thinking about the call he'd taken on his mobile phone just before he set out. It was from Efe, sounding hurried and anxious. There had been 'a turnup for the books', as he called it, which meant that Leonora Simmonds had changed her mind and was going to allow the Walsh pictures to be housed wherever he, Reuben, thought best. When Efe told him about the real creator of the pictures, he was overwhelmed and wanted to discuss it further, but it was clear that Efe was eager to get off the phone and said only that he'd asked the parking staff to watch out for Reuben's car. Details of the revelations would have to wait.

'I might get there early,' Reuben had said. 'I'd like to walk in those lovely gardens for a while. Would that be OK?'

Reuben had been assured that the gardens were at his disposal.

He'd left London early to beat the traffic and was just beginning to get the hang of the white BMW he'd hired. Beside him on the passenger seat was the perfect birthday present. It was, he knew, unique.

Reuben had not been looking forward to his meeting with Leonora. Persuasion, charm assaults, bringing pressure to bear—he hated anything that forced him to be something other than what he naturally was: a quiet man who hated the limelight. 'Strong and silent', his ex-wife called him once, but that was a long time ago and now, at the biblical age of three score years and ten, he could no longer claim strength as a distinguishing characteristic. He'd been ready to put his case to Leonora as forcefully as he could, but he wasn't sorry that none of that would now be necessary. Now, his gift was a way of thanking her, rather than a kind of bribe. I'm on my way to Willow Court, Reuben said to himself as the green and gold countryside slid past at high speed. He couldn't help feeling optimistic and younger than he had for years.

This is the best bit of any social occasion, Rilla said to herself, as she lay in the bath. The part before it begins. Expectation. Anticipation. Deferred gratification. As she closed her eyes and thought about Sean's kisses, she felt her whole body become as warm and liquid as the water that surrounded her. Talk about deferred gratification! This delaying of pleasure meant that she was in an almost permanent state of sexual excitement. Stop thinking about Sean, she told herself. This is Leonora's day.

Rilla got out of the water and wrapped herself in a towel the size of a small blanket. On the way back to her bedroom, she noticed that the door of the nursery was open. Oh God, she thought. Not Douggie again. She felt irritated at Fiona. Why the hell couldn't she keep track of her kid. Rilla went to see what he might have got up to.

'Beth! What are you doing here? I thought it was Douggie. Why aren't you getting ready?'

'Sorry, Rilla. I just wanted a place to think quietly for a bit.' She was kneeling on the floor, looking at the dolls.

'Something wrong?'

'Well, not wrong exactly.' Beth sighed. 'I suppose I can tell you, though Efe doesn't want anyone to know yet. Fiona's done a runner.'

'I'm amazed! I didn't think she'd have the nerve. But why did she choose this exact moment?'

'She found a message on Efe's phone. An obscene message, from what I've heard. Did you know that Efe was cheating on her?'

'I hadn't thought about it. But it seems in character.' Rilla frowned. 'Look at this, Beth! These are the real dolls. The ones Maude made for Leonora. The ones we were never allowed to play with. How astonishing! Mother must have put them here. I wonder why.' She picked up the little girl doll and looked at her, then put her back carefully.

Beth sat back on her heels. She took the father doll and put him to stand at the dining-room window, looking out. Rilla was wondering whether she ought to say something when Beth said, 'I've had my mind changed, Rilla. These few days. I don't think we've been together for so long and at such close quarters since we were kids. I think I had a distorted opinion of him.' There was a slight trembling in her voice.

Rilla looked at her daughter. 'Oh, Beth, no. You love him, don't you? Efe. You really, really love him. I never knew. I'm so sorry. I'm always too caught up in my own things to notice. Poor darling.'

'I *did* love him but I don't now. Not in the way I used to. I've been a bloody fool. I mean, even after he married Fiona, I sort of hoped. That one day he'd just say, *No, it's you I really love, Beth. I've made a terrible mistake*. But he didn't, of course. And I've been so horrible to Fiona. I hated her, for no reason except that Efe loved her. Poor thing. He might have loved her once, but he doesn't exactly seem brokenhearted, does he? More concerned with the Maude Walsh revelations.'

'Oh, Beth, it's not fair! I wanted you to have a lovely time at this party.'

Beth got to her feet and smiled. 'I intend to. Efe will never spoil anything for me ever again. I don't know why I came in here. I think I just wanted to remind myself . . . maybe that real life isn't as easily arrangeable as doll's house life. I'm going to get ready now. But I can come in later and put your hair up. Would you like me to?'

'Oh, darling, would you?'

'Sure. I'll come and do it when I'm dressed.'

Beth left the room with such a light step that Rilla wondered whether there was something else Beth should have told her. She made her way to her own room and sat down at the dressing table. I'll ask her when she comes to do my hair, she said to herself as she massaged moisturiser into her face and neck. She had just sprayed Vivienne Westwood's *Boudoir* all over her body when someone knocked on her door.

'Come in,' she called, and there was Gwen, dressed in a track suit and looking harassed. 'What's the matter?'

'I've just spoken to Efe, Rilla. Do you know what's happened?'

'No, Gwen,' she lied. Gwen might be put out to realise that Rilla knew something about her son before she did. 'It isn't Mother, is it?'

Gwen shook her head. 'It's Fiona. She's left him. Left Efe, I mean. He wouldn't tell me why. I don't know what I'll do.' She sat down on the edge of the bed and took out a hanky.

'Gwen, please don't cry. I'm sure they'll work something out.'

'What if they don't? What if she never goes back to him? Oh, it's not Fiona. It's not even Efe. If he wants to risk his marriage with sordid affairs, that's his business, but it's Douggie. I may never see him again, Rilla. I couldn't bear that.' She started crying again. 'I'm so sorry, Rilla, I didn't mean to burden you like this.'

'Don't be silly, Gwen, you can burden me all you like, but you *will* see Douggie. I'm sure Fiona won't keep him away from you. Even if they *do* divorce, Efe will get visitation rights and you can make sure he brings

Douggie here whenever he has him. Efe won't want to look after Douggie on his own. He'll need you. Really he will.'

Gwen looked happier. 'Yes, I suppose he might.'

'And in any case,' Rilla added, 'you don't know she's gone for ever. She might just want to give Efe a bit of a shock. She might well be back.'

'That's true. I hadn't thought of that.' Gwen stood up. 'Thanks for letting me witter on. I must go and do a repair job on my eyes.'

After Gwen left the room, Rilla thought how surprising everyone was. She'd never have guessed that her sister was so besotted with Douggie. Poor Gwen. For a while, she considered the chances of Fiona going back to Efe but then she thought, What the hell! Why should I worry about such things today? Time enough for family problems tomorrow. I'm going to a party, dammit. She turned her mind to the question of earrings. Dangly crystal drops or gobstopping baroque pearls?

As Reuben Stronsky drove through the gates of Willow Court, he looked down the avenue of oaks to the house. What a sensational view, he thought. If only it were in London instead of here in the boondocks, then turning the house into a museum would be a distinct possibility.

He parked the BMW in the area that had been set aside for parking. As he got out of the car, he remembered the first time he'd come to this house, as a visitor among others, years ago now. The pictures had hit him right between the eyes and he'd been haunted by them ever since.

A young man was approaching. 'Good morning, sir. We've been expecting you.'

'Thank you. I'm rather on the early side, I'm afraid. I'm going to walk about for a while and then it's drinks on the terrace, am I right?'

'Yes, that's right, sir. At about eleven, I believe.'

'I'll be there,' Reuben said.

The young man disappeared in the direction of the house. Before Reuben locked the car up, he put the parcel under a blanket in the boot. He wasn't going to go up to the house clutching the present. It was important that Leonora received it without any distractions. He'd go and get it later on, when the party was over.

As Reuben began to walk towards the gardens, he took out his mobile phone from a pocket in his jacket and punched in Efe's number. 'Efe, is that you?' he said. 'This is Reuben. I'm in your car park right now.'

Efe expected to be alone at breakfast, but to his surprise Leonora was sitting at the table in the kitchen, drinking tea and looking rather frail in her dark blue dressing gown. He was used to seeing his grandmother dressed, made-up, with her pearl earrings in place. She's old, Efe thought. Really old. He noticed, perhaps for the first time, the wrinkles round her eyes, the blue veins standing out on the backs of her hands.

'Happy birthday, Leonora!' he said, and came over to give her a kiss.

'Thank you, darling. I've just come down for a cup of tea before getting ready for the party. I'm rather excited.' She smiled at Efe, and oddly, she suddenly looked not like an old woman but more like a kid.

Efe hesitated. He knew he ought to tell her about Fiona, but part of him was seriously considering lying. Saying something about her still not feeling well, not in a state to go to the party.

'Something's the matter, Efe, isn't it?' said Leonora. 'I know it is, so there's no point looking away. And don't lie to me, please. I don't need to be protected. I've always known when you're lying.'

'Wouldn't dream of it, Leonora. There *is* something, actually. I was going to tell you later. I didn't want to spoil the party.'

'Tell me.'

'It's Fiona. She's left me. That's it. She's taken Douggie and gone.'

Leonora was silent for a moment. Then she said, 'Do you want to go after her? I won't mind if that's what you feel you have to do.'

'Certainly not! I wouldn't miss your party for the world. Besides, it's up to her to come back, not up to me to go chasing her all over the country.'

'I'm touched, darling. But, Efe'—Leonora's voice became sharper—'perhaps that attitude has something to do with why Fiona left in the first place? What about Douggie? Surely you want him back?'

'I'll get him back, don't you worry,' Efe said, privately wondering how on earth he would look after Douggie on his own.

'Anyway, thank you for telling me, Efe. I'm sorry Fiona will miss the party. She was looking forward to it, I think.'

'More fool her, then, for going. I refuse to worry about her today. Today is your day, Leonora. It's got to be fun from start to finish.'

'Well. I'd better go and get my glad rags on then. I shall see you on the terrace for drinks.'

'Right,' said Efe, and when Leonora left the room, he turned his attention to his mobile phone.

Getting-up noises were coming from upstairs. That was Chloë, shouting something as she ran along the corridor. He helped himself to another slice of toast. It would be ages before they all sat down to lunch and he intended to start drinking very soon. It wasn't every day that your wife left you. He was missing Fiona, wasn't he? Of course I am, he thought. And Douggie. I really am missing him. It's just because there's so much else going on here that I'm not completely miserable. Reuben is here. He's walking round the grounds. He'll be coming to the terrace at eleven and I'll introduce him to Leonora. Efe intended to circulate for most of the afternoon, but he was longing to see Melanie again. There would, surely, be some time for them to sneak off somewhere.

His mind turned to their last meeting, which was three weeks ago. Far too long. He remembered that they'd barely managed to shut the door of the back room of Melanie's shop behind them before she'd started to tear his clothes off. She'd been waiting for him, so she was naked under her thin dress. Efe put the remains of his toast down, suddenly overcome with desire. He had intended to try Fiona's number again, to talk some sense into her, but this wasn't the right time. He was going to be in the money now, thanks to the revelations about Maude Walsh. He wondered whether that would influence Fiona in any way and decided that it wouldn't. No, if Fiona came back it would be because she couldn't bear to live without him. She needed him, he knew that, and he was reasonably sure of being able to win her round. The only thing he had to work out was whether he wanted to.

'You look great,' said Chloë, peering over her mother's shoulder into the dressing-table mirror.

Gwen was wearing a bronze linen dress and sapphire earrings. She smiled gratefully up at her daughter. 'So do you,' she said gallantly, though she thought Chloë's dress looked like a nightie.

'This dress is a nightie,' Chloë said. 'I found it in a secondhand shop. It's beautiful fabric. I can't believe anyone would wear it to bed.'

The fabric was apricot satin. There was a panel of lace set into the bodice and it occurred to Gwen that Leonora used to possess a garment very like this long ago. She hoped that her mother wouldn't make some remark.

Gwen smiled at Chloë. 'I'm so grateful for the way you told Leonora about Maude's message, by the way. You were very discreet and thoughtful and it can't have been an easy conversation.'

'No, it wasn't.' Chloë went to the bed, and lay across it, Gwen noticed, in exactly the same way she used to do as a little girl. 'Leonora went so pale, and then she just sobbed and sobbed and it was awful. I didn't know what to do really, so I just hugged her. She's dead thin, and I could feel how . . . how fragile she was.'

'That's splendid of you, Chloë. No one else could have done that as well as you. Really, Leonora's always adored you, hasn't she?'

'Well, whatever she thinks about some things I do and everything I wear, she never gets on my case in the same way that you do, Mum.'

'I do not get on your case, as you put it. It's just that sometimes I think certain things you do are a bit . . . well, off.'

'I can't help it, Mum. That's me. I'm not like Beth. I do love her to bits but she is little Miss Perfect, isn't she?'

'I wouldn't have you be anything like anyone else at all, Chloë darling. I love you. You know that, don't you? Even though I don't say it nearly enough. And I'm not exactly a tolerant mother, am I? I expect you wish you had a mother like Rilla.'

'No, of course I don't,' said Chloë. 'Though Rilla's a smashing aunt.'

'And I'm very proud of you too,' Gwen added. 'Your tree in the hall is lovely. I don't remember whether I've told you how much I love it.'

'OK, Mum,' she said. 'Ta very much. But we're beginning to sound like people in a soap, don't you think?'

Gwen was about to answer when there was a knock at the door. She said, 'Come in.'

'Hello, darlings!' Rilla said. 'It's only me and Beth. Are you ready? Oh, you both look gorgeous. Let's all go down together and find Mother.'

'God, Rilla, you've rather overdone it with the perfume, haven't you?' Gwen wrinkled her nose.

'Don't be a bore, Gwen,' said Rilla lightly. 'I'm not going to get into any spats this morning, so you can say what you like.'

'Wow, Beth!' said Chloë. 'That dress is fantastic. You look amazing.'

'So do you,' said Beth. She was in a plain sheath of heavy red silk. Her only jewellery was a pair of long agate earrings.

Gwen added, 'It's lovely. A wonderful colour for you.'

'I think,' Rilla said, 'that we should go and find Leonora and wish her happy birthday and prepare for the fray.'

They went downstairs two by two, Beth and Chloë first, followed by Gwen and Rilla. Gwen said, 'It's going to be all right, isn't it? The party?'

'It'll be sensational,' Rilla answered. 'Don't worry about a thing.'

That must be her, Reuben thought, looking across the lawn that stretched like green velvet for about a hundred yards to the terrace. Leonora Simmonds. There was something regal in her carriage. She was sitting up very straight, while guests stood and talked all around her.

Then Reuben saw that Efe was sitting on a chair very close to Leonora's, talking to her. She listened for a moment and seemed surprised and then looked around. This was the signal Reuben had been waiting for. He and Efe had arranged for Leonora to be forewarned. It would have been unkind to catch her quite unprepared. He made his way over the grass and up the flight of steps to the terrace. Then he found himself in front of her, and her clear blue eyes were looking straight into his.

Before he could say anything, she smiled at him and said, 'Mr Stronsky? Welcome to Willow Court.'

Reuben took off his Panama hat and bowed from the waist. 'It's a great honour and a pleasure to meet you, ma'am,' he said.

'Efe, bring Mr Stronsky a glass of champagne.' Leonora patted the chair beside her as he stood up. 'Sit down and tell me all your plans.'

'It looks choreographed, doesn't it?' Beth was talking to Chloë and Philip and Alex and watching the guests on the lawn below the terrace. She had a champagne glass in one hand and her gaze was fixed on a stick-thin woman with surprisingly large breasts and a wide, red mouth who had squeezed herself into the tightest of white dresses.

'That's Melanie,' said Alex, noticing the direction in which she was staring. 'Eye-catching or what? Look at Efe.'

'I've heard of body language,' said Philip, 'but that's taking it a bit far.'

Efe had one arm draped round Melanie's shoulder and showed no sign of leaving her in order to circulate among the other guests. Beth saw James approaching the couple. He said a few words in Efe's ear and Efe moved away at once, but not before he'd given Melanie's bottom an affectionate pinch. Her laughter was audible to them all.

'Efe is clearly devastated by Fiona not being here,' said Alex.

'Clearly,' said Beth and burst out laughing herself. The champagne was getting to her as well.

Leonora could tell from the happy murmurings coming from the other tables that the food had been a complete success. The mozzarella and basil fritters, the salmon crêpes, the chocolate mousse cake, had come and gone. She'd eaten every mouthful set before her, but she hadn't tasted anything properly. There was too much to look at. There was also the matter of the speech she had undertaken to make, telling everyone about Maude Walsh. How she detested speaking in public.

She looked round the table at her family. As it turned out, Fiona's absence was fortuitous. It meant that Reuben could sit with them. He had been quite a surprise to Leonora. *American Millionaire* made her think of someone fat and red-faced in a big hat and he was the exact opposite: thin, and tall and quiet, with a shock of white hair. His eyes were very dark and his manners were impeccable.

Nanny Mouse was enjoying herself. Miss Lardner sat next to her, making sure that she ate a little, but for the most part, the old lady just looked about her with the air of a child at the circus, her eyes wide with wonder. Sean was on her other side and talked to her all the time, which was angelic of him.

'Mother!' said Gwen, breaking into her thoughts. 'They're bringing the birthday cake in. Look!'

All the guests were craning to see the cake, which was being taken round the marquee on a sort of lap of honour. Leonora had vetoed candles. She had no intention of being seen puffing out air in public. The huge tray progressed round the marquee, and applause broke out as everyone realised that the icing was a perfect reproduction of a painting from the Walsh Collection: the portrait of Leonora as a young girl, sitting on the edge of a bed, wearing a lilac dress. Everyone started talking at once, so that James had to stand up and call for silence.

'Thank you, everyone. It's time for the cutting of the cake. Beautiful as it is. And I am going to call on Leonora to say a few words but before we do all that, let's sing to a great lady. Happy birthday, Leonora.'

'Happy Birthday' had always been one of Leonora's least favourite songs, but she smiled graciously while the assembled company tried, without much success, to fit 'dear' plus her name into the notes provided by the music. As soon as it was over, she stood up.

'You're very kind,' she said, and took a deep breath.

Leonora became aware of the applause, and of Gwen putting a knife into her hand. 'Wonderful speech, Mother,' she whispered. 'You must cut the cake now.'

Leonora bent forward to make the first stroke. She made a wish, just as she used to do when she was a girl. Please, let everyone be happy, she thought, and then instantly chided herself for being stupid. Everyone couldn't possibly be happy. She amended it in her head: please let everyone be as happy as they can be, whenever they can. That was better.

The singing broke out again as Bridget and two helpers came to remove the cake so that it could be cut into more than seventy pieces. The tune this time was 'For She's a Jolly Good Fellow'.

'What an inadequate song,' said Reuben, leaning in to whisper in her ear. 'You deserve something grander, more dignified, Mrs Simmonds.'

'Please call me Leonora,' said Leonora. Reuben Stronsky, she decided, was a real gentleman.

Beth walked round to the kitchen garden to get away from the party. Alex was photographing the revellers down by the lake, and in the gazebo. Many people had left already, but there were still enough to make it worth his while. The lunch had been perfect in every detail, and she could see Gwen relaxing as one delicious course after another had come and gone. Everyone seemed to be having a marvellous time.

She walked up the path towards the shed. It seemed to her exactly the right place to go to get away from the party for a while. She went up to the door and was just about to open it when she heard a noise from inside. She glanced in at the small, dusty window.

She couldn't see very well, but there was a pale flash of legs moving and long black hair was spread out over the work table in the corner. There were grunts and moans and Melanie's ringing voice giving the game away. 'Oh, Efe, Efe, yes . . . yess.'

Beth ran away down the path between the lettuces and carrots towards the house, trying to put what she'd just seen out of her mind. Poor Fiona, she thought. He really doesn't give a shit about her. Efe looks after his own desires, and that's that. She was happy to notice that thinking about Efe didn't cause her any pain. Every element of desire had gone. What remained was concern and affection and family loyalty. What astonished her now was the strength of her feelings towards Alex. How could she have been so blind for so long?

'You were a star,' Rilla said to Sean. 'Looking after Nanny Mouse all day long. A real treasure.' They were sitting in the alcove, smoking. This, Rilla thought, is where it started.

'You can drop fag ends among the roses today,' Sean said. 'Leonora's had such a busy day she'll never notice.'

'Oh, yes, she will. You don't know my mother. But it was a lovely party, wasn't it? I thought that chocolate mousse cake was the best thing of all. I wonder if Bridget would give me the recipe. And Gwen looks much more relaxed now that the party's over.'

'There's still lots to be done on the film,' Sean said. 'I'm going to have to come down here next Wednesday, and interview Leonora again.'

'What about Monday and Tuesday? What are you doing then?'

'Well, Monday's a bank holiday but I have to go into the office on Tuesday, of course.'

'Of course. But what about after work? Will you come and have dinner with me, on Tuesday night?'

'I was hoping you'd ask.'

'I'm asking.' She turned to kiss him.

'Someone might see us,' he murmured rather halfheartedly.

'I don't care if they do,' said Rilla. 'Kiss me.' After some moments, she murmured, 'On Tuesday night, remember to bring your toothbrush.'

Gwen looked towards the marquee. All the tables would be folded away soon, and she was happy to think that the washing-up and clearing away were going to be seen to by someone else. Soon, it would be just the family left at Willow Court. She began to walk through the Wild Garden towards the lake, feeling as though she were letting out a breath she'd been holding for much too long. She bent down and took off her sandals and left them lying on the grass. The Wild Garden was not the place for high heels and party dresses. Gwen wished she was wearing trousers. I'm alone, she thought, for the first time in days. It's bliss.

As she approached the lake, she saw someone—a woman—sitting on the old tree stump. The swans had gathered there, too. Gwen was surprised at how disappointed she felt to find that she wouldn't after all be on her own. And then she noticed that the woman was Rilla.

'Rilla?' she said tentatively. 'Are you all right?'

'Hello, Gwennie. Of course I'm all right. Why shouldn't I be?'

'I'm just surprised that you chose to come to the lake all by yourself.'

'It's a test,' said Rilla. 'I was here with Sean and it wasn't so bad. So I thought I'd give it a go on my own. It was Mother's doing really. She . . . she explained to me properly what happened when Mark died. She made me feel . . . well, a little less guilty that I wasn't here.'

'We've never spoken about it either, have we?' said Gwen. 'I should have looked after you more, I know, but there were the children . . .' She bit her lip, remembering that hideous time, when Efe kept waking in the night with bad dreams, and Alex stopped talking altogether for a few weeks. If she hadn't had Chloë to look after, she would have gone mad.

'You didn't do anything wrong, Gwen,' Rilla said quietly. 'I've never blamed you in the least, and now, well, let's just say that everything's clearer now and I'm here, aren't I? Dealing with it, as Beth would say.'

Rilla stood up and started walking. Gwen fell into step beside her.

'It was a super party,' Rilla said, in a tone that marked a change of subject, a lightening of the atmosphere.

'No disasters, thank heavens.'

'And I don't know if you've noticed,' Rilla went on, 'but Beth and Alex are always together, aren't they?'

Gwen smiled. 'They've always been friends, from childhood.'

'Not that sort of close, Gwen. I mean . . . Well, I came across them in the kitchen yesterday and they'd been kissing.'

Gwen stopped and stared at Rilla. 'Are you sure?'

'Positive. What do you think about that?'

'I don't know.' Gwen thought abut it for a moment. 'God, Rilla, might we become in-laws as well as sisters? It's quite odd, isn't it?'

'I think,' said Rilla, 'that our children are lucky to be spared any surprises in the mother-in-law department.'

Their laughter broke the silence of the late afternoon.

Almost everyone had gone home. It was six o'clock and the last visitors were drifting towards the car parking area. Beth was upstairs fetching her jacket. She and Chloë and Philip and Alex were going to the pub. They'd decided unanimously that they needed a change from Willow Court. On her way downstairs, she saw Efe standing at the door of his room.

'Hi, Efe,' she said, trying hard to eradicate from her mind the image of him and Melanie in the shed. 'All alone?'

'Come in for a bit, Beth,' he said. She could hear from his slurred speech that he'd drunk far too much. 'Chat to me. I'm feeling miserable.'

She looked at her watch.

'Not got the time?' he said. 'No time for poor old Efe, eh?'

'Oh, God, Efe!' she said. 'If you're going to be pathetic, I'm off.'

'No, I won't be pathetic. Promise. Just come in and have a chat.'

She went into the room and sat down on the chair by the window.

'You could come and sit here on the bed with me,' Efe said.

'Why would I want to do that, Efe?'

'She's gone, Beth. Fiona. And now you're going. But you've always been the one all my other women had to measure up to.'

How ironical, Beth thought. I loved him so much. How come it's all evaporated so quickly? It had, though. Now all she felt for Efe was a kind of affectionate pity, mixed with something like contempt.

'I've got to go, Efe,' Beth said, a little more gently.

'You all bloody leave, don't you? Fiona left.'

'You're not exactly missing her though, are you?' Beth said. 'Melanie looked as though she was doing a grand job of cheering you up.'

'Just a good shag, that's all she is, Beth. I can talk to you. I can't talk to anyone else. Not Fiona and not Melanie. You. I think I love you best, Beth. Yes, I definitely do. Come over here.'

'No, Efe,' she said, as firmly as she could. 'You don't love me best. I don't know what you think I can do for you, but I'm off now. I'm going to the pub with Alex. So I'll see you tomorrow, I suppose.'

'Alex! Stolen you from under my nose. Bastard. I'll have a word with him. Tomorrow.' He sank back onto the bed and covered his face with one arm. 'Piss off, Beth. Piss off back to Alex.'

'Bye, Efe,' she said and left the room. He'd sleep it off and might even forget all about what he'd said to her. Too late, she thought. He's said it far too late. She ran downstairs to find Alex.

'We won't discuss business now, Leonora,' said Reuben. 'It's your birthday. But I'm seriously thinking of some kind of twinning arrangement. A small gallery here, just down by the gazebo, maybe even built in the same style . . . you know, a lot of glass and white wrought iron . . . and another one over in the States. We'll talk about it tomorrow.'

They were sitting on the bench under the magnolia tree in the Quiet Garden. The shadows were creeping over the grass. It would soon be dusk.

'I'm so grateful to you, Reuben, for everything.'

'For what?' Reuben said. 'I feel privileged to be part of your celebration. This is a most beautiful place.'

'I love these evenings at the end of summer,' Leonora said. 'Autumn's coming and you can feel it, can't you?'

'Yes, I guess you can, but it's still a long way off. Hard to imagine such a thing as winter on a day like today.'

He put a small parcel in Leonora's hand. 'Let me tell you the story of this gift,' he said. 'I was in Paris a few weeks ago, hunting about as I always do among the bookstalls on the Left Bank. And I found this at the bottom of a large pile of secondhand books.'

Slowly, Leonora unwrapped the package. Inside was a small, framed picture. The pastel portrait of a young woman, leaning on the parapet of a bridge in Paris. There was Notre Dame sketched in behind her.

'Is it Maude? How astonishing! She's beautiful,' Leonora said. 'She's happy! Maybe in love. That's what she looks like. A happy woman in love.'

'That's right. But you haven't noticed the signature.'

'I can't quite make it out, without my glasses. Who's the artist?'

'Ethan Walsh. This is a genuine Ethan Walsh. One of the very few. I figure he did it while they were living in Paris. Can you believe the serendipity? That I should come across it like that? I think it's amazing.'

Leonora was silent for a long time, staring at her mother's face, young, carefree, full of love for the man who was putting her likeness down on paper. Ethan. Not cruel then. Not bitter at Maude's superior talent. Not deceiving anyone but telling the world how much he loved this woman in front of him. This was her mother before Willow Court became her prison. There was nothing in the face in this picture that foreshadowed hair floating on dark water behind a screen of willow branches; nothing of pain, or anger or despair.

'Thank you, Reuben. I can't think of anything in the whole world I'd have liked better. I only have sad memories of my mother but you've given me another Maude. And also, something good about my father to hold on to while I take in what he did. He must have loved her very much, don't you think, when he did this? Even though it changed later.'

'Sure he did,' said Reuben. 'He loved her a whole lot. I think we should go in now, Leonora, don't you? It's getting late.'

'You go, Reuben. I'll come in a minute. And thank you.'

Leonora watched him leave the garden. She half closed her eyes, and found that she was looking at the border where the late-summer flowers were nearly over. The memory came to her out of nowhere. Maude, sitting on a small stool, with a sketchbook in her hand. The flowers, the folds of her mother's skirt. I'm so close to her. It must have been one summer when I was very small, Leonora thought. I can recall how she smelt, of sun and lily of the valley, and she had a hat with a wide brim and a mauve ribbon. I can remember everything about that moment. She smiled. She had retrieved a picture of her mother to set against the bad images that filled her head. Maybe later, she said to herself, I will recall other things, different glimpses of Maude's life.

Leonora went on sitting under the magnolia tree holding the portrait in her lap until the sun dipped below the top of the garden wall. Then she stood up and made her way back to the house.

ADÈLE GERAS

Adèle Geras was born in Jerusalem and spent her early childhood in a number of different countries because her father worked for the Colonial Service. 'Before I was eleven, I'd lived in Cyprus, Nigeria and North Borneo, and later my parents were sent to the Gambia and Tanganyika (now Tanzania), where I used to join them from boarding school in England during the summer holidays. When I was away at school, my parents—in particular my father—sent me books of all kinds, pointing out the best bits, so putting all sorts of treasures into my hands.' Adèle read French and Spanish at St Hilda's College, Oxford, and after graduation held a variety of jobs ranging from actress and singer to teaching French in a girls' school in Manchester.

In 1976 Adèle became a full-time author and has been writing books for children and young adults ever since. 'People have been asking me for years when I'd write a "proper book",' says Adèle, 'meaning one that doesn't appear on the children's book list. It is a comment that leaves me speechless and aghast, as though writing children's books were a mere practise ground—which it is not.'

Facing the Light is the author's first adult novel and she came to write it almost by accident. 'I was invited by a friend in publishing to submit a synopsis for a "sweeping women's novel". I emailed her one page and she

liked it so much that she asked me to write a chunk of the text. All the time I was writing the book, it was known as "The Chunk" and I still think of it as that sometimes. When it was eventually bought as part of a two-book deal, I was—as they say in footballing circles—"over the moon".

'When I embarked on *Facing the Light*, I wanted to write the sort of book that welcomes readers into its world. I knew that the story would be set in one place, with a family gathered together for an important celebration. I think place is perhaps the most important inspiration for anything I write. It's the element I remember best from everything I read, and Willow Court with its lakes and gardens came to me first.'

For Adèle Geras, home for the past thirty-five years has been in Manchester, where she and her husband raised their two grown-up daughters. Although busy working on her second novel, she is still writing books for children. It's a heavy workload but one that she loves. 'I can truthfully say that the time I spend writing flies by because I'm having such a good time. It's my sincere hope that my readers get equal pleasure from reading my books.'

Jane Eastgate

BIRTHRIGHT

Nora Roberts

A life can be changed in a second.
It happened to Suzanne Cullen,
thirty years ago, when her three-
month-old daughter, Jessica, was
stolen from her.
From that moment on, Suzanne has
never given up hope that one day
she will find her daughter. Then,
one night, as Suzanne watches
a television news report,
Jessica's face appears . . .

PROLOGUE

DECEMBER 12, 1974

DOUGLAS EDWARD CULLEN had to pee: his three-year-old bladder was full to bursting. He danced, in exquisite torture, from the toe of one of his red shoes to the other.

The mall was full of noise, the blasts of Christmas music that added to his impatience, the shouts of other children, the crying of babies.

He knew all about crying babies now that he had a little sister. Jessica wasn't crying. She was sleeping in the buggy and looked like a doll baby in her red dress with the white frilly junk on it. But sometimes Jessie cried and cried and her face got all red and scrunched up. When that happened, Mama got too tired to play with him. Sometimes he didn't like having a little sister who cried and made Mama too tired to play.

But most of the time it was OK. He liked to look at her and watch the way she kicked her legs. And when she grabbed his finger, really tight, it made him laugh. Grandma said he had to protect Jessica because that's what big brothers do. He'd worried so much about it that he'd sneaked in to sleep on the floor beside her cot just in case the monsters who lived in the closet came to eat her in the nigh-time.

But he'd woken in his own bed in the morning, so maybe he'd only dreamed he'd gone in to protect her.

They shuffled up in line and Douglas glanced uneasily, at the smiling elves who danced around Santa's workshop. They looked a little bit mean and mad—like Jessica when she was crying really loud.

Mama crouched down and spoke to him softly. When she asked if he had to pee, he shook his head. He was afraid if they went to the toilet they'd *never* get back in line and see Santa. Then the line moved, people shifted, and he saw Santa.

He was big. His beard was very long. You could hardly see his face. And when he let out a big, booming *ho, ho, ho*, the sound of it squeezed Douglas's bladder like mean fingers.

He was a big boy now. He wasn't afraid of Santa Claus.

Mama tugged his hand, told him to go ahead. Go and sit on Santa's lap.

He took a step forward, then another, on legs that began to shake. And Santa hoisted him up. *Merry Christmas! Have you been a good boy?* Terror struck Douglas's heart like a hatchet. The big man in the red suit held him tight and stared at him with tiny, tiny eyes.

Screaming, struggling, Douglas tumbled out of Santa's lap, hit the platform hard. And wet his pants.

Mama was there, pulling him close, telling him it was all right. His breath was still coming in hard little gasps as he burrowed into her.

She gave him a big hug, lifted him up so he could press his face to her shoulder. Still murmuring to him, she turned. And began to scream.

Clinging to her, Douglas looked down. Jessica's buggy was empty.

ONE

THE ANTIETAM CREEK DEVELOPMENT project came to a rude halt when the blade of Billy Younger's digger unearthed the first skull.

Scooping up a dirty, empty-eyed skull along with the rich soil, having it leer at him in the white blast of midsummer sunlight was enough to have 233-pound Billy scream like a girl.

When he'd regained his coherency, he reported to his foreman, and his foreman reported to Ronald Dolan. By the time the county sheriff arrived, several other bones had been exhumed by curious labourers. The medical examiner was sent for, and a local news team arrived. Word spread. There was talk of murder, mass graves, serial killers. Eager fingers squeezed juice out of the grapevine so that when the examination was complete, and the bones were deemed very old, a number of people weren't sure if they were pleased or disappointed.

But for Dolan, who'd already fought through petitions, protests and injunctions to turn the pristine fifty acres of boggy bottomland and woods into a housing development, the age of the bones didn't matter. Their very existence was a major pain in his ass. And when two days later Lana Campbell, the transplanted city lawyer, crossed her legs and gave him a smug smile, it was all Dolan could do not to pop her in her pretty face.

'You'll find the court order fairly straightforward,' she told him, and kept the smile in place. She'd been one of the loudest voices against the development. At the moment, she had quite a bit to smile about. 'The County Planning Commission has given you sixty days to file a report and to convince them that your development should continue.'

'I know the ropes, sweetheart. Dolan's been building houses in this county for forty-six years.'

'The Historical and Preservation societies have retained me. I'm doing my job. Members of the faculty from the University of Maryland archaeology and anthropology departments will be visiting the site. As liaison, I'm asking you to allow them to remove and test samples.'

'Attorney of record, liaison.' Dolan, a strongly built man with a ruddy, Irish face, leaned back in his desk chair. Sarcasm dripped from his voice. 'Busy lady.' He hooked his thumbs in his braces. He always wore red braces over a blue work shirt, part of the uniform, as he thought of it. Part of what made him one of the common men, the working class that had made his town, and his country, great.

'We're both busy people, so I'll come straight to the point.' Lana was dead sure she was about to wipe that patronising grin off Dolan's face. 'You can't proceed on your development until the site is examined and cleared by the county. Samples need to be taken for that to happen. Any artefacts excavated won't be of any use to you. Cooperation in this matter would, we both know, go a long way towards shoring up your PR troubles.'

'I don't look at them as troubles.' He spread his big, working man's hands. 'People need homes. The community needs jobs. The Antietam Creek development provides both. It's called progress.'

'Thirty new homes. More traffic on roads not equipped to handle it, already overcrowded schools, the loss of rural sensibilities and open space. But that's another matter,' she said before he could respond. 'Until the bones are tested and dated, you're stuck.' She tapped a finger on the court order. 'Dolan Development must want that process expedited. You'll want to pay for the testing. Radiocarbon dating.'

'Pay—'

Yeah, she thought, who's the winner now? 'You own the property. You own the artefacts.' She'd done her homework. 'You know we'll fight against the construction, bury you in court orders and briefs until this is settled. Pay the two dollars, Mr Dolan,' she added as she got to her feet. 'your attorneys are going to give you the same advice.'

Lana waited until she had closed the office door behind her before letting the grin spread across her face. She strolled out, took a deep breath of thick summer air as she gazed up and down Woodsboro's Main Street. This was *her* town now. Her community. Her home. And had been since she'd moved there from Baltimore two years before. It was a good town, steeped in tradition and history, fuelled by gossip, protected from the urban sprawl by distance and the looming shadows of the Blue Ridge Mountains. Coming to Woodsboro had been a huge leap of faith for a born-and-bred city girl. But she couldn't bear the memories in Baltimore after losing her husband. Steve's death had flattened her. It had taken her nearly six months to find her feet again, to pull herself out of the sticky haze of grief and deal with life.

And life demanded, Lana thought. She missed Steve. There was still a hole in her where he'd been. But she'd had to keep breathing, keep functioning. And there was Tyler. Her baby. Her boy. Her treasure.

She couldn't bring back his daddy, but she could give him the best childhood possible. He had room to run now, and a dog to run with. Neighbours and friends, and a mother who'd do whatever needed to be done to keep him safe and happy. She checked her watch as she walked. it was Ty's day to go to his friend Brock's after preschool. She'd given Brock's mother, Jo, a call in an hour. Just to make sure everything was all right.

She didn't look small-town. Her wardrobe had once been selected to suit the image of an up-and-coming lawyer in a major urban firm. She might have hung out her sign in a little rural dot of less than 4,000 people, but that didn't mean she couldn't continue to dress for success.

She wore a summer suit in crisp blue linen. The classic tailoring complemented her delicate build and her own sense of tidiness. Her hair was a straight swing of sunny blonde that brushed the jawline of a pretty, youthful face. She had round blue eyes that were often mistaken for guileless, a nose that tipped at the end and a deeply curved mouth.

She swung into Treasured Pages, beamed at the man behind the counter. And finally did her victory dance.

Roger Grogan took off his reading glasses and raised his bushy silver eyebrows. He was a trim and vigorous seventy-five, and his face made Lana think of a canny leprechaun.

'You look pretty full of yourself. Must've seen Ron Dolan.'

'Just came from there. You should've come with me, Roger.'

'You're too hard on him. He's just doing what he thinks is right.'

When Lana merely angled her head, stared blandly, Roger laughed.

'Didn't say I agreed with him. He doesn't have the sense to see if a community's this divided over something, you need to rethink.'

'He'll be rethinking now,' Lana promised. 'Testing and dating those bones is going to cause him some major delays. And if we're lucky, they're going to be old enough to draw a lot of attention—national attention—to the site. We can delay the development for months. Maybe years. The longer the development's delayed, the more Dolan loses. And the more time we have to raise money. He might just reconsider selling that land to the Woodsboro Preservation Society.' She pushed back her hair. 'Why don't you let me take you to lunch? We can celebrate today's victory.'

'Why aren't you letting some young guy take *you* out to lunch?'

'Because I lost my heart to you, Roger, the first time I saw you.' It wasn't far from the truth. It made him chuckle, nearly made him blush. He'd lost his wife the same year Lana had lost her husband. He often wondered if that was part of the reason for the bond that had forged between them so quickly. He admired her sharp mind, her stubborn streak, her absolute devotion to her son. He had a granddaughter right about her age, he thought. Somewhere.

'I've got books to catalogue—just in. Don't have time for lunch.'

Roger dealt in rare books, and his tiny shop was a small cathedral to them. It smelt, always, of old leather and old paper.

'This is beautiful,' Lana said, picking a book up and tracing a finger over the leather binding. 'Where did it come from?'

'An estate in Chicago.' His ears pricked at a sound at the rear of the shop. 'But it came with something even more valuable.' The door between the shop and the stairs to the living quarters on the first floor opened. Lana saw the pleasure light up his face, and turned.

He had a face of deep valleys and strong hills. His hair was very dark brown with gilt lights in it. There was a rumpled mass of it that brushed the collar of his shirt. The eyes were deep, dark brown, and at the moment seemed a bit surly. As did his mouth. It was a face, Lana mused, that mirrored both intellect and will. Smart and stubborn, was her first analysis. But perhaps, she admitted, it was because Roger had often described his grandson as just that.

The fact that he looked as if he'd just rolled out of bed and hitched on a pair of old jeans as an afterthought added sexy to the mix. She felt a pleasant little ripple in the blood she hadn't experienced in a long time.

'Doug.' There was pride, delight and love in the single word. 'Wondered when you were going to wander down. Good timing, as it happens. This is Lana. Lana Campbell, my grandson, Doug Cullen.'

'It's nice to meet you.' She offered a hand. 'We've missed each other whenever you've popped back home since I moved to Woodsboro.'

He shook her hand, scanned her face. 'You're the lawyer.'

'Guilty. How long are you in town?'

'I'm not sure.'

A man of few words, she thought, and tried again. 'You do a lot of travelling, acquiring and selling antiquarian books. It must be fascinating.'

'I like it.'

'It must be satisfying for both of you, to share an interest, and a family business.' Since Douglas looked bored by the conversation, Lana turned to his grandfather. 'Well, Roger, since you've blown me off, again, I'd better get back to work. Nice meeting you, Doug.'

'Yeah. See you around.'

When the door closed behind her, Roger let out a steam-kettle sigh. "See you around"? That's the best you can do?'

'There's no coffee. Upstairs. No coffee. No brain. I'm lucky I can speak.'

'Got a pot in the back room,' Roger said in disgust, and jerked a thumb. 'That girl's smart, pretty, interesting, and,' he added as Doug moved behind the counter and through the door, 'available.'

'I'm not looking for a woman.' The scent of coffee hit his senses and nearly made him weep. He poured a cup, burned his tongue on the first sip and knew all would, once again, be right with the world. He sipped again, glancing back at his grandfather. 'Pretty fancy for Woodsboro.'

'I thought you weren't looking.'

Now he grinned, and it changed his face from surly to approachable. 'Looking, seeing. Different kettle. I didn't know she was your girlfriend.'

'If I was you're age, she damn well would be.'

'Grandpa, age doesn't mean squat. I say you should go for it. OK if I take this upstairs? I need to go clean up, head out to see Mom.'

Callie Dunbrook sucked up the last of her Diet Pepsi as she fought the Baltimore Beltway traffic. She'd timed her departure from Philadelphia—where she was supposed to be taking a three-month sabbatical—poorly. But when the call had come through, requesting a consultation, she hadn't considered travel time or rush-hour traffic.

She'd been out of the field for seven weeks. Even the whiff of a chance to be back in again drove her as ruthlessly as she drove her old and beloved Land Rover.

She knew Leo Greenbaum well enough to know he wasn't a man to ask her to drive to Baltimore to look at some bones unless they were very interesting bones.

God knew she needed another project. She was bored brainless writing papers for journals, lecturing. Archaeology wasn't classroom and publishing to Callie. To her it was digging, measuring, boiling in the sun, drowning in the rain, sinking in mud and being eaten alive by insects. Heaven.

She wore her hair long because it was easier to pull it back or bunch it up under a hat—as it was now—than to worry about cutting and styling it. She also had enough healthy vanity to know the straight honey-blonde suited her.

Her golden-brown eyes were long, the brows over them nearly straight. As she approached thirty, her face had mellowed from cute to attractive. When she smiled, three dimples popped out. One in each tanned cheek, and the third just above the right corner of her mouth.

The gently curved chin didn't reveal what her ex-husband had called her rock-brained stubbornness. But then again, she could say the same about him. And did, at every possible opportunity.

She tapped the brakes and swung, with barely any decrease in speed, into a parking lot, hopped out into a vicious, soupy heat.

The building's receptionist glanced over, saw a woman with an athletic body, an ugly straw hat and terrific wire-framed sunglasses.

'Dr Dunbrook for Dr Greenbaum.'

'Sign in, please.' She handed Callie a visitor's pass.

Callie rode the elevator up to the second floor, where Leo was waiting for her and kissed her—the only man of her acquaintance not related to her who was permitted to do so.

'Looking good, Blondie. How was the drive?'

'Vicious. Make it worth my while, Leo.'

'Oh, I think I will. How's the family?'

'Great. Mom and Dad're beating the heat up in Maine. How's Clara?'

Leo shook his head. 'She's taken up pottery. Expect a very ugly vase for Christmas.' He opened a door and gestured Callie in. 'Take a look at this.' He walked behind his desk, unlocked a drawer and drew out a bone fragment in a sealed bag.

Callie took the bag and examined the bone within. 'Looks like part of a tibia. Given the size and fusion, probably from a young female. Very well preserved. This is from western Maryland, right? Civil War country. This predates that. It's not from a Rebel soldier boy.'

'It predates the Civil War,' Leo agreed. 'By about five thousand years.'

When Callie's head came up, he grinned at her like a lunatic. 'Radiocarbon-dating report,' he said and handed her a file.

'Hot dog,' she said.

Rugged, rolling hills riotously green with summer spilled into wide fields thick with row crops. Outcroppings of silver rock bumped through the green like gnarled knuckles and rippling finger bones. It made Callie think of those ancient farmers, carving their rows with primitive tools, hacking into that rocky ground to grow their food. To make their place.

It was a good place, she decided, to work.

The sun sheened over the hip-high corn and gave it a wash of gold over green and gave a young chestnut gelding a bright playground for romping. Cows lolled in the heat behind wire or split-rail fences.

The road twisted and turned to follow the snaking line of the creek, and she drove ten miles without passing another car. When the road opened up again, she punched it, flying by a roll of farmland, a roadside motel, a scatter of homes, with the rise of mountains ahead.

Houses increased in number, decreased in size as she approached Woodsboro's town line. She slowed, got caught by one of the two traffic lights the town boasted, and was pleased to note one of the businesses tucked near the corner of Main and Mountain Laurel was a pizza parlour. A liquor store stood on the other corner.

Reviewing Leo's directions in her mind, she made the turn on Main and headed west. Structures along the main drag were neat, and old. Streetlights were old-timey carriage style, and the sidewalks were bricked.

She noted a café, a hardware store, a small library and a smaller bookstore, several churches and a couple of banks. She made a right when the road split, followed its winding path. Woods were creeping in. Thick, shadowy, secret.

She came over a rise, with the mountains filling the view. And there it was. She pulled to the side of the road by the sign announcing: HOMES AT ANTIETAM CREEK—A Dolan and Sons Development.

There was wide acreage of bottomland, and from the looks of the earth mounded early in the excavation, it was boggy. The trees—old oak and towering poplar—ranged to the west and south and crowded round the run of the creek as if guarding it from interlopers.

Part of the site was roped off, and there the creek had widened into a good-sized pond. On the little sketch Leo had drawn for her, it was called Simon's Hole. She wondered who Simon had been and why the pond was named for him.

On the other side of the road was a stretch of farmland, a couple of weathered outbuildings, an old stone house and nasty-looking machines.

Lifting her camera, she took a series of photos, and was just about to hop the construction fence when she heard, through the summer silence, the sound of an approaching vehicle.

With her sleek blonde hair, the breezy yellow trousers and top, the woman who slid out of the flashy red car looked like a sunbeam.

'Dr Dunbrook?' Lana offered a testing smile.

'That's right. You're Campbell?'

'Yes, Lana Campbell. I'm so glad to meet you. When we heard the bones were thousands of years old—'

'"We" is the preservation organisation you're representing?'

'Yes.' She pushed back a wing of hair with her fingertip, and Callie saw the glint of her wedding band. 'The Historical and Preservation societies in the county and a number of residents of Woodsboro and the surrounding area banded together to protest against this development. The potential problems—'

Callie held up a hand. 'You don't have to sell me. Town politics aren't my field. I'm here to do a preliminary survey of the site—with Dolan's permission,' she added. 'To this point he's been fully cooperative.'

'He won't stay that way.' Lana's lips tightened. 'He wants this development. Can you tell me something about the process? What you'll be doing?'

'Right now I'm going to be looking around, taking photographs, a few samples. No reason not to see what's right here.' Callie slithered down into a six-foot hole and began to dig, methodically, while Lana stood above, wondering what she was supposed to do.

She'd expected an older woman, someone weathered and dedicated and full of fascinating stories. Someone who'd offer unrestricted support. What she had was a young, attractive woman who appeared to be disinterested, even cynical, about the area's current battle.

'Um. Do you often locate sites like this? Through serendipity.'

'Mmm-hmm. Accidental discovery's one way. Natural causes—say, an earthquake—are another. Or surveys, aerial photography, subsurface detections. Lots of scientific ways to pinpoint a site. But serendipity's as good as any.'

'Aren't you going to bring in a team? I understood from my conversation with Dr Greenbaum—'

'Teams take money, which equals grants, which equals paperwork. That's Leo's deal. Dolan's footing the bill, at the moment, for the prelim and the lab work.' She didn't bother to look up. 'You figure he'll spring for a full team, the equipment, the housing, the lab fees for a formal dig?'

'No.' Lana let out a breath. 'Oh God, is that another bone? Is that—'

'Adult femur,' Callie said. None of the excitement that was churning in her blood was reflected in her voice.

'Are you going to take it into the lab?'

'No. It stays. I take it out of this wet ground, it'll dry out. I need proper containers before I excavate bone. But I'm taking this.' Delicately, Callie removed a flat, pointed stone from the damp wall of earth. 'Give me a hand up.'

Wincing only a little, Lana reached down and clasped Callie's filthy hand with her own. 'What is it?'

'Spear point.' She crouched again, took a bag out of her pack and sealed the stone, labelled it. 'This looks like rhyolite to me. Could be this was a camp—Neolithic campsite. Could be it was more. People of that era were starting to settle, to farm, to domesticate animals.'

If she'd closed her eyes, she could have seen it in her mind. 'They weren't as nomadic as we once believed. Ms Campbell, from this very cursory study, I'd say you've got yourself something real sexy here.'

'Sexy enough for a grant, a team, a formal dig?'

'Oh yeah. Nobody's going to be digging footings for houses on this site for some time to come. You got any local media?'

The light began to gleam in Lana's eyes. 'A small weekly newspaper in Woodsboro. A daily in Hagerstown. They're already covering the story.'

'We'll give them more, then bump it up to national.' Callie studied Lana's face as she tucked the sealed bag in her pack. 'I bet you come across real well on TV.'

'I do,' Lana said with a grin. 'How about you?'

'I'm a killer. Dolan doesn't know it, but his development was a non-starter five thousand years ago.'

'He's going to fight you.'

'He's going to lose, Ms Campbell.'

'Make it Lana. How soon do you want to talk to the press, Doctor?'

'Callie.' She pursed her lips and considered. 'Let me touch base with Leo, find a place to stay. That motel outside of town'll do for a start. Where can I reach you?'

'My cellphone.' Lana scribbled down the number. 'Day and night.'

'What time's the evening news?'

'Five thirty.'

Callie looked at her watch, calculated. 'Should be enough time. If I can move things along, I'll be in touch by three.'

She started back towards her car. Lana scrambled to catch up. 'Would you be willing to speak at a town meeting?'

'Leave that to Leo. He's better with people than I am.'

'Callie, let's be sexist.'

'Sure.' Callie leaned on the fence a moment. 'Men are pigs whose every thought and action is dictated by the penis.'

'Well, that goes without saying, but what I mean in this case is people are going to be more intrigued and interested in a young, attractive *female* archaeologist than a middle-aged man who works primarily in a lab.'

'Which is why I'll talk to the TV crew. And don't shrug off Leo's impact. He's got a passion for digging that gets people stirred up.'

'Will he come in from Baltimore?'

Callie looked back at the site. Pretty flatland, the charm of the creek and the sparkle of the pond. The green and mysterious woods. Yes, she could understand why people would want to build houses there. She suspected they had done so before. Thousands of years before.

'You couldn't keep him away.' She was already yanking out her cell-phone and dialling Leo when she drove away. 'Leo. We struck gold. I had a femur and a spear point practically fall in my lap. We need security, a team, equipment, and we need that grant. We need them all a.s.a.p.'

'I've already pulled the chain on the funds. You can take on some students from the university but they want first crack at studying some of the artefacts. And I'm doing some fast talking with the Natural History Museum. I've got a buzz going, Blondie, but I'm going to need a hell of a lot more than a couple of bones and a spear point to keep it up.'

'You're going to get it. It's a settlement, Leo. I can feel it. And the soil conditions? Hell, they couldn't be much better. We may have some hitches with this Dolan. We need some big guns to get his cooperation. Campbell wants to call a town meeting. I drafted you for that.'

'When?'

'Sooner the better. I want to set up an interview with the local TV. It's midsummer. We've only got a few months before we'll have to pack it in for the winter. Media exposure puts the pressure on Dolan. He doesn't step back and let us work, he refuses to donate the finds or pushes to resume his development, he comes off as a greedy asshole with no respect for science or history.'

She pulled into the motel's lot, parked and, shifting the phone, grabbed her pack. With that slung over her shoulder, she pulled out her cello case. 'I'll take the students, use them for grunts until I see what they're made of.'

She yanked open the door of the lobby, stepped up to the desk. 'I need a room. Biggest bed you got in the quietest spot. Get me Rosie,' she said into the phone. 'And Nick Long if he's available.' She dug out a credit card, set it on the counter. 'They can bunk at the motel just outside of town. Hummingbird Inn, on Maryland Route 34. Get me hands, eyes and backs, Leo. I'm going to start shovel tests in the morning. I'll call you back.'

At four o'clock, dressed in clean olive-green trousers and a khaki-coloured shirt, her long hair freshly shampooed, Callie once again pulled to the shoulder of the site.

The camera crew was already setting up for the outside broadcast. Callie noted Lana Campbell was there as well, clutching the hand of a towheaded boy who had the kind of cherubic face that spelt trouble.

Dolan stood directly beside his business sign. Callie assumed he was Ronald Dolan because he didn't look happy.

The minute he spotted Callie, he broke off and marched towards her.

'You Dunbrook? What the hell's going on here?'

'Dr Callie Dunbrook.' She gave him a full-power smile. 'Local TV asked for an interview. I always try to cooperate. Mr Dolan'—still smiling, she touched his arm as if they were compatriots—'you're a very lucky man. The archaeological and anthropological communities are never going to forget your name. I just want to shake your hand.' She took his, pumped. 'And thank you for your part in this incredible discovery.'

'Now you listen here—' He started to bluster again, but she hurried off to introduce herself to the camera crew.

'Slick,' Lana murmured. 'Very slick.'

'Thanks.' She studied the little boy. 'Hi. You the reporter?'

'No.' He giggled, and his mossy-green eyes twinkled with fun. 'You're gonna be on TV. Mommy said I could watch.'

'Tyler, this is Dr Dunbrook. She's the scientist who studies old things.'

'Bones and stuff,' Tyler declared. 'Like Indiana Jones. Did you ever see a dinosaur?'

Callie winked at him. 'I sure have. Dinosaur bones. But they're not my speciality. I like human bones. You have Mom bring you by some time and I'll let you dig. Maybe you'll find some.' She ran her hand over his sun-shot hair. 'See you later, Ty-Rex.'

Suzanne Cullen experimented with a new recipe. Her kitchen was equal parts science lab and homey haven. Once she'd baked because she enjoyed it and because it was something a housewife did. She'd often laughed over the suggestions that she open her own bakery. She was a wife, then a mother, not a businesswoman. She'd never aspired to a career outside the home.

Then, she'd baked to escape her own pain. To give herself something to occupy her mind other than her own guilt and misery and fears. And all in all, she'd found it a more effective therapy than all the counselling, all the prayers, all the public appearances.

When her life, her marriage, her world had continued to fall apart, baking had been a constant. Suddenly, she *had* wanted more. She had needed more.

Suzanne's Kitchen had been born in an ordinary, even uninspired room in a neat little house a stone's throw from the house where she grew up. She'd sold to local markets at first, and had done everything—the buying, the planning, the baking, the packaging and delivery—herself.

Within five years, the demand had been great enough for her to take her products county-wide. Within ten, she'd gone national.

Though she no longer did the baking herself, and the packaging, distribution and publicity were handled by various arms of her corporation, Suzanne still liked to spend time in her own kitchen, formulating new recipes. She lived in a big house snuggled well back on a rise and guarded from the road by woods. And she lived alone.

At fifty-two, she was a very rich woman who could have lived anywhere in the world, done anything she desired. She desired to bake and to live in the community of her birth.

When the five-thirty news came on, she caught the mention of Woodsboro on the television and, picking up her glass of wine, turned to see. Callie's face filled the screen, Suzanne blinked, stared, and stepped closer to the screen.

Her heart began to thud, painfully, against her ribs as she looked into dark amber eyes under straight brows. Her skin went hot, then cold, and her breath grew short and choppy. She shook her head. Everything inside it was buzzing like a swarm of wasps. She couldn't hear anything else, could only watch in shock as that wide mouth moved.

And when the mouth smiled, quick, bright, and three shallow dimples popped out, the glass in Suzanne's hand slid out of her trembling fingers and shattered on the floor at her feet.

TWO

SUZANNE SAT IN THE LIVING ROOM of the house where she'd grown up. Her hands were clutched in her lap, white knuckles pressed hard against her belly as if she were protecting the child who'd once lived in her womb.

Douglas sat on the edge of a BarcaLounger that was older than he was. His stomach was as tight and tangled as his mother's fingers.

The air smelt of the cherry tobacco from his grandfather's pipe, a warm scent that always lingered there. With it was the cold yellow odour of his mother's stress. It had an essence that was strain and fear and guilt, and slapped him back into the terrible days of his childhood when it had permeated everything.

His grandfather gripped the remote with one hand and kept his other on Suzanne's shoulder, as if to hold her in place. 'I didn't want to miss the report,' Roger said, then cleared his throat. 'Asked Doug to run home here and set the VCR as soon as Lana told me about it. Didn't watch it yet.'

'Play it, Daddy.' Suzanne's voice hitched. 'Play it now.'

Roger started the tape. The hand on Suzanne's shoulder began to knead.

'Fast-forward through—here.' Suzanne snatched the remote, slowed the tape to regular speed when Callie's face came on-screen. 'Look at her. God. Oh my God.'

'Sweet Jesus,' Roger murmured. Like a prayer.

'You see it. It's Jessica. It's my Jessie.'

'Mom.' Douglas's heart ached at the way she said it. *My Jessie*. 'She's got the colouring, but . . . that lawyer, Lana. She looks as much like Jessie might as this woman does. Mom, you can't know.'

'I *can* know,' she snapped out. She stabbed the remote, froze the screen as Callie smiled. 'She has her father's eyes. Jay's eyes—same colour, same shape. And my dimples. Three dimples, like me. Like Ma had.'

'There's a strong resemblance.' Roger felt weak. 'The colouring, the shape of the face. Those features.' Something was rising up in his throat that felt like equal parts panic and hope. 'The last artist projection—'

'I have it.' Suzanne leapt up, grabbed the folder she'd brought with her and took out a computer-generated image. 'Jessica, at twenty-five.'

Now Douglas rose as well. 'I thought you'd stopped having those done.'

'I never stopped.' Tears wanted to spill but she forced them back with the iron will that had got her through every day of the last twenty-nine years. 'I stopped talking to you about it because it upset you. But I never stopped looking. I never stopped believing.' She pushed the picture into his hands. 'Look at your sister.'

He held the photo as the pain he'd shut down, through a will every bit as strong as his mother's, bit back at him. It made him helpless. It made him sick. 'A resemblance,' he continued. 'Brown eyes, blonde hair.' Unlike his mother, he couldn't live on hope. Hope destroyed him. 'How many other girls, women, have you looked at and seen Jessica? I can't stand watching you put yourself through this again. You don't know anything about her. How old she is, where she comes from.'

'Then I'll find out.' She took the photo back with hands that were unsteady. 'If you can't stand it, then stay out of it. Like your father.'

She knew it was cruel, to slash at one child in the desperate need for the other. She knew it was wrong to strike out at her son while clutching the ghost of her daughter to her breast. But he would either help, or step aside. There was no middle ground in Suzanne's quest for Jessica.

'I'll run a computer search on my laptop back at the store.' Douglas's voice was cold and quiet. 'I'll get you what information I can.'

'I'll come with you.'

'No.' He could slap just as quick and hard as she. 'I can't talk to you when you're like this. Nobody can. I'll send you what I find.'

So, she was the right age, Doug thought as he scanned the information from his search. The fact that her birthday was listed within a week of Jessica's was hardly conclusive, though his mother would see it as proof.

He could read a lifestyle into the dry facts. Upper-middle-class moneyed suburban. Only child of Elliot and Vivian Dunbrook of Philadelphia. Mrs Dunbrook had played second violin in the Boston Symphony Orchestra before her marriage. She, her husband and infant daughter had relocated to Philadelphia, where Elliot Dunbrook had taken a position as surgical resident.

She'd grown up in privilege, had graduated first in her class at Carnegie Mellon, gone on to get her master's and, just recently, her doctorate.

She'd pursued her career in archaeology while compiling her advanced degrees. She'd married at twenty-six, divorced not quite two years later. No children. She was associated with Leonard Greenbaum and Associates, the Paleolithic Society, and several universities' archaeology departments. She'd written a number of well-received papers.

What he could see was a woman who'd been raised by well-to-do, respected parents. Hardly baby-napping material. But his mother wouldn't see that, he knew. She would see the birthday and nothing else. Just as she had countless times before.

Sometimes, when he let himself, he wondered what had fractured his family. Had it been that instant when Jessica disappeared? Or had it been his mother's unrelenting, unwavering determination to find her again?

Or was it the moment when he himself had realised one simple fact: that by reaching for one child, his mother had lost another.

He would do what he could. He attached the files, emailed them to his mother. Then he buried himself in a book.

There was nothing like the beginning of a dig, that time when anything is possible and there is no limit to the potential of the discovery. Callie had a couple of fresh-faced undergraduates that came along with a small grant from the university. She'd take what she could get. She would have Rose Jordan as geologist, a woman she both respected and liked. She had Leo's lab, and the man himself as consultant. Once she had Nick Long pulled in as anthropologist, she'd be in fat city.

She worked with the students, digging shovel samples, and had already chosen the two-trunked oak tree at the northwest corner of the pond as her datum point. With that as her fixed reference they'd begin measuring the vertical and horizontal location of everything on the site. She'd completed the plan of the site's surface the night before, and had begun to plot her three-foot-square divisions. Today they'd start running the rope lines to mark the divisions. Then the fun began. Rain the night before had turned the ground soggy and soft. Her boots were already mucked past the ankle, her hands were filthy and she smelt of sweat.

For Callie, it didn't get much better.

She glanced over at the toot of a horn, and this time the interruption had her grinning. She'd known Leo wouldn't be able to stay away for long. 'We're finding flakes in every shovel sample,' she told him. 'My theory is we're in the knapping area there.' She gestured to where the two students continued to dig and sieve the soil. 'Rosie will verify rhyolite flakes. They sat there, honing the rock into arrowheads, spear points, tools. Go a little deeper, we'll find discarded samples.'

'She'll be here this afternoon. How are the students doing?'

'Not bad. The girl, Sonya, she's got potential. Bob, he's willing and able. And earnest. Really, really earnest. I'm going to put him on community relations, let him give visitors a lecture on what we're doing, what we're looking for.'

'I'll take that for you today.'

'Thanks, Leo. I'm going to need containers. I don't want to start pulling bones out of the ground and have them go to dust on me once they're out of the bog. I need equipment. I need nitrogen gas, dry ice. I need more tools, more hands.'

'You'll have them,' he promised. 'The great state of Maryland has given you your first grant on the Antietam Creek Archaeological Research Project.'

'Yeah?' She grabbed his shoulders as the delight burst through her. 'Yeah? Leo, you're my one true love.' She kissed him noisily on the mouth.

'Speaking of that.' He patted her dirty hands, stepped back. 'We're going to have to discuss another key member of the team. While we do,

I want you to remember we're all professionals.' He cleared his throat. 'The anthropological significance of this find is every bit as monumental as the archaeological. Therefore, you and the head anthro will need to work together as coheads of the project.'

'Well, hell, Leo, what am I, a diva? I don't have a problem sharing authority with Nick.'

'Yes, well . . .' Leo trailed off at the sound of an approaching engine. 'You can't always get what you want.'

Shock came first, racing with recognition as she spotted the brawny four-wheeler in demon black, then the ancient pick-up truck pulling a dirty white travel trailer painted with the name DIGGER.

'Callie . . . before you say anything—'

'You're not going to do this.' She had to swallow. Emotions, too many, too mixed, too huge, slammed through her.

'It's done.'

'Aw, Leo, no. Goddamnit, I asked for Nick.'

'He's not available. The project needs the best, Callie. Graystone's the best.' Leo nearly stumbled back when she spun towards him. 'Personal business aside, Callie, you know he's the best. Digger, too. Adding his name to yours greased the grant. I expect you to behave professionally.'

She showed Leo her teeth. 'You can't always get what you want.'

She watched him jump out of the four-wheeler. Jacob Graystone, all six feet, one and a quarter inches of him. His hair, a straight-arrow fall of black, spilled out beneath an old brown hat. A plain white T-shirt was tucked into the waistband of faded Levi's. And the body beneath them was prime. Long bones, long muscles, all covered in bronzed skin that was a result of working outdoors and the quarter of his heritage that was Apache.

He turned, and though he wore dark glasses, she knew his eyes were a colour caught, rather beautifully, between grey and green.

He flashed a smile—arrogant, smug, sarcastic. All of which, she reckoned, fitted him to the ground. He had a face too handsome for his own good, or so she'd always thought. Those long bones again, sharp enough to cut diamonds, the straight nose, the firm jaw with the hint of a scar. Her pulse began to throb and her temples to pound. Casually, she ran a hand down the chain round her neck, assured herself it was tucked under her shirt.

He even walked smugly, she mused, in that damn cowboy swagger. It had always irritated the hell out of her.

His companion stepped out of the truck. Stanley Digger Forbes. A hundred and twenty-five pounds of ugly.

'Graystone.' She inclined her head.

'Dunbrook.' His voice was a drawl, a warm and lazy slide of words that brought images of deserts and prairies. Deliberately she looked away from him. One look at Digger made her lips curve. He was grinning like a hyena, his smashed walnut face livened by a pair of spooky black eyes and the glint of his gold eyetooth.

He wore a gold hoop in his left ear, and a dirty blond rat's tail hung beneath the bright red bandanna tied round his head.

'Hey, Dig, welcome aboard.'

'Callie, looking good. Got prettier.'

'Thanks. You didn't.'

He gave her his familiar hooting laugh. 'That girl with the legs?' He jerked his chin towards the students. 'She legal?' Despite his looks, Digger was renowned for being able to score dig groupies as triumphantly as a batter connecting with a high fastball. He sauntered off towards the shovels.

'OK, let's run through the basics,' Callie began.

'No catching up?' Jake interrupted. 'No small talk?'

'There's no point in wasting time bullshitting about old times.'

'Digger's right. You're looking good.' She was. Just the sight of her blew through him like a storm. She wore the same clunky watch, pretty silver earrings. Her mouth was just a bit top-heavy, and naked. She never bothered with paint on a dig. But she'd always slathered cream on her face morning and night no matter what the living conditions. Just as she'd always made a nest out of whatever those living conditions might be. A fragrant candle, her cello, comfort food, shampoo that had the faintest hint of rosemary.

Ten months, he thought, since he'd seen her. And her face had been in his mind every day, and every night. 'Word was you were on sabbatical.'

'I was, now I'm not. You're here to co-coordinate, and to head up the anthropological details of the project now known as Antietam Creek.'

She angled away as if to study the site. The truth was it was too hard to stand face to face with him. To know they were both measuring each other. Remembering each other. 'We have what I believe to be a Neolithic settlement. Radiocarbon testing on human bones already excavated are dated at five thousand, three hundred and seventy-five—'

'I've read the reports, Callie. You got yourself a hot one. Digger can set up camp here. I'll get my field pack, then you can show me around. We'll get to work.'

She drew a deep breath when he strode back towards his four-wheeler. She counted to ten. 'I'm going to kill you for this, Leo. Kill you dead.'

But they worked well together. And that, Callie thought as she showered off the grime of the day, was one more pisser. They challenged each other, professionally, and somehow that challenge forced them to complement each other. It had always done so.

She loved his mind, even if it was inside the hardest head she'd ever butted her own against. His was so fluid, so flexible, so open to possibilities. The problem was they challenged each other personally, too. And for a while . . . for a while, she mused, they had complemented each other.

But mostly they'd fought like a pair of mad dogs.

When they weren't fighting, they were falling into bed. When they weren't fighting or falling into bed or working on a common project they . . . baffled each other, she supposed.

It had been ridiculous for them to get married. She could see that now. What had seemed romantic, exciting and sexy in eloping like a couple of crazy teenagers had turned into stark reality. And marriage had become a battlefield with each of them drawing lines the other had been dead set on crossing. Of course, his lines had been absurd, while hers had been rational. But that was neither here nor there.

They hadn't been able to keep their hands off each other. And her body still remembered, poignantly, the feel of those hands.

But then, it had been painfully apparent that Jacob Graystone's hands hadn't been particularly selective where they wandered. The bastard.

That brunette in Colorado had been the last straw. Busty, baby-voiced Veronica. The bitch.

And when she'd confronted him with her conclusions, when she'd accused him in plain, simple terms of being a rat-bastard cheater, he hadn't had the courtesy—the *balls*—to confirm or deny.

What had he called her? Oh yeah. *A childish, tight-assed, hysterical female*. She'd never been sure which part of that phrase most pissed her off, but it had coated her vision with red. The rest of the argument was a huge, boiling blur. All she clearly remembered was demanding a divorce—the first sensible thing she'd done since laying eyes on him. And demanding he get the hell out, and off the project, or she would.

Had he fought for her? Hell no. Had he begged her forgiveness, pledged his love and fidelity? Not a chance.

He'd walked. And so—what a coincidence—had the brunette.

Still steaming from the memory, Callie stepped out of the shower. Then closed a hand round the ring she wore on a chain round her neck.

She'd taken the wedding ring off—yanked it off, she recalled, as soon as she'd received the divorce papers for her signature. But she hadn't been able to let it go as she'd told herself she'd let Jacob go.

He was, in her life, her only failure.

She told herself she wore the ring to remind herself not to fail again.

She pulled off the chain, tossed it on the dressing table. If he saw it, he'd think she'd never got over him. Or something equally conceited. She wasn't going to think about him any more. She was going to see if Rosie wanted to hunt up a meal.

She pulled open the bedroom door and nearly ploughed into the woman who was standing outside it. 'Sorry. Can I help you?'

Suzanne's throat snapped shut. Tears threatened to overflow.

'Didn't mean to startle you,' Callie said when the woman only continued to stare. 'Are you looking for someone?'

'Yes. Yes, I'm looking for someone. You . . . I need to speak with you. You don't know me. I'm Suzanne Cullen. It's very important that I speak with you. Privately. Please. Five minutes.'

There was such urgency in the woman's voice, Callie stepped back. 'Five minutes. Look, you'd better sit down. You don't look very well.' The fact was, Callie thought, the woman looked fragile enough to shatter into pieces.

'Thank you.' Suzanne lowered to the side of the bed. She wanted to be clear, she wanted to be calm. She wanted to grab her little girl and hold on to her so tight three decades would vanish.

'I need to ask you a question. It's very personal, and very important.' Suzanne took a deep breath. 'Were you adopted?'

'What?' With a sound that was part shock, part laugh, Callie shook her head. 'No. What kind of question is that? Who the hell are you?'

'On December 12th, 1974, my infant daughter Jessica was stolen from her buggy in the Hagerstown Mall.' She spoke calmly now. She had, over the years, given countless speeches on her ordeal.

'I was there to take my son, her three-year-old brother, Douglas, to see Santa Claus. There was a moment of distraction. A moment. That's all it took. She was gone. We looked everywhere. The police, the FBI, family, friends, the community. Organisations for missing children. She was only three months old. We never found her. She'll be twenty-nine on September 8th.'

'I'm sorry.' Annoyance wavered into sympathy. 'I'm very sorry. I can't imagine what it must be like for you, for your family. If you have some idea that I might be that daughter, I'm sorry for that, too. But I'm not.'

Suzanne opened the portfolio carefully. 'This is a picture of me when I was about your age. Will you look at it, please?'

Reluctantly, Callie took it. A chill danced up her spine as she studied the face. 'There's a resemblance. That sort of thing happens, Ms Cullen.'

'Do you see the dimples? Three? You have them.'

'I also have parents. I was born in Boston on September 11th, 1974.'

'My mother.' Suzanne pulled out another photo. 'Again, this was taken when she was about thirty. You see how much you look like her. And, my husband.' Suzanne drew out another photo. 'His eyes. You have his eyes—the shape, the colour. Even the eyebrows. Dark and straight. When I saw you on television, I knew. I *knew*.'

Callie's heart was galloping, a wild horse inside her breast, and her palms began to sweat. 'Ms Cullen, I'm not your daughter. My mother has brown eyes. I know who my parents are.'

'Ask them.' Suzanne pleaded. 'Look them in the face and ask them. If you don't do that, how can you be sure? If you don't do that, I'll go to Philadelphia and ask them myself. Because I know you're my child.'

'I want you to leave.' Callie's knees were starting to shake.

Placing the photographs on the bed, Suzanne rose. 'You were born at four thirty-five in the morning, at Washington County Hospital in Hagerstown, Maryland. We named you Jessica Lynn.' She set another picture on the bed. 'That's a copy of the photograph taken shortly after you were born. Have you ever seen a picture of yourself before you were three months old?' She paused a moment, then stepped to the door. Indulged herself by brushing her hand over Callie's. 'Ask them. My address and phone number are with the pictures. Ask them,' she said again and hurried out.

Trembling, Callie shut the door, leaned back against it.

It was crazy. The woman was sad and deluded. And crazy. She probably saw her daughter in every face that held any remote resemblance.

It didn't mean anything. It was insane to think otherwise.

Her parents weren't baby thieves, for God's sake. They were kind, loving, interesting people. The sort who would feel nothing but compassion for someone like Suzanne Cullen. The resemblance, the age similarity, they were only coincidences.

Ask them. How could you ask your own parents such a thing? Hey, Mom, did you happen to be in the mall in Maryland around Christmas in '74? Did you pick up a baby along with some last-minute gifts?

At the knock on the door she whirled round, yanked it open. 'I told you I'm not . . . What the hell do you want?'

'Share a beer?' Jake clanged the two bottles he held. 'Truce?'

'I don't want a beer, and there's no need for a truce. I'm not interested enough to have a fight with you, therefore, a truce is moot.'

'Not like you to turn down a free beer at the end of the day.'

'You're right.' She snagged one, then booted the door. It would have slammed satisfactorily in his face, but he'd always been quick.

'Hey. Trying to be friendly here.'

'Get lost, Graystone. I'm not in the mood.' She turned her back on him and spotted her wedding ring on the dressing table. Shit. Perfect. She stalked over, laid a hand over it and drew the chain into her fist.

He sauntered towards the bed as she jammed the ring and chain into her pocket. 'What's this? Looking at family pictures?'

She spun round and went pale as ice. 'Why do you say that?'

'Who's this? Your grandmother? Never met her, did I? Then again, we didn't spend a lot of time getting chummy with each other's families.'

'It's not my grandmother.' She tore the photo out of his hand. 'Get out.'

'Hold on.' He tapped his knuckles on her cheek, an old habit that had tears burning the back of her throat. 'What's wrong?'

She wanted to pull the cork and let it all pour out. 'It's none of your business. I have a life without you. I don't need you.'

His eyes went cold, went hard. 'You never did.' He walked to the door. He glanced at the cello case in the corner, the sandalwood candle burning on the dressing, the laptop on the bed and the open bag of Oreos beside the phone. 'Same old Callie,' he muttered.

'Jake?' She stepped to the door, nearly touched him. Nearly gave in to the urge to pull him back. 'Thanks for the beer.'

She felt like a thief. It hardly mattered that she had a key to the front door. She was still sneaking in at two in the morning.

Callie hadn't been able to settle after Suzanne Cullen's visit. She hadn't been able to eat, or sleep, or lose herself in work.

Not that she believed she'd been that baby. Not for a minute.

But she was a scientist, a seeker, and until she had answers she knew she'd pick at the puzzle like a scab until it was uncovered. Even if that meant going into her parents' house in Philadelphia when they were away, even if it meant searching their files and papers for some proof of what she already knew.

She was Callie Ann Dunbrook.

The house was dark but for a faint gleam in the first-floor window of her mother's sitting room. Her parents would have set the security system, putting the lights on a changing pattern of time and location while they were in Maine. They were sensible, responsible people.

They liked to play golf and give clever dinner parties. Her father liked to potter around the garden. Her mother played the violin and collected antique watches. He donated four days a month to a free clinic. She gave music lessons to underprivileged children.

They'd been married for thirty-eight years, and though they argued, occasionally bickered, they still held hands when they walked together.

She knew her mother deferred to her father on major decisions, and most of the minor ones. It was a trait that drove Callie crazy. She was often ashamed of herself for viewing her mother as weak, and for viewing her father as just a bit smug for fostering the dependence. But if these were the biggest flaws she could find in her parents, it hardly made them baby-snatching monsters.

Feeling foolish, guilty and ridiculously nervous, Callie let herself into the house. She moved down the wide hallway and into her father's study. She hesitated there, wincing a bit as she looked at his lovely old mahogany desk. She still felt like an intruder.

She walked to the first of the filing cabinets. Anything she needed to find would be in this room, she knew. Her father took care of the finances, the record keeping, the filing. She began to search. The medical records were precisely organised. She flipped past the folder marked for her mother, the one marked for her father, and drew out her own.

She noted the childhood inoculations, the X-rays on the broken arm she'd suffered when she'd fallen out of a tree. There was her tonsillectomy in June 1983. The dislocated finger when she'd been sixteen.

But she found no hospital records of her birth. No paperwork from paediatric exams for the first three months of her life.

Didn't mean anything. Her breathing quickened. He just filed them elsewhere. A baby file. Or he put them with her mother's medical records.

Yes, that was it. He'd kept the documentation of her pregnancy and had kept his daughter's earliest records with that. To close the event. She scanned through, trying to pick up key data without actually reading what she considered her mother's private business.

She found the reports and treatment for the first miscarriage in August 1969. She'd known about it, and about the one that followed in the fall of '71.

Her mother had told her how they'd sent her into a clinical depression. And how much finally having a healthy baby girl had meant to her.

And here, Callie noted with a shudder of relief, here was the third pregnancy. The ob-gyn had been concerned, naturally, with the diagnosis of incompetent cervical Os that had caused the previous miscarriages, had prescribed medication, bed rest through the first trimester.

The pregnancy had been carefully monitored by Dr Henry Simpson. She'd even been admitted to the hospital during her seventh month owing to concerns about hypertension, but she'd been treated, released.

And that, to Callie's confusion, was where all documentation of the pregnancy ended. The paperwork picked up nearly a year later with a sprained ankle. It was as if her mother's pregnancy had stopped in its seventh month.

There was a knotted ball in her stomach as she rose again, returned to the files. She opened the next drawer, thumbed through looking for more medical records. And when she found no folder that fitted, she crouched and started to open the bottom drawer. Found it locked. Refusing to allow herself to think, she searched through her father's desk for the key.

When she didn't find it, she took his letter opener, knelt down in front of the drawer and broke the lock.

Inside she found a long metal fireproof box, again locked. This she took back to the desk, sat. For a long moment she simply stared at it, wishing it away.

She could put it back, stick it in the drawer and pretend it didn't exist. Whatever was inside was something her father had gone to some trouble to keep private. What right did she have to violate his privacy?

And yet wasn't that what she did every day? She violated the privacy of the dead, of strangers, because knowledge was more sacred than their secrets.

'I'm sorry,' she said, and attacked the lock with the letter opener.

She lifted the lid, and began.

In the first week of the eight month of her pregnancy, Vivian Dunbrook's foetus had died in the womb. Labour was induced, and she delivered a stillborn daughter on June 29, 1974.

Less than two weeks later, a hysterectomy, recommended due to cervical damage, was performed. The patient was treated for depression.

On December 16, 1974, they adopted an infant girl whom they named Callie Ann. A private adoption, Callie noted dully, arranged through a lawyer. The fee for his services was $10,000. In addition, another fee of $250,000 was paid through him to the unnamed biological mother. The infant was examined by Dr Peter O'Malley, a Boston paediatrician, and deemed healthy.

Her next examination was a standard six-month checkup, by Dr Marilyn Vermer, in Philadelphia, who had continued as the infant's paediatrician until the patient reached the age of twelve.

'When I refused to go to a baby doctor any more,' Callie murmured and watched, with some surprise, as a tear plopped on the papers she held.

'Jesus. Oh Jesus.' It couldn't be real. It couldn't be true. How could two people who'd never lied to her about the most inconsequential matter have lived a lie all these years?

'What the hell do you mean she's taken the day off?' Jake shoved his hat back and fried Leo with one searing look.

'She said something came up.'

'Yeah, yeah. And it would be just like her to flip off this project because she's ticked I'm on it.'

'No, it wouldn't. You know she doesn't play that kind of game.'

'OK.' It was worry that had anger gnawing at Jake. 'Something was wrong with her last night. She wouldn't talk about it. But she had some pictures out. Looked like family shots to me. Would she tell you if something was wrong with her family?'

Leo rubbed the back of his neck. 'I'd think so. She only said she had some personal business, that it couldn't wait.'

'She got a guy?'

'How the hell do I know? She doesn't tell me about her love life.' Leo aimed a bland look. 'I can't repeat what Callie's said to me about you. I don't use that kind of language.'

'Cute.' Jake stared off towards the pond, his eyes shielded by his dark glasses. 'Whatever she's said, whatever she thinks, if she's in some sort of trouble, I'll get it out of her.'

'If you're so damned concerned, why the hell did you get divorced?'

Jake lifted his shoulders. 'Good question, Leo. Damn good question.'

He'd fallen for her, and fallen hard, the first time he'd seen her, Jake admitted. It had been terrifying and annoying. *She* had been terrifying and annoying. He'd been thirty, unencumbered—unless you counted Digger—and planning to stay that way. He didn't answer to anyone, and certainly had no intentions of answering to some curvy little archaeologist with a mean streak.

God, he'd loved that mean streak of hers.

Sex had been as stormy and fascinating as their bickering. But it hadn't solved his problem. She'd given him her body, her companionship, the challenge of her contrary mind. But she'd never given him the one thing that might have settled him down. Her trust. She'd never trusted him.

For months after she'd booted him, he'd consoled himself that it was her blatant lack of faith that had ruined everything. Just as for months he'd held on to the conviction that she'd come crawling after him.

Stupid, he could admit now. Callie never crawled. And as time passed, he'd begun to see that maybe, perhaps, possibly, he hadn't handled everything quite as adeptly as he could have. Should have.

It didn't really shift the blame away from her, which was exactly where it belonged, but it did open the door to considering another approach.

That current still ran between them, he acknowledged. If the Antietam project offered him a channel for that current, he'd use it.

He'd use whatever came to hand to get her back.

Callie hadn't expected to sleep, but just after dawn she'd curled up on top of the bed in her old room. She'd woken a full four hours later at the sound of the front door slamming, and the bright call of her name.

'Callie!' Sheer delight lifted Vivian's voice as she rushed through the doorway. 'I was so surprised to see your car in the drive. When did you get here?'

'Last night.' She didn't lift her head. She wasn't ready to look at her mother's face. 'I thought you and Dad were in Maine.'

'We were. We decided to come home today instead of Sunday. Baby . . .' Vivian lifted Callie's chin. 'What's wrong? Aren't you feeling well?'

'Just a little groggy.' Her mother's eyes were brown, Callie thought. But not like her own. Her mother's were darker, deeper. 'Is Dad here?'

'Yes, of course. He's taking a look at the tomato plants.'

'I need to talk to you. To both of you. Just give me a minute to throw some water on my face. I'll be right down.'

When she came out of the bathroom and went downstairs, Vivian was in the hallway, clutching her husband's hand. How perfect they look together, Callie thought.

They'd lied to her, every day of her life.

'Callie. You've got your mother in a state.' Elliot gave her a hug. 'What's wrong with my girl?' he questioned, and had tears burning her eyes.

'I didn't expect you back today.' She stepped out of his arms. 'I thought I'd have more time to figure out what to say. Now I don't.'

'Callie, are you in trouble?'

She looked at her father's face, into his face, saw nothing but love and concern. 'I don't know what I am,' she said simply, and walked across the hallway into the living room. There she turned, took one deep breath. 'I need to ask you why you never told me I was adopted.'

Vivian made a strangled sound. 'Callie, where did you—'

'Please don't deny it. Please don't do that.' She could barely get the words out. 'I'm sorry, but I went through the files.' She looked at her father. 'I broke into the locked drawer, and the security box inside. I saw the medical records, the adoption papers.'

'Elliot.'

'Sit down, Vivian. Sit down.' He pulled her to a chair, lowered her into it. 'I couldn't destroy them. It wasn't right.'

'But it was right to conceal the facts of my birth from me?'

Elliot's shoulders slumped. 'It wasn't important to us.'

'Wasn't—'

'Don't blame your father.' Vivian reached up for Elliot's hand. 'He did it for me,' she said to Callie. 'I made him promise. I made him swear. I needed . . .' She began to weep, slow tears streaming down her face. 'Don't hate me, Callie. Oh God, don't hate me for this. You were my baby the instant you were put in my arms. Nothing else mattered.'

'A replacement for the baby you lost?'

'Callie.' Now Elliot stepped forward. 'Don't be cruel.'

'Cruel?' Who was this man, staring at her out of sad, angry eyes? Who was her father? 'You can speak to me of cruel after what you've done?'

'What have we done?' he tossed back. 'We didn't tell you. How can that matter so much? Your mother needed the illusion at first. She was devastated. She could never give birth to a child. When there was a chance to adopt you, to have a daughter, we took it. We loved you, love you, not because you're like our own, because you *are* our own.'

'I couldn't bear the thought of people looking at you and seeing you as a substitute,' Vivian managed. 'We moved here, to start fresh. Just the three of us. And I put all of that away. It doesn't change who you are. It doesn't change who we are or how much we love you.'

'You pay for a black-market baby. You take a child stolen from another family, and it doesn't change anything?'

'What are you talking about?' Elliot's face filled with anger. 'That's a vicious thing to say. Whatever we've done we don't deserve that.'

'You paid a quarter of a million dollars.'

'That's right. We arranged for a private adoption and money speeds the wheel. We agreed to the fee, agreed that the biological mother should be compensated. To stand there and accuse us of *buying* you, of stealing you, denigrates everything we've ever had as a family.'

'Last night, a woman came to my room. She'd seen the news report I did on my current project. She said I was her daughter. That on December 12th, 1974, her infant daughter was stolen. From a mall in Hagerstown, Maryland. She showed me pictures of herself at my age, of her mother at my age. There's a very strong resemblance. Colouring, facial shape. The damn three dimples. I told her I wasn't adopted. But I was.'

'It can't have anything to do with us.' Elliot rubbed a hand over his heart. 'That's insane. We went through a lawyer. A reputable lawyer who specialised in private adoptions. We had recommendations from your mother's obstetrician. We'd never be a party to kidnapping, to baby brokering. You can't believe that.'

She looked at him, at her mother, who stared at her out of swimming eyes. 'No. No,' she said and felt a little of the weight lift. 'No, I don't believe that.'

'I don't know if you can ever forgive me,' Vivian began.

'I don't think you understand, Mom.' Callie crouched down by her mother's chair. 'I have to know the facts. I can't see the whole picture until I have the pieces of it to put together. We're a family. Nothing changes that, but I have to know the facts.' She lowered herself to sit cross-legged on the floor. 'First I need to understand . . . about adoption. Did you feel it made you, me . . . *us* less valid?'

'However a family is made is a miracle,' Elliot responded. 'You were our miracle.'

'But you concealed it.'

'We wanted a child.' Vivian's fingers tightened on Elliot's. 'We so very much wanted a child. When I had the first miscarriage, it was terrible. I can't explain it to you. The sense of loss and grief and panic. Of . . . failure. And when I miscarried again. I was . . . I felt . . . broken.'

Callie touched Vivian's hand. 'I know. I understand.'

'They gave me pills to get me through the depression.' She managed a watery smile. 'Elliot weaned me off them. He kept me busy instead. He pulled me out of the pit. I wanted to try again. Elliot wanted to wait a little longer, but I was determined. I got pregnant again. I was so happy. And I was careful. This time I got past the first trimester, and it looked good. I felt the baby move. Remember, Elliot?'

'Yes, I remember.'

'I bought maternity clothes. We started decorating the nursery. There were some problems with my blood pressure, serious enough in the seventh month for them to hospitalise me briefly. But it seemed like everything was all right until . . .'

'We went in for an examination,' Elliot continued. 'There was no foetal heartbeat. Tests showed the foetus had died.'

'It was a little girl,' Vivian said quietly. 'Stillborn. So beautiful, so tiny. I held her, and for a while I told myself she was only sleeping. But I knew she wasn't, and when they took her away, I fell apart.'

'She was in a deep state of depression. The stillbirth, the hysterectomy. The loss, not only of another child but any hope of conceiving again.'

How old had she been? Callie thought. Twenty-six? So young to face the loss. 'I'm so sorry, Mom.'

'Elliot brought up the possibility of adoption. I didn't want to listen, but he laid it out in stark medical terms. There would not be another pregnancy. If we wanted a child, it was time to explore other ways of having one. Did I want a child, or did I just want to be pregnant? If I wanted a child, we could have a child. I wanted a child.'

'We went to an agency—several,' Elliot added. 'There were waiting lists. The longer the list, the more difficult it was for Vivian.'

'My new obsession.' She sighed. 'I thought of myself as expecting. Somewhere there was a child that was mine. And every delay was like another loss.'

'She was blooming again, with hope. I couldn't stand the thought of that bloom fading, of watching that sadness come into her again. I spoke of it to Simpson, her obstetrician. He gave me the name of a lawyer who did private adoptions. Direct with the birth mother.'

'Marcus Carlyle,' Callie said, remembering the name from the files.

'Yes,' Vivian said, steadier now. 'He was wonderful. So supportive, so sympathetic. The fee was very high, but that was a small price to pay. He said he had a client, a young girl who'd had a baby and realised that she couldn't care for her properly. He would tell her about us; if she approved, he could place the child with us. He said he would let us know within weeks.'

'It seemed like fate,' Elliot explained.

'He called eight days later at four thirty in the afternoon. When I answered the phone, he said, "Congratulations, Mrs Dunbrook. It's a girl." I broke down and sobbed. He said it was moments like this that made his job worth while.'

'You never met the birth mother.'

'No.' Elliot shook his head. 'The only information given was medical history, and a basic profile. We went to his office the following day. There was a nurse, holding you. You were sleeping. The procedure was we didn't sign the papers until we'd seen you, accepted you.'

'You were mine as soon as I saw you, Callie,' Vivian said. 'The instant. She put you in my arms, and you were my baby. Not a substitute, not a replacement. Mine. I made Elliot promise that we'd never refer to the adoption again, never tell you or anyone. Because you were our baby.'

'It was so vital to Vivian's state of mind,' Elliot said. 'She needed to close away all the pain and disappointment.'

'But the family?' Callie began.

'Were just as concerned about her as I was,' Elliot answered. 'And just as dazzled by you, as completely in love. We just set that one thing aside. Then, we moved here; no one knew, so why bring it up? Still, I kept the papers, though Vivian asked me to get rid of them. It didn't seem right to do that.'

'Callie.' Composed again, Vivian reached out. 'Mr Carlyle was a reputable lawyer. We wouldn't have gone through anyone we didn't absolutely trust. My own obstetrician recommended him. These men were—are—compassionate, ethical men. Hardly involved in some sort of black-market baby ring.'

'This woman's baby was stolen on December 12th. Three days after that, your lawyer calls and says he has a baby girl for you. The next day, you sign papers, write cheques and bring me home.'

'You don't know her baby was stolen,' Vivian insisted.

'No, but that's easy enough to verify. I have to do this. The way my parents raised me makes it impossible for me to do otherwise.'

'If you confirm the kidnapping'—Elliot's heart shuddered as he spoke—'there are tests to determine if there's a biological connection.'

'I know. I'll take that step if it's necessary.'

'I can cut through the red tape so you'll have the results quickly.'

'What will you do if . . .' Vivian couldn't finish the sentence.

'I don't know.' Callie blew out a breath. 'I don't know. I'll do what comes next. You're my mother. Nothing changes that. Dad, I need to take the paperwork, start checking out everyone involved. Dr Simpson, Carlyle. Did you get the name of the nurse who brought me to his office?'

'No.' He shook his head. 'Not that I remember. But I can track down Simpson for you.'

'Let me know as soon as you find out. Whatever happens, I'm still going to love you. But there's a woman who's in considerable pain over the loss of a child. She deserves some answers.'

Doug didn't know the last time he'd been so angry. To find out that his mother had gone to this Callie Dunbrook. Humiliating herself, tearing open scars, dragging an outsider into a personal family tragedy.

The way Woodsboro worked, it wasn't going to take long for the Cullen family history to be dug up and discussed endlessly all over again. So he was going to see Callie Dunbrook himself. To ask her not to speak of his mother's visit with anyone—if it wasn't too late for that. To apologise for it.

He wasn't going to get a better look at her, he assured himself. As far as he was concerned Jessica was gone. Long gone. And if she did come back, what was the point? She wasn't Jessica now. If she was still alive, she was a different person, a grown woman.

Whatever way it worked, it was only more heartache for his mother.

He pulled over to the side of the road by the construction fence. As he stepped out of the car, a short man in mud-brown attire broke away from a group and walked to meet him.

'How's it going?' Doug said for lack of anything else.

'It probably looks a bit confusing right now, but in fact, it's the early days of a very organised archaeological dig. Human bones nearly six thousand years old were discovered by a digger operator—'

'Yes, I know. I thought there was a Callie Dunbrook heading this up.'

'Dr Dunbrook's the head archaeologist on the Antietam Creek Project, with Dr Graystone as head anthropologist. We're segmenting the area,' Leo continued, 'measuring off squares. Each square will be given a number for reference. As we dig, we destroy the site. By documenting each segment, with photographs and on paper, we maintain its integrity.'

'Uh-huh. Is Dr Dunbrook here?'

'I'm afraid not. But if you have any questions, I can assure you either I or Dr Graystone can answer them.'

Couldn't just walk away now, Doug realised. Questions were expected. 'So, what's the point? I mean, what do you prove by looking at old bones?'

'Who they were. Who we were. Why they lived here, how they lived. The more we know about the past, the more we understand ourselves.'

'I don't feel I have much in common with a six-thousand-year-old man.'

'He ate and he slept, he made love and he grew old. He wondered. Because he wondered, he progressed and gave those who came after a road to follow. Without him, you wouldn't be here.'

'Got a point,' Doug conceded. 'Anyway, I just wanted to take a look. I used to play in those woods as a kid. Swam in Simon's Hole in the summer.'

'Why do they call it Simon's Hole?'

'The story is some kid named Simon drowned there a couple of hundred years ago. He haunts the woods, if you're into that kind of thing.'

Lips pursed, Leo took off his glasses. 'Who was he?'

Doug shrugged. 'I don't know. Just a kid.'

'There's the difference. I'd need to know. Who was Simon, how old was he? What was he doing here? It interests me. By drowning here, he changed lives. The loss of anyone, but particularly a child, changes lives.'

A dull ache settled in Doug's belly. 'Yeah. You got that right. I won't hold you up any longer. Thanks for your trouble.'

It was just as well she hadn't been there, Doug told himself as he started back to his car. What could he have said to her, really?

Another car pulled up behind his. Lana jumped out, gave him a cheery wave. 'Hi there. Taking a look at Woodsboro's latest claim to fame?'

He placed her. Hers wasn't a face a man forgot quickly. 'Bunch of holes in the ground. I don't know how it's any better than Dolan's houses.'

'Oh, let me count the ways.' Her hair tossed in the breeze. 'We're already starting to get some national attention. Enough that Dolan won't be pouring any concrete slabs any time soon. If ever. Hmmm.' Her lips pursed. 'I don't see Callie.'

'You know her?'

'Yes, we've met. Did you take a tour of the site?'

'No.'

'Are you naturally unfriendly, or have you just taken an instant dislike to me?'

'Just naturally unfriendly, I guess.'

'Well, that's a relief.'

She took a step away, and, cursing under his breath, Doug touched her arm. He wasn't unfriendly, he assured himself. Private was different from unfriendly. But rude was rude, and his grandfather was very fond of her.

'Look, I'm sorry. I've got some things on my mind.'

'It shows.' She took another step, then turned back quickly. 'Is something wrong with Roger? I'd have heard if—'

'He's fine. He's just fine. Got a thing for him, have you?'

'A huge thing. I'm crazy about him. Did he tell you how we met?'

'No.'

She paused, then laughed. 'OK, don't nag, I'll tell you. I wandered into the bookstore a few days after moving here. I was setting up my practice, I'd put my son in day care, and I couldn't seem to hold two thoughts together. So I went for a walk and ended up in your grandfather's place. He asked me if he could help me with anything. And I burst into tears. Just stood there, sobbing hysterically. He came round the counter, put his arms round me and let me cry all over him.'

'That's just like him. He's good with strays.' Doug winced. 'No offence.'

'None taken. I wasn't a stray. I knew where I was, how I'd got there and where I needed to go. But at that moment it was all so huge, so heavy, so horrible. And Roger held on to me, and mopped me up. There's nothing in the world I wouldn't do for Roger.' She paused again. 'Even marry you, which is what he'd like. You could ask me to dinner. It'd be nice to have a meal or two together before we start planning the wedding.' The look on his face was so perfect, so priceless, so utterly filled with male horror, she laughed until her sides ached. 'Relax, Doug, I haven't started buying place settings. Yet. I just thought it fair to tell you, if you haven't figured it out, that Roger's got this fantasy in his mind about you and me. He loves us, so he figures we're perfect for each other.'

He considered. 'Nothing I say at this point could possibly be the right thing to say. I'm shutting up.'

'Just as well, I'm running behind.' She started towards the fence, glanced back with a brilliant smile. 'Why don't you meet me for dinner tonight? The Old Antietam Inn. Seven o'clock? My treat.'

He frowned after her. 'You always this pushy?'

'Yes,' she called back. 'Yes, I am.'

Moments after Lana got back to her office, Callie walked into it. 'I need to talk to you.'

'Sure. Come on in, Callie. Have a seat.'

Callie walked to the window. 'If I hire you, whatever we discuss is confidential.'

'Of course.'

'I'm looking for a lawyer. Marcus Carlyle. He practised in Boston between 1968 and 1979.' That much she'd been able to find out by cellphone on the drive back down. 'After '79 he closed his practice. That's all I know. I also know that at least part of his practice included arranging private adoptions.'

She took a folder out of her bag, leafed through and set her adoption papers on Lana's desk. 'I want you to check on this, too.'

Lana noted the names. 'Are you trying to find your birth parents?'

'No.'

'Callie, I can initiate a search for Carlyle. I can, with your written permission, attempt to cut through some of the privacy blocks on adoptions in the seventies and get you some answers on your birth family. I can do both of those things without any more information than what you've given me. But I can do them quicker if you give me more.'

'I'm not prepared to give you more. Yet. I'd like you to find out what you can about Carlyle. To locate him if possible. And to find out about the process that led to this adoption. I've got some digging to do myself in a couple of other areas.'

Jake cruised into Woodsboro. When he spotted Callie's Land Rover parked in front of the local library, he swung to the kerb himself. He parked on top of her bumper—just in case she decided to run out on him—then got out and sauntered up the concrete steps into the old stone building. He saw Callie running a microfiche at a table.

He walked up behind her, read over her shoulder.

'Why are you looking through thirty-year-old local papers?'

She nearly jumped out of her chair. 'What the hell are you doing sneaking up on me that way?' she demanded.

'What's your interest in a kidnapping in 1974?'

'Back off, Graystone.'

'Cullen. Jay and Suzanne Cullen. Suzanne Cullen—something familiar about that name. "Three-month-old Jessica Lynn Cullen was taken from her buggy at the Hagerstown Mall yesterday,"' he read. 'Christ, people suck, don't they? They ever find her?'

'I don't want to talk to you.'

'Too bad, because I'm not going to let up until you tell me why this business has you so upset. You're on the verge of tears here, Callie.'

'I'm just tired.' She rubbed at her eyes like a child.

'OK.' He wouldn't have to make her angry, he realised. Good thing, as he didn't have the heart for it. 'I'll take you back to the motel.'

'I don't want to go back there. God. I need a drink.'

'Fine. We'll dump your car back at the motel, then go find a drink.'

The Blue Mountain Hideaway was a spruced-up roadhouse tucked back from the road several miles outside of the town proper. Some men Callie took to be locals sat at the bar having an after-work brew. From the work boots, caps and sweaty T-shirts, she pegged them as labourers. Maybe part of Dolan's construction crew. Their heads swivelled round when Callie and Jake walked in.

She slid into a booth. 'I don't know what I'm doing here.' She looked at Jake, really looked. But she couldn't read him. That had been one of the problems, she thought. She'd never been quite sure what he was thinking. 'What the hell is this?'

'Food and drink.' The waitress came over. 'A couple of burgers, well done, with fries, and two of whatever you've got on draught.'

Callie started to protest, then just shrugged and went back to brooding again.

She didn't just look tired, she looked worn. He wanted to take her hand, close it in his and tell her that whatever was wrong, they'd find a way to fix it.

And that was a sure fire way to get his hand chopped off at the wrist.

Instead he leaned towards her. 'This place remind you of anything? That dive in Spain, when we were working the El Aculadero dig.'

'What, are you stupid? This place is nothing like that. That had some weird music going, and there were black flies all over the damn place.'

'Yeah, but we had a beer there. Just like this.'

She shot him a dry look. 'Where didn't we have a beer?'

'We had wine in Veneto, which is entirely different.'

That got a laugh out of her. 'What, do you remember all the alcoholic beverages we've managed to consume?'

'You'd be surprised at what I remember.' The laugh had loosened the knot in his stomach. 'I remember you toss off all the covers at night. And how a foot rub makes you purr like a kitten.'

She said nothing as their beers and burgers were served. He was trying to cheer her up. She couldn't figure why he'd bother. 'How come you're not bitching at me for being away from the field today?'

'I was going to get to it. I just wanted a beer first.' He grinned at her.

'I had something I had to do. It couldn't wait—' She broke off as the men who'd been at the bar swaggered up to the table.

'You two with those assholes digging around by Simon's Hole?'

Jake squeezed bright yellow mustard on his burger. 'That's right. In fact, we're the head assholes. What can we do for you?'

'You can get the hell out, quit messing around with a bunch of old bones and shit and keeping decent men from making a living.'

Callie sized up the men. The one doing the talking was fat, but it was hard fat. The other had that alcohol-induced mean in his eyes. 'So, you guys work for Dolan?'

'That's right. And we don't need a buncha flatlanders coming in and telling us what to do.'

'There we disagree.' The pleasant tone, the casual moves, gave the impression of a man not interested in a fight, or prepared for one. Those who believed that impression, Callie knew, did so at their peril. 'Since it's unlikely either of you know dick about archaeological investigation or anthropological study, or any of the associated fields such as dendrochronology or stratigraphy, we're here to take care of that for you.'

'You think throwing around twenty-dollar words is gonna keep us from kicking you out of town, you better think again. Asshole.'

The guys still had a chance, Callie calculated, as long as Jake wanted to eat in peace more than he wanted the entertainment of a bar fight.

Jake shrugged, picked up a fry. 'The fact is, my associate here has a black belt in karate and is mean as a snake. I should know. She's my wife.'

'Ex-wife,' Callie corrected. 'But he's right. I'm mean as a snake.'

'Which one do you want?' Jake asked her.

'I want the big one.' She looked up at the men with a cheerful grin.

'OK, but I want you to hold back,' Jake warned her. 'Last time—that big Mexican? He was in a coma for five days.' He nudged his plate away. 'You guys all right with doing this outside? I hate having to shell out for damages every time we bust ass in a bar.'

They shifted feet, bunched and released fists. The big one sneered. 'We're telling you the way it is. We don't fight with pussies and girls.'

'Suit yourself.' Jake waved a hand at the waitress. 'Can we get another round here?' He lifted his burger, bit in with every appearance of enjoyment, as the men, muttering insults, stalked to the door.

'They don't mean anything.' The waitress set fresh beers on the table, scooped up the empties. 'Austin and Jimmy, they're just stupid is all, but they don't mean anything. It was mostly the beer talking.'

'No problem,' Jake told her.

'Mostly, people are real excited about the doings out there by Simon's Hole. But there's some's got a problem with it. Dolan hired extra crew, and they got laid off when the work stopped.'

'Beer talks loud enough,' Jake said when the waitress left them alone, 'it can be a problem. Digger's camped out on the site, but we may want to think about adding a little more security. We've got the field plotted, and the segments are logged into the computer. We started removing the overburden.'

She winced at that. She'd wanted to be there when the team removed the topsoil. 'You got the college kids doing the sieving?'

'Yeah. I sent today's report to your computer. Look, Callie, tell me what's wrong. Tell me why instead of being in the field you were in a library reading about a kidnapping that happened in 1974. The same year you were born.'

'I didn't come here to talk about it. I came to have a beer.'

'Fine, I'll talk about it. Last night there were photographs on your bed. You're upset. You say they're not family photos, but there's a strong resemblance. Today, you're researching the kidnapping of a baby girl same age as you. What makes you think you might have been that baby?'

She didn't speak. She'd known he would put it together. Give the man a hatful of jumbled details and he'd make them into a cohesive picture in less time than most people could solve a crossword puzzle.

And she'd known she'd tell him. The minute he'd found her in the library, she'd known he was the one person she would tell.

She just wasn't ready to analyse why.

'Suzanne Cullen came to my room,' Callie began. And told him everything. 'So . . . there will have to be tests,' she finished. 'To verify identity. But it's reasonable to make the supposition that Suzanne Cullen is correct.'

'You'll need to track down the lawyer, the doctor, anyone else involved in the adoption and placement.'

She looked at him then. This, she realised, was one solid reason she could tell him. He'd never burden her with the sympathy or outrage on her behalf. He'd understand that to get through it, she'd need to pursue the practical. 'I've started that. My father's tracking down the obstetrician.

I ran into a block on the lawyer, so I hired one of my own to dig there. Lana Campbell, she's the one representing the preservation people.'

'The lawyer had to know, so he's your datum point. I want to help you.'

'Why?'

'We're both good at puzzles, babe. But together, we're the best out there.' He pushed his plate aside, reached over and took her hand. His fingers tightened when she tried to jerk it free. 'Don't be so damn prickly. Hell, Dunbrook, I've had my hands on every inch of your body and you get jumpy because I've got your fingers.'

'I'm not jumpy, and they're my fingers.'

'You think you stopped mattering to me because you cut me loose? It occurs to me that we got to be a lot of things to each other, but we never got to be friends. I'd like to take a shot at it, that's all.'

If he told her he'd decided to sell Avon products door to door, she'd have been no more surprised. 'You want us to be friends?'

'I'm offering to be your friend, you blockhead. I want to help you find out what happened. We've got two priorities.' He rubbed his thumb over her knuckles. 'The dig, and your puzzle. We've got no choice but to work with each other on the first. Why not do the same on the second?'

'We'll fight.'

'We'll fight anyway.'

'True, very true.' That didn't bother her nearly as much as the urge she was resisting to curl her fingers into his. 'I appreciate it, Jake. I really do. Now let go of my hand. I'm starting to feel goofy.'

As they walked outside, she blinked, in some surprise, against the strength of the sun. She pulled out her sunglasses, then pursed her lips when Jake yanked a sheet of paper from under his windshield.

'"Go back to Baltimore; or you'll pay,"' Jake read. He balled up the note, tossed it in the car. 'I think I'll run out and check on Digger.'

'*We'll* go out and check on Digger.'

'Fine.' He climbed in, waited for her to slide into the seat beside him, leaned over, pressed his lips to hers.

She had an instant of pure shock. How could all that heat still be there? How *could* it? And cutting through the shock was a quick primal urge to move in, wrap around him and burn alive.

Before she could, he was easing back, turning the key in the ignition.

She set her teeth, more furious with herself than with him. 'Keep your hands and your mouth to yourself, Graystone.'

'I still like the taste of you . . . Wait. Speaking of taste. Suzanne Cullen. Suzanne's Kitchen?'

'Huh?'

'I knew it was familiar. Hell, Cal. Suzanne's Kitchen. Chocolate chip cookies. Macadamia nut brownies.' He made a low sound of pleasure. 'Quiet—I'm having a moment.'

'Suzanne Cullen is Suzanne's Kitchen? Son of a bitch. I have to go and see her, Jake. I have to go and tell her we have to take tests. I don't know how to handle her.'

He touched a hand to hers. 'You'll figure it out.'

Doug was trying to figure out how to handle himself, where Lana Campbell was concerned.

She was already at the table when he got to the restaurant, and was sipping a glass of white wine. She was in a summer dress—soft, sheer, simple instead of the slick business suits he'd seen so far.

She smiled when he sat across from her. 'I wasn't sure you'd show up.'

'If I hadn't, my grandfather would have disowned me.'

'We're so mean, ganging up on you this way.'

'Why *are* you ganging up on me?'

'Roger because he loves you, and he can't see how you can have a good life unless you find the woman you're meant to share it with.'

'Which would be you.'

'Which would be me,' she agreed. 'Because he loves me, too. And he worries about me being alone, raising a child without a father. He's an old-fashioned man, in the best possible definition of the term.'

'That explains him. What about you?'

She took her time. 'I haven't dated very much since my husband died. But I enjoy people, company, conversation. I thought I'd enjoy having dinner out with an attractive man.'

'How did your husband die?'

She paused only a moment, but it was just long enough for Doug to see the grief come and go. 'He was shot in a convenience-store robbery.'

'I'm sorry.'

'So am I. It was senseless. And it was very horrible. One moment my life was one thing, and in the next instant it was another.'

'Yeah, I know how that goes.'

'Do you?' Before he could respond, she reached across the table, touched his hand. 'I'm sorry. I forgot. Your sister. I suppose that gives us something traumatic in common. Let's hope we have some other, more cheerful mutual connections. I like books. Do you actually read, or do you just buy and sell?'

'It'd be pointless to be in the business of books if I didn't value them for what they are.'

'What do you like to do, besides read and hunt for books?'

'That takes up most of my time.'

If talking with him was going to be like pulling teeth, she thought, she'd just get out the pliers. 'You must enjoy the travel.'

'It has its moments.'

'Such as?'

He looked over at her, his face mirroring such obvious frustration, she laughed. 'I'm relentless. You might as well give up and tell me about yourself. Let's see . . . Do you play a musical instrument? Are you interested in sports? Do you believe Lee Harvey Oswald was a lone gunman?'

'No. Yes. I have no definitive opinion.'

'Caught you.' She gestured with her fork. 'You smiled.'

'I did not.'

'Oh, yes, you did. A very nice smile, too. Does it hurt?'

'Only a little. I'm out of practice.'

She picked up her wineglass and chuckled. 'I bet we can fix that.'

He enjoyed himself more than he'd expected. She was . . . intriguing, he supposed, as they walked out of the restaurant. She was a bright, interesting woman who'd been strong enough to face up to a terrible personal blow and carve out a fulfilling life. He had to admire that, as he hadn't done nearly so well in that area himself.

Added to that, it was certainly no hardship to look at her. God knew looking at her, listening to her, being drawn out by her had taken his mind off his family situation for a few hours.

'I had a good time. I'd like to do it again.' When they reached her car, she tossed her hair back, aimed those blue eyes at him. 'Next time, you ask,' she said, then rose on her toes and kissed him.

He hadn't been expecting that, either. He tasted the wine they'd shared. The light tones of the scent she wore hazed over his mind. Then she eased back, and left his head spinning. 'Good night, Doug.'

It took him nearly a full minute to pull two coherent thoughts together. *Oh, Grandpa, what have you got me into*?

Callie elected to work the site both horizontally and vertically. This would give the team the ability to discover and study the periods of inhabitation, while simultaneously slicing through time to note the changes from one period to another in a different segment of the dig.

She needed the horizontal method if she was going to verify and prove that the site had once been a Neolithic village. And she needed Jake for that, too. An anthropologist of his knowledge and skill could identify and analyse those artefacts and ecofacts from the cultural viewpoint.

Digger was already working at his square, his hands as delicate as a surgeon's as they finessed the soil with dental probes and fine brushes. Rosie was one square over, her pretty toffee-coloured skin sheened with sweat. Her hair was a tight black buzz over her skull. The two college students carted buckets of soil over to the sieving area. Leo and Jake manned the cameras for the moment. Callie chose the far end of the first grid, away from the group and nearest the pond. She needed to concentrate, to think only about the work, one specific square.

When she uncovered bone, she continued to record, to brush the earth away, to pour it into the pail. Sweat dripped down her face. Then she sat back on her heels, lifted her head and looked over the site.

As if she'd spoken, Jake stopped his own work and began to cross the field. The he stopped, looked down, squatted beside her.

Deep in the boggy soil, the remains told a story without words. The larger skeleton with the smaller turned close to its side, tucked there in the crook of the elbow.

'From the size of the remains, the infant died in childbirth or shortly after. The mother, most likely the same. They buried them together,' Callie said. 'That's more intimate than tribal. That's family.'

'Leo needs to see this. If they had the culture to inter this intimately, these two aren't alone here.'

'No, they're not alone. This is a cemetery.'

Had they loved each other? she wondered. Did the bond forge that quickly—mother to child, child to mother? Had Suzanne held her like this, moments after she'd taken her first breath? And yet wasn't it the same bonding when Vivian Dunbrook had reached out to hold close and safe the infant daughter she'd longed for? What made a daughter if it wasn't love? And here was proof that the love could last thousands of years. Why should it make her so horribly sad?

'We'll need a Native American consult before we disinter. I'll call.'

'But these need to come up. Ritual and sensibilities aside, they need to be treated and preserved or they'll dry out and fall apart.'

Thunder rumbled. 'Nothing's going to dry out today. That storm's going to hit.' Jake rubbed a thumb over the back of her hand. 'Don't be sad.'

Deliberately she turned away from him. 'It's a key find.'

'And hits a little close to home right now.'

'That's not the issue.' She couldn't let it be.

The storm broke, just as Jake had predicted. It gave her the chance to hole up in her motel room and sketch her vision of the settlement. The knapping area, the huts, the graveyard. If she was right, she expected they'd find the kitchen midden somewhere between areas D-25 and E-12.

When the phone rang, she answered it absently. The minute she heard her father's voice her focus shattered.

'I tracked down Henry Simpson. He's retired now, relocated in Virginia. I spoke with him briefly. I said you were interested in finding out a bit more about your birth parents. I hope that was all right.'

'It seems the simplest way.'

'He couldn't tell me much. He thought Marcus Carlyle had relocated. He told me he'd see if he could find out where.'

'I appreciate it. I know this isn't easy for you, or Mom.'

She couldn't go back to work now, she thought after she hung up. The only way to move forward was to do what came next. She called Suzanne.

Callie slid out of the car and arrived on the front porch, dripping. The door opened immediately. Suzanne was wearing slim black trousers with a tailored blouse in aqua. At her side was a black labrador. 'Please . . . come in out of the rain. Sadie's harmless, but I can put her away if you want.'

'No. She's OK.' Callie stood awkwardly, one hand stroking the dog's head while Suzanne stared at her. 'We need to talk.'

'Yes. Of course. I made coffee.' Suzanne gestured towards the living room. 'I'm so glad you called. I didn't know, exactly, what to do next.'

'I was adopted in December 1974. It was a private adoption. My parents are law-abiding, loving people, Mrs Cullen—'

'Please, could you, would you call me Suzanne at least?'

For now, she thought, as she sat down. Just for now.

'It was a private adoption,' Callie continued. 'A lawyer placed a baby girl with them for a very substantial fee.'

'You told me you weren't adopted.' Suzanne spoke from the sofa.

'They had reasons for not telling me. Reasons that have nothing to do with anyone but themselves. If I was the child stolen from you—'

'You know you are.' *Jessica. My Jessie.* Everything inside her wept. Determined not to let her hands shake, she picked up the coffee pot and poured.

'There are tests we can take to determine the biology.'

Suzanne breathed in deeply. 'You're willing to take them?'

'We need to know. You deserve to know. I'll do what I can to find the answers. I don't know if I can give you more than that. I'm sorry.'

'I'll take the tests.' Tears were in Suzanne's voice, thickening it. 'And Jay, your . . . my ex-husband.' She battled with the tears because they blurred her vision. She had to see her child. 'My life changed in that moment I turned my back on you. A minute,' Suzanne said as calmly as she could. 'Maybe two. And my life changed. So did yours. I want a chance to know who you are, to share some part of those lost years with you.'

'All I can give you right now are answers. How, why, hopefully who. But none of that will turn things back and make me your daughter again.'

This was *wrong*, Suzanne thought. 'If you feel that way, why did you come? You could have ignored me, or insisted there wasn't an adoption.'

'I wasn't raised to lie, or to ignore someone's pain. But you're looking for a kind of reunion I can't give you, a kind of bond I don't feel.'

Every healing scar on Suzanne's heart opened. 'What do you feel?'

'Sorry. I feel sorry for you, and your family. And for mine. Part of me wishes you'd never seen me on the news, because the minute you did, you changed my life again.'

'I'd never do anything to hurt you.'

'I'm afraid almost anything I do is going to hurt you.'

'Maybe you could tell me something about yourself. Something you've done or wanted to do. Just . . . something.'

'I found bones today.' When Suzanne blinked, Callie worked up a smile, picked up a cookie from the coffee tray. 'At the dig. I believe what we have was a Neolithic settlement by the creek bed.'

'If I came out to the site, would you show me what you do?'

'Sure. Did you make these?' She held up the half-eaten cookie.

'Yes. Do you like them? I'll give you a box to take with you. I—'

'They're great.' It was a kind of reaching out, Callie thought. The best she could do for now. 'I've been eating your baked goods for years.'

'Really?' Tears wanted to swim again, but Suzanne willed them back. Pleasure shone in her eyes instead. 'I like knowing that. You're very kind.'

'No, I'm not. I'm single-minded, easily irritated, selfish and driven.'

Suzanne laughed. 'I have something I'd like to give you.' She rose, walked to a side table and picked up a box. 'They're letters. I wrote you a letter every year on your birthday.'

'We don't know yet for certain if you wrote them to me.'

'We both know.' Suzanne sat down again, set the box in Callie's lap. 'It would mean a lot to me if you'd take them. You don't have to read them, but I think you will. You're curious about things or you wouldn't do what you do. So you're bound to wonder about, well, about this.'

'OK. Look, I've got work,' Callie began, and rose.

'There's so much I still want to—'

Even as Suzanne sprang to her feet, Sadie let out a happy bark and scrambled towards the door. It opened and Doug stepped in. 'Cut it out.' With an exasperated laugh, he pushed the cheerful canine off and glanced up. A thousand things raced through his mind.

'Doug.' Suzanne's hand fumbled to her throat. This is . . . Oh God.'

'Callie Dunbrook. I was just leaving. I'll . . . be in touch,' Callie said to Suzanne. Though her heart was drumming she kept herself composed as she brushed by Doug, opened the door and made the sprint to her car.

'Why did you come here?'

She shoved the wet hair out of her eyes and turned to see Doug standing beside her in the rain. Electric tension snapped around him, nearly visible.

'It wasn't to piss you off. I don't even know you.'

'My mother's in a difficult frame of mind right now. She doesn't need you adding to it by dropping by for coffee and cookies.'

'As it happens, that's not why I came. I don't want to upset your mother. I don't want to mess up your life. But we all need some answers.'

'Every couple of years since Suzanne's Kitchen went national, someone's come along telling her she's her long-lost daughter. Your line of work, that runs on grants and endowments, right?'

She lifted her chin, stepped forward until her boots bumped his shoes, and spoke directly into his face. 'Fuck you.'

'I won't let anyone hurt her. Not ever again.'

'Let me remind you, Doug, *she* came to *me*. Out of the goddamn blue, and now my life's turned upside-down.'

'She doesn't mean anything to you.'

'That's not my fault either.' But the guilt had weight. 'Or hers. If you're worried about your inheritance, relax. I don't want her money.' She turned, popped up into the Land Rover, slammed the door.

By the time she got back to the motel, her temper had reached its peak. Even as she opened the door the phone rang. She snatched it up. 'Dunbrook, what?'

'Well, don't bite my head off,' Lana told her. 'I just called to give you an update. But if you're going to snarl at me, I'll just up my hourly rate.'

'Sorry. What have you got?'

'I'll come there. Give me a half-hour.'

'Shit.' Callie slammed down the phone and someone knocked at the door. 'Great, just great.' She yanked open the door and glared at Jake. 'Doesn't anyone have something better to do than bug me?'

He stepped inside. 'I've just dipped into the local gossip pool. Frieda, my waitress, tells me Dolan's already heard about today's find. He went ballistic, ranting about taking us to court. Claiming we're making it all up—that we're in league with the preservation people and this whole thing is a ploy to screw his development. People are also saying the site's cursed. You know, the graves of the ancients disturbed by mad scientists.'

'So we have a cursed site, a pissed-off developer and need to have the Native American consult supervise our work. We're still short-handed, and the field's going to be a mud pit tomorrow thanks to this rain.' She paced. And grinned. 'I love this job.'

'Where'd you take off to?' He tapped the oversized shoebox at the foot of the bed with his toe. 'Buying footwear? You gone female on me, Dunbrook?' He flopped down on the bed, crossed his feet at the ankles.

She grabbed the box, then set it down on the dressing table. 'Letters. Suzanne Cullen wrote them to her daughter every year on her birthday. Jesus, Jake.If you could've seen her face when I went to see her. All that *need*. And just as I was leaving, her son came in. Blasted me, like I'd just pushed myself off in that damn buggy all those years ago to screw up his life. He actually accused me of being after her money.'

'How long will he be hospitalised?'

The comment made her feel marginally better. 'You've got siblings, right? One of each. Do you fight over your parents like dogs over a bone?'

'We just fight,' he said. 'It's the nature of the relationship. I can kick my brother's ass, but anybody else tries to, I kick theirs and twice as hard. And if anything happened to my kid sister, I guess I'd go crazy.'

'I was his kid sister for three months. What kind of bond is that?'

'Visceral, Cal. Instinctive. Added to that, he's the boy child, the older, and it was, most likely, verbalised that it was his job to look out for you.' He paused. 'He failed. Now he's a man and as the only son, I'd imagine he's transferred those duties to his mother. You're both outsider and lost child. He's in a hell of a primal fix.'

'Sounds like you're sticking up for him.'

'Merely outlining the basic theories. Now, if you were to come over here, crawl all over me and ask me to go and beat him up for you . . .'

The knock on the door had her jerking her thumb towards it. 'Out.'

But Jake simply linked his fingers behind his head and settled in.

Lana shook out an umbrella as she nipped inside. 'Miserable out there,' she began. 'Oh.' She spotted Jake stretched out on the bed. 'Sorry, I didn't realise you had company.'

'He's not company, he's an annoyance working his way up to millstone. Jake Graystone, Lana Campbell.'

'How's it going?'

Millstone or Graystone, he looked very much at home. 'Listen, Callie, if this is a bad time we can set up an appointment for tomorrow.'

'This is as good a time as any. Except it's a little crowded in here.'

'Plenty of room.' Jake patted the bed beside him.

'What I have to discuss with Callie comes under the area of privilege.'

'It's OK,' he told her. 'We're married.'

'Divorced.' Callie slapped at his foot. 'If you found something out, you can talk in front of the moron. He knows the set-up.'

'Well, I got some information on Marcus Carlyle. He did indeed practise law in Boston during the time period you gave me. Prior to that he practised first in Chicago, fourteen years, then in Houston for thirteen. Subsequently in Boston, where he remained about ten years, then he relocated to Seattle where he practised another seven years.'

'Guy gets around,' Jake commented.

'Yes. He closed his practice in 1986. That's where I've lost him for now. I can keep looking, or I can hire an investigator. It'll cost you considerably more. Before you decide,' she continued before Callie could speak, 'you need to know what else I found out.' Lana opened her briefcase, took out Callie's adoption papers. 'These papers were never filed.'

'What do you mean they weren't filed?'

'I mean there was no adoption. No legal proceeding through any court in Boston, or Massachusetts for that matter. There's no record, anywhere, that Elliot and Vivian Dunbrook adopted a child on this date, any date prior or any date subsequent to the one on these papers.'

'What the hell does that mean?'

'It means that Marcus Carlyle did not file the petition with the court. The case number listed on the petition, and the final decree, is bogus.'

Callie stared at the papers. 'This doesn't make any sense.'

'I might make sense of it if you told me why you hired me to find this lawyer.'

Jake got up, took Callie by the shoulders and moved her to the bed. 'You want her to know?' She managed a nod.

He had a way, Callie thought, of lining up the facts, laying them out cleanly, concisely. It was like listening to a synopsis of an event that had nothing to do with her. Which, she supposed, was his intention.

'Callie,' Lana said. 'I have to ask you one vital question, and I need you to set your emotions aside before you answer. Is it possible Elliot and Vivian Dunbrook were involved, in any way, with the kidnapping?'

'My mother feels guilty if she has a book overdue at the library. They had nothing to do with it. Couldn't have. And I saw their faces when I told them about Suzanne Cullen. They're as much victims as she is.'

As you are, Lana thought, but nodded. The Cullen baby, she thought again. Douglas Cullen's sister. Roger's granddaughter. How many lives were going to be turned round yet again?

'I don't want you spending time looking at them when you could spend it finding this son of a bitch,' Callie continued. She tossed the papers on the bed. 'He not only stole babies, he sold them. No way I was the only one. We'll have to substantiate that. Hire the investigator.'

'All right. I'll take care of it tonight. Callie, do the Cullens know?'

'I went to see Suzanne today. We're arranging for tests to confirm.'

'I should tell you. I have a personal relationship with Roger Grogan. Ah, Suzanne Cullen's father,' Lana explained when Callie's face went blank. 'We're friends, good friends. And I had a date with Douglas Cullen last night.'

'I thought you were married.'

'I was. My husband was killed almost four years ago. I'm interested in Doug on a personal level. Is that a problem for you?'

Callie rubbed her hands over her face. 'Small towns. I don't know what difference it makes, as long as you remember who you're representing. Your boyfriend thinks I'm after his mother's money.'

'One date doesn't make him my boyfriend,' Lana said mildly. 'I'm going to do some more digging and get the investigator started. I'll need you to stop by the office some time tomorrow. Hopefully, I can give you an update.' She picked up her umbrella. 'Goodbye, Jake.'

'Lana.' Because she seemed the type for it, he opened the door for her. When he closed it, he hesitated. He wasn't quite sure what to do about, or for, Callie. She'd put on a good front with Lana, but he could see under it to where she was shell-shocked and unsure. And unhappy.

'I don't know what I'm going to tell my parents.' She blurted it out, then just lifted her hands, let them fall. 'What can I tell them?'

'Nothing.' He walked to her now. 'No point in telling them anything else until you have more facts. Why don't you try holding on to me for a minute. You never tried that one before.'

'I don't—' But he slid his arms round her, pulled her in. After a moment's resistance, she laid her head on his shoulder, breathed deeply.

The spot just under his heart fluttered. Settled. 'That's the way.'

She closed her eyes. He was right, she supposed, she hadn't tried this one before. It wasn't so bad. 'Is this another friendship deal?'

'Yeah. Well, that and the possibility you'll get hot and want to have sex. Let's see.' He nipped at her ear, then her jaw.

She pressed her body to his, and felt their hearts slam together. The instant hunger, his, hers, was a kind of relief. She was still whole, still real. She was still Callie Ann Dunbrook.

And, she thought, she still wanted things that weren't good for her.

Then his lips rubbed hers in a whisper that spoke more of affection than passion. 'It's still there, Callie.'

'That was never our problem.'

He could still taste her, that unique flavour that was Callie. She was inside him like a virus. There was nothing he could do about it. Worse, he'd come to the conclusion, months ago, there was nothing he wanted to do about it.

He wanted her back, and he was damn well going to get her back. Taking her to bed wasn't the answer—and wasn't that too damn bad. She finally needed him. And he needed to show both of them he wouldn't let her down. No matter how much he wanted her, they weren't going to haze the situation with sex this time round. He'd help her through this mess she was in. Then they'd start over.

They'd done some work over pizza and it had got her brain functioning again. She could see what she needed to do. She'd have Lana arrange for a local lab to draw her blood and ship the sample to her father's associate in Philadelphia. And just to keep Douglas Cullen throttled back, she'd have Lana draft out some legal document waiving or refusing, whatever it needed to be, any claim to any portion of Suzanne Cullen's estate.

She closed her eyes, opened herself to the music as she drew out Bach. Her mind could rest with the music. Flow with it. Quiet. Here was comfort, the mathematics and the art, blended together into beauty.

Soothed, she set the cello aside and climbed into bed. Five minutes later she was picking up the box Suzanne had given her.

So, she had a curious nature, she told herself. She'd just read through the letters. They would give her a better sense of the woman, and very possibly another piece of the puzzle.

My darling Jessica,

Today you're one year old. It doesn't seem possible that a whole year has passed since I first held you. There are times when I think it really has been a dream. Times when I hear you crying and start towards your room. But then I remember, and I don't think I can stand it.

My own mother made me promise I would write this note. I don't know what I would have done without my mother these past months. I wonder if anyone really understands what I'm going through but another mother. Your daddy tries, and I know he misses you, so much, but I don't think he can feel this same emptiness.

I'm hollow inside. There are times I think I'll just crumble away. Part of me wishes I could, but I have your brother. Poor, sweet little boy. He's so confused. He doesn't understand why you're not here.

I know you'll come back soon. Jessie, you have to know we'll never,

never stop looking. All of us. Mama and Daddy, Grandpa and Grandma, Nanny and Pop. All the neighbours, and the police. Don't ever think we let you go. Because we never did. We never will.

You're right here in my heart. My baby, my Jessie.

I love you. I miss you. Mama.

She folded the pages neatly and switched off the light. And she lay in the dark, aching for a woman she barely knew.

Callie spent most of the next day on the painstaking task of uncovering the skeletal remains. The latest find had prised two graduate students out of the university. She had her photographer in Dory Teasdale, a long, leggy brunette. And her finds assistant in Bill McDowell, who didn't look old enough to buy beer but had five seasons on three digs under his belt.

She found Dory competent and enthusiastic, and tried to ignore the fact she was the same physical type as one Veronica Weeks. The woman who'd been the last straw in the shattering of her marriage to Jake.

'Got another one.' Jake nodded towards the lanky man standing with Digger. 'Itinerant, got his own tools. Name's Matt Kirkendal. Seems to know his ass from a line level.'

'Hands are hands,' Callie stated. 'Stick him with Digger for a couple of days. What do you think of the new grad students?'

'Girl's easy to look at.' He caught the look Callie shot him, ignored it. 'The guy's an eager beaver because he wants to impress you.'

'He does not.'

'Serious crush. I know just how he feels.'

The latest find had also brought more press. Callie gave an interview to a reporter from the *Washington Post*. 'The adult bones are female. Between the ages of twenty and twenty-five. And see here, this is interesting. There was a break in the humerus. Most likely in mid-childhood. Despite the injury she was in good health, meaning she wasn't shunned from the tribe. They cared for their sick and injured. That's illustrated in the way she and her child were buried: not just together. They were arranged here with her holding the child. This indicates compassion, even sentiment. Certainly ceremony. They mattered to someone.'

'There are some who object to the exhuming and studying of the dead.'

'You can see the care we take in what we do here. The respect given. They have knowledge. If we don't study, we're not honouring her. We're ignoring her.'

'What can you tell me about the curse?'

'I can tell you this isn't an episode of *The X-Files*.'

She worked another hour, steadily, silently. As she reached for her camera Jake came over to join her. 'What is it?'

'It looks like a turtle carapace. It's tucked between the bodies.' Callie began the painstaking task of excavating the carapace. As she carefully lifted it free, she heard the rattle of stones inside.

'It's a toy,' she murmured. 'They wanted her to have a toy.'

Jake took the rattle. 'It's likely her father made this for her before she was born. Her birth was anticipated. And her loss, mourned . . . Listen, Leo just got off the phone with Dolan. Dolan's threatening to go after an injunction to block us from removing anything from the site. If he's smart he can spin it so he's against disturbing the graves of the dead.'

'Then how does he plan to build houses?' she enquired.

'Good question. The main thing is he wants the dig stopped. He owns the land. He can block us from removing artefacts if he pushes hard enough.'

'Then we push back, harder.'

'We're going to try reason and diplomacy first. I've got an appointment with him tomorrow.'

THREE

WHEN CALLIE STEPPED OUT of her motel room the following morning, she saw red. Crude, vicious graffiti crawled over her Land Rover, in paint as bright and glossy as fresh blood.

GRAVE-ROBBING DOCTOR BITCH! it announced. GO HOME!

Fury was only a quick step away from shock. She stormed back inside her room, grabbed the phone book and looked up the address of Dolan and Sons.

She slammed the door again just as Jake opened his. 'How many more times do you plan to slam the door before . . .' He trailed off when he saw her car. 'Well, shit. You figure Austin and Jimmy?'

'I figure I'm going to find out.'

Minutes later, she squealed to a stop in front of Dolan's Main Street office. A pleasant-looking woman unlocked the office door from the inside. 'I'm sorry. We're not open for another fifteen minutes.'

'Dolan. Ronald Dolan.'

'Mr Dolan's on site this morning, up on Turkey Neck Road.'

It took her twenty minutes.

As she swung onto a private lane, she could hear the sounds of construction. Several large men, already sweaty, were at work.

She spotted Dolan and strode towards him. 'Austin and Jimmy,' she snapped out. 'The dickhead twins. Where are they?'

He shifted his weight, scanned the paint splattered over her car. 'You got a problem with any of my men, you got a problem with me.'

'You got a couple of mental giants named Austin and Jimmy on your payroll, Dolan. And this looks like their work to me.'

Something moved in his eyes. And he made a very big mistake. He smirked. 'I've got a lot of people on my payroll.'

'You think this is amusing?' She lost what tenuous hold she had on her temper and gave him a light shove. Work around them ceased. 'You think malicious destruction of property is a goddamn joke?'

He jabbed a finger in her face. 'I think when you're somewhere you're not wanted, doing something a lot of people don't want you to do, there's a price to pay.'

She slapped his hand aside. 'If you think this sort of malicious, juvenile behaviour is going to scare me away, you're more stupid than you look.'

Someone sniggered, and Dolan's face went beet red. 'You've come whining about a little paint to the wrong man.'

'You call this whining? You're the one who's going to whine, Dolan, when I stuff your head up your ass.'

That announcement caused a flurry of catcalls from the men. What she might have done next was debatable, but a hand clamped on her shoulder, hard. 'I think Mr Dolan and his band of merry men might have more to say to the police,' Jake suggested. 'Why don't we go take care of that?'

He pulled Callie back. 'Consider the fact that there are about a dozen men armed with power tools and really big hammers.' He kept his voice low as he steered her towards her Land Rover. 'And consider that they'll elect to use them on me first, as I'm not a woman. And shut up.'

She shrugged his hand off, yanked open the door, slammed it, then sent mud splattering as she reversed.

She drove half a mile, then pulled over to the side of the road. Jake stopped behind her. 'I didn't need help,' she stormed.

'You made a tactical error. You confronted him on his turf while he was surrounded by his own men. Hell, Dunbrook, you know more about psychology than that.'

She sighed. 'I hate when I get that mad. So mad I can't think straight.

I'm going to hate this, too.' She looked back at him. 'You were right.'

'Wait. I want to get my tape recorder out of the car.'

'If you're going to be a smart-ass, I won't finish thanking you.'

'I get a "you were right" *and* a thankyou? I'm going to tear up in a second.'

'I should've known you'd milk it.'

He'd come after her, she thought. And in her heart she knew he'd have mopped up the construction site with anyone who'd laid a hand on her. It made her feel just a little too warm and gooey inside.

'We should call the law. How'd you know where I was, anyway?'

'Went by Dolan's office, asked the still pale and trembling assistant if a woman with fire spurting out of her ears had been in. The rest was easy.'

When Lana pulled up to the site that afternoon, she had Tyler with her.

'If I find bones, can I keep them?'

She went round to unstrap him from his safety seat. 'No.' She boosted him on her hip, walked to the gate and stifled a gasp when she saw the graffiti on Callie's Land Rover.

'Well, what have we got here?' Leo wiped his hands on his khakis and walked over to greet them. 'You look like a young archaeologist.'

'I can dig. I brought my shovel.' Ty waved his red plastic shovel.

'This is Tyler. Ty, this is Dr Greenbaum. I hope it's all right. Callie said I could bring him by some time. He's been dying to come back.'

'Sure it is. Want to come along with me, Ty?'

Without a moment's hesitation, Ty reached out, leaning from his mother's arms into Leo's.

'Well, I've been replaced.' Lana shook her head, then skirted mounds and buckets on her way towards the square hole where Callie worked.

'Hey, pretty lady.' Digger stopped work to give her a wink. 'Anything you want to know, you just ask me.' He was standing in another square, but leapt out nimbly to catch her attention. He smelt, Lana noted, of peppermint and sweat and looked a bit like an animated mole.

'Ah . . .'

'Digger, stop hitting on my lawyer,' Callie called out. 'Lana, get away from him. He's contagious.'

Lana looked down at Callie's work. 'What happened to your Land Rover?'

'I figure one of Dolan's men. I let him know it this morning.'

Lana angled her head. 'Need a lawyer?'

'Not yet. The county sheriff's looking into it.'

'Hewitt? More tortoise than hare, but very thorough.'

'But since you're here, I've got a question. Why do people iron jeans?'

Lana glanced down at her carefully pressed Levi's. 'To show respect for the manufacturer's work. And because they show off my ass better.'

'Good to know. I see Leo's dragooned Ty-Rex.'

Lana straightened and glanced over to where Tyler was happily digging in a small pile of earth with Leo beside him. 'He's in heaven. While they're occupied, I need to talk to you.'

'Figured. Let's take a walk. I need to stretch my legs anyway.'

'I have a little more information on Carlyle. While practising in Chicago and Houston, Carlyle represented couples in over seventy adoptions. Duly decreed through the court. This most certainly comprised the lion's share of his practice *and* income. During his time in Boston, he was the petitioners' council in ten adoptions.'

'Which means?'

'Wait. During his practice in Seattle, he completed four adoptions. Through the court,' Lana added. 'We're now under one per year.'

'So he found it far more profitable to steal babies than to go through the system.' They walked into the trees that ranged along the river. 'It's a reasonable hypothesis, but there's just not enough data to prove it.'

'Not yet. But there'll be a trail. No matter how careful he was.'

'I don't want to involve other families. How can we tell them the child they raised was stolen from another family? That they never legally made that child theirs? It's not their fault that this bastard twisted something as loving and honourable as adoption into profit and pain.'

His profit, Lana thought. Your pain. 'Shall I call off the investigator?'

'No. Keep him focused on finding Carlyle. She wrote me letters.' Callie paused. 'Suzanne wrote me letters every year on my birthday. And she saved them in a box. I read one last night. It broke my heart, and still it doesn't *connect* to me. Not the way she needs it to. She's not my mother. Nothing's ever going to make her my mother.' She shook her head. 'But there has to be payment made. We find Carlyle, and he has to pay. He and whoever else was part of it. I can do that for her.'

'I don't know what else you can do other than what you're doing. And what you're doing is both very kind and very brave.' Lana slid some paperwork out of her shoulder bag. 'The statement refusing any part of Suzanne or Jay Cullen's estates. You need to sign it, where indicated. Your signature needs to be witnessed.'

Callie nodded. 'Leo'll do it. Then I want you to take a copy of this and deliver it, personally, to Douglas Cullen.'

'Thanks a lot,' Lana replied. 'That's going to really help me get him to ask me out.'

'If he blows you off because of me, he's not worth your time anyway.'

'Easy for you to say. You've got a guy.'

'If you're talking about Graystone, you're way off. That's over.'

'Pig's eye.'

Callie stopped. 'Is that a legal term?'

'Let's call it an honest observation, with a touch of harmless envy. He's gorgeous.'

'Yeah, he's got looks.' She shifted her attention to where he crouched with Sonya over a section drawing. 'We've got a primal thing. Sex was—well, we were damn good at it. We didn't seem to be much good for each other outside the sack.'

'Yet you told him about this.'

'He caught me at a vulnerable moment. Plus you can trust Jake with a confidence. And he's a demon on details. Never misses a trick.'

He missed with Ronald Dolan. He'd tried every angle he could think of during their late-afternoon meeting. Charm, science, patience, humour. Nothing budged Dolan from the trench he'd decided to stand in.

'Mr Dolan, the fact is the County Planning Commission put a hold on your development, and for good reason.'

'A few weeks and that ends. Meanwhile I've got a bunch of people out there tearing up my property. And a lot of people around here don't like the idea of you messing with graves. All we've got is your word they're thousands of years old.'

'The bones, the artefacts and ecofacts so far excavated and dated substantiate that a Neolithic village existed along Antietam Creek. We're talking about a find of enormous scientific and historical impact.'

'Doesn't change the fact whenever those bodies were put there, they weren't asking to be dug up and put under some microscope. Ought to have enough respect to let the dead rest in peace, that's my feeling on it.'

'If that's the case, how do you intend to proceed with your development?'

'We'll put up markers.' He could afford to cull out an acre, section it off, even put in fancy stones to spotlight a bunch of bones. The one thing he couldn't afford to do much longer was sit and wait.

'We've yet to determine the full area we suspect is a Neolothic cemetery,' Jake pointed out. 'Where the hell are you going to put the markers?'

'I'll get my own survey, and we'll do the right thing. You got some Indian—excuse me, *Native American*—coming out to say some mumbo jumbo and give you the go-ahead. Well, I can get me a Native American out here who'll protest any tampering with those bodies.'

Jake leaned back. 'Yeah, you probably could. But we'll trump you on that score. It so happens I'm a quarter Indian, excuse me, Native American, myself and I have contacts you couldn't dream about. And while some may feel the graves should be left undisturbed, more are going to feel sympathetic to the sensitivity with which we handle the project than to the idea of having those graves paved and sodded over so you can see a profit on your investment. You take us on, Dolan, and the press is going to bury you long before the courts decide who's right.'

A mile and a half out of town, in a house Dolan had custom built, Jay Cullen sat with his ex-wife and stared at Callie Dunbrook on video. He felt, as he always did when Suzanne pushed the nightmare in front of him again, a tightness in his chest, a curling in his belly.

He was a quiet man. He'd graduated from the local high school, had married Suzanne Grogan, the girl he'd fallen in love with at first sight at the age of six, and had gone on to earn his teaching degree. For twelve years, he'd taught maths at his alma mater. After the divorce, after he'd been unable to stand Suzanne's obsession with their lost daughter, he'd moved to the neighbouring county and transferred to another school. He'd found some measure of peace. Though weeks might go by without him consciously thinking of his daughter, he never went through a day without thinking of Suzanne.

'She was adopted four days after Jessica was taken. A private adoption. She sat where you're sitting right now and explained to me that after some research, she felt it necessary to have tests done. I'm not asking you to agree with me, Jay. I'm asking you to agree to the tests.'

'What's the point? You're already convinced she's Jessica.'

'Because she needs to be convinced. And you, and Doug—'

'Don't drag Doug through this again, Suz. For God's sake.'

'This is his sister.'

'This is a stranger. We're never getting Jessica back, Suzanne. No matter how hard you try to turn back the clock.'

'You'd rather forget it. Forget her.' Bitterness clogged her throat.

'That's right. I wish to God I could forget it. But I can't. I can't forget, but I can't let it drive my life the way you do, Suzanne.'

'You gave up.' It was tears now, cutting through the bitterness.

'That's not true.' But his anger had already dissolved in weariness. 'I didn't give up, I accepted. I had to. But I'll have the tests. Just tell me what you need me to do.'

Full of the thrill of his time at the dig, Tyler broke away from his mother as they came into the bookstore. 'Look, Grandpa Roger, look what I got!

It's a part of a spear, an *Indian* spear. Maybe they killed people with it.'

'Ty's very bloodthirsty these days.' Lana caught a movement out of the corner of her eye. 'Hello, Doug.'

'Lana.' He studied the boy. Pretty kid, he thought. Looked like his mother. Absently, Doug ran a hand over Ty's tumbled hair. 'Are you going to be an archaeologist?' he asked.

'I'm going to be . . . what's the other one?' he asked Lana.

'Paleontologist,' she supplied.

'I'm going to be that 'cause you get to find dinosaurs.'

'Doug, do you have a minute?' Lana asked.

'Sure.'

'Leave the big guy with me,' Roger offered. 'Doug, why don't you take Lana in the back, get her a nice cold drink?'

'OK.' He gave Ty a tap on the nose. 'See you later, Ty-Rex. What?' he demanded as Lana made a choking sound.

'Nothing. Thanks Roger.' She followed Doug into the back room.

'So.' She brushed back her hair as he dug in the mini-fridge for drinks. 'I guess you didn't enjoy yourself as much as I did the other night.'

He felt a little finger of unease tickle its way up his spine. 'I said I did.'

'You haven't called to ask if you could see me again.'

'I've been tied up.' He held out a Coke. 'But I thought about it.'

'If you're going to ask me out, I'd like you to do it now.'

'Why?' He felt his neck muscles tighten when she only arched her brows. 'OK, OK. Man. You want to go out tomorrow night?'

'Yes, I would. What time?'

'I don't know.' He felt like he was being squeezed. 'Seven.'

'That'll be fine. Now that we've settled that, I should let you know I'm Callie Dunbrook's lawyer.'

'Excuse me?'

'I'm representing Callie Dunbrook in the matter of establishing her identity.' Lana opened her briefcase, took out legal papers. 'I drew up these papers, per her request. She instructed me to give you a copy.'

He didn't reach out. He had to fight back the urge to hold his hands behind his back. First she manoeuvres him into a date—date number two, he amended. Then she drops the bomb. And all without breaking a sweat. 'Did you come in here to wrangle another date or to serve me with legal papers?'

She pursed that pretty sex-kitten mouth. 'I guess the word "wrangle" is accurate enough, if unflattering. However, I'm not serving you with papers. I'm providing you with a copy, per my client's request. And if you're uncomfortable with seeing me socially while I'm representing

Callie, I'll respect that, even though I consider it stupid and shortsighted. Do you want to retract your request for a date tomorrow at seven?'

'Then I'd be stupid and shortsighted.'

She smiled, very, very sweetly. 'Exactly. And of course, you'd deprive yourself of my stimulating company.' She held out the papers again.

Without his reading glasses he had to squint, but it didn't take him long to get the gist. Lana watched his face harden, those dark eyes narrow and glinting as he read. Odd how temper sat so sexily on a certain type of man.

He lowered the papers and that angry glint blasted her. 'You can tell your client to kiss my ass.'

She kept her expression bland. 'I'd prefer you relayed that yourself. But before you do, I don't think it's a breach of client confidentiality to tell you that my impression of Callie is of a strong, compassionate woman who is trying to do what's right for everyone involved.'

'I don't care.'

'Maybe you don't.' Lana closed her briefcase. 'But you might find it interesting that when Callie met Ty she called him Ty-Rex. Just as you did. I'll see you tomorrow. Roger has my address.'

Callie was working with Jake, wrapping exhumed bones in wet cloths and plastic to preserve them, when she heard a car door slamming. 'Douglas Cullen.'

'Is that so?' Jake straightened as Callie did, measured the man, as Callie did. 'He doesn't look very brotherly at the moment.'

Doug stalked up to her. Saying nothing, he yanked the legal papers out of his back pocket. He held them out so she could see what they were, then ripped them to pieces.

Nothing he could have done would have earned her anger—or her respect—quicker. 'You're littering on our site, Cullen.'

'You're lucky I didn't stuff it in your mouth then set fire to it.'

Jake stepped forward. 'Why don't you pick up the pieces and try it.'

'Those papers are an insult to me, and to my family.'

'Oh yeah?' Her chin didn't just come up, it thrusted. 'Well, accusing me of being after your mother's money was insulting to me.'

'It was.' He glanced down at the scraps of paper. 'I'd say we're even.'

'No, we'll be even when I tramp around where you work and cause a stink in front of your associates. Meanwhile, get lost. Or I might just give in to the urge to kick your ass and bury you in the kitchen midden.' She smiled when she said it—a big, wide, mean smile. And the dimples winked out.

'Christ. Jesus Christ.' The ground shifted under his feet. His face went so pale, his eyes so dark, she worried he might topple over at her feet.

'What the hell's wrong with you?'

'You look like my mother. Like my mother with my father's eyes. You've got my father's eyes, for God's sake. What am I supposed to do?'

The baffled rage in his voice, the naked emotion on his face were more than her own temper could hold. It dropped out of her, left her floundering. 'I don't know. I don't know what any of us . . . Jake?'

'Why don't you take this into Digger's trailer? I'll finish up here.'

Shoulders hunched, Callie stalked towards Digger's trailer. She didn't wait to see if Doug followed. She swung inside, stepped expertly over, round and through the debris to reach the mini-fridge. 'We've got beer or water.'

'This is a dump.'

'Yeah, Digger gave his servants his lifetime off.'

'Is Digger a person?'

'That's yet to be scientifically confirmed. Beer or water?'

'Beer.' He stared at her. 'I'm sorry. I don't want you to exist. That makes me feel like scum, but I don't want all this pouring down on my family, on me. Not again.'

The absolute honesty had her re-evaluating him. Under some circumstances, she realised, she'd probably like him. 'I don't care for it myself.'

'I want my mother to be wrong. But I can't look at you and believe she's wrong this time.'

If she was walking through an emotional minefield, Callie realised, so was he. 'No, I don't think she's wrong. We'll need the tests to confirm, but there's already enough data for a strong supposition.'

'She's never got over it. I think if you'd died, it would have been easier for her. The uncertainty, the need to believe she was going to find you, every day, and the despair, every day, when she didn't. It changed her. It changed everything. I lived with her through that.'

'Yeah.' He'd lived his life with it. 'And I didn't.'

'You didn't. It broke my parents apart. In a lot of ways, it just broke them. She built a new life, but she built it on the wreck of the one she had before. I don't want to see her knocked off again, wrecked again.'

'She wants her daughter back, and nothing is going to make that happen. I can only give her the knowledge, maybe even comfort, that I'm alive, that I'm healthy, that I was given a good life with good people.'

'They stole you from us.'

'No, they didn't. They didn't know. And because they're the kind of people they are, they're suffering because now they do know.'

'You know them. I don't.'

She nodded now. 'Exactly so.'

He got the point. They didn't know each other's family. They didn't know each other. It seemed they'd reached a point where they would have to. 'What's your first clear memory?'

'My first?' She considered, sipped her beer. 'Riding on my father's shoulders. At the beach. Martha's Vineyard, I'm guessing.'

'Mine's waiting in line to see Santa at the Hagerstown Mall. The music, the voices, this big-ass snowman that was kind of freaky. You were sleeping in the buggy. You had on this red dress. Mom had taken off your cap because it made you fussy. You had this duck-down hair. Really soft, really pale. You were basically bald.'

She felt a connection to that little boy that made her smile at him as she tugged on her messy mane of hair. 'I made up for it.'

'Yeah.' He managed a smile in return as he studied her hair. 'I kept thinking about seeing Santa. I had to pee like a racehorse, but I wasn't getting out of line for anything. Then it was my turn, and Mom told me to go and sit on Santa's lap. I was petrified. When he picked me up, I freaked. Started screaming, pushing away, fell off his lap and made my nose bleed.

'Mom picked me up, holding me, rocking me. I knew everything was going to be all right then. But she started screaming, and you were gone.'

He'd been three years old, she thought. Terrified. Tramautised, and riddled with guilt. So she handled him the way she'd want to be handled. She leaned back. 'So, you still scared of fat men in red suits?'

He let out an explosive laugh. And his shoulders relaxed. 'Oh yeah.'

It was after midnight when Dolan moved to the edge of the trees and looked on the site that he'd carefully plotted out into building lots. Antietam Creek Development, he thought. Good, solid, affordable houses: his legacy to his community.

It wasn't right, he thought. Damn Historical and Preservation societies had already cost him more time and money than any reasonable man could afford.

For all he knew, Lana Campbell and her tree huggers had arranged this whole fiasco just to pressure him to sell them the land at a loss. For all he knew these damn hippie scientists were playing along, making a bunch of bones into some big deal.

He'd got the idea when that smart-ass Graystone had been in his office, trying to throw his weight around. Big scientific and historical impact, his butt. Let's see what the press had to say when it heard some of that big impact were deer bones and ham bones and beef bones.

With satisfaction, he looked down at the garbage bag he'd carted from the car he'd parked a quarter of a mile away. He'd show Graystone a thing or two.

And that bitch Dunbrook, too. He was a goddamn pillar of the community, not some asshole teenager with a can of spray paint. He wasn't going to let that go.

He had men depending on him for work, and those men had families depending on them to bring home the bacon. He was doing this for his community, Dolan thought righteously as he crept out of the woods.

He walked quietly towards one of the squares, glancing nervously at the trailer, then at the trees when he thought he heard a rustling. Most tended to steer clear of the woods at Simon's Hole. Not that *he* believed in ghosts. Yet his hand trembled as he reached in the bag, closed his hand over a cool, damp bone.

He heard the sounds again—a plop in the water, a shifting of brush. 'Who's out there?' His voice was shaky. 'You got no right to be creeping around. This is my land. I've got a gun, and I'm not afraid to use it.'

He darted forward, caught the toe of his shoe and went down hard.

He cursed himself, shoved to his knees. Nobody there, he told himself. But when the shadow fell across him, he didn't have time to scream. The pain from the blow to the back of his head lasted seconds only.

When his body was dragged to the pond, Dolan was as dead as the young boy named Simon who had drowned before Dolan was born.

FOUR

DIGGER WAS SOAKING WET and smoking the Marlboro he'd bummed from one of the sheriff's deputies in great, sucking drags. 'I just jumped right in. Didn't think, just went. Had him half up on the bank there before I saw how his skull was crushed. No point in mouth-to-mouth.'

'You did what you could,' Callie comforted. 'You should go and get dry.'

'They said they'd have to talk to me again. Never did like talking to cops.' He lowered himself to the ground right there to stare at the faint fingers of mist that rose up from Simon's Hole.

Callie signalled Rosie to sit with him, then walked over to Jake. They studied the area. The sheriff and three deputies had already run crime-scene tape. Dolan's body was exactly where Digger had left it, sprawled face down on the trampled grass beside the pond. She could see the unnatural shape of the skull, the depression formed from a blow, she speculated. Good-sized stone, brought down from behind.

There were light impressions of Digger's bare feet leading straight to the pond, then others—deeper, wider apart—that clearly showed his race back to the trailer. And there was a green bag on the ground, animal bones spilled out of it.

'He must've come out, figuring he'd salt the site with animal bones. Give us some grief,' she said quietly. 'Then somebody bashed his head in. Who the hell would do that?'

'I don't know. But a murder on-site's going to do a hell of a lot more to delay or stop the dig than planted deer bones.'

Her mouth opened and closed before she managed to speak. 'Hell, Jake, you're thinking somebody killed Dolan to screw with us? That's just crazy.'

'Murder's crazy,' he countered. Instinctively Jake put a hand on her shoulder, uniting them, as Sheriff Hewitt, a tall barrel of a man, walked towards them.

'Dr Dunbrook.' He nodded. 'Can I ask you what you did yesterday?'

'I got to the site just before nine. I worked that segment most of the day.' She gestured to the area, now behind crime tape.

'Alone?'

'Part of the day alone, part of the day with Dr Graystone. I took a break, about an hour, midday. Ate lunch and worked on my notes right over there.' She pointed to a couple of camp chairs in the shade by the creek. 'We worked until nearly seven, then I went back to my room. Alone.'

'Did you go out again?'

'No. Look, you already know about my confrontation with Dolan yesterday, at his job site. But I don't kill somebody for vandalising, or for knowing somebody who vandalised. If you're looking for an alibi, I don't have one.'

'She never left her room,' Jake said and had both Callie and the sheriff turning towards him. 'Mine's right next door. You started playing the cello at about eleven. Played the damn thing for an hour.'

'I spoke with Mr Dolan yesterday afternoon, in response to your complaint.' Taking his time, Hewitt reached in his pocket, pulled out a notebook. He licked his index finger, turned a page. 'When you and the deceased argued yesterday, did you physically assault him?'

'No, I—' She broke off, grabbed hold of her temper. 'I shoved him, I think. A little push.'

'You had a set-to with Dolan yourself yesterday.' Hewitt turned to Jake.

'I did. He wanted us gone, which is why, I assume, he came out here last night.' Jake sent a meaningful look towards the green bag. 'If he'd known anything about what we're doing here, he'd have known this was useless.'

'I can't say I know a hell of a lot about what you're doing either, but I can tell you you're not going to be doing it for the next couple of days, at least. I need you, all of you, to stay available.'

'We're not going anywhere,' Callie replied.

Hewitt turned another page. 'I swung by the hardware store in Woodsboro yesterday. Seems somebody bought a couple of cans of red spray paint.'

'Somebody?' Callie echoed.

'I had a talk with Jimmy Dukes last night.' Hewitt's face moved into a sour smile. 'And his friend Austin Seldon. Didn't take long for them to confess to it. Now I can charge them, lock them up for it, if that's how you want it done. Or I can see to it they pay to have your car fixed up again and come on round here to give you an apology face to face.'

'When I get an estimate on the paint job, I want a certified cheque in my hand within twenty-four hours. They can keep the apology.'

When the medical examiner arrived, Callie and Jake moved away.

'As they're not going to let us work today,' Callie said. 'I've got some personal business I need to take care of.'

'Right.' Jake took her arm. 'I'm going with you.'

'You don't even know where I'm going.'

'So tell me.'

'I'm going to Virginia to see this Dr Simpson. I don't need company.'

'But I doubt you want to drive to Virginia inside that nasty graffiti.'

She hissed out a breath. 'Damnit.' But because he had a point, she climbed into his car. 'If you're driving, I'm in charge of the radio.'

Henry Simpson lived in an up-market suburban development Callie was certain Ronald Dolan would have approved of. The lawns were uniformly neat and green, the houses on them as trim as soldiers standing for inspection. 'If I had to live here, I'd shoot myself in the head.'

'Nah. You'd paint your door purple, put pink flamingos in the front yard and make it your mission to drive your neighbours insane.'

'Yeah. It'd be fun. That's it, the white house with the black Mercedes.'

'Oh, thanks, that really narrows it down.'

She had to laugh. 'On the left, next drive.'

Jake pulled into the drive and shut off the engine. They got out of the car and walked up the pathway to the door.

The woman who answered the bell was middle-aged and had found a way to bloom there. 'You must be Callie Dunbrook. I'm Barbara Simpson. I'm so glad to meet you.' She offered a hand. 'And you're . . .'

'This is my associate, Jacob Graystone,' Callie told her. 'I appreciate you and Dr Simpson agreeing to see me on such short notice.'

'Why, it's no problem at all. Please come in, won't you? Hank's just cleaning up from his golf game. Why don't we sit in the living room? Just make yourselves comfortable. I'll bring in some refreshments.'

There was a huge, exotic flower arrangement on the lake-sized glass coffee table. Callie's work boots were sunk into wall-to-wall carpeting.

'No kids,' Jake said as he dropped down on the leather sofa.

'Dad said he had a daughter from the first marriage. This, um, Barbara is his second wife. They got married after my parents moved to Philadelphia. Then Simpson moved to Virginia. Lost touch.'

At that moment, Henry Simpson came in. He had a smooth golfer's tan and a little soccer ball-sized paunch under his summer-knit shirt.

'Vivian and Elliot's little girl, all grown up. I haven't seen you since you were a few months old. God, I feel creaky.'

'You don't look it. This is Jacob Graystone. My—'

'Another archaeologist.' Simpson took Jake's hand and pumped. 'Fascinating. Please, sit. So it's Dr Callie Dunbrook. Your parents must be very proud.'

'I don't know how much my father told you when he contacted you this morning to ask if you'd see me.'

'He told me enough. Enough to concern me. I have to be honest with you, Callie, I believe this woman who approached you is mistaken. Marcus Carlyle had a very good reputation in Boston. I would never have referred your parents to him otherwise.'

'Why did you recommend Carlyle, specifically?' Callie asked.

He picked up the glass of lemonade Barbara served. 'I met him at a patient's home during a dinner party. He was well spoken, amusing, compassionate, and appeared to be committed to helping families form. That's how he put it. Forming families. He impressed me.'

'Did you recommend him to others?'

'Yes. Three or four other patients, as I recall.' He hesitated. 'We became what you could call professional friends. The man I knew could not possibly be involved in kidnapping, Callie.'

'Maybe you could just tell me about him.'

Simpson paused. 'He was a dynamic man, with a fine mind, exquisite taste, distinguished bearing. He took a great deal of pride in his work.'

'What about his own family,' Callie pressed. 'People he was close to—personally, professionally.'

'Professionally, I couldn't really say. Socially, we knew or came to know dozens of the same people. His wife was a lovely woman, a bit vague. Of course, it did become common knowledge that he enjoyed the company of other women.'

'He cheated on his wife.' Callie's voice went cold.

'There were other women.' Simpson shifted uncomfortably. 'Apparently his wife elected to look the other way when it came to his indiscretions. Though they did eventually divorce.' He leaned forward. 'This child who was stolen was taken from Maryland. You were placed in Boston. I don't see how the two events could be connected.' He shook his head, gently rattled the ice in his glass. 'How could he know, how could anyone, that there would be an opportunity to steal an infant at that time and place, just when an infant was desired in another place?'

'Are you still in contact with Carlyle?' Jake asked him.

Simpson leaned back. 'No, not since he moved out of Boston. Marcus was considerably older than I. He may very well be dead.'

Callie leaned back against the seat in Jake's car and shut her eyes. 'He doesn't want to believe it. He still thinks of Carlyle as a friend. The brilliant, dynamic adulterer.'

'And you were thinking that description sounds familiar.'

So he hadn't missed that, she thought. Yet she couldn't work up the spit for a fight. Moreover, she just couldn't drag herself back over that old, rocky ground.

'I can only be pulled in so many directions at once.'

He fought back the resentment. He'd promised to help her, he reminded himself. He was hardly doing that if he buried her under his own needs.

'Let's do this. We just walked out of the house. Neither one of us said anything yet.'

Surprise had her asking a simple question. 'Why?'

He reached out, rubbed his knuckles over her cheek. 'Because I . . . I care about you. Believe it or not.'

She wanted to drag off her seat belt, crawl over and into his lap. But she would never give in to her desires. 'OK, we just got in the car. My first comment is: Even though he doesn't want to believe me, I've made another person miserable and worried and guilty. And he gets to be miserable and worried and guilty over the other patients he recommended Carlyle to. Just in case they're in the same situation. Then you figure, gee, how many people did *those* people pass to Carlyle?'

'I've been thinking that would be a vital element of his business. Client word of mouth. Affluent, infertile clients who network with other affluent, infertile clients. And you get your product—'

'Jesus, Graystone. Product?'

'Think of it that way,' he countered. 'He would. You get the product from another pool altogether. Lower to middle income. People who can't afford to hire private investigators. Young working-class parents. Or teenage mothers, that kind of thing. And you'd go outside your borders.'

'He'd have to have some sort of network himself. Contacts. Most people tend to want infants, right? You need to target them.'

'Now you're thinking.' And the colour had come back in her face, he noted. 'You'd need information, and you'd want to make sure you were delivering a healthy baby.'

'Hospital contacts. Maternity wards. Doctors, nurses, maybe Social Services if we're dealing with teenagers or low-income couples.'

'And Jessica Cullen was born?'

'In Washington County Hospital, September 8th, 1974.'

'Might be worth checking some records, finding Suzanne's obstetrician, maybe jarring her memory some.'

'Maybe I am still hot for you.'

'I can pull off at a motel if you really need to jump me.'

'That's incredibly generous of you, but I still have a little self-control left. Just drive. But, Graystone?'

He glanced over, saw her studying him. 'Dunbrook?'

'You don't piss me off as much as you used to.'

He caressed her hand. 'Give me time.'

At seven, Lana was folding laundry. She'd vacuumed every inch of the house and had, to his bitter regret, shampooed the dog. She'd done everything she could think of to keep her mind off Ronald Dolan.

It wasn't working.

She'd said terrible things to him. She'd thought worse things than she'd said. Now he was dead.

The dog went barrelling by her as she lifted the basket to her hip. He set up a din of barks, attacking the front door seconds before someone knocked. Lana opened the door. She blinked at Doug as both Tyler and the dog flew at him.

'Stop it! Elmer, down! Tyler, behave yourself.'

'I got him.' To Tyler's delight, Doug scooped him up under his arm like a football. 'Looks like they're trying to break for it.'

'Oh, Doug, I'm so sorry. I completely forgot about tonight.'

'Hear that?' He turned Ty. 'That's the sound of my ego shattering.'

'I don't hear nothing.'

'Anything,' Lana corrected. 'Please, come in. I'm just a little turned around. Ty, would you take Elmer up to your room for a few minutes?'

Doug set Ty on his feet. 'Nice place,' he said.

'Thanks.' She looked distractedly around the now spotless living room. 'It just went out of my mind. Everything did after I heard about Ron Dolan. I was horrible to him.' Her voice broke as she set the clothes basket down. 'Just horrible. He was a decent man, with a wife, children, grandchildren. He believed he was right as much as I—'

'Hey.' He put his hands on her shoulders. 'Beating yourself up over doing your job doesn't accomplish anything. You need to get out of here for a while. So let's go.'

'I can't. I'm not good company. I don't have a sitter. I—'

'Bring the kid. He'll like what I had in mind anyway.'

The last place Lana expected to spend her Saturday night was in a batting cage. 'No, no, you don't want to club somebody with it. You just want to meet the ball.' Behind her, Doug leaned in, covered the hands she gripped on the bat.

'I've never played baseball. Just some catch with Ty in the front yard.'

'Don't try pulling your deprived childhood on me as a bid for sympathy. You're going to learn to do this right. Just watch for the ball. Your only purpose in life will be to meet that ball with this bat. You're the bat and the ball.'

'Oh, so this is Zen baseball.'

'Ha-ha. Ready?'

She caught her bottom lip between her teeth, nodded. And hated herself for squealing as the ball flew towards her.

'You missed it, Mommy.'

'Strike one. Let's try again.' This time Doug kept her trapped between his arms and guided the bat as the ball pitched towards them.

The knock of bat on wood, the faint vibration in her arms from the contact, made her laugh. 'Do it again.'

She knocked several more, all to Tyler's wild cheers. Then testing, she leaned back, looked up so her lips nearly grazed Doug's jaw. She waited until his gaze shifted down to hers. 'How'm I doing?' she murmured.

'You're never going to play in the major league, but you're coming along.' He laid a hand on her hip, then stepped back. 'OK, Ty, you're up.'

Lana watched them, the man's big hands over her child's small ones on a fat plastic bat. For a moment her heart ached viciously for the man she'd loved and lost. And for a moment, she could almost feel him standing beside her, as she sometimes did when she watched their son sleep late at night. Then there was the muffled crack of plastic on plastic, and Ty's bright and delighted laughter rang out. The ache faded.

There was only her child, and the man who guided his hands.

It took three days before the site was cleared for work. They were no closer to finding Dolan's killer. And Callie knew when she brushed and probed at the earth that she was exploring the place where a man had been killed.

'You were never happier than when you had a pile of earth and a shovel.'

She turned her head, and felt her heart give a quick lurch as she saw her father. 'It's a dental pick,' she said, and held it up. Then she set it aside, boosted herself out of the hole and tilted her head up to kiss his cheek. She brushed her hands on the butt of her jeans. 'Is Mom with you?'

'No.' He glanced around. 'You look pretty busy around here.'

'We're making up for lost time. We had to stop everything on-site for three days until the police cleared the scene.'

'Police? Was there an accident?'

'No. There was a murder.'

'*Murder?* My God, Callie. One of your team?'

'No. No.' She squeezed his hand, and the initial awkwardness she knew they'd both felt dropped away. 'Let's get some shade. It was the guy who owned the land here, the developer. Somebody bashed in his skull. Probably a stone. Right now we don't know who or why. It's likely it was someone with a grudge. From what I gather, he had as many enemies as friends, and the sides were divided over this development.'

'What happens now, with your project?'

'I don't know. We're taking it a day at a time. Graystone's called in a Native American consult to approve the removal of remains.' She gestured towards Jake and the stocky man beside him.

He looked at the man who'd been his son-in-law. The man he barely knew. 'And how are you dealing with working with Jacob again?'

'It's OK. He's being less of a pain in the ass than he was. Which, in turn, makes me less of a pain in the ass. But you didn't drive all the way down from Philadelphia to see the project or ask me about Jake. You got the results of the blood tests.'

'They're very preliminary at this point, Callie, but I . . . I thought you'd want to know.'

The Earth did not stop spinning on its axis, but in that one moment Callie's world took that final lurch that changed everything. 'I already knew.' She took her father's hand, squeezed it hard.

'I realise you'll need to tell the Cullens. I thought you might want me to go with you when you do.'

'You're such a good man. I love you so much.'

'Callie—'

'No, wait. I need to say this. Everything I am I got from you and Mom. And this can't . . . I'm sorry for the Cullens. I'm desperately sorry for them. And I'm angry, for them, for you and Mom, for myself. I don't know what's going to happen. That scares me, Daddy.' She pressed her face to his chest.

He gathered her in, tears choking him. 'I want to fix this for you. My baby. But I don't know how.'

She let out a trembling breath. 'I have to deal with it. Like a project. I can't just look at the surface and be satisfied. I have to see what's under it.'

'I know.' He dug his handkerchief out of his pocket. 'Here.' He dabbed at her cheeks. 'I'll help you. I'll do everything I can to help.'

Jake watched them. He'd known, just as Callie had known, the minute he'd seen Elliot. And when she'd broken down, cried in her father's arms, it had ripped at his gut. He watched the way they stood now, with Callie's hands on his face. Trying to comfort each other, he thought. There was a tenderness between them he'd never experienced in his own family. Graystones, he thought, weren't adept at expressing the more gentle of emotions. He'd never doubted his parents loved each other, or their children, but he wasn't sure he'd ever heard his father actually say 'I love you' to anyone. He'd shown love by seeing there was food on the table, by teaching his children, by the occasionally affectionate headlock or pat on the back.

Maybe that was why he'd never got comfortable telling Callie the things women wanted to hear. That she was beautiful. That he loved her. That she was the centre of his world and everything that mattered.

He saw her walk towards the creek. Elliott looked over at Jake. Jake met him halfway.

'Jacob. How are you? I'd like to tell you that both Vivian and I were very sorry when things didn't work out between you and Callie.'

'Appreciate that. I'd better tell you that I know what's going on.'

'Good. It helps knowing she's got someone to lean on right now.'

'She won't lean. That's one of our problems. But I'm around anyway.'

She knew it was a cop-out, she knew it was cowardly. But Callie had Lana call Suzanne and set up a conference, in her office for the following day. In the meantime she was stuck in a twelve-by-fourteen-foot room with a single window, a rock-hard bed and her own churning thoughts.

She dropped down on the bed, opened the shoebox. She didn't want to read another letter. She was compelled to read another letter.

Happy birthday, Jessica. You're five years old today.

Are you happy? Are you healthy? Do you, in some primal part of your heart, know me?

Both your grandmothers came by this morning. They wanted to take me out. We'd go to the outlets, they said. We'd have lunch.

I was angry. Couldn't they see I didn't want company or laughter or outlet malls? I wanted to be alone. I hurt their feelings, but I didn't care.

There are times all I want to do is scream and scream and never stop. Because today you're five years old, and I can't find you.

I baked you a cake and I drizzled it with pink icing. It's so pretty. I put five white candles on and I lit them and sang 'Happy Birthday' to you.

I can't tell your daddy about it. He gets upset with me, and we fight. Or worse he says nothing at all. But you and I will know.

When Doug came home from school, I cut him a slice of it. He looked so solemn and sad as he sat at the table and ate it. I wish I could make him understand that I baked you a cake because none of us can forget you. But he's just a little boy.

I haven't let you go, Jessie. I haven't let you go.

I love you, Mama

Love, she thought as she put the box away, was so often thorny with pain. It was a wonder the human race continued to seek it.

But maybe loneliness was worse.

She couldn't stand to be alone now. She slanted a look at the wall between her room and Jake's. Even the idea of it cheered her up enough to have her smiling, perhaps a bit wickedly as she opened her cello case, rosined her bow, and struck the first notes.

It took only thirty seconds for him to pound a fist on her door.

Taking her time, she braced her instrument on the chair and went to answer. He looked so damn sexy when he was pissed.

'Cut it out.' He gave her a little shove. 'I mean it.'

'I don't know what you're talking about. And watch who you're shoving.' She shoved him back, harder.

He slammed the door at his back. 'Look, you only play that *Jaws* theme to annoy me. You know it creeps me out.'

His eyes were sharp and green, that handsome rawboned face livid.

He was, she thought smugly, hers for the taking.

'Anything else?'

He ripped the bow out of her hand, tossed it aside.

'You don't scare me. You never did.'

He hauled her up to her toes. He could smell her hair, her skin. Lust crawled along with temper in his belly. 'I can change that.'

'You know what, Graystone? It burned your ass that I had a mind of my own. You couldn't tell me what to do then, and you sure as hell can't now. So take a hike.'

'It wasn't your mind that burned my ass, it was your pig-headed, ego-soaked streak of pure bitchiness.' He caught her fist an instant before it ploughed into his guts. They grappled a moment.

Then they fell on the bed.

Thank God, thank God, was all she could think when he flipped her, when his body pinned hers, when his mouth rushed down to take. She arched against him, her mind screaming for more. And her hands streaked over him to take it.

They rolled again, gasping for breath as they fought off jeans. The momentum had them pitching off the side of the bed, landing on the floor with a thud. Even as the fall jarred and dazed her, he was driving into her.

She couldn't speak; she couldn't stop. Each violent thrust fired in her blood until her body was a mass of raw nerves. The orgasm seemed to tear up from her toes. For one instant she saw his eyes, vivid and clear above her. Even as they glazed, as she knew he was falling out of himself, they watched her.

She'd rolled over on her stomach and lay flat out on the floor. He lay beside her, staring up at the ceiling. A second-rate motel room, Jake thought, an argument, mindless sex. Did certain patterns never change?

He'd wanted to give her more. God knew he'd wanted to try to give them both more. But maybe, when it came down to it, this was all there was between them. And the thought of it broke his heart.

'Feel better now?' he asked as he sat up to reach for his jeans.

She turned her head, looked at him with guarded eyes. 'Don't you?'

'Sure.' He stood, hitched on his jeans. 'Next time you're in the mood for a quickie, just knock on the wall.' He saw emotion flicker over her face before she turned her head away again. 'What's this? Hurt feelings? Come on, Dunbrook, let's not pretty this up. You pushed the buttons, you got results. No harm, no foul.'

'That's right.' She wished for him to go. Wished for him to crouch down and scoop her up, to hold on to her. Just to hold on to her.

She waited until she heard the door close, until she heard his open next door. Shut. Then for the second time that day, she wept.

Callie told herself she was steady when she took a seat in Lana's office the next afternoon. She wasn't

'This is a difficult situation,' Lana said. 'For you, most of all.'

'I'd say it's tougher on the Cullens.'

'No. Tug of war's harder on the rope than the people pulling it.'

Unable to speak, Callie pressed her fingers to her lids. 'Thanks. Thanks for getting it, for not just being the objective legal counsel.'

'All right.' Lana sat behind her desk. 'We're still working on tracking Carlyle after he left Seattle. But we have found something else.'

'Which is?'

'His son, Richard Carlyle, who lives in Atlanta. He's a lawyer.'

'Isn't that handy?'

'My investigator reports he's clean. Squeaky. He's forty-eight, married, two children. He's practised in Atlanta for sixteen years, primarily in real estate. There's nothing to indicate he lives above his means. He would have been nineteen, twenty, when you were taken. There's no reason to believe he was involved.'

'But he must know where his father is.'

'The investigator's prepared to approach him on that matter, if that's what you want.'

'I do.'

'I'll take care of it.' Lana's intercom buzzed. 'That's the Cullens. Are you ready?'

It was a strange moment, seeing what would have been her family had fate taken a different turn. She tried to look at Jay Cullen without staring. He looked . . . pleasant, she decided. Very like the fiftyish maths teacher she knew him to be.

Lana stepped forward, her hand outstretched. 'Thank you for coming, Mrs Cullen, Mr Cullen, Doug. Sit down, please. As you know, I'm representing Callie's interests in the matter of her parentage. Recently, certain questions and information have come to light regarding—'

'Lana.' Callie braced herself. 'I'll do this. The preliminary results on the tests we agreed to have taken are in. These are pretty basic. One of the tests, standard paternity, is really a negative test. It will show if an individual isn't the parent. That isn't the case here. The results so far give a strong probability that we're . . . biologically related. Added to those results is the other information and the—'

'Callie.' Doug kept his hand on Suzanne's shoulder. 'Yes or no?'

'Yes. There's a margin for error, of course, but it's very slight. We can't know conclusively until we locate and question Marcus Carlyle, the lawyer who handled my adoption. But I'm sitting here looking at you, and it's impossible to deny the physical similarities. It's impossible to deny the timing and the circumstance. It's impossible to deny the scientific data gathered to date.'

'Almost twenty-nine years.' Suzanne's voice was hardly more than a whisper, but it seemed to shake the room. 'But I knew we'd find you. I knew you'd come back.'

'I—' Haven't come back, Callie wanted to say. But she didn't have the heart to say the words out loud as the tears spilled down Suzanne's cheeks and she flung her arms round Callie.

'It's all right now.' Suzanne stroked Callie's hair, her back. She crooned it, softly, as she might to a child. 'It's going to be all right now.'

How? Callie fought a desperate urge to break away from the hold and just keep running until she found her life again.

'Suze.' Jay touched Suzanne's shoulder, then drew her gently away.

'Our baby, Jay. We found our baby.'

'Mrs Cullen, why don't you come with me?' Lana slipped a hand under Suzanne's arm. 'You'll want to freshen up a bit. Why don't you come with me?' she repeated.

Jay waited until the door closed, then turned to Callie. 'But we haven't, have we?' he said quietly. 'You're not Jessica.'

'Mr Cullen—'

'The biology doesn't matter. You know that—I can see it on your face. You're not ours any more. And when she finally understands that—' His voice broke, and she watched him gather the strength to finish. 'When she finally comes to grips with it, it's going to be like losing you all over again.'

Callie lifted her hands. 'What do you want me to do?'

'I wish I knew. You, um, didn't have to do this. Didn't have to tell us. I want . . . I don't know if it makes sense to you or not—but I need to say that I'm proud that you're the kind of person who didn't just turn away.'

She felt something loosen inside her. 'Thank you.'

'I need some air.' He walked quickly to the door. 'Doug,' he said without looking back. 'Take care of your mother.'

Callie dropped back in her chair. 'Do you have something profound to say?' she asked Doug.

He walked over, sat down, leaning forward with his hands dangling between his knees. His gaze was sharp on her face. 'All my life, as long as I can remember, you've been the ghost in the house. Every holiday, every event, even ordinary days, the shadow of you darkened the edges. There were times, plenty of times, I hated you for that.'

'Pretty inconsiderate of me to get myself snatched that way.'

'If it wasn't for you, my parents would still be together. If it wasn't for you, everything I did growing up wouldn't have had that shadow at the edges. I wouldn't have seen the panic in my mother's eyes every time I was five minutes late. I get the impression you had a pretty good childhood. Easy, normal, but not so fancy you got twisted around by it.'

'And you didn't?'

'No, I didn't have easy or normal. If I do a quick, two-dollar analysis, it's probably what's kept me from making a life, up until now. But maybe that's why I'm going to be able to handle this better than any of the rest of you. Easier to deal with flesh and blood than it was with the ghost.'

'Jessica's still a ghost.'

'Yeah, I get that. You wanted to push her away when she hugged you, but you didn't. You didn't push my mother away. Why?'

'I don't have any problem being a bitch, but I'm not a heartless bitch.'

'Hey, nobody calls my sister a bitch. Except me. I loved you.' The words were out before he realised they were there. 'I was only three, so it was probably the way I'd have loved a puppy. I hope we can try to be friends.'

His eyes were direct, she thought. And a deep brown. Mixed with the turmoil she saw in them was a kindness she hadn't expected.

'It's not as hard to deal with having a brother as it is . . .' She shot a glance towards the door.

'Don't be too sure. I've got time to make up for. Such as, what's with Graystone? You're divorced, right, so why's he hanging around?'

She blinked. 'Are you kidding?'

'Yeah, but I might not be later.'

Callie opened her mouth, then shut it again as the door opened. Lana brought Suzanne back in. 'I'm sorry, I didn't mean to fall apart that way. Where's Jay?' she asked, looking around.

'He went outside, for some air,' Doug told her.

'I see.' And her lips thinned. 'But this is a happy day.' She took Callie's hand as she sat down. 'We know you're safe and well. You're here.'

'We don't know how, we don't know why. We don't know who.'

'What's important is you're here. We can go home. We can go home now and . . .'

'What?' Callie demanded. Panic snapped into her. 'Suzanne. I can't make up for all you lost. I can't be your little girl. I can't give up what I am to be what you had. I wouldn't know how.'

'You can't ask me to just walk away, to just close it off, Jessie—'

'That's not who I am. We need to find out why. You never gave up,' she said as Suzanne's eyes filled again. 'That's something we have in common. I don't give up either. I'm going to find out why. You can help me.'

'I'd do anything for you.'

'Then I need you to take some time, to think back. To remember. Your doctor when you were pregnant with me. The people in his office, the people you had contact with during the delivery. The paediatrician and his office staff. Who knew you were going to the mall that day? Make me a list,' Callie added. 'I'm a demon with lists.'

'Yes, but what good will it do?'

'There's got to be a connection somewhere between you and Carlyle.'

'The police . . .'

'Yes, the police,' Callie said with a nod. 'The FBI. Get me everything you can remember from the investigations. Everything you have.'

'I will. Of course I will. But I need some time with you. Please.'

'We'll figure something out. Why don't I walk you down to your car?'

'Go ahead, Mom.' Doug walked to the door, opened it. 'I'll be right there.'

He closed the door behind them, leaned back on it as he looked at Lana. 'Sort of takes "dysfunctional family" to a whole new level.'

She let out a breath. 'How are you doing?'

'I don't know yet. I just sat here and had a conversation with . . . with my sister. The second one I've had in the last few days. Before that, the last time I saw her, she was bald and toothless. It's all just a little surreal.'

'And they all need you to varying degrees.'

He frowned, turned back towards her. 'I don't think so.'

'It was very obvious to this objective observer. And it explains to me why you keep going away, and why you keep coming back. Why don't you take a break from all this tonight. Come over. I'll fix you a home-cooked meal.'

He didn't know if he'd ever seen a prettier woman. Or one who managed to have a soothing way about her even as she pushed a man into a corner.

'I'm not planning to stay. You need to know that.'

'I was offering to grill some chicken, not let you move in.'

Jay was staring at the pot of geraniums on the porch when Callie brought Suzanne out. His gaze went to Suzanne's face first, Callie noted. 'I was just coming back up. I needed a moment to clear my head.

Suzanne.' He reached out to touch her arm, but she moved back in a gesture as clear as a slap.

'You walked away.' Deliberately, Suzanne turned, pressed her lips to Callie's cheek. 'Welcome home. I love you. I'll wait in the car for Doug.'

'I'll never make it up to her,' he said softly. 'Or you.'

'You don't have anything to make up to me.'

He turned to her then, though he kept a foot between them, kept his hands at his sides. 'You're beautiful. It's the only thing I can think of to say to you. You're beautiful. You look like your mother.'

He started down the steps just as Doug came out of the door.

'You're going to be in the middle of that.' Callie nodded at the car.

'I've been in the middle of that all my life. Look, I wasn't going to ask anything, but will you go by some time and see my grandfather? The bookstore on Main.'

She massaged her temples. 'Yeah. OK. Doug—maybe we can have a beer some time. We can give that being friends a try, and you can fill me in on Cullen family dynamics. I don't know where to step around them.'

He gave a short laugh. 'Join the club. Family dynamics? We'd better get a keg.'

She watched him get in the car, then started towards her own, spotting Jake leaning on the hood. Deliberately, she took out her sunglasses, put them on as she walked up to him. 'Does your being here mean you're not mad at me any more?'

'I wouldn't go that far.'

'Maybe I used you, but you didn't exactly put up a fight.'

He took her arm before she could stalk by him. 'We used each other. Was it rough in there?'

'Could've been worse. I don't know how, but I'm sure it could've been. What the hell are you doing here, Jake? Riding to the rescue?'

'No.' He plucked the keys from her, 'Driving. We rented a house.'

'Excuse me?'

'Our own little love nest, sugarplum.' He started the car. 'The motel rooms are too small, and too inconvenient. The team needs a local base. You, me and Rosie need more room to work. Dory, Bill and Matt will be bunking there, too. And we got us a pair of horny kids from West Virginia this afternoon, Chuck and Frannie. He's got some digs under his belt, and he's working on his master's. Anthro. She's green as grass, but willing to do what she's told.'

She propped her feet on the dashboard. 'Well, we need the hands.'

'We do indeed. We also need storage and a kitchen. And,' he added, 'you need a base here after the season. We've got other digging to do.'

'We?'

'I said I was going to help you.'

She frowned as he turned off the road onto a bumpy gravel lane. 'I don't know what I'm supposed to make of you, Jake. One minute you're the same annoying jackass you always were, and the next you're an annoying jackass who's trying to be nice. You gaslighting me?'

He only smiled and gestured by jerking up his chin. 'What do you think?'

The house was big, and sheltered by trees. Part of the creek snaked alongside. The grass brushed her ankles as she walked towards the front.

'We got a six-month lease that comes in cheaper than the motel.'

She liked the feel of the place, but wasn't ready to admit it.

'Got the key?'

Jake unlocked the door, then scooped her off her feet. 'Never did carry you across the threshold.' He closed his mouth over hers for ten hot, humming seconds.

'Cut it out. And we didn't have a threshold.' Her stomach muscles were balled into a knot, and she shoved against him. 'The hotel room in Vegas where we spent our wedding night doesn't count.'

'We can move in tomorrow.'

'Fine.' She walked through the living room onto the deck. 'Quiet here.'

'It won't be once we're in it.' He laid a hand on the base of her neck. 'Why don't you let it out, Callie? Why do you have such a hard time letting anything out but your mad?'

'I don't know. She fell apart, Jake. She just went to pieces up there in Lana's office. She was holding on to me so tight I could barely breathe. I started thinking, what would I be like if none of this had happened? If she hadn't turned away for that few seconds, and I'd grown up . . . here.'

When she started to move away, Jake tightened his grip, held her in place. 'Just keep talking. Pretend I'm not here.'

'That minor in psych's showing,' she told him. 'I just wondered, that's all. What if I'd grown up Jessica? Jessica Lynn Cullen would have a keen fashion sense. She thinks she'll go back to work when the kids are older, but for now she's president of the PTA and that's enough for her. Or maybe she's Jessie. She'd have been a cheerleader, married her college sweetheart. She keeps scrapbooks and works part-time, retail, to help supplement the income. She's got a kid, too, and enough energy to handle all the balls she has to juggle.'

'Is she happy?'

'Sure. Why not? But neither of those women would spend hours digging, or know how to identify a six-thousand-year-old tibia. They sure as hell wouldn't have married you. You'd have scared the shit out of them. And for all those reasons, including having the bad judgment to marry you, I'm glad I didn't turn out to be either one of them. I could think that even when Suzanne was sobbing in my arms. All I could think was I'm glad I'm who I am.'

FIVE

CALLIE WORKED LIKE A DEMON, logging ten-hour days in the sweltering August heat, probing, brushing, detailing. At night she composed reports, outlined hypotheses, studied and sketched sealed artefacts before they were shipped to the Baltimore lab. She had a room of her own, with a sleeping-bag tossed on the floor. She didn't spend much time downstairs in what they called the common area. It was, she'd decided, just a little too cosy. As most of the team spent evenings in town or at the site, Rosie tended to make herself scarce—obviously and regularly—leaving Callie alone with Jake.

It was just a bit too much like playing house. The fact was, she realised, she'd never got over Jacob Graystone. He was, unfortunately, the love of her life. The son of a bitch.

She wondered where she and Jake might have ended up if they'd taken time to be friends. What if they'd stuck it out? They might have found something worth keeping.

She hadn't trusted him, she admitted now: he'd had a reputation with women. Nor believed he loved her as much as she loved him. And that had made her crazy. Because if she loved him more, it gave him the power. So she'd pushed, determined to make him *prove* he loved her. And every time he'd come up short, she'd pushed harder. But who could blame her? The close-mouthed son of a bitch had never once said the words. Thank God the whole thing had been his fault.

She glanced at her watch and slipped downstairs to see what she could grab for her habitual midnight snack. She didn't switch on any lights: she'd always had good instincts where food was concerned.

'Why are you skulking around in the dark?'

'I'm not. I'm moving quietly in consideration of others as I seek food.'

He was wearing nothing but black boxers. She wasn't going to mention it or complain. Even an ex-wife was entitled to enjoy the view. He had some build on him, she thought. Lanky and tough at the same time, with a few interesting scars to keep it from being too pretty.

'Come and take a look at this,' he told her and started out of the kitchen.

There was a drawing on his worktable. He'd taken their site survey and had created a settlement. Men, women, children going about their daily lives. A small hunting party walking into the trees, a woman with a baby nursing at her breast, the men in the knapping area making tools and weapons. There was a sense of order and community. Of tribe, Callie noticed. And most of all, of the humanity Jake was able to see in a broken spear point or a shattered clay pot.

'It's terrific. It's the kind of thing that reminds us why we do it. I wish I could draw like this.'

When he touched her hair, she shifted away and stepped out onto deck. The trees were silvered from the moon, and the air was warm and soft and still. She heard him step out behind her. 'Jake, do you ever . . . When you stand on a site, do you ever feel the people we're digging down to? Do you ever hear them?'

'Of course.'

She laughed, shook back her hair. 'Of course. I always feel so privileged when I do, then after, when it passes, I just feel dopey. I've never said anything about it. A woman acts foolish in the field, starts talking about hearing the whispers of the dead, guys are going to dismiss her.'

'I don't think so.' He touched her hair again. 'One thing I never did was dismiss you.'

'No, but you wanted me in the sack.'

'I did.' He brushed his lips over the back of her neck. 'Do. But I was nearly as aroused by your mind. I always respected your work, Cal.'

'We're not going to have a repeat of the other night.'

'No.' He scooped her hair to the side and nibbled his way to her ear. 'This time it's going to be different. You know what we never did?'

A hot tongue of lust licked along her skin. God, she'd missed feeling like this. 'I don't think we skipped anything.'

'Yeah, we did.' His arms came round her waist. 'We never romanced each other. I never seduced you.'

Her hand closed tight over his, squeezed. 'There's someone out there,' she whispered.

She felt his body stiffen. He kept his lips close to her ear, as if still nibbling. 'Where?'

'Two o'clock, about five yards back, in the cover of the trees.'

He didn't question her. He knew she had eyes like a cat. Still holding her, he tilted his head so he could scan the dark, gauge the ground. 'I want you to get pissed off, push away from me and go inside. I'll come after you.'

'I said we're not doing this. Not now, not ever.' She turned on her heel and strode back into the house.

'You're not throwing that in my face again.' He stormed in behind her, gave her a light shove to keep her moving, and grabbed a pair of jeans on the way. 'Make sure all the doors are locked,' he ordered, and slapped off the lights in his office. 'Then go upstairs. Stay there.'

'For God's sake, Jake, what do you think you're going to do?'

'Listen to me. Somebody killed Dolan just a few miles from here. What I'm not doing is taking any chances. Lock the goddamn doors, Callie. If I'm not back in ten minutes, call the cops.' He eased open the back door, scanned the dark. 'Lock it,' he repeated, then slipped out.

She was out of the front door barely a minute after Jake was out of the back, a can of insect repellent in her hand. She heard an owl hoot, a pair of mournful notes. In the distance a dog was barking in incessant yelps. And something else, something larger, crept in the shadows.

She thumbed off the cap on the can, heard a sudden storm of movement back towards the house. Even as she braced to spring forward and give chase, a gunshot exploded.

Everything stilled in its echo—the barking, the mournful owl. In those seconds of stillness, her own heart stopped.

It came back in a panicked leap, as she shouted for Jake. She ran, her fear and focus so complete she didn't hear the movement behind her.

The force of a blow sent her flying headlong into the trunk of a tree.

Jake raced towards the sound of Callie's voice. When he saw her, crumpled in a sprinkle of moonlight, his legs all but dissolved.

'Callie. Oh God.' He hauled her into his lap. There was blood on her face, seeping from a nasty scratch over her forehead. But her pulse was strong, and his searching hands found no other injury.

'OK, baby. You're OK.' He rocked her, holding tight until he could battle back that instant and primal terror, picked her up, then carried her through the woods towards the house. She began to stir as he reached the steps. 'Hurts,' she mumbled.

'Don't you pass out again. Don't you do it.' He carried her back to the kitchen, set her down on the counter. 'Sit where I put you, breathe slow. I'm going to get something to deal with that granite skull of yours.'

'Someone came up behind me, shoved me—' She broke off, jerked straight. 'The gunshot. Oh my God, Jake. Are you shot? Are you—'

'No.' He grabbed her hands before she could leap down from the counter. 'Hold still. Do I look shot to you? I saw a bullet hit a tree about five feet to my left.' He ran water onto a cloth. 'Hold still now.'

'Someone shot at you.'

'I don't think so. I think they shot at the tree. Now look at me. How's your vision? Dizziness? Nausea?' he asked her.

'I'm OK.'

'It couldn't have been just one guy. You were down and out a good fifty feet from where I was when he plugged the tree.'

'And he came up behind me,' she agreed.

'You screamed.'

'I called out in concern when I thought you'd been shot.'

'You screamed my name.' He positioned himself between her legs. 'I always liked that.'

'I called out,' she corrected, but her lips twitched. 'Austin and Jimmy?'

'If it was, they've upped the ante. I guess we call the cops.'

But they didn't move, not yet, just continued to look at each other. 'Scared me,' Callie said after a moment.

'Me too.'

She put her arms out, drew him in. 'If anybody gets to shoot at you, it's going to be me.'

'And I'm, obviously, the only one entitled to knock you out cold.'

Oh yeah, she thought as she kept her cheek pressed to his. The irritating son of a bitch was the love of her life. Just her bad luck. 'You know, what you were talking about before we were so incredibly rudely interrupted? How you never seduced me? I never seduced you either.'

'Callie, you seduced me the minute I laid eyes on you.'

She let out a half-laugh. 'I did not.'

'You never believed it.' He eased back, touched his lips to her cheek. 'I could never figure out why. I'll call the sheriff, then get some painkillers.'

'I can get them.'

'Why can't you let me take care of you? Even now, when you're hurting.'

Baffled, she started to scoot down. Then stopped herself. She wasn't sure of the steps of this new dance they seemed to have begun, but at least she could try to find the rhythm.

'Look, maybe you could give me a hand down. If I jar something, I think my head'll fall off.'

He lifted her down to the floor. Gently, she noted. He'd been gentle several times that night—more in that single night than she could recall him being with her since they'd met. He reached over her head, took the bottle of pills out of the cabinet. 'Here.'

'Thanks. You know what, I think I need to sit down.' She did, right on the floor, as much to see how he'd react as for necessity.

She saw it, that quick concern that raced over his face before it closed down again. 'You dizzy?'

'No. It just hurts. I'll just sit here, take drugs, wait for the cops.' Thoughtfully, she shook out pills as he went to the phone. She wasn't sure what this new aspect of Jacob Graystone meant. But it was interesting.

Callie didn't trust herself to dig on three hours of patchy sleep.

She'd put off going by Treasured Pages as Doug had asked, and it was time to stop procrastinating. She understood why he'd asked it of her, and she could admit to her own curiosity about another member of the Cullen family. But what was she supposed to say to the old guy?

There was a woman at the counter when Callie walked in, and a man behind it with wild grey hair and a white shirt with creases so sharp they could have cut bread. Callie saw the instant shock run over his face.

The woman glanced at Callie, frowned. 'Mr Grogan? Are you all right?'

'Yes, yes, I'm fine. Sorry, Terri, my mind wandered there. Why don't you leave these with me for a few days and I'll call you with a price?'

'OK. I'd appreciate that, Mr Grogan. Bye.'

Roger waited until the door shut. 'I'm going to put the Closed sign up, if that's all right with you.'

'Sure. Ah, Doug asked me if I'd come by.'

'Would you like to come into the back? Have some coffee?'

'Sure. Thanks.'

He didn't touch her, or make any move to take her hand. He didn't stare or fumble. And his ease put Callie at hers.

'This is a nice place. Comfortable. I've always thought of bibliophiles as stuffy fanatics who keep their books behind locked glass.'

'I've always thought of archaeologists as strapping young men who wear pith helmets and explore pyramids.'

'Who says I don't have a pith helmet,' she countered and made him laugh.

'I wanted to come out to the site, to see your work. To see you. But I didn't want to . . . push. It's so much for you to deal with all at once. How did you hurt your head?'

She tugged at the fringe she'd cut to hide the scrape and bruise. 'I guess this isn't doing the job after all.' She started to tell him something light, something foolish, then found herself telling him the exact truth.

'My God. This is madness. What did the sheriff say?'

'Hewitt?' She shrugged. 'What cops always say. They'll look into it. He's going to talk to a couple of guys who hassled me and Jake. Some morons named Austin and Jimmy. They want us off the project. And they're not alone.'

'The development is no longer an issue. Kathy Dolan contacted me last night. That's Ron's widow. She wants to sell the land to the Preservation Society. There will be no development at Antietam Creek.'

'Just speculation, but could someone have killed Dolan so his wife would be pressured into selling?'

'I can't imagine that. There were a lot of people who thought highly of Ron, and a lot who didn't. But I don't know one of them who'd crack his head open and dump him in Simon's Hole.'

'I could say the same thing about my team. I should get back to them.' But she didn't rise. 'Can I ask you a question first? A personal one?'

'Of course you can.'

'Suzanne and Jay. What happened between them?'

He let out a long breath, sat back. 'We were normal people, living ordinary lives. This sort of thing isn't supposed to happen to normal people living ordinary lives. But it did, and it changed us. It changed Suzanne and Jay. The stress broke something in her, and broke something between her and Jay neither knew how to mend. Finding you was Suzanne's entire focus. She hounded the police, she went on television, talked to newspapers, to magazines. It was a transformation. It drove Jay into himself even as it drove Suzanne out. Suddenly this young woman was an activist. And when she wasn't actively working to find you, she was horribly depressed. Jay wasn't able to keep up, not the way she needed him to.'

'It had to be hard on Doug.'

'It was. Being caught between the two of them. They tried.' He touched her then, had to. He laid his fingertips lightly on the back of her hand. 'They're both decent, loving people who adored their son.'

'Yes, I understand that.' And because she understood, she turned her hand over, hooked her fingers with Roger's. 'But they couldn't rebuild that ordinary life when a piece of it was missing. He still loves her.'

Roger pursed his lips. 'Yes, I know. How do you?'

'Something he said when she was out of the room. The way he said it. I'm sorry for them, Mr Grogan. But I don't know what to do about it.'

'Nothing you or anyone else can do. I don't know the people who raised you, but they must be decent and loving people.'

'Yes, they are.'

'For everything they gave you, I'm grateful.' He cleared his throat. 'But you were also given something at birth from Suzanne and Jay. If you can accept that, can value that, it can be enough.'

She looked down at their joined fingers. 'I'm glad I came in today. If you feel like it, you could ride out to the site with me. I'll give you a tour.'

'That's the best offer I've had in a long time.'

Callie was just setting out her tools the next morning when Lana pulled up. She tipped her sunglasses down as she got closer and winced as she studied Callie's forehead. 'Ouch. I have some news that's not going to make you any happier. Carlyle's son isn't being forthcoming. He told the investigator he doesn't know where his father is.'

'I want the investigator to keep at it.'

Lana nodded. 'You went to see Roger yesterday. There was someone in the store when you were there. She recognised you. It's a small town, Callie. People know people, and people remember. The talk's already getting up some steam that you're Suzanne and Jay's lost daughter. I thought you should know so you can decide how you want to handle it.'

'Does Suzanne know?'

'I've got an appointment with her in an hour.'

'I need that list. The names of her doctor, the nurses, whoever shared her hospital room when she delivered. I haven't wanted to push her about that.'

'But you'd like me to.' Lana nodded. 'No problem.'

'Get me Carlyle's son's address and phone number. I might be able to convince him to talk to us.'

Suzanne listened to everything Lana had to say. She provided a neatly organised computer-generated list of names from the past. She remained absolutely calm as she showed Lana to the door. Then she whirled round at Jay. 'I asked you to be here this morning because Lana said it was important to speak with both of us. Then you say nothing.'

She walked past him towards the kitchen. 'Just go, Jay. Just go.'

He nearly did. She'd said that to him years before. Just go, Jay. And he had. But this time he strode after her, taking her arm. 'You shut me out then, and you're shutting me out now. What do you want, Suzanne?'

'I want my daughter back! You won't do anything about it. You barely spoke to her in Lana's office. You never touched her.'

'She didn't want me to touch her. Do you think, do you really think that this isn't killing me? I grieved, Suzanne, and I hurt. But you didn't see, you didn't hear. There was nothing for you but Jessie. You couldn't be my wife, you couldn't be my lover. You couldn't even be my friend because you were too determined to be her mother.'

The words were like sharp arrows thudding into her heart. He'd never said this sort of thing to her before. Never looked so angry, so hurt. She wrenched free. 'You closed off from me when I needed you most.'

'Maybe I did. But so did you. I needed you, too, Suzanne, and you weren't there for me. I wanted to try to keep what we had together, and you were willing to sacrifice it all for what we lost.'

'She was my baby.'

'Our baby. Goddamnit, Suze, *our* baby. We lost our daughter. But I lost my wife, too. I lost my best friend, I lost my family. I lost everything.'

She swiped at tears. 'I need to go out and see Jessica—Callie.'

'No, you're not to. If you go out there you'll push her that much further away. Because if you don't let her draw the lines you're going to lose her a second time. She doesn't love us. I hate saying it to you. But if I don't it'll only hurt you more.'

'I want her to come home.' Wrapping her arms tight round her waist, Suzanne rocked. 'I want her to be a baby again so I can just hold her.'

'I wanted that, too. I know you don't believe me, but I wanted that with all my heart. Just to . . . just to touch her.'

'Oh God, Jay.' She lifted her hand, brushed a tear from his cheek with her finger. 'I'm sorry. I'm so sorry.'

'Maybe, just this once, you could hold me instead. Or let me hold you.' He slipped his arms round her. 'Just let me hold you, Suzanne.'

'Oh, Jay.' Going with her heart, she touched her lips to his cheeks. 'I know you're right, about her coming to us. But it's so hard to wait.'

'Maybe it wouldn't be so hard if we waited together.'

It took some manoeuvring. It always did when it came to Douglas, Lana thought. But she'd not only engineered another date, but had talked him into letting her meet him in the apartment over the bookstore.

She wanted to see where he lived, however temporary. And she thought they might start working on defining what they had going between them.

He called out a 'Come in' when she knocked on the outside entrance.

'I'll be out in a minute,' he shouted from the next room.

'No hurry.' It gave her time to poke around. There were a few mementos scattered about. A baseball trophy, books, and prints of Mucha's *Four Seasons*, a Waterhouse mermaid, and Parrish's *Ecstasy* and *Daybreak*. A man who put fancy on his walls and kept a high-school trophy was a man worth getting to know better. To get started, she walked to the bedroom doorway.

He was working at a laptop. He wore, to her fascination, tortoiseshell glasses. She felt a little curl of lust in her belly and stepping behind him, trailed her fingers through all that dark hair.

He jerked, swivelled round in the chair and stared at her through the lenses. 'Sorry. Forgot. Are you early?'

'No, right on time.' He seemed just a bit nervous to have her there, in his bedroom. And because he did, she felt powerful. 'No hurry, though. The movie doesn't start for an hour.'

'An hour. Right.' She still had on her lawyer suit. Pinstripes. What was there about pinstripes on a woman? 'We were going to eat first.'

She ran her hands over his chest. 'Hungry?'

'Oh yeah.'

'What're you in the mood for?' she asked, then laughed when he crushed his mouth to hers.

She wound herself round him. Surrounded him, was all he could think, as her taste, her scent, her shape dazzled his senses. 'Let me . . .'

'I intend to.' Her heart was thudding: she loved the feel of it—that hard pump of life. She eased back to give his hands room to work. 'The glasses were the kicker, you know.'

'I could say the same about the pinstripes. They just kill me. But why don't we . . .' He tugged the jacket off her shoulders, let it catch at her elbows. 'That's a nice look for you,' he told her and assaulted her throat with his teeth.

Her arms were pinned and her flesh exposed. There was something dark and erotic about that quick change of control, about surrendering that moment of power to him. Then she was under him on the bed. He drew the skirt over her hips, down and away. She wore stockings that stopped at the thigh with little bands of lace, and a white satin thong.

He slowly tasted her lips, her throat, then her breasts.

Her hands stroked over him—his hair, his shoulders, his back. As she sighed into him, she tugged his shirt up, drew it over his head, tossed it aside. And the slide of flesh to flesh made her tremble.

Patient, she thought dreamily, and oh so thorough. Here was a man who sought to give as much as he took, to please as well as to take pleasure. One who could make her body quiver and her heart stand still.

And because of it, she arched to offer him more. Moaned his name when his lips, his hands grew more impatient. Sensations tumbled through her, too quickly now to separate. She fought with the button of his jeans. 'Doug,' she whispered, and guided him to her.

He watched her lashes flutter, and the pulse beat in her throat as her head arched back. As the pleasure built stroke by slow, deep stroke. He knew she clung, as he did, to that last slippery edge of reason. When he felt her clutch around him, he lowered his mouth to hers again and took the fall.

'Doug? I have one thing to say about this. Mmmmm.'

He grinned at her. 'How'd I manage to miss you whenever I came to town?'

'Now you're going to miss me whenever you leave town.'

Because that rang true, entirely too true, he rolled away and got up. 'There's a library I need to assess,' he said. 'In Memphis.'

'Oh.' She sat up, kept her tone very casual. 'When are you leaving?'

'A couple of days. I'm coming back right after I'm done. I don't think it's a good idea for me to be away with all that's going on.'

She nodded. 'I have to agree. Your family needs you.'

'Yeah. And another thing.' He looked down at her aroused. 'I'm not finished with you yet.'

They made love again, then curled up together in contented silence.

Neither of them stirred when the sounds of sirens wailed. 'It'll be hot in Memphis. Are you going to Graceland while you're there?'

'No. I'm there to do a job, not to pay homage to The King.'

'You could do both.' She angled her head. 'You should go, just for the experience. Then you should buy me something incredibly silly.' She kissed the tip of his nose. 'I have to go.'

He didn't want her to go, and the urge to pull her back, hold her to him, with him, was more than a little frightening. 'Want to try for the movies again, when I get back?'

It pleased her he'd asked first this time. 'Yes.' As she started to rise, the cellphone in her briefcase across the room began to ring.

He saw the instant fear flash into her eyes as she scrambled up. 'It must be Denny, the babysitter.' She tore open the briefcase and grabbed the ringing phone. 'Hello? Denny, what . . . What? My God. Yes. Yes, I will.'

'Tyler. What's wrong with Tyler?' Doug demanded.

'Nothing. He's fine. Ty's fine. God, Doug. My office is on fire.'

Callie heard about the fire at six fifty the following morning when Jake shook her out of sleep. 'Go away or I'll kill you.'

'Wake up, Dunbrook. Your lawyer's office burned down last night.'

'What?' She blinked up at him. 'Lana? Where is she?'

'She's OK. The local news reported no one was in the building when the fire started. Arson's suspected. They're investigating.'

'Arson? Well, who the hell would . . .' She trailed off. 'She's my lawyer. Records of our search would have been in that office.'

'You got it. Maybe somebody doesn't like the idea of you digging up information about what happened to you.' He touched a fingertip to the raw skin on her brow.

'I'm going to Atlanta.'

'You want to tackle Carlyle's son, face to face. There's a Delta flight to Atlanta in just over two hours, with a couple of seats.'

She looked at him as she reached for jeans. 'I only need one seat.'

'Good thing, as that's all you're getting. I'm in the other one. I'm coming, Callie,' he said before she could speak. 'I'm not going to let anything happen to you.'

Richard Carlyle stood behind his desk. He was tall and well built. When he extended his hand Callie noted the monogrammed cuffs. The Rolex. She remembered Henry Simpson describing Marcus Carlyle as a handsome, dynamic man of exquisite taste. Like father, like son.

'Ms Dunbrook, Mr Graystone. How can I help you?'

'It's very important that I locate your father,' Callie said.

'I see.' He steepled his fingers, and over them his face lost its polite interest. 'As this is the second enquiry about my father in the last few days, I have to assume they're connected. I can't help you, Ms Dunbrook.'

'He arranged for babies to be stolen, transported, then sold to childless couples who paid him large fees without being aware of the kidnappings. He drew up fraudulent adoption papers in these cases, which he never filed with any court.'

Richard stared at her without blinking. 'That's ludicrous. And I'll warn you such an allegation is slanderous as well as preposterous.'

'It's neither when it's the truth. It's neither when there's proof.'

'What proof could you possibly have?'

'Myself, for a start. I was stolen as an infant and sold to a couple who were clients of your father. The exchange was made in his Boston office.' Callie reached in her bag. 'Copies of the adoption papers, never filed with the court. Copies of the fees your father charged. Copies of the initial tests run to substantiate that I am the biological daughter of Jay and Suzanne Cullen, whose infant daughter was stolen, December '74. Police reports,' she added, nodding at the pile of papers. 'Newspaper accounts.'

Richard's fingers trembled lightly as he began to go through the file.

'I'm not going to stop until I have the answers. Where's your father?'

'I haven't seen my father in more than fifteen years,' Carlyle shot back angrily. 'If I knew where he was, I wouldn't tell you. I intend to look into this personally, but I don't believe there's any validity in your allegations. The man I knew was a mediocre father, a failure as a husband and a difficult human being. But he was a good lawyer, with a dedication to the institution of adoption. He helped create families. He was proud of that.'

'Proud enough to play God?' Callie put in.

'I said I'd look into it. If you'll give my assistant numbers where you can be reached, I'll be in touch.'

Jake got to his feet before Callie could speak. 'It's strange, isn't it, Carlyle, to have your perception of your family, your sense of self shaken in one blinding moment?' He took Callie's hand. 'That's exactly what happened to her. So you look into it. And you remember this: We'll find him. Because nobody's going to get away with making Callie unhappy.'

She didn't say anything to him until they were outside. 'That was some closing speech, Graystone. I haven't thought much about being unhappy.'

'I made you unhappy. That's something I've thought about quite a bit.'

'We made each other unhappy.'

He turned her face to his. 'Maybe we did. But I know one thing for sure. I was happier with you than I was without you.'

'Damnit, Jake,' was all she could say.

'Figured you should know. Being a smart woman you'll be able to conclude I prefer being happy to unhappy. So I'm going to get you back. Now, let's give him a few days. I say we go back to work, on the site and on the list of names Suzanne gave you.'

She gave in to impulse, touched his face. Maybe she was an idiot, she thought, but she, too, was happier with him than she was without him.

'You're back.' Bill McDowell trotted up to Callie. 'I was kind of hoping I could work with you.'

She reminded herself she was here to teach as well as dig. Enlightenment was as essential as discovery. 'We'll see about it tomorrow.'

'Awesome.' He jogged off to get his trowel.

'You know, you can get a rash having your butt kissed that much,' Jake commented.

'Shut up. He's just eager. Starting next week, we're only going to have Sonya at weekends. She starts classes full-time.'

'What about Dory?'

'She's arranging a sabbatical. She doesn't want to leave the dig. Chuck and Frannie are staying on. Matt and Bill, too. We're going to lose a couple of the itinerants, the undergrads. Leo's working on replacements.'

'If we're going to be short-handed, let's keep those hands busy while we've got them.'

They separated, Jake to work on what they'd termed 'the hut area', and Callie back to the cemetery, where she could work in her own bubble of silence, painstakingly excavating the distant past as her mind carefully turned over the known elements of her own.

William Blakely, Suzanne Cullen's obstetrician, retired twelve years after delivering her of a healthy baby girl. He died of prostate cancer fourteen years later, survived by his wife, who had been both his office manager and his nurse.

Blakely's receptionist had also retired, but had moved out of the area. She intended to visit the widow, track down the receptionist and the delivery-room nurse and Suzanne's paediatrician.

Meticulously, she brushed the soil from the jawbone of a skull. 'Who were you?' she wondered aloud.

She started to reach for her camera, glanced over when it wasn't there.

'I've got it.' Dory crouched down, framed in the skull.

'We're trying to get a poker game together for tonight. Interested?'

'Yeah, but I've got to work.'

'You haven't taken a night off since I started on the dig. And when you're not on-site, you're travelling. In and out of Atlanta yesterday, a day in the lab—'

'How'd you know I went to Atlanta?'

Dory flinched at the snap in Callie's voice. 'Rosie mentioned it. She said you and Jake had to fly to Atlanta on business. Sorry.'

Callie waited until she was gone, then boosted out of the hole.

'What's up?' Rosie asked her.

'Did you mention to anyone that I was in Atlanta yesterday?'

'Yeah, your not-so-secret admirer was pretty bummed when you weren't here. I told him you had some business south. I might've told someone else. Was it a secret mission?'

'No.' She rolled her shoulder. 'Just jumpy, I guess.' She frowned over to where Bill worked. 'Has he asked you anything else about me?'

'Yeah, if you've got a boyfriend.'

'A boyfriend? Give me a break.'

'He shoots sulky glares at Jake when he's absolutely sure Jake's not looking. And gooey ones at you. It's sweet. Be nice to him.'

That made her think about perceptions, about team dynamics and gossip. She decided to go after the next pieces of her puzzle without Jake.

Lorna Blakely had steel-grey hair, wore bifocals and housed four cats.

She kept the screen door locked and peered suspiciously through it.

'I'd like to speak with you about one of your husband's patients. Suzanne Cullen. Do you remember her?'

'Of course I remember her. I'm not senile. She was a nice young woman, had pretty babies. One got kidnapped. Terrible thing.'

'Yes, ma'am. That's what I'd like to talk to you about.'

'You the police? That must've been thirty years ago.'

'No, I'm not the police.' How much, Callie wondered, could she trust her instincts? They told her that this tiny woman wasn't the type to black-market babies. 'Mrs Blakely, I'm the baby who was kidnapped. I'm Suzanne Cullen's daughter. If I could ask you some questions it might help me figure out what really happened.'

'Why the devil didn't you say so in the first place?' Lorna pushed open the screen. She led the way into a small living room.

'Would you remember, when your husband was treating Suzanne through her pregnancy, if anyone asked questions about her?'

'The police asked questions back when it happened. Wasn't a thing we could tell them. Wil'm was heartsick over it. That man loved his babies.'

'What about the others who worked in your husband's office?'

'Had a receptionist, another nurse. Hallie. She was with us ten years.'

'What about Karen Younger, the receptionist?'

'Moved to Houston. Got two grandchildren now.'

'I wonder if I could have her address, and Hallie's? There were people at the hospital, too. One of the delivery-room nurses was with Suzanne for both deliveries. Would you remember her name?'

Lorna puffed out her cheeks. 'Might've been Mary Stern, or Nancy Ellis. Can't say for sure, but Will'm asked for one of them most often. You check with Betsy Poffenberger. She worked there more than forty years. Nothing she doesn't know about anybody or anything goes on there.'

'Lorna Blakely sent you?' Betsy sat on her front porch with a pair of binoculars close at hand. 'Old bitty. Never did care for me.'

'She thought you might be able to tell me who was in the delivery room with Suzanne Cullen when her daughter was born. Maybe who her room-mate was during her stay. The names of the nurses and staff working the maternity wing. That sort of thing.'

'Felt sorry as could be for Mrs Cullen when that happened. Everybody did. Alice Lingstrom was head nurse on the maternity floor. She's a particular friend of mine. She and Kate Regan and me, we talked about it plenty, over breaks and at lunch. Kate worked in Administration. Can't say I recall what was what right off, but I could

find out. I still got ways,' she said with a wink. 'Guess I could do that.'
'Thank you.' Callie wrote down her cellphone number. 'You can reach me on this. I'd appreciate any information at all.'
Betsy peered up at Callie's face. 'You kin to the Cullens?'
'Apparently.'

The poker game was under way when Callie got back. She turned towards the stairs with the hope of getting up them and into her room unnoticed. But Jake appeared to have radar where she was concerned.
'Why did you sneak off?' He propelled her through the door.
When they reached the creek, she pulled her arm free. 'I had some legwork I wanted to do alone. I'm not having the team gossiping about us because we're always together.'
'Fuck gossip. Did it occur to you that I'd worry?'
She saw, very clearly, that he had. 'I'm sorry.'
'You apologised. It's a day of miracles.' He took her face in his hands, pressed his lips to hers.
When she didn't kick him, shove him, he drew her closer. He deepened the kiss, let his fingers slide back into her hair.
Callie couldn't remember him ever kissing her in quite this way, with patience, and with care. As if she mattered a very great deal.
'What's going on with you?' she murmured against his mouth.
'That's my question.' He eased back.
She nearly refused to tell him, then realised that was simply a knee-jerk reaction. You demand, she thought, I refuse. And we end up nowhere.
'Why don't we sit down?' And she sat on the bank and told him.

SIX

CALLIE SAT CROSS-LEGGED on the ground, filling out a find sheet. When a shadow fell over her, she turned her head. It was a jolt to see Suzanne. It was almost like looking at an older version of herself.
'I heard you on the radio this morning. You made it sound fascinating. so I thought it was time I had a look for myself. I hope it's all right.'
'Sure.' Callie got to her feet. 'What do you think?'

'It's tidier than I imagined somehow. And more crowded.'

'We're able to pull in a lot of volunteers at the weekends.'

'Yes, so I see,' she said, smiling over at where little Tyler scooped a trowel through a small pile of soil. 'Starting them young. And every find tells you something about who lived here, and how. If I understood your radio interview.'

'That's right. You have to find the past in order to understand the past.' She paused as her words echoed back to her. 'I'm trying to do that.'

'Yes, I know you are.' Suzanne touched a hand to Callie's arm. 'You're uncomfortable with me, and that's partly my fault for going to pieces the way I did in Lana's office that day. Jay gave me a hell of a lecture over it. I'm going to *try* not to put that kind of pressure on you again. I want to get to know you, Callie. I know you're trying to . . . reconstruct. Betsy Poffenberger called me this morning. She said she wanted to make sure it was all right with me to give you information, but what she wanted was to pump me for it. I didn't tell her anything, but people are starting to put things together.'

'I know. Are you all right with that?'

She pressed a hand to her stomach. 'I'm jittery all the time. But I can handle it. I'm stronger than I've given you reason to think.'

'I've read some of your letters. I think you're one of the strongest women I've ever known.'

'Oh. Well.' Eyes stinging, Suzanne looked away. 'That's a lovely thing to hear from a grown daughter. I'd really like you to tell me about your work here. I'd really like to understand more about it, and you.'

'I'm working this section.' Needing to make the effort, Callie took Suzanne's arm, turned her. 'We're establishing that this area was a Neolithic settlement. And this section their cemetery. As we excavate bones—bones are my speciality, by the way . . .'

Jake watched Callie give Suzanne a tour of the site. He could gauge Callie's emotional state by her body language. She'd closed in immediately upon seeing Suzanne, then had gone on the defensive, from there to uneasy, and now to relaxed.

He turned as Ty raced over, followed by Lana. He was clutching a bone in his grimy fist.

'Look! Look what I got. I found a bone.'

Jake chuckled at the low and essentially female sound of disgust Lana tried to muffle. 'Let's have a look. Why don't we ask the expert?'

'It's a bone!' Ty called out as Callie walked over with Suzanne.

'It certainly is.' Callie stepped close, examined it thoughtfully.

'From a dead person?' Ty asked.

'A deer,' she said and watched his face fall in disappointment. 'It's a very important find,' she told him. 'Someone hunted this deer so the tribe could eat. Maybe a young boy, not much older than you. And you have this to remember him. I'll show you how to clean it and label it.'

He reached out, and Callie reached for him. For a moment she and Jake held the child together. Something fluttered in her belly as their eyes met. 'Ah, maybe you could explain the site to Suzanne from the anthropological level,' she said. 'Ty and I have—ha-ha—a bone to pick.'

'It's a strange world, isn't it?' Suzanne said when Callie carted Tyler off. 'You're my son-in-law. More or less. And since I don't know the circumstances of your relationship with Callie, I don't know if I should be mad at you or disappointed in you or sorry for you.'

'I probably deserve a little of all three.' He thought for a moment, then dug his wallet out of his pocket and took out a snapshot.

'I can't give it to you,' he said. 'It's the only one I've got. But I thought you might like to see it. Wedding photo. Sort of. We drove out to Vegas and got it done in one of those get-hitched-quick places.' Callie had chosen siren red for her wedding dress. The dress was short, skimpy and strapless. Jake wore a dark suit and a tie with a green and blue parrot on a red background. His arms were round her. They were both grinning like idiots, and looked ridiculously happy.

'You look terribly in love,' Suzanne managed. She looked over as a car pulled up. 'It's Doug.' She started towards the fence, then pulled up short when she saw her son nip Lana at the waist and kiss her. 'Oh.' Suzanne pressed a fist to her heart as it lurched. 'Well. I didn't see that one coming.'

'Problem?' Jake asked her.

'No. No,' she decided. 'Just a surprise.' She saw Ty race over, still waving the deer bone. When Doug crouched down to look at it, Suzanne pressed that fist a little harder against her heart. 'A very big surprise.'

Doug studied the bone, listened to Ty chatter, then shook his head. 'This is very cool. I don't know if you're going to want what I've got in here when you've got something like this.' Doug pulled out a palm-sized tyrannosaurus.

'It's a T-rex! Thanks!' Ty fell on Doug's neck in gratitude. 'It's the best! Can I go and bury it and dig it up again?'

'You bet.' Ty sprinted off to the spoil pile. 'That seems to be a hit.' He looked back to see Lana grinning at him. 'Want a present?'

He reached in the bag again, watched her mouth fall open as he pulled out her gift. 'An official electric-blue, guitar-shaped Elvis fly-swatter. After considerable search and debate, this was the silliest thing I could find.'

'It's perfect.' Laughing, she threw her arms round his neck.

Callie had just called for the team to gather up their tools when the last visitor arrived. She watched Betsy Poffenberger lever herself out of a blue Camry.

Bill McDowell jogged over. 'A bunch of us are going to camp out here tonight. Grill up some dogs, have some beer. Just hang out. You gonna?'

'I don't know.' She was already walking away. 'Mrs Poffenberger?'

'You didn't mention you were Suzanne Cullen's girl.'

'Does that make a difference?'

'Sure it does. It's just like a mystery story. Well, I talked to Alice and Kate, and Alice, she remembered that it was Mary Stern who was the delivery-room nurse when Suzanne Cullen's babies were born. Got a couple of other names for you.' She took out a sheet of paper. 'Mary Stern is living down in Florida now. Sandy Parker here, she died in a car crash about five years ago. She was on the night shift. Now this one, this Barbara Halloway. She wasn't on staff more than a year.'

'Thank you, Mrs Poffenberger. I'm sure this will help.'

'Snooty young thing,' she continued. 'Had her sights set on bagging a doctor. Got one, too, up north somewhere.'

'Thank you. I'll be sure to let you know what I find out.'

Callie tucked the paper in her back pocket, stepped back from the fence as Betsy climbed in her car and Jake sauntered up. 'I've got names. At least a dozen names.'

Bill McDowell got a little drunk. It didn't take more than a single beer to manage it, but he had two, just to be sure he'd stay that way awhile. Callie wasn't going to come back to the site that night. Disgusted, disappointed, he got to his feet, swaying. 'Gotta piss. You mind?'

'Don't mind a bit,' Digger said. 'Don't fall in the pond and drown yourself.'

Bill staggered away from the tents, away from the company. What the hell did he want to stay here for when Callie was at the house?

The blow had him sprawling face down. He moaned once, as he was rolled towards the pond, but was already sliding under the pain when his head slipped under the water.

'OK, here's the basic grid.' Jake had Callie as the central point, with her parents on one side, the Cullens on the other. Henry Simpson, Marcus Carlyle, Richard Carlyle, the Boston paediatrician, the names of their known staff were listed on her parents' side, and the names from the lists Suzanne Cullen and Betsy Poffenberger had provided, on the other.

'You're the single known connection, but there must be others.'

'I'll type in the known data on each of these names,' Callie said. 'You go and make more coffee.' She smirked as he stalked out. He hated making coffee. They were falling back into old patterns, she thought, but they weren't fighting as much, or jumping between the sheets at every opportunity. That . . . restraint, added an appealing tension. She ordered her mind to clear so she could concentrate on the data she was bringing up on the Net. Then she yawned as she noted the article on Henry Simpson. 'What the hell good is a stupid fluff piece on some charity golf tournament?' She started to bypass it, then made herself stop. Just like sieving the spoil, she reminded herself.

She nearly missed it. Her eyes had moved on before her brain registered the information. Her finger jerked on the mouse, then scrolled back.

'We're out of milk,' Jake announced as he came back in. He lowered the pot as she turned her head and he saw her face. 'What did you find?'

'A connection. Barbara Simpson, née Halloway.'

'Halloway. Barbara Halloway. The maternity-ward nurse.'

'We sat in their house. We sat in their house and they dripped shock and sympathy. I need to go to Virginia, face them with this.'

'As soon as we get more data on her, we'll go. We'll go together.'

She lifted a hand, closed it over his. 'He held my mother's hand. He used my father's grief. I'm going to hurt them.'

'Damn right. Let me take over there for a while.'

'No, I can do it. I need to do it,' she said, gripping his hand when she saw the shutter come down over his face. 'I need to do it for my parents, for the Cullens. For myself. But I don't know if I can if you step back.'

'I'm not going anywhere.'

'There are a lot of ways of stepping back from someone. I could never make you understand that. You close up, and I can't find you.'

'If I don't close up, you slice me in two.'

'I don't know what you're talking about. I never hurt you.'

'You broke my heart.'

'I did not. No, I didn't. You . . . you left me.'

'Bullshit, Callie. I'll tell you exactly what happened—fuck!' He balled his hands into fists as the phone on his desk shrilled.

He snatched it up. 'Graystone.' And froze. 'Bill McDowell. He's dead.'

Callie sat on the ground just beyond the dig. The air held the faintest chill when the breeze fluttered. Fall, it seemed, was already moving into the mountains.

She'd rushed out of the house with Jake minutes after the phone call, with Rosie and Leo right behind them. They'd beaten the police to the scene by ten minutes. But they'd still been too late for Bill McDowell.

Now she could only watch and wait.

Other members of the team sat or stood around. 'I don't think I can take it. I don't think I can stand it.' Sonya turned her head. 'I don't see how he can just be dead. I didn't even see him go over to the pond.'

'I heard Digger say something like, "Don't fall into the pond and drown." I laughed.' Dory's breath caught on a sob. 'I just laughed.'

Bob shifted his feet. 'We were always laughing at him.'

'I want to go home.' Sonya began to cry. Dory put both arms round her.

Let them cry together, Callie thought. She just didn't have any tears.

She could hear voices trailing off as people broke camp. And cars leaving. She would have preferred both quiet and solitude. But Leo would never have agreed to her staying on-site alone. Jake was the only person whose company she could stand through this kind of night.

'You don't think Bill fell into the water.'

Jake's eyes were as careful and cool as his voice. 'Everybody said he was drunk. Why didn't they hear the splash? Why didn't he call out when he fell? Water's cold, slap you sober enough, if you fell in.'

She nodded. 'Two men end up dead in the same little body of water outside the same town, on the same dig, within weeks of each other. Anybody thinks that's just a coincidence is nuts. And you're not subscribing to the popular local theory that the site's cursed.'

He smiled a little. 'No. Someone killed Dolan for a reason. Someone killed McDowell for a reason. How are they connected?'

Callie dropped onto the sofa, tucked up her legs. 'The dig.'

'That's the obvious link. Go a segment over and there's you. Aren't you so distracted now that you're not thinking about Barbara Halloway? If somebody killed that kid, it was because he was handy. Because he was separated from the group just long enough.'

'He's dead because someone wants to stop me. He's dead, and I couldn't bother to give him a minute of my time today.'

'Come on, come here.' He sat down on the thin cushions of the sofa and pulled her closer. 'You should try to get some rest. Stretch out,' he ordered, and nudged her down until her head rested in his lap.

She was silent for a moment, listening to the night sounds, absorbing the quiet sensation of having his hand stroke over her hair.

Had he touched her that way before? Yes, she thought. Yes, he had. Why hadn't she paid more attention to those small gestures? Did she need words so much that she'd ignored the quieter, simpler signs of affection?

'I don't want to be alone.' She wasn't speaking just of tonight, but of all the nights without him. 'I thought I did, but I don't.' She rose, sliding up, body to body, until her arms were chained round his neck. 'Be with me.' She covered his mouth with hers.

She was trembling, he realised. Part fear, part need, part exhaustion. He gathered her closer. 'Tell me you need me. Just once.'

'I do need you. Touch me. You're the only one who ever really could.'

'This isn't the way I wanted it to be.' He skimmed his lips along her jaw as he lowered her to the narrow couch. 'For either of us. But maybe it's just the way it's meant. Don't think. Just feel.'

His fingers were warm as they trailed over her. Her belly quivered as they stroked down and flipped the button on her ancient trousers.

His lips pressed lightly, just above her waist, and made her moan. When his mouth came back to hers in a kiss of lingering sweetness, she went pliant under him. A surrender, he realised. Both of them surrendering in a way they never had before. Her heart was thudding thickly, and her breath was slow and ragged. Having her now erased every lonely hour without her.

They watched each other as he slid inside her, watched as they began to move together. He saw her eyes blur, both pleasure and tears.

'Stay with me.' He crushed his mouth to hers. 'Stay with me.'

So she stayed with him. And was with him still when they shattered.

When Doug stepped into the kitchen, he saw the man he thought of as Callie's ex-husband leaning against the stove, while he whipped what looked like a garden fork in a mixing bowl.

'Sorry to interrupt.'

Jake kept beating the eggs. 'Callie's in the shower.'

'Oh. Guess I figured you'd all be up and around by now.'

'Late start today. Coffee's fresh. Milk too. Just picked it up on the way back from the dig this morning.'

'You were working all night?'

'No.' Jake stopped beating the eggs and turned to flip the bacon in the skillet. 'I thought you'd come by to see how she was doing. But I don't guess you've heard.'

'What do you mean how she's doing? What happened?'

Instant concern, Jake noted. Blood could run thick. 'One of our team drowned last night. In Simon's Hole. Somebody killed him,' he added quietly. 'I think two people are dead because Callie's digging up the past—one that doesn't have anything to do with the site. She'll be down in a minute so I'll cut to the point. I don't want her alone, not for so much as an hour. When I can't stick with her, you will.'

'You think someone's going to try to hurt her?'

'I think the closer she gets, the more they'll do to stop her.'

'Doug!' Callie said as she came in. 'Um. How's it going? I heard you were out of town.'

'I got back yesterday. I came by the site but you were busy. I just dropped by to give you something I picked up in Memphis.' Doug handed her a small brown bag. 'Just a little souvenir from Graceland.'

'You went to Graceland! I always wanted to go to Graceland. I have no idea why. Wow, look at this, Graystone. It's an official Elvis beer mat.' She took a step towards Doug, hesitated. what the hell was she supposed to do? Should she kiss him, punch him on the arm? 'Thanks.' She settled for patting his shoulder. 'Have you had breakfast? Why don't you stay? There's plenty, right, Jake?'

'Sure.'

'Grab a plate,' she told him, filling the toaster.

'Leo told me to come straight back,' Lana announced as she walked in. 'Doug, I saw your car outside. I guess you heard what happened.'

'Grab two plates,' Callie told him. 'Do we need a lawyer?'

'Leo has some concerns. I'm here to alleviate them. The legal concerns anyway. As to the rest'—she lifted her hands—'It's awful. I don't know what to say. I spoke with Bill just yesterday afternoon. I don't really think I could eat. I just want to speak with Leo.'

'When I cook, everybody eats,' Jake announced. 'You'd better get a seat before the horde takes them all. How many we got, Dunbrook?'

'Rosie and Digger are at the site. So counting our guests here, we'll be eleven for breakfast this morning.'

They came in and out, in various states of dress and undress.

Callie concentrated on the meal. She didn't bother to tune in as Lana went over the legal ground with Leo.

'People might make us stop,' Sonya commented.

'The Preservation Society has bought the land,' Lana told her. 'I can promise you that none of us blames your team for what happened.'

'He died when we were all just sitting there.' Sonya sniffed.

'In many cultures, many societies,' Jake said, 'you show respect for the dead by honouring their work. We'll dig.'

'I don't mean to stir up trouble,' Dory began. 'I just wondered what would happen if Bill's family sues. How would that kind of legal trouble affect the grant? Could it be pulled?'

'Let me worry about that,' Lana told her. 'My advice is to go on. Cooperate with the police, and with the media.'

'We're also going to employ a strict buddy system.' Leo pushed his plate aside, reached for his coffee. 'Nobody wanders into the woods at any time alone. We're not losing anyone else. I think it's best if we take today off. Anyone who's remaining should be ready to work tomorrow.'

'I've got some personal business in Virginia today.' Callie glanced at Jake. 'Dory and the West Virginia turtledoves can relieve Rosie and Digger this afternoon. We'll put Bob and Matt and Digger on the night shift. I'll have a daily schedule worked out by tomorrow.'

She went into Jake's office to print out the article on Simpson, to make a file folder for the lists, the chart. 'What's in Virginia?' Doug asked.

'Who. Someone I need to talk to.'

'Is this about . . . Does it have to do with Jessica?'

'Yeah. I'll let you know what I find out.'

'I'll go with you,' he said then shifted aside as Lana nudged through. 'What's this about?'

'I've got some information I need to check out.'

She frowned at her watch. 'Let me call Roger, see if he can handle Ty until we get back.'

'What is this "we"?' Callie demanded.

'I think it's what you refer to as a team. I'm the legal portion of that team. Let me just make that call, then you can fill me in on the drive.'

Callie couldn't even manage to take the wheel, and had to settle for sitting shotgun in Jake's SUV instead of her own.

'How long was Simpson your mother's doctor?' Lana unearthed a legal pad from her bag and began taking notes.

'I don't know. At least since 1966.'

'And he wasn't married to Barbara Halloway at that time?'

'No, I think that was closer to 1980. He's got a good twenty years on her.'

'And according to your information, she worked at Washington County Hospital from July or August of '74 until the spring of the following year, and was on the maternity floor when Suzanne Cullen was admitted. In the spring of the following year, she relocated. You don't know where?'

'I'm going to find out where, and you can bet your ass that at some time between spring of '75 and 1980, she spent time in Boston.' She shifted to look into the back seat. 'She was still working in Hagerstown when Jessica Cullen was kidnapped. You don't forget something like that. But when we talked to them, it was all news to her.'

'It's circumstantial.' Lana continued to write. 'But I agree.'

'Circumstantial, my ass. Halloway was one of Carlyle's organisation.

One of his key medical contacts. An obstetrics nurse. She gets word that he's in the market for an infant, preferably female. Suzanne Cullen delivers a baby girl who fits the bill.'

'She'd have been the one to take her,' Doug said quietly. 'She'd have been the one in the area, the one with the opportunity to keep tabs on my parents, on us.'

'My parents said a nurse brought me to Carlyle's office,' Callie agreed.

'Obviously, she needs to be questioned.' Lana drew several circles round Barbara Halloway's name on her pad. 'But isn't it more likely she'd talk in an official interview with the authorities than to you?'

'After we talk to the Simpsons, I'll give Sheriff Hewitt everything I have. For all the good it does.' Noting Doug's fingers linked with Lana's, Callie swivelled further round. 'So, you guys sleeping together yet?'

'Where the hell do you get off asking that?' Doug demanded.

'I'm just trying the sister hat on for size. How's the sex anyway?'

'Cut it out,' said Doug.

'Starting to think it wasn't such a bad thing when somebody grabbed me out of that buggy, huh?'

'I'm wondering how I can talk them into kidnapping you again.'

'I'd just find my way back now. You're awful quiet, Graystone.'

'Just enjoying watching you needle somebody besides me for a change. Almost there, Doug.'

'Remember, I'm in charge,' Callie said when Jake pulled in the driveway. 'You three are back-up.'

She climbed out of the car, walked to the front door, pressed the bell.

She heard nothing but the late-summer twitter of birds.

'Let me check the garage.' Jake walked off.

'They could be out, Sunday lunch, tennis game,' Lana suggested.

'No. They know what's going on. They know I've been talking to people who might remember Barbara.'

'Garage is empty,' Jake reported.

She slapped a fist on the door. 'They couldn't have known I was coming. Not this fast.'

Jake scanned the houses across the street. 'We fan out, knock on some doors and politely ask after our friends the Simpsons.'

'OK.' Callie said. 'We'll go in couples. Couples are less intimidating. We were supposed to drop by for drinks with Barb and Hank. Now we're worried we've got the wrong day or that something's wrong.'

By the time Jake rang the bell on their third stop, they had their story and routine down smooth as velvet frosting. The woman answered so quickly, he knew she'd watched their progress from house to house.

'I'm sorry to bother you, ma'am, but my wife and I were wondering about the Simpsons. We were supposed to drop by for drinks,' he said to the woman. 'But they don't answer the bell.'

'All four of you having drinks with the Simpsons?'

'Yes, my brother and I are old family friends of Hank's and Barb's,' Callie said. 'My brother just got engaged. That's actually why we were coming by for drinks. Just a little celebration.'

'I don't see how you're going to celebrate when they're out of town.'

Callie's hand tightened on Jake's. 'Out of town? But they didn't mention a trip when I talked to them a couple of weeks ago.'

'Spur of the moment,' the woman provided. 'I happened to see them loading up the cars when I came out to get the morning paper. Dr Simpson said they'd decided to drive up to their place in the Hamptons, spend a few weeks. Seemed strange to me, them taking both cars. Took enough luggage for a year, if you ask me. They were out here around ten this morning, loading up—and Barbara, you never see her up and around on a Sunday morning before noon. Must've been in a hurry to get on the road.'

'It's a long drive to the Hamptons,' Callie noted. 'Thanks. We'll have to catch up with them later.' They started back across the street. 'Do you think they went to the Hamptons?' she said under her breath.

'No. And I don't think they're coming back. But they'll leave some sort of trail. We'll find them.'

The long drive back only to relay the scattered pieces of the puzzle to the county sheriff, leaving everything very much as it had been at the start of the day, was another disappointment.

There should've been something more to be done. Something else.

Callie sat down at her computer and began a personal time line from the date of her birth, through all the significant dates in her life up to the trip back to Virginia, which brought her to the present.

Once you had the events, you had a pattern, she thought. And sitting back, she saw one element of the pattern. From the day she'd met him, Jake had a connection to every major point in her life.

Absently, she reached for a cookie and found the bag empty.

'I've got a stash in my room.'

She jolted, jerked round to see Jake leaning against the doorway. 'Damnit, stop sneaking around, spying on me.'

'You're feeling pretty beat up, aren't you, baby?'

Her stomach slid towards her knees at the slow, soft sound of his voice. 'Don't be nice to me. It drives me crazy.' She turned away, opened the file again. 'It's just a time line, trying to establish a pattern. Go ahead.' She got up so he could have the desk chair and plopped down onto the floor. 'The highlights and lowlights of my life.'

'You slept with Aiken? The Egyptologist? What were you thinking?'

'Just never mind, or I'll start commenting on all the women you've slept with.'

'You don't know all the women I've slept with. I'm going to shoot this file to my laptop. I'll download it later, play with it.'

'Fine, great. Do what you want.' Why did she want to cry? Why the hell did she want to cry? 'You always did anyway.'

He sent the file to his email, then got up and walked to her. 'You always thought so.' He sat down beside her, trailed his fingers over her shoulder. 'I didn't want to leave that day in Colorado.'

Ah, yes, that was why she wanted to cry. 'Then why did you?'

'You made it clear it was what you wanted. You said you wanted a divorce.'

'Yeah, and you jumped on that quick, fast and in a hurry. You and that six-foot brunette were out of there like a shot, and I got a divorce petition in the mail two weeks later.'

'I didn't leave with her. You never trusted me, Cal. You never believed in me, in us, for that matter.'

'I asked if you'd slept with her. You refused to deny it.'

'I refused to deny it,' he agreed, 'because it was insulting. It still is. If you believed that I'd break a vow to you, that I'd break faith with you over another woman, then the marriage was a bad joke.'

She had her own wounds. 'Just once I wanted you to fight *for* me instead of with me. I wanted that, so I'd know what you never told me.'

'What? What didn't I tell you?'

'That you loved me.'

She didn't know whether to laugh or weep at the shock on his face.

'That's bullshit, Callie. Of course I told you.'

'Not once. You never once said the words. "Mmm, babe, I love your body" doesn't count, Graystone. "Oh that, yeah, me too." I'd get that sometimes when I said it to you. But you never said it to me. Obviously you couldn't. Because one thing you're not is a liar.'

'Why didn't you say all this before? Why didn't you just ask me if I loved you?'

'Because I'm a girl, you big stupid jerk.' She pushed to her feet, headed for the door.

'Don't.' He didn't move, didn't rise and didn't raise his voice. Surprise, because everything in their history indicated he would do all three, stopped her. 'Don't walk out. Let's at least finish this part without turning away from each other. You didn't ask,' he continued quietly, 'because in our culture, verbalisation of emotions is as important as demonstrations of emotions. If you'd had to ask, the answer had no meaning.'

'Bingo, Professor.'

'Because I didn't tell you, you thought I slept with other women.'

'You came with a track record. Jake the Rake.'

'Damnit, Callie. I was never unfaithful to you. Being accused of it . . . It hurt. So I got mad, because I'd rather be mad than hurt.'

'You didn't sleep with her?'

'Not her, not anyone else. There was no one but you.'

She had to sit down again, so merely slid down the door. 'She left her bra in our room. Half under the bed,' Callie continued. 'And I thought, our bed. He brought that bitch to our bed.'

'I didn't. I can only tell you I didn't. Not in our bed, not anywhere. Not her, Callie, not anyone, since the first time I touched you.'

'OK.'

'OK?' he repeated. 'That's it? Why didn't you tell me about this when it happened?'

'Because I was afraid if I showed you the proof you'd admit it. If you'd said, yeah, you slipped but it wouldn't happen again, I'd've let it go. So I got mad,' she said with a sigh. 'Because *I'd* rather be mad than hurt, too.'

He moved to sit in front of her so their knees bumped. 'We've been making some progress on being friends this time.'

'I guess we have.'

'We could keep doing that. And I can work on remembering you're a girl while you work on trusting me.' And maybe he could show her a part of himself he'd never thought to share before. 'You know, we never got around to taking that trip west to see my family after we got married. My parents make a good team, a reliable unit. But I don't remember ever hearing either one of them say they loved the other. If I were to phone my parents and tell them I loved them, they'd both be embarrassed. We'd all be embarrassed.'

She felt a warm, unexpected wave of tenderness for him, and brushed his hair away from his face. 'We always talked about our feelings in my house. I doubt a day went by when I didn't hear my parents say I love—to me or to each other. Carlyle did a better job than he could possibly know in connecting the Cullens and the Dunbrooks.'

'What do you mean?'

'Big emotions, verbalised. I'll show you.'

She got up, took the shoebox out of her duffle, handed him a letter.

Dear Jessica,

Happy birthday, sweet sixteen. How excited you must be today. My little girl is a young woman. I look at young women your age, and I think, oh, how lovely and bright and fresh they are. How thrilling it is for them to be on the brink of so much. And how frustrating and difficult. I think about what I'd like to say to you. The talks we might have about your life and where you want it to go.

I know we'd quarrel. I'd give anything just to be able to fight with you, have you storm up to your room and slam the door. I would give anything for that.

Every day and every night, Jessie. You're in my thoughts, my prayers, my dreams. I miss you.

I love you. Mom

'She loved me. Not just the baby she'd lost, but whoever I was. She loved me enough to write that. To give all those letters to me so I'd know I was loved.'

'Knowing you can't love her back.'

'Knowing I can't love her back,' Callie agreed. 'Not this way. Because I have a mother who I did all the things with that Suzanne wrote of wanting to do with me.' She shook her head. 'What I'm trying to say is my mother could have written that. Vivian Dunbrook could have written that kind of letter to me.

'I already have some of the answers. I know where I come from. And I know I can get through this. Because the time line isn't finished until I can give the woman who wrote that letter the rest of the answers.'

SEVEN

DOUG KNOCKED, then decided it was doubtful anyone could hear him over the noise rolling out of Lana's house. Cautious, he opened the door, poked his head in. The dog was barking like a maniac, the phone was ringing, something blasted on the living-room TV and Tyler was wailing.

He could hear Lana's frustrated and close-to-strident voice trying to cut through the din. 'Tyler Mark Campbell, I want you to stop this minute.'

'I wanna go to Brock's house. I don't like you any more.'

'You can't go to Brock's house because I don't have time to take you. And I don't like you very much right now either, but you're stuck with me. Now turn off that television and go up to your room.'

Doug nearly stepped back outside again. None of his business.

'You're mean to me,' Tyler sobbed. 'If I had a daddy he wouldn't be mean to me. I want my daddy instead of you.'

'Oh, Ty. I want your daddy, too.'

He supposed that was it—the child's pitiful sob, the absolute misery in Lana's voice, that pushed him in the door. 'Hey, what's all this?'

She turned. He'd never seen her look less than perfectly groomed, he realised. Now her hair was standing in tufts, her eyes were damp, her feet were bare, and there was a coffee stain splattered over the front of the 'World's Best Mom' T-shirt she wore. He'd been attracted to the stylish, organised attorney. Seduced by the warm, confident woman. Intrigued by the widowed single mother who seemed to effortlessly juggle all the balls in the air. And to his utter astonishment, he fell in love with the messy, frustrated, unhappy woman with toys scattered at her feet.

'Sorry.' She forced a smile. 'We're in bedlam at the moment—'

'She yelled at us.' Ty flung himself at Doug. 'She said we were bad. Can I go home with you?'

'No, you may not go anywhere, young man, but to your room.'

'Why don't you go and answer the phone?' Doug suggested to Lana, jerking his head towards the shrilling phone. 'Give this a minute.'

'I don't want you to . . .' Be here. See this. See *me*. 'Fine,' she snapped.

Doug switched off the television and, carrying Ty, opened the door, whistled for the dog. 'Had a rough morning, haven't you, slugger?'

'Mommy spanked my butt. I don't like her when she's mean.'

'She get mean a lot?'

'Nuh-uh. But she is today.' He lifted his head, aimed a look that managed to be woeful, hopeful and innocent all at once. 'She doesn't like me any more. I put the bad guys in the toilet and it flushed over. But we didn't mean it.'

'Oh boy.' How did a man resist a package like this? He'd gone all his life walking down his own path, satisfied to be alone. Now there was this woman, this boy, this idiot dog. And they all had hooks in his heart.

'Your mom was trying to work.'

'Brock's mom doesn't work.'

His own voice echoed back to him as he'd complained or sulked because his mother had been too busy to give him her undivided attention. *Too busy for me, are you? Well, I'm going to be too busy for you.*

How stupid was that? Hell of a note, he thought, when a four-year-old's tantrum causes an epiphany in a man past thirty.

'Brock's mom isn't your mom. Nobody's more special than your own mom. Nobody in the world.' He held Ty close. 'But you've got a really great mom. It said so on her shirt.'

'She's mad at me. Grandma helped me buy the shirt for Mommy's birthday, and Elmer jumped and made her spill coffee all over it. And when he did, she said a bad word. She said the *S* word.' Remembering it had his lips curving again. 'She said it *two* times. Really loud.'

'Wow. She must've been pretty mad. But we can fix that. Want to fix it?'

Ty sniffed, wiped at his nose with the back of his hand. 'OK.'

Lana had just finished the call when she heard the door open. Tyler came in, clutching a ragged bouquet of black-eyed Susans. 'I'm sorry I did the bad stuff and said the mean things. Don't be mad any more.'

'Oh, Ty.' Weepy, she dropped to her knees to drag him close. 'I'm not mad now. I'm sorry I spanked you and yelled at you. I love you so much.'

'And I'm not going to kill the bad guys in the toilet any more.'

'OK.' She pressed her lips to his brow. 'We're OK. Go ahead and pick up your things, then I'll put the *Star Wars* video on for you.'

'OK! Come on, Elmer!' He raced off with the dog scrambling after him.

Lana pushed at her hair, though it was hopeless, and got to her feet. She walked into the kitchen, where Doug was sipping a mug of coffee.

'I'm sorry you walked in on all that.'

'You mean that I walked in on all that normal?' He thought of his mother again, with some shame. 'One person has to hold all the lines, occasionally some of the lines get snagged.' He lifted a mangled shoe off the counter. 'Which one of them chewed on this?'

She sighed as she filled a vase with water. 'Damn dog nosed it right out of the shoebox while I was trying to deal with the flood in the bathroom.'

'You should've called a plumber.' He bit back a laugh when she bared her teeth at him. 'Oh, you did. I'll take a look at it for you.'

'Doug, I appreciate it, I really do. I appreciate your taking Ty out of the line of fire until I calmed down, and helping him pick the flowers, and offering to stand in as emergency plumber, but it's not your job to fix the toilet. I don't want you to think I expect that sort of thing just because we're dating.'

'How about if you start expecting that sort of thing because I'm in love with you?'

The vase slid out of her fingers and hit the counter. 'What? What?'

'Happened about fifteen minutes ago, when I walked in and saw you.'

'Saw me.' Stupefied, she looked down at herself. 'Saw *this*?'

'You're not perfect. That's a big relief. It's intimidating to think about being with someone for the long haul—which is something I've never tried with anyone before—if she's absolutely perfect. But she spills coffee all over herself and doesn't get round to brushing her hair, yells at her kid when he deserves it, that's worth thinking about.'

'I don't know what to say.' What to think. What to do. 'I'm not . . .'

'Ready,' he finished. 'So, why don't you just tell me where the plunger is, and I'll see what I can do.'

'It's, ah . . .' She waved a hand overhead. 'Already up there.'

When he walked out, she braced a hand on the counter. He'd fallen in love with her because of coffee stains and messy hair. Oh God, she realised as her heart fluttered, she was in trouble.

This time when the phone rang, she picked it up absently. Minutes later, she was streaking upstairs where Doug, Ty and the dog all huddled round the toilet. 'Out. Everybody out. I have to shower. Doug, forget everything I just said about not expecting, because I'm about to take terrible advantage of you.'

He glanced at Ty, then at her. 'In front of witnesses?'

'Ha-ha. Please, I beg you, take Ty downstairs, scoop up everything that doesn't look like it belongs in the home of a brilliant attorney. Stuff it in a closet. Put the dog out back. Ty, you're going to Brock's after all.'

'But I don't wanna now—'

'Come on, pal.' Doug started the scooping with Ty. 'We'll have a man-to-man talk about the futility of arguing with a woman when she has a certain look in her eye.'

Lana was jumping out of the shower when Doug gave a cursory knock and walked in. 'What's going on?' he demanded.

'Richard Carlyle just called from the airport. He'll be here at noon. I have to look like a professional instead of a raving lunatic. I have to contact Callie, go through the files again.' She grabbed a slate-blue jacket. 'I have to call Jo—Brock's mother—and see if he can go over there for a couple of hours. Then I'm going to impose on you to drive him over.'

'I'll drive him over, but I'm coming back.'

Lana opened the door. Her voice was coolly polite. 'Mr Carlyle? I'm Lana Campbell.' She offered a hand. 'I'd like to thank you for coming all this way to speak with us. I believe you've met both Dr Dunbrook and Dr Graystone. This is Douglas Cullen. Please sit down, Can I get you coffee, or something cold.'

'I won't be here that long.' But he took a seat. 'I checked on the documents Dr Dunbrook and her associate left in my office. While it's true that the papers for the adoption by Elliot and Vivian Dunbrook of the infant girl were not properly filed—'

'They were fraudulent.'

'They were not properly filed. This oversight might very well have been the fault of the court, a law clerk, an associate or assistant.'

'I hardly find that valid'—Lana took a seat as well—'as the petition for adoption and the final decree were both signed by all parties and bore what appears to be a forged court seal. And the exchange—fee for child—was made in your father's presence.'

'A number of infants were placed through my father's practice. And many people worked on the cases he took. To accuse him of taking part in this sort of heinous baby bartering is ridiculous.'

'If you're so sure he wasn't involved, why don't you ask him?'

'I'm afraid that's just not possible. He's dead. My father died ten days ago. In his home on Grand Cayman. I've just returned from there.'

Callie felt the bottom drop out from under her. 'We're supposed to just take your word that he died? So conveniently?'

'He'd been ill for some time.' He opened his briefcase. 'I have copies of his medical reports, his death certificate and his obituary. You can easily have them substantiated.' Carlyle got to his feet. 'It's over, Dr Dunbrook. He can't answer your questions, explain or defend himself. And I won't see my family punished. I'll show myself out.'

Jake heard the deep, sorrowful sound of the cello. Callie was sulking.

He walked round to the kitchen where Dory was working at the table. 'We found some great stuff today. The hand axe Matt dug up was amazing,' she offered.

'Yeah, a good find.' He opened the refrigerator, reached for the wine.

'I'm, ah, coordinating Bill's notes. I thought somebody should.' She looked up at the ceiling. The music was soft and distant, almost like the night sounds whispering through the open window. 'That's pretty, but so damn sad. She's really talented. Still, it's kind of weird. An archaeologist who hauls a cello around to digs so she can play Beethoven.'

'Yeah, she just couldn't play the harmonica like everybody else. Don't work too late.' He carried the wine and two glasses upstairs. He knew what it meant when Callie had her door closed, but he ignored the signal and opened it without knocking. She sat in a chair, facing the window as she drew the bow over the strings.

'Go away, Jake.'

In response he sat down on the floor, poured the wine and drank.

Irritation flickered over her face, then smoothed out. She set the bow again, then played the two-toned warning notes from *Jaws*.

He made it for nearly thirty seconds before his skin began to crawl. 'Cut it out.' But he had to laugh. 'You're such a bitch.'

'Damn right. Why won't you go away?'

'Last time I did that, I stayed mad, sad and lonely for the best part of a year. This time I'm not going away. I know what you're thinking.'

'The bastard's dead, and I'll never look him in the eye and tell him who I am. Simpson and his wife are gone, and I don't have the time and money to track them down.'

'Whatever price Carlyle'd pay wouldn't change what he did. What you do now, for the Cullens, your parents and for yourself, is what counts.'

'What *am* I going to do, Jake? I can't be Jessica for Suzanne and Jay. I can't ease the guilt my parents feel for their part in all this. The one thing I felt I could do was get down to the answers.'

'What answers do you need?'

'How many others are there? Others like me, others like Barbara Halloway? Do I look for them? It's only prolonging the anxiety for my parents, and the unhappiness for the Cullens. I'd get some personal and intellectual satisfaction from finishing the pattern. When I weigh that against everything else, it's just not heavy enough.'

She bent over to pick up her glass of wine. 'Two people are dead, but I can't be sure they're connected to this now. I can't even be certain Lana's fire's a part of it. By all accounts Carlyle was old and sick. He sure as hell didn't bop up to rural Maryland and kill two people, shoot at you, knock me unconscious and burn down Lana's office.'

'Must've made a hell of a lot of money selling babies over the years.' Jake studied the wine in his glass. 'Enough to hire the kind of people who kill, knock women out and burn down buildings.'

'Why do you want me obsessing on this?'

'I don't. You won't stop obsessing until you finish it.'

'I can't figure out what you're looking for.'

'Want a surprise? I want you to be happy. Because . . .' He paused, drank deep. 'I love you more than I realised.'

She felt the shock of it, and the thrill, blast straight through her heart and down to her toes. 'You need to guzzle wine before you can say that?'

'Yeah. Give me a break, I'm new at this.'

Later, when she lay sprawled beside him, her breath still choppy, her skin slicked with sweat, she smiled into the dark. 'Feeling pretty happy.'

He traced the curve of her hip, her waist, with his hand. 'It's a start.'

'I want to tell you something.' She sighed. 'I don't know a couple more devoted to each other than my parents. But it was my mother who had the need. She gave up her music, moved away from her family, made herself into the perfect doctor's wife because she needed my father's approval. It was her choice, I know that. But I always looked at her as a little less. I always promised myself I'd never put myself second for anyone. I'd never need someone so much that I couldn't be a whole person without him.'

'I never wanted you to give anything up.'

'No. But I was terrified I would anyway. I didn't want to need you, because that made me weak and you strong. And I was already crazy because I loved you more than you loved me, and that gave you the edge.'

'So it was a contest?'

'Partially. The more I felt at a disadvantage, emotionally, the more I pushed you. I wanted you to prove you loved me.'

'And I never did.'

'No, you never did. And I wanted to hurt you—because I didn't think I could. You can barely choke out that you love me. I'm afraid to love you. What the hell are we supposed to do?'

'Sounds like a match made in heaven to me.'

Let the dead stay dead, Callie thought as she gently brushed soil from the finger bones of a woman who'd stayed dead for thousands of years. She wanted to walk away. What the hell was her responsibility anyway—here, or to somewhere she'd been for three months of her life? Why should she risk herself, her happiness, maybe even the lives of others just to know all the facts about something that could never be changed?

'Take five.' Jake'd been watching her for several minutes, measuring the weariness and the despair that had played over her face.

'I'm done. I'm just done. I want to go back home.' There were tears in her throat. 'I want to feel normal.'

'OK.' He drew her against him. 'We'll take a few days. Let me get in touch with Leo.'

She drew back, tried to steady herself. And saw Suzanne pull to the side of the road. 'Oh God. That's perfect. That's just perfect.'

'Callie.' Suzanne actually seemed happy as she came through the gate. 'Jake. I thought Jay would beat me here, but I see he's running late.'

'I'm sorry. We were supposed to meet for something today?'

'No. We just wanted to . . . Well, I won't wait for him. Happy birthday.' She held out a gift bag.

'Thanks, but it's not my birthday until . . .' Realisation came with a quick jolt. Jessica's birthday.

'I realised you might not think of it, but I've waited a long time to wish you a happy birthday in person.'

She saw no sorrow or regret on Suzanne's face. Only a joy that left her unable to turn away. 'Well.' She stared down at the bag.

'I made you a cake. I don't mind telling you that not everyone gets a cake baked in Suzanne's actual kitchen by Suzanne's actual hands these days. There's Jay now. Do you have a few minutes?'

'Sure.'

'I'll have him get the cake out of the car for me. Be right back.'

Callie stood, the shiny bag dangling from her fingers. 'How is she doing this? How is she making it a celebration?'

'You know why, Callie.'

'Because my life matters to her. It never stopped mattering.' She looked down at the gift bag, then back towards the bones of a long-dead woman. 'She's not going to let me walk away.'

'Babe.' He leaned down to kiss her. 'You were never going to let yourself walk away. Let's go and have some cake.'

The team descended on the cake like locusts on wheat. Maybe, Callie thought as she heard the laughter, it was just what they'd all needed to push away the guilt and depression over Bill's death.

She took the wrapped package Jay offered her. 'Suzanne will tell you picking out gifts isn't my strong point.'

'Car mats. For our fourth anniversary.'

He winced. 'And I've never lived it down.'

Amused, Callie finished ripping off the wrapping. They seemed so easy together. 'Well, this beats car mats.' She ran her hand over the cover of a coffee-table book on Pompeii. 'It's great. Thanks.'

'If you don't like it, you can—'

'I do like it.' It wasn't so hard to lean over, touch her lips to his cheek. Much harder to watch him struggle to control his stunned gratitude.

She picked up the gift bag, riffled through the matching tissue paper for the jewellery box.

'They were my grandmother's.' Suzanne's fingers twined with Jay's as Callie drew out the single strand of pearls. 'She gave them to my mother on her wedding day, and my mother gave them to me on mine. I wanted you to have them. Even though you never knew them, it's a link.'

'They're beautiful. I do appreciate it.' Callie looked back towards the square in the ground where ancient bones lay waiting. Jake was right, she thought. She'd never be able to walk away.

She put the pearls back gently in the box. 'One day you'll tell me about them. And that's how I'll know them.'

Callie worked on her laptop at the site until dark, then stretched out to stare up at the stars and plot out her next workday in her mind. Matt and Digger were to relieve her and Jake at two. There was an utter peace here, in the night, in the open.

She could hear the faint scratch of Jake's pencil over paper. 'Why didn't you make a living out of that? Out of, you know, art?'

'Not good enough. Not to mention it wouldn't have been macho enough for me when I started college. Bad enough I never intended to work the family ranch, but then to work at becoming a painter? Hell, my old man would've died of embarrassment.'

'He wouldn't have supported you?'

Jake flipped a page on his sketch pad and started on another. 'He wouldn't have stopped me, or tried to. But he wouldn't have understood. I wouldn't have either. Men in my family work the land, or with horses, with cattle. I was the first in my family to earn a college degree.'

'I never knew that.'

He shrugged. 'Just the way it is. Sending me to college was a sacrifice.'

'Are they proud of you?'

He was silent for a moment. 'The last time I was home, I guess about five, six months ago, I just swung by. Didn't let them know I was coming. My mother put an extra plate on the table. Well, two, one for Digger. My father came in, shook my hand. No fatted calf, if you get me. But later on, I happened to glance at the shelf in the living room. There were two books on anthropology there, mixed in with my parents books. It meant a lot to me to see that, to know they'd been reading about what I do.'

'That's the nicest story you've ever told me about them. Any water in the cooler?'

'Probably.' He shifted to open it. But he stayed turned away for so long, she kicked him in the ankle.

'Is there or not?'

'Yeah.' He turned back. 'Somebody's in the woods with a flashlight.' He spoke in the same casual tone as he handed her the bottle of water.

Her eyes stayed locked with his for a beat, then shifted over his shoulder. She watched the beam of light move through the trees.

'Why don't you go in the trailer, call the sheriff?'

'Why?' Slowly, Callie uncapped the water bottle and took a drink. 'Because if I do, you'll head out there without me. We'll check it out first. Dolan and Bill were both alone. If whoever's out there is looking to repeat the performance, he'll have to deal with two of us.'

'All right. We stay together. Agreed?'

Jake switched on the flashlight, aimed it at the oncoming beam. As that beam turned fast to the west, both he and Callie rushed forward.

'He's heading towards the road.' Instinctively Callie veered in the same direction, plunged into the trees. 'We can cut him off.' Then the beam they chased switched off.

She closed her eyes, concentrated on sounds. And heard the fast slap of feet on ground. 'He changed directions again.' She pointed.

'We'll never catch him. He's got too much of a lead. Stupid for him to be out here with a light to begin with. A moron could figure one of us would spot it.'

Even as he said the words, their import struck both of them. Seconds later, the first explosion split the air. 'The trailer.' Jake watched the tongue of flame shoot skywards. 'Son of a bitch.'

Callie came out of the trees at a dead run, thinking only of reaching the fire extinguisher in her car. Her body hit the ground with an impact that jarred bones as Jake fell on top of her. 'Propane!' he shouted.

And the world exploded.

Heat swooped over her, a burning hand that seared her skin and stole her breath. Tiny points of flame showered down like rain. Debris followed like shrapnel, thudding to the ground in twisted, flaming balls.

When Jake rolled off her, she shoved up to her knees. Smouldering wreckage lay scattered around them, and what was left of the trailer burned madly. She leapt towards Jake as he tore off his smoking shirt.

'You're bleeding. Let me see how bad. Are you burned?'

'Not much.' Though he wasn't entirely sure of that. But the searing pain in his arm was from a gash, not from burns. 'Better call nine-one-one.'

'You call.' She wrenched the phone out of her back pocket. 'I'll get the first-aid kit out of the Land Rover.'

She scrambled up, tore off in a run. Calm, she ordered herself as she yanked the door open. But she remembered how he'd shielded her head with his arms. Her body with his body.

She grabbed the first-aid kit and a bottle of water and ran back.

He was sitting where she'd left him. He'd told her to go in the trailer, he remembered. 'You didn't go in the trailer like I told you to. If you had—' He put his good arm round her, and they helped each other to their feet. 'Looks like it's our lucky night.' He let out a huge sigh. 'Digger's going to be pissed.'

Any records and specimens that had been stored in the trailer until they could be transported were gone. Hours of painstaking work destroyed in a heartbeat. Fire fighters, cops, emergency workers trampled over the site. It would take weeks to repair the damage, to calculate the loss. To start again.

'Whoever was in the woods was a diversion.' The anger was beginning to sharpen Callie's voice now, replacing the shaky shock. 'He drew us away so someone else could fire the trailer.'

Hewitt studied the smouldering heap. 'But you didn't see anybody?'

'No, we didn't see anybody. We were a hundred feet away, in the trees. We'd just started back when we heard the first explosion.'

'The propane tanks.'

'The first one. It sounded like a damn cannon, and then the hero here tackled me. Then the second one blew. But whoever was in the woods was heading back towards the road. Probably had his ride parked close by.'

'I'm thinking so,' Hewitt agreed. 'I don't believe in curses, Dr Dunbrook, but I do believe in trouble. And that you've got.'

'It's connected, to everything I told you about Carlyle, the Cullens. It's just a way to scare me off this site, away from Woodsboro, away from the answers.'

'Sheriff.' One of the deputies trotted up. 'You'd better see this.'

They followed Hewitt towards the pond, to the section where Callie had worked. Lying in the ruler-straight square was a department-store mannequin dressed in olive drab chinos and shirt. Round its neck hung a hand-lettered sign that read R.I.P.

Callie balled her hands into fists at her sides. 'Those are my clothes. The son of a bitch has been through my things.'

EIGHT

IT WOULDN'T HAVE BEEN difficult to get into the house, Jake thought, yet again. The fact that the police had found no signs of forced entry meant nothing. Someone had been inside, selected Callie's clothes.

Someone had left them a very clear message.

He had no doubt that whoever had blown up the tanks would have done so even if Callie had been in the trailer.

Carlyle was dead. The Simpsons? He considered them. Both were fit, fit enough, he imagined, for one of them to have taken a quick sprint through the woods while the other dumped the effigy in the trench, then set a small charge on the tank. But his gut told him Barb and Hank were as far away from Callie and Woodsboro as they could manage.

They'd known just when to run, he remembered. And he had a feeling he knew how.

He walked towards the driveway as Doug pulled up. 'Where is she?'

'Asleep. Appreciate you getting here so fast.' He told Doug about the effigy of Callie, left in the ancient grave.

'Can you get her away from here?'

'Oh yeah, absolutely. If I sedate her. They stood in silence for a moment. 'She's dug in here now,' Jake said at length. 'She won't budge until she finds what she's after.'

'I can go to Boston. Ask some questions. But when I'm gone, I'm not here to look out for my family, or for Lana and Ty. I can ask my father and my grandfather to move in with my mother for a few days. But Lana's alone out there.'

'How would she feel about a houseguest? Digger could bunk there. If I needed somebody to look out for my family, that's who I'd ask. Your main problem will be your lady might fall in love with him.'

'That's reassuring. It has to still be going on, doesn't it? If we don't find the answers, it's never going to stop.'

Callie was still sleeping when Jake went up to her bedroom. He lay down beside her. Then he dropped off the edge of fatigue into sleep.

He woke on a blast of pain when he rolled over on his bad arm. And saw Callie was gone. He sprang up and bolted from the room. The silence of the house had him shouting her name before he was halfway down the stairs.

When she rushed out of his office, he didn't know whether to laugh at the annoyance on her face or fall to his knees and kiss her feet. 'Where the hell were you? Where the hell is everybody?'

'I'm working on your computer.'

'Where's the team?'

'Spread out. On-site, waiting to let us know when the cops clear it. At the college, using some of the equipment, in Baltimore at the lab.'

'Then let's get started.' He headed out of the room. 'We're going to look through their things.' He hefted Chuck's backpack from the corner of the living room, dumped it on the table and unzipped it.

'We've got no right to do this, Jake.'

'Question.' He stopped what he was doing long enough to look at her. 'Who knew we were heading to Virginia the other day?'

She lifted her shoulders. 'You and me, Lana and Doug.'

'And everybody in the kitchen when we were talking about schedules. Everybody who heard you say you had some personal business in Virginia.'

She sat down, hard. 'My God.'

'Busybody across the street said they were loading up about ten. We were getting up from the table right around nine. It only took a phone call, telling them you were coming and to get the hell out.'

No longer reluctant, she searched through the contents of the backpack, then started on Frannie's. They found a notebook wrapped up in a T-shirt.

'It's a diary.' Callie sat cross-legged now and began to read. 'Starts on the first day they joined the dig. Huh, she thinks you're really hot.'

'Yeah?'

She scanned words, flipped pages. 'Rosie's nice. Patient. Dory: snooty and superior. Sonya's friendly, but kind of boring.'

She paused, scowled. 'I am not scary and bossy.'

'Yeah, you are. What else does she say about me?'

'Bob's got a dumpy ass and sweats too much. Bill . . .' She had to pause, gather herself. 'She thinks Bill's smart, but too much of a geek. A lot of daily minutiae. And . . . then there's a run-down of what happened to Bill. Nothing new.' Still, she jumped when the phone rang.

'We're cleared,' she said to Jake when she hung up. 'We need to get out to the site.'

'OK.' He began repacking Frannie's gear. 'But we're going to go through the others first chance we get.'

It only took Doug a day and a half to track down what he considered a reasonable lead: Maureen O'Brian, who had worked at the country club where both Carlyle and his first wife had been members.

'Goodness, I haven't seen Mrs Carlyle for twenty-five years,' Maureen said. 'I did her nails every week, Monday afternoons, for three years.'

'Did you know her husband?'

'Of him, certainly. He wasn't good enough for her, if you ask me."

'Why do you say that?'

Her mouth went prim. 'A man who can't be faithful to his wedding vows is never good enough for the woman he made them to. His side piece, she'd come into the salon now and then herself.'

'You knew her?'

'One of them anyway. This one was married herself, and was a doctor of all things.. Dr Roseanne Yardley. My friend Colleen did her hair.' She smirked. 'Not a natural blonde.'

Natural or not, she was still blonde when Doug found her finishing her rounds at Boston General. Tall, stately, that sweep of hair perfectly coiffed, Roseanne had a clipped, Bostonian voice. 'Yes, I knew Marcus and Lorraine Carlyle. I really don't have time to discuss old acquaintances.'

'My information is that you and Marcus were more than acquaintances.'

She strode into a small office, moved directly to the desk and sat behind it. 'What do you want?'

'I have evidence that Marcus Carlyle headed an organisation that profited from fraudulent adoptions by kidnapping infants and selling them to childless couples. And that he used and employed members of the medical profession in his organisation.'

She didn't even blink. 'That's perfectly ridiculous.'

Doug didn't budge, even when she pushed to her feet. 'My sister was stolen when she was three months old and days later sold to a couple out of Carlyle's Boston office. I have proof of that. I have evidence linking another Boston doctor to that event.'

Very slowly, she sat down again. 'What doctor?'

'Henry Simpson. His current wife was one of the obstetrics nurses on duty the night my sister was born, in Maryland.'

'If this is true, if any portion of this is true, I don't see how my regrettable affair with Marcus has anything to do with it.'

'Accumulating data. How long were you involved?'

'Nearly a year.' Roseanne sighed and sat back. 'He was twenty-five years older than me, and quite fascinating.'

'Did you ever discuss your work, your patients?'

'I'm sure I did. I'm in paediatrics. A major part of Marcus's practice was adoption. We were both dedicated to children. I certainly don't remember him ever trying to draw specific information from me, and none of my patients was kidnapped.'

'But some were adopted?'

'Of course. That's hardly surprising.'

'Tell me about him. Why did the affair end?'

'He was a very calculating man, and one with no sense of fidelity. You may find that odd as we were having an extramarital affair, but I expected him to be faithful while we were. When I discovered he was having another affair while we were involved, I broke it off. Learning he was cheating on me with his young secretary was just a bit too much of a cliché. I heard she was one of the few from his practice here Marcus took with him when he went to Seattle.'

'Do you know anything about Carlyle or her since?'

'I heard he divorced Lorraine, and I was surprised when he remarried that it wasn't the secretary.' She tapped her pen. 'You've intrigued me, Mr Cullen. Enough that I may ask a few questions in a few quarters myself. Leave me a number where you can be reached.'

Doug settled into his hotel room, searched a beer out of the minibar and called Lana. There was some noise, some giggling, then a very warm female laugh. 'Hello?'

'What was that?'

'Doug? I was hoping you'd call.' Something that sounded like an ape, followed by hysterical childish laughter drowned out her voice. 'God, it's a madhouse in there. Digger's cooking. He's a very reassuring, not to mention entertaining presence. He's wonderful with Ty. Thus far, though it's a struggle, I've been able to resist my lust for him. Though he warns me it's a losing battle.'

Doug dropped down on the bed, scratched his head. 'I've never been jealous before. It's lowering to have my first experience with it over a guy who looks like a garden gnome.'

She laughed, then lowered her voice. 'I suppose I should ask you what you've found out.'

'Enough to know Carlyle liked women, and more than one at a time. I've got a gut feeling the secretary is a key link. I'm going to try to focus in on finding her.'

Callie was irritable, jumpy and distracted. Intellectually, she knew her reaction was exactly what they wanted. But the core of the problem was not knowing who *they* were. There was no one to fight, and no place for her to gather and channel her anger.

She took a long, critical study of herself in the little hand mirror from her pack.

She'd looked worse, she decided. But she'd sure as hell looked better. Maybe she'd give herself a facial. Rosie always had plenty of girl stuff in her pack. She started down to the kitchen then stopped halfway when she saw Jake at the door, and her parents on the other side.

They made an awkward tableau, she thought. How many times had they actually met, face to face? Twice? No, three times, she corrected.

'Well, this is a surprise.' She tried to keep her voice easy and bright, but the tension inside her, around her, was thick enough to drink.

'We'd've been here an hour ago if your mother hadn't insisted we stop for this,' Elliot said.

'A birthday cake. We could hardly come to wish you a happy birthday and not bring a cake. I know it's not till tomorrow, but I couldn't resist.'

Callie's smile felt frozen, but she reached out for the box.

'We thought you might like to go out to dinner. We've got a room in a hotel just over the river. We're told the restaurant's very good.'

'Well, I . . .'

'I can lock the cake up somewhere,' Jake offered. 'Otherwise, it'll be a memory when you get back.'

'Like I'd trust you around baked goods. I'll hide it. And you'll have to come with us.'

'I've got work . . .' he began.

'Me too. But I'm not turning down a free meal away from the horde, and I'm not leaving you with this cake. I'll be down in ten,' she told her surprised parents, then hurried out with the cake.

Jake drummed his fingers on his thigh. 'Listen, I'm going to cut out. I know you want some time alone with Callie.'

'She wants you to come.' There was such simple bafflement in Vivian's voice, Jake nearly laughed. 'So you'll come.'

'Mrs Dunbrook—'

'You'll need to change your shirt. And wear a jacket. A tie would be nice. Go on and change. We'll wait.'

'Yes, ma'am.'

Elliot waited until they were alone to lean down and kiss his wife. 'That was very sweet of you.'

'I don't know how I feel about it, or him, but if she wants him, she gets him. That's all there is to it.'

The shirt needed to be ironed, Jake discovered. Trying to remember if the shirt had been laundered after the last wearing, he sniffed at it. OK, points for him. It didn't smell. Yet.

He'd probably sweat through it before they got to the entrée.

Then he ran a hand over his face and remembered he hadn't shaved in days. He grabbed his kit and stomped off to the bathroom to take care of it.

A guy shouldn't have to put on a damn jacket and shave to have dinner with people who were going to look at him like the suspicious ex-husband.

He was scraping the razor through lather when the knock sounded. 'What?'

'It's Callie.'

He shoved the door open, one-handed, then grabbed her and yanked her in. 'Get me out of this.'

Her brows winged up. 'Get yourself out of it.'

'Your mother won't let me.'

Her heart warmed. 'Really?'

'She made me change my shirt. It's wrinkled. And I don't have a tie.'

'It's not that wrinkled, and you don't need a tie.'

'You put on a dress.' He batted it out, a vicious accusation.

'You're nervous about having dinner with my parents.'

'I'm not nervous.' He cursed when he nicked his chin. 'I don't see why I'm having dinner with them. They don't want me horning in.'

Look how sweet he was, she thought. Just look at the sweetness she'd ignored. 'Are we trying to get somewhere together, Graystone?'

'I thought we were somewhere.' Then he paused, rinsed off the blade. 'Yeah, we're trying to get somewhere.'

'Then this is part of it. It's a part I can't skip over again.'

At the restaurant they talked about the dig. A topic that seemed safest all round. Though no one mentioned the deaths, the fires.

'I don't think Callie's ever mentioned what got you into this kind of work.' Elliot approved the wine, and glasses were poured.

'Ah . . . I was interested in the evolutions and formations of cultures.' Jake ordered himself not to grab for his glass and glug wine like medicine. 'What causes people to form their traditions . . .'

And the man wasn't asking for a damn lecture. 'Actually, it started when I was a kid. My father's part Apache, part English, part French Canadian. My mother's part Irish, Italian and German and French. That's a lot mixed into one. So how do you get there? All those pieces have a trail back. I like following trails.'

'And you're helping Callie follow hers now.'

Everything stilled for a moment. He could feel Vivian stiffen beside him, saw Callie lift a hand, lay it on her father's in a gesture of gratitude.

'Yeah. She doesn't like help, so you have to badger her.'

'We raised her to be independent, and she took it very much to heart.'

'You didn't intend her to be stubborn, hardheaded and obstinate?'

'I call it being self-sufficient, confident and goal-orientated.' Callie broke off a piece of bread, nibbled. 'A real man wouldn't have a problem with it.'

He passed her the butter. 'Still here, aren't I?'

She buttered a piece of bread, handed it to him. 'Got rid of you once.'

'If you'll excuse me a minute.' Vivian pushed back from the table. As she rose, she laid a hand on Callie's shoulder, squeezed.

'Ah . . . I'll go with you. What?' she hissed.

Inside the rest room, Vivian took out her compact. 'You're twenty-nine years old. You're in charge of your own life. But I'm still your mother.'

'Of course you are. Nothing changes that.'

'And as your mother, I exercise the right to stick my nose into your business. Are you and Jacob reconciled?'

'Oh. Well. Hmmm. I don't know if that's a word that will ever apply to me and Jake. But we're sort of together again. In a way.'

'Are you sure this is what you want?'

'He's always been what I wanted,' Callie said simply. 'I can't explain why. We didn't put much work into the first time.'

'You had good sex. Please.' Vivian leaned back against the basin when Callie registered surprise. 'I've had plenty of good sex myself. You and Jacob have a strong physical attraction to each other. He's good in bed?'

'He's . . . he's excellent.'

'That's important.' Vivian turned to the mirror, dusted powder on her nose. 'But equally important, from my point of view, is that he's sitting out there with your father. He came here with us tonight, and he didn't want to. That tells me he's willing to work. You make sure you shovel your own load, and the two of you may just have something.'

'I messed it up so bad the first time.'

'I'm sure you did. But I'm also absolutely certain he messed up more.'

Callie grinned. 'I love you, Mom.'

Callie waited for his comments on the drive home, then finally asked. 'So? What did you think?'

'Good. I haven't had prime rib in months.'

'Not the food, you moron. My parents. Dr and Mrs Dunbrook.'

'Good, too. Holding up their end. It takes a lot of spine to do that.'

'They liked you. And you held up your end, too. So thanks.'

'I did wonder about this one thing.'

'Which is?'

'Are you going to get two birthdays every year? If I'm supposed to come up with two presents, it's really going to tick me off.'

'I haven't seen one yet.'

'I'll get round to it.' He pulled in the lane, bumped up the narrow gravel road.

She got out of the car, stood for a moment in the cooling night air. 'Love's a lot of work, so I'm told. So we'll work.'

He took her hand, lifted it to his lips. Dangling from his thumb and index finger was a bracelet, glittering gold, sparkling from the complex etchings cut in a complex Byzantine design. 'Happy birthday.'

She traced her finger over the gold. 'It's . . . Jeez, Jacob. Wow.'

'If I'd known a bauble would shut you up, I'd've buried you in them a long time ago.'

'You can't spoil it with insults. I love it.'

He took her hand again, walked her to the house. He could hear the sounds of the television as he eased the front door open. 'Crowded in there. Let's go straight up.'

She stepped into her room. 'Where the hell did that come from?'

The bed was in the centre of the room. It was old, the iron headboard painted silver. There were new sheets on the mattress, and a hand-lettered sign propped on the pillow:

HAPPY BIRTHDAY, CALLIE, FROM THE TEAM.

'Wow.' Delighted, she hurried over to sit on the side of the bed and bounce. 'This is great. I should go down and thank everyone.'

Grinning, Jake closed the door. 'Thank me first.'

Maybe it was the new bed, or the sex. Callie's mood was strong and bright. She felt so in tune with her team—and so guilty at the memory of searching backpacks—that she gave everyone birthday cake for breakfast and was delighted to see Leo wander into the kitchen.

'Happy birthday.' He set a package down on the counter. 'And I want to make it clear that I had nothing to do with it.'

Callie poked the box with her index finger. 'It isn't alive, is it?' She pulled out a shallow, somewhat square-shaped dish glazed in streaks of blue, green and yellow.

'Wow. It's a . . . what?'

'I said I had nothing to do with it,' Leo reminded her.

'Ashtray?' Rosie ventured.

'Too big.' Bob looked over her shoulder to study it. 'Soup bowl?'

'Not deep enough.' Dory pursed her lips. 'Serving bowl, maybe.'

'You could put, like, potpourri in it. Or something,' said Fran.

'Dust catcher,' was Matt's verdict.

'Art,' Jake corrected. 'Which needs no other purpose.'

'There you go.' Callie turned it over to show the base. 'Look, she signed it. I have an original Clara Greenbaum. Thanks, Leo.' It was, very possibly, the ugliest thing she'd ever seen.

'Potpourri.' Rosie gave her a bolstering pat on the shoulder.

'What are you going to call it when you thank her?' Jake wondered as they started out to the car, to get to work.

'A present.'

Suzanne wiped her nervous hands on the hips of her slacks. She steeled herself, squared her shoulders, lifted her chin and opened the door to Vivian Dunbrook.

'Mrs Cullen. Thank you so much for seeing me.'

'Please come in.'

'Such a beautiful spot.' Vivian stepped inside. If there were nerves, they didn't show in her voice. 'Your gardens are wonderful.'

'A hobby of mine.' Back straight, face composed, Suzanne led the way into the living room. 'Please, sit down. Can I get you anything?'

'No, please, don't trouble.' Vivian chose a chair, ordered herself to sit slowly and not just collapse off her trembling legs.

She could be just as cool, Suzanne told herself. Just as classy and polite. She sat down, crossed her legs, smiled. 'Are you in the area long?'

'Just a day or two. We wanted to see the project . . . Oh, this is awkward. I thought I knew what to say, how to say it. I practised what I would say to you. But . . .' Emotion clogged Vivian's voice. 'But now, I don't know what to say to you, or how to say it. I'm sorry? What good is it for me to tell you I'm sorry? It won't change anything, it won't give back what was taken from you. And how can I be sorry, all the way sorry? How can I regret having Callie. I can't even imagine what you've been through.'

'No, you can't. Every time you held her, it should've been me holding her. I should've told her bedtime stories and worried late at night when she was sick. When you took her to school the first day and watched her walk away from you, it should have been me who felt so sad and so proud. And I should've been allowed to feel that sense of loss when she went off to college. That little empty space inside.' Suzanne fisted a hand over her heart. 'The one that has pride at the edges of it, but feels so small and lonely inside. But all I've ever had was that empty space.'

They sat, stiffly, in the lovely room, with the hot river of their bitterness churning between them.

'I can't give those things back to you.' Vivian kept her head up. 'And I know, in my heart, that if we'd learned this ten years ago, twenty, I would've fought to keep them from you. To keep her, whatever the cost.'

Suzanne leaned forward as if poised to leap. 'I gave her life.'

'Yes. I'll never have that bond with her, and I'll always know you do. So will she, and it will always matter to her. She'll never be completely mine again.' She paused, fighting for composure. 'I can't possibly understand how you feel, Mrs Cullen. You can't possibly understand how I feel. But I ache because neither of us can know what Callie's feeling.'

'No.' Suzanne's heart quivered in her breast. 'We can't. All we can do is try to make it less difficult. I don't want her hurt.'

'I . . . I should go, but I wanted to give you these.' Vivian touched the bag she'd set down beside the chair. 'I went through the photographs in our albums, made copies of what I thought you'd like to have.'

She rose, picked up the bag and held it out. Staring at it, Suzanne got slowly to her feet. There was a fist round her heart, squeezing so tight. 'I wanted to hate you,' she declared. 'I wanted you to be a horrible woman. How could I have wanted my daughter raised by a horrible, hateful woman?'

'I know. I didn't want to hear you speak of her with so much love. I wanted you to be angry and cold. And fat.'

Suzanne let out a watery laugh. 'God. I can't believe how much better that makes me feel.' She let herself look into Vivian's eyes. She let herself see. 'I don't know what we're going to do.'

'No, neither do I.'

'But right now, I'd really like to look at the pictures. Why don't we take them to the kitchen? I'll make coffee.'

While they spent two emotional hours going through Callie's pictorial history, Doug once again sat in Roseanne Yardley's office.

'I spent some difficult hours thinking of what you told me. You won't get to Lorraine,' she said. 'Richard will block you there. But . . .' She slid a piece of paper across the desk towards him. 'To the best of my information that's Marcus's secretary's location. I can't promise it's accurate or up to date.'

He glanced down, noted that Dorothy McLain Spencer was reputed to live in Charlotte. 'Thank you.'

'If you find her, I'd like to know.' She rose. 'Marcus said once that helping to place a child in a loving home was the most rewarding part of his job. I believed him. I would swear he believed it, too.'

Lana found herself smiling the minute she heard Doug's voice over the phone. 'Where are you?'

'On my way to the airport. I've got a line on Carlyle's secretary, so I'm heading to Charlotte to check it out.' He gave her the hotel he'd booked. 'Pass that on to my family, will you? Anything going on I should know about?'

'I'm going to be able to move back into my office in a week. Two at the most. On the arson, they know how, but not who. Same goes, to date, for the trailer. We miss you around here.'

'That's nice to know. I'll call once I check into the hotel. When I get back, I'm taking Digger's place. He's out, I'm in. Non-negotiable.

'A challenging phrase to a lawyer.' She was still smiling when she hung up. Then immediately picked up the phone again to put the plan that had formed in her mind into action.

'Time for a lunch break, chief.'

With her face all but in the earth, Callie gently blew soil away from a small stone protrusion. 'I've got something here. Stone.'

Rosie sat back on her heels to open Callie's tea jug. 'Thing's still full. Want a lecture on dehydration?'

'I've been drinking the water. I don't think this is a tool, Rosie.'

Since she'd poured out tea already, Rosie drank it before hopping down to take a look. 'Definitely been worked.'

Callie brushed at the loosened dirt, went back to probing.

'I'm drinking your tea. I'm not going back for my Gatorade.' With a sandwich and drink, Rosie sat down again, watched the stone shape grow. 'You know what that looks like to me?'

'I know what it's starting to look like to me.' Excitement was beginning to skip down her spine. 'Hell, Rosie. It's a day for art.'

'It's a goddamn cow. A goddamn stone cow.' Rosie rubbed her eyes as her vision blurred. 'Whew! Too much sun. You want some pictures?'

'Yeah, let's use the trowel for scale.' She was reaching for her clipboard when she realised Rosie hadn't moved. 'Hey, you OK?'

'Little woozy. Weird. I think I'd better . . .' But even as Callie reached out, Rosie collapsed forward against her.

'Rosie? Hey! Somebody give me a hand.' She braced herself, held the weight while the team and visitors gathered in.

'Everybody move back. I'm a nurse.' A woman pushed through. With one hand monitoring Rosie's pulse, she lifted one of Rosie's eyelids to check her pupils. 'Call an ambulance.'

Jake strode into the emergency room. 'Callie, what did they say?'

'They asked me a bunch of questions. They're not telling me anything. They took her back there somewhere.'

'Call your father. He's a doctor. They'll tell him things they might not tell us.'

'God, I should've thought of that myself. I can't think,' she added as she pulled out her phone. She stepped outside with it, breathed slow and steady as she called her father.

'He's coming,' she told Jake. 'He's coming right away.' She reached down, gripped his hand when she saw the nurse come back.

'You need to help us. You need to tell me what kind of drugs she took. The sooner they know that, the quicker they can treat her.'

'She didn't take any drugs. She doesn't take drugs. Jake?'

'She doesn't use,' he confirmed. 'I was working ten feet away from her most of the morning. She never left the area until lunch break.'

'She didn't take anything. She ate half a sandwich, drank a couple of glasses of iced tea. Then she said something about having too much sun, felt woozy . . . It was my tea. She drank my tea.'

'Was there something in the tea?' the nurse demanded.

'I didn't put anything in it. But . . .'

Jake yanked out his phone. 'I'm calling the police.'

She sat outside on the kerb with her head on her knees. She didn't look up when her father sat beside her. 'She's dead, isn't she?'

'No. No, honey. They've stabilised her. She's very weak, but she's stable. She ingested a dangerous dosage of Seconal.'

'Seconal? Could it have killed her?'

'Possibly. I want you to come home with us, Callie.'

'I can't.' She pushed to her feet. 'Don't ask me.'

'Why?' Angry now, he rose, hurried after her, grabbed her arm. 'This isn't worth your life. You're ten pounds lighter than your friend. The dosage she took could have killed you.'

'I won't be safe until all of it's uncovered. I'm afraid none of us will.'

'It was one of our team,' Jake said flatly, the anger too deep to show.

Callie sighed. 'Yeah, it was one of ours. I had the damn jug on the kitchen counter with the lid off. Everybody knows that's my jug, and most days I work solo, at least through to lunch break. Whoever did it knows my pattern.'

'We're going to take the team apart. One by one. We not only keep the project going, we keep the team intact until we find the one responsible. We'll use the mummy's-curse angle. Start the rumour. Some local rednecks want to pay us back for screwing up the development, and they've been sabotaging the project. We make them believe we believe it, convince them we have to stick together. While whoever's done this thinks we're off on that angle, we narrow the field.'

'Bob was on the team before I knew about the Cullens.'

'We can put him on a secondary list. We don't eliminate anyone until we have absolute proof.' He brushed the back of his knuckles over her cheek. 'Nobody tries to poison my wife.'

'Ex-wife. We need to bring Leo in on this.'

They agreed the plan with Leo, then called the rest of the team in for a kitchen-table meeting. Callie passed out beer while Leo started things off with a booster speech.

'But the police wouldn't tell us anything.' Jittery, Frannie looked at face after face, never lighting on one for more than a fingersnap. 'They just asked a lot of questions. Like one of us made Rosie sick on purpose.'

'We think somebody did.' At Callie's statement, there was absolute silence. 'We put a lot of people out of work,' she continued. 'And some of those people are pretty steamed about it. Somebody set a fire in Lana Campbell's office. Why?' She waited a beat and, as Frannie had, watched faces. 'Because she's the Preservation Society's lawyer and largely responsible for us being here. Somebody torched Digger's trailer, blew the hell out of some of our equipment, some of our records.'

'Bill's dead,' Bob said quietly.

'Maybe it was an accident, maybe it wasn't.' Jake studied his beer and was aware of every breath around him. 'But it added to the disturb-the-graves-and-face-the-curse deal laymen like to spook each other with. Bad shit happens, they can start gossiping that the project's cursed.'

'Maybe it is.' Dory pressed her lips together.

'Spirits don't dump barbiturates in jugs of iced tea.' Callie folded her arms. 'People do. And that means we're going to have to keep the dig clear of all outsiders. We stick together. We take care of each other. That's what teams do.'

Jake stretched a hand out over the table. Callie laid hers on his. One by one, others put their hands out until everyone was connected. And Callie knew she held hands with a murderer.

NINE

THE CALL FROM THE FRONT DESK announcing the delivery of a package from Lana Campbell interrupted Doug as he was plotting out his approach. He grabbed his room key and went down to retrieve it.

And there she was. He lifted Lana right off her feet and caught that pretty mouth with his. 'Some package! Where's Ty?'

She kissed him. 'You say exactly the right things. He's spending a couple of days with his grandparents in Baltimore. Why don't we go up to your room? I've got a lot to tell you.'

He hauled her bags up to his room.

'I wanted Ty tucked away right now, and I felt Digger would do more good with Callie and Jake than with me. I also felt you deserve a sidekick.'

'I'd say I got top of the line, sidekick-wise. You know one of the first things I noticed about you, Lana?'

'No. What?' She stood very still while he unbuttoned her blouse.

'Soft. Your looks, your skin, your hair. Your clothes.' He slid the blouse away. 'A man's just got to get his hands on all that soft.' He trailed a finger down the centre of her back to the hook of her slacks.

'Maybe you should put the Do Not Disturb sign out.'

'I did.' He lowered his mouth, nuzzled her throat.

She let herself go, let the anxiety and excitement of the past hours melt away. The long, loving stroke of his hands over her warmed her skin. Her blood, her bones. So she sighed his name when his lips came back to hers. And yielded everything. When he filled her, body and heart, she spoke his name. Just his name.

Spent, sated, he held onto her. The temptation was great to simply drag the covers over their heads and shut out everything else.

'I want time with you, Lana. Time that's not part of anything else.'

She rubbed her cheek against his shoulder. 'I'm sorry, I'm going to spoil the mood. Something happened yesterday.' She told him about Rosie, watched his relaxed expression chill, then heat. 'Callie knows whoever laced the tea was one of her own team. She won't be careless. We have to leave it to her to handle that end. We'll handle this one.'

'I've got a list of Spencers—the secretary's last name—out of the phone book, and I've been running Internet searches. I'm down to six who might work. The others have lived here too long to fit. I've got a city map: I was working out how best to approach them.'

'There's something to be said for the more direct approach. Just go and knock on doors and ask if we're speaking to Marcus Carlyle's former secretary.'

'Stop and think for a minute.' He followed her as she went into the bathroom. 'We don't know what we're dealing with. You've already had your office destroyed, been scared enough to send Ty away. Think about him if something happens to you.'

She stepped under the shower. 'You're trying to scare me, and that's the right button to push, but I can't and won't live that way. It took me two months after Steve was killed to work up the courage to go into a goddamn convenience store. But I did it because you can't constantly be afraid of what might happen. If you do, you lose control of what *is* happening, and all the joy and pain it holds for you.'

'Damn.' He pulled off his jeans, stepped into the shower behind her, wrapped his arms round her waist. 'You don't leave me room to argue.'

She patted his hand, then stepped out before her hair got wet. 'I'm a professional. I'll start plotting our route.'

But when he came out to join her, she wasn't working on anything. Instead she stood by the desk holding a little Boston Red Sox baseball cap in her hands. 'You got this for Tyler.'

'Yeah, I thought he'd get a kick out of it. When my grandfather used to travel, he'd always bring me a baseball cap or a toy. Some little thing.'

'He asked when you'd be back.'

'Yeah?'

It was the instant delight in Doug's voice that struck her first. Instant, natural and true. Her heart tripped. 'Yes, he did. And he'll love this.'

'I didn't forget you either.'

Lana stared as he produced a can of Boston baked beans. When he dropped it into her hand, grinned at her, her heart not only tripped, it fell with a splat. She began to weep.

'Oh, Lana, don't cry. It was a joke.'

'I never believed I'd feel anything this strong again.' She had to sit, steady herself. 'I didn't want to feel like this again. Because when you do, there's so much to lose. It would've been so much easier, so much easier if I could have loved you a little. If I could've been content and have known you'd be good to Ty. Good for him.'

'Somebody told me that you can't live your life worrying about what could happen, or you miss what's happening.'

She sniffled. 'Clever, aren't you?'

'Always have been. I will be good to Ty.' He sat beside her. 'I'll be good to you.'

'I know it.' She laid a hand on his knee. 'I can't change Ty's name. I can't take that away from Steve.'

Doug looked down at her hand. At the wedding ring she continued to wear. 'OK.'

'But I'll change mine.'

He looked up, met her eyes. The flood of emotion was so huge, it almost swamped him. 'You know, this is starting to tick me off. First, you beat me to asking for a date, then you seduce me before I make my move. And now you propose to me.'

'Is that your way of saying I'm pushy?'

'No, it's my way of saying I'd like to ask you this time. Marry me, Lana.'

'I'd love to, Douglas.' She rested her head on his shoulder, sighed. 'Let's get this job done so we can go home.'

They had a nice working rhythm, Lana decided. They looked like a very safe, all-American couple, which was why those first three doors had opened to them so easily.

House number four was rosy old brick with a white verandah and a vintage Mercedes sedan in the drive.

There was an estate agent's sign in the yard.

'It's on the market. Interesting. Pulling up stakes?' Doug considered. 'Nobody but you and my family know we're here, but somebody knew I was poking around in Boston.'

'Mmm. It certainly gives us a logical way inside: house-hunting. We'll be the Beverlys from Baltimore. We're relocating here.'

They walked towards the house, holding hands. They rang the bell. After a short wait a woman in a slim beige suit answered.

'May I help you?'

'I hope so,' Lana said. 'I apologise for intruding, but my husband and I saw the house was for sale. We're looking for a house in the area. I wonder if it might be convenient to see the inside right now? Or could we make an appointment for later today or tomorrow?'

'You're just moving to Charlotte?'

'We will be,' Doug confirmed. 'From Baltimore. It is a really beautiful house. Just what we are looking for.'

'I have a little time if you want a look.'

'I would love it.' Lana started towards the main parlour behind her.

'What fabulous windows. And the fireplace! Does it work?'

'Yes, it's fully functioning.'

'Wonderful craftsmanship.' Lana ran a finger over the mantel and got a closer look at the photographs scattered over it. 'Oh, is this your daughter?'

'Yes.'

'She's lovely. Are these floors original?'

'Yes.' As Mrs Spencer glanced down, Lana signalled Doug to join her at the fireplace. 'Yellow pine.'

'Are you retired, Dorothy?'

There was a flicker of confusion, of suspicion, as she turned back to Lana. 'Yes, for some time now.'

'And did you pass your interest in the business to your daughter? The way you passed your name. Do they call you Dory, too?'

She stiffened and saw out of the corner of her eye that Doug blocked the hallway door while Lana stood by the French doors. 'Dot,' she said after a moment. 'Who are you?'

'I'm Lana Campbell, Callie Dunbrook's attorney. This is Douglas

Cullen, her brother. Jessica Cullen's brother.'

'How many babies did you help to sell?' Doug demanded.

'I don't know who you are or what you're talking about. I want you out of my house. If you don't leave immediately, I'll call the police.'

Doug stepped to the side, picked up the phone. 'Be my guest.'

She snatched the phone, spun away to the far side of the room. 'Get me the police. Yes, it's an emergency. I want to report a break-in. There's a man and woman in my house, refusing to leave. Yes, they're threatening me, and they've made upsetting statements about my daughter. That's right. Please hurry.'

She clicked the phone off.

'You didn't give them your name or address.' Lana started forward, threw up her hands as Dorothy heaved the phone at her.

'Nice save,' Doug commented when she made a fumbling catch. He took both Dorothy's arms, pushed her into a chair. 'Hit redial.'

'Already did.'

It rang twice before she heard a breathless voice say, 'Mom?'

She hung up. 'She called her daughter.' She punched numbers quickly.

'Dunbrook.'

'Callie, it's Dory. We found Dorothy Spencer. We found Carlyle's secretary. Dory's her daughter. And Dot Spencer just called her. She knows.'

'All right. I'll call you back.'

'She'll be OK,' Lana told Doug as she disconnected. 'She knows who and what to look for now. Dory won't get away,' she added as she walked towards Dorothy. 'We'll find her, just as we found you. She's a murderer.'

'That's a lie.' Dorothy bared her teeth.

'You know better. Whatever you and Carlyle did—you, him, Barbara Halloway, Henry Simpson—you didn't resort to murder. But she did.'

'Whatever Dory's done was to protect herself, and me. Her father.'

'Carlyle was her father?' Doug asked.

Dorothy sat back as if perfectly at ease, but her right hand continued to open and close. 'Don't know everything, do you?'

'Enough to turn you over to the FBI.'

'Please.' With a careless shrug, Dorothy crossed her legs. 'I was just a lowly secretary. How could I know what he was doing? And if you ever prove he was, you'll have a harder time proving I was involved.'

'Barbara and Henry Simpson can implicate you. They're happy to.' Doug smiled to add punch to the lie. 'Once they were promised immunity, they had no problem dragging you in.'

'That's not possible. They're in Mex—' She broke off, tightened her lips.

'Talk to them lately? They were picked up yesterday, and they're already building a case against you.'

'Just tell me why,' Doug demanded. 'Why did you take her?'

'I took no one. That would've been Barbara. There were others, of course.' She drew a breath. 'I want to call my daughter again.'

'Answer the questions, we'll give you the phone.' Lana set it in her lap, folded her hands over it.

Dorothy stared at the phone. Lana saw the genuine worry. She's afraid for her daughter, she thought. Whatever she is, she's still a mother.

'Why did he do it?' Doug pressed. 'I'm asking you why he did it.'

'It was Marcus's personal crusade—and his very profitable hobby.'

'Hobby,' Lana whispered.

'He thought of it that way. There were so many couples with healthy bank balances who couldn't conceive. And so many others who were struggling financially who had child after child. One per couple, that was his viewpoint. He handled a number of adoptions, legitimate ones. They were so complicated, so drawn out. He saw this as a way to expedite.'

'And the hundreds of thousands of dollars he earned from the sale of children didn't enter into it.'

She sent Lana a bored look. 'Of course it did. He was a very astute businessman. Why weren't you enough for your parents?' she asked Doug. 'In a way, they were surrogates for another couple who desperately wanted a child and had the means to support that child very well. Loving people in a stable relationship. That was essential.'

'You gave them no choice.'

'Ask yourself this: If your sister was given the choice today, who would it be? The people who conceived her, or the parents who raised her?'

There was conviction in her voice now. 'Ask yourself that question, and think carefully before you continue with this. If you walk away, no one else has to know. No one else has to be put through the emotional turmoil. If you don't walk away, you won't be able to stop it. All those families torn apart. Just for your satisfaction.'

'All those families torn apart,' Lana said as she rose, 'so Marcus Carlyle could make a profit from playing God.'

She handed Doug the phone. 'Call the police.'

'My daughter.' Dorothy sprang to her feet. 'You said I could call my daughter.'

'I lied,' Lana said and took great personal satisfaction in shoving the woman back into her chair.

A few hundred miles away, Callie scrambled out of a six-foot hole even as she clicked off her cellphone. It was temper that propelled her up and out when she spotted Dory briskly crossing the field towards the cars and trucks parked on the side of the road.

Callie shot off in a sprint, leaping over a stunned Digger.

It was his instinctive shout that had Dory whipping her head round. Their eyes met, one thudding heartbeat. Callie saw it—the rage, the acknowledgment, the fear—then Dory broke into a run.

Through the buzzing in her ears, Callie could hear other shouts. But that was all distant, down some long, parallel tunnel. Her focus had fined down to one goal. She saw nothing but Dory. And she was gaining.

Neither woman slowed pace, as Callie ploughed her body into Dory's. They rolled over dirt, grappling, clawing. Callie scented blood, tasted it, then kicked in blind fury as she was lifted straight up into the air. She could see nothing but the woman on the ground, people gathering round.

'Stop it! Goddamnit, Callie, stop or I'm going to have to hurt you.'

'Let go of me. Let go! I'm not finished.'

'She is.' Jake tightened his hold, struggled to get his own wind back. 'From the looks of it, I'd say you broke her nose.'

'What?' The mists were clearing; the wild rage began to level. Blood was spilling out of Dory's nose, and her right eye was already swollen. 'She's the one,' Callie panted out. 'Move aside, Jake. I'm not going to hit her again, but I've got something to say to her.' Everyone else dropped into silence. 'The tackle was for Rosie.'

'You're crazy.' Dory moaned and wept.

'The nose, that's for Bill. The black eye, we'll give that to Dolan.'

Dory held up her blood-smeared hands as if in plea to the rest of the team. 'I don't know what she's talking about.'

'She killed Bill. And she put Rosie in the hospital.' Her hand snaked out, grabbed Dory by her torn shirt before anyone could stop her. 'You're lucky Jake pulled me off.'

'Keep her away from me,' Dory pleaded as she cringed back.

'You're sure about this, Callie?' Leo demanded.

'Yeah, I'm sure.'

'Well.' Leo sighed. 'Let's call the police and sort this out.'

Jake dabbed antiseptic on the claw marks along Callie's collarbone. He'd moved her away from the rest of the team, leaving them tending to Dory. He glanced over his shoulder, noted that Bob was patting Dory's shoulder and Frannie offering her a cup of water. 'She's convincing everybody you went after her out of the blue.'

'Doug and Lana have Dorothy Spencer in Charlotte. That's enough of a connection to convince Hewitt to take her in for questioning.'

'She's not here alone.'

Callie hissed out a breath. 'I wasn't thinking. I just acted. But damnit, Jake, she would've got away. She was heading for the cars.'

'I'm not arguing with that. You stopped her; she had to be stopped. We can count on Doug and Lana to give the Charlotte cops the picture. We've got more pieces, and we'll put them together until we have the whole picture.'

Sheriff Jeff Hewitt folded a piece of gum into his mouth. He kept his attention on the deputy who helped Dory into another cruiser for transportation to the ER.

'It's an interesting story, Dr Dunbrook, but I can't arrest a woman for murder on your say-so. I'm going to be talking to her further. I'm going to be talking to the Charlotte police and the FBI. I'm going to do my job.' He shifted his attention, studied her bruised face. 'Might be a good idea if you let me do it, instead of trying to do it for me.'

She soaked a symphony of bruises in the tub, took a painkiller and stewed. Then she took her herbal tea into Jake's office, sat down on the worktable beside him. 'I feel sort of let down. I'm counting on the police and FBI to nail it, but it's like I've dug down, layer by layer, and I see pieces of what's under there, but I can't seem to make the whole thing out. And something tells me the whole thing isn't going to be what I wanted to find in the first place.'

'A good digger knows you can't choose what you find.' He picked up her hand, examined the scraped knuckles, wiggled her fingers. 'How's this feeling?'

'Like I ploughed it into bone at short range several times.'

Still, she used it to pick up the phone when it rang. 'Dunbrook. Sheriff Hewitt.' She rolled her eyes derisively towards Jake, then froze.

'They lost her.' She set the phone down carefully before she could give in to rage and heave it through the window. 'She just walked out of the hospital when the deputy was distracted. Nobody remembers seeing her leave, nobody knows where she went.'

Doug swung by his mother's. The phone, he decided, wasn't the way to tell her what they'd learned.

He walked in the front. He hadn't paid enough attention to the life his mother had made for herself, he admitted. How she'd built a business, created a home. Not only had he ignored what she'd managed to do, he'd resented it.

'Mom?

'Doug?' Her voice carried down the stairs. 'You're back! I'll be right down.'

He heard the click of heels on wood—quick, brisk, female.

'Wow,' he managed. 'What's up with you?'

'Oh. Well. Just . . . nothing really.'

She blushed. He didn't know mothers *could* blush. And apparently he'd forgotten how beautiful his own mother was. Her hair was swept around her face, and her lips and cheeks were attractively rosy. But the dress—midnight blue and sleek—was the killer.

'Where are you going?'

'I have a date.'

'A what?'

'A date.' Flustered, she hurried into the kitchen, made coffee and circled cookies on a plate, just as she had when he'd come home from school. 'I'm going out to dinner. With your father.'

'Excuse me?'

She set the plate down. 'I said I have a dinner date with your father.'

He sat down. 'You and Dad are . . . *dating*?'

'Just a casual dinner.'

'There's nothing casual about that dress.' Shock was slowly making room for amusement, and trailing just behind was a nice warm pleasure.

'It looks all right? I've only worn it to a couple of cocktail events.'

'It looks amazing. You look amazing. You're beautiful, Mom. I should have told you that every day. I should've told you I love you, every day. That I'm proud of you, every day.'

'Oh, Douglas.' She lifted a hand to her heart as it soared, and tears filled her eyes. 'There goes the thirty minutes I spent on my face.'

'I'm sorry I didn't. I'm sorry I couldn't. I'm sorry I didn't talk to you because I was afraid you blamed me.'

'Blamed you for . . .' Even as the tears spilled over, she lowered her cheek to the top of his head. 'Oh, Douglas. No. My poor baby,' she murmured. 'I let you down in so many ways.'

'No, Mom.'

'I know I did. But for you to think that. Oh, baby. I promise you, not once—even at the worst—did I blame you. You were just a little boy.' She pressed her lips to his brow. 'I love you, Doug, and I'm sorry I didn't tell you, every day. I shut you out. I shut your father out. Everyone. Then when I tried to open up again, it was too late.'

'It's not too late. Sit down, Mom. Sit down.' He held her hands as she lowered into the chair beside him. 'I'm going to marry Lana Campbell.'

'You—oh my God.' More tears spilled over as she began to laugh. 'What are we drinking coffee for? I have champagne.' She got up, pulled three tissues out of a box on the counter.

'Later. Later when we're all together.'

'I'm so happy for you. I like her very much. And her little boy—' She broke off. 'Oh my, I'm a grandmother.'

'I'm crazy about him. There are some other things I need to tell you. About Jessica.'

'Callie.' Suzanne sat down again. 'We should call her Callie.'

'Where would she go?' Callie paced Jake's office. 'Would she risk trying to get out of the country, head down to the Caymans? Her father's dead.'

'There might be money there,' Lana offered.

'We've established Carlyle was ill,' Callie went on. 'If they were still marketing babies, it's unlikely he played a central role. If they weren't still in the business, why go to such lengths to stop me from tracking him down? If and when I gathered enough information to interest the authorities, he'd be gone.'

'Logically, his connections feared exposure'—Jake continued scribbling on a pad—'possible prosecution and imprisonment.'

Lana motioned towards the door that connected to the living area. 'She didn't do this by herself.'

'It's not one of them,' Callie replied. 'Bob and Sonya were here before any of this started. They're clear. Frannie and Chuck come as a set. She didn't know a hell of a lot, but he did. No way this is his first dig. I'd say the same about Matt. He's too knowledgeable about the procedure.'

'We've had others come and go since July, and we can't be sure about them. But this core group's probably solid.' Taking his pad, he moved over to the time-line chart.

'I believe the police will find her, just as they'll track down the Simpsons.' Lana lifted her hands. 'Then they'll gather up the rest. You've already broken the back of the organisation. You have your answers.'

'There's more. Still more underneath. I haven't got it all.' Callie stopped pacing to stand behind Jake. 'What're you doing?'

'Blending time lines. Yours, Carlyle's, Dory's. The date of Carlyle's first marriage, the birth of his son, his move to Boston.'

'Big gap between the marriage and the arrival of the bouncing baby boy,' Callie commented. 'Lana, do you have the data on his adoption practice before Boston handy?'

'I can look it up. I brought all my file disks. May I use your computer, Jake?'

'Go ahead. Be interesting, wouldn't it, to have a look at the first Mrs Carlyle's medical records?'

'Mmm. You can't be sure, yet, that's Dory's real date of birth.'

'Bound to be close enough. She's about your age, Cal. Makes her around twenty years younger than Richard Carlyle. According to my maths, Carlyle would've been over sixty when she was born.'

'Sexagenarian sperm's been known to get lucky,' Callie commented, studying the grid Jake was creating. 'How old's Dorothy?'

'Well into her fifties,' Lana said. 'Maybe ten years older than Carlyle junior. The first adoption petition I find was filed in '46. Two that year.'

'Two years after the marriage,' Callie murmured. 'Long enough. He'd been in practice, what, six years before he developed an interest in adoptions?' She studied the entire chart, watched the pattern form. 'It's a big leap,' she said to Jake.

'A logical hypothesis based on available data.'

'What is?' Doug stepped up to the chart.

'Richard Carlyle was the first infant stolen by Marcus Carlyle. But not for profit. Because he wanted a son.'

Doug shoved his glasses further up his nose. 'You get that from this?'

'Just take a look at it,' Callie insisted. 'He shifts the focus of his practice two years after his marriage, six years after he began his career. What if he and his wife were having problems conceiving? He develops a personal interest in adoption, researches it, gets to know all the ins and outs.'

'Then why not just adopt?' Lana put in.

Jake shrugged. 'His known history of infidelity indicates a man who uses sex, and who sees his prowess as part of his identity.'

'Not being able to conceive a child would damage his ego.' Doug nodded. 'He's not going to let it be known he may be shooting blanks.'

Callie held up a hand. 'But he wants a child—a son. He'd want to know exactly where that child came from. He wouldn't tolerate the rules they had back then of sealing records on birth parents. And he's looking around. Look at all these people who have children. Much less worthy than he. Less financially secure, less important. Less.'

Lana swivelled her chair round. 'It fits his profile.'

'He's been representing adoptive parents for years now. He knows the routine, he knows doctors, other lawyers, agencies,' Jake continued. 'He finds birth parents who may fit his criteria. Then with or without a private arrangement with those birth parents, he takes his son. I'll bet my

CD collection there'll be no adoption petition or decree on Richard Carlyle filed in the courts.'

'Shortly after, he relocates to Houston. And because it worked, he saw it as a means to meet the needs of other worthy, childless couples. His way.' Doug nodded. 'And to profit from it.'

'Then Richard found out,' said Callie. 'It caused a rift between father and son. Marcus treated his mother shabbily, and perhaps because she didn't give him a son the more traditional way, this increased or caused his infidelities.'

'They didn't divorce until Richard was twenty.' Jake tapped his fingers on the time line. 'The year Dory was born.'

'The marriage suited Carlyle. But now his son's grown and discovered the truth. The family's fractured. The marriage is over.'

'And Carlyle's had an illegitimate child with his secretary. That'd be a slap in the face for mother and son.' Doug picked up the coffeepot. 'It's an interesting theory, but I don't see how it helps locate Dory.'

'There's another layer.' Callie turned to the time line again. It all seemed so clear to her now. Just brush that last bit of dirt away and everything was right there. 'Look at the dates again. The move from Boston to Seattle. About as far away as you can manage. Why? Because your secretary, who you've been intimate with, who knows your criminal activities, has just told you she's pregnant. But not with your child. With your son's.'

'Dorothy Simpson and Richard Carlyle?' Lana leapt up.

'A young, impressionable boy—maybe one who's just discovered he's not who he thought he was. He's shaken,' Callie surmised. 'He's vulnerable. And he's angry. The older, attractive woman. If he knows his father's been with her, it only adds to the pull. "I'll show that bastard." Dorothy staring at thirty. She's been working for—and sleeping with—Carlyle for a long time. She'd be tired of being the other woman and getting nothing out of it. Here's the son. Young, fresh. Another hook into Carlyle.'

'More logical to believe it was the younger Carlyle who impregnated her, than the older,' Jake said. 'He's sixty and, according to known data, had never before conceived a child.'

'Carlyle wasn't protecting his estranged, dying father,' Callie concluded. 'He was protecting his daughter.'

'The question was, where would she go?' Jake drew a circle round Richard Carlyle's name on the chart. 'To Daddy.'

'You run this theory by the cops, they're going to think you're crazy or brilliant.' Doug blew out a breath. 'But if they're open to it, and they toss it at Dorothy, she might slip.'

'If we're right, this has been going on for three generations,' said Callie. 'Whether or not Richard took an active part, he knew. There's something even more hideous about passing down this, well, evil, from father to son to daughter. How could he be a part of perpetuating it, of covering it up, of profiting from it?'

Jake crossed to her, traced his fingers gently over her bruised cheekbone. 'You found what you were digging for, Cal.'

'Yeah. And I have to put it on display. I don't have a choice.'

She turned as the phone rang. 'It's two in the morning. Who the hell's calling? Dunbrook.'

'Hello, Callie.'

'Hello, Dory.' Callie grabbed a pencil, scrawled on the wall by the phone. *Call the cops. Trace the call*. 'How's the nose?'

'It hurts like a bitch. And believe me, you're going to pay for that. I've got your mother, Callie.'

The blood stopped pumping through her veins. 'I don't believe you.'

There was a horrible laugh. 'Yes, you do. Don't you wonder which mother? Don't you want to find out? How much are you willing to pay?'

'Tell me what you want and I'll get it.'

'I want my mother!' Her voice spiked. The wild rage in it curdled Callie's stomach. 'Are you going to get her for me, you bitch?'

'They're only questioning her.' As she began to shake, Callie gripped the counter. 'They might have let her go by now.'

'Liar! Another lie about my mother and I'll use this knife I'm holding on yours.'

'Don't hurt her.' Terror clawed icy fingers down her spine. 'Tell me what you want me to do and I'll do it.'

'Call the police, and she's dead. Understand?'

'Yes. No police. Can I talk to her?'

'You'll talk to me. We'll talk about payment, about what you're going to have to do. Just you and me. You come alone or I'll kill her. Simon's Hole. You've got ten minutes or I start cutting her.'

'Cellphone,' Jake said the minute she hung up. 'They're going to try to triangulate.'

'No time. She gave me ten minutes to get to the pond. I can barely make it now. She's got my mother. She's going to kill her if I don't come. Now and alone. For God's sake, I don't even know which one she's got.'

Jake pulled a knife from his boot. 'Take this. I'll be right behind you.'

'You can't. She'll—'

'You have to trust me.' He took her in his arms. 'There's no room, no time for anything else. You have to trust me. I'm trusting you.'

She stared into his eyes and made the leap. 'Hurry,' she said and ran.

She made it in nine minutes.

'Dory! I'm here. I'm alone. Don't hurt her.'

She walked towards the water, saw a light flash, spun towards it.

'Stop right there. Did you call the cops on the way?'

'I didn't. I won't risk my mother just to punish you.'

'You've already punished me. And for *what*? To prove how smart you are? Marcus Carlyle was a great man. Even dead he's better than you.'

'What do you want me to do?'

'Suffer. Stay where you are.' Dory stepped back, into the shadows. Seconds later a form rolled forward, halfway to the edge of the pond.

Callie saw a glint of blonde hair, a hint of pale skin.

'You stay back or I'll kill her.' She held up a gun. 'Look, I said I had a knife, but this looks like a gun. In fact, it looks like the same gun I used to nearly put a hole in your very sexy ex-husband. It would've been easy. I'd already killed Dolan. That was sort of an accident. But I hit him harder than I meant to. Seemed the best thing was to dump him in Simon's Hole. I hoped you'd get blamed for it, but that didn't work out.'

I'll be right behind you, Jake had said, she remembered. Trust him.

'You burned down Lana's office.'

'Fire purges. You should never have hired her. You should never have started poking around in something that didn't *matter* to you. I could kill you.' She lifted the gun, trained it on Callie's heart. 'Then it would be over for you. But that's just not good enough. Not any more.'

'Why Bill?' Callie inched forward as Dory stepped back.

'He was handy. And he asked too many questions. He kept wanting to know about my training. Just couldn't mind his own business. Just like you. Why, look what I found.' She shoved with her foot again, and another bound figure rolled towards the water. 'Running rings round you. See? I've got both your mothers.'

Jake came in from the east side of the woods, quiet and slow, without a light. The sound of voices made his heart trip, but he forced himself not to run towards them. He was armed with only a kitchen knife.

He shifted direction, moving through the dark towards the voices. And stopped, heart hammering, when he saw the human outline. Signalling for silence, he crept closer. Two figures, two men. Callie's fathers were bound to the two-trunked oak tree, gagged. Their heads sagged onto their chests.

'Probably drugged,' he whispered. 'Cut them loose.' He passed the knife to Doug. 'Stay with them. If they come to, keep them quiet.'

'For Christ's sake, Jake, she's got both of them.'

'I know it.'

'I'm going with you.' He closed a hand over his father's limp fingers, then gave the knife to Digger. 'Take care of them.'

Callie's heart went numb. The mother who had given birth to her, the mother who had raised her. Now both their lives depended on her. 'You're right. You've run rings round me. But you didn't do this alone. Where's your father, Dory? Can't you face it, Richard?'

'Figured that out, did you?' Grinning widely, Dory gestured with her free hand. 'Come on out, Dad. Join the party.'

'Why couldn't you leave it alone?' Richard stepped out beside his daughter. 'Why couldn't you let it stay buried?'

'Is that what you did? Just accepted? Never looked?'

'He did it for the best. He gave me a good life. I walked away from him and what he was doing.'

Her palms were sweating, and they itched for the knife in her boot. She could kill to save her mother—her mothers—she could kill without hesitation. 'And that was enough? You did nothing to stop it.'

'I had a child of my own to think of. A life of my own.'

'But you didn't raise that child. Dorothy did. With plenty of influence from Marcus.'

'I was barely twenty. What was I supposed to do?'

'Be a man.' Out of the corner of her eye, she watched Dory watching Richard. 'Be a father. But you let him take over. He twisted her, Richard. Can you protect her now, knowing she's killed?'

'She's my child. Nothing that's happened was her fault. It was his. All you need to do is go away for a few weeks,' Richard said. 'Disappear long enough to stall the police investigation so that I can get Dory somewhere safe. So I can arrange for Dorothy's release. Without you, they lose their most vital link. That's all you have to do.'

'Is that how she talked you into spying on the house, into helping her blow up the trailer? Is that how she convinced you to help her to do this tonight? Are you so blind you can't see she's only interested in causing pain? In revenge?'

'Nobody else has to get hurt,' he insisted. 'I just need time.'

Dory shook back her hair. 'She wanted my grandfather to pay. My mother to pay. But she'll pay now.' Crouching, she held the gun to one blonde head.

'Dory, no!' Richard shouted even as Callie sucked in air to scream.

'Which one will you save?' She shoved the other figure into the water.

'If you dive in after her, I'll shoot this one. If you try to save this one, the other drowns. Tough call.'

'Dory, for God's sake.' Richard lurched forward, only to freeze when she swung the gun at him.

'Stay out of this. Hell, let both of them drown.' She shoved the limp body into the pond, then aimed the gun at Callie. 'While you watch.'

'Go to hell.' Braced for the bullet, Callie prepared to dive.

She sensed the movement, barely registered it as Jake rushed out of the trees. She was in the air, over the water, when she heard the shot.

She felt the sting, but she was in the water, swimming desperately to where she'd seen the first of her mothers slide under. She still didn't know which one. She'd never save them both.

She filled her lungs with air and plunged. She was blind now, diving deep into the black, praying for any sign of movement, any shape.

Her lungs burned, her limbs went heavy and weak in the cold water, but she pushed down, further down. And when she saw the glimmering shadow, gritted her teeth and kicked with all her strength.

She grabbed hair, pulled. Her lungs and muscles screaming, she hauled the dead weight up. White lights danced in front of her eyes. When her air gave out, she flailed. Weakened, floundering, she began to sink.

Then she was rising up again as hands pulled her towards the surface.

She broke through, choking. Still she shoved weakly at Jake as he towed them both towards the bank.

'No. The other one. The other went in a few feet up. Please.'

'Doug's in. It's all right. Get her up. Let's get her out. Take her!'

More hands grabbed for her as she started to crawl her way out.

She rolled towards the unconscious figure. Saw Suzanne's face.

'Oh God, oh God.' She cast one desperate look towards the pond.

'Hold on.' Jake dived back into the water.

'Is she breathing?'

'Let me.' Lana pushed her aside. 'Lifeguard, three summers.'

Matt held the gun now, trained on Dory as she lay face down on the ground. Richard sat beside her, his head in his hands. 'Cops're coming,' he said as the sirens cut the air. 'Ambulance, too. We called both.'

'My mother.' Callie looked towards the pond, back towards Suzanne. Then simply collapsed to her knees when three heads broke the surface.

'She's breathing,' Lana called out.

'Somebody cut these ropes off her.' Trying not to weep, Callie crawled over to help pull Vivian to shore. 'Cut those goddamn ropes off her.'

A hand took Callie's wrist. 'We got yours,' Doug managed.

Callie reached out. 'We got yours.'

Shortly after dawn, Callie walked into the hospital waiting room and shook Lana gently by the shoulder.

'What? Oh God. Must've dozed off. How are they?'

'Everyone's doing fine. My father and Jay are being released. They want to keep my mother and Suzanne for a few more hours at least.'

'How are you?'

'Grateful. More than I can say. I appreciate everything you did, right down to getting the dry clothes.'

'No problem. We're family now. I guess in more ways than one.'

Callie crouched down. 'He's a really good man, isn't he? My brother.'

'Yes, he is. He cares very much about you. You've got a family here.'

'I didn't know it was Suzanne I was pulling up. I had to make a decision. Go after the one who'd been in the longest.'

'She might have died if you hadn't made that decision. That makes it the right one. How's the shoulder?'

Callie worked it gingerly. 'Pretty sore. You know how they say it's just a flesh wound? Whole different perspective on that when it's your flesh. Lana, when this comes out, there'll be others like me.'

'Yes. Some will want to dig, discover. Others will want to leave it buried. You did what was right for you, and by doing it, you stopped it from going any further. Let that be enough for you, Callie.'

'The single person most responsible was never punished.'

'Can you believe that when you do what you do? Do you really think it all ends with bones in the ground?' Lana looked down at her hand, at the finger where her wedding ring had once been. She'd taken it off, had put it—lovingly—away. And when she had, she'd felt Steve watching her. Lovingly. 'It doesn't,' she said.

Callie thought of how often she heard the murmurs of the dead when she worked. 'So, my consolation is, if there's a hell, Marcus Carlyle is frying in it?' She considered a moment. 'I think I can live with that.'

'You go home, too.' Lana patted her arm.

On the drive back, Callie kept her eyes closed. 'I've got a lot to say to you,' she told Jake. 'You came through for me, in a big way. And I knew you would. I wanted you to know that I knew you would.'

She opened her eyes when she felt the car stop. Blinking, she stared at the field. 'What the hell are we doing here? This isn't the time for work.'

'No, but it's a good spot.' He got out, waited for her to join him. Taking her hand, he walked to the gate. 'I've got some things to say to you, too. I want you back, Callie. All the way back. Only better. I'm not going to let you go again. I'm not going to let you let us go again. I heard that shot, saw you go into the water.' He broke off, turned away. 'That could've been it. I can't wait any more to settle this between us. I need you to love me the way you did before things got away from us.'

'That's stupid, Graystone.'

'The hell it is.'

'It's stupid because I never stopped loving you, you big jerk. No you don't.' She threw up a hand when she saw the gleam in his eyes. 'This time you get down on one knee, and you ask.'

'You want me to get down on my knees?' He was sincerely horrified.

'Yes, I do. Oh yeah. Assume the position, Graystone, or I walk.'

'All right, all right. Damnit.' Scowling, he knelt.

'You're supposed to take my hand and look soulful.'

'Oh, shut up. Are you going to marry me, or what?'

'That's not the way to ask. Try again.'

'Mother of God.' He huffed out a breath. 'Callie, will you marry me?'

'You didn't say you love me.'

'You're really getting a charge out of this, aren't you?'

'The biggest.'

'Callie, I love you.' And the smile that warmed her face loosened the tightness in his chest. 'Damnit, I loved you from the minute I looked at you. It scared me to death, because for the first time there was a woman who could hurt me. I walked away because I was sure you'd come running after me. Didn't happen. I won't walk away again. I love you.'

She blinked at tears. 'I won't walk either, Jake. I won't expect you to know what I need or want. Or assume I know what you're feeling or thinking. I'll tell you. I'll ask you. And we'll find the way. Got a ring?'

'Are you kidding me?'

'A ring's appropriate. But, luckily for you, I happen to have one.' She pulled the chain from under her shirt, lifted it off and spilled it, and her wedding band, into his hand.

He stared at it with emotion storming through him. 'This looks pretty familiar.'

'I didn't take it off until you showed up here. I asked Lana to bring it with her when she got the dry clothes from the house.'

'You wore this the whole time we were separated?'

'Yeah. I'm a sentimental slob.'

'That's a coincidence.' He tugged a chain from under his shirt, showed her the matching band.

'It's not going to be Vegas this time. We'll have a real wedding. And we're buying a house. Some place we can try to plant roots.'

'No kidding?' He laid his forehead on hers. 'A home. And, Callie, I want kids.'

'Now you're talking. Our own tribe, our own settlement.'

'I love you.' He kissed each of her dimples. 'I'll make you happy. And you love me. Crazy about me.'

'Apparently.'

'That's good. Because there's this one thing. The wedding is sort of, superfluous, seeing as we're still married.'

'Excuse me?'

'I never signed the divorce papers.'

She gaped at him. 'You didn't sign them? We're not divorced?'

'Nope. Here, put this back on.' She let him slide the ring on, then took his and did the same. And when he swept her off her feet, carrying her through the gate as a groom might a bride over the threshold, she laughed.

She looked over his shoulder at the work yet to be done, the past yet to be uncovered. They'd dig it out, she thought.

Everything there was to find they'd find. Together.

NORA ROBERTS

Nora Roberts is the youngest child of a family of five, and was born in Silver Spring, Maryland, in the USA. 'My parents were always telling us stories about their courting days. And, like the best stories, they were always embellished.' Perhaps inspired by her parents' own love story, Nora married at seventeen and had two sons, Jason and Dan. She and her husband built a cabin on the top of a hill in western Maryland and Nora settled down to a contented life of motherhood, gardening, canning fruits and vegetables, and making her sons' clothes. 'I even macramééd two hammocks. I needed help!'

That help was to come in the form of a blizzard which, in February 1979, left Nora stranded at home for a week with her six- and three-year-old sons—who were unable to get to kindergarten—and a dwindling supply of chocolate. Nora found herself slowly going crazy, and, to relieve the frustration, started to write one of the many stories that had been buzzing around in her head for years. 'Immediately, I knew this was it,' she recalls, and persevered through half a dozen rejection letters until *Irish Thoroughbred* was accepted for publication by Silhouette in 1981. For Nora Roberts a new career was born but unfortunately, her husband found it difficult to come to terms with

her success and their marriage broke up.

Four years later, her first best-selling novel, *Playing the Odds,* was published, and it was around this time that Nora Roberts hired a carpenter, Bruce Wilder, to build some bookshelves in her home and he asked her out on a date. 'I hadn't dated since high school, so I was nervous,' admits the publishing world's queen of romantic novel-writing. 'But I figured since he'd been in and out of my house for weeks, he couldn't be an axe murderer or I'd have been dead already. So I said yes and he cooked me this wonderful dinner at his house. When he finally moved in, I thought he wouldn't last five minutes with the kids, but we've been married for seventeen years now.'

Over those years, Nora Roberts has established herself as a publishing phenomenon in the United States, having written more than 150 novels, sixty-nine of which have been best sellers. One fascinating Nora Roberts statistic is that if all her books were placed top to bottom, they would stretch across the United States from Los Angeles to New York five times! 'It's amazing, isn't it?' she says. 'I started writing as a way to save my sanity and fell into a job I love.'

Jane Eastgate

Jill Mansell

Nadia Knows Best

Jay Tiernan is Nadia's knight in shining armour. She is sure of it. First he rescued her from her snowbound car, then he offered her the job of her dreams—designing new gardens for the houses he renovates.

The next chapter in the fairy-tale is the one in which Nadia and her knight fall in love—just how hard can that be?

Chapter One

'OOOOOHH . . . EEEE . . .' To her horror Nadia realised she was having a Bambi moment. A scary, drawn-out, Bambi-on-ice moment in fact. Except unlike Bambi she couldn't make it stop simply by landing with a bump on her bottom.

The car carried on sliding in slow motion across the perilously snow-packed road. Despite knowing—in theory—that what you were meant to do was keep your foot *off* the brake and steer *into* the skid, Nadia's hands and feet were frantically doing all the wrong things because steering into a skid was like trying to write while you were looking in a mirror and—oh God, *wall*—

Cccrunchh.

Silence.

Phew, still alive, hooray for that.

Opening her eyes, Nadia unpeeled her trembling gloved hands from the steering wheel and mentally congratulated herself on not being dead. The car was tilted at a bit of an odd angle, thanks to the ditch directly in front of the wall, but despite the best efforts of the snow she hadn't actually been going fast enough to do spectacular amounts of damage to either it or herself.

Then again, what to do now?

Bracing herself against the cold, Nadia clambered out of the grubby black Renault and inspected the crumpled front wing.

Her face screwed up against the stinging onslaught of low-flying snowflakes, she hopped back into the car. She had her mobile. She could ask the police to come and rescue her . . . except chances were they might want to know where she was. Hmm. Maybe phone home then, and at least let the family know she was in a ditch, in a blizzard, somewhere in deepest darkest Gloucestershire. Or, more accurately, deepest *whitest* Gloucestershire. Although it would be dark soon enough.

This dilemma was solved neatly enough by the discovery that her phone was dead, which narrowed the options down to two. Should she leave the car and trudge off through the ever-deepening snow in search of civilisation? Or stay here and hope that somebody—preferably in a Sherman tank or a helicopter—might come along and rescue her?

Since civilisation could be miles away and her feet still ached like mad from dancing last night, Nadia reached over to the back seat for her sleeping-bag, wriggled into it like a giant worm and settled down to wait.

Poor old Laurie, he'd missed a brilliant party. Nadia smiled to herself. She wondered how hot it was right now in Egypt, and if he'd managed to squeeze in a visit to Tutankhamun's tomb before flying on to Barcelona.

Gosh, she was hungry. Easing a hand from the cocoon of her sleeping-bag, she flicked open the glove compartment. A packet of Rolos and a half-empty bag of wine gums. Should she ration herself, like people trapped on mountains, to one Rolo a day? Or give in to temptation and guzzle the whole lot at once?

Compromising, Nadia ate three Rolos and half a dozen wine gums, then switched on the car radio for company just in time to hear a DJ cheerfully announce that there was plenty more snow on the way.

That was the thing about Sherman tanks, they were never around when you needed them.

Less than half an hour later—though it seemed more—Nadia let out a shriek and abruptly stopped singing along with Sting to 'Don't Stand So Close To Me'. Actually, it was an appropriate song. The person who had tapped on her window was pretty close.

Male or female? Hard to tell with that hat pulled down over their face. Wrapped up in a Barbour, thick sweater and jeans, it was either a man or a hulking great six-foot-plus woman.

Nadia opened the window and promptly wished she could have been wearing something more alluring than a green nylon sleeping-bag.

'Are you OK?'

He had dark hair, light brown eyes and snowflakes decorating his black, spiky eyelashes.

'I'm fine. Really warm. Skidded off the road,' Nadia explained, fairly idiotically given the novel angle at which she was sitting.

He inclined his head. 'I noticed.'

Nadia peered at the empty road behind him. 'Did you crash too?'

'No, I abandoned the car before that happened. It's at the bottom of the last hill. Look, there's a village half a mile ahead. Do you want to walk with me?'

Nadia hesitated. Hang on, a complete stranger in the middle of nowhere, seemingly perfectly normal until he reappeared with madness in his eyes and a sharp axe? How many times had she seen *that* film?

'How do you know there's a village?' She didn't want to struggle through the blizzard on a whim.

The mad axe-murderer seemed entertained by the wary look in her eyes. Smiling, he patted the pocket of his waxed Barbour. 'I have a map.'

'I feel like a refugee,' Nadia muttered as they trudged along the narrow lane, the snow squeaking underfoot. She was carrying her rolled-up sleeping-bag under one arm and her overnight case in the other.

'You look like a refugee.' Glancing across at her, he broke into a grin and held out an arm. 'Here, let me carry those.'

She knew his name now. Jay Tiernan. He'd introduced himself while she'd been struggling to extricate herself from the sleeping-bag. Thankfully, Nadia handed him her bag. Her nose was a fetching shade of pink, her eyes were watering and her toes numb. Ranulph Fiennes needn't worry about competition—she'd be hopeless in the Antarctic.

'You lied,' Nadia panted forty minutes later. 'That wasn't half a mile.'

'Never mind, we're here now.'

Nadia peered through the tumbling snowflakes at the deserted single street. There were no lights on in any of the cottages. Nor were there any shops. Just a postbox, a bus shelter and a phone box. And a pub.

'The Willow Inn,' Jay announced, squinting at the dilapidated sign. 'We'll try there.'

After several minutes of hammering on the wood, they heard the sound of keys rattling and bolts being drawn back.

'Blimey,' slurred the landlord, enveloping them in a cloud of whisky breath. 'Mary and Joseph and the little baby Jesus. Fancy bumping into you in a place like this.'

Nadia, clutching her rolled-up sleeping-bag in her arms, realised he thought she had a baby in there.

'Hi,' Jay began. 'We wondered if—'

'Shut, mate. Closed. Six o'clock we open.'

'Look, the roads are blocked, we've had to abandon our cars, we've been walking for *hours*,' Nadia blurted out. 'We need somewhere to stay.'

As a rule, batting her eyelashes and widening her big brown eyes had the desired effect, but the landlord was clearly too far gone for that.

'Don't do board and lodging neither.' Wheezing with laughter he said, 'There's a stable down the road, you could try there.'

Nadia briefly wondered if bursting into tears would help.

Jay said, 'We'd pay you, of course.'

The landlord's bloodshot eyes promptly lit up. 'Hundred quid.'

'Fine.'

'Cash, mind. Up front.'

Solemnly, Jay nodded. 'It's a deal.'

The power cut that had left every house in the street in darkness was still going strong at nine o'clock that evening. The pub, illuminated with flickering candles, had gradually filled up with locals driven out of their homes by the lack of TV, as well as half a dozen other stranded drivers.

Dinner, also thanks to the power cut, was thick chunks of bread toasted over an open fire, doorsteps of cheese, pickled onions the size of satsumas and stale digestive biscuits.

'A candlelit meal, what could be more romantic?' Jay indicated their rickety wooden table. 'Never let it be said I don't know how to give a woman a good time. Pickled onion?'

Nadia smiled; he had a nice voice. She'd always been a sucker for a nice voice. 'No thanks. We need to sort the room thing out. You can't sleep down here.'

With only fifteen pounds in her purse, it had been left to Jay to come up with the rest of the money for the only spare bedroom. When Pete had shown them the chilly room, taken up almost entirely by a lumpy, unmade double bed (A hundred pounds? Bargain!), Jay had murmured, 'It's OK, I'll sleep downstairs.' But that had been before the others had arrived, turning the small bar into a makeshift refugee camp. It wasn't fair to take the room Jay had largely paid for.

'You should have the bed,' Nadia told him. 'I'll be fine down here.'

'You might be fine, but you won't get any sleep.'

'I'd feel guilty otherwise.'

'We could both sleep in the bed,' said Jay.

Nadia hesitated. It was the most practical solution, of course. It was just a shame he couldn't have been nice-but-comfortingly-ugly, rather than nice-and-definitely-attractive. *Dangerously* attractive, in fact.

Not that she'd be tempted to do anything naughty, but she didn't want Jay thinking she might be tempted.

'Just sleep.' Nadia met his gaze. 'No funny business. We'd have all our clothes on. And I'd be in my sleeping-bag,' she added for good measure.

'Absolutely.' Jay's mouth had begun to twitch.

'I have a boyfriend,' Nadia explained firmly, 'and we love each other.'

Jay nodded, to show he understood. 'Me too.'

Gosh, weren't gay men lovely? Nadia thought delightedly as they lay in bed together two hours later. You could relax and chat away about anything at all, secure in the knowledge that there was no underlying agenda. She'd told Jay about her job at the garden centre, her family in Bristol and last night's party in Oxford.

Now he was asking her about Laurie. Only too happy to oblige, Nadia propped herself on one elbow and said, 'Oh, he's just brilliant, the best boyfriend in the world. He's a model.' She added with pride, 'Last month he was on the cover of *GQ*.'

'I'm impressed.' Jay smiled. 'So how did you two meet? At some fantastically glitzy party? Did Madonna and Guy invite you to dinner and there he was? Or did he just turn up at the garden centre one day in desperate need of a clematis?'

'Ho ho. Actually, we've known each other since we were kids. He lived over the road from us. Laurie taught me how to ride a bike with no hands, I taught him how to shoplift Pick 'n' Mix from Woolworth's . . .'

'*Cider With Rosie* meets *Bonnie and Clyde*.' Jay raised an eyebrow. 'So you've been together how long? Since you were *seven*?'

'Oh no. We were just friends then. I went away to college at eighteen then Laurie was off the following year. When he came back two years ago we took one look at each other and it hit us both like a brick.' Nadia clapped her hands together. '*Bam*, just like that. And we've been together ever since.'

'I'm confused. So when did the modelling thing start?'

'I entered him for a competition,' she explained. 'One of those daytime TV programmes was offering a prize of a contract with a top modelling agency. I just stuck a photo in an envelope and posted it off without telling him. A month later they phoned and told him he'd been shortlisted for the final. He went mental! He thought modelling was for poofs—ooh, sorry, but he did.'

'That's OK.' Jay inclined his head.

'Anyway, we managed to persuade him that it *wasn't*,' Nadia hastily emphasised, 'and Laurie finally agreed to go up for the final. Mainly to shut me up, I think. But then he won the competition and that was it, the agency put him on their books and the whole thing took off. Before, he'd been training as a stockbroker and hating every minute. Now he's travelling all over the world doing magazine shoots and ad campaigns. It's just brilliant, a whole new career.'

'Thanks to you,' Jay said mildly. He paused. 'Ever regret it?'

'Why would I regret it? We might not see as much of each other as before, but he comes back whenever he can. We still love each other.

And it's not going to last for ever. By the time you hit thirty, you're over the hill. We talk to each other all the time. He's been in Egypt for the last few days, shooting an ad campaign for Earl jeans.' Nadia plumped up her pillow and changed the subject. 'Anyway, your turn now. Tell me all about your boyfriend.'

The candle on the bedside table flickered, sending an eddy of shadows across the wall.

'Actually, I'm not gay,' said Jay.

'So why did you tell me you were?'

'To relax you.' His eyes were bright with amusement. 'And it worked.'

'That's cheating,' Nadia groaned. 'I trusted you. You lied to me.'

'OK, I'm sorry.' Laughing, Jay held up his hands. 'But it did stop you panicking about spending the night in bed with a strange man who might try to seduce you, didn't it?'

'You could at least have waited until the morning before telling me you were straight.'

'I was going to. Until you asked me about my boyfriend. Anyway, you don't have to worry,' said Jay. 'I'm still not going to even try to seduce you. So you're perfectly safe.'

'Right. Well, that's good.' Nadia wriggled down into her sleeping-bag, affecting indifference but secretly she preferred him gay. Just because she'd never be unfaithful to Laurie didn't mean she couldn't be attracted to a good-looking man.

'You could ask me about my girlfriend if you like,' Jay prompted.

'Go on then, tell me about her.'

He winked. 'We broke up a couple of months ago.'

Typical. 'See?' Nadia heaved a sigh. 'You're doing it already. You wouldn't have said that if you'd still been gay.'

'Oh, come on, don't get all defensive. I said I wouldn't try to seduce you, didn't I?'

'But now you're flirting with me,' Nadia complained.

'So? I'm allowed to flirt. You were doing it earlier,' he pointed out, 'when you thought I was gay.' Jay's dark brown eyes glinted at her with amusement.

'I was not.' Feeling herself blushing, she was glad of the dim light. 'Why would I want to?'

Oh crikey, was he right? She hadn't even realised.

'And now you aren't doing it,' he went on. 'You're back-pedalling like mad. Which has to mean you like me at least, ooh'—he held out his hand, the thumb and forefinger half an inch apart—'this much.'

Not fair, not *fair*.

'If I didn't like you that much, I wouldn't be here. Then again, you might snore.'

'Not at all. I'm the perfect gentleman in bed.' He flashed a wicked grin. 'No one's ever regretted spending the night with me.'

Nadia didn't doubt it for one second. He was great company, confident and charismatic. If she weren't involved with Laurie, let's face it, she'd be tempted to go for it. Why not, after all? Here they were stranded in a snowbound pub. No one else need know . . .

Oh good grief, she was actually imagining how it would feel to slide her hand up beneath that thick dark blue sweater of his . . . What was the matter with her? She was just a shameless hussy, stop it, stop it, *stop it*.

She had Laurie. Who could ask for more?

Appalled with herself, Nadia leaned over and blew out the flickering candle. Thankful that Jay wasn't able to read her mind—and horribly afraid that he could—she said, 'I'm going to sleep now. Good night.'

The following morning, clomping downstairs in her boots, Nadia discovered an arctic wind whistling through the empty pub and the front door gaping open. Everyone had gathered outside to applaud the snowplough that was shooting great plumes of snow up into the air as it made its stately way along the main street.

Nadia found Jay among the crowd. 'We're saved. We shan't have to eat each other, that's a relief. How am I going to get my car out of the ditch?'

'Don't worry. The cavalry have arrived.' Jay indicated the tractor trundling along in the wake of the snowplough. It slowed to a halt outside the pub and a burly farmer type jumped down.

'Passed some cars back there, in need of a tow.' Spotting Nadia's hopeful face he said, 'One of them yours, love? Want some help?'

She could have kissed him. Her fiftysomething knight in a filthy tractor! This was village life for you, Nadia thought gratefully. Everyone pulled together, helping each other out.

'Oh, I do,' she said. 'Mine's the black Renault, this is so *ki*—'

'No problem, love. Any time. That'll be fifty quid.'

Talk about highway robbery. Country people weren't lovely at all.

'Just don't say cash,' Nadia warned the greedy selfish mercenary farmer. 'I can do a cheque.'

'Got a guarantee card?' The farmer was nothing if not blunt.

'Who shall I make the cheque out to, Dick Turpin?' Nadia replied.

'Have you out of there in a jiffy, love.' The farmer winked at her, unabashed. After all, business was business. Sudden blizzards were always a nice little earner.

The Renault had been hauled out of the ditch, dented but otherwise unharmed. Jay had arrived at the scene on his way back to his own car.

'It's been nice meeting you.' Jay's eyes crinkled at the corners as he looked down at Nadia as she revved the engine. 'Could have been nicer still, but never mind.'

Nadia nodded. In the cold light of day, she knew that if she'd given in to temptation last night, she'd be feeling twisted with guilt by now.

'Thanks for everything, Jay. Bye.'

'That boyfriend of yours is a lucky bloke.' Jay rested his hand briefly on the roof of the car. 'Tell him I said so.'

For a moment Nadia wondered if he was about to bend down and give her a goodbye kiss on the cheek. She realised she was holding her breath. Just a sociable peck, not full-frontal snogging, was absolutely fine . . .

Well, it would have been, if it had happened.

'Drive carefully now,' said Jay. 'And don't skid into any more ditches.'

'Yes, boss. You too.' Nadia grinned. 'See you around.'

Why did people always say that, when they knew they wouldn't?

The flight from Barcelona to Bristol Airport had landed fifteen minutes ago and Nadia was hopping impatiently from one foot to the other at the arrivals gate. Any second now, the first passengers would begin to emerge through the sliding smoked-glass doors. There were butterflies in her stomach—huge, excitable tropical butterflies rather than the sedate English kind—and adrenaline was sloshing through her body like free beer at a student party.

Nadia gazed, transfixed, as an ultra-smart businesswoman tip-tapped out on ultra-high heels, followed by a gaggle of holidaymakers, then a frazzled-looking girl in her twenties with a screaming baby and a toddler in tow.

At the sound of a shout behind her, the girl turned and let out an exclamation of relief as Laurie raced through the doors clasping a battered toy giraffe.

'I found it on the floor by the luggage trolleys.'

'That's why she was yelling. I didn't even realise she'd dropped it. Thank you so much.' The girl's face was alight with gratitude.

'No problem.' Laurie flashed his trademark broad smile and Nadia, watching them from six feet away, realised that this was why she loved him. He was kind and thoughtful and would help anyone.

And here he was now, coming towards her, holding out his arms.

'Nad!'

Mushy with love, she threw her own arms round him then felt her feet leave the ground as he lifted her up and swung her round. Then he was kissing her.

'I've missed you so much.' Hugging her tightly, then taking a step back, Laurie surveyed her and said, 'God, you look fantastic.'

'So do you. Messy, but fantastic.' Grinning, she put a hand up to his slept-on sunstreaked blond hair, then cupped the side of his gold-stubbled jaw. For a professional model, Laurie had no vanity whatsoever. He was wearing baggy black trousers that looked like jumble sale rejects. The pale grey sweater with holes in the elbows had once belonged to his father. His trainers were state-of-the-art and filthy.

'I know, I know. I'm a mess.' Laurie's green eyes widened with good-natured resignation; he was well used to being fussed over by highly strung editors and frenetic casting agents. 'Let's go. How is everyone? Is that damn parrot still alive?'

Harpo, who belonged to Nadia's grandmother Miriam, had a long-standing love-hate relationship with Laurie.

'Of course he's alive.' As Laurie expertly heaved his bags over one shoulder, Nadia said, 'He's missed you like mad.'

'Did he get my card?' Laurie had sent Harpo a postcard of a parrot in a mini deckchair with a tiny knotted hankie on his head.

'We tied it to his cage. He pecked holes in it, said something about gross exploitation and cruelty to parrots.'

'That's because he has no sense of humour,' Laurie said loftily

They headed for the short-term car park, catching up on each other's news. When they reached Nadia's Renault, Laurie paused to admire the dented front wing.

'Not bad.' He bent to take a closer look. 'So there you were, upside-down in the ditch, when this complete stranger turns up and persuades you to spend the night with him?'

Nadia, her arm still wrapped round Laurie's waist, pinched him beneath the ribs. 'He came and rescued me. I was so grateful, I thought the least I could do was sleep with him . . . *ouch*.'

'Very funny.' Grinning, Laurie pinched her in return. 'Come on, let's get out of here.'

'Like them.' Nadia tilted her head up to watch as a plane soared skywards. Laurie's eyes followed.

'That'll be me tomorrow. Off to Paris.' He sounded resigned.

Nadia gave him a hug. 'Not until tomorrow night. We've got a day and a half.'

Laurie looked down at her. With a half-smile he said, 'I know.'

Nadia, who was driving, felt an ill-defined squiggle of unease during the twenty-minute drive back to North Bristol. On the surface they were both chattering away, but beneath the surface lay an undercurrent warning her that something was up. She kept waiting for the feeling to go away, but it didn't. Finally she pulled into the driveway of her family's house, having narrowed it down to two possibilities.

'OK, let me just say this. Did you think I was serious when I told you that I'd spent the night with that chap at the pub? I mean, d'you think I might actually have had sex with him? Because I didn't, I swear. I just said it as a joke.'

'Of course I know that. I didn't think you were serious.' Looking distinctly uncomfortable, Laurie raked his fingers through his streaky hair.

Nadia braced herself. OK, now she had to put the second question to him. 'So have you? Met someone else, I mean?'

'No. I haven't. I'd never do that to you.'

Phew. Well, that was a relief.

'But something's wrong,' she persisted.

'Nothing's wrong. I'm fine.'

The words were great, just what she wanted to hear. Sadly, they were coming from the mouth of the world's poorest liar. Laurie might not be seeing anyone else, but he certainly wasn't fine.

'Laurie, you can't pretend there isn't something wrong, just *tell* me—'

'Here he is, back at last! Darling boy, let me have a good look at you!' Miriam flung open the passenger door and clasped Laurie's face between her thin hands. Huge diamonds flashed on her fingers, and for a slender seventy-year-old woman she had a surprisingly firm grip.

But when it came to seventy-year-olds, Miriam Kinsella was hardly par for the course. She could wear couture clothes or ancient corduroy trousers and men's shirts with equal panache. Her glossy black hair was fastened in a bun and, as ever, her dark eyes were heavily accentuated with kohl liner. As the inside of the car filled with Guerlain's *L'Heure Bleue*, Nadia was reminded that Miriam might spend an entire day gardening, but she wouldn't dream of doing it without first spraying on her favourite perfume.

'Beautiful as ever,' Miriam pronounced, having deposited a crimson lipstick mark on Laurie's thin, tanned cheek. 'Now, come along inside. Are you hungry? Your father's still at the clinic but he'll be back soon.'

Edward Welch, Laurie's father, was a neuropsychiatrist. Now sixty-six and no longer employed by the NHS, he had retained a consulting room at one of Bristol's private clinics where he saw patients twice a week. It kept his own brain active, he maintained, gave him something to do other than the *Telegraph* crossword.

And lust helplessly after Miriam, thought Nadia as her grandmother led the way into the house. Following the death of his wife, Josephine, five years earlier, Edward's feelings for Miriam had rapidly become apparent to all of them.

The only fly in the ointment had been Miriam's steadfast refusal to return Edward's feelings. As far as she was concerned, he was a wonderful man and a dear friend. They enjoyed each other's company and were invited everywhere together, but Miriam had made it clear there could be no more to their relationship than that. And Edward had been forced to accept it. Being Miriam's friend and a sizable part of her life was infinitely preferable to not being her friend and being excluded from her life.

'Now, let's feed you up.' Bustling into the kitchen, Miriam threw open the king-sized fridge. 'There's some chicken casserole left over from last night, or . . .'

'Miriam, I'm taking Nadia out to dinner. Markwick's,' he added when Nadia raised her eyebrows. 'Table's already booked.'

Markwick's was one of her favourite restaurants. Nadia wondered if it was the equivalent of the guilty husband buying his wife roses and chocolates. From a petrol station. Then again, maybe she wasn't being fair; Laurie was always taking her out to gorgeous restaurants.

She just didn't have a good feeling about it this time.

Still, whatever it was would have to wait a few hours. Miriam was here now, and Edward would be back soon, followed by Clare and Tilly—Laurie wasn't just hers, he was a part of the whole family.

When James Kinsella had married Leonie it had been, possibly, the first truly impulsive action of his life. At the age of twenty-one, halfway through his accountancy training, it had been while he was driving home from work one evening that he'd spotted her walking across the Downs in Clifton, thumbing a lift. Appalled, James had stopped his car and informed her that hitchhiking was a dangerous thing to do.

Laughing at his earnest expression, Leonie had thrown back her long blonde hair and said, 'Are you dangerous?'

James had replied, 'Of course not, but the man in the next car to stop might be.'

Cheekily, she had yanked open the passenger door, climbed in and said, 'Better give me a lift then, before he turns up.'

Five months later, they'd been married. James had never met anyone like Leonie before. She was fearless, a true free spirit, with a breathtaking zest for life. And James was utterly enthralled.

It didn't take long, though, for James to discover that free spirits don't necessarily make great mothers. When Nadia was born, Leonie launched into her earth-mother phase, but it didn't last. Shortly before Nadia's first birthday, James came home from work to be greeted by his wife thrusting their daughter into his arms, yelling, 'Why did nobody ever tell me being a mother was going to be so bloody *boring*?'

It had taken all James's energy to calm her down and persuade her not to walk out on them. Somehow they managed to stagger on for another year and a half. Then Leonie discovered to her horror that she was pregnant again. Clare was born and the situation went from bad to worse. She loved her children but was unable to cope with their incessant demands. Leonie felt as if she was trapped in an airless Perspex cube.

It was while she was in Canford Park one late spring morning, having taken Nadia and Clare along to commune with the tadpoles and baby frogs in the pond, that she met Kieran Brown. He was an out-of-work actor, and utterly charming. A fortnight later she packed her bags and ran off to Crete with him.

Witnessing the extent of James's shock and desolation—and having inwardly predicted from the start that her son's marriage would come to a sticky end—Miriam had promptly taken charge and insisted that he and the children move in with her. A wealthy widow, her house was large enough, and helping to look after Nadia and Clare would give her something to do. At forty-seven, Miriam had the energy of a twenty-year-old. And the children adored her.

Since James couldn't begin to imagine how else he might manage, he had accepted his mother's generous offer. The children adapted to the changes with gratifying ease. It had, he decided with heartfelt relief, been the right thing to do. In a couple of years, maybe, the difficulties might ease and they would find a place of their own.

Twenty-three years on, it hadn't happened yet, and in the meantime, their unorthodox family set-up had expanded to include Tilly, when Leonie had arrived at the house with a fatherless one-year-old and departed shortly afterwards, without her.

'You're not eating,' said Laurie. 'Come on, try the duck. It's fantastic.'

'I don't want to try the duck.' Nadia kept her voice low; this was Markwick's after all. 'I want you to try telling me the truth.'

Laurie reached across the table, his fingers closing around hers. 'Can't we just enjoy the meal?'

'Obviously not, if I can't even swallow a mouthful of it. Laurie, either you tell me what's wrong or I stand up on this chair and scream.'

The look on her face told Laurie all he needed to know. 'OK.'

Laurie hesitated, pushing his fingers through his hair.

'OK.' Another pause. 'I think we should call it a day. We hardly ever see each other. It's not fair on you.'

It was like plunging into an ice-cold swimming pool that you'd expected to be warm. There was a high-pitched ringing in Nadia's ears.

'Not fair on me, or not fair on you?' Nadia couldn't believe she was managing to get the words out.

'Neither of us.' Laurie shrugged unhappily. 'I'm sorry, I'm so sorry. But it's for the best. Everything's different now. Our lives have changed . . . You haven't done anything *wrong*,' Laurie said helplessly. 'It's just . . . oh Nad, you must know what I mean. This isn't anything to do with you.'

Struggling to get her bearings, Nadia said, 'When were you planning on breaking the news? Tomorrow afternoon, on the way back to the airport? My God, I can't believe we're here having this conversation. I thought we were happy and all this time you've been gearing yourself up to do this.' Nadia shook her head in disbelief. 'How long ago did you decide?'

'Nad, please, I feel bad enough as it is. Over the last few weeks, I suppose.' Laurie was looking thoroughly miserable.

'A few *weeks*? Oh, great. So a fortnight ago, when I was telling that bloke how fantastically happy we were together, you were already planning to dump me! Do you have any idea how stupid that makes me feel?'

'Look, I'm sorry. I thought this was the best way. We can't carry on like this, never seeing each other. The agency's got me working nonstop for the next eight months.' Laurie struggled to explain. 'All over Europe, Australia, Japan, the States . . .'

'Fine. You don't have to explain.' Then a thought occurred to her that made her feel sick. She marvelled at Laurie's selfishness. 'But we were going to spend the night together. We'd have made . . .' no, not made love, '. . . we'd have had sex, and you'd have known it was for the last time, but *I* wouldn't. Well, that's a really thoughtful finishing touch.'

'Nadia, this isn't easy. I'm only doing it because it's for the best.'

That old line again. 'Oh, do me a favour,' Nadia hissed across the table. 'You're dumping me because you want to shag your way around Paris and Milan and New York, because you're a jet-setter now and jet-setters only have sex with It-girls and supermodels.'

'It's not that,' said Laurie.

'Isn't it? I don't really care anyway.' Of course, this was a massive lie. Nadia dropped her head. No more Laurie. It was just an unfathomable concept. She badly wanted to cry now. Furiously and violently. But she was buggered if she'd give Laurie the satisfaction.

Raising her head, Nadia looked at him from beneath her eyelashes.

'OK, it's over. But you were still going to sleep with me tonight.' Nadia waited, holding his gaze. 'What a shame we're both going to miss out on the last time.' Another pause, followed by a tiny playful smile. 'Well? Do you still want to?'

It was as easy as asking a five-year-old if he wanted to open his Christmas presents a week early. She saw the spark of relief in his eyes as he reached across the table and squeezed her hand.

'Of course I still want to,' said Laurie.

Feeling powerful for the first time that evening, Nadia rose to her feet and said icily, 'Well, that's a real shame, because you *can't*.'

Chapter Two

HOW PEOPLE'S LIVES could change in the space of fifteen months, thought Nadia as she queued up at the supermarket check-out with a basket containing a bottle of hair detangler—yes, it was still uncontrollably curly, no change there—and a tube of Immac. This was her precious day off and how was she spending it? Detangling her hair, defuzzing her legs and watching the woman ahead of her in the queue idly leaf through a copy of this week's *OK!* magazine.

Thanks to her sister, Nadia already knew that there was a photograph on page twenty-seven of Laurie in a dinner jacket, arriving at the Oscars with one of the nominees for Best Supporting Actress. Clare, who read every glossy magazine going, had spotted the picture of the smiling couple yesterday and had thoughtfully rushed downstairs to show Nadia just how much Laurie's life had changed.

'Imagine! The Oscars! With a girl like that! Bet she didn't get that dress in Top Shop. And they describe him as a model-turned-actor.'

Nadia had briefly been tempted to batter her sister to death with the iron in her hand. But Clare wasn't being deliberately cruel. It just wouldn't occur to her that Nadia might not want to see her ex-boyfriend pictured in a magazine with some sensational-looking new girl.

Oh yes, Laurie was living a whole new charmed life now. He hadn't been home for months. He had fallen into acting when his agency had sent him to appear in a pop video. At a party several weeks later, he'd met a director who recognised him from the video and cast Laurie in his new movie. Hollywood parties are stuffed to the gills with aspiring actors desperate for their big break. Laurie, who didn't even want one, got his. The movie part had been small, but he acquitted himself with honours. Knowing his luck, Nadia thought drily, by this time next year he'd be the one nominated for an Oscar.

'She used to go out with Johnny Depp.' Clare was drooling over the accompanying article. 'Hey, how cool is that? You've slept with someone who slept with someone who slept with Johnny Depp.'

'I could always singe your ears,' Nadia offered, holding up the iron.

'Ooh, *touchy*.' Clare turned to Harpo in his cage. 'You'd think she'd be flattered, wouldn't you, Harpo? What's Nadia got, eh? What's Nadia got?'

It had taken her hours to teach him this one.

'Brrrkkk,' Harpo squawked in return. 'Nadia's got a fat arse.'

Leaving the supermarket, Nadia made her way along Princess Victoria Street past the art gallery and the shoe shop. Charlotte's Patisserie loomed ahead, their white chocolate éclairs luring her towards them.

'Nadia!'

So wrapped up in the heavenly prospect of biting into a squishy, silky-smooth éclair that she barely registered her name being called, Nadia yelped in alarm as a hand came to rest on her shoulder.

Oh God, had she accidentally shoplifted something from the supermarket? Had a burly store detective chased her down the street?

'Oh, it's you!' Relief broke over her like a wave.

Jay Tiernan was shaking his head with amusement. 'I saw you walking past the art gallery. Well, I was almost sure it was you. This is amazing, I was just thinking about you the other day.'

'Really? Why?' Flattered, Nadia pulled her stomach muscles in.

'My sister-in-law pranged her car. Smashed the front wing, just like you did. Your face,' he went on cheerfully, 'when I put my hand on your shoulder. You jumped a mile.'

'Yes, well. I thought you were a store detective.'

Jay raised his eyebrows. 'You've been *stealing*?'

'No! I just—'

'Something decent, I hope—*oh*.' Having whisked her carrier from her grasp and briskly surveyed the less-than-glamorous contents, he shook his head sorrowfully at Nadia. 'You really don't have any idea how to shoplift, do you? This is hopeless, hopeless!'

'Very funny.' Taking the bag back from him, Nadia said, 'What are you doing in Bristol anyway?'

'I moved down from Oxford a few months ago. And right at this minute—well, up until thirty seconds ago, I was standing in front of two paintings like *this*'—he struck a pose of chin-rubbing indecision—'trying to choose which one to buy.'

'In the Harrington Gallery?' Nadia realised that this was where he must have been when he'd spotted her going past the window.

'Yes.' Jay took her arm. 'Come on. This has to be fate. You can help me decide.' He paused. 'Unless you're in a desperate hurry to get home.'

Nadia shook her head in a free and easy manner. 'No hurry.'

'Quite sure about that? Promise me you're not growing werewolf legs as we speak?' Raising his eyebrows, Jay glanced at the carrier bag containing the offending tube of depilatory cream.

Nadia shot him a sunny smile. 'Oh, that's not for me. Whenever I meet a man who thinks he's really hilarious, I like to sneak into his house at night and squeeze Immac into his bottle of shampoo.'

As Jay pulled her inside, Nadia chose not to mention just how well she knew the Harrington Gallery. Not well, as in sleeping with the owner, but she'd been dragged along to a fair few preview nights in her time.

'This one,' Jay announced, stepping in front of the first painting. Moments later she found herself being swivelled by the elbows to her left and planted before a second canvas. 'Or this one?'

Nadia opened her mouth to speak, then shut it again.

It just had to be, didn't it?

The painting on the right was a towering dramatic mountainscape featuring a lot of grape-coloured sky with the occasional shaft of sunlight breaking through the clouds. Very moody. Almost biblical. That is, until your gaze was gradually drawn to the bottom left-hand corner, where a couple were kissing in an old-fashioned red telephone box. The painting, on sale for £750, was by an artist she hadn't heard of. The second one, priced at £520, had been painted by Clare, her sister.

Clare's style was quirky, offbeat and character-led, like Beryl Cook without the acres of fat. This particular work, executed in bold watercolours overlaid with ink, depicted a wedding reception complete with naughty pageboys, lecherous bridegroom, gossiping guests and the bride's mother passed out with one hand clutching a bottle of Pomagne and her head on the table. The bride, meanwhile, was at the door legging it with one of the waiters. The painting was titled *Happy Ever After*.

'Well?' said Jay, at her side.

'Hmm.' Thoughtfully, Nadia studied her sister's painting from all angles. Behind his desk at the far end of the gallery, Thomas Harrington spotted her. Catching his eye, Nadia indicated with a faint shake of her head that she'd prefer him not to come and greet her like an old friend.

'Which one?' Jay prompted in her ear.

'Honestly?'

'Honestly.'

Nadia recalled Clare's remarks earlier as she'd ogled the photos of Laurie. 'Since you ask, I prefer the one with the phone box.'

'Really?'

'It's unexpected. You don't see it at first. The other one's more all-over funny, a bit slapstick.' As guilt belatedly kicked in, Nadia amended, 'Then again, it's still good. And cheaper.'

'Oh well, that's it then. If I choose it now I'd look like a lousy cheapskate.' Turning to Thomas Harrington, Jay said cheerfully, 'I'll just have to take the one with the phone box.'

When Jay had done the credit card thing and Thomas Harrington had murmured in her ear, 'It's no skin off my nose, but your sister's going to beat you to a pulp if she gets to hear about this,' Nadia allowed herself to be led away to a pavement café for a drink to celebrate.

'So tell me what you've been doing with yourself. Are we safe out here, by the way?' Jay indicated the magazine rack standing outside the newsagents across the narrow street. 'Your boyfriend's not likely to leap from the pages of *GQ* and lay one on me?'

Oh God, how she had boasted about her wonderful relationship, about the deep love she and Laurie had had for each other.

'That was ages ago. We broke up. And if you smirk,' she added as the corners of Jay's mouth began to twitch. 'I'll pour salt in your coffee. We just aren't together any more and I'm fine about it. How about you?'

'I'm fine about it too.' Hastily he covered his coffee with his hand. 'And I'm not smirking. It's just really nice to see you again.'

The next time Nadia looked at her watch, a whole hour, incredibly, had gone by. She had learned that Jay was now living here in Clifton, in Canynge Road. He was in property development and buying up and renovating neglected houses in the area, then selling them on at a profit.

'And how's your job going? Weren't you working in a garden centre?'

'Out at Almondsbury. Yes, I'm still there. It's great, I love it.'

This was a massive exaggeration. Her job was OK, verging on the tedious. The plants and flowers themselves were fine, but when customers came back complaining that the pot of fuchsias they'd bought three years earlier had just died—as if she'd personally doused them with cyanide—well, it was enough to make you wonder if some people should be allowed to buy plants in the first place.

'You love it,' Jay echoed thoughtfully. He paused. 'That's a shame.'

'Why?' Nadia sat up a bit straighter. 'I don't love it that much.'

'OK. On a scale of one to ten. How much do you love your job?'

'Two,' Nadia promptly replied.

Jay let out a low whistle. 'You're right, you don't love it that much.'

'I didn't want to sound like one of those people who whinge on about their boring job but can't be bothered to get off their fat backside and find something better.' Even though, basically, this described her situation to a T.

'But you know a lot about gardening?' said Jay.

'I know everything. I'm Charlie Dimmock in a bra.' How that woman ever managed to work without one was a mystery to her. 'Why?'

Jay shrugged. 'Maybe nothing. I need a gardener, that's all.'

He needed a gardener? Hey, say no more.

'I can fit that in, no problem. In my spare time,' Nadia explained eagerly. 'How big is it?' Oops. As the actress said to the bishop.

Looking as if he were trying not to smile, Jay leaned back in his chair. 'When I buy a wreck of a house and do it up, it generally has a wreck of a garden to go with it. I need someone to transform it into something superb. I'm talking clearance, re-landscaping, planting, the lot.'

'I could do that!' Nadia sat up. 'I did landscaping at college.' Crikey, Jay had talked about fate earlier. This really *was* fate. 'I'm a hard worker and I wouldn't let you down.' She was aware of sounding disgustingly eager.

Jay hesitated, evidently reluctant to hand her the job on the spot. 'I put an ad in the local paper last week. I've had quite a few responses.'

'Maybe,' Nadia said promptly, 'but none of them have slept with you and I have. That has to count for something.'

Damn, damn, she *knew* she should have had sex with him.

From the look of amusement in Jay's brown eyes she could tell he was thinking the same thing. Nadia silently cursed her faithfulness. If she didn't get this job it would all be Laurie's fault. Him and his lousy promises that they'd be together for ever. God, she wished she could hate him as ferociously as he deserved.

'Do you have a garden you could show me?'

It would have been nice if the house could have been empty, but Nadia's home seldom was. Doing her best to sound businesslike, she led Jay into the kitchen and announced, 'Gran, this is Jay Tiernan, he needs a gardener so I've brought him here to show him what I can do. Jay, this is Miriam Kinsella, my grandmother. And Edward Welch, our neighbour.'

Miriam and Edward were watching the racing on television while finishing a late lunch of garlic bread, Milano salami and a bottle of Barolo. Swivelling round on her chair, Miriam waggled her fingers at Jay.

'Won't shake hands, mine are all messy and garlicky. Well, I can see why Nadia would want to work for you. Will you have a glass of red, Jay? Come along, pull up a chair and join us. Darling, *well done*,' she stage-whispered to Nadia. 'And those *eyes*. Just what you need to cheer you up, wherever did you find him?'

Nadia briefly closed her eyes and wished the good fairy could have granted her a nice normal apple-cheeked grey-bunned, apron-wearing grandmother. It was a good job she loved Miriam. Otherwise she would have been forced to lock her in the attic years ago.

Jay was grinning broadly.

'Two more glasses,' Miriam instructed Edward, who she tended to treat like a butler.

'No, don't bother'—Nadia shook her head—'we're not staying. Just five minutes in the garden, then Jay has to leave.' Hastily, she led Jay through to the garden. 'Sorry. My grandmother does have her good points, I just can't think of any right now.'

'Doesn't bother me.' Crossing the terrace, Jay stood with his hands on his hips and surveyed the grounds stretching before him.

In a curving amphitheatre of mature trees—beech, ash and cedar—free-form beds of ostrich fern, Oriental poppies and delphiniums bordered the emerald lawn. From the lily pond on the left, a winding stream snaked down to a larger pond in the bottom right-hand corner of the garden. Everything was planted to look as though it hadn't been deliberately planted at all—the gardening equivalent of a supermodel sporting just-got-out-of-bed hair that had actually taken five stylists three hours to achieve. Nadia had slogged her guts out to create this garden and as far as she was concerned it was perfect. But would Jay think so?

Finally he spoke. 'You did all this?'

'Every last inch of it myself,' Nadia told him with pride, 'down to carrying these flagstones.' She stamped her heel against the pale honey Cotswold stone covering the terrace.

'I'm impressed,' said Jay.

Phew. Nadia exhaled. 'So, do I get the job?'

'I still have other people to see. The appointments are all set up.'

'Cancel them,' said Nadia. 'You don't need them. You've got me.'

'I shouldn't.' Jay glanced at her, then broke into a grin. 'But what the hell. OK.'

Yesss! A quick-thinking decision-maker, unconcerned with breaking the rules and letting other people down. In other words, absolutely not the kind of person *ever* to get romantically involved with. The sensible part of Nadia's brain carefully noted this fact down. The hopeless part gave a happy shiver of anticipation and wondered what her new boss looked like naked.

Because she was almost sure he fancied her. You could generally tell.

'Excellent,' Nadia said happily.

'So?' A female voice behind her nearly made Nadia jump off the wooden bench. 'What have you done with him?'

Damn, Clare had said she'd be out this afternoon.

'Done with who?'

'I've just been told'—Clare's tone was arch—'that you have a rather spectacular man out here with you. Naturally, I had to come and see this vision for myself. So where is he? Buried in the compost heap? Tied to a tree? Manacled to the lawn mower and locked in the shed? Nad, how many times have I told you, this isn't the way to stop a man running out on you, they have to *want* to stay.'

'He's gone to the loo, and as soon as he comes back we're leaving.'

Keen to be gone, Nadia jumped to her feet and said, 'I'd better find—'

'Oh, here he is!' Having leapt up with even more alacrity than Nadia, Clare exclaimed, 'We thought you'd escaped! Hi!'

Clare was already introducing herself and mentally giving Jay Tiernan the once-over. She'd never been what you'd call shy.

'I've just seen the painting in your sitting room,' Jay announced. 'Why didn't you tell me you already had one by the same artist?'

Sometimes you do something silly on the spur of the moment, like persuading a virtual stranger not to buy one of your sister's paintings, because what's the chances of her ever getting to hear about it?

Sadly, in Nadia's case, it took about six seconds.

Puzzled, Clare said, 'In our sitting room?'

'The door was open and I spotted it on the wall.' Jay smiled at her while Nadia sent frantic telepathic messages instructing him to Stop Right There. 'I bumped into Nadia in Clifton this afternoon and dragged her into the Harrington Gallery. Couldn't decide between two paintings. She told me which one to buy.'

Clearly, those telepathic signals hadn't worked. Stumbling over her words, Nadia said hastily, 'Oh no, that's not true, I didn't *tell* you—'

'And?' Clare interrupted. Her eyes were glittering. 'Which painting did she say you should buy? The one by the artist whose work is hanging in our living room?' Horrible elongated pause. 'Or the other one?' As if she hadn't figured it out already.

'The other one.' Now it was Jay's turn to hesitate. 'Er, sorry, have I put my foot in it? Is the artist a friend of yours?'

'You complete cow!' roared Clare. 'How *could* you?' Turning to face Jay, she bellowed, '*I* painted those pictures. What did I ever do to deserve this from my own sister?'

What had she ever done? Ha, only about a million things.

'OK, OK, maybe I should have told Jay I knew you. But then he'd have felt he had to buy your painting. He asked me which one I preferred,' Nadia said hurriedly, 'and I told him the truth.'

'You bitch!' Clare's eyes blazed as she spun back round to face Jay. 'She's jealous, that's all it is. Because I can paint and she can't. Nadia spends her days selling plastic gnomes and humping sacks of gravel into the boots of people's cars. She can't even keep a boyfriend, they all leave her. That's another reason she's jealous of me. If I were you I'd get out quick, and thank your lucky stars you found out what she's like before it's too late.' And with that she stalked off into the house.

'Well,' said Jay finally. 'That was . . . interesting.'

'Sorry.' Nadia gritted her teeth. She couldn't think of anything else to say. Keen to avoid any further contact with her family, she led him round the side of the house to where her car was parked on the drive.

As she fumbled with the keys, the sitting-room window was flung open and Harpo screeched, 'Nadia's got a fat arse!'

Jay looked startled. 'Good grief. Is that your sister?'

'My grandmother's parrot.'

And then Clare's voice came bellowing through the same window: 'She's desperate to get married and have babies, you know!'

OK, enough. 'Excuse me a moment.' Nadia abruptly wheeled round. She stormed through the front door, slamming it hard behind her.

'Ow!' shrieked Clare, clutching the side of her face. She lunged forward but Nadia was too quick for her. Like the SAS, she was in and out in less than five seconds.

'Sorry about that.' Jumping into the driver's seat, she started the engine.

Jay replied with amusement, 'I don't think you are.'

'Well. She deserved it. Sometimes only a really good slap will do. Anyway, it wasn't true,' said Nadia. 'About me being desperate to get married and have babies. Not that it's relevant,' she added hastily.

This would have been an appropriate moment for Jay to have told her that she didn't have a fat arse either—because she *didn't*—but all he did was nod. Nadia drove him back to his car in silence.

As he lifted the bubble-wrapped painting off the back seat, she said, 'I expect you've changed your mind now about giving me the job.'

'One thing,' said Jay. 'Why did you persuade me to buy this painting?'

'I liked it more.' Nadia paused. 'And also Clare was having a dig at me this morning about my ex-boyfriend. She knew she was getting on my nerves and she was really enjoying it. But I really do prefer that painting.'

He nodded. 'OK.'

'OK what?'

'Better hand in your notice at the garden centre.'

Nadia exhaled with relief, a huge smile spreading unstoppably across her face. 'Oh, thank you! You're sure?'

'Hey, I have a brother, I know what it's like. We used to fight all the time.'

'Used to? You don't still fight?'

Jay shook his head. 'Not any more. Here, give me a ring in the next day or two.' He passed her a business card from his wallet.

Clutching it like a winning lottery ticket to her chest, Nadia said fervently, 'You won't regret this. I promise not to slap any of your clients.'

'Glad to hear it,' said Jay. 'And it might be an idea to check the seal on that bottle of hair remover. Make sure it hasn't mysteriously got squeezed into your shampoo.'

Nadia knew she was going to enjoy working for him. Still beaming like an idiot, she headed for her car.

'One other thing,' Jay called out.

She turned back. 'What?'

'The parrot was wrong.'

The letter had arrived this morning. Sitting at her dressing table, Miriam carefully unfolded it and read it for the third time.

This was the trouble with the world today. Everyone had access to computers and the computers knew too damn much about everything. It had all been so simple fifty-odd years ago. If you wanted to disappear, you just moved to another part of the country, put the past firmly behind you and made a new life for yourself.

And it *had* been a happy life, she'd made sure of that. What was the point of dragging all this old stuff up now?

Raising her head, Miriam gazed at her reflection in the bevelled mirror. It was the eyes, of course, that had given her away. The rest of her body was showing all the normal signs of wear and tear. But her eyes had remained the same.

Bloody Edward, this was all his fault. He had been invited to perform the official opening of a new research institute in Berkshire. When a press photographer had taken their picture together and asked for her name she had given it to him without a second thought. Who could have imagined that someone might spot her face in the newspaper and then track her down through some voting register on the internet?

Miriam heaved a sigh of irritation mingled with fear. Tempting though it was simply to rip the letter up and throw it in the bin, she knew she couldn't do that. Carefully she picked up her fountain pen, copied the sender's home address onto the front of the envelope and crossed out her own. In big capitals she wrote: RETURN TO SENDER. NOT KNOWN AT THIS ADDRESS. Then she slid the letter back into the torn-open envelope and Sellotaped it shut. At least the return address on it was Edinburgh, a nice safe distance away.

Twice a week, instead of catching the bus home at four o'clock, Tilly had after-school activities. On Tuesdays she had French club and on Fridays it was netball. Following these, she would walk from school to the newsagents, a hundred yards down from the office where James worked. She always bought something small, chewing gum or TicTacs, to give herself authorised customer status. Then, she would flip through the magazines. Having decided that Tilly wasn't yet another shoplifting adolescent, the woman who worked in the shop allowed her to browse in peace until James appeared to buy his copy of the evening paper and take her home.

The teenage problem pages were what Tilly liked best. It was always comforting to read about other people's less-than-perfect lives. Compared to some, she'd actually got off quite lightly.

The other items she was drawn to were the true-life stories in the women's magazines, the ones where mothers revealed how they had risked their lives in some way in order to save their children. Masochistically, Tilly devoured these tales of maternal devotion. She was unable to stop herself fantasising that maybe one day the same thing might happen to her. Say she needed a kidney transplant or something, and Leonie was the only match, but there was a real danger she wouldn't make it through the operation, Leonie would still insist on going through with it, because, 'Darling Tilly, you're the most important thing in the world to me, all I care about is getting you well again!' And eventually she'd pull through and they'd live happily ever after, just like the brave, loving families in the true-life magazines.

Well, everyone was allowed to have fantasies, weren't they?

Tilly carried on carefully turning the pages of *Take-A-Break*, while other customers came and went. She knew that the woman who worked there was called Annie, because a lot of the regular customers greeted her by name. She was old, probably in her forties, Tilly guessed, but she had a kind face, a ready smile and haphazardly tied-back blonde hair that couldn't appear to make up its mind whether to be curly or straight.

Tilly turned as the bell above the door went *ting*, expecting it to be James. But a jovial man in workman's clothes came into the shop. Tilly watched him buy an angling magazine and a lottery ticket, and listened to him banter with Annie about last week's ticket being faulty.

'You must get fed up with people saying that,' Tilly ventured when the man had left.

'Tell me about it.' Annie rolled her eyes in a long-suffering manner. 'And they always think they're being so witty and original. You just have to smile and play along. But they're nice people,' she hastily amended. 'It's just a bit of fun. Better than not bothering to talk at all.'

'I like it in here,' said Tilly. 'It's friendly. I mean, as long as you don't mind me waiting here?'

'Don't be daft. Of course I don't mind. Here's your dad now,' said Annie, glancing up as James came through the door.

'OK, pigeon? Ready to go?'

Tilly loved it when James called her pigeon, almost as much as she loved the way he flung a fatherly arm round her shoulder. She waited at his side while he dug into his pocket for change and picked up a copy of the *Evening Post*.

'Come on then, let's get home.'

'Bye,' said Annie.

Turning, Tilly gave a little wave and said shyly, 'See you soon.'

'So who is he?' Clare demanded, appearing in Nadia's bedroom doorway. 'Apart from a complete wuss so incapable of making up his own mind that he has to get a girl to do it for him?'

But from her tone of voice, Nadia knew this was Clare's way of indicating that she was prepared to forgive her. Probably because she was going out with Piers tonight and wanted to borrow something to wear.

'His name's Jay Tiernan. He's my new boss. He's a property developer.'

Making her way over to the wardrobe, Clare began idly flicking through the clothes hanging there. 'Fancy him?'

'No!'

Clare smirked. That was the irritating thing about having a sister, they could always tell.

'I don't,' Nadia insisted, going a bit red.

'He's probably married,' announced Clare, the expert. 'And gets up to all sorts. This isn't bad.' Clare was pulling out a lime-green top with velvet edging. The price tag was still pinned to the label. 'Can I wear it tonight?'

Nadia sighed. Trade-off time. Clare had done the reconciliation bit. Now, in return, Nadia had to let her borrow the top. 'OK.'

'Great. And next time you bump into some bloke in the street who drags you into an art gallery, spare a thought for your family, OK? I'm only a poor struggling artist.'

This definitely wasn't true. Clare was a bone-idle artist who'd never struggled in her life. But Nadia let it go.

'He isn't some bloke I just bumped into in the street. Remember when I got caught in the snowstorm last year? He was the one I had to share a room with in the pub.'

A slow smile spread over Clare's face. 'Get out of here! Ha, so that's how you got this new job. You slept with the boss.'

Harpo was shuffling along the window seat in the sitting room when the telephone began to ring. 'Get the bloody phone,' he squawked.

'Get it yourself, that'd be a help,' Miriam muttered. There was an air of tension about her as she snatched up the receiver. Tilly saw her hesitate before saying brusquely, 'Yes?'

The next moment her grandmother visibly relaxed. 'Yes, yes, of course she is, I'll put you on. Tilly darling, it's your mother.'

Blimey, Tilly thought. This had to be the first time Miriam had been relieved to hear Leonie's voice on the phone. Normally she reacted as though a tramp had spat in her face.

Leonie was an erratic communicator, sometimes leaving three months between calls. At other times, chiefly when she had a new man to rave about, she might ring her youngest daughter twice in a week.

This time, true to form, Leonie had apparently met a wonderful guy and she'd never *ever* been happier. His name was Brian, Tilly learned, he was something in the music industry and, best of all, he had a thirteen-year-old daughter, wasn't that just wild? Brian couldn't wait for the four of them to meet up and all get to know each other.

It was with muddled emotions that Tilly eventually hung up the phone. Pleasure that her mum actually wanted her to meet Brian and his daughter. Fear that they wouldn't like her. And unease, because her mother's relationships were always so fragile that the slightest knock could cause everything to end up going horribly wrong. Again.

'OK, darling?' Miriam patted the sofa next to her.

'Mm.' Tilly nodded and sat down, biting her thumbnail. 'Mum's coming down soon with her new boyfriend. He's bringing his daughter with him. She's the same age as me.' Tilly paused. 'Her name's Tamsin.'

'Tilly and Tam. Sounds like one of those American sitcoms.'

Tilly smiled, because her grandmother could always make her feel better. Miriam wasn't afraid of anyone or anything.

'Come on, cheer up. I'm sorry I can't pretend to like your mother.' Miriam kissed the top of her head. 'But she does have her good points.'

Startled, Tilly said, 'Does she?'

'Darling, my son James was always a sensible boy. Then he lost his mind, went completely bonkers for a while and married your mum. But thanks to her, we have three beautiful girls.' Breaking into a smile, she ruffled Tilly's fine, dark blonde hair.

Yes, thought Tilly, but only two of them are his.

'Give us a kiss,' squawked Harpo. Tilting his head to one side he added bossily, 'No tongues.'

Miriam heaved a sigh. 'I'm going to strangle Clare.'

In the taxi on her way home, Clare was forced to admit that things weren't exactly going according to plan. When she'd first met Piers a couple of months ago at a party, he'd definitely been attracted to her. And she'd liked him a lot too.

Usually all her relationships followed a pattern. The men liked her more than she liked them. She enjoyed being the one in control. And the fact that her boredom threshold was low meant that she always tired of them first. When she ended the affair, they were devastated, while she moved on to the next challenge. Like Madonna. So why wasn't it working this time? Why was Piers treating her like this? And why was it having the effect of making her more keen on him, instead of less?

In the back of the cab Clare fretfully pulled at the hem of her lime-green top—would those Vindaloo stains ever come out?—and ran through the events of the evening. They'd arranged to meet at Po Na Na on Whiteladies Road at eight o'clock and, humiliatingly, Piers hadn't arrived until almost nine. Yet while she'd known she *should* walk out at eight fifteen, she hadn't been able to bring herself to do it. When he did finally turn up, she should have chucked a drink in his face before stalking off. But somehow she'd found herself thinking, 'It's OK, he's here now, that's all that matters.'

Clare bit her lip. It was as if Piers had cast a spell on her, with his light, lazy, upper-class drawl, his caustic sense of humour and that floppy public-school hair. Oh, and maybe the electric-blue Ferrari.

From Po Na Na they had moved on to the Clifton Tandoori, even though she wasn't wild about Indian food. When she'd objected, Piers had called her a party pooper and announced that he was in desperate need of a curry. Then, later, when he'd playfully flicked a fork at her, spattering beef Vindaloo sauce over her top, he'd mocked her attempts to clean it off with a napkin and said, 'All this fuss, it's like watching a 1940s housewife. Next thing we know, you'll be darning socks.'

But it was always said with humour, rather than nastiness. And mysteriously Clare found herself making allowances for his behaviour, telling herself that he didn't mean it, it was his upper-class upbringing.

Piers was an Old Etonian. He was twenty-five and a financial adviser. He had a chiselled face, wicked navy-blue eyes and extremely wealthy parents in Surrey. He also had an early start at work tomorrow, which was why instead of spending the night at his Clifton flat, Clare had found herself being deposited in a taxi at eleven thirty and sent home.

'Charge it to my account,' Piers had casually informed the taxi driver, making Clare feel like a prostitute.

Except they hadn't even had sex. Well, they had of course. Lots and lots of truly fantastic sex. Just not tonight.

It was one of the reasons he so intrigued her, Clare realised. The fact that he could so effortlessly take or leave her. Clare wasn't stupid. She knew Piers was playing a game with her to keep her interested. Sooner or later she'd show Piers who was really in charge, make him—

'Here we are, Latimer Road. What number, love?'

'The one at the end. Three streetlamps down, on the left.'

He slowed to a halt beneath the third streetlamp. 'There you go.'

'Thanks.' The interior light came on as Clare opened the rear door.

'A good long soak in Ariel,' said the overweight driver.

'What?'

He nodded at her chest. 'Curry stains. That's your best bet.'

Bloody know-all cab drivers. He needn't think he was getting a tip.

Chapter Three

WHEN NADIA DREW UP outside the house in Clarence Gardens on Monday morning, Jay Tiernan was already standing on the pavement waiting for her. Which was deeply unfair, seeing as it was only ten to nine and he'd said he'd meet her there at nine o'clock. She'd wanted to arrive first, create a good impression.

Now all she had to rely on was her clipboard.

Stepping out of the car, Nadia tucked the brand-new clipboard efficiently under her arm and made her way over to him.

'You're looking pleased with yourself,' Jay observed.

She said brightly, 'I'm in a good mood. Can't wait to start my new job.'

'Come on, I'll show you round. Just try not to slap anyone, OK?'

The house was a Victorian, detached, five-bedroomed property in the process of being completely renovated by Jay's team of builders—Bart, Kevin and Robbie. Nadia was relieved to note that they didn't appear to be the leering, catcalling, whwoarr-darlin' types. Bart and Kevin were a father-and-son act and Robbie, who was in his twenties, seemed painfully shy. They continued working away, as Jay showed her the house and then the garden.

If there had once been a lawn, it was no longer remotely visible. The weeds were at waist height and the area closest to the house was littered with rubbish.

'Well?' Jay was watching her survey the carnage. 'Are you scared?'

'You're joking. I love it. This is like being asked to give Hagrid the makeover of his life.' And turning him into George Clooney.

Jay smiled. 'The aim is to put it on the market in six weeks.'

'I can do that.' Hoping she could, she wiped her damp palms on her jeans. 'Right, I'll make a start. I'll need a truck by Wednesday morning to take away the first load of waste.'

'I'll arrange that.'

'Once I see what the ground's like, I'll be able to draw up a plan,' said Nadia. 'Then we'll discuss how much you want to spend.'

It was a shame she couldn't use her super-efficient clipboard to knock up a quick garden plan on the spot, but there was no point while it was still in this much of a state.

Which was lucky really, seeing as she'd forgotten to bring a pen.

Three hours later, Robbie came out to the garden and mouthed something to her. Switching off the chainsaw, Nadia pushed her goggles to the top of her head and dragged off her protective gloves. Who said gardening wasn't glamorous?

'Sorry, couldn't hear you,' said Nadia.

'Erm . . .' Robbie hesitated like a boy in a school play who's forgotten his lines. 'Um, we've just boiled the kettle. Bart wondered if you'd like a cup of tea.'

'Oh, fantastic.' She beamed over at him, willing him to relax.

Inside the house the kitchen was pretty much gutted, but there was a kettle plugged into a socket. Next to it on the dusty floor sat a box of tea bags, an opened carton of milk, a bag of sugar and a grubby teaspoon. Having pointed them out to her, Robbie vanished without another word.

Right.

'OK, love?' Moments later, Bart appeared in the doorway clutching a tobacco pouch and a vast mug of tea. He was in his mid-fifties at a guess, with very little hair and a friendly face. 'You've bin workin' your socks off, haven't you? Blimey, like the *Texas Chainsaw Massacre* out there. Must have worked up a thirst by now.'

'I have,' said Nadia. 'Are there any more mugs?'

'Didn't you bring your own? Oh well, no problem.' Glugging back his tea, Bart gave his own mug a brisk upside-down shake then wiped it briefly on the brick-dust-stained T-shirt stretched over his stomach. Holding it out, he said generously, 'You can use mine.'

Was this some kind of test? Bravely, Nadia took the chipped mug, dropped a tea bag into it and filled it from the just-boiled kettle. She was truly one of the boys now.

'Have you worked for Jay long?'

'Four months, me and Kevin. Ever since he moved to Bristol. Robbie joined us two months ago.'

'Robbie seems quite . . . quiet.'

'Ah, he's a nice enough lad. Don't have a lot to say for himself, but he's a good worker. Got a degree in physics,' Bart added, between puffs of his spindly hand-rolled cigarette.

'And Jay? What's he like? I mean, is he a good boss?'

'Oh, he's all right. You don't mess Jay about, he won't mess you about. Works hard.' Bart coughed and chuckled. 'Plays hard too. You know the kind, single bloke with an eye for the girls. That mobile phone of his sees some action, I can tell you. Sometimes they even turn up where we're working, trying to track him down. He's a good businessman, mind. Knows how to make money. That's why he'll be pleased he took you on. Bet you're a lot cheaper than a poncy landscape gardening company with glossy colour brochures and a website.'

Was she supposed to take this as a compliment? Nadia finished her tea and smiled. 'Thanks.'

The top shelf of the magazine rack wasn't Annie's favourite section of the shop. She hated it when men came in and bought porn magazines. But the latest issue of *Playboy* had been delivered and it was her job to display them. She waited until the shop was empty, then hauled the stool out, climbed onto it and began stacking *Playboy*s on the top shelf.

The shop door swung open just as the wasp swooped into Annie's field of vision. Letting out a squeak of alarm she batted it away. Incensed, the wasp veered round in a circle and promptly dive-bombed her like a mini Spitfire. Annie ducked and took a panicky step back.

'Steady on,' said a male voice, but Annie was way beyond steadying herself. Her foot groped for support that was no longer there. The pile of glossy magazines slithered from her grasp as with an undignified shriek she tumbled to the ground, hitting the sweet display behind her. Mars bars, tubes of Fruit Pastilles and boxes of TicTacs came showering down, like painful confetti.

'Stay where you are, don't move,' ordered the same male voice.

Swivelling her head round, Annie saw that it belonged to the father of the girl who sometimes waited in the shop for him to finish work.

'I'm OK.' Momentarily she closed her eyes. 'I think.'

'You're bleeding.' He crouched down beside her. 'Look at your leg.'

Opening her eyes, Annie looked and flinched. Not so much at the sight of the blood seeping from her knee through a large hole in her navy tights, but at the copies of *Playboy* strewn around her, each one fallen open to display women with pumpkin-sized breasts. Mortified by the nakedness surrounding her, she attempted to wave her helper away.

'I'm fine, really. It's just a scratch. Was it the *Evening Post* you were after?' A daft question, seeing as this man called in every evening without fail for an *Evening Post*.

'Never mind that, let's get you sorted out.'

'The magazines,' Annie murmured, her cheeks flushing.

'I'll take care of them.' Adopting a businesslike manner, he swiftly closed each gaping magazine, gathered them up and stuffed them on the bottom shelf of the magazine rack behind a bunch of *Woman's Weeklys*. The door clanged open and his daughter rushed in.

Her eyes widened as she spotted her father on his knees, retrieving Fruit Pastilles and TicTacs from beneath the sprawled legs of the woman who worked in the shop.

Annie struggled to sit up a bit straighter. 'I fell off the stool. Your dad's helping me clear up.' At least the *Playboys* were out of sight.

'Are you hurt?' The girl moved towards them, adding hopefully, 'Did you break your leg? I've got my first-aid badge.'

'Watch what you say,' her father murmured under his breath. 'She'll have you trussed up like a chicken before you can say Jamie Oliver.' His dark eyes met Annie's and she broke into a smile.

'My leg's fine,' she told his daughter. 'It's just a graze.'

The man helped Annie to her feet. Her bottom hurt quite a lot—she'd have a massive bruise there tomorrow—but Annie kept this information to herself. She limped over to the desk. There was a packet of plasters in the drawer beneath the cash register; with a tissue she dabbed carefully at the blood through the hole in her wrecked tights.

'Here, let me.' With the air of a ward sister, the girl whisked the plasters from her, peeled the backing from one and placed it over the cut.

'There.' The girl stepped back, pleased with her handiwork.

'Excellent, Tilly.' Her father paused, glancing at his watch, then at Annie. 'You close up at six, don't you? Are you OK to get home or can we offer you a lift?'

'Oh! That's really kind of you.' Annie was touched by the offer, and sorely tempted. Literally. But she shook her head. 'No, I'll be fine. But thanks, anyway.'

Once Tilly and her father had left, it was time to start closing up for the night. When that was done, Annie hauled her carrier bags of shopping through from the back room, triple-locked the door and set off for the bus stop. Her bottom felt like Mike Tyson's punch bag. As Annie hobbled along, she winced as each step sent a jolt of pain radiating out from the base of her spine. She wished the bus stop was nearer.

Then a car pulled up just in front of her and the passenger window was buzzed down.

'You're limping,' Tilly announced sternly. 'You can hardly walk.'

Leaning over and reaching behind Tilly's seat, her father pushed open the rear door and said, 'Come on, jump in.'

Jumping anywhere was beyond her, but Annie managed to heave both her carrier bags and herself onto the Jaguar's roomy back seat.

'Thank you. It hurt more than I thought. I think I jarred my spine.'

'So, where are we going?' Tilly's father sounded cheerful.

'Kingsweston.' Annie prayed it wasn't out of his way. 'Thanks, um . . .'

'His name's James,' said Tilly. Helpfully she added, 'Mine's Tilly.'

'And I'm Annie.'

'Like Little Orphan Annie! Are you an orphan?'

'Tilly!' In the rearview mirror, Annie saw the girl's father raise his eyebrows in despair.

'What? I'm only asking.'

'Well, kind of. I lost my father years ago. And my mother died in January. But I think I'm probably too old to count as an orphan.'

'Why? How old are you?'

More eye-rolling in the mirror.

'Thirty-eight,' said Annie.

'Oh.' Tilly sounded surprised. 'I thought you were more than that.'

'Yes, well.' Gravely Annie said, 'I've had a hard life.'

'I lost my father too,' Tilly announced. 'He walked out on my mum when I was a baby.'

'Oh.' Annie was taken aback. 'I thought—'

'That James was my dad? No.' Tilly shook her head. 'Not even my stepdad. It's a bit complicated. But he's just like a real dad,' Tilly added. 'Makes me do my homework, moans about my taste in music, all that sort of thing.'

Drily, James observed, 'Years of practice with your sisters.'

Now Annie was definitely confused, but in typical teenage fashion, Tilly was now digging a CD out of her rucksack and the remainder of the journey was spent listening to American rap, with James intermittently complaining that he couldn't understand a word and what was wrong with a nice tune you could sing along with?

Swivelling round in the passenger seat, Tilly said, 'See what I mean about being just like a real dad?'

'Mine used to say the same about my David Bowie LPs,' said Annie.

Tilly frowned. 'What's an LP?'

In the rear mirror, James gave Annie a sympathetic, see-what-I-have-to-put-up-with look.

They had reached Kingsweston. Smiling, Annie said, 'Just up here on the right, the little row of cottages. Mine's the one on the corner.'

Nadia was pleased with herself. She'd done a really good plan of the garden last night. She had even bought a brand-new set of top-of-the-range felt-tips in order to create the requisite blaze of colour.

And Jay Tiernan, annoyingly, wasn't here to appreciate it.

He was a busy man, Nadia realised that. As well as organising the electricians, plumbers and carpenters, he was liaising with estate agents and solicitors, preparing to sell this house when it was finished and already on the lookout for the next house to buy. This meant he was out and about a lot. Which was fine, but it would have been less annoying if he didn't spend so much time with his mobile switched off.

'Still no luck, love?' Bart came outside as she was jabbing at the buttons of her own phone.

Nadia shook her head. 'He said he'd organise a truck.' She gestured at the mountain of garden waste piled up next to the side gate. 'I don't know if he's fixed something up or not.'

'If he said he would, he probably did.' Bart began to roll a cigarette.

'But what if he hasn't? And I've got my plans here for him. I need him to see them before I start the next phase.' Her corkscrew hair bounced around her shoulders as she shook her head in disbelief. 'Why does he always have to have his bloody phone switched off?'

The expression on Bart's face told her exactly what he thought Jay might be up to. Lighting his roll-up, he took a long drag.

'Like I told you, he's a busy chap. Popular with the ladies. Had a bit of a thing going with the woman who sold him the last place we done up. Dunno if he's still seeing her, but if he isn't there'll be someone else.'

Was Bart subtly letting her know that any hint of flirtation from Jay should be taken with a wagonload of salt? Speaking of wagons . . .

'I'm not interested in his love life.' Nadia's tone was clipped. 'I just want all this rubbish cleared away, and I need Jay to approve the plans.'

'Tell you what,' Bart said soothingly. 'Why don't you take your lunch break? Maybe he'll be here by the time you get back.'

Nadia was away for twenty minutes. By the time she returned with her rolls, crisps and Snickers bar, Jay had been and gone. *Allegedly.*

'Just missed him, love,' said Bart. 'He turned up just after you left.'

Dismayed, Nadia said, 'Are you serious?'

'I told him what you needed. He gave the clearance company another ring and they'll be here by one o'clock. Oh, and he's taken the garden plans with him, but he says you can make a start on the terrace.'

Nadia felt like a six-year-old beginning to have suspicions about Father Christmas. Had Jay really been here, or was Bart only saying it to humour her? What if Bart had stuffed her painstakingly constructed plans into the bottom of his rucksack?

When the truck arrived shortly after one o'clock, Nadia wondered if Bart had phoned them himself.

Miriam and Edward were sitting in Edward's back garden when he proposed to her. Again.

Miriam briefly closed her eyes, wishing he wouldn't do this to her.

'I'm serious,' said Edward, removing the folded-up *Daily Telegraph* from her hands and placing her Biro on the garden table. 'I don't see what the problem is. I love you and I want you to marry me.'

'And I want you to stop asking me.' Miriam's spine stiffened instinctively; her shoulders went back. 'We're fine as we are.'

'I like to do things properly. Properly means getting married.'

'Well, that isn't going to happen.'

Edward couldn't force her to change her mind. But he wasn't happy with the situation. Heaving a sigh, he walked stiffly over to the far wall, ostensibly to admire the rambling roses basking in the afternoon sunlight.

Miriam, watching him, wondered how he would react if she told him the real reason why she refused to marry him. Ironically, she suspected he wouldn't even care, once he got over the initial shock. But not allowing herself to marry him was the punishment she had meted out to herself after . . . well, after *the thing* had happened. Even more ironically, Edward was standing in the exact spot where it had happened.

The next day, Thursday, was hot but showery. Nadia, stripped to a vest and shorts, worked through the rain to level the ground where the French windows at the back of the house led out onto the garden. Raindrops dripped steadily from the ends of her corkscrew curls. She looked appalling but didn't care. There was nobody around to see what a fright she looked. Nobody who counted, anyway.

Jay's mobile was still switched off. For all she knew, he could be in New Zealand now.

He turned up at twelve thirty, carrying her folder of plans.

'These are fine. Go ahead. I've set up an account at the garden centre, so you can chalk up anything you need.' No friendly greeting. No 'Hi, how are you, sorry I missed you yesterday.' He wasn't even smiling.

Nadia stopped digging and leaned on her shovel.

'Are you OK?' she asked Jay. He seemed offish and distracted.

'Of course I'm OK,' he replied coolly. It was like suddenly being faced with Jay Tiernan's scary bank-managerish twin brother, the one who was in fact a cyborg. Maybe this was just the way things were going to be, now that she was actually working for him.

Fair enough, but Nadia thought he could have called her garden plan something more constructive than just *fine*. 'May I make a comment?'

Jay glanced at his watch, then shrugged. 'Go ahead.'

'It's none of our business what you get up to during the day, but you can't leave your phone switched off. I was trying to reach you yesterday and I couldn't. It's unprofessional. We need to be able to contact you.'

Jay, his expression as hard and detached as an Indian chief's, said, 'There's such a thing as using your initiative. If you were that desperate, you could have organised another truck. Anyway, I have to go. Tell Bart I'll speak to him tomorrow about the electrician.'

And without another word he was gone. Moments later Nadia heard the sound of his car's engine starting up.

What the hell was going on here? He couldn't have been less interested in her complaint if she'd been an ant on the heel of his boot. Was Jay Tiernan a bastard who had formerly masqueraded as a nice person? Or was he none-too-subtly pointing out to her that if she fancied him she may as well stop it right now because she was wasting her time?

The next morning Nadia scooped up the just-delivered post on her way into the kitchen. Clare was already up, which was either an outright miracle or meant that she'd only just come home after last night. Miriam was making coffee and James was buttering toast.

Dealing the letters out like a poker hand, Nadia recited, 'Bill, bill, junk mail, bill. Something for you, Gran, a fat one. Here, catch.'

Miriam caught it, her heart in her mouth. But it was OK, nothing to worry about, just one of Emily Payne's irritating round-robin letters.

'Ooh, this looks more exciting, Dad.' Nadia waggled the heavy cream envelope enticingly under his nose. 'Mm, heavy paper and addressed with real ink.'

James knew at once what it was. Several other people at work had received theirs in the post yesterday. Taking a cup of coffee from Miriam, he slid the invitation under the saucer.

'Come on, Dad, what's in the envelope?' Behind him, Clare draped her arms round his shoulders.

'I'll open it later.'

'Tell you what, why don't I open it now?' With a grin, she whisked the envelope out from beneath the saucer and, ripping it open, studied the embossed card inside. She wrinkled her nose in disgust. 'A dinner party at Cedric and Mary-Jane's—God, nightmare. I'd rather eat dog food.'

James entirely agreed. Cedric Elson was his boss, head of Elson and Co, Chartered Accountants. Mary-Jane was his liposuctioned wife. And their dinner parties were the bane of James's life.

'It says James and partner,' Clare pointed out.

'I told them I don't have a partner.' James sighed. 'Mary-Jane said I should make the effort and find one. But I don't know anyone to invite.'

Out in the hall, Tilly was on her knees stuffing trainers and a PE skirt into her already bulging rucksack. Pausing for a second, she heard Clare say, 'Get someone from an agency. One of those escort girls, a really stunning one. That'll make everyone sit up and take notice.'

'I'm not hiring someone from an agency.' James sounded resigned.

'You can take Eliza,' said Miriam.

'Not Eliza.' James's groan was audible even out in the hall. It wasn't the first time he'd been threatened with Edward's secretary.

'Oh, James, don't pull that face, you don't have to marry the woman. It's only a dinner party. You have to take someone,' Miriam persisted.

'I'm going to be late for work.' Tilly heard a chair being scraped back.

Out in the hallway, James picked up his briefcase and car keys before dropping a kiss on Tilly's bent head.

'Bye, pigeon. See you later.'

'Hi, how are you?' Annie greeted Tilly with a warm smile when Tilly came into the shop at twenty past five.

'OK. Is your knee better?'

'Oh, it's fine.' The bruise on her bottom was really colourful, but Annie didn't mention this. 'Chewing gum?'

Tilly nodded and pulled her money out of her rucksack. She passed the coins over to Annie and took a deep breath.

'Look, I hope this isn't rude, but do you have another half?'

Annie frowned. 'Another half of what?'

'You know, like a partner, husband, boyfriend . . .'

'Oh.' Annie broke into another smile. 'Well, no, not really.'

'What does not really mean?'

'Um, it means . . . no.' Taken aback, Annie said, 'Why?'

'Just wondered.' Cheerfully, Tilly unwrapped the packet of Wrigley's Extra. 'So, if a man asked you to go along with him to his boss's dinner party next Saturday night, there wouldn't be anything to stop you?'

Annie's heart rate increased, like an ancient car suddenly being urged to break the speed limit.

'Well, that would depend on the man and what he was like.'

'But if he was really nice, you'd say yes?' Tilly's eyes were bright.

'Ah . . . well, I suppose so, in theory.'

'That's great. Brilliant.' Behind her, the door swung open and James came in, sending Annie's out-of-practice heart into Ferrari mode. James picked up his usual paper, dropped the right money onto the counter, flashed her a smile and said, 'Busy day?'

Annie unstuck her tongue from the roof of her mouth. 'Quite busy.'

'Right, we'd better be off.' Playfully James tapped his rolled-up newspaper between Tilly's skinny shoulder blades. 'Come along, you.' Over his shoulder he added casually, 'Have a good weekend.'

The shop door swung shut behind them. Annie called, 'You too.'

It was like waking up on the morning of your birthday and watching the postman walk straight past your front gate.

'You didn't.' James blanched. 'Tell me this is a joke, Tilly. Please.'

On their way back to the car park Tilly had casually dropped her bombshell. James abruptly stopped walking; this was awful, just awful.

'It's not a joke, it's perfect. Annie's a really nice person. Come on, I've done all the hard work. All you have to do now is officially ask Annie. You already know she's going to say yes.'

If there had been a brick wall handy, James would have banged his head against it.

'Tilly, I know you're trying to help, but this isn't how it's done. For heaven's sake, I don't even know the woman.' Closing his eyes briefly, James realised that when he'd burst into the shop ten minutes ago, Annie must have been expecting him to raise the subject. What a mess, what a complete and utter balls-up.

'I'll have to explain to her,' James said wearily. 'You stay here.'

When he arrived back at the shop, Annie, her cheeks flushed, said hesitantly, 'Hello again.'

James wished he only had something simple to do, like saw off his own legs. Mentally bracing himself, he plunged straight in. 'OK, look, Tilly's just told me what she said to you. I had no idea she'd been planning something like this. I'm so sorry,' said James, 'it must have put you in an awkward situation. I do apologise. Anyway,' he rushed on, 'please, forget she said anything. And, um, sorry again.'

Annie tucked her unstyled fair hair carefully behind her ears and said, 'Right. OK.'

'Well.' James knew he should be leaving, but couldn't quite figure out how to do it without seeming rude. 'I mean, I know Tilly's only trying to help, but she doesn't understand. You know how it is with these work-related dinner parties. Everyone else is married, so they expect you to turn up with someone too, because otherwise you'll have completely messed up their seating plan. I mean, imagine the horror of eleven guests instead of twelve at dinner, it just doesn't bear thinking about.'

'Mad,' Annie agreed, her smile slightly forced. 'Goodness, is it ten to six already?' She began counting busily through the newspapers piled up on the counter.

Taking his cue to leave, James turned. He reached the door, then turned again. He might have solved one problem but there was still the dilemma of who he could take along to Cedric's dinner party.

'Of course, if you wanted to come with me, that would be great. Not because you're too polite to say no, but because you think you really might enjoy it . . . um, well, no, don't worry . . .'

'I'd like to go with you,' said Annie. Surprising herself.

'Really?' James couldn't quite believe he'd done it. 'It might not be much fun.' He felt it only fair to warn her.

'We could make it fun,' said Annie.

It was six thirty on Friday evening and the builders were long gone, but Nadia was still working. Taking advantage of the improved weather, she was preparing the ground for the paved terrace.

The side gate clicked open and Jay appeared, wearing a dark grey

T-shirt, black jeans and dark glasses. He looked like Darth Vader, only less cheerful.

'Hi,' said Nadia. She wondered if he'd forgotten how to smile.

'I thought you'd have left by now.'

'Just finishing off. Is that allowed?' She said it lightly, hinting that it would be fine to make some form of light-hearted comment in return. Jay didn't appear to notice.

'Of course it's allowed. I just dropped by to see how the work was progressing.' He was studying the repainted window frames at the back of the house.

Nadia said, 'I'm sorry, have I done something wrong?'

'What?' The opaque lenses swung in her direction.

'Me. Done something wrong. I must have done.' She semi-shrugged. 'You used to be . . . different.'

'Don't worry about it.' Jay impatiently jangled his keys. 'Just need to check inside, then I'll be off. See you Monday.'

Fifteen minutes later, Nadia packed up for the night, letting herself out through the side gate. Jay's car was still parked across the road.

Making her way down the short drive, she turned and glanced back at the house. There he was, standing at the living-room window, talking on his mobile phone. So he did occasionally deign to switch it on. Nadia only hoped the recipient of the call appreciated how honoured they were to be actually speaking to him in person.

It would have been nice to think that he was behaving like this because he'd resorted to the treat 'em mean, keep 'em keen strategy of courtship. Sadly, Nadia knew he wasn't. Oh well, at least it was Friday. Her first week working for Jay Tiernan was over. Or the eerily lifelike cyborg currently passing himself off as Jay Tiernan. If she was still working for him in December, the staff Christmas party was sure to be a riot.

Nadia reached the end of Clarence Gardens before remembering that she was low on petrol. Turning the car, she set off back up the road.

It happened completely without warning; they came out of nowhere like two speeding furry bullets zinging across the road. Nadia let out a shriek of horror and jammed her foot on the brake. A nightmare split-second later came the ominous thud of body-on-bumper impact.

With a squeal of tyres, the Renault slewed to a violent halt. Sickened and shocked, Nadia stumbled from the car and pressed a shaking hand to her mouth. A cat, a short-haired ginger one, lay on its side in the gutter. It was quite dead.

'Oh no, oh no,' Nadia sobbed, tears streaming down her cheeks as she dropped to her knees.

'It's OK,' said a reassuring voice in her ear. It was Jay crouching beside her, feeling beneath the cat's furry jaw for a pulse.

'It's not OK. I killed someone's cat.' Nadia heaved a sob, shaking her head in revulsion at what she'd done.

'There was nothing you could do,' said Jay. 'He ran into the road, chasing after the other cat. I saw it from the window. Come on, don't cry. It really wasn't your fault.'

Nadia wiped her wet cheeks with the back of her hand, but the tears were still coming. Quite astonishingly, Jay's arm was round her shoulders and he was actually being concerned and caring. Almost . . . *nice*.

'Oh God, it's really dead.' Lifting the animal gently onto her lap, Nadia began to stroke it. She reluctantly turned over the disc bearing the cat's name and saw an address engraved on the other side.

'Felstead Avenue,' Jay read aloud. 'That's the road behind this one.'

'Right.' Nadia nodded, feeling sick. 'I'll tell the owner. What number?'

'Fourteen, but you're not doing it alone. I'll come with you.'

'OK.' She managed a wobbly smile. 'You're being really nice.'

Jay raised an eyebrow. 'Don't sound so surprised. I'm not an ogre.'

Clearly, Jay didn't realise he'd been weird and distant for the past week.

'OK, I'm ready.' Nadia mentally girded her loins—whatever that actually meant. 'Let's go.'

'Well,' she said ten minutes later. 'That's . . . that. That bloody man couldn't have cared less.'

The man who had opened the front door of 14 Felstead Avenue had been balding, middle-aged and brusque. OK, so the cat had copped it. Hardly surprising, since the daft thing had never had any road sense.

She almost wished now that the cat's owner had been a tearful old lady.

'I bet he won't even have it buried. He'll just chuck it in his wheelie bin. Honestly, some people shouldn't be allowed to keep animals.'

'Look, how about a brandy to calm you down?'

A drink would be lovely, just what she needed—

Jay's phone began to ring. In his hurry to answer it, he missed her nod. Nadia watched his expression change. After several curt whens, yeses and rights, he hung up.

'Sorry, I have to go. Are you all right to drive home?'

Nadia nodded. Just as well, really.

'OK. Bye.'

And that was it, he was gone. Into his car and out of sight.

So was he nice, or wasn't he? She still didn't know.

It was Saturday lunchtime and sunlight streamed in through the sloping windows on the top floor of the house. Clare sat back on her stool and surveyed the painting so far. The scene was of a gaggle of overexcited women in hugely ornate hats, enjoying a day at the races. She was going to call it *All Of A Flutter*. In the foreground she had a gloriously seedy-looking bookie leering as he eyed up the ladies in their skimpy skirts.

When Clare was in the mood to paint, she could keep going for hours. But today she was too distracted. Yesterday Piers had been away at a conference in London, and now it was midday and he still hadn't rung her.

Clare gazed moodily out of the window. She'd never been the type to phone a boyfriend, because she'd always known they'd phone her. But it was starting to look as if she might have to call Piers, because he didn't appear to be ringing her and how else could she get to see him? She swirled her paintbrush in a jar of turps and picked up the phone.

'Yeah?'

'Hi, it's me.' *Boing, boinngg* went Clare's intestines as she heard his voice. 'Just wondered what you were up to.'

She'd practised this line. It was nice and casual, free of whininess and suitably laid back. Not for her the fretful 'you-said-you'd-call-me' accusations, oh no. Instant turn-off.

'Hi, you.' Piers sounded as if he was lying in bed, smiling. 'I was just thinking about you.'

Don't sound flattered, don't simper.

'How was London?'

'Oh, not so bad. Pretty knackering really. How about you?'

'Oh, ended up at a *wild* party in Failand last night.' Clare was buggered if she'd tell him she'd stayed in and watched *Frasier*. 'I'm fairly shattered myself, don't feel like doing anything too energetic this afternoon . . .' She paused.

Piers yawned. 'Me neither. There's rugby on the telly—that's enough exercise for me.'

'Rugby?' Clare loathed rugby with a passion. 'I love rugby! Tell you what, I could bring over a bottle of wine if you fancy some company.'

Was that pushy, over-keen, pathetically eager? No, of course it wasn't. She was making a relaxed, spur-of-the-moment suggestion, that was all.

'OK. If you like.' Piers sounded surprised but not displeased. 'But don't bother with wine. Pick up some beers instead.'

Clare switched off the phone with a flourish. There, that hadn't been so hard, had it? Piers had been delighted to hear from her, and now she was going to spend the rest of Saturday with him.

Clothes, Clare thought joyfully, bounding over to her wardrobe.

Clothes for a relaxing afternoon *à deux* in front of the TV. Something casual, of course. But sexy. Jeans? No. Skirt and strappy top? Definitely not. What did she have that he hadn't already seen her in? Apart from her dressing gown and slippers.

And her mac.

Emerging from the shower, Clare roughly blow-dried her hair, made up her face and slipped her feet into high-heeled pink mules. Then, letting the towel in which she was wrapped drop to the floor, she sprayed herself with Dior's *Eau Svelte* and reached into the wardrobe for her mac.

Striking a pose in front of the full-length mirror, Clare surveyed herself. Oh yes. Perfect. Saucy but innocent, sexy but fun. This was a great mac. Pale pink PVC on the outside, lined with fake fur on the inside, it came to just above the knee. With the buttons done up and the belt tightly tied at the waist, nobody would ever know you weren't wearing anything underneath.

Hefting the Thresher's bag into her arms, Clare climbed the steps and pressed the buzzer outside Piers's flat.

'Yup?' Piers's voice came through the speaker on the entry phone.

'It's me.'

'Hello, you.' His voice softened. 'Come on up.'

As she climbed the stairs to his second-floor flat, there was an odd smell, that she couldn't place. It wasn't until Piers opened his front door and the full force of the smell rushed out to greet her that Clare recognised it. The air was thick with the acrid stench of alcohol-fuelled male bodies. Through the open living-room door Clare could see them draped across furniture and stretched out on the floor.

'What's going on? When did they get here?' Horrified, she took a step back.

'Last night. They persuaded me to meet them at the club when I got back from London. Then we all came back here and crashed out,' Piers said with a boyish grin. 'Here, let me take these.' He seized the carrier bag and pulled out the lagers. 'Just what we need, hair of the dog.'

Clare wanted to stamp her feet in frustration. This was the opposite of what she'd been looking forward to. 'Are they going home now?'

'You must be joking. The rugby starts in ten minutes.' As he said it, Piers began to nuzzle her neck. 'God, you smell gorgeous.'

Unlike the rest of your guests, Clare thought sourly. Oh hell, why did this have to happen?

'Come on.' Piers pushed her through to the living room and held the Thresher's bag aloft like a football trophy. 'Look! Lager and . . . ugh, wine.' He turned to Clare. 'We're lads, we don't drink wine.'

'It's for me,' said Clare.

'I'm a woman trapped in a lad's body,' announced Eddie, one of Piers's closest friends. 'Don't fret, petal, I'll have a glass of wine. Clare, come over here and sit by me.' He patted the sofa across which he was sprawled.

Eddie was a big groping lech whose hands wandered at the slightest opportunity. It would have taken him less than ten seconds to discover that she was naked under her mac, and declare it to the room at large.

'I'm fine over here.' She picked an uncomfortable chair next to the window, well away from Fast Eddie.

'Take off your coat,' said Piers, opening a lager. 'Aren't you hot?'

'Of course she's *hot*,' leered Eddie.

'I'm not, actually. I'm cold. I'll keep my coat on, thanks.'

The next ninety minutes became a personal battle. Telling herself that as soon as the stupid rugby game was over, everyone would leave, Clare vowed to sit it out. Or, more accurately, sweat it out. The sun poured through the window and perspiration trickled down her back. All around her, men were roaring encouragement at the TV screen, knocking back the beers.

When the match finally ended, Eddie rose to his feet. 'Right, I'll go and pick up some more booze.'

No, no, *no*. Scarlet-cheeked with heat and indignation, Clare cornered Piers in the kitchen. 'Can't you make them go?'

Piers looked surprised. 'I can't do that. Angel, these are my friends.'

'I thought we were going to relax and have some time alone together.'

Piers appeared genuinely mystified. 'You should have said.'

Now she really wanted to cry. 'I had a special surprise for you, too.'

'You did? What is it?'

Clare gave him an 'are-you-mad'? look. 'You're not getting it now. I'm going home.'

Piers shrugged. 'OK.'

Why didn't she hate him for treating her like this? Even now, if he begged her to stay, she probably would. Except that was the thing about Piers, he never did beg.

'Hey, hey, what's going on out here?' Eddie barged into the kitchen.

'I'm just leaving,' Claire said coldly, as she turned and made for the kitchen door.

'Leaving?' He mimed horror, clasping his big hands to his chest. 'But you can't leave. I can't bear it,' Eddie wailed melodramatically.

His hand, shooting out, grabbed the back of her mac. As he yanked her towards him, Clare let out a squeak of fear and tugged the hem of the mac back down to her knees. She was a split second too late.

A slow, idiotic grin spread over Eddie's face. 'Oh, wow. Hello, baby!' He leered at her, Austin Powers style. 'Or should I call you Sharon? Did I really just see what I thought I saw?'

Piers, whose view had been blocked by Eddie, said, 'Saw what? And who's Sharon?'

'Sharon Stone.' Eddie gave his friend a hefty nudge. 'You remember, in *Basic Instinct*.' His grin broadening, he turned back to Clare. 'So that's why you kept your coat on.'

Their laughter followed her all the way down the staircase. Hot tears of humiliation were scalding her eyes by the time she reached the street. A taxi came along and she flagged it down.

'Blimey, love, thought it was gonna rain, did you? You must be boiling in that get-up.' The driver swivelled round as she cranked open the window. 'I'm tellin' you, you'll feel a lot better if you take that coat off.'

The annoying thing about electronic organisers was that Nadia didn't know how to work them.

Jay had left behind his Psion on the newly installed worktop in the kitchen before disappearing for the afternoon. Picking it up, Nadia gave it a shake, just in case this was all it needed in order to fall open and magically start spilling out riveting items of gossip about his private life. Then, hearing footsteps on the stairs, she hurriedly stuffed the Psion into her bag. If Bart spotted it, he might volunteer to drop it round to Jay's house on his way home from work.

And there was no need. She was quite capable of doing that herself.

She pulled into Canynge Road at just gone six o'clock. Jay's car was there, which was good. Not that she had any kind of hidden agenda or anything. It was just interesting to see where other people lived.

When Jay opened the door he seemed surprised to see her, as if he'd been expecting someone else. 'Oh, hi. What's this about?'

Not the most enthusiastic of welcomes, but Nadia gave him one of her sunniest smiles anyway. She held up the Psion. 'I found it in the kitchen.'

'Right. Thanks.' Nodding with relief, Jay took the organiser from her.

For heaven's sake, why wasn't he inviting her in? Expectantly, Nadia said, 'That's OK, it wasn't too far out of my way.'

'Look, I'd ask you inside but I'm actually just on my way out.'

'Oh no, no, that's fine, I can't stop anyway. I have to pick up my sister and take her to buy a . . . hamster. She's going to call him Gerald.'

It was pretty startling, listening to the words coming out of her own mouth. Jay looked taken aback too.

'Your sister the artist?'

A hamster. Why? Why?

'Not Clare. My other sister,' Nadia hurriedly explained. 'She's thirteen.'

Nadia hurried back to the car. While she was unwrapping a chewing gum she noticed a taxi pulling up outside Jay's house, from which a woman with long blonde hair emerged. She looked to be in her early thirties and beautiful in an unsmiling ice-queen kind of way. Honestly, talk about miserable. She needed someone to tell her a joke. Then the taxi pulled away, and Nadia saw what she hadn't been able to see before.

The woman was pregnant.

Startled, Nadia watched her turn and climb the steps to Jay's front door, then ring the bell and wait. When the door opened, she looked at Jay and briefly said something before walking past him into the house. The door then closed behind them.

Nadia sat back in her seat, dumbfounded. If the blonde was Jay's girlfriend—especially his pregnant girlfriend—wouldn't they have heard about her before? He'd never even hinted he was involved with someone.

Then again, what if she were his ex-girlfriend? That would explain why she wasn't looking too cheerful. God, and who could blame her?

Stop it. Nadia gave herself a mental telling-off. Just because a pregnant woman had disappeared into Jay's home didn't automatically mean the baby was his. She could be his cleaning lady, or a piano teacher—

The front door opened again.

Jay had his arm round the pregnant woman and was carrying a small overnight case. As he unlocked his car and helped her into the passenger seat, he gave her hand a squeeze.

Well, thought Nadia. Probably not his piano teacher then.

Chapter Four

'BUT I DON'T WANT a hamster,' said Tilly the following evening. 'I hate hamsters, they're like rats.'

'OK,' Nadia conceded. 'But you have to promise me something. If a strange man ever starts asking about your hamster, just pretend you have one called Gerald.'

'You're weird,' said Tilly.

'I know. But I'm very lovable. Blimey, what's Michael Schumacher doing coming to our house?' Nadia peered out through the living-room window as something testosterone-fuelled roared up the drive.

'It's for me.' Clare's voice sang out from upstairs. 'It's Piers. Can someone let him in?' This was Clare's way of letting everyone know she was far too cool to be ready on time.

Pulling open the front door, Nadia came face to face with someone who clearly thought he was great. Irresistible, in fact.

'Hi, Clare'll be down in a minute.' Nadia had never seen him before, but instinctively she suspected that she didn't like Piers. 'Come through to the living room.'

Tilly, twisting round on the sofa, beamed hello at him. 'She can never make up her mind what to wear.'

'You're telling me.' Piers winked at Nadia. 'And sometimes she doesn't wear anything at all.'

Nadia gave him a blank look.

'Didn't Clare tell you about Saturday?' Piers started to laugh.

There was the sound of thunderous footsteps on the staircase, then Clare breathlessly catapulted into the living room.

'Ready! Let's go!'

As the electric-blue Ferrari made its way down Whiteladies Road, Clare revelled in the way people turned and stared.

After the humiliating events of Saturday afternoon, she had given serious thought to finishing with Piers. But when he'd phoned her on Monday he couldn't have been more charming or apologetic. Plus, Clare couldn't blame him for the actions of one idiotic friend.

Which was why she'd agreed to see him tonight, and was now extremely glad she had. Piers was on his best behaviour, having arrived to pick her up exactly on time and looking sensational in the rich-boy navy suit that went so well with his eyes. They looked like a couple out of a glossy magazine, Clare thought joyfully.

'D'you have a brush in there?' Piers nodded at her beaded clutch bag.

'Yes, do you want to borrow it?'

'I meant for you.' He sounded amused. 'I prefer your hair down.'

Clare bit back the automatic retort that it was her hair and she'd spent ages putting it up. But Piers had an eye for these things and if he thought she looked better with her hair down, it probably did look better down.

Taking the brush out of her bag, Clare began unpinning the chignon.

'Good girl. By the way'—he slid his hand experimentally up her bare thigh—'are you wearing anything under that slinky dress?'

'Big knickers. Very big knickers. And I have to be back home tonight,' she added, to show him she wasn't a pushover.

Piers looked hurt. 'You can't go home. I want you to stay at my place.'

Clare smiled to herself, pleased to be back in charge.

'Well. We'll see.'

Tilly watched from her bedroom window, a mixture of fear and excitement squirming in her stomach. It was Saturday, it was midday, and any minute now her mother would be pulling into the driveway along with her new boyfriend and her new boyfriend's daughter: Brian and Tamsin. Tilly prayed she'd like them.

As the car came bouncing up the drive, Tilly took a deep, steadying breath. What if they didn't like her?

'Oh, my baby, come here, give me a hug, look how you've *grown*.' Bracelets jangled as Leonie flung out her arms. She was wearing a floaty, pointy-hemmed dress, silver earrings as big as saucers and woody-spicy perfume. 'Just look at you,' Leonie mock-scolded, holding her at arm's length. 'So skinny! I hope you're eating properly.'

'Of course I'm eating properly.' Tilly tucked her hair behind her ears, feeling mousy and plain. With her long Clairol-blonde hair, heavily made-up eyes and bright clothes, Leonie looked marvellously exotic in a flashy, fairground kind of way.

'Darling, this is Brian.' Linking her arm through Tilly's, Leonie swung her round. 'And Brian's daughter, Tamsin. You two, this is Tilly, my beautiful baby girl. Now why don't you all get to know each other while I pop inside for a quick chat? Then we can go.'

Tilly hated it when Leonie introduced her to people then promptly abandoned her with them. Feeling awkward, she turned to the other occupants of the car. Brian had long hair that was thinning on top and he was wearing a leather waistcoat, as befitted someone in the music business. Tamsin was startlingly pretty with sparkly green eyes and a heart-shaped face. Her denim jacket was covered in scrawled writing and she was sitting cross-legged on the back seat with a Walkman in her lap.

'Hi,' said Tilly in desperation.

'All right?' Brian was busy tapping his fingers against the steering wheel, drumming along to an invisible beat.

'Are you a vegetarian?' said Tamsin.

'Um, no.' Tilly wondered if this would make Tamsin hate her.

'Oh.' The girl sounded amused. 'You look like one.'

Things got easier over lunch in a busy pizzeria on Park Street. Leonie was on vivacious form, keeping the conversation going. Relaxing, Tilly decided that Tamsin wasn't so bad after all; she was less scary than she'd first appeared. Brian seemed OK too, although he didn't actually say much. He did, however, have a couple of old friends in Bristol whom he was anxious to look up.

'So what we thought, darling, is we'd pop off and see them for an hour or two, when we leave here,' Leonie explained. 'That gives you and Tamsin some time together to really get to know each other, and we'll meet the two of you back here at . . . ooh, five o'clock?'

It was like being set up on a blind date. Not that she'd ever been on one. With a jolt of dismay, Tilly said, 'What do we do until then?'

'Darling, you're teenagers, what do girls your age normally do on a Saturday afternoon? Go shopping! Have fun together!'

'Can't.' Tamsin gloomily sucked her ice-cream spoon. 'No money.'

'We'll give you money,' Leonie announced. 'See you back here at five.'

'Ten pounds each.' Tamsin shook her head in disgust as the two of them emerged from the restaurant.'Won't even keep me in cigarettes.'

'It's better than nothing.' Tilly thought ten pounds was quite a lot.

'I like your mum, though,' Tamsin said. 'She's good fun, isn't she?'

'I suppose.' Tilly couldn't help feeling fobbed off. For the last fortnight she'd been mentally preparing for her mother's visit, and it was practically over already. By seven o'clock, Leonie would be making 'let's-go' noises. By seven thirty they'd be gone.

Tamsin offered her a Marlboro Light. 'Isn't it a bit weird, you living with some bloke who isn't even your dad?'

'No.' Tilly was instantly on the defensive. 'I like it. I'm happy where I am. And I suppose I've got used to Mum not being around. She was never a mother-type mother.'

'You're lucky. Mine is, and it's a complete nightmare. She's so strict you wouldn't believe it. Nag, nag, nag, do your homework, clean your room—it did my head in. That's why I came to live with my dad.' She shook back her hair, clearly pleased with herself. 'He lets me do whatever I like.'

Their trawl around the shops didn't last long. When Tamsin discovered that Tilly's school was only fifteen minutes' walk away, and that the first eleven were playing cricket against Bristol Grammar, she insisted they went along to watch the game.

Tilly wrinkled her nose; cricket was unbelievably dull. 'What for?'

'Look, it's your duty to cheer them on. And check out the talent. Oh, come on, it'll be a laugh,' Tamsin urged.

On the way to the school, they had to pass the newsagents where Annie worked. Tilly had spent her money on nail varnish and two hair scrunchies, and now, with only forty pence in her pocket, she was regretting it. She could've murdered a can of Coke.

'Want to go in here?' Tilly paused as they drew level with the shop.

'Sure. I like newsagents.' Tamsin grinned at her. 'We can wave at ourselves on the CCTV.'

'I don't think this one has CCTV.'

Annie was behind the counter, leafing through a copy of *Hello!*.

'You caught me out.' Beaming at Tilly, she pointed to the photo she'd been studying, of a glamorous hairdo. 'I'm getting mine done straight after we've closed here.' Tonight was Annie's big dinner date with James. 'This is the kind of thing I'm after, but it's so embarrassing taking a photo along, isn't it?' Annie closed the magazine. 'I'll just ask them to put my hair up. So, what are you doing here on a Saturday?'

'We're going along to watch a cricket match at the school.' Glancing over her shoulder, Tilly said, 'This is Tamsin. My . . . um, friend.'

To her horror, as she turned, she saw Tamsin hurriedly stuffing something into her jeans pocket . . . Tilly couldn't believe it.

'Er, I'll have some orange TicTacs please,' Tilly said, far too loudly.

Ignoring Tilly, Annie said calmly, 'Maybe you should put those back.'

'Excuse me?' Tamsin raised her eyebrows. 'Put what back?'

Oh God, oh God. Tilly began to sweat.

'Those pens.' Annie's gaze didn't waver from Tamsin's face. 'The ones you just put in your pocket.'

'Pens? Why would I want a bunch of stupid pens?' Tamsin looked at her as if she were mad. 'Tilly, ready to go?'

Tilly was rooted to the spot and in a state of anguish. She wanted to cover her eyes like a three-year-old and pretend she wasn't here.

'See this?' Annie gestured to the sign on the wall, announcing that Shoplifters Would Be Prosecuted. 'It's true. Now come on, just—'

'Who's going to catch me if I run out of here now?' Tamsin smirked.

Annie said evenly, 'I know which school you go to.'

'And that's where you're wrong, because I don't even live in Bristol. So you'll never find me.' Tamsin's eyes were bright with triumph.

'Put them back,' Tilly blurted out.

'Oh, for God's sake, this is pathetic.' Heaving an exaggerated sigh, Tamsin dragged the pens from her pocket and flung them back into their box on the stationery shelf. 'There, happy now?'

Tilly turned back to Annie. 'I'm sorry. I'm so sorry.'

'Not your fault,' Annie said quietly.

'Could you . . . um, not mention this to James?'

Annie hesitated, then nodded. 'OK.'

By five o'clock, Tilly was officially confused. After the hideous scene in the newsagents, it had become obvious that Tamsin was Seriously Bad News. Except . . . an hour later, she had flirted so effectively with the boys from school that purely by association Tilly had rocketed into the top ten of girls worth talking to.

'That was pretty cool.' Tamsin sounded pleased with herself as they headed back to the pizza restaurant. In possession of at least a dozen mobile phone numbers, she could afford to be smug.

'They're dorks.' Tilly flicked back her hair as if it was worth flicking back. But secretly she was envious.

'Maybe. Who cares? They fancied me rotten. Don't tell my dad about the shop thing, OK?'

'OK.'

When Leonie and Brian dropped Tilly back home at seven o'clock, Leonie gave her a patchouli-scented hug and said, 'I *knew* you two would get on.'

'Well . . .'

'Brian's asked me to marry him. Isn't that fantastic?'

Dutifully, but with a sinking heart, Tilly echoed, 'Fantastic.'

Annie Healey wiped the steam from her bathroom mirror and regarded her soft-focus reflection with a mixture of fear and anticipation.

Not fear, that wasn't the right word. Apprehension, maybe. Or just general anxiety.

Actually, no, it was fear. How pathetic to be this scared when all she was doing was going out to dinner with a man. But she was just so horribly out of practice.

When he arrived at seven o'clock to pick her up, James was looking very smart and not a little uneasy himself. As he helped her into the car, Annie said, 'Look, I feel it's only fair to warn you that I'm very nervous.'

Straightening, James adjusted his spectacles. 'You are? Oh, I'm sorry.'

'Don't take it personally.' Annie shook her head. 'I'd be the same with anyone. You see, I'm not used to doing this. It's been a long time.'

James climbed into the driver's seat and stuck the key in the ignition. 'Me too.'

'I bet my time's longer than your time.'

James smiled. 'We don't have to be at the Elsons' until eight o'clock. Shall we stop somewhere and have a drink first?'

'Definitely,' said Annie with relief.

They sat out in the garden of a pretty pub in Easter Compton.

'By the way'—James cleared his throat—'you're looking very nice this evening. Sorry, my daughter told me I had to say that when I came to pick you up, and I forgot. But it's true,' he hastily amended. 'You really do look nice. I . . . er, like your hair as well.'

Annie self-consciously touched her hair, which the hairdresser had back-combed and pinned into an ambitious chignon. She was terrified to move her head in case the whole lot came tumbling down. Her dress wasn't helping matters either. When she'd tried it on in the shop, it had looked amazing, as glittery and gorgeous as a mermaid's tail. How could she possibly have known that the moment you sat down those triangular sequins would stick into your flesh like knives?

'Go on then,' James prompted. 'Tell me how long it's been since you did this.'

Here we go. 'Fourteen years,' said Annie, and waited for him to spit his drink all over the table.

But all James did was nod. 'Oh well, I can beat that. Seventeen years for me.'

Blimey. It was Annie who was shocked. 'Look at us, we're a right old couple of dinosaurs! What happened to you, then?'

'Well, it's complicated. My wife walked out on me and my daughters twenty-three years ago. She's led a fairly chaotic life ever since. When she broke up with Tilly's father she needed a roof over her head so we let her move back in for a while. Then, when she took off again, she left Tilly with us.'

'You're kidding,' gasped Annie. 'People leave gloves behind . . . they don't leave *children*.'

'Leonie's in a league of her own. She felt she couldn't cope with Tilly. Actually'—James hesitated—'she gave us the choice. Either we took Tilly, or Tilly went into care. Well, there was no decision to make. We already loved her.'

Annie was deeply shocked. 'Does she still see her mother at all?'

'Intermittently. When it suits Leonie. She came to see Tilly today, in fact. Brought her latest boyfriend and his daughter up from Brighton to introduce them. The girls are pretty much the same age, apparently.'

Right. Annie nodded as all became clear. She was also touched by James's attitude; only a truly decent man would bring up a child for whom he was in no way responsible. The simple way he had said, 'We already loved her,' had brought a lump to her throat.

'Tilly's a credit to you. She's a lovely girl.'

'Tilly's a credit to herself.' James spoke with genuine warmth. 'She'd have been a lovely girl whoever brought her up. Anyway, can I be nosy and ask about you?'

'Ask away. But I'm not very exciting.' Annie's eyes sparkled. Now that they were sitting down together actually having a conversation, her nervousness had lessened dramatically. She was feeling far more comfortable.

Apart from the sequins, obviously.

'My mother had a stroke,' she said matter-of-factly. 'Fourteen years ago. She needed someone to move in with her, and I did. Last year she died. All the time Mum was ill, I was too busy looking after her to meet anyone who might . . . you know, become important. I don't regret it, but this is why I'm embarrassingly out of practice.'

'Did you really not mind?' said James.

'No.' Annie shook her head and smiled. 'How could I mind? She was my mum.'

It was ten to eight and their glasses were empty. James rose to his feet. 'Another drink?'

'Don't we have to be there by eight?'

'I don't want to go. I'd much rather stay here, talking to you.'

It was what Annie wanted too, but she had a highly developed guilt gene. 'They'll be waiting for us. We have to go.'

'Why do you keep doing that?' With a crooked smile, James imitated her wiggle.

Damn, he'd noticed. 'Death by sequins.' Annie was rueful. 'They're digging into my legs and—ouch! What was *that* for?'

James had just hit her. *Bam*, right on top of her head.

Economically, James said, 'Wasp.'

'Oh God, did you get it? I'm allergic to wasps!' Annie let out a squeak of fear as she heard the ominous sound of buzzing emanating from the depths of her hairdo. She shouted, 'Get it out, get it out!'

The wasp was trapped in a mass of lacquered back-combing. Squeezing her eyes shut, she felt James yank out the grips, separating her hair like David Bellamy venturing intrepidly through the jungle.

The next moment James flung the wasp away into the bushes.

'There, gone.'

'Thank God for that.' Annie shuddered with relief. 'Last time my arm swelled up like the Elephant Man's. You saved my life.'

'But not your hair.' James sounded regretful. 'I'm sorry.'

Gingerly, she put her hands up to her head. 'But I don't have a hairbrush.' Recalling the incident in the newsagents, she added ruefully, 'Honestly, what is it with me and wasps?'

The drive back to Kingsweston was a painful journey for Annie.

'It's no good, I'll have to change out of this dress. These sequins are killing me.'

James looked concerned. 'I hope you didn't buy it specially.'

'Not at all,' Annie lied as they pulled up outside her cottage. 'Come on in. I'll be as quick as I can. Make yourself at home, and ring your boss and tell him we're running late.'

Upstairs, in the bathroom mirror, she discovered just how much of a disaster her hair was. She began brushing the sticky tendrils.

Finally all the hairspray was out and her hair was back to its normal shoulder-length no-style. Annie unzipped her dress. Oh, the bliss of freedom from spiky sequins. The only other smart-enough outfit she owned was a simple black shift, high-necked and sleeveless. Annie quickly put it on and added a rope of real-looking pearls.

'You look lovely,' said James when she reappeared downstairs. 'Remind me again, why do we have to go to this dinner party?'

'Because your boss will sack you if you don't.' Annie pulled open the front door. 'Come on. Things are never as bad as you think they are going to be.'

This was true, of course. Sometimes they turn out worse.

Cedric and Mary-Jane lived in a sprawling brand-new house cunningly designed to resemble an old farmhouse. Mary-Jane answered the door. In her late forties, she did her level best to pass for a twenty-six-year-old. With her jacked-in waist and jacked-up face, and teeny-tiny stiletto-shod feet, she looked like Barbie's grandmother.

'At last, at last!' Mary-Jane trilled, ushering them inside.

'James, good to see you.' Cedric came to greet them. 'And this is . . . ?'

'Annie Healey.' As he spoke, James became aware that Mary-Jane was sizing up Annie's appearance and finding it lacking.

'*Sweet* little necklace,' Mary-Jane murmured.

'Welcome, Annie.' Cedric puffed enthusiastically on his King Edward cigar. 'Now come along through and meet everyone; it's a pleasure to finally meet one of James's lady friends. Have you been together long?'

James tensed, but Annie said cheerfully, 'Oh, for a while. This is a beautiful house you have here.'

'Thank you, my dear. Now, what can I get you to drink?'

As they sat down to eat, it became apparent that Cedric was charmed by Annie and Mary-Jane wasn't taking it well. Over their first course, Mary-Jane turned the conversation to jewellery, showed off her latest four-carat solitaire, then asked Annie where she'd bought her pearls.

'Claire's Accessories. Four pounds,' Annie said happily.

Mary Jane smirked. 'Heavens, don't they bring you out in a rash?'

Worse was to come. As they were being served the main course, Ray Hickson snapped his fingers and said, 'Got it!'

Ray was a fellow accountant of the sharp-suited, sleazeball kind, who James had never liked.

'I knew I knew you from somewhere.' Ray addressed Annie with a triumphant gleam in his eyes. 'Hang on a sec.' Producing his wallet, Ray slid out a tenner and waved it at Annie. 'Give us twenty Benson and Hedges and a copy of the *FT*.'

James suppressed the urge to reach across the table and punch him.

'Sorry, I'm afraid we're closed,' said Annie. Turning to Cedric, who was looking perplexed, she calmly explained, 'I work in a newsagents.'

'How extraordinary!' Mary-Jane started to laugh. 'Is that how you two met? James, I had no idea you were involved with a shop assistant!'

James reddened with outrage on Annie's behalf.

Gallantly Cedric said, 'My sister worked in a shop once.'

Mary-Jane snorted with laughter. 'Darling, that was Asprey's.'

Discreetly, James excused himself and left the room.

He returned two minutes later, clutching his hand. 'Cedric, I'm sorry, we're going to have to leave. There was a wasp in your bathroom and it stung me. I'm allergic to wasp stings.' Breathing heavily and holding out his hand, palm up, James showed them the puncture mark surrounded by a small raised reddened area. 'If I don't take my medication in time, I could be in trouble. Annie, I'm afraid you'll have to drive me home.'

It was pretty scary, driving a make of car she'd never driven before. As soon as they were safely out of sight of Cedric and Mary-Jane's faux-Tudor monstrosity, Annie slowed the Jag to a halt and said admiringly, 'Quick thinking, Batman. But I don't know how you managed it.' Intrigued, she reached for his hand and examined the palm in the dim glow of the interior light. 'This looks exactly like a real wasp sting.'

When she looked up, James's mouth was twitching. 'It *is* a wasp sting.'

'Oh my God, it's from the wasp that was caught in my hair, isn't it? You got stung when you grabbed it—and never even told me.'

'It's no big deal. I'm not really allergic to wasp stings,' said James as they both climbed out of the car and swapped seats.

'Right.' Assertively, James restarted the car. 'Are you still hungry? I know a great Indian restaurant in Redland.'

'Will they mind that I work in a newsagents and my pearls aren't real?'

James, pulling away from the kerb, said, 'So long as you haven't drunk fifteen pints of lager, they'll welcome you with open arms.'

The look on James's face when he put his head round the kitchen door told her all Miriam needed to know.

'What time do you call this?' she demanded, secretly delighted that he'd obviously had a good time. It was as if marriage to Leonie had unnerved him to such a degree that he hadn't been able to bring himself to risk dating again.

James pulled a face. 'Ten past one. Don't tell me I'm grounded.'

Miriam said, 'So you had a good time at the dinner party after all?'

'I had a good time,' James agreed. 'It's been a really great evening.'

'With the woman from the newsagents Tilly set you up with?'

Unlike Mary-Jane Elson, Miriam wasn't poking fun. Feeling happier than he had in a long time, James said, 'Annie,' and felt the back of his neck heat up. It was like coming out of a decades-long hibernation.

Watching him, Miriam was reminded that she had felt the same way once, about the writer of the letter she'd had such trouble replying to tonight. The second letter had arrived this morning. The gist of it, basically, was that he didn't believe he had made a mistake before.

In a small corner of her heart she still loved him. The rest of her wished he was dead.

Slightly ashamed to be thinking such a thing—but not ashamed enough to stop thinking it—Miriam said, 'Tell me what Annie's like.'

'Down-to-earth. Straightforward. She's a good person,' said James. 'Kind. Easy to be with.' He paused. 'And she's honest. Like you, really.'

'Oh, that's me all right.' As she flashed a smile, Miriam wondered how James would react if he knew the truth. 'I'm just an all-round saint.'

'I'm not stupid, you know,' Tilly announced. 'I know what you're up to.'

Nadia looked bemused as Tilly chucked her school bag into the back of the car and jumped into the passenger seat.

'What? All I did was offer to pick you up after school while Dad's away. What's wrong with that?'

Tilly raised her eyebrows. 'Remind me, which of us is thirteen?'

Precocious little brat.

'So do you want a lift, or not?'

'Lift please.'

'And how about an ice cream? I've been working my socks off and I'm hot.' Casually Nadia said, 'Where's that newsagents you usually go to?'

Equally casually, Tilly said, 'There's a garage just up here on the left.'

'Oh, come on,' begged Nadia, 'don't be so mean, I just want to see her! Just tell me which one she works in.'

'Up past the traffic lights, on the right.'

Over the years Nadia had seen James being set up on blind dates and nothing had ever come of them. This time, clearly, things were different. Following his initial outing with Annie Healey on Saturday night, they had seen each other on Sunday evening and *again* on Monday evening. This morning, Tuesday, James had driven up to Liverpool for a two-day conference, having arranged to meet up with Annie on Thursday night.

Bursting with curiosity, Nadia was longing to see her dad's new girlfriend for herself.

The woman serving behind the counter had wavy fair hair, loosely tied back in a ponytail, and friendly blue eyes.

Tilly said, 'Nadia, this is Annie Healey. Annie, meet Nadia, my sister.'

Thinking how much less stressful for Annie a chance encounter would be than a deliberately pre-planned one, Nadia put on her surprised-but-delighted face and said, 'Really? How lovely to meet you!'

'You too.' Annie flushed slightly, but she was smiling.

'We came in because Nadia was desperate for an ice cream.' Tilly then added happily, 'And to check you out.'

Fantastic.

'She wasn't supposed to say that,' Nadia apologised to Annie.

'It's OK, I don't mind.' Annie was sympathetic. 'I'd be curious too.'

Hugely relieved to discover that she liked Annie Healey, Nadia said, 'Our mother's had so many boyfriends I can hardly be bothered to meet them any more. But with Dad it's different, he . . . um . . .'

'I know, he told me. And here I am.' Annie pulled a face and gestured self-deprecatingly at her green nylon overall. 'I hope you weren't expecting Nicole Kidman.'

'Here you go.' Tilly, who had been delving into the chest freezer, pushed a Magnum into Nadia's hand.

'When Dad's back from his conference, you must come round for dinner one evening,' Nadia told Annie. 'Meet everyone properly. But now we really have to go,' she added, because the poor woman was still looking apprehensive, like an interviewee about to be grilled by Jeremy Paxman. 'I've parked on double yellows.'

'We're not parked on double yellows,' Tilly complained as they made their way back to the car.

'It was a white lie, to get us out of there. Sometimes it's easier to fib.' Meaningfully Nadia added, 'Like pretending I didn't know who Annie was, until you opened your big mouth. What's that noise?'

Tilly glanced over her shoulder. 'Boys from our school, mucking about.' They were fourth-formers. Everybody knew these fourteen-year-olds were a law unto themselves.

Everyone except Nadia.

'Somebody's on the ground. They're hitting him!' Outraged, Nadia grabbed Tilly by the sleeve.

'Just leave them. Don't interfere,' begged Tilly. 'It'll be embarrassing.'

'Even more embarrassing when you hear on the news that a schoolboy was kicked to death in the street and no one bothered to do anything about it. *Hey!*' shouted Nadia, breaking into a run and dragging Tilly along in her wake. 'You lot! Leave him alone!'

'Ooh, I'm so scared,' mocked one of the teenagers, grinning insolently. 'Watch out, boys, it's Batman and Robin.'

Tilly was mortified. It was all right for Nadia, piling in where she wasn't wanted, she didn't have to face them in the playground tomorrow.

'I said *stop it*!' roared Nadia, when one of the fourth-formers aimed another kick at the boy sprawled on the ground.

'It's not Batman and Robin,' one of the others jeered, 'it's Clint Eastwood. Look, he's got his Magnum.'

That cracked them up. They promptly began licking imaginary ice creams and snarling, 'D'you feel lucky, punk? C'mon, make my day.'

'Get out of here, all of you, or I'll call the police,' bellowed Nadia and, laughing, they turned and scooted off on their skateboards.

'It's OK, they've gone,' Nadia told the curled-up heap on the ground. Nadia shoved the uneaten Magnum into Tilly's hand. Bending down, she rested a hand on his trembling shoulder. 'Come on, up you get.' Nadia heaved the boy into a sitting position. He was of smallish build, with rumpled dark hair, a thin face and a rip in the knee of his school trousers. There were a couple of grazes on his arm, and he had a swollen, cut lip. 'Honestly, those thugs, how could they do this to you?'

'How could *you* do this to me?' hissed the boy, who Tilly now recognised. He was new to the school. She had noticed him at break times, sitting on his own. Now, pushing Nadia away, he rose painfully to his feet and used his shirtsleeve to wipe the blood from his mouth.

'I'm never going to live this down now,' he muttered, 'being rescued by a couple of *girls*. Can you imagine how humiliating that is?'

Nadia gazed at him, open-mouthed. 'But . . . they were—'

'Kicking me, I know. And it would have been all over in a couple of minutes. But not any more, oh no.' Vehemently the boy shook his head. 'They won't let me forget this in a hurry.' He turned and limped away.

Nadia looked as if she'd just been slapped.

Tilly gave a what-did-you-expect shrug. 'Told you not to get involved.'

It was the hottest day of the year so far and Nadia was stripped to a cropped white halter-neck vest and denim shorts, with her hair tied up in a messy topknot. The sun was blazing down and her tan was coming along nicely.

Levelling the soil before laying down the patio stones was back-breaking work. Thirsty too. Pausing to uncap her bottle of water, Nadia glugged back a couple of tepid mouthfuls and pulled a face. Never mind, there was more in the house.

She was standing at the kitchen window, guzzling down ice-cold water from the mini fridge that Jay had brought along for them to use when she saw a taxi pull up outside. The passenger got out and Nadia abruptly stopped drinking. It was the pregnant woman she'd seen arriving at Jay's house the other day. This time she was wearing loose white maternity trousers and a man's dark blue shirt. She wasn't looking happy.

As Bart and the boys were working upstairs in the bedrooms, Nadia opened the front door. At close quarters she looked even more miserable, pale and drawn, her shoulders slumped in defeat.

Had Jay dumped her? Had he told her he'd do his bit financially, but that any kind of relationship between them was out of the question?

'I'm looking for Jay. Is he here?'

'Sorry, he isn't.'

'Any idea where he is?'

Nadia shrugged and shook her head. 'He doesn't always tell us. Have you tried his phone?'

'It's switched off.' The woman's expression was bleak and Nadia felt a surge of compassion.

'That thing's always switched off. Look, can I take a message?'

Nosy? Moi?

The woman looked absolutely wretched. 'No. I'll just keep trying his phone. But if you do see him, tell him it's urgent. I'm on my way to the hospital now.' As she spoke, the woman's ringless left hand moved to her stomach. 'He has to get there as soon as he can.'

Oh God, don't say she was actually in labour!

'Of course I will.' Nadia nodded vigorously. 'And your name is . . . ?'

Well, she could hardly refer to her as the miserable pregnant one.

'Belinda.'

Nadia's smile was reassuring. 'No problem, I'll definitely tell him.'

'Thanks.' The woman made her way back to the waiting taxi.

Jay turned up an hour later. By the time Nadia had rushed in from the garden, he was deep in conversation with Bart and the boys.

'Jay, could I—'

'Hang on a sec.' Jay held up a hand to stop her. 'Let me just get this sorted out first.'

Agitated, Nadia blurted out, 'But you need to get to the hospital. Belinda was here. It's very urgent, you have to go right away.'

That got his attention. She watched the colour drain from Jay's face.

'Belinda was here?' Was that guilt in his eyes?

'She's gone straight there in a taxi. You'd better hurry,' said Nadia.

Bart let out a low whistle when Jay had left. 'What was that all about? Who's Belinda?'

'She's nine months pregnant,' Nadia told him. 'And not very happy with our boss.'

'Bugger me,' whistled Bart.

Tilly saw him in the afternoon as they passed each other in the corridor on the way to their respective classes. Glancing up and accidentally catching her eye, he hastily looked away. One of the boys behind him, also recognising Tilly, jeered, 'Hey, Davis, aren't you gonna say hello to your girlfriend?'

Appalled to realise she was blushing, Tilly shot the boy a filthy look, which only amused him all the more.

'Oi, Robin, where's Batman today?' Darting across the corridor he aimed a skilful kung-fu-style kick at the hem of her pleated school skirt. 'Got your pants on over your tights, I hope, Boy Wonder. Phwoarr, very sexy . . .' Tilly's skirt flew up to reveal sturdy navy knickers '. . . NOT.'

Any attempt at retaliation was pointless. Tilly gave him another killer stare then stalked off down the corridor in disgust. Honestly, it was times like this that made you almost look forward to double physics.

He was loitering casually, waiting for her when school finished at three thirty. Tilly knew this because of the way he ignored her totally as she walked past him at the school gate.

As she made her way down the road to the bus stop, Tilly sensed him behind her. Finally, when there was no longer anyone else from school in sight, he caught her up.

'Look, I'm sorry.'

He loped along beside Tilly, hands stuffed into trouser pockets, narrow shoulders hunched. 'It wasn't your fault, OK? And I'm sorry Moxham's having a go at you now.'

Tilly shrugged. 'He'll get bored soon enough. What's your name?'

'Davis.'

Tilly hid a smile. 'I meant your first name.'

'Oh. Calvin.'

'*Calvin?*' Crikey, talk about embarrassing. She'd thought hers was bad.

'My friends call me Cal. Well,' he amended, 'the friends I *used* to have. Since we moved down here, everyone's called me Davis.'

Tilly realised it couldn't be much fun, having to start all over again at a new school; people saw you observing from the sidelines and it didn't occur to them that at your last school you might have been Mr Dazzlingly Popular, the life and soul of the party.

'You can call me Cal if you like,' Calvin announced. 'Or Calvin. Or Davis. Up to you.' For a moment it seemed likely that he might actually smile. 'Multiple choice.'

'OK.' He wasn't what you'd call fantastically good-looking or anything, but he wasn't ugly. Just . . . average, Tilly concluded. 'I'm Tilly.' Glancing over her shoulder, she added, 'And this is my bus.'

'Right.' Cal watched her jump onto the bus. 'See you around.'

Nadia arrived for work early the next morning. It was going to be another stunning day and to celebrate she had stopped off at the mini supermarket on the way. Nestling in a bag on the seat beside her were four Galaxy truffle ice creams to treat the workers. Nothing for Jay because . . . well, she didn't think he deserved one. Then again, there was every chance they wouldn't see him. Babies didn't pop out like bars of chocolate from a vending machine.

But as she climbed out of the car, a double-parked post van pulled away revealing Jay's car parked behind it.

Noiselessly, she unlocked the front door and made her way through to the kitchen. So far there was no sign of Jay. Nadia inched open the fridge door and prepared to slide the bag into the freezer section without—

'What are you doing?'

'Ouch!' yelped Nadia as the spring-loaded door of the freezer compartment snapped back, catching her fingers. 'I was putting stuff in the fridge, that's all.' Jay looked terrible. His face was drawn, his eyes heavily shadowed. Dark stubble covered his chin and he didn't appear to have slept. 'Um . . . is everything all right?'

'To be honest, no.'

In the time she'd known him, Jay had always been In Control, capable of handling anything at all. Now, for once, he appeared defeated.

Unnerved, Nadia said, 'Did she have the baby?'

'What? Oh . . . no. It's not due for another month.'

Right.

When he didn't elaborate, Nadia said cautiously, 'Look, it's none of my business, but if you want to talk about it . . .'

'Yes.' This time Jay nodded. Slowly he repeated, 'Yes, I think I do.'

'Does she want you to marry her?'

Jay smiled briefly. As if he'd forgotten how to.

'Belinda is my sister-in-law.'

Blimey. He was in deeper trouble than she'd imagined.

'It's not my baby,' said Jay. 'Belinda's married to my brother, Anthony.' He paused and glanced out of the window, visibly collecting himself before carrying on. 'She was married to my brother Anthony,' he amended. 'He died last night.'

They sat outside on the stone steps leading down to the garden. Seated next to her, Jay explained about Anthony's earlier brush with cancer, the radiation therapy and punishingly aggressive doses of chemo.

'The doctors warned him not to raise his hopes but Anthony was convinced he'd beaten it for good. Six months later, Belinda found out she was pregnant. They'd thought the treatment would leave him infertile. You've never seen a happier couple.'

Picking up a small stone, Jay turned it over and over between his fingers before lobbing it into the levelled earth. 'Then a few weeks ago the cancer came back. This time it was everywhere, in his bones, in his liver, in his lungs. Anthony didn't have a chance. He went into a coma yesterday. And then he died at eleven o'clock last night. He was thirty-two.'

'I'm so sorry.' She meant not just the usual condolences, but for thinking bad things of Jay all this time. He'd spent every spare minute of the last few weeks visiting his brother in the hospital—no wonder his phone had been turned off. Desperately ashamed, Nadia said, 'We hadn't any idea. You should have said something.'

'I probably should,' Jay agreed. 'But I didn't want to. I made the mistake of telling my neighbour a while back. Since then, every time I've pulled up outside my house, she's been there with her caring face on, asking me how Anthony's doing. I started to dread the sight of her. In fact, that's why I haven't been home. When we left the hospital, I came here instead. It's been easier,' he explained, 'knowing that you didn't know anything about it. Being treated like a normal human being.'

'Where is Belinda now?'

'Her parents drove up from Dorset last night. They've taken her back to stay with them until the funeral. I'm organising everything,' said Jay.

'And I had such a go at you,' Nadia groaned, 'because we could never get hold of you. I can't believe you just let me do it.'

'I'll be more reachable from now on. I won't need to keep my phone switched off. Apart from when we're actually in the church, of course.'

He was trying to cheer her up, which only made Nadia feel worse. Humbly, she said, 'Um . . . do you want an ice cream?'

'No thanks, I have to get to the register office.'

'Sure.' Nadia watched him stand up, brushing the dust from his trousers as he prepared to leave. At last she knew why he'd been so offish and abrupt ever since she'd come to work for him, and so completely unlike the Jay Tiernan she'd met in the wilds of Gloucestershire.

Everything suddenly made sense.

As if reading her mind, Jay said, 'You never know, once things get back to normal I might turn out not to be the boss from hell after all.'

'I won't count my chickens.'

Nadia only said it to make him smile. The trouble was, things weren't likely to get back to normal, were they? Not for a while at least. Belinda hadn't even had the baby yet.

Chapter Five

IT HAD BEEN James's idea to hold a barbecue. He wanted to introduce Annie to his family, and this seemed the best way to do it. The weather had been fantastic all week. Barbecues were casual, informal affairs. Everyone could relax and enjoy themselves.

At least that had been the plan before Leonie had turned up.

Hearing a car pull up outside and thinking it was Piers, Clare raced across the hall and yanked open the front door.

'Mum!' She stared in alarm at Leonie. 'What are you doing here?' Clare was puzzled. She knew Tilly was due to be spending the weekend in Brighton but the plan had been for her to catch the train down there tomorrow morning.

'It's a surprise, darling! Tilly mentioned on the phone that you were having a little get-together this evening and Brian had to take Tamsin to some ghastly school function, so I just thought why not pop on down? Come along now, give your mother a kiss. And Nadia as well, look at you! Honestly, it wouldn't kill you to be a tiny bit more welcoming.'

Clare was torn. If she'd come all this way, could they actually refuse to let her in? Plus, Clare wasn't particularly looking forward to meeting this Annie person. When you were used to having your dad all to yourself, the thought of him suddenly finding someone was . . . well, a bit yukky, to be frank. What's more, hadn't it even occurred to everyone that she might be after his money? James had a good job, financial acumen and a hefty shares portfolio. Annie Healey worked in a newsagents and clearly wasn't in the higher tax bracket. She was bound to regard their father as a catch.

And speaking of catches, where was bloody Piers?

Behind her, Nadia said flatly, 'This isn't a good idea, Mum. Dad's bringing his new girlfriend over. She might feel a bit awkward—'

'Oh, that's ridiculous, why on earth should it be awkward?' Leonie trilled with laughter. 'I left James over twenty years ago, for heaven's sake. I'm hardly likely to be jealous, am I?'

Tilly's footsteps sounded across the oak floor. 'Gran says the barbecue's ready to start cooking stuff and can someone fetch the steaks—oh!'

'My *baby*,' Leonie exclaimed, enveloping Tilly in a hug. 'Isn't this a lovely surprise?'

At that moment they heard another car turn into the drive. Make this be Piers, make this be Piers, Clare silently prayed. But it wasn't, of course. It was James's dark blue Jaguar. He'd been to pick up Annie.

Nadia saw the look of barely contained horror on her father's face as he spotted his ex-wife in the doorway.

'James, you're looking just as handsome as ever.' Leonie threw out her arms and left her daughters standing in the doorway. Greeting her ex-husband with enthusiasm, she then turned and said gaily, 'And you must be Annie, how lovely to meet you!'

'Leonie, what are you doing here?' James's voice was level.

'I was missing Tilly. She mentioned the barbecue. The girls said I might make things awkward for Annie, but I told them we'd be fine. And now we are fine, aren't we?' Leonie gazed brightly from James to Annie.

Nadia sighed, realising that they were going to be stuck with Leonie for the rest of the evening. She had skin thicker than a brontosaurus.

'It's gone seven.' Nadia gave Clare a nudge. 'Are you sure Piers is coming?'

Clare, through slightly gritted teeth, said. 'Of course he is.' She'd kill him if he let her down again.

Out in the garden, chiefly for Tilly's sake, everyone was behaving in a civilised fashion and acting as if Leonie was an invited guest.

Well, fairly civilised.

'What would you like on your steak, Leonie? Tomato sauce? Mustard?' Beaming, Leonie took the plate from Miriam.

'Just as it is, thanks. Everything looks gorgeous.' As unflappable as ever, she went on, 'Clare, darling, you've got a face on you like a wet Wednesday in Wigan. Whatever's wrong, my angel?'

'Nothing's wrong.'

'Boyfriend was supposed to be turning up,' Miriam cut in, 'and he hasn't. Mr Unreliable,' she added. 'If you ask me, he needs getting rid of.'

'He isn't unreliable.' Clare felt bright spots of colour spring to life in her cheeks. 'He's probably just been held up.'

'Could have phoned,' said Edward, who was busy pouring drinks. 'If I'm held up, I let people know.'

Clare rolled her eyes. 'I think I need the bathroom,' she said.

In the deserted living room, Clare used the ordinary phone to dial her mobile. Those outside would be able to hear it playing its jaunty tune. After several bars, Clare hung up and pretended to answer her own phone, wandering back out onto the terrace.

'Oh no, how awful . . . Piers, of course I don't mind. You stay there as long as you have to. Yes, yes, I love you too. OK, ring me tomorrow. Bye.'

There, ha. Gwyneth Paltrow, eat your skinny heart out.

'That was Piers,' Clare said pointlessly. 'He's in Surrey. His grandmother died suddenly this morning. He tried to ring me earlier but he was stuck on the motorway and the battery was flat on his phone. Poor Piers, he's trying to comfort his mother and apologising to me for not turning up . . .'

'Oh, darling, that's such a shame,' said Leonie. 'Honestly, old people are so selfish, aren't they? You never know when they are going to drop dead.'

Annie wasn't having a great time. Beforehand, the prospect of meeting James's family had been scary, if only in a five-out-of-ten kind of way. Now it was turning out to be more eight-out-of-ten. Tilly, who she'd thought she could count on to be on her side, was clearly torn by the arrival of her mother. Leonie, while perfectly polite on the surface, had a disconcerting habit of saying things in a jokey fashion, then glancing at people so as to signal that she hadn't been joking really. Nadia, who would have been an ally, was busy helping Miriam with the barbecue. Edward seemed nice enough, but Annie couldn't begin to imagine what kind of conversation she might hold with a consultant neuropsychiatrist.

'Annie, you *must* try the kebabs, they're fantastic. Ooh, careful, bit hot. So whereabouts exactly *do* you work?'

This was what Clare had been doing, urging Annie to try the kebabs, or the king prawns, or the roasted peppers, then asking her a question the moment her mouth was full. Anxious not to appear rude, Annie was then obliged to chew frantically and swallow far too soon. She just hoped it didn't look as painful as it felt, like in *Tom and Jerry* when Tom gulped down a fish sideways and you could see the head and tail bulging out either side of his neck.

'It's the newsagents on Quorn Street,' she finally managed to say.

Clare pulled a rather-you-than-me face. 'God, is it awful?'

'I like it there,' said Annie.

'And you live in Kingsweston? Is yours one of those big houses by the green?' There was a glittery look in Clare's eyes. She was a pretty girl, enviably slim in jeans and a midriff-baring black T-shirt, with long dark hair falling down her back. But she was definitely having a dig.

'No,' said Annie. 'One of the small cottages next to the phone box.'

Clare raised her plucked eyebrows. 'Have you tried the scallops yet? Here, you must try a scallop. So why did Dad have to come and pick you up this evening? Is there something wrong with your car?'

Wondering if anyone had ever given her the slap she deserved, Annie said calmly, 'I don't have a car.'

'No car? Heavens, you poor thing! Still, it must be nice being driven around in Dad's Jag.'

'Clare.' James, just back from switching on the lights around the terrace, shot her a look of warning.

'What?' Apparently mystified, she shook her head.

Moments later Miriam emerged from the house clutching a bowl of potato salad in one hand and the cordless phone in the other, saying sympathetically, '. . . and I'm so sorry to hear about your grandmother.'

Annie watched the colour drain from Clare's face.

'I can't hear you, dear. Speak up.' Miriam raised her voice. 'Say that again? Oh, right. Well, that's good. Here's Clare, I'll pass you over to her.'

Mutely Clare held out her hand for the phone.

'Darling, fantastic news, Piers's grandmother has been miraculously resurrected. She's absolutely fine. You might need to shout though. Almost sounds as if Piers is ringing from some crowded pub.'

Clare couldn't believe it. Bloody Piers, how could he do this to her? 'Yes?'

'Clare, hey, sorry I couldn't make it, got held up in Clifton. We're all at the Happy Ferret, if you fancy joining us.'

'No thanks.' Clare spat the words out; she'd never been so ashamed.

Annie had cheered up considerably. The way Miriam had winked at her as she'd passed the phone over to Clare had helped a lot. Now, with the sky darkening and the citronella candles flickering away in their water bowls, Annie settled back into a chair on the terrace. Music was drifting out through the living-room windows and Miriam and Edward were dancing on the terrace. James was turning the last of the kebabs on the glowing barbecue. Leonie kicked off her shoes, grabbed Clare's wrist and dragged her up to join in the dancing. Tilly, sitting on the stone steps with her arms wrapped round her knees, watched them.

'Top up,' Nadia announced, pouring wine into Annie's almost empty glass. Shaking back her curls and collapsing onto the chair next to her, she said, 'So, are we not so scary as you thought?'

Annie smiled. 'I've enjoyed myself.' Well, most of it. 'I think your sister Clare thinks I'm a gold-digger and I really wish she didn't.' Earnestly, Annie added, 'I promise you, I'm not interested in your dad's money.'

'Don't take any notice of Clare, she's in a strop because of this so-called boyfriend of hers. Posh Piers.' Nadia pulled a face. 'Unlike the rest of us, Clare isn't used to being mucked about by men.'

'How about you?' said Annie.

'Oh, my last proper boyfriend dumped me almost eighteen months ago. Edward's son,' Nadia added, nodding towards Edward and Miriam.

'Gosh,' said Annie, sympathetically. 'Must be awkward.'

'Not really. Edward doesn't talk about Laurie when I'm around. Anyway, he's in America now, which makes things easier.'

Since the break-up, Laurie's flying visits to his father had been few and far between and Nadia had always made a point of making herself scarce during these times. It wasn't that she was still bitter, she just didn't see why she should feel obliged to be amicable and pretend they were still jolly good friends. Because it did still hurt, deep down.

'And you've not met anyone else since then?'

'Well, no, but I haven't given up yet. They can just run faster than me, that's all. Once I learn to use a lasso, they won't be able to get away.' She twirled a lasso above her head and aimed it at James as he headed towards them, bearing yet another plate of food.

Leonie had been to the loo and was on her way back outside when the front doorbell rang.

Harpo squawked, 'Somebody get the bloody door.'

Since there was no one else around, Leonie did as Harpo suggested.

Blimey. And very nice too.

Smiling playfully up at the visitor, Leonie said, 'Let me guess. You're the bad boy.' Leonie ushered him into the hall. 'Oh yes, I've been hearing all about you.' She wagged a finger at him. 'Still, at least you're here now. I'm Leonie by the way. Clare's mother. Come along through.'

'I think we may have our wires crossed,' said the visitor. 'I just wanted a quiet word with Nadia.'

Since he wasn't moving, Leonie said, 'Aren't you Piers?'

'No. Jay Tiernan.'

'And you're a friend of Nadia's? Now this *is* interesting,' Leonie teased.

'And why so *formal*?' she went on, brushing her hand against the lapels of his dark suit. 'I mean, it's a very *nice* suit, but not what most men would wear to a barbecue.'

'It was my brother's funeral this afternoon,' said Jay. 'I haven't—'

'Stop!' Leonie shouted in triumph. 'We've already had death-of-a-close-relative, you can't just copy someone else's excuse,' she chided. 'That's *so* unoriginal. Come on now, try and think up one of your own.'

'Sorry,' said Jay. 'OK, just tell her my watch stopped and that's why I'm late. Now, could you go and find Nadia and let her know I'm here?'

In the hall, Jay was looking handsome but strained, as though the day had taken its toll. Thanks to several glasses of wine, Nadia was able to give him a hug. Nothing erotic, just one of those brief poor-you ones.

A burst of laughter filtered through from the garden and Jay turned away. 'I didn't realise you had a party going on. I'll just leave—'

'No you won't.' Nadia put a hand out to stop him as he moved towards the front door. 'What made you come here?'

Jay hesitated, then shrugged. 'The last guests left half an hour ago. Belinda's parents have taken her back to Dorset again. I gave a couple of people a lift home and it turned out they live not far from here. So I just stopped by on the off chance that you might be free to join me for a much-needed drink.'

It was horribly inappropriate, but Nadia couldn't help it. A little knot of lust was busily forming in the pit of her stomach, because with those shadowed eyes and that dark stubble and the sexily loosened tie around his neck, Jay really was looking fantastically attractive. Of course he didn't want to be at home on his own, after the traumas of the day. He needed someone to take his mind off all that and cheer him up. And she was just the girl to do it.

'I'd love to go for a drink,' said Nadia. 'Just give me two minutes.'

'You look different,' Jay commented as he led the way through to his kitchen. He reached into the fridge for a bottle of Meursault.

'That's because you've never seen me in a dress before. Thanks,' said Nadia as he handed her a brimming glass. Pouring an equally large one for himself, he downed half of it in a matter of seconds.

'Are you sure that's the way Oz Clarke says to do it?'

Jay shrugged. 'Right now, I'm not bothered what it tastes like. I just want to blur the edges of a truly godawful day.' He showed her into the living room. 'Have a seat.'

The room was huge, high-ceilinged and unfussily decorated. The walls were covered with dark blue wallpaper, the carpet and curtains were cream and the navy sofas squashily comfortable. Above the fireplace hung the telephone box painting. Nadia, sinking into one of the sofas, watched Jay shrug off his jacket, remove his tie and fling them onto the back of another chair. Then he topped up his glass and drank some more.

Blimey, at this rate he'd be out cold in thirty minutes.

'Come and sit down,' said Nadia, feeling sorry for him. She meant come and sit down in the general sense, i.e. on any chair or sofa in the vicinity, but Jay took it as an invitation and joined her on the sofa.

'D'you know what gets me? It's all so fucking unfair. Two brothers, one's single, the other married with a baby due. The single one used to smoke, the married one never did. The single one enjoys a drink, doesn't go to the gym and has eaten more than his share of junk food. Needless to say, the married one's always taken good care of his body. So which one of them dies of cancer? The married brother, of course.'

Nadia said, 'Are you telling me you wish it had been you?'

'I'm not that noble. I'm just saying that, statistically, it should've been. Guilt trip, I suppose. I'm still here and Anthony's gone.'

'That's normal.' Nadia nodded wisely. She'd watched enough episodes of *Oprah* to know that.

'I know. But it doesn't stop me feeling guilty. Bet you're glad you came here now,' Jay added drily.

'I'm fine. Don't worry about me.'

Over the course of the next hour, they talked about Anthony. And death. And whether brothers were better than sisters. And what heaven would be like if you could design it yourself. And where the corkscrew had disappeared to.

By eleven o'clock a second bottle was empty. 'You came to work for someone you thought you knew, and got a completely different person instead. I did feel guilty about that.' Jay touched her bare arm and all the little hairs on the back of it instantly leapt to attention. 'But things should start to improve. Give me a while and I should get back to normal.'

'You mean you'll stop being an ogre?' Nadia thought about easing her arm away, but it didn't seem to want to move.

'Was that what I was? Really, an ogre?'

'No. Well . . . no.' She shook her head, because to be fair he hadn't been. 'But you're right about not being what I was expecting.'

'I'm sorry.' Jay's smile was rueful, his hand still in contact with her forearm. Idly, without even realising it, his fingers were stroking her overheated skin. Oh, it was such a heavenly feeling. It would be churlish to move, surely. She was here to cheer him up.

'What are you thinking?' said Jay.

Ha, not going to tell you *that*. 'Nothing.'

'You must be thinking something. Go on,' Jay prompted, taking another drink.

Nadia's gaze was drawn to the hand holding the glass. 'Nice watch.'

Jay's mouth twitched. 'No, you weren't.'

'OK, clever clogs, why don't you tell me what I'm thinking?'

This time he smiled properly. Their eyes met.

'Fine. I'll tell you. But only telepathically. I'll tell you what you're thinking, then what I'm thinking, then you can tell me if I'm right.'

'And we do all this telepathically?'

Jay nodded, his gaze fixed on hers. Dark brown eyes with wickedly long black lashes. Tanned skin surrounding them, showing paler laughter lines at the outer corners. Unable to tear her gaze away, Nadia knew exactly what was going through his mind:

You want to sleep with me.

I *don't*.

Oh yes you do. And I want to sleep with you, so why are we wasting time?

'Well?' Jay's mouth was twitching once more at the corners, his eyebrows lifting enquiringly as he spoke. 'What's the verdict?'

Not giving him the chance to back off, Nadia reached over and hooked her hand behind his neck. Pulling him towards her, she kissed him gently at first, then harder. Joyfully, she felt Jay respond.

Gosh, he was a gorgeous kisser. His arms were round her, his warm hands moving against her back—

Rrrrring rrrring, sang the phone on the table in front of them.

'Bloody hell,' Jay muttered under his breath. Heaving a sigh, he broke away. 'Any other day, I'd ignore it . . .'

'But not today. Go on, pick it up.'

After a couple of minutes, he said loudly, 'Hang on a moment, Aunt Maureen, I just need to switch something off in the kitchen . . .'

Covering the mouthpiece, he turned to Nadia. 'It's my mother's sister. She's eighty-three and lives in a nursing home in Toronto. Her doctors wouldn't allow her to fly over for the funeral. She's extremely upset about Anthony.'

A lump sprang into Nadia's throat. 'Don't worry about me,' she told Jay as he headed for the door. 'You go ahead, I'll be fine.'

No longer smiling, he shot her a look of gratitude and left the room.

Was this how mating dogs felt when they got a bucket of cold water unceremoniously chucked over them? Nadia sat up straight and pulled the hem of her dress down. Every ounce of desire had drained out of her. How could they have even considered doing anything so selfish? Jay's brother was dead, his funeral had taken place just a few hours ago. Romping around on a sofa was . . . God, it was all wrong. Jay was in a vulnerable state. Nadia cringed, deeply ashamed of herself.

The desire may have gone, but the four glasses of wine were still swimming around in her veins. That was the incredible thing about alcohol; if you were excited it heightened the excitement. If you were sitting there doing nothing, the effect was soporific.

Since getting up and going home would be plain rude, Nadia kicked off her shoes and curled her legs up on the sofa. It was a really comfortable sofa, which helped. And the velvet cushions under her head were blissfully squidgy . . .

Arriving back home at seven thirty, Nadia had banked on the rest of the household being asleep. Her breath caught in her throat as she saw Tilly, loading an overnight bag into the back of her mother's new car.

Leonie, emerging from the house, exclaimed, 'Darling, there you are, we were all wondering where you'd got to. Oh dear, last night's clothes . . . act like a pushover and men will treat you like a pushover. It's not the way to gain their respect.'

Sometimes, Nadia marvelled, her mother really was beyond belief.

'I didn't act like a pushover.'

Lowering her voice Leonie added reprovingly, 'Nor is it setting a good example to your sister.'

'I slept on the sofa,' said Nadia, and Leonie, laughing merrily, pointed up at the sky.

'Ooh, look, flying pig.'

'Mum,' Tilly groaned. 'Please don't.'

'Don't what? I'm just trying to give Nadia some advice. I don't like to see my daughter looking cheap. Remember, darling. Don't ring him and ask when you are going to see him again. Men can't stand being pestered.'

'I know when I'm going to see him again,' Nadia reminded her mother. 'He's my boss. I'll see him at work on Monday morning.'

'That's something else you should never do. Get involved with your boss.' Leonie switched on the ignition. 'That's just asking for trouble.'

'It's for you,' said Miriam, handing the phone to Nadia.

'You should have woken me. I would've driven you home.' Her stomach tightening with pleasure. *See? I didn't phone him, he phoned me.*

Nadia replied, 'I was up early. Sorry about falling asleep on your sofa.'

'And I'm sorry I abandoned you. Poor old Aunt Maureen,' said Jay. 'She was on the phone for over an hour. I couldn't not speak to her.'

'Of course you couldn't. Really, it's OK.'

'Anyway, thanks for last night.'

'Thanks for what? I didn't do anything.' *The phone rang, remember?*

'You know what I mean.' Jay sounded as if he was smiling. 'Look, what are you doing tonight?'

Nadia's heart broke into a canter.

'Um . . .' A vivid mental image of Leonie flashed into her mind, tut-tutting and shaking her head in disapproval. Irritated, Nadia took a deep breath and attempted to banish the unwanted image.

But all the same she'd realised that sleeping with him so soon after Anthony's funeral would be a mistake. Seeing him again this evening would still be too soon. It never hurt to keep men hanging on.

Finding it hard to believe that she was actually taking Leonie's advice, Nadia said quickly, 'I'm busy tonight. And tomorrow.'

'Oh, right. That's a shame.'

'But maybe next weekend . . .' Out of the corner of her eye Nadia saw Miriam smiling broadly. 'I mean, I think I'm probably free then . . .'

'OK. Well, we'll talk about it later in the week,' said Jay.

The phone rang again twenty minutes later as Nadia was polishing off a doorstep of toast and Marmite. Clare, who had belatedly surfaced and was moodily stirring a mug of coffee, leapt up. 'Yes,' she said, eagerly.

Her shoulders sagged as someone who clearly wasn't Piers replied.

'Hang on. I'll get her.' Clare waved the phone feebly at Miriam. 'Gran, for you.'

Miriam was at the sink, scrubbing last night's barbecue racks. She glanced over her shoulder. 'Who is it?'

'Don't know.' Clare shrugged, uninterested. 'He didn't say.'

Miriam seized the phone. 'Hello?'

Pause.

'I'm sorry, who is this?'

Looking up, Nadia saw her grandmother's spine stiffen.

Miriam switched off the phone.

'What was *that* about?' Nadia demanded.

Miriam, returning her attention to the sink, said, 'Hmm? Oh nothing. I ordered some bath towels from John Lewis and they've come in.'

Clare and Nadia exchanged glances. Bath towels. Of course.

'If Piers phones you up,' Nadia addressed Clare, 'you want to tell him to take a running jump.'

Clare rattled irritably through the pages of the newspaper in search of the horoscope. 'Just let me handle things my way, OK?'

The metal barbecue racks clattered onto the drainer. Miriam, snapping her rubber gloves off, turned and stalked out of the room.

'Whoever that was, he's rattled Gran.' Clare raised her eyebrows. 'You don't think she's been having an affair, do you?'

This wasn't likely. Miriam didn't have enough spare time for an affair.

'Don't change the subject.' Nadia was stern. 'You and Piers. He's messing you about.'

Clare hesitated, clearly torn between maintaining a brash façade and needing to confide in someone, even if it was only the sister she spent most of her life bickering with.

'Oh God, I *know*.' With a howl of despair, Clare abruptly buried her face in her hands. 'The thing is, I really like him. I can't help it, I just *do*.'

Upstairs, Miriam sat on the bed and dialled the number she'd obtained by calling 1471. He picked up on the first ring.

'Miriam? Is that you?'

'Now listen to me. I never want you to call this number again. You have your own life and family and I have mine. I don't want to see or to speak to you. It's all in the past. I'm serious.' Miriam heard her voice begin to crack and waver. 'Just leave me *alone*.'

'Brilliant, you're here.' Tamsin hugged Tilly like a long-lost best friend. 'Welcome to the house of no-fun. I've been bored out of my skull. Come on, I'll show you where you're sleeping. This is going to be so cool!'

Tamsin's bedroom was large and south-facing, with two single beds and posters of pop stars on every wall.

Bouncing onto her own bed, Tamsin slid a packet of cigarettes out from beneath the pillows and flung open the window. 'Want one? Oh, go on, live a little. God, aren't parents the pits? I've been grounded since Monday. One minute they're moaning that I'm under their feet the whole time. Then last Sunday I went out with some friends and came home a bit late and they went completely mental, said I wasn't to mix with people like that. I'm telling you, it's doing my head in. Still, never mind, you're here now.'

'Right,' Tilly said uncertainly.

'Look at the two of you.' Leonie gazed fondly at them from the doorway. 'Getting on like a house on fire, just like a couple of sisters.'

Tamsin, kneeling behind Tilly on the bed, fashioning her hair into intricate plaits, gave her a prod between the shoulder blades.

'Um, could me and Tam go and get a McDonald's later?' Tilly said it as though the thought had just occurred to her.

'Well . . . did Tamsin tell you she's been grounded? Last Sunday she didn't come home until half past one in the morning.'

Half *one*? Good grief, thought Tilly.

'I could stay here,' Tamsin helpfully suggested, 'while Tilly goes. But then I don't suppose she'd want to go on her own. Poor old Tilly, it's like she's being punished when she didn't even do anything wrong.'

'Ha, worked like a dream,' Tamsin crowed, kissing the ten pound note as they headed towards the town centre.

'We have to be back by two o'clock.'

'Don't fuss! As long as we're together, they won't mind if we're a bit late. You're my chaperone. My very own Mary Poppins.'

Except Mary Poppins was in control, thought Tilly.

'You're late,' said Brian, and Tilly felt her palms grow sweaty.

'Tilly wanted to look around the shops,' Tamsin lied easily. 'Dad, relax, we're here now. It's only half past three.'

'They're fine, darling,' Leonie chimed in. 'Didn't I tell you there was nothing to worry about? Look at them, they've had a lovely time.'

A lovely time sitting in the not-very-clean bedsit belonging to one of Tamsin's new-found friends. One of the friends her father disapproved of, it went without saying. Jif—*Jif!*—sported beige dreadlocks, many tattoos and a quite staggering amount of facial jewellery. They hadn't really done much at the bedsit, just listened to music and smoked a lot. It had actually been rather boring, not that Tilly had told Tamsin this.

That evening they went out to a family-friendly pub where an Abba tribute band were playing. 'You must be joking,' Tamsin exclaimed when Brian teasingly suggested a twirl on the floor. 'God, music for old fogeys.'

Leonie wrapped an arm round Tilly's thin shoulders. 'Enjoying yourself, darling?'

Tilly nodded and smiled, and Leonie gave her a hug. Tilly, flushing with pleasure, thought, look at us, me and my mum having a nice time together. It gave her a warm Ready Brek glow in her stomach.

On Wednesday morning, Miriam announced to Edward that she was going shopping. She drove across town and parked the car outside the firm of solicitors she'd picked out of the phone book.

'Christine Wilson,' she told the receptionist. 'I have an appointment at eleven with David Payne.'

The offices were dull and in need of redecoration. David Payne, in his mid-forties, matched them perfectly.

'Right, Mrs Wilson. Perhaps you'd like to tell me why you're here.'

Miriam explained her situation. When she'd finished, David Payne sat back and shook his head.

'Oh dear,' he sighed, tapping his pen on the desk. 'This could be messy. Very messy indeed. I'm afraid prison can't be ruled out.'

Miriam nodded. 'So what do you suggest I do?'

'Not a lot you can do, at the moment. As far as you and this gentleman are concerned, the ball is pretty firmly in his court.'

Miriam tried hard not to feel sick; she almost wished she hadn't come now. This was turning out to be scarier than she'd thought.

Willing herself not to look at her watch—damn, too late—Nadia wondered if she'd blown her chances with Jay. It was ten past five on Thursday afternoon and there had still been no mention of their date. She'd been waiting for him to say something for four whole days now. She was beginning to understand why Clare agreed to see Piers the instant he'd phoned her on Monday. The more Jay didn't ask her out, the more Nadia wanted him to.

Frustrated, she shoved her heel down on the spade and carried on turning over the soil in what would eventually be a flowerbed. And now—her watch was almost taunting her—it was a quarter past five. She took off her watch and stuffed it in her bra. What if Jay *had* changed his mind? How dare he! Men shouldn't be allowed to say they were going to ask you out then go back on their word.

Some time later, Jay's voice behind her made Nadia jump.

Well, not really, because she'd heard him making his way across the terrace, but she pretended he'd made her jump. It never did any harm to give your boss the impression you were engrossed in your work.

'What?' She raised her head.

'I said it's almost six o'clock. Everyone else has left.'

'Almost six? Sorry. I just wanted to finish this bed.'

'Dinner on Saturday?' said Jay.

'Sorry?' Inside her chest, her heart did a tiny victory hornpipe.

'Saturday evening. Unless you have other plans.' Jay raised his eyebrows. 'Because if you have, that's OK, I'll just—'

'Saturday's great! No other plans,' Nadia blurted out.

'Fine.' Jay nodded. 'I'll pick you up, shall I? Eight o'clock?'

'Eight o'clock, perfect.' Nadia paused. 'I thought you'd forgotten.'

'What made you think that?'

'It's Thursday afternoon.' Honestly, was he thick?

'Oh, right. Well, you've kept me waiting.' Jay's look of amusement sent lustful quivers darting down her spine. 'I thought it was my turn to do the same to you.'

'Will you two *please* be quiet?' With a sigh, Tilly flung open Nadia's bedroom door. 'I can't hear the TV.'

'Yes, boss, no, boss, sorry, boss.' Clare mock saluted before breaking into song once more.

'You sound worse than Harpo. He's cringing downstairs with his wings over his ears. Just turn the music down a bit, will you?'

'Aye aye, boss. Nad, turn the music down.' Clare was applying lip gloss. Spotting Nadia in the mirror she yelped, 'Those are *my* earrings. I was going to *wear* those earrings.'

'They look better on me. Anyway, I let you borrow my belt. Ooh, is that a car outside?'

As a diversionary tactic, it worked like a charm. Clare shot over to the window. Tilly, rolling her eyes, left the room. Nadia, smugly finishing off her hair in the mirror, experienced that warm glow of anticipation you get when you just know a truly great night lies ahead. In honour of the occasion, she had even—sluttishly but sensibly—slipped a spare pair of knickers and her toothbrush into her handbag.

It was seven thirty and Miriam had already left with Edward for the theatre. James was out too, with Annie. Piers had rung to let Clare know he was on his way over. And at eight o'clock Jay would be here.

'Hoooo!' Clare let out a squeal of excitement at the sound of tyres on gravel. This time a car really had arrived. 'It's Piers!'

'Break a leg,' said Nadia, as Clare skipped to the door.

'Break both yours,' Clare gaily called back, already on her way down the stairs. In those heels, it was a miracle she didn't.

Having primped to the limit, Nadia made her way down to the living room ten minutes later. Tilly was stretched out across the sofa, peeling a satsuma and watching *Blind Date*.

'Sure you're going to be all right here on your own?' Nadia gave Tilly's bony ankle an affectionate rub; only since her thirteenth birthday had she been allowed to stay in the house alone. Tilly raised her eyebrows.

'I'm going to finish up the tub of Snickers ice cream and watch whatever I want to watch on TV without being interrupted.'

'OK. But no cocaine, no bingeing on tequila and no wild parties.'

'Are salt and vinegar crisps allowed?'

'No more than two packets.' Reaching over, Nadia ruffled her hair.

'Oh, we're lucky to have you. Come here and give your big sister a kiss.'

'Phew, you stink.' Tilly wriggled out of reach. 'What're you trying to do to the man, chloroform him?'

Instantly Nadia scrambled into a sitting position. 'Oh God, is it too strong? The bottle kind of slipped as I put it on—bugger, it *is* too strong.' She sprang to her feet, panicking slightly as the giveaway tick-tock sound of a cab outside reached them.

Rushing to the downstairs cloakroom Nadia seized the nailbrush. Dragging it through the soap, she frantically brushed her wrists then ran them under the tap. Gingerly she scrubbed at her—ouch—neck, then splashed on cold water to rinse away the soap and vigorously towelled herself dry. Well, not quite; the front of her white top was splattered with water—but on such a warm night it would evaporate soon enough.

Rrrrrinnggg.

'The man of your dreams is here,' Tilly sang out, a bit too loudly for Nadia's liking. 'Is it safe to let him in or has the smell not gone yet?'

'I'll get it.' Nadia skidded across the hall and pulled the door open.

Oh good grief.

'Nadia.' Laurie's green eyes surveyed her with affection. He shook his blond head at her in long-time-no-see admiration. 'You look fantastic. Is this a private wet T-shirt competition or can anyone join in?'

Chapter Six

THE SECONDS SEEMED to stretch into hours. Nadia tried to breathe and found she couldn't; the air was stuck in her lungs. Not Jay. Laurie. *Laurie*, who she'd spent the best part of eighteen months trying to forget. Damn, she'd practically turned not thinking about Laurie into an art form. And now here he was on her doorstep and giving her the kind of look she remembered so well.

Finally he said, 'Who else is in?'

'Um . . . nobody.'

Behind her Tilly wailed indignantly, 'Oh, thanks a *lot*,' before throwing herself into Laurie's outstretched arms. 'It's so great to see you again!' She had idolised Laurie from babyhood. 'What are you doing here?'

As he hugged her, Laurie's eyes met Nadia's. 'I'm back. For good.'

Nadia couldn't speak.

'There weren't any lights on over the road so I came straight here. All my stuff's outside in the porch. OK if I bring it in?'

Tilly helped him lug the various bags into the hall. Then, glancing at Nadia's shell-shocked expression, she said chirpily, 'Well, I've got geography homework. If anyone needs me, I'll be in my room.'

They went into the living room.

'Well?' said Laurie.

'Well what?'

'Nad, I'm sorry. I can't believe what I did and I'm really, truly sorry.' His expression was deadly serious.

Nadia's fingers and toes were now numb. 'And?'

'I was an idiot. I made a horrible mistake. I can see that now. Hollywood's a shit place to live. The film industry's crap. I couldn't stand it a minute longer, the people out there just aren't *real*, they're *hollow*. They're offering me bigger and better jobs but I'm just not interested in doing them any more.' Laurie's mouth twitched. 'What's happened to your neck anyway? Has Clare been trying to strangle you?'

'Too much scent. I was scrubbing it off.' Jay would be here any minute now. Nadia began to panic.

'Girls' night out?'

'What makes you so sure it's not a man?'

'Dad told me you weren't seeing anyone,' Laurie said easily.

Nadia felt her short fingernails digging into her palms. 'Well, I'm seeing someone tonight. And he's a man.' Oh yes, definitely a man.

Laurie shrugged good-naturedly. 'I'll just wait here until you get back.'

Oh, fantastic.

'Don't look at me like that.' Laurie was smiling again in that heart-melting, rueful way of his. 'Nad, I know this has all been a bit of a shock. No pressure, obviously, but we do have to talk. You go out on your date. Have a great time. I'll keep Tilly company until you get home.'

Tilly, who'd been eavesdropping shamelessly *and* peeping out of the landing window, came galloping down the staircase.

'He's here! Off you go. Me and Laurie'll have a brilliant time.' She looked eagerly at Laurie. 'Do they have Monopoly in America?'

'They do. They also have geography homework.' He grinned.

'I don't really have geography homework.' Tilly tut-tutted at his naiveté. 'I was being discreet.'

'Nobody in this family knows the meaning of the word. Come on, I'll teach you now. We don't want to scare off Nadia's date.'

Nadia, her heart in her throat, waited until the living-room door was firmly closed. Although she knew it was coming, the front doorbell when it rang still made her jump. Oh God, how could this be happening to her?

And then Jay was there on the doorstep, smart in a suit and eyeing the luggage on the floor behind her with amusement.

'Somebody leaving home?'

'Harpo.' From somewhere, Nadia dredged up a flip remark as she reached for her handbag. 'He says we drive him mad and he's going back to Madagascar.' Through the closed living-room door they heard Harpo squawk raucously.

Nadia's brain was too full to concentrate on anything. The restaurant Jay took her to was buzzy and fun, but even ordering from the menu was beyond her. Laurie was back. Laurie was back and he was telling her he'd made a terrible mistake.

'Nadia?' Jay raised his eyebrows at her and she realised the waiter was waiting with pad and pen poised. 'Um . . . I'll have the same as you.'

Big mistake. Nadia flinched when their first courses arrived. How could Jay even think she'd like whitebait?

'So, are you going to tell me what this is about?'

'Sorry?' Oh God, those fish, still with their heads on and their eyes in. Nadia couldn't even bear to look at them.

Jay sat back in his chair. 'Listen, much as I'd like to put it down to the excitement of being here with me, somehow I don't think it's that. Are you OK?'

'I'm sorry. I just forgot they served whitebait with the eyes still in.'

Jay clearly didn't believe her. His dark eyes were fixed on her face, silently daring her to fob him off. 'What's really wrong?'

Exhaling, she pushed the scary whitebait away. 'The suitcases. They belong to Laurie. He came back tonight.'

Silence. At their table, if nowhere else. All around them, laughter and lively conversation and the clink of cutlery carried on regardless.

'He came back,' said Jay. 'To *you*?'

'No. Back from the States. He says he's sorry. He seems quite, um . . .'

'Keen?'

Nadia shook her head, then nodded, then shook it again.

Helplessly, she said, 'I don't know. He only turned up ten minutes before you did. I'm a bit . . .'

'Confused?'

'Could you stop finishing my sentences?' said Nadia.

'Somebody has to. Do you want me to take you home?'

'Yes, please.' Nadia waited for him to settle the bill. What there was of it. Oh well, nobody could say she wasn't a cheap date.

'Not my home,' she told Jay as they left the restaurant. 'Yours.'

'Look.' They were in Jay's car, roaring up Park Street. Jay sounded resigned. 'I was looking forward to tonight.' With a brief sideways glance in her direction he added, 'I think you were too.'

Unable to speak, Nadia nodded. There was a lump in her throat. Fumbling in her bag for a hankie—oh God, *mustn't cry*—she pulled out the spare knickers by mistake and hastily shoved them back in.

'But you need to sort yourself out. Make up your mind what you want. If I took you home with me now, you'd be thinking about him.'

He was right. Nadia's vision blurred with tears. She found herself torn between two men.

Nadia cleared her throat, blinked hard until the lights of Park Street swam back into focus, and said, 'So what do you think I should do?'

'You can't ask me.'

'I am asking you.'

'Fine.' Jay's tone was curt. 'I think you should tell your ex-boyfriend he has a bloody nerve to think you'd even *consider* taking him back. I think you should tell him to fuck off back to LA and never bother you again.'

'But I can't do that.'

'Of course you can.' Jay was scornful. 'Come on. Where's your pride? He dumped you once. What's to stop him doing it again?'

'Who says I'm going to take him back? I haven't said I will! He just turned up tonight.'

'Don't get stroppy. You asked me what I thought and I told you. What you decide to do now is up to you.'

They drove the rest of the way in chilly silence. Jay pulled up outside the house and kept the engine running.

'Sorry,' Nadia said awkwardly.

'Not your fault.' The curtness of his tone managed to indicate that actually it was.

'Right. Bye then.'

'Go away,' Tilly wailed in outrage as she entered the sitting room. 'You're too early. We were having *fun*.'

'Too bad, Cinderella.' Nadia gave her scruffy ponytail a tug. 'One of your ugly sisters has come home, and it's time you were in bed.'

Tilly and Laurie had been playing Pictionary; the carpet around them was littered with discarded, scribbled-on sheets of paper. Pulling a face, Tilly lightning-sketched a miserable-looking gooseberry.

'Go on.' Laurie gave her a hug. 'I'll still be here tomorrow.'

As Tilly put her arms round Nadia and kissed her good night, she stage-whispered, 'Isn't it great? You're so *lucky*.'

Nadia managed a smile. Lucky wasn't how she was feeling right now.

'We weren't expecting you back before midnight,' said Laurie when they were alone.

'I nearly didn't come back at all.'

'Come on, sit down.' He patted the sofa next to him. 'But you changed your mind.'

Nadia didn't sit down. Or tell him Jay had refused to let her stay.

'Hey.' Laurie's voice softened. 'I'm sorry if I messed up your date. I didn't know, did I?'

'Suppose not. I'm having a cup of tea, d'you want one?'

Laurie followed her into the kitchen, watching her faff about with mugs and spoons and tea bags. His hair was blonder, his tan deeper; even his eyes were greener than she remembered.

'Are you wearing coloured contact lenses?' Nadia blurted out.

Laurie looked appalled. 'You're not serious. *Me?* No coloured contacts. No botox. No dodgy implants.'

'Glad to hear it.' Turning to the tea-making, which felt as complicated as carrying out open-heart surgery, Nadia managed to spill sugar all over the worktop. Damn. 'Do you still take . . . ?'

'Oh yes.' He was grinning at her now. 'I think I was the only person in Hollywood who did. You should have seen the look on people's faces. Funny how it's fine to shove cocaine up your nose, but'—he mimed horror—'to actually put *sugar* in your *tea* . . .'

'So they wouldn't have been too impressed with your deep-fried Mars bars,' Nadia remarked.

'One more reason to get out of there.' He shrugged. 'So have you made up your mind yet?'

'About deep-fried Mars bars? Well, I couldn't eat more than three in one go, but—'

'You know what I'm talking about,' Laurie interrupted, and a shock of electricity zip-zapped down Nadia's spine. 'Us,' said Laurie. 'I'm sorry. I know I shouldn't pressure you. But I just wondered if you'd decided anything yet. Now that the initial shock's worn off.'

Worn off? Good grief, she hadn't even *begun* to get to grips yet with the initial shock. Nadia thrust one of the mugs at him.

'If I told you to go away and leave me alone, would you do it?'

'No.' Laurie smiled and shook his head. 'I'm going to stay *until* you change your mind.'

'What makes you think I would?'

'I just do.'

'Confident,' said Nadia.

'I don't mean that in a big-headed way,' Laurie hurriedly explained. 'We were brilliant together, Nad. You know we were. As soon as you forgive me for being a twat, we can be brilliant again.'

'I don't believe it!' exclaimed Miriam, when she and Edward arrived back at ten thirty.

You and me both, Nadia thought as Miriam flung her arms round Laurie.

'Well, this is a surprise.' Edward cleared his throat. 'How long are you home for?'

'I'm back for good, Dad.'

Miriam raised an enquiring eyebrow at Nadia. Nadia shrugged, feeling wrung out.

'Back for good?' Edward sounded concerned. 'Is anything wrong?'

'Something *was* wrong,' Laurie agreed. 'Don't worry, I'm not in trouble. I just came to my senses. As soon as Nadia here forgives me and takes me back, everything will be all right.' Simply, Laurie added, 'I love her.'

Nadia squirmed, aware of all eyes upon her. This was what she'd dreamed of for so long.

Miriam gave him another hug. 'And how does Nadia feel about this?'

Annoyed that they now appeared to be discussing her as if she wasn't even there, Nadia said, 'Nadia isn't making any decisions right now. In fact, Nadia's going to bed.'

'Stubborn,' whispered Miriam. 'Always been stubborn. Remember when she pushed over the Christmas tree because she couldn't get the fairy to sit properly on the top? Oh well.' She squeezed Laurie's tanned arm. 'If anyone can talk her round, darling, it's you.'

Nadia couldn't believe it. 'This has *nothing* to do with Christmas fairies.'

'Sweetheart, admit it, you can get temperamental. You'd spent two hours decorating that tree. When you knocked it down you smashed all the baubles.'

'*So?*' Nadia spread her arms in despair.

'Darling, I'm just saying that sometimes you do something impulsive and live to regret it.' Miriam's tone was soothing. 'It's called cutting off your nose to spite your face.'

Nadia had a terrible night's sleep. Having gone off to bed in a bit of a huff, she'd spent the next few hours tossing and turning and listening to the noisy celebrations continuing downstairs. James, returning at midnight from his evening out with Annie, had joined in. The boy was back and everyone was delighted. When he and Edward finally left at around three, she'd heard Miriam saying reassuringly, 'Don't worry about Nadia, she'll come round soon enough. She's missed you dreadfully, you know.'

Gritting her teeth, Nadia had only just resisted the urge to yell out a Harpo-style epithet. If anyone else had treated her that badly, her family would have united against him. But the fact that it was Laurie apparently meant all was forgiven.

Did that mean she was supposed to forgive him too?

Did she *want* to?

What was Jay doing now?

Well, he'd be out for the count, obviously. Let's face it, the chances that he was lying awake fretting about *her* were an unequivocal nil.

'I just heard,' bellowed Clare, flinging open the bedroom door and launching herself onto the bed.

'Owww,' Nadia groaned.

'I just got home and Dad told me. Come on, wake *up*.' Clare prodded her annoyingly in the ribs. 'Tell me everything!'

Rolling over, Nadia shielded her eyes from the sunlight pouring through the window. 'What time is it?'

'Ten o'clock. And according to Miriam, Laurie's going to be here at ten thirty. Apparently you're going shopping with him.'

'Shopping.' This was all far too much. 'To buy what?'

'What do runaway boyfriends generally buy when they want to win you back? A bloody great engagement ring.'

'*What?*'

Clare flashed a triumphant grin. 'Only joking. He's after a house.'

Nadia didn't need Clare to regale her with details of the night she'd spent with Piers—the spark in her eyes and her irritating Tigger-on-springs demeanour were enough to let Nadia know it had been fantastic.

But Clare told her anyway, perching on the window seat in the bathroom and shouting above the roar of the shower.

'. . . he's so gorgeous . . . we had such a brilliant time . . . ' Clare bellowed happily. 'He's really realised he can't mess me about any more. I told him, any more bullshit and I'd be off. That brought him to his senses. So how did it go with thingy last night? Jay?'

'Not good.' Nadia began rubbing de-frizzing serum into her ringlets.

'Oh well, never mind. You've got Laurie now.' As far as Clare was concerned, it was as simple as buying a new budgie when your old one dropped off its perch.

'What if I don't want Laurie now?'

'Are you mad? Why wouldn't you want him? Coming back like this. It's just so romantic! Don't you realise how lucky you are?'

When Laurie arrived twenty minutes later, Clare hurled herself at him like an overexcited puppy.

'Ha!' Triumphantly she pulled away. 'I've just kissed someone who's kissed someone who's kissed Johnny Depp.'

'Blimey.' Laurie looked impressed. 'Who'd you just kiss?'

'You, you berk!' Clare punched him on the arm. 'You were at the Oscars with that actress who used to go out with him.'

Grinning, Laurie shook his head. 'Our agents set it up. We'd never even met before. I literally didn't touch her. Our job was to pose for the press like *this*.' He placed the palm of one hand an inch from the small of her back, tilted his head towards hers and flashed his teeth at an imaginary camera lens. 'Her dress was on loan from some swanky designer. No physical contact allowed in case I marked it with my nasty sweaty hands.'

'Don't look nasty to me.' Clare beamed. 'God, I still can't believe you're back. How on earth could you not enjoy being in LA? You must have met loads of famous people.'

'Of course I did. But just because they're famous doesn't make them fun. Besides, I missed Nadia. Where is she, anyway?'

Nadia, who'd been loitering in the hall, took a deep breath and stepped into the kitchen.

'*Ooof*,' Nadia gasped as she lost her footing at the top of the staircase. Next moment she was tumbling down the stairs. 'Ouch, that *hurt*.'

It was eleven thirty on Sunday morning. If yesterday had gone ahead according to plan, she might still be lying in Jay's bed now. Instead, she was here looking round the third property of the day, an empty four-storey house in Redland. The estate agent had given them the keys. Laurie, rushing down behind her, said urgently, 'Don't move. Lean back against me. Nothing broken?' His face was white with concern. 'Are you sure?' He was crouching beside her.

Nadia nodded and slowly flexed her hips. 'Jarred my back a bit, but the rest of me's fine.'

'I could have told you that.' Unable to resist the quip, Laurie placed her arm round his shoulders. 'Come on then, let's get you up. Lean on me.' Carefully he hauled her upright. 'Are you sure you're OK?'

'I'm sure. Don't make a fuss.' Disconcertingly, his face was only inches from hers. 'You can let go of me now.'

His green eyes fixed on hers, as honest and heart-wrenching as ever. 'Do you have any idea how much I want to kiss you?'

Nadia felt her stomach wrestling itself into knots.

'But I'm not going to,' said Laurie. 'Not until you really want me to.'

'Oh.' Nadia took a step back. Being kissed was one thing; actually admitting you *wanted* to be kissed was quite another.

'We haven't seen the ground floor yet.'

The rooms on the ground floor were huge, helped along by the lack of furniture. Standing at the drawing-room window overlooking the garden, Laurie said lightly, 'What d'you think?'

'Laurie you're the one buying the house. You have to decide.'

He winked. 'It has to be somewhere you like, though. If we get back together, you'll be living there. Eighty-foot garden. Big enough for you?'

'Too big for you,' Nadia retorted, because Laurie was to horticulture what Princess Anne was to pole-dancing. And this house was priced at three seventy-five, for crying out loud. It was a ludicrous amount of money for him to shell out on a whim.

'And you can really afford it?'

'I can really afford it.'

Gosh.

'And I like this place. I mean, picture this garden in five years.' Laurie gestured expansively through the window. 'A swing over there, under the apple tree. One of those baby trampolines, a couple of tricycles . . .'

'Aren't you a bit old for a tricycle?' said Nadia.

'It's what I want to happen. You, me and a houseful of kids.' Laurie broke into a grin at the look on her face. 'OK, three kids. Three's fine, if that's all you want.'

'What are you going to do, now you're back?' Abruptly she changed the subject. 'Job-wise, I mean. Would you go back to stockbroking?'

Laurie pulled a face. 'Something else, preferably. Anyway,' he went on carelessly, 'I'm not even thinking about that yet. There's money in the bank and I'm taking the rest of the summer off to enjoy myself.'

'You must have enjoyed yourself over there too,' said Nadia. Well, the question had been niggling away at her all morning, waiting to be asked. 'You had girlfriends, didn't you?'

'A couple.' Laurie grew serious. 'What are you asking, how many girls I slept with? OK, three. None for the first five months, by the way. Then I realised I couldn't live like a monk for the rest of my life. But no serious relationships. How about you?'

'God, hundreds. A different man every night,' said Nadia.

'Right. And were any of them . . . you know, serious relationships?'

'Only a couple of dozen.'

'A couple of dozen,' said Laurie. 'Well, that's not so bad. That's manageable competition. So I'm still in with a chance, then?'

'Mr Modest-as-ever,' Nadia observed.

'Not modest,' said Laurie. 'Just optimistic. I have hope. After all'—he flashed his irresistible smile—'you haven't said no yet.'

It was Monday morning, and Nadia's back was giving her serious gyp. Clattering down a flight of stairs, bashing her spine against every step, had resulted in pretty spectacular bruising. Surveying the stacked-up paving stones for the patio at Clarence Gardens without enthusiasm, she unscrewed the top of her water bottle and took a swig. That hurt too.

And there was no sign of Jay, which was a disappointment. Nadia'd planned to compare her reaction the moment she saw him with her reaction when Laurie had come over yesterday morning. Rely on her body's instincts to tell her what she needed to know. Except her body was probably going to be too busy going *ooh, ouch* to tell her anything helpful right now. Oh well, hey ho. On with the job she was being paid to do. Maybe after the first few paving stones her muscles would loosen up.

When the side gate clicked open an hour later, Nadia felt her heart begin to gather speed. Colour rushed to her cheeks and her stomach clenched tighter than a three-year-old clutching a sweet.

'For heaven's sake.' With difficulty, she straightened up and wiped her dusty, perspiring hands on her shorts. 'What are you doing here?'

'Miriam said you crawled down to breakfast on all fours. I thought you might appreciate a hand. So here I am, dressed for work and ready to help.'

'I don't think that's a good idea. What if Jay turns up?'

Laurie shrugged. 'May as well do something useful with these muscles.' One of the clauses in his agent's contract, Nadia had learned, was that Laurie had been obliged to spend a minimum of fourteen hours a week working out in a trendy LA gym.

'If you want to be useful,' she said, 'you could go to the chemist and pick up some paracetamols.'

'Hey, I nearly forgot.' Laurie delved into the front pocket of his bashed-up jeans. He had brought a tube of Deep Heat.

'Come on, pull your T-shirt up. It'll help.'

Nadia's mouth went dry. 'I'll do it.'

'Don't be a baby. Anyway, you couldn't reach.' Taking hold of her T-shirt, Laurie lifted it to bra level and surveyed her bruised back. He shook his head in sympathy. 'OK, don't worry. I'll be gentle.'

While she held her breath, closed her eyes and thought of . . . well, something else, he carefully smoothed the smelly cream into her skin.

'There, all done.' Stepping back, Laurie dropped the T-shirt back into place. 'Now, why don't you go and get the paracetamols? And pick up something for lunch? I'll get on with laying the stones.'

It made sense. The ground was all ready, and Laurie was more than capable of laying the stones. But . . .

'Look, forget why I came back,' Laurie said patiently. 'Just think of us as friends. If we were friends and I needed help, you'd help me, wouldn't you?'

'Maybe.' Nadia tried to imagine them as just good friends. As they had been once, years ago.

'Right, so that's all we are. Stop being so bloody stubborn and let me get on with the job.'

'OK. Thanks. Paracetamols.'

Laurie, already picking up the first paving slab with ridiculous ease, said, 'And lunch.'

Jay knew at once who the stranger was. For a minute he watched unobserved from the French doors as Laurie Welch got on with the job in hand. Finally, straightening up and pulling his T-shirt over his head, Laurie turned and spotted him.

'Where's Nadia?' said Jay.

'Gone to pick up a few things. She hurt her back yesterday. I'm helping out.' Laurie's voice was friendly. 'If that's OK with you.'

'Fine with me,' Jay lied.

'You're the boss, I take it.'

'That's right.' There was a spade propped up against the wall. Jay wondered if bashing Laurie over the head with it and burying his body in the garden would be an option.

'I'm the ex-boyfriend. Laurie Welch.' Wiping his palms on his jeans, Laurie came over to shake hands.

Jay said, 'How did Nadia hurt her back?' and immediately regretted it. Did he really want to know?

'We were looking at houses. I took her to see one in Redland and she fell down the stairs.'

'Right. Which house in Redland?' Jay kept up with what was happening on the property market.

'Clarendon Road. Five bedrooms, fantastic garden. We liked it. Plenty of room for . . . well, you know. We both know we want kids, so not much point in buying a penthouse flat.'

Laurie was enjoying himself. Having arrived back in England in the nick of time, he had no doubt at all that Nadia would come round before long. OK, so she had developed a bit of a crush on this boss of hers, but Laurie was confident that he'd win in the end; he didn't regard Jay Tiernan as a serious threat. And it was such fun subtly letting him know that.

'You know, I was ready to put an offer in yesterday, but falling down the stairs might have put Nad off the place.' The gate clicked and Laurie's gaze shifted away from Jay's. 'Here she is now.'

Jay turned and saw Nadia carrying two Waitrose bags.

'I was just telling Jay about your accident. Show him your bruises.'

'There's no need, I'm sure he believes—'

'See?' Before Nadia was able to protest, Laurie had swivelled her round and pulled up her T-shirt. His tanned fingers moved lightly over her back, tracing the outlines of the swollen, purple bruises.

'I'm fine,' Nadia protested, flushing as she covered them once more. 'Look, I need to get this stuff inside.' Nadia glanced at Jay. 'Could I have a word?'

Jay didn't move. 'Fire away.'

She gave him a don't-muck-about look. 'In private.'

Bending down with difficulty, Nadia put the snacky lunch food and drinks into the fridge and prayed the blast of cold air would remove the heat from her cheeks. Jay was standing behind her in the doorway.

Slowly straightening up, Nadia turned and mumbled, 'Sorry. I didn't ask Laurie to come here and help me. He just turned up.'

'Just as well he did. He's making a pretty good job of that patio.'

'I know. But it's an awkward situation.'

There was a pause. Upstairs in the master bedroom, they heard Bart and Kevin hammering away at the skirting boards.

Finally Jay spoke. 'It's not awkward. Look,' he said evenly, 'you work for me. We get on well. You know as well as I do that if Laurie hadn't come back when he did, things would have gone further.'

Nadia's arms prickled with goose bumps.

'Possibly.'

'Bullshit.' Jay's eyes glittered with amusement. 'Definitely. But how long would we have lasted? A week? A month? A decade?' He shrugged. 'That's the trouble, isn't it? We don't know and we're not going to get the chance to find out. It's slightly disappointing, but it's not a catastrophe.'

'Right.' Nadia felt the goose bumps subside in defeat. So, not pistols at dawn then.

'If you didn't want him back, you'd have told him by now. The two of you have a history,' Jay went on. 'Long term, you've decided, he's probably a safer bet than I am. The devil you know, versus the devil you only work for. That's fine. I can handle it. I'm not going to lock myself in my house and drink myself to death.'

Nadia ventured a smile and said, 'Well, good.'

'Meeting girls is easy. All it takes is a trip to a wine bar. You see someone you like the look of, you get chatting. Mission accomplished.'

'Wine bars? That's where it all happens?'

'Not always. You can meet girls anywhere. At the gym,' said Jay. 'Or the squash club. Or at auctions, parties, art galleries . . . Once I even found one crashed in a ditch.'

Oh, very droll. Now he was making jokes about the situation. Nadia was inwardly miffed; clearly she was far less important to him than she'd imagined. Then again, as Jay had pointed out, he was the devil she didn't know.

'I'd better get back to work,' Nadia said awkwardly.

Tilly arrived in the school cafeteria in a state of shock. As she queued up with her tray, she spotted Cal sitting on his own in a far corner, eating his way through a mountain of chips.

When the tray was filled, Tilly made her way over. Warily Cal looked up; sharing a table with a girl was asking for trouble. But Tilly was too preoccupied to care. Plonking her tray down opposite him, she breathlessly announced, 'You'll never guess what.'

'My mother says that. It drives me nuts.' Cal smiled slightly to soften the accusation. 'It can mean one of the neighbours has dropped down dead in the garden or the price of carrots has gone up by two pee.'

'Sorry. Suzy Harrison's in hospital. She had her appendix out last night.'

Cal raised his eyebrows.

'She had the leading part in next week's school play. You know, Sandy in *Grease*? Mrs Durham auditioned for a new Sandy this morning, and I've got the part!'

'Wow, that's great.' Cal was duly impressed.

'It's scary.' Tilly attempted to fork up a twirl of wet spaghetti but it splashed back down onto her plate. Her stomach was in knots anyway. She shivered with a mixture of elation and fear. 'It's only eight days away. I've got so many *lines*. What if I can't learn them in time?'

'You'll be fine.' Cal calmly dunked a chip into the pool of tomato ketchup on his plate. 'If you like, I could help you.'

'Really? That'd be brilliant.' Reaching down for her school bag, Tilly said, 'I've got the script right here—'

'Not now.' Cal jerked his head meaningfully in the direction of one of the rowdier tables, where a group of his classmates had just spotted him with Tilly. 'After school, OK? I'll meet you at the gates.'

Cal had a real talent for voices.

Tilly was deeply impressed. 'Why didn't you audition?'

They were in the park, lying on their stomachs under one of the chestnut trees. Cal was reading all the other parts, changing his voice according to whichever character he was playing. All Tilly had to concentrate on were Sandy's lines.

'Can't sing. Can't dance,' Cal told her.

'I'm scared everyone will laugh at me. What if they all start sniggering because I'm not pretty enough?'

He looked at her, and Tilly realised she sounded as if she was angling for a compliment. She cringed, not wanting Cal to humour her.

'You'll have the costume on, and heaps of make-up. You'll scrape through.' Cal broke into a grin. 'Or, you could make all the audience wear blindfolds.'

The butterflies in her stomach melted away. Tugging a single stem of couch grass out of the ground, Tilly waggled it in his ear.

Cal abruptly stopped laughing. 'Oh shit, people from school.'

Following the line of his gaze, Tilly saw a group of fourth-year girls sauntering in their direction. Fourth-year girls weren't as alarming as fourth-year boys, but it was a close-run thing.

'I'd better go,' muttered Cal.

'No, don't.' Without meaning to, she laid a hand on his arm.

'What are you two up to?' The leader of the girls approached them, her friends trailing in her wake. Her name was Janice Strong and she wore an astonishing amount of mascara.

'Cal's helping me learn some stuff.'

Janice's tarantula eyelashes shielded her eyes as she lit a cigarette. 'What kind of stuff?'

'I'm in the school play. I need to learn my lines.'

'Aren't you supposed to know them by now?' Janice peered down at the script lying open on the grass, with Tilly's lines highlighted in Day-Glo pink. 'Bloody hell, you got the part of Sandy? You're taking over from Suzy Harrison?'

Tilly nodded, tensing up inside and waiting to be scornfully informed that she wasn't pretty enough. But Janice started to laugh. 'Ace! That cow Colleen Mahoney went up for it this morning. She was certain she'd get the part. Bloody good for you.'

The next moment, Janice and her acolytes had dropped down onto the grass next to them and Tilly found herself being offered a Silk Cut.

'Cheers.' Tilly took it and prayed she wouldn't splutter.

'*Cal*'s reading all the other parts,' Tilly explained. 'He's great at it.'

Playfully, Janice nudged Cal's thigh with her outstretched toes. 'Come on then, *Cal*. Let's hear you.'

Tilly saw him mentally weighing up the available options; either run away and risk ridicule or stay and read and risk more ridicule. Finally Cal turned the page of the script and launched into Rizzo's attack on Sandy, his American accent spot on.

At the end, Janice and her friends whistled and clapped.

'Brilliant,' Janice exclaimed. She was gazing at Cal with new respect.

An ice-cream van had trundled into the park. As it came to a jangly halt fifty yards away, Cal said, 'I'm going to get an ice cream.'

'One for me?' Janice batted her eyelashes as he rose to his feet.

'Sorry, I've only got a pound.'

By the time Cal had queued up and returned with two Magnums, Janice and her gang had left.

'I thought you only had a pound,' said Tilly as he handed her one of the Magnums.

'I lied.'

Tilly sat up and ripped off the wrapper. Cracking the outer layer of chocolate with her teeth, she took a heavenly bite.

'I think Janice fancies you. She told me you were cool.'

His eyes sparkling, Cal said, 'Do you think I'm cool?'

Tilly felt a hot sensation flower inside her rib cage. Was this flirting?

'You bought me a Magnum. Can't get much cooler than that.'

'Darling, that's fantastic news.' Miriam gave Tilly a hug. 'But next Tuesday, what a *shame*. We'll be away.'

Tilly's face fell. On the way home in the car, James had regretfully broken the news that next week he would be stuck at some works conference in Sheffield. And now Miriam and Edward were flying off to Venice for a week's holiday.

'I've got six tickets,' Tilly fretted.

Nadia, fresh from her bath and bundled up in her dressing gown, said, 'Well, I'll definitely come. I love *Grease*.'

'That's why you've got such a big bum.' Clicking her tongue at Harpo, Clare said cheerfully, 'What's Nadia got, Harpo? What's Nadia got?'

'Gotta pick a pocket or two,' cackled Harpo.

'That bird's losing it.' Clare shook her head. 'He's got Alzheimer's.'

'And Laurie will want to come,' Nadia persisted.

'Oh Lord, Laurie's driving us up to Heathrow on Tuesday.' Miriam shook her head in apology.

'It's OK.' At this rate Tilly was going to be about as popular as the bride who arranges her wedding for the day of the FA cup final.

'Clare's coming,' said Nadia, widening her eyes meaningfully at Clare. 'Aren't you?'

'Wouldn't miss it for the world. I'll just chuck away my ticket to see Robbie Williams in concert, shall I?' Not having spotted Tilly's trembling chin, Clare was making one of her ill-timed jokes.

'How about Annie?' Nadia was getting desperate now.

'I already asked her. But she can't close the shop before six, and that's when the show starts.' Tilly's eyes brimmed with tears. Her voice rising, she said, 'Suzy Harrison's dad works in New York and he was flying back specially for the show. But that's fine, don't worry about it, I'll be—'

'Tilly.' Miriam couldn't bear it. 'Sweetheart, it's OK, we'll cancel Venice.'

'You can't c-cancel a h-holiday.' Tilly wiped her wet cheeks.

Nadia slipped unnoticed from the room. Upstairs, she looked up her mother's number and punched it out.

'Tuesday, Tuesday,' mused Leonie, when Nadia had finished explaining. 'Hmm, I don't see why not. Sounds like fun!'

Nadia heaved a sigh of relief. 'Fantastic. Could you ring Tilly in five minutes? Just ask her how her day's been, then take it from there?'

The transformation in Tilly was instantaneous. Coming off the phone, she threw her arms round Miriam, clinging to her like a koala.

'It's OK, Gran, you can go to Venice. Mum's coming to see me in the show! They're going to drive up on Tuesday afternoon—all three of them! Isn't that brilliant?' Tilly looked as if she might burst with pride. 'Sorry if I was a pain before.'

Miriam fondly stroked her uncombed blonde hair. 'Darling, I'm so glad. You're never a pain.' Miriam's heart contracted with love.

Tilly couldn't stop beaming now. 'They'll probably want to stay here for the night.' Tilly was busy conjuring up happy family images. 'It's OK if they stay here, isn't it?'

'Of course they can stay,' Miriam told Tilly.

Five people, Tilly thought joyfully. Six seats. She would give her last ticket to Cal. Tamsin would be so impressed.

The next morning dawned greyish but dry, perfect turf-laying weather. At nine o'clock the lorry arrived, the turf was swiftly unloaded and Nadia prepared to get down to business. No sign of Laurie. No sign of him last night either. Did that mean he was tiring of his attempt to win her over? Had her refusal to fall into his arms, not to mention his bed, caused him to lose interest? Nadia, her mouth dry, wondered if he'd gone out and found himself a more accommodating girlfriend.

Oh good grief, had he?

Lining up the first strip of turf, Nadia knelt and prepared to unroll it.

If she'd *known* there was a time limit—

'Are you stuck?'

The truck driver who'd delivered the turf hadn't shut the garden gate behind him, which was why she hadn't heard Laurie arrive. Turning, Nadia felt a rush of—what? Relief? Love? *Don't get carried away*. He was here, that was all that mattered for now.

'Actually, my back's loads better today.' Leaning back she rotated first one shoulder then the other.

'Good. Fancy a wedding on Saturday?'

'Meaning what?' Not what she thought he meant, surely.

'I rang Nick Buckland last night. You remember Nick?'

Nadia nodded. Laurie and Nick had trained together to become stockbrokers. With his average looks and ebullient character, Nick had always maintained that if he was ever going to land himself a gorgeous woman, he'd need to make a serious pile of cash.

'And. Can you believe it? He's getting married on Saturday.'

'Good for him.' Nadia's cheeks reddened. 'I always liked Nick.'

'Oh dear.' Laurie surveyed her with wicked amusement. 'Did you think I was asking you to marry me on Saturday? Anyway, last night was his stag night. We met up and had a few drinks at the Alpha Bar.'

'Who's Nick marrying?'

'A girl called Sophie. I met her when she and her friends turned up around eleven. She's lovely,' said Laurie. 'Tall, thin, pretty and blonde. They make a great couple. And they invited us along to the wedding. Nick sends his love, by the way. He can't wait to see you again.'

It would be nice to see Nick too. Nadia wondered if Laurie had been chatted up by any of the girls at the Alpha Bar last night. It was a glitzy place, where the female clientele weren't renowned for being shy.

'So you had a good time at the Alpha Bar?'

Damn, Laurie was giving her one of his looks. That was the trouble with old boyfriends; he knew her too well.

'You mean did I get flirted with and chatted up while I was there?'

Nadia shrugged. 'You don't have to tell me.'

'Of course I was flirted with.' Laurie rolled his eyes. 'But I'm not interested in being hit on by girls in bars There's only one reason why I came back here. And you know what that is.'

'OK.' Out of the corner of her eye, Nadia saw Bart's portly figure moving about behind the French doors. Hardly the moment for a romantic . . . um, moment. Pushing her hair back from her forehead, she said, 'I think Bart's wondering why it's taken me forty minutes to lay three feet of turf.'

'But you'll come to Nick's wedding on Saturday?'

'Yes.' Nadia smiled; of course she'd go to Nick's wedding.

Together they began unrolling the lengths of turf. After a minute or two, Laurie said, 'By the way, Jay was at the Alpha Bar last night.'

Nadia dropped the turf. 'What was he doing there?'

'The usual.' Laurie was busy pressing edges together to disguise the join. 'Why do single men generally go to places like the Alpha Bar?'

Nadia was now unrolling turf at a rate of knots. It was completely irrational to feel betrayed, but somehow she did. 'Who was he with?'

'Well, he seemed to be getting on pretty well with a couple of girls.'

A couple! 'So what happened?'

'You mean, did he pull? Haven't the foggiest. We left just after midnight, went on to the Alexander Club. Nick ended up dancing on one of the tables with a feather bra tied round his head. Pete got a photo of him. He's planning to slip copies into every Order of Service booklet in the church. You can sleep with him if you want.'

Nadia thought she must have misheard.

'Sleep with Pete? I don't even know him!'

'He's Nick's best man. He's good fun, you'd like him.' Laurie paused. 'But that wasn't who I meant.'

Nadia swallowed.

'Jay Tiernan?' Laurie said helpfully. 'The chap you were on the verge of getting involved with when I came back?'

'Who told you that?'

'Oh, come on, I'm not stupid. Plus, Clare may have mentioned it in passing.'

Sisters, who'd have them?

'You're torn. You can't help wondering what you might be missing if you choose me. So find out,' said Laurie. 'Sleep with him, then decide.'

'This is ridiculous.' Nadia shook her head. 'You can't be serious.'

'If that's what it takes, I'm completely serious. I think I'll win in the end. But I don't want to spend the rest of my life with someone who's always wondering, deep down, if she made the right choice.'

'What if I decided I'd rather be with him than with you?'

'That's a risk I just have to take. But at least then we'd know.'

Chapter Seven

THE WEDDING CEREMONY was proceeding without a hitch. Beautiful blonde Sophie had arrived bang on time, her smile dazzling. Nick, paunchier than the last time Nadia had seen him, had remembered to peel the price stickers off the soles of his new shoes for the kneeling bit. Nobody had burst in at the crucial moment to object to the ceremony taking place.

'You may kiss the bride,' proclaimed the vicar.

'Whmmph.' Nadia muffled the sob by burying her face in Laurie's hankie. She couldn't help it; Nick and Sophie were in love. Nick, normally so bawdy and cynical, looked as if he might be on the verge of tears himself. This was all he wanted in the world. Oh bugger, and now her mascara really was starting to run.

'We could do this.' Laurie's mouth was almost touching her ear.

A shiver zipped down Nadia's spine. 'Do what?'

'This. The whole church bit. All you have to do is say yes.'

Nadia gazed straight ahead at Nick and Sophie ecstatically kissing each other. She couldn't breathe. That could be us, she thought.

'I want to marry you,' Laurie went on.

Talk about shameless, thought Nadia. He was taking advantage of her while she was in a vulnerable state.

'Have you ever thought about becoming a double-glazing salesman?'

When the service was over, the bride and groom led the exit from the church. The people in the front pews peeled off row by row, following them outside. Nadia and Laurie, five pews back, left their seats when the time came and made their way down the aisle.

Nadia admired the posies of white rosebuds and stephanotis attached to the ends of each of the pews. Spotting a woman in an ornate orange hat the size of a satellite dish, she wondered how much it had cost. Oh, but there was someone with far better taste, a tall redhead wearing a knee-length old-gold silk jacket over a peachy-yellow dress of the same material. The colours were stunning together, complementing the girl's auburn hair perfectly. Now that was the way to make an impression on—

Oh, *good grief*. The redhead's companion was Jay.

How? How could he be here? *How?*

The redhead was chattering away in a vivacious fashion. Next to her, Jay nodded and smiled as if agreeing with whatever she'd just said. Then his gaze shifted and came to rest on Nadia. He nodded again briefly, then carried on listening to the redhead.

Laurie, following her line of vision, said, 'Hey, look who's here!' Grinning, he waved at Jay. 'That's one of the girls he was with at the Alpha Bar the other night. She must be one of Sophie's friends. She was out on the hen night.'

The reception was being held at the Holborn Hotel, famed for its views over the suspension bridge. It was a really nice hotel, rather posh, quite grown-up. Everyone was mingling in the hotel garden, drinking champagne and socialising.

Nadia, in contrast, was having a hard time behaving like a grown-up. She longed to stick out her foot next time Redheaded Girl wandered past, and trip her up. She couldn't help it; Redheaded Girl was annoying her intensely. The way she threw back her head and laughed whenever Jay said something even remotely amusing. The way she kept picking invisible bits of fluff off the lapels of his jacket.

'Nadia! Brilliant to see you again. You're looking fantastic!' Nadia found herself enveloped in a bear hug that quashed all the air out of her lungs. Nick had never known his own strength.

But he was right, Nadia thought, she *was* looking fantastic. The dark blue spaghetti-strapped top Clare had bought last week went brilliantly with her own indigo-and-silver long floaty skirt from Monsoon. For once her hair had done as it was told. She just hoped Nick wasn't the only person here who'd noticed she looked gorgeous.

'You too,' Nadia told him. 'And now you're married! I can't believe it.' Over Nick's sturdy shoulder she watched Jay refilling Redheaded Girl's glass. He was wearing a dark grey suit and—oops, quick, look away.

'You'll be next.' Beaming all over his face, Nick said, 'When Laurie told me the two of you were back together—'

'We aren't back together,' Nadia interjected. Bloody hell, what had Laurie been telling him?

'I didn't say that.' Next to her, Laurie shook his head. 'I didn't. I just said we were seeing each other again. In a purely platonic way. Until I can persuade Nadia to change her mind.'

'He did. Absolutely right.' Nick nodded vigorously. 'But you will change your mind, won't you?' He clutched Nadia's hands. 'I know he's an ugly bugger, but he's not so bad, deep down. Go on. If you two tie the knot we'll be able to have married-couples dinner parties like proper grown-ups. With matching cutlery, the works.'

'That's a great reason to get married.' Nadia nodded thoughtfully. 'Thanks, I'll bear it in mind.'

'Do I know you?'

Nadia turned and came face to face with Redheaded Girl.

Oh shit.

'Sorry? No, I don't think so.' She'd just said sorry. How British.

'Oh. That's odd.' The girl's tone was challenging rather than friendly. 'It's just that you keep looking over at me. All the time.'

'I don't keep looking over at you.' This was actually true. She was looking over at Jay. The problem was, every time he turned his head in her direction, she was forced to glance hastily away and pretend to be gazing transfixed at something or someone else instead. 'Well, if I've been looking at you, it wasn't deliberate. I didn't realise I was doing it.'

Redheaded Girl tilted her head to one side. 'I hear you work for Jay.'

'That's right.' Nadia didn't normally dislike people practically on sight, but for Redheaded Girl she'd make an exception.

'Do you have a thing for your boss?'

Oh, for crying out loud, where *was* Laurie? Now that she could actually do with having him around, he'd disappeared.

'No.' Perspiring, Nadia shook her head.

'It's just that I thought it might explain why you keep looking over. Because you want Jay and you're jealous that I have him and you don't.'

Nadia was outraged. How dare this horrible girl be right?

'That's not true.' With a huge effort she kept her voice calm.

'Well, I'm glad to hear it.' The girl's smile didn't reach her cold eyes. 'Because I'm thirty-three and I've spent a long time waiting for a man like Jay to come along. He's just what I'm after, and I plan to hang on to him.'

Nadia bumped into Jay in the corridor on her way back from the loo.

'How did you get invited to Nick and Sophie's wedding?' Three glasses of Moët had loosened her tongue.

'I bumped into the girls at the Alpha Bar. Andrea used to share a flat with Sophie. She didn't have a partner for the wedding, so she asked me if I'd like to come with her.'

'She's thirty-three,' said Nadia, hoping for a glimmer of shock.

Jay looked amused. 'I know. She told me.'

Bugger. 'She's been waiting ages for someone like you to come along.' Nadia wondered if they'd already slept together.

'Thanks. The garden's looking good, by the way.'

Irritated, she said off-puttingly, 'Andrea likes you. A lot.'

'Well, good.' Jay's brown eyes shone with amusement. 'I didn't go along to the Alpha Bar to meet women who'd hate me.'

Outside, a gong sounded.

'Saved by the gong,' said Jay.

Nadia bristled. 'Saved from what?'

'I'm sorry, I thought this was an interrogation.'

Nadia gave up. The trouble with sparring with Jay was that you never won. He had an infuriating habit of having an answer for everything.

'People are going in to eat. I'd better get back to Laurie.'

'And I'll go and find Andrea,' Jay said easily.

Andrea and her shrieking, thirty-three-year-old ovaries, Nadia thought with derision. God, if they were sharing a table with Andrea and Jay, it would be pepper pots at twenty paces.

They weren't sharing a table. Thankfully, the next couple of hours whizzed by. Meeting up with Laurie's old stockbroking pals and their other halves was great fun. Their table was one of the rowdiest in the room. Bottles were emptied with a flourish and speedily replaced. Nadia had a stitch in her side from laughing.

Actually, when you were laughing this hard, a stitch was the least of your worries. Nadia stood up and said, 'Back in a minute.'

She was in much-needed mid-wee when the door to the ladies' loo opened. High heels clattered across the marble-tiled floor. Two lots of heels. One set tap-tapped into the cubicle two down from her own, while the other set headed for the basin. Nadia heard the sound of a make-up bag being unzipped.

'So who's Hannah seeing now?' This from the girl in the cubicle.

'She went out with Toby the other night. He took her to dinner at that new place on Chandos Road.'

Dinggg, Nadia's ears pricked up. Was that Andrea's voice?

'No sign of her getting back with Piers then?'

Piers? Piers who?

'Ha, she wishes! Piers is up to his old tricks again.' The voice that possibly belonged to Andrea was scornful. 'He's been seeing this girl, some arty type. Total pushover, according to Piers. But when I saw him at Boom on Sunday he was all over Felicity Temple-Stewart.'

Nadia's brain was racing. Sunday, Sunday . . . Clare hadn't seen Piers on Sunday. He'd told her he was visiting his sister in Oxford. Slowly, silently, Nadia tugged up her knickers then lowered herself to the floor of the cubicle.

'Anyway, how are things going with you two?' This from cubicle girl, now washing her hands. 'Very nicely, by the look of things.'

Nadia held her breath. Now she really had to know. Crouching on her hands and knees, she ducked her head down and to one side.

'Very nicely indeed. I think my lottery ticket's come up—*aaarrgh!*'

Andrea, having glanced in the mirror, had spotted a pair of dark eyes peering out from under the closed cubicle door behind her. She had let out a high-pitched shriek and spun round.

'Get up!' Andrea shouted. 'Get up and get out here! What the bloody hell d'you think you're playing at?'

Awkwardly, Nadia stumbled to her feet.

'You!' jeered Andrea, when Nadia emerged from the cubicle.

Her friend said, 'Andy? Who is this?'

'She works for Jay. She's a . . . gardener.' Andrea made it sound like maggot-eater. 'She's jealous of me because I'm with Jay and she isn't. And now she's crawling around on a toilet floor, eavesdropping on us.' Her mouth twisted into a triumphant smile. 'Classy. I can't wait to tell Jay about this.'

Sophie seemed so nice, Nadia couldn't imagine what she'd been thinking of, sharing a flat with someone as poisonous as Andrea. The deeply annoying thing was, if Andrea had been a nice person, she could have found out all about Piers. But she'd rather cut out her tongue than ask her now.

'Tell Jay what you like. Doesn't bother me. Except I wouldn't get your hopes up too high, if I were you. He's pretty crap in bed.'

Pleased with herself, Nadia headed for the door.

Well, what could she do now, other than launch into the rest of the reception with a vengeance?

By this time the disco was already belting out Duran Duran's greatest hits. Determinedly not looking—even for a millisecond—in the direction of Jay and Andrea's table, Nadia danced with Laurie, then with Laurie's ex-boss, with Laurie again.

The DJ, slowing down to give the older contingent a breather, began to play something hideous by Celine Dion. When Laurie turned automatically towards their table, Nadia hauled him back.

Understandably, he looked shocked. 'You don't want to dance to this.'

'I do.' Nadia swung herself against him and Laurie grinned.

Nadia wound her arms round his neck. Laurie was a good dancer, and he was looking great in his suit. In fact Laurie was looking great, full stop. He was by far the most beautiful man in the room. He had the best hair, Nadia decided, running her fingers through it as they danced. The best eyelashes. And the very, *very* best cheekbones . . .

Hmm, maybe she was the tiniest bit tipsy.

Leaning her head on Laurie's shoulder, Nadia risked a speedy glance in Jay's direction. OK, bit juvenile, but she so wanted to know if he was watching her. In an envious fashion, preferably.

Except he wasn't. He was bloody writing something on a napkin while Andrea sat beside him with her body language on show. She was smirking away like a *Countdown* winner.

Celine Dion gave way to Michael Bolton.

'You know'—Laurie's tone was conversational—'a lesser man than me might think his luck was in.'

Mortified, Nadia realised that she'd been indulging in some shameless hip-grinding.

'It's not you, it's Michael Bolton. He has that effect on me.'

Nadia ordered her hips to behave themselves. After Michael Bolton they danced along, rather more decorously, to something by Westlife. When they eventually returned to their table, Laurie disappeared to the bar in search of more drinks.

There was no sign anywhere of Jay and Andrea.

Nadia was hot, her face undoubtedly shiny. In search of a tissue, she reached for her bag and encountered a napkin laid over the zip.

Unfolding it, she saw that the napkin had been written on. There, in Jay's unmistakable slanting scrawl, were the words: *No I'm not*.

'Don't forget, you have to be there by six or you won't be able to get in.'

It was eight o'clock on Tuesday morning and Tilly was all of a jitter. Today was her Big Day. School, followed by final rehearsals, followed by make-up and preparation, followed by The Show Itself.

'You'll be brilliant.' Nadia gave her a squeeze. 'I can't wait for tonight.'

'You won't be late, will you?' Tilly's eyes were huge in her pale face.

'We'll be there. *Early*,' Nadia added.

'All ready?' James came into the kitchen carrying his overnight case. He was dropping Tilly at school before setting off for Sheffield.

'Ready.' Tilly leapt to her feet, hauling her rucksack over her shoulder.

Miriam kissed Tilly. 'Off you go, darling. I'm so sorry we're going to miss the show. You'll be a sensation, I just know it.' Miriam hugged her hard, her conscience jabbing at her. She had persuaded Edward that a week in Venice would be fun, when in reality all she was doing was running away from further letters and phone calls.

'We'll be thinking of you,' she told Tilly.

Nadia's car was booked into the garage in Westbury for its MOT. At eight thirty, Miriam was following Nadia to the garage, then giving her a lift into work. At three o'clock Laurie was driving Miriam and Edward up to Heathrow. At five o'clock, Nadia would finish work, change into the clothes she had brought with her, then wait for Clare to pick her up at five fifteen and drive her to Tilly's school.

It had all been planned like a military campaign.

At twenty past eight the telephone shrilled. Nadia snatched it up.

'Darling, it's me. This show thing of Tilly's. It is tonight, isn't it?'

How absolutely typical of Leonie not to be sure.

'Yes, it's tonight. The show starts at six and—'

'The thing is, darling, we're not going to be able to make it after all.'

Nadia froze. Was her mother *serious*?

'We've just been asked to a party and it's not the kind of invite you turn down! This chap used to be a member of Status Quo, darling, can you imagine? So could you just let Tilly know and wish her good luck? I'm sure she'll understand.'

'She won't.' Nadia was discovering the true meaning of the expression 'making your blood boil'. 'Mum, you promised to come and see her. You *have* to be there. You seriously want me to tell Tilly that you won't be coming to see her in the show because you'd rather go along to some has-been's party?'

'He isn't a has-been,' Leonie retorted crossly. 'And, let's face it, we're talking about a school production, hardly the London Palladium. But OK, if it'll make you any happier . . . we'll make up some other excuse instead. I know,' Leonie went on cheerfully, 'we'll say we've all gone down with a really nasty bug. Tilly can't argue with that.'

'Blimey, love, you scrub up a treat.' Bart bumped into Nadia as she emerged from the newly refurbished bathroom, having done her make-up and changed into a strappy red dress and high heels.

'Thanks, Bart.' Nadia grinned.

'Got a hot date then?' As he expertly rolled a cigarette, Bart glanced out of the landing window and broke into a nudge-nudge leer. 'Don't worry, love, we won't tell Laurie. Mum's the word.'

Peering out of the window, hoping to see Clare, she watched Jay emerging from his car. 'I'm not waiting for Jay,' she told Bart. 'My sister's picking me up.'

Aware that her last contact with Jay had been the note he'd left, informing her that actually he wasn't rubbish in bed, Nadia nipped back into the bathroom. He wouldn't be here long.

At five twenty, the builders trooped off home. Jay was still upstairs. Nadia, by this time in the kitchen drumming her fingers on the work-top, rang home and listened to the phone go unanswered. Well, that was good. It had to mean Clare was on her way.

'What are you doing? I didn't know you were still here.' Jay appeared in the kitchen doorway. 'Your car isn't outside.'

'It's in the garage, getting an MOT. Clare's picking me up.'

'Off somewhere nice?'

'School concert. Tilly's starring in *Grease*. Excuse me.' Getting seriously twitchy now, Nadia fumbled in her bag for her mobile and pressed redial. At home the phone continued to ring unanswered.

'I can give you a lift,' Jay offered as she punched out the number of Clare's mobile. It was switched to the answering service.

'She should be here any moment. I can't believe she's doing this.' Nadia began to feel sick; surely Clare wouldn't let Tilly down. 'Leonie was meant to be coming as well, but she cancelled this morning.'

By twenty to six there was still no sign of Clare.

'Come on.' Jay ushered Nadia into his car.

'I'm going to kill her.'

'But not until after the show.'

Nadia's hands were shaking so much she could barely fasten her seat belt. 'I've got five tickets,' she fumed, 'for the front row. And I'm going to be the only one sitting there.'

'Would it help if I offered to go with you?'

Too wound up to care how she sounded, Nadia heaved a sigh and said, 'I suppose you're better than nothing.'

The corners of Jay's mouth twitched. 'Thanks.'

By ten to six the school hall was buzzing and crammed with people. Easing their way through the crowds, they found their allotted seats. The end one was occupied by Cal Davis, with whom Tilly had recently become so friendly.

As Nadia greeted him, a hand touched her arm. Swinging round, she saw Annie looking out of breath but triumphant.

'Oh, thank God.' Nadia hugged her. 'But how did you get here?'

'Your grandmother phoned James. James rang me. I closed the shop at five thirty and ran all the way. At least I can fill an empty seat.'

'Hi, Cal!' a chirpy voice sang out, and Nadia turned to see two girls looking delighted to see him. 'Exciting, isn't it? Lucky you, in the front row. We're stuck right at the back.'

Something about the girls rang a bell in the back of Nadia's mind. Tilly had relayed the story of their encounter with her in the park.

'We've got two spare seats. Want to sit with us?'

'Hey, cool!'

Eighty minutes later, the final curtain fell and the audience rose to their feet as one, clapping and cheering and whistling.

The curtains lifted once more and the cast stepped forward to take their bows. There was a lump in Nadia's throat as Tilly was invited to step forward and the roars of approval rose to a climax. Tilly beamed down at her guests. Apart from the opening moments of the show, when she'd fluffed a couple of lines, she had played the part of Sandy to perfection. The evening had been a triumph.

'I only came along to fill an empty seat.' Next to Nadia, Jay had to raise his voice in order to be heard. 'But I'm glad I did. Tilly was brilliant.' He paused, then said, 'I feel like a proud father.'

The head teacher appeared on stage once everyone had taken their bows, to announce that as soon as *all* the chairs had been stacked *neatly* at the back of the hall, the bar would be open. Parent volunteers began serving warm white wine and an assortment of soft drinks.

'You don't have to stay,' she whispered to Jay. 'You'll hate this bit. Tilly and I can get a cab home.'

He looked astounded. 'You must be joking. This is Tilly's big night. I wouldn't miss it for the world.'

By the time Tilly reappeared, changed back into her own clothes, Jay had bought a round of drinks.

'You were ace,' Janice said enthusiastically. 'Wicked. Wasn't she, Cal?'

'Oh yes.' Cal smiled his quirky smile at Tilly. 'Totally wicked.'

'You were fantastic,' Nadia said, 'the star of the show.'

'I wish Mum could have been here. But even though she was ill, she still managed to organise flowers. That was thoughtful of her, wasn't it?'

Don't say a word, don't say a word.

'But what happened to Clare?'

The six million dollar question. Nadia couldn't bring herself to tell any more lies. 'I don't know, sweetheart. She just didn't turn up.'

Tilly looked worried. 'D'you think she's had an accident?'

Not yet.

'Well,' said Jay, when they'd dropped Annie off at the cottage and watched her disappear into her house. 'Do you want to go somewhere for a drink, or get home?'

Nadia had slipped Tilly twenty pounds and left her to celebrate with her new-found friends over a pizza on the Gloucester Road. Tilly had promised to share a taxi with Cal and be home by eleven.

'I need to see Clare.' And tear her hair out by the roots.

'OK.' Jay swung the car round. 'Where's Laurie tonight?'

'London. He drove Miriam and Edward to Heathrow, then arranged to meet up with an old friend from the agency.' Nadia said warily, 'Are you still seeing thingy? Andrea?'

'Yes, thanks.' Jay looked amused. 'Despite what you told her.'

'Sorry. She annoyed me. She made assumptions I didn't like.'

'I hate it when that happens. People making assumptions about me. Especially when they're not true.'

Oh dear. Touché. Feeling her pulse accelerate, Nadia recalled she had Laurie's permission to sleep with Jay. Not that she needed his permission, seeing as she was still officially single and free to sleep with whoever she liked. And if she did decide to go for it, what better time than tonight? Laurie wouldn't be back from London for hours. Best of all, it would drive Andrea insane . . .

'I need to get home,' Nadia said firmly.

Some things were more important than annoying somebody else's annoying new girlfriend. She had to beat the living daylights out of Clare.

Nadia surveyed the driveway. Clare's car was there.

'I'd invite you in,' she said, 'but . . .'

'I know. I might not be able to handle the sight of all that blood.'

As Nadia let herself in, all the rage came flooding back. If Jay hadn't been around to give her a lift, she might have missed the show herself. Had Clare even bothered to think about how Tilly would have felt if *none* of her family had turned up?

There were lights on upstairs. Nadia stormed up.

Clare's room was messy but empty.

The bathroom door was shut. What if Clare had slipped in the shower and spent the last five hours lying unconscious with a fractured skull?

Nadia tried the handle. The bathroom door was locked.

'Clare? Are you in there? *Clare? Open the door!*'

Nothing. Oh God. You read about accidents like this in the papers.

Rattling the handle again, Nadia bellowed, '*Clare!*'

More silence. Then . . .

'Leave me alone.'

'*What?*' Nadia stared at the door in disbelief, terror instantly replaced by boiling rage.

'Where the *hell* have you been?' Nadia roared, hammering on the door. 'You were supposed to pick me up, you missed Tilly's show, and you couldn't even be bothered to *phone* me! You're unbelievable, you know that? Open the bloody door this minute.'

Moments later the key turned in the lock and the door swung open. And Nadia was stopped in her tracks by the pitiful sight before her. She'd never seen Clare looking so awful, puffy-eyed, pinch-faced and . . . well, a complete mess.

'Don't tell me, this is about Piers. It just has to be,' Nadia sneered.

Clare stumbled past her out of the bathroom, heading back to the sanctuary of her room. Nadia followed close behind.

'He's dumped you, hasn't he?' Her voice was tinged with satisfaction. Now, at last, Clare knew how it felt. 'You self-centred bitch, you could still have phoned me. Tilly's your *sister*. . .' The words were tumbling out fast, turbo-charged by rage and Clare's breathtaking selfishness.

'Shut up!' screamed Clare, hurling something small at her. It bounced painlessly off Nadia's chest and dropped to the floor.

Nadia peered down at it. 'What's that?' She said it, although she already knew.

'What d'you bloody think it is? I'm pregnant.' Clare buried her face in her hands and collapsed on the bed.

Oh God.

Bending, Nadia retrieved the white plastic stick thing. One blue line. Two blue lines.

'Does Piers know?'

'He went berserk.' Clare snatched a handful of tissues from the box next to the pregnancy stick. Fresh tears began to roll down her cheeks. 'He doesn't even think it's his,' Clare said helplessly. 'He thinks I've been sleeping around, but I haven't. He also thinks I did it on purpose, to trap him. But I *didn't*.'

'How long have you known?'

'Seven hours? At lunchtime today, when I was flicking through my diary, I realised my period was late. Only two days, but I'm never late. After that I couldn't concentrate. In the end I thought I'd pop to the chemist and pick up a testing kit, just to put my mind at rest.' Clare paused, said brokenly, 'Except it didn't.'

'God.' Nadia couldn't imagine how Clare must have felt.

'I'm sorry, I'm really sorry about not picking you up or getting to

Tilly's school thing. And I know I should have phoned you. But I just couldn't.' Clare began to tremble. 'I rang Piers at work, but he'd taken the afternoon off, so I went round to his flat but he wasn't at home either. So then I drove round all the bars in Clifton until I found him.'

'With a girl,' guessed Nadia.

'No. With his horrible friend Eddie. Well, there were girls there,' Clare amended. 'But they weren't *with* them. Just chatting at the bar.'

Nadia hadn't mentioned the conversation she'd overheard at the wedding. But all she did was nod. 'Go on.'

'I told Piers I had to talk to him. I managed to get him to come and sit in my car. And that's where I told him.' Clare took a deep, shuddering breath. 'Oh God, it was a nightmare. He said he never wanted to see me again. He tried to write me out a cheque for an abortion and when I ripped it up he called me a stupid little tart. Then, just as I was getting really hysterical, a traffic warden came along and said I was parked on double yellows and I had to move my car. So that was it. Piers jumped out and legged it back into the pub.'

'He's a tosser.' Nadia shook her head. 'A complete and utter tosser.'

'I know. But maybe when he's had a chance to think about it, he'll change his mind,' Clare pleaded. 'He might wake up tomorrow feeling—'

'Like a tosser,' Nadia said firmly. 'Because that's all he is, and you know it. Let's face it, he isn't going to change his mind.'

'Oh God.' Clare started crying again, hopelessly and noisily. 'What am I going to do? I don't know what to *doooo*.'

Nadia put her arms round Clare, who clung to her, sobbing 'Sshh, come on, it'll be OK.'

'How can it be OK?' Clare sniffed. 'I'm pregnant and my boyfriend's dumped me. It can't get any worse than this.'

'Look, you don't have to have this baby.' Despite squirming inwardly as she said it, Nadia forced herself to sound matter-of-fact.

'Have an abortion, you mean?' Dully, Clare shook her head. 'No.'

Astounded, Nadia said, 'You want to have the baby?'

Clare was running her fingers through her tangled hair.

'Of course I don't want to. I'm twenty-three, for crying out loud. But I couldn't get rid of it, I just can't do that.' She sniffed again. 'Like mother like daughter. Leonie had kids she didn't want. Now I'm about to do it. Maybe it's genetic.'

Miriam had issued strict instructions that any post arriving while she was away and addressed to her should be left in the top drawer of the dresser in the hall. Now, she slid open the drawer. Everyone else was out. The holiday had been wonderful, but Edward was still pressing her to marry him. Once or twice she'd been tempted to tell him everything. But she couldn't bring herself to go through with it.

There was quite a stack of mail. Miriam sifted through each item in turn, her spirits rising. No handwritten envelopes and nothing from Edinburgh. Maybe he'd given up at last.

Then she reached it, beneath the glossy cellophane-wrapped brochures. Miriam stared at the Jiffy bag bearing her name and address, in that all-too-familiar handwriting. Oh God, what now?

It was a videotape.

She made her way through to the living room, slotted the tape into the video and pressed PLAY. Her heart began to gallop as the TV screen flickered, then cleared. Black and white. Old cine film, recorded over fifty years ago, now transferred to video.

Miriam watched, almost in disbelief. She remembered the day—how could she ever forget it?—yet she'd never seen this film before. She couldn't even recall the name of the person who had been wielding the bulky cine camera. Was it Geoffrey? Gerald? They had looked forward to seeing the results. But Geoffrey or Gerald had disappeared shortly afterwards to carry out his stint of National Service.

And now, fifty-two years later, Miriam watched the day unfold. There she was, wearing a dress that looked pale grey on the video but which had in fact been a glorious lime green. Laughing into the camera without a care in the world.

It had been such a happy day. Carefully Miriam identified everyone else captured by the camera. Most of all, she studied the man who had sent her the video, the man who had turned her life upside-down once before and was now threatening to do the same again.

It was impossible not to wonder what he looked like now.

With a shudder, Miriam hoped to God she wouldn't find out.

Feeling like a boxer psyching himself up before a fight, Clare made her way downstairs. Miriam was back and dinner was about to be served. Tonight was the night Clare was going to make her announcement.

About to head out to the garden, where she could hear voices, she glanced out through the French windows and promptly shot into reverse.

Bursting into the kitchen where Nadia was mashing potatoes, Clare hissed, 'What's *she* doing here?'

'Who? Annie?' Nadia resumed her energetic mashing. 'Tilly's brought back the video of the school show. We've all got to watch it after dinner. Tilly persuaded Annie to come along and see it too. Don't look at me like that,' she went on, because Clare was scowling like a teenager. 'Annie's nice.'

'I'm telling Dad and Gran about the baby. It's none of her business.'

Nadia sighed. Clare was still wary of Annie, reluctant to welcome her into the family. It was frustrating when their father was clearly so happy.

'You might be glad of her. Dad's less likely to go mental.'

'We don't need someone like her worming her way into our family.'

For heaven's sake. Nadia finished piling the mashed potato into a serving dish and plonked it into Clare's hands.

'It's the hormones getting to you. Now take the dish through to the dining room and call everyone inside. And . . . try and break it to them gently,' Nadia pleaded. Clare had a talent for making an awkward situation worse.

'Oh, don't nag.' Clare tried to sound irritated, but her insides were in too much of a knot. She managed a weak smile. 'It'll be OK. It's only a baby, after all, not the end of the world.'

Nadia served up the chicken casserole, everyone helped themselves to broccoli and buttered carrots, and James poured the wine. It was, on the surface, a normal, happy, noisy gathering. Miriam was regaling them with tales of Venice.

'Clare, more chicken?' Noticing that she'd almost cleared her plate, James pushed the dish towards her. 'You must be hungry.'

Nadia's toes scrunched up in anticipation, wondering if she'd take this as her cue. ('Well, that's probably because I'm eating for two now!')

'Starving.' Clare helped herself to more casserole. 'Thomas Harrington rang me this afternoon. He's putting on a show next week and one of the other exhibitors has had to pull out.' She spread her arms, ta-dah style. 'So I'm in! Isn't that fantastic? Twelve paintings and loads of media coverage. I just know this is going to be my big break.'

Nadia breathed out slowly. Clare was doing the good news, bad news routine, softening them up before delivering the killer blow.

James, beaming with pride, said, 'Brilliant news.'

Clare was basking in the approval, visibly happy, then Nadia saw her take a deep breath.

'And there's something else,' Clare began, her voice trembling slightly.

Nadia felt the urge to dive under the table.

'Isn't everything just great?' Tilly exclaimed. 'First me in my show, and now Clare has one too! Gran, can we watch my tape as soon as dinner's over? I'm so excited, I can't wait for all of you to see it!'

'Darling, of course we can,' said Miriam.

'Honestly, they were all so good, so professional.' Annie chimed in with enthusiasm. 'None of the others was as good as Tilly, of course.'

Clare shot Annie a look of disdain, muttering, 'Pass the sick bag.'

Nadia tensed. Annie went red. James said icily, '*What* did you say?'

'Nothing.' Clare pressed her lips together.

But Tilly was furious. 'You couldn't be bothered to turn up for the show. Now you're not even interested in watching the video. You're even more horrible than I thought.' Tilly's voice rose.

'Yes, Clare,' Miriam joined in, 'you're being extremely rude.'

With an edge of sarcasm, Clare said, 'I wonder why.'

'I know why.' Tilly looked at Clare. Finally she turned to Miriam at the head of the table. 'It's because she's pregnant.'

A fork clattered onto a plate. Nadia drained her glass. Like Wimbledon spectators, everyone's gaze swivelled in unison across to Clare.

'Oh no.' Her heart sinking, Miriam said, 'Tell me this isn't true.'

Tossing back her long hair in defiance, Clare glared at Tilly. 'It is true. And how the bloody hell did *you* find out?'

'I overheard you and Nadia talking about it yesterday.'

'I was about to tell all of you, until Bigmouth here stuck her oar in. Anyway, everyone knows now. Can someone pass the mashed potato?' Clare's words were casual but her blue eyes glittered with unshed tears.

'Oh, Clare, how could you be so stupid,' Miriam sighed. 'How happy is Piers about this?'

'He's not.' Clare was defiant. 'We broke up. I don't need him anyway. I didn't mean this to happen, but it has. And I'll manage.'

'You're going to have the baby?' said James.

'Yes. It deserves a chance, OK? Think back, Dad. When Leonie found out she was pregnant with me, I don't suppose she was too thrilled, was she? It would have been easier for her not to have gone through with it. But she did. And I'm glad about that.' Clare's eyes swam. 'Because I'd rather be here than not here. Even now,' she added, her voice starting to waver. 'And I wouldn't call this the best night of my life.'

There was a long silence. Then Miriam said gently, 'Oh darling.'

Clare burst into tears.

As Miriam jumped up and enveloped her in a hug, Clare sobbed, 'I'm s-sorry, it was an accident. I'll look after it, I p-promise.'

'Sweetheart, don't cry. We'll manage. Sshh, there there, it's all right.'

Clearly feeling horribly out of place, Annie rose to her feet and said, 'Why don't I clear away the plates?'

'I can't believe I was so stupid,' Clare sobbed. 'I really loved him. I thought he loved me. I've been such an idiot.'

'Everyone makes mistakes.' Miriam's tone was soothing, her hands rubbing Clare's heaving shoulders. If only you knew, she thought.

'And I won't be a nuisance, I promise. I'll move out.'

Everyone knew this was about as likely to happen as Rod Stewart announcing he was gay.

'Plenty of time to think about that,' James said gruffly.

Annie had finished clearing the plates. Hovering in the doorway she said hesitantly, 'Shall I . . . um, bring in the pudding?'

Her tone brisk, Miriam nodded at Annie and gave Clare a buck-up pat on the back. 'Pudding. Yes, of course we're having pudding. And after that we'll all watch Tilly's video.'

A plane droned overhead. Pointing skywards, Clare said, 'Shouldn't we wait until Steven Spielberg gets here? He'd hate to miss it.'

Chapter Eight

STRAIGHTENING UP, Nadia surveyed the border she had just planted with mahonia, nicotiana and mignonette. How she loved those names. They sounded like a troupe of can-can dancers at the Moulin Rouge. Behind them, Himalayan honeysuckle covered the stone wall. She still had a serious amount of watering to do if the plants weren't about to keel over and die in the current heatwave.

Speaking of keeling over, she could do with a drink herself.

'Looking good.' Jay greeted her in the kitchen.

Aware that she was hot and sweaty and streaked with soil, Nadia said, 'Hardly, I'm a mess.'

'I meant the garden.'

Oops. Serves me right.

'Tea?' Jay grinned, to soften the blow. He filled the kettle and switched it on, then watched Nadia scrub her hands in the sink.

'Actually, I've got something for you.' Nadia dried her hands and dug into her jeans pocket. Retrieving the glossy invitation, she handed it over. 'Sorry it's crumpled. You don't have to go if you don't want to. Clare just said it would be nice if you could come along.'

Jay studied the invitation.

'And buy a painting, I imagine.' Drily he added, 'Preferably something of hers this time.'

'That's up to you. Anyway, it should be a good show. Hi, Robbie.' Nadia broke off, realising that Robbie was hovering uncertainly in the doorway. 'I'm just making tea. Want some?'

Robbie nodded. Still as shy and awkward as ever, he far preferred to communicate non-verbally.

'Thursday,' said Jay. 'I think I can manage that. I like her work.'

'Robbie, here you are.' Nadia had made the teas in true builder's fashion. Tea the colour of Frank Bruno, that was how they liked it.

Jay's invitation lay on the worktop. Gazing intently at it, then turning to Nadia—but managing not actually to catch her eye—Robbie said awkwardly, 'Um . . . could I have one of those?'

'Well . . . um,' Nadia prevaricated. This was awkward. Clare had specified that only wealthy, glamorous and preferably highly photogenic people should receive invitations. 'The thing is,' Nadia said apologetically, 'I don't have any more invitations.'

Robbie pointed. 'There's one sticking out of your pocket.'

'Oh!' Stalling for time, Nadia stammered, 'I d-didn't know you were interested in art, Robbie.'

'I'm not. But my brother likes it. He's always going to art galleries.'

Robbie's brother. Nadia pictured him, as painfully shy as his sibling, slipping through the glittering crowd, hoovering up all the canapés and free drinks. Then, mercifully, melting away again. No harm done. Bugger it, how could she refuse Robbie?

'OK. Of course he can have one.' Overcompensating for her guilt with a bright smile, Nadia handed him the invite with a flourish.

'Well,' said Jay, when Robbie had shuffled out of the kitchen, 'I thought that went very well.' He was still laughing at her.

'Clare's going to kill me,' Nadia groaned. 'It's supposed to be a glittering occasion, packed with beautiful people.'

Jay raised a dark eyebrow. 'Was that a compliment?'

'Actually, Clare said beautiful if possible.' Nadia smiled sunnily at him. 'Failing that, filthy rich.'

Thursday night. Seven o'clock. The Harrington Gallery was lit up and bursting with guests. Clare and the two other exhibiting artists were being photographed for the local paper.

With her glossy dark hair swinging loose around her shoulders and her high-necked, sleeveless pink dress skimming her tanned body, Clare was easily the most photogenic of the three. As she flashed a dazzling smile for the camera, anyone could be forgiven for envying and admiring her talent and stunning looks. Nadia, watching from the far end of the gallery, marvelled at the façade Clare was able to present.

As instructed, the guests had dressed for the occasion. Everyone seemed to be chatting animatedly and helping themselves to canapés. Some of them were even bothering to glance at the paintings on view.

Laurie looking scruffily gorgeous as usual in his dark suit, conversing easily with a stern, rather plain, middle-aged woman. As he said something else and gestured towards one of Clare's works, the woman broke into a delighted smile. No one was capable of resisting Laurie's charms.

'Spotted him yet?' murmured a voice in her ear, and Nadia jumped, almost spilling her drink. It was Jay. She hadn't seen him arrive.

'Spotted who?' Heavens, it was hard to sound casual when you didn't feel it.

'Robbie's brother.'

'Oh, right. Well, no sign so far.' Nadia pulled a wry face. 'I had to tell Clare in the end. She said if he's even remotely embarrassing, it's my job to kick him out.' Her attention was momentarily diverted by a glamorous brunette sporting a football-sized bump under her shirt. 'By the way, I've been meaning to ask you. How's Belinda?'

'Not too bad.' Jay paused. 'Missing Anthony, of course.'

'You must miss him too.'

He nodded. 'Sometimes I forget. When Anthony's football team got beaten three nil on Saturday, I actually picked up the phone to ring him.' With a wry smile, Jay added, 'Actually, he'd probably be glad he didn't live to see their pitiful performance.'

'Come on,' said Nadia, 'let's get you another drink.'

Jay stayed where he was. 'One more thing. Why are you over here and Laurie's over there? Have you finished with him?'

B-bump b-bump went Nadia's heart. She breathed in Jay's aftershave, fresh and tinged with lime.

'You have to be a couple before you can finish with someone.'

Jay's gaze didn't waver. 'Isn't it about time you made up your mind?'

God, this was like being on *The Weakest Link.* Of course it was. But it wasn't as simple as that.

'I want another drink.' Nadia began to move away. 'Are you going to buy a painting?'

'I'm not sure.'

'Why not?'

'The thing is, there are a couple I like, but I can't decide. Over there.' With his glass, he indicated the paintings.

'Come on then, let's go and have a look. If you faff about, someone else'll get there first and you'll miss out on both of them.'

A small smile lifted the corners of Jay's mouth. A dry, know-all smile with a hint of challenge.

'Exactly.'

Damn, thought Nadia with resignation. She'd walked right into that.

'This one's definitely my favourite,' said Annie. 'Look at the expressions—don't you just love the little boy hiding under the table?'

The evening was turning out to be far less intimidating than Annie had feared. Everyone was cheerful and friendly, and the paintings meant there was always something to talk about. Especially where Clare's pictures were concerned, each with its own cast of characters and a story to tell.

The man she'd been chatting with glanced at the brochure in his hand. 'Clare Kinsella. She's a clever girl, I'll say that for her.'

'She is.' Annie nodded in agreement as James reappeared with a fresh drink for her, and said, 'Oh, thanks, darling.' Then she blushed, because she'd never actually called him darling before. It had just popped out.

'Dad, Dad.' Behind James, Clare tugged his arm. 'Three paintings sold already, isn't that amazing? And an agent's offered to represent me in New York!'

The man next to Annie said, 'Sorry, I didn't realise.' Genially he added, 'You must be incredibly proud of your daughter.'

Before Annie could react, Clare had swung round. 'Oh, please,' Clare half-laughed in disbelief, 'you have to be kidding. You didn't seriously think she was my mother!'

'Sorry.' The man blinked, taken aback by her vehement reaction.

'I mean, do we even *look* alike?' Clare gestured at Annie, with her wavy fair hair, plump curves and mortified expression. 'Apart from anything else, she's not even old enough to be my mother. She just looks it.'

'Clare.' James was apoplectic.

Annie turned and fled out of the gallery.

Into the shocked silence, James said furiously, 'You've gone too far this time.'

'I don't care.' Awash with hormones, Clare defiantly stood her ground. 'She's after you, Dad. I just want her to leave our family alone.'

James's voice was icy. 'Nobody's going to tell me to stop seeing Annie. She's welcome at our house any time and I won't tolerate you speaking to her in that way. In fact,' he concluded, 'I think it's high time you moved out.' James turned and left, following Annie out of the gallery.

'Oh, for God's sake,' Clare sighed under her breath.

'Family tiff,' observed the man who had caused the ruckus.

Irritated, Clare surveyed him. He was incredibly ugly, with the face and neck of a toad. He wore a hideous purple velvet suit with an ultra-shiny gold waistcoat. He was also perspiring freely and the neckline of his emerald-green shirt was damp with sweat. When he stuck out his pudgy hand, she forced herself to shake it. Yurgh, wet.

'Malcolm Carter,' said the toad. 'I like your work.'

Double yurgh, was he leering at her? Clare, who had been leered at by ugly men before, said briskly, 'Well, I should be mingling.' Honestly, she'd gone to all the trouble of ensuring that only the right people received her invitations; clearly the other exhibitors hadn't been so fussy.

Malcolm blinked. 'You could always mingle with me. Speak to me nicely and I might buy something.'

What a creep. Clare wondered whatever possessed a middle-aged man to put on a purple velvet suit and think he looked good in it.

'Look, I'd love to stay, but I need to see that man over there.' Vaguely she indicated Jay.

Groping inside his jacket, Malcolm pulled out a card. 'Here, keep this anyway. We should get together soon. Dinner maybe, next week.'

'Absolutely.' Clare flashed her most insincere busy-artist smile, the one involving almost more teeth than she possessed. 'Bye!'

'New boyfriend?' said Jay.

'You're so funny. I just had to get away from him.' Clare shuddered at the thought of being snogged by Mr Toad and his repulsive toad-like tongue. 'So, are you going to buy one of my paintings? Go on, you know you want to.' Rolling her eyes, she said mournfully, 'I'm going to need every penny I can scrape together.'

'Nadia told me. How are you feeling?'

Clare hesitated. To be honest, now that the initial shock had worn off, the prospect of a baby was no longer as horrifying as it had been. She had bought herself a book entitled *You And Your Baby*, and had even felt quite maternal towards the diagrams of foetuses at different stages of development, even though most of them looked like E.T. It was all very new and strange, yet at the same time curiously moving . . .

Except this wasn't the image she wanted to project tonight.

'Pretty crappy.' Clare shrugged bravely. 'But selling more pictures would definitely cheer me up.'

'I'm not going back in there,' said Annie, 'so don't even waste your breath if that's why you've come after me.'

'Don't be daft.' James had found her finally, waiting at the bus stop opposite the church. She was dry-eyed but trembling and clearly upset.

'She really doesn't like me. Well, I don't like her either. I'm sorry, James, but that's it. Your daughter is a spiteful cow. And here's my bus, so—'

'You're not getting on the bus. I'm taking you home,' James said firmly. 'Clare's gone too far. I've told her she has to move out.'

The bus trundled to a halt, the doors swishing open.

'She'll still be your daughter,' said Annie. 'And I'm catching this bus.'

'No, you aren't.'

The driver, watching the exchange with interest, said, 'Getting on?'

'Yes.' Annie attempted to wrench free from James's grasp.

'No,' said James.

They glared at each other.

The bus driver, who had young children, said with exaggerated patience, 'Right, I'm going to count to three. One . . . two . . .'

'Let me *go*,' Annie panted.

'I'm never going to let you go.' Without even realising what was about to come out of his mouth, James added, 'I love you.'

'. . . three,' concluded the driver, and the doors swished shut.

'There's no point,' said Annie, scrabbling in her pocket for a tissue as tears began to leak from her eyes. 'It's never going to work. Clare wants me out of your life and she's not going to stop until she gets her way.'

'That's not going to happen,' James insisted. 'I won't *let* it happen. Come on.' James took her firmly by the hand and led her to his car.

Ten minutes later they reached Annie's cottage. The sun was setting now. The look of sadness on Annie's face clutched at James's heart.

'I don't think we should see each other any more,' she said quietly. 'It's too difficult, too . . . complicated. Easier to end it now, before—'

'No, listen to me.' Vehemently, James shook his head. 'I love you. And I want us to be together, more than anything. You're the best thing that's *ever* happened to me.'

'Don't, please don't.' Annie rubbed at her brimming eyes with the scrumpled damp tissue.

'Let's go inside.' James climbed out of the car, gazing pointedly at a nosy neighbour peering out of her bedroom window. The moment Annie had managed to fit her key into the lock, he bundled her over the threshold and kissed her, hard.

'You're not making things easy for me,' Annie protested, when she was free to speak again. 'I'm only trying to do the sensible thing.'

'Bugger being sensible,' declared James, who had spent the last forty-odd years being sensible and now couldn't for the life of him imagine why. 'I'm not letting you go and that's that.'

Annie couldn't speak. James had just told her that he loved her. Theirs had been a ridiculously chaste romance to date. All they had exchanged so far had been kisses. She had been grateful. Young people these days might leap into bed with each other at the drop of a G-string, but she had never been able to do that. Love was important to her. And now she was ready to take their relationship further.

Except what was the point, when the relationship was doomed?

'James. Please.' Falteringly, she tried to explain. 'I've seen this happen before. If the children aren't happy, no one can be. The family just gets torn apart and everyone ends up miserable.'

'I love you,' murmured James. *Third* time, oh God, he must really mean it. 'I want to be with you,' he went on.

Annie melted; how was it possible to feel so loved and so unhappy at the same time? It was hopeless, a no-win situation. And James wasn't helping, kissing her neck like that. The thin strap of her turquoise dress slid down and Annie shakily exhaled, each kiss setting her skin on fire.

Oh, who was she kidding? Of course she wasn't unhappy.

'Not fair,' she whispered, trembling with lust and anticipation as the second strap slipped off.

'Just trying to cheer you up.' James smiled and pulled her closer. Hmm, he was definitely managing that.

Annie gave up and kissed him back.

'Only if you want to,' he added. Dear James, so gentle and diffident, as considerate of her feelings as ever.

'I want to,' Annie solemnly assured him. Leading him towards the stairs, she added with a mischievous smile, 'In fact, I insist on it.'

'I don't know what's happened to Dad and Annie.' Nadia was puzzled. 'They've vanished. I hope nothing's wrong.'

'Probably just got bored.' Clare shrugged. 'God, what a bloody waste of an evening this has been.'

It was nine o'clock, and everyone was starting to leave.

'Don't say that. It hasn't.'

Truculently, Clare snapped, 'Of course it has. Total disaster. I sold three paintings, that's all. *Three*, for crying out loud. And your so-called friend was a fat lot of use.' Her gaze narrowed as Jay headed towards them.

'Just came to say goodbye,' he cheerfully announced. 'Great show.'

'Thanks so much for coming,' said Clare. 'I'm so glad you enjoyed yourself. Even if you didn't buy a single painting. Still, at least you got some free drinks out of it, that's the important thing.'

'Look, I'm not going to buy a picture I only *quite* like.' Refusing to rise to the bait, Jay said reasonably, 'I'd rather wait. Maybe we could talk about a commission. Not now, obviously . . .' He indicated his watch.

'Oh, *obviously* not now. We're all *far* too busy. In fact you'll have to excuse me, I think Thomas wants a word.' Clare turned and stalked off.

'Oh dear,' said Jay. 'Not happy. But I'm not buying something just because I feel sorry for her. That would be the ultimate insult.'

Nadia sighed. He was right.

'See you tomorrow.' Jay turned to leave. Over his shoulder he added, 'At least Robbie's brother didn't turn up.'

Nadia made her way over to the desk where Thomas Harrington was talking to Clare. Lurking next to Thomas was the short plump man in the purple velvet suit.

'Great news,' Thomas exclaimed, beaming at Nadia. 'Clare's just sold two more paintings! We have a collector here with a truly discerning eye! Have you met Malcolm Carter, Nadia? Malcolm, this is Clare's sister.'

'How d'you do? Clare has a great talent. I'm just inviting her to dinner,' Malcolm told Nadia. 'I'd like to discuss her plans for the future.'

Clare's tightly clenched jaw said it all. Nadia guessed exactly what was going through her head. It was school discos all over again, being violently self-conscious and aware of the fact that the slow music had started and everyone was paired up but you. Then, lumbering towards you with a determined glint in his eye, comes the ugliest boy in the school . . .

Actually, that was me, Nadia realised. She doubted it had ever happened to Clare.

'I've just bought two of your paintings,' Malcolm pointed out. 'So how about Thursday?' Malcolm was nothing if not persistent.

'Thursday. Um . . .'

'Or Friday. Or Wednesday. Whichever night suits you best.'

'D'you know what I really hate?' Clare demanded. 'I really hate it that those other two exhibiting artists sold more than me. If you bought another painting, I'd be level with Phil.' Perkily, she beamed at Malcolm. 'So how about it? And we'll have dinner any night you like.'

Nadia squirmed; sometimes, Clare was beyond belief.

Malcolm studied Clare for several seconds without speaking. Then he smiled, and it occurred to Nadia that he was actually a lot shrewder than Clare was giving him credit for.

'You drive a hard bargain. I hope you're worth it.'

'Of course I am.' Her expression was serene. 'So, which painting?'

He turned and pointed. 'The cinema queue.'

'I love that one, Great choice,' enthused Thomas Harrington, still scarcely able to believe that Clare's audacious demand had been met.

Malcolm Carter handed his card over to Thomas. When the transaction had been concluded, he shook Clare's hand. 'It's a pleasure doing business with you. I'll see you on Thursday. Eight o'clock at my house.'

Clare smiled. 'And I'm sure you won't mind if I bring my sister along.'

Oh great, thought Nadia, drag me into it.

Malcolm inclined his head and said pleasantly, 'I'd be delighted. Actually'—he turned to Nadia—'I believe you know my brother, Robbie.'

'Trust you to make things complicated,' murmured Annie, rolling over onto her side in bed. Her whole body was tingling and alive. The last hour had been, without question, the most perfect of her entire life.

'I'm not letting you go.' To prove it, James's arms tightened round her. 'Nothing's going to come between us. I just won't let it happen.'

The Clare problem was still there. It wasn't going to go away.

'We'll still see each other,' she told James. 'But I don't want to see Clare. I'd rather just keep out of her way. You can visit me here,' she said with a smile. 'I'll be your mistress.'

'I'm single. You're single. We shouldn't need to sneak around.'

'Come on. It'll be fun.' Playfully, Annie tweaked one of his dark chest hairs. 'If you ask me, having to sneak around is what keeps affairs going. It's the excitement factor. You don't have a chance to get bored.'

'I'm never going to get bored with you.' James kissed her. 'That's a promise. I love you. Did I mention that?'

'May have done. I wasn't really paying attention.' Annie cupped his dear face in her hands; how could she have thought, even for a second, that giving up James was an option?

Malcolm Carter lived in a modern apartment in Capricorn Quay on Bristol's waterfront. The third-floor apartment overlooked the harbour. Having welcomed them into his home, Malcolm had left Nadia and Clare out on the balcony with drinks while he put the finishing touches to dinner.

'Just be nice to him,' Nadia warned now.

'He gives me the creeps. And I'm not even hungry. We don't need to be here.' Clare was truculent. 'He's bought the paintings.'

'At least be polite. He might buy more if you don't antagonise him.'

'He looks like a toad. And he fancies me. Ugh,' said Clare with a shudder of disgust.

'Dinner's ready, girls.' Malcolm appeared on the balcony and Nadia prayed he hadn't overheard. 'If you'd like to come on through.'

The glass dining table was laden with food. Around the walls,

Malcolm's art collection was displayed. No expert, Nadia nevertheless recognised a couple of big names.

'This salmon mousse is fantastic.' Nadia ate with enthusiasm. 'And I *love* that painting.'

'Beryl Cook. I started buying her stuff fifteen years ago. Cost twenty times that now.' Malcolm was wearing a shiny lime-green shirt today, and tight magenta trousers. Proudly, he added, 'I have an eye.'

For art, maybe. Nadia thought it was a shame it didn't extend to his wardrobe. Nevertheless, she was impressed.

'And you think Clare could sell like that?' This was exciting!

'Possibly. We'll have to see how she goes. Some of that work she did for the exhibition was dashed off in too much of a rush.' Malcolm turned his attention to Clare. 'That's why they didn't sell.'

'How kind of you to point that out,' Clare drawled.

Nadia kicked her. 'It's true. You *were* churning them out.'

'Everyone finished? Let me have your plates.' Malcolm rose.

'Patronising git,' Clare muttered while he was out in the kitchen.

'He's trying to help you,' Nadia hissed back.

'Here we go!' Emerging from the kitchen with a steaming casserole dish, Malcolm announced, 'It's a lamb tagine. Speciality of the house.'

Clare clutched her stomach. She shook her head and said, 'I'm sorry, I'm going to have to go home.'

Nadia stared at her. This was Clare all over, it epitomised her total selfishness. If she wasn't happy with a situation, any excuse would do to get her out of it. That she was inconveniencing anyone else wouldn't even occur to her.

'You can't go,' said Nadia.

'I need to. I feel really ill. Sorry.' Clare was getting to her feet. 'I just couldn't eat a thing. Nadia, you have to drive me home now.'

'It's fine.' Malcolm nodded at Nadia. 'It's not her fault if she's ill.'

If being the operative word, Nadia thought savagely.

'Your lovely food,' Nadia apologised. 'After all the trouble you went to.'

'I didn't. The caterers delivered it. Hope you feel better soon,' Malcolm called after Clare as she rushed from the flat.

'I'm really sorry,' Nadia told Malcolm.

'It's OK.' His face creased into a rueful toad-like smile. 'By the way, your sister was wrong about one thing. I don't fancy her. I'm gay.'

'Blast,' said James, putting down the phone and coming into the kitchen. Annie was making the sauce to go with their steaks. 'That was New York. They need some papers faxed through urgently. They're at the office. I'm going to have to go in.' James paused. 'What d'you want to do?'

Breaking into a smile, Annie realised that this was why she loved him. One of the many reasons, anyway. He was so considerate.

'I'm fine. I'll carry on getting dinner ready. How long will you be?'

'Thirty minutes. Shouldn't take more than that. Are you sure?'

Annie kissed him lingeringly on the mouth. With everyone else out for the evening, she'd been persuaded to come to the house tonight, to watch the latest Bond film just out on DVD. They were quite safe, James had assured her. No Clare. And it actually felt deliciously illicit.

'Absolutely sure. By the time you get back I'll have dinner ready.'

'You're unbelievable,' Nadia said furiously. 'That poor man.'

'Oh, stop going on. Anyway, I *do* feel ill. I've got a stomach ache.'

'Bullshit.' Nadia gripped the steering wheel. Clare had always been the same, the world's biggest hypochondriac.

'I have. It really hurts!'

'Probably because you ate a pound of grapes last night. Right, we're home.' Nadia pointedly left the engine running. 'Bye.'

Clare looked at her. 'Where are you going?'

'I'm going to catch up with some friends at the Comedy Club.' The way Clare hesitated meant that Nadia knew, just *knew*, she was about to ask if she could come along too. 'And no,' Nadia said bluntly, before Clare had a chance to open her mouth, 'you're not coming with me. You can stay at home and go to bed. That's what sick people do.'

Clare watched the car disappear. She'd been about to ask Nadia to stay with her, because she did actually feel unwell, despite having exaggerated the symptoms in order to get out of creepy Malcolm's flat. She did have a kind of stomach ache, more of a rumbling gripey sensation than actual pain. Experiencing it again now, Clare turned towards the house. So what if she had eaten a lot of grapes yesterday? The *You And Your Baby* book had said that food cravings began at around six weeks' gestation. She felt inordinately proud. Imagine, yesterday she'd experienced her first proper pregnancy craving.

Letting herself into the house, Clare was expecting it to be empty. Miriam and Edward had gone to the theatre in Bath. Tilly was out with Cal. And James's dark blue Jaguar was missing from the driveway. But there was a smell of cooking in the air.

Ouch, stomach. That *did* hurt.

'Did you forget the office keys? *Oh.*' Annie stopped abruptly in the kitchen doorway. She was wearing an apron and clutching a whisk.

Brilliant, thought Clare. Just what I need. She surveyed Annie with contempt. 'Cooking dinner. How cosy. Have you moved in and nobody remembered to tell me?'

Recovering from her initial shock, Annie stood her ground. 'I only came here this evening because your father told me you were out.'

'Really? Well, now I'm back.' Doggedly ignoring the uncomfortable sensation in her stomach, Clare stalked past her into the kitchen. 'I do still live here, but I'm looking for another place just as fast as I can. Bet you can't wait,' she added, pouring herself a glass of water from the bottle in the fridge.

Annie deliberately turned her back on James's nightmare daughter and began to stir the pan of sauce on the stove. Clare took the hint and stalked out of the kitchen. Shaking slightly, Annie heard her stomp up the stairs. Then the bathroom door slammed shut.

Moments later the hairs on the back of Annie's neck rose as a high-pitched shriek rang out upstairs.

Annie froze. God, what now? Then she heard another noise, less of a shriek, more of a groan. Alarmed, she rushed out to the hall and called out, 'Are you OK?'

No reply.

Then Annie head a low-pitched moan, like the sound of an animal in pain. Racing up the stairs, she hammered on the bathroom door.

'Clare? What's wrong?'

Still nothing. By this time truly terrified, Annie beat the door again. 'Clare, please. Can you hear me?'

Moments later, to her intense relief, the door was finally unlocked.

The moment Annie saw Clare's ghostly pallor and distraught expression, she knew what had happened.

'I'm bleeding,' Clare whispered, cradling her stomach. 'Oh God, this can't be happening . . . I don't want to lose the baby . . .' She slumped against the wall. Annie caught her.

'OK, come on, let's get you into bed. Which is your room?'

Helplessly, Clare nodded in the direction of the door at the far end of the landing. Together they made their way slowly towards it. Annie helped Clare onto the bed.

'Let me call the doctor.' Annie straightened up, but Clare's hand gripped her wrist.

'Don't leave me. Please don't leave me on my own. I'm sorry I was so horrible to you. But . . . I'm so scared. I don't want to lose my baby.' Tears rolled down her cheek.

Having finally managed to extricate herself, Annie was back moments later with the phone. The NHS Direct adviser told her to keep Clare in bed and monitor the situation. Tomorrow morning she should see her doctor. Basically, there was nothing else that could be done. If miscarriage was going to happen, it would.

'Oh God,' Clare groaned, in despair. 'I just can't believe it. Three weeks ago I was crying because I didn't want to be pregnant. And now here I am, crying because I don't want to lose it.'

Feeling sorry for Clare had until tonight been something Annie would have put on a par with bumping into Elvis in Asda. Now, she simply gathered the girl into her arms and let her sob.

'Thanks. You're being really kind,' Clare gulped, some time later. 'I've been such a cow. I didn't want you taking Dad away from us, and I didn't want anyone trying to be our stepmother.'

'I wasn't planning on doing either of those things,' said Annie.

'Well, I'm sorry.'

'That'll be your dad.' Annie rose to her feet as the front door slammed downstairs. 'Let me speak to him.'

Two minutes later James burst into the bedroom, his face white and strained. Hugging Clare, he said, 'Oh, sweetheart. I'm so sorry. Maybe it just wasn't meant to be.'

'I know.' Deep down, Clare did know that. 'Dad? Annie's been really great.'

'She *is* really great.' James stroked his daughter's tousled hair.

Clare nodded. 'When you've finished eating, could she come up here and sit with me?'

'I'm sure she will, if that's what you want.'

The house in Clarence Gardens was finished at last and on the market. Inside, following the departure of the decorators yesterday, the smell of fresh paint lingered. The windows gleamed and the official For Sale sign had gone up.

Nadia was outside watering when Andy Chapman, the estate agent, arrived at midday with the first potential buyers. Nadia was still busy drenching the parched nicotianas when everyone appeared on the sunbaked terrace.

'Well, this is just charming.' The wife turned to her portly husband. 'Isn't it, Gerald? I can just see us sitting out here.' To Andy she added, 'It's been very well designed.'

'Nadia designed the garden,' Andy explained.

'You mean you did all this yourself? By heck, and you're only a slip of a thing,' the husband exclaimed. This was what was so heavenly about men who weighed at least twenty stone, Nadia decided. As far as they were concerned, anyone under ten stone counted as a slip of a thing. 'Is she included in the price?' Guffawing at his own joke, Gerald turned back to Nadia. 'Tell you what, love, we could keep you here, in the spare bedroom, in exchange for keeping the garden up to scratch.'

'Any time,' Nadia joked back. 'I'd live here like a shot.'

Too late, she saw the wife give her husband an anxious nudge, terrified that he may be taken up on it.

'I'd like to see the kitchen again,' the woman announced to Andy, before Nadia could start haggling over terms and conditions.

'Seemed pretty keen,' Andy observed ten minutes later, having despatched the potential buyers and come back out onto the terrace for a cigarette. 'Could be promising. Anyway, next one's due any minute.'

'He's already here,' said Jay, emerging through the French windows onto the terrace with Laurie in his wake.

Nadia's fingers tightened round the garden hose she was in the process of winding up.

'Mr Welch. Right on time. *Excellent*,' Andy declared, stepping forward to shake Laurie's hand with enthusiasm.

The expression on Jay's face was unreadable. Laurie grinned at Nadia. 'No need to look so shocked. I can buy it if I want, can't I?'

Only taken aback for a millisecond. Andy said, 'You two know each other?'

'I've asked Nadia to marry me,' Laurie replied easily. 'Just trying to get her to make up her mind.'

Andy could barely contain his delight. 'And what were you saying not ten minutes ago? That you'd live here like a shot? Sounds like a perfect arrangement to me.'

There was a knot in Nadia's stomach. Laurie and her together. It had been her dream for years. Yet suddenly she was no longer so sure . . .

'Nad? Why don't we take a look round?'

'You've already seen the house,' she told Laurie coolly.

'Not since it's been finished. Come on.' As he reached for her hand, Nadia noticed the absence of the zing of electricity she'd come to associate with his touch.

Jay's phone beeped. He glanced briefly at the text message on the screen and snapped it shut.

'Right, I'll leave you to it. Have to go.'

'You took Malcolm's advice on board then.' Nadia studied the fairground scene taking shape on the canvas. 'This is tons better.'

Clare, painting in the garden, glanced over her shoulder at Nadia. She knew it was better too. Maybe turning into a nicer person was making her a better artist. She'd even heard herself admiring Annie's new dress yesterday.

'Thomas at the gallery said Malcolm's pretty well-respected on the art scene,' Clare admitted. 'He reckons any advice Malcolm offers, I should take.' Quickly she added, 'But he still looks like a fat toad,' because there was such a thing as being *too* nice.

'So. How are you feeling?' Collapsing onto the grass, Nadia popped the tab on a can of lager and offered up the other one.

'Fine.' As she opened the can, Clare realised that it was true. Let's face it, while having the miscarriage hadn't been nice, maybe it wasn't a tragedy for this to have happened.

'I'm twenty-three,' she told Nadia. 'I want children one day. But I'd much rather have them with someone who isn't a complete arsehole.'

'Absolutely.' Nadia nodded in agreement. 'And you couldn't find anyone more arseholey than Piers. You're well out of it.' Wriggling out of her T-shirt, Nadia flopped down in suncatcher mode in her lime-green lace bra and white shorts.

'Crikey, what's up with Tilly?' Clare said, as Tilly, looking shell-shocked, headed across the lawn towards them.

Nadia patted the grass next to her. 'Tilly, sit down. Are you OK?' She saw that Tilly was trembling. 'Who were you talking to on the phone when I came through?'

'Mum.'

Typical. What was Leonie up to now?

Aloud, Nadia said, 'And?'

'She wants me to go and live with her in Brighton. For good.'

It wasn't so much the unexpectedness of the invitation that had Nadia lost for words, it was the look on Tilly's face. Were those tears of horror swimming in Tilly's huge blue eyes? Or tears of joy?

'This is fantastic,' Nadia breathed as the auctioneer called the assembled crowd to attention. 'How can everyone else look so calm? What if I scratch my ear and buy a house by mistake?'

'Just don't scratch your ear,' Jay murmured.

'But I might not be able to help it! I'm feeling very twitchy. And itchy.'

'You've probably got fleas,' whispered Jay. Pulling Nadia in front of him, he held both her hands firmly down at her sides.

Phew, that was exciting. She felt his breath on the back of her neck, and the heat from his body against her spine. Even better was the knowledge that, in all honesty, there wasn't any need for him to be doing this, because they both knew she wouldn't really accidentally bid for a house.

The attraction was still there, Nadia thought happily. On both sides. And maybe the time had come at last to do something about it.

'Now we come to Lot Seven,' said the auctioneer, and Nadia felt her heart break into a clumsy gallop, because this was the one Jay was after.

'Highcliffe House. Just off the Downs in Sneyd Park,' the auctioneer continued. 'A detached Georgian property requiring refurbishment but retaining many original features. I'll start the bidding at two hundred . . . two twenty . . . two forty . . . two sixty . . .'

Overwhelmed by the speed of the bidding, Nadia's head swivelled around the room as she attempted to pick out the other bidders. God knows how the auctioneer managed it; some of them were dipping their heads by no more than a fraction of an inch. Close behind her, she knew Jay was doing the same.

'Sold,' said the auctioneer, with a delicate tap of his gavel. 'For five hundred thousand pounds.'

'Who got it?' Nadia twisted round, her heart in her mouth.

'I did,' said Jay. His mouth twitched. 'I always get what I want. Well, almost always.'

Nadia's stomach did an excited bunny-hop.

'Mr Tiernan?' The auctioneer raised his eyebrows, indicating that Jay should make his way over to the desk by the entrance.

'Fancy a drink when I'm done?' Jay said lightly.

Fancy a drink? She could do with a whole vineyard.

'Why not?' Nadia smiled.

Oh crikey, it was looking like make-your-mind-up time.

Jay took her to Crosby's, a busy, buzzy bar on Whiteladies Road in Clifton. He ordered a bottle of Veuve Clicquot to celebrate.

'Here's to the new project,' he said, raising his glass. 'Yours too.'

Nadia chinked glasses with him. 'My next garden.'

Jay's plan was to turn Highcliffe House into four flats and the surrounding grounds into a communal garden. It was larger than the one she'd just finished, but in less of a mess than Clarence Gardens.

'Five hundred thousand pounds,' marvelled Nadia. 'That's a lot.'

'I'd have gone up to five forty.'

Gosh. He'd probably sell the apartments for over £300,000 apiece. Speculate to accumulate and all that. You must need nerves of steel in Jay's business, not to mention the ability to keep a cool head. And he was cool, thought Nadia. It was an attractive quality in a man. Then again, having a body like his didn't do any harm. Or eyes like that. Or a wicked smile so dangerous it should definitely be made illegal—

'What?' said Jay. Oh God, and here he was, doing it again.

'Just wondered where you got your shirt,' Nadia lied. 'It's my dad's birthday soon. He might like something like that.'

'Try again.'

'What?'

'The truth, this time.'

'OK, he probably wouldn't like it but I'm desperate to liven him up.'

'Come on, you know what I'm talking about,' said Jay, and Nadia's mouth went dry.

Oh, she did, she did.

Then his mobile burst into life.

Taking a gulp of champagne, Nadia thought, don't answer it.

Less than two minutes later she thought, *shit*.

Jay slid the phone back into his pocket. 'That was Belinda's mother. Belinda's having the baby.'

Nadia nodded. She'd already heard him say, 'I'm setting off now. I'll be there by ten.' Which was, frankly, not what she wanted to happen.

'You're going down to Dorset?'

'I promised Belinda I would,' Jay said evenly. No longer smiling, it was clear that the birth of his brother's child would be an emotional, bittersweet experience.

'Just as well you had time for only one glass.'

'I'm sorry.' Jay's mouth twitched. 'This seems to keep happening, doesn't it? If Anthony was still alive, I'd have something to say to him about his timing.'

Jangling his keys, Jay said, 'Better make a move. I'll drop you home.'

Nadia gave herself a brisk mental shake. 'No need, I'll be fine.' It was only eight o'clock, still warm and sunny outside. It would be an easy walk back across the Downs.

'Sure?'

'Absolutely.' She did her best to breathe normally as Jay dropped a fleeting goodbye kiss on her cheek.

He pulled out his sunglasses. 'I'm going to be an uncle.'

'You'll have to set a good example,' said Nadia. 'Think only pure thoughts, do only good things.'

'How dare you?' Jay's dark eyelashes cast shadows on his razor-sharp cheekbones as he smiled briefly down at her. 'You know perfectly well I've never had a pure thought in my life.'

Chapter Nine

TILLY WAS IN BED trying to work through her muddled train of thoughts. She'd never been more confused in her life.

It was eleven o'clock in the morning. Outside her bedroom window the sun blazed down; it was another glorious day. Everyone else had gone out, giving her the peace and quiet she needed to think things through. She was utterly torn. She may love her mother, but she didn't want to live with her. This was her home. She was happy here, happy with her school and her friends—especially Cal—and her family.

But was her family happy with her? They weren't even really her family. James and Miriam may have brought her up, but she wasn't related to them. And what if they didn't love her quite as much as she'd always imagined? What if they were secretly hoping she *would* go and live with her mother? Tilly blinked back tears. Of course, they hadn't said as much. They never would. But they had their own lives to lead. James had Annie now, and they were so happy together. As for Miriam, surely she'd done more than her share over the years.

Hot tears dripped down Tilly's cheeks. When she'd told her family about Leonie's plan, she had expected them to react with horror and dismay. She'd waited for Miriam to announce, 'What absolute nonsense! Darling, of *course* you're not moving to Brighton, you're staying here with us where you belong.' But it hadn't happened like that. Taking the news calmly Miriam had stressed that it was her decision. If she wanted to live with Leonie, then that was absolutely fine. Not that they wanted to lose her, because of course they'd all miss her dreadfully, but at the same time Leonie was her mother. They would understand. Hugging her, James had said much the same thing. So had Nadia and Clare, which had come as the biggest shock of all.

Tilly rubbed her eyes. Well, basically, she didn't have a lot of choice. Everyone might be telling her she did, but it wasn't actually true. Like it or not, she was going to have to move to Brighton and live with Leonie, Brian and Tamsin. New school, new people.

Pushing back the duvet, Tilly stumbled out of bed. She still had a couple of hours to kill before meeting Cal at two thirty. Tomorrow,

Leonie was driving up to talk to Miriam and James about the move and to take Tilly back with her for a few days. It would make sense to get her things together now.

Tilly crammed jeans, trainers, various tops and underwear into her sports bag. Having closed the bag with difficulty, Tilly promptly opened it again, stuffed in a nightie and and set to wrestling with the zip again.

Her nightie proved to be the straw that broke the camel's back.

'Oh bum.' Tilly gazed in dismay at the broken zip.

The loft was a bit of a memory lane. Thankful that there were no Indiana Jones-style cobwebs, Tilly eased her way past her own cot, dismantled now and propped against the water tank. James could never bear to throw anything away. He'd lugged her old tricycle up here, and the musical mobile that had hung in her bedroom for years.

Squeezing between piled-up crates of gramophone records and old books—honestly, had James never heard of Oxfam?—she spotted Miriam's cases over in the far corner.

There, that one would do. Miriam wouldn't mind. Reaching for the squashy tan leather case, she hauled it over the others then made her way back towards the trapdoor.

Back in her own room, Tilly unzipped the case.

But how strange. Why on earth would Miriam have left a videotape in there? Surely it couldn't be one of those rude ones? Of course it couldn't. Good grief, Miriam would never have anything to do with mucky videos. Her all-time favourite film was *Casablanca*. In fact, this probably was a copy of *Casablanca*.

Except it wasn't.

Idle curiosity had got the better of Tilly and now she was wishing she'd never gone up into the loft in the first place.

Rocking backwards and forwards with her arms wrapped tightly round her ribs, Tilly watched the flickering black and white images on the screen and wondered if she was going completely mad.

How could she be seeing what she was seeing on this video? It was just bizarre. Tilly knew what Robert Kinsella, Miriam's husband and James's father, looked like. There were photographs of him dotted around the house. This made no sense at all.

Because the man she was watching certainly wasn't Robert Kinsella.

Jay phoned Nadia the following morning.

'Hi,' she said happily. 'How are you?'

'Shattered. It's hard work, you know, this giving birth business.'

'You poor thing, I hope you had loads of painkillers.'

'Gas and air. Pethidine. I passed on the epidural.'

'Well done you. And?'

'A boy. Daniel Anthony. Eight pounds six ounces, fit and healthy, blue eyes, dark hair.' Jay paused. 'And absolutely huge balls.'

Nadia laughed. She couldn't help it, he sounded so perplexed.

'He'll grow into them. How's Belinda?'

'Emotional. Happy. She swears he's the image of Anthony, but you know what newborn babies are like. They all just look red and squashed to me. Anyway, I'll be home this evening. If you're free, do you fancy dinner?'

'Could do.' Nadia flushed with pleasure.

'Look, I don't know what time I'll be back, so I'll give you a ring.'

Leonie would be arriving any minute now. Feeling like a dog bracing itself for a visit from the vet, Tilly lugged her bag downstairs.

'Darling, you can't use that! The zip's broken,' Miriam exclaimed. 'Why don't I pop up to the loft and find you a proper case?'

'I'm fine.' Having returned her grandmother's case, along with the bewildering videotape, to the attic, Tilly had crammed all her stuff back into her old sports bag and fastened it with a sturdy belt.

It was hard to meet Miriam's gaze. Tilly was painfully aware that she had no right to ask prying questions. She was the cuckoo in the Kinsella nest, a cuckoo about to be gently nudged out.

'Oh, sweetheart.' Enfolding Tilly in her scented embrace, Miriam said, 'We'll miss you so much if you decide to go. You do know that, don't you? The house just won't be the same without you.'

That was the thing about Miriam, she was so believable. When she said stuff like this, it sounded as if she really and truly meant it.

'Anyway.' Miriam glanced out of the window as a car came crunching up the gravel drive. 'Sounds as though Leonie's arrived. Do you want to go and meet her, while I get the drinks organised?'

In the kitchen, Edward was already arranging glasses on a tray.

Miriam brushed away a tear. 'Bloody hell, Edward, I can't bear the thought of Tilly going to live with that wretched woman. If I had my way I'd tell Leonie to clear off and never come near us again. But she's Tilly's mother, and if it's what Tilly wants . . . oh, sod it, I know I mustn't influence her, but it's so hard to try and stay impartial. I want to *shoot* Leonie.'

'I know, I know.' Edward put his arms round Miriam. 'But Tilly has to make up her own mind.'

'She's only thirteen!'

'All the more reason why she probably wants to go. And shooting

Leonie really wouldn't help. Tilly might not appreciate the gesture.' Edward had a neuropsychiatrist's sense of humour. He couldn't help it.

Pulling herself together, Miriam took a steadying breath. 'Right, I'll take the tray. Can you bring the rest?'

'*The Mummy Returns*,' murmured Clare as Leonie came sauntering towards them with her arm round Tilly's shoulders. 'Here we go.'

'Now remember what I said,' Miriam warned. 'No slanging matches. It's the last thing Tilly needs.'

'Crikey.' Gasping, Nadia peered into the drink Edward had poured her. 'Any tonic in this gin?'

'We're going to need something to line our stomachs,' said Miriam grimly. 'Edward, there's dolcelatte and ciabatta in the larder. And don't forget the olives.'

For a millisecond Nadia thought Edward was about to tell Miriam to fetch her own bloody olives. But all he said, drily, was, 'Just call me Jeeves.'

'Darlings, here we all are,' Leonie exclaimed, descending on them and kissing her elder daughters. 'Isn't this lovely? I was just telling Tilly how excited Tamsin is. We just can't wait to have her home with us!'

'If she decides she wants to go,' Nadia said evenly, because Tilly was looking like a trapped rabbit.

'Oh, nonsense, of course she wants to. Don't you, darling?' Leonie patted Tilly's arm, then dug into her raffia shoulder bag. 'Here, I've brought some brochures about Tilly's new school. No James?' she added, glancing around the table.

'Dad had a meeting. He'll be here by four.'

Leonie swivelled round on her chair at the sound of the garden gate clicking open. 'Laurie, how heavenly to see you again!' Leaping to her feet, she greeted Laurie with characteristic enthusiasm.

'I just came to tell Dad he's had a call.' As Laurie spoke, Edward returned with a second tray of food. 'A Professor Spitz rang from Boston. He'll phone back in an hour.'

Edward nodded. Ernst Spitz was an old colleague.

'Stay and have a drink, Laurie.' Leonie tugged him down next to her. 'How's that daughter of mine treating you? Has she come to her senses?'

Nadia gritted her teeth. Her mother adored Laurie and couldn't understand why she hadn't taken him back in a flash. Leonie thought that flitting from one man to the next was a completely normal thing to do.

'Still working on her,' said Laurie with an easy grin. 'She's making me wait. It'll happen.'

Nadia felt her shoulders stiffen. Laurie's confidence was annoying too. 'I'm seeing someone else tonight.' Defiantly she took another swig of her drink.

'Jay? Well, good.' Spinning the cap off the vodka, Laurie poured himself a couple of inches and topped it up with orange juice. 'I told you you should. Get him out of your system.'

Leonie said excitedly, 'You mean the one with the dead brother!'

'And more notches on his bedpost than Jack Nicholson,' said Laurie.

'Ah, but that's what makes them so irresistible.' Leonie gave a pleasurable shiver. 'You can't beat a good bad boy.'

Turning to Clare she went on brightly, 'How's that naughty chap of yours? Piers, isn't it?' Leonie was the only one here who didn't know about her brief pregnancy.

'At last.' Miriam sighed with relief as they all heard the front door slam. 'Here's James.'

It's going to be fun, everything's going to be great, Tilly told herself as she headed back up the garden and into the house. Her mother had said so, she kept stressing how marvellous it would be, especially with someone her own age to play with.

'It's just what Tilly needs,' Leonie had explained to James. 'You should see the two of them together, they're as thick as thieves!'

Which, what with Tamsin's shoplifting skills, was actually quite funny, except it scared Tilly rigid. Anyway, look on the bright side. She and Tamsin could talk about teenage girlie stuff together. Plus, Tilly reminded herself, her mother genuinely wanted her there.

Right. Ice cubes.

She was busy clattering ice into a tall glass jug when the doorbell went. Tilly went to answer the front door.

A man she didn't know was standing in the porch.

At least she thought she didn't know him, but there was something distantly familiar about his face.

The visitor had to be around Edward's age, and despite the heat was wearing an expensive-looking suit, dark blue shirt and striped tie.

Clutching the jug of ice cubes to her chest she said warily, 'Hello?'

'Hello there. I'm here to see Miriam Kinsella. Is she around?'

Tilly wondered who he was.

'She is expecting me.' As if sensing her doubt, the man said charmingly, 'Miriam and I are old friends.'

Remembering her manners, Tilly said, 'She's out in the garden.'

She led the way through the house. At the French windows, the man paused. 'There she is,' he murmured, gazing at Miriam. He shook his head in admiration. 'Hasn't changed a bit.'

Out of curiosity, Tilly said, 'When did you last see her?'

He smiled. 'How long since I last saw Miriam? Fifty-two years.'

Blimey. More than half a century. The good old black and white days, marvelled Tilly.

The next moment, prompted by this thought, she realised where she knew him from. Oh, good Lord.

'Come on,' said the man, guiding her forward. 'Time to say hello.'

Miriam glanced up and felt a chill settle around her ribs. Oh no, it couldn't be, it couldn't possibly be.

Miriam's heart felt as if it had been physically wrenched out of her body and plunged into ice-cold water. She'd spent months mentally bracing herself for something like this, but now it was actually happening she knew she was hopelessly unprepared.

'Miriam.' The man standing before her nodded and smiled slightly.

'Charles.' Hideously aware of curious eyes upon her, Miriam held out her hand for him to shake.

Ignoring it, Charles bent and kissed her on each cheek. 'No need to look so terrified. I don't have a gun.'

He had now gained everyone's attention. Miriam pushed back her chair and said, 'Maybe we should talk in private.'

'I'd prefer to do it here.' Charles stood his ground. 'Out in the open, so to speak. I think your family deserve to know, don't you?'

Curtly, Edward said, 'What's this about?'

Miriam's face was white, her knuckles clenched. 'You can't just barge in here—'

'I did tell you I'd be paying a visit. In my last letter, remember?'

Miriam remembered the last letter. She had thrown it into the bin without reading it. Closing her eyes, she shook her head.

'Well,' said Leonie. 'I'm intrigued! Are we going to sit here like this all afternoon or is some kind soul going to put us out of our suspense?'

'My name is Charles Burgess.' The man remained standing. 'Miriam and I were married in 1950.'

James put down his drink. 'Mum? Is this true?'

Miriam nodded.

'Well, that's not so terrible, is it?' said James, wondering what all the drama was about. 'Plenty of people get divorced.' James frowned. 'My parents married in 1952. That's only two years after—'

'Our wedding,' supplied Charles Burgess. 'But that's the thing, you see. We never divorced. Which I'm afraid makes your mother a bigamist.'

A wisp of white thistledown drifted idly over the gathered bottles and glasses. A bee settled briefly on the table, then flew off again.

The silence was abruptly broken by a snort of laughter. 'Sorry, sorry, but this is just too funny for words. Miriam, my mother-in-law, a bigamist! She dumped her husband, upped and left and married someone else! And when you think of all those years of grief Miriam's given *me*.'

'Leonie.' James flashed her a warning glance.

'But it was fifty years ago, so basically who gives a toss?'

'Actually, I give a toss,' said Charles Burgess.

Gazing down at her hands, Miriam saw that they were shaking. Defiantly, she reached for her drink and gulped it down.

'I married Miriam because I loved her,' Charles continued. 'I thought we loved each other. For richer or poorer, until death do us part. When I said those words, I meant them.'

Miriam couldn't look at him; she had meant them too. Meeting Charles Burgess at the age of eighteen had been an all-consuming experience. Everyone else had wanted Charles but she had been the one he'd chosen to marry. The trouble was, the fact that he was no longer single hadn't stopped the other girls chasing him. Particularly beautiful, predatory Pauline Hammond.

Seeing them together that Friday afternoon, Miriam had died inside. There had been rumours before then, of course, endless hints dropped and warnings given. She had done her best to ignore them, but at that moment she'd known the truth, because sometimes you just *did*. This was how it would always be with Charles. A philanderer didn't change his spots. All the old feelings of jealousy surged up now, as caustic and wounding as though they'd never been away.

In less than an hour, Miriam had packed and left.

'I came home from work one day and she was gone,' Charles said now, addressing the assembled group. 'And so had a fair amount of our money. That was below the belt, Miriam.'

'Why was it below the belt?' Miriam bridled. 'We were married. It was our money, not just yours.'

'You destroyed my life,' Charles continued. 'I loved you, Miriam. I couldn't stop looking for you. Everywhere I went, I'd catch a glimpse of a dark-haired girl and think it was you. But it never was. And every time I thought I was getting over you, something would happen to knock me back. Did you enjoy the wedding video, by the way?'

Miriam couldn't speak.

Frowning, James said, 'What video?'

'It's up in the loft.' Tilly's voice was small. 'Hidden in one of the cases.'

Everyone except Miriam turned to stare at Tilly, who shrank down in her chair and examined her bitten fingernails.

'I'm not a crying man,' Charles said evenly, 'but when I sat down and watched that cine film, I cried.'

Miriam looked at him. 'How touching. Did Pauline Hammond cry too?'

'Miriam.' Charles shook his head. 'I never had anything to do with that girl. Either before or after you disappeared. Never.'

Anger rose up in her. 'I saw you, that Friday afternoon. I came to your office and saw you with her. I was watching through the glass door, Charles. You were holding her. You were kissing the top of her head.'

'Because she'd just had a call from the hospital, telling her that her mother was dead. She was distraught,' said Charles Burgess. 'Her mother was hit by a car and killed. I took Pauline to the infirmary. When I got home I would have told you. Except I couldn't, because by then you were gone.'

Miriam couldn't breathe. 'Is that true?'

'I never lied to you then, and I'm not lying now. I spent the next ten years trying to find you,' said Charles. 'And I never stopped loving you. My wife died two years ago,' Charles announced. 'That means we're both free to give it another go. I want you back, Miriam. You loved me once. I can make you love me again.'

'Your wife died,' she echoed. 'So you did divorce me?'

Charles shook his head. 'After seven years, I had you declared dead.'

Heavens, imagine that, thought Miriam. I'm officially dead.

'Look, you can't just turn up like this and say you want her back,' Laurie exploded.

For a split second Miriam was tempted to retort, 'Why not? You did.'

'Miriam isn't free.' Laurie indicated Edward, who didn't react. 'This is my father. He and Miriam are . . . a couple.'

Which wasn't strictly true, thought Miriam with a pang of guilt. Maybe they were a couple emotionally, but not in the physical sense.

Charles Burgess nodded and said, 'Dr Welch, that's right, I saw the photograph of you with Miriam in the paper. Sorry. But Miriam was mine first. The two of you aren't married. If you were,' he added, 'I wouldn't have come.'

'But they're together,' Laurie insisted. 'They have been for years.'

'All the more surprising, then, that they haven't married.'

'That is none of your business,' Laurie angrily retorted. 'Anyway, you're wasting your time. Miriam isn't interested.'

'You don't know that. She might be. All I'm asking for is the chance to find out,' said Charles Burgess. 'I'm staying at the Swallow Royal.

Miriam, I'd like you to join me for dinner this evening. Seven thirty. You owe me that much, at least.'

'And what if she says no?' persisted Laurie.

'I'll go straight to the police. Miriam will be arrested and charged with bigamy and theft. Trust me, I'd make sure the case went to trial,' Charles promised equably, 'and Miriam could end up in prison.'

At long last, Edward spoke. 'Feel free,' he said coolly, causing everyone to stare at him in disbelief. Pushing back his chair and smoothing the front of his shirt, he rose to his feet. 'You're absolutely right. I've been asking her to marry me for years and she's always said no. Looks like I've been wasting my time.'

'Edward,' Miriam gasped, 'that's not true! You can't—'

'On the contrary, I can. Now, if you'll excuse me.'

Leonie showed Charles out of the house.

Unable to face her family, Miriam said, 'We need more gin,' and headed for the kitchen.

Leonie was there already, switching on the kettle.

'Well, this is a turn-up.' Leonie's bright eyes danced. 'You of all people, a bigamist. And a thief!'

'Leonie, please don't.' Miriam's tone was curt, belying the swirl of emotions she was experiencing.

'Not to mention the other business. Poor old Edward, still not having the faintest idea why you won't marry him. Oh God, and did you see the way he pressed his hand to his chest as he stood up? For a second there I thought it was going to happen all over again. First Josephine, then Edward. I mean, ironic or what?'

Close to despair, Miriam snapped, 'Will you keep your voice down?'

'Oh, come on, relax. I can't believe you've never told Edward. I mean, it's not as if you did it on purpose. And he was as much to blame as you.'

The kitchen door swung open. In the doorway stood Laurie and Nadia. All the colour had drained from Nadia's face.

Evenly, Laurie said to Miriam, 'She can't believe you've never told Edward what?'

Nadia had to sit down. She couldn't believe what she was hearing. Aided and abetted by Leonie—and because she no longer had a lot of choice—Miriam was spilling out the whole story. It was no secret that Laurie's parents hadn't had the happiest of marriages. Josephine's only enjoyment in life had come from making Edward miserable, while all the time she had revelled in her status as the wife of an eminent neuropsychiatrist and had flatly refused even to contemplate divorce.

Edward, at the end of his tether, had turned to Miriam for support. Within months they had fallen in love and embarked on a discreet affair.

'But not discreet enough,' Miriam admitted resignedly. 'She found out and called me over to the house. While Edward was at work she confronted me out in the garden. It was awful, she was screaming at me, and calling me terrible names. And because I knew I deserved it, I didn't retaliate, but that only made Josephine more furious. Then . . . oh God, all of a sudden she made this gasping noise and clutched her chest. Then she just slumped to the ground and that was it.' Miriam's dark eyes filled with tears. 'She was dead.' She paused, unable to meet Laurie's narrowed gaze. 'Leonie was visiting. She heard Josephine shouting and came over to see what was going on; she heard everything else too. We rang 999 and I made her promise never to tell anyone about the argument. I didn't want Edward to feel any worse than I knew he already would.'

Nadia was in shock. Laurie's face was utterly expressionless. First James, then Tilly and Clare had by this time joined them in the kitchen and were listening with equal disbelief.

Miriam finally summoned the courage to look at Laurie. 'I'm sorry.'

'I used to respect you,' Laurie told Miriam. He shook his head in disgust. 'What a difference a day makes. And someone had better pay a visit to my father. It doesn't seem fair, somehow, that he should be the last to know.' Another pause. 'Do you want me to tell him exactly how his wife died?'

Miriam closed her eyes and shook her head. 'I'll do it myself.'

'Let's get out of here,' Laurie muttered when Miriam had disappeared over the road and Leonie had borne Tilly off to Brighton.

Nadia clung to the passenger seat as Laurie drove at high speed, rocketing through the narrow lanes. When they pulled up outside a wisteria-clad country hotel on the outskirts of Winterbourne he said, 'Sorry, I can't face going home tonight. Is this OK?'

Nadia nodded and squeezed his hand. Feeling desperately sorry for him, she could only guess at his sense of betrayal.

'I keep picturing it, you know.' He glanced sombrely at Nadia. 'My mother arguing with Miriam. When someone dies, you imagine it happening, you go over and over it in your mind. Now it feels like I have to start all over again.'

'Come on.' Nadia's tone was soothing. 'Let's get you booked in.'

Laurie looked distraught. 'You're not going to leave me here? I could really do with the company. I mean, no funny business.'

Nadia's heart went out to Laurie. How could she abandon him now, after a day like today? She said, 'D'you think they sell toothbrushes?'

'God, I'm shattered. To be honest, all I want to do is sleep.'

This, of course, turned out to be a big lie. What Laurie had really wanted to do was sleep with *her*.

And under the circumstances, Nadia thought some time later when it was all over, how could she have refused?

'See?' Laurie murmured. 'I knew you could make me feel better.'

Then his mouth closed over hers once more, warm and sweetly familiar, and Nadia gave herself up to the sheer pleasure of it. Their bodies fitted together so well, just as they always had done. Making love with Laurie had always been magical.

'What?' said Nadia, realising that he was gazing down at her.

Laurie's green eyes sparkled. 'Aren't you glad we came here now?'

'Are you telling me you deliberately planned this?'

'Of course not.' Vehemently Laurie shook his head, then broke into an unrepentant grin. 'But, OK, I admit it, as soon as we pulled up outside this place it did occur to me that this could be my big chance.'

Nadia smiled too, because that was the thing about Laurie; he'd always been honest.

'And now there are just two things I have to say. Firstly, I love you.' Laurie kissed her again, his gold-blond hair flopping over his forehead. 'And secondly, I'm bloody starving.'

'There's a restaurant downstairs.' Nadia squirmed helplessly as he began to nuzzle the part of her neck where he knew she was ticklish.

'Boring. I wouldn't be allowed to ravish you between courses. I think we're probably safer having dinner up here.'

'Less likelihood of being arrested,' Nadia agreed.

When he'd finished ordering dinner, Laurie gazed soberly at the phone in his hand. 'I should call Dad. But I just can't. Not tonight.'

'Don't then.' Whisking the phone from him, Nadia rapidly punched out her own home number. 'They're all adults, let them sort out their own mess—hi, it's me. Laurie and I are staying at Hutton Hall. He needed to get away for a bit. We'll be back tomorrow, OK? Call me if anything drastic comes up.'

Reaching for the phone, Laurie added, 'But only if it's really drastic. All in all, we'd prefer not to be disturbed.'

At the other end of the line, Clare let out a squeal of delight. 'You finally did it. About bloody time too.'

Laurie grinned. 'I know. Luckily, I was worth waiting for.'

Worth waiting for, oh crikey . . . It had just occurred to Nadia that Jay had said he'd call.

Her phone was in her bag on the dressing table, and switched on. Nadia realised if Jay had called, she would definitely have heard it ringing. Actually, it was just as well he hadn't rung; she'd only have had to turn him down. Leaping out of bed with one man to rush off with another probably wasn't considered good etiquette.

Nadia's phone wasn't in her bag. Wandering out into the garden to clear away the debris of the afternoon's drinks party, Clare heard the familiar chirpy ringtone and spotted the mobile lying under the table.

Clare abandoned the glasses and answered it. 'Hello?'

'At last. I've been leaving messages for the last hour. Why didn't you call me back?'

Recognising the voice, Clare said jauntily, 'Because this isn't Nadia. You're lucky enough to be talking to her beautiful, far more talented sister. Not that you deserve to be,' she went on, 'seeing as you still haven't bought a single one of my dazzling masterpieces.'

'I was thinking about that. We may be able to come to an arrangement.' Jay was sounding cheerful. 'Can I have a word with Nadia?'

'She's not here. All kinds of weird stuff has been happening today, you wouldn't believe it. Anyway, Nadia's gone off with Laurie, to stay in some posh country house hotel. She rang not long ago from their room, and let me tell you, they weren't reading the Gideon Bible. Now, what kind of an arrangement?'

There was a pause. Then Jay said, 'What?'

'You said we could come to an arrangement. Look, I'm not doing anything this evening, so why not come round and we'll talk about it?'

'Well, er . . .'

'Oh, go on,' Clare wheedled. 'I just hate being here on my own. And if you're good, I'll tell you all about Miriam being a bigamist.'

'So there you go,' Clare concluded some time later, having spilled every last bean to Jay Tiernan. 'And she's having dinner with the long-lost husband right now. Another drink?'

'No, thanks. I can't stay long.' As Jay shook his head, Clare wondered why she'd never realised before quite how attractive he was. Except . . . well, she *had*, of course, but you didn't contemplate tangling with anyone your sister might have earmarked for herself.

But now Nadia had chosen Laurie. And Jay Tiernan was gorgeous.

Refilling her own glass, Clare shot him a challenging smile. 'So, what kind of a commission are we talking about?'

'Well, Nadia tells me you do portraits.'

'I do.' Clare nodded with pride.

'My mother arranged for me and Anthony to be painted when we were babies, and I was wondering if you could do the same. My nephew was born this morning. Could you manage that, working from photographs?'

Sensing that he didn't entirely trust her—portrait work was, after all, a particular skill—Clare leapt to her feet. 'Come on, follow me. I'll show you some of my stuff.'

Upstairs in her room, she pulled out sketch pads and thrust them into his arms.

'These are good,' said Jay. 'The only thing is I want it to be a surprise for Belinda, but some people aren't keen on family portraits in oils. I don't want her feeling obliged to hang the bloody thing on the wall simply because she knows it cost a lot of money.' As he spoke, his gaze wandered over to Clare's easel, where the current work-in-progress was drying. 'That's very nice.' Her fairground painting, was, if she said so herself, one of her better ones.

'It's going to be called *Taken For A Ride*.' Assuming a businesslike air, Clare said, 'OK, I have a suggestion. I could do you the portrait in oils or gouache for five hundred pounds, but you get a far better result with a pencil sketch. Why don't we do it that way? Then, if Belinda isn't wild about it she doesn't have to feel guilty, because I'll do the pencil drawing for free.' Triumphantly Clare added, 'That way, you'll have all that lovely money left over to buy one of my fabulous paintings.'

Jay regarded her with amusement. '*Taken For A Ride*?'

'Not at all, I call it a bargain.'

Finally he nodded. 'OK. You've got yourself a deal.'

'You won't be disappointed.' Clare shivered with pleasure as her bare arm not-quite-accidentally brushed against his. Closing the sketch pad and throwing it onto the bed, she said invitingly, 'Shall we celebrate with another drink?'

'Better not. I should be getting back.' Jay smiled.

When they reached the front door, Clare paused. Reaching to open the door, she felt her cropped top ride up to expose even more of her torso. Tugging it back down resulted in a tantalising glimpse of tanned cleavage and fuchsia-pink bra. Clare grinned in apology, then leaned back against the open door and smiled her best temptress's smile up at Jay.

'Well, I'll drop those photos over in the next few days.'

'Pleasure doing business with you.' Tilting her face up to his, Clare gave Jay the perfect opportunity to drop a kiss on her parted lips.

'Tell Nadia I'll call her tomorrow.' Jay skilfully manoeuvred himself past her bare midriff.

The hotel restaurant was the kind of glamorous, sedate place where people murmured to each other and took care not to scrape their cutlery against the plates. The clientele were pretty sedate, too, and elegantly turned out.

Glimpsing her reflection in the mirror-lined walls, Miriam thought how well she and Charles blended in. No one would ever guess why they were here.

'Why are you smiling?' said Charles.

'Oh.' Miriam shook her head. 'It just makes you think, doesn't it? If we look ordinary, can you imagine the kind of secrets this lot must be harbouring?'

Charles put down his fork. 'You've never looked ordinary in your life. You haven't changed a bit.' He paused. 'Miriam, I'm serious about this.' Reaching across the table, Charles seized her hand. 'I know I'm seventy-two with my hair turning grey and my joints starting to play up, but inside here'—he held her palm against the front of his crisp shirt—'it's the same as it ever was. The moment I saw you, my heart beat faster. It did it then, and it's still doing it now. When you disappeared, you made a monumental mistake, and I think you know it.' His expression softened. 'It's those giveaway big brown eyes of yours. You never could hide anything from me.'

'Except myself. And rather a lot of money,' Miriam reminded him, which made Charles shout with laughter and diverted attention away from the fact that what he'd been saying was unnervingly true.

Edward was charming and well-educated, a true gentleman in every way. But he didn't make her feel the way she did being here with Charles. Beneath the classic black Jean Muir silk-knit, her body was fizzing away like a twenty-year-old's.

'Well?' Charles was still holding her hand. 'Am I right?'

'When I left, I did everything I could to put you out of my mind,' Miriam said slowly. 'I was devastated, but I told myself I was better off without you. And I haven't had an unhappy life,' she went on. 'Robert was a wonderful man. I have a terrific family. I know I've given Edward a hard time, but we've been happy too. We really have.'

Well, apart from the bit where his wife found out about us and dropped dead . . . and the fact that in order to punish myself I've never since that day allowed Edward back into my bed.

Charles shook his head. 'It's the future I'm interested in. I want to spend the rest of my life with you.'

Shakily Miriam smiled, though her eyes were suddenly bright with tears. To think that her entire life could have been so different.

'I never stopped loving you,' said Charles Burgess.

Miriam was eighteen again, her heart racing crazily and the butterflies swirling en masse in her stomach. Heavens, poor Charles, what had she done to him? She'd been so convinced that he'd been having an affair with Pauline Hammond that it had never occurred to her that she might have made a terrible, *terrible* mistake. And what was she to do now? Well, Edward would no longer want anything to do with her, that was for sure. Not after today.

'What are you thinking?' said Charles.

Miriam was thinking that maybe she did owe it to Charles to try again. And if they were to try, she would be able to spare her family the shame of her bigamy being exposed.

Her voice breaking with emotion, Miriam whispered, 'It's good to see you again, Charles.'

The lines around his eyes deepened as he broke into a smile. 'My dear. Not half as good as it is to see you.'

'You can't tell me what to do, you're not my mother!'

'I can tell you not to steal money from my purse.'

'God, I hate you!'

The vicious argument between Leonie and Tamsin had carried on like this for some time. Appalled, Tilly had been forced to witness the battle from the sidelines. Finally, Brian had arrived home and frog-marched his daughter to her room.

Twenty minutes later, he had emerged with Tamsin and made her apologise to Leonie. Afterwards, as Leonie had dropped Tilly off at the station, she'd said, 'Never mind, darling, it'll be so much better once you're here. Having you to keep an eye on her will make all the difference.'

Tilly really didn't see how it could. Tamsin had never taken a blind bit of notice of anything she said.

Now, she was arriving back in Bristol to pack up her belongings and say goodbye. On Saturday morning, Leonie would be driving up to collect her. Tilly wondered if anyone would actually miss her. Probably not. They seemed to have more than enough to occupy them just now. The train pulled into Temple Meads station and squealed to a halt. Tilly had made a point of telling Clare what time she'd be getting in but there was no sign that the hint had been taken. Hauling her sports bag over her shoulder, Tilly made her way out of the station and headed for the row of bus stops. It was starting to rain, the grey clouds overhead matching her mood.

'Whaaa!' Tilly shrieked as a pair of hands covered her eyes. Spinning round, she saw Cal grinning at her and threw her arms round him. 'Oh my God, you made me jump! How did you know I was here?'

'Rang the house. Your sister told me which train you'd be on.'

Oh Cal, dearest Cal. She was going to miss him. Terrified that she was about to cry, Tilly beamed at him.

'Come on, let's go back to my place. Are you free?'

'I'm all yours,' Cal teased, and Tilly had to look away hurriedly.

When they reached Latimer Road, everyone was out.

Except Harpo, of course, who greeted Tilly with a ribald, Barbara Windsorish cackle followed by a wolf whistle.

'You've been watching too many *Carry On* films,' Tilly told him.

'Oooh, matron,' squawked Harpo, lovingly nipping her fingers as she fed him a raisin.

'Hey.' Cal moved towards her as Tilly's face abruptly crumpled. 'Don't cry. He didn't mean to hurt you.'

'It's not Harpo.' The dam had burst without warning. Tilly sank to her knees, burying her head in her hands. 'It's just . . . oh God . . . I don't want to leave. I *love* this family. I don't want to move to Brighton.'

Kneeling on the floor next to her, Cal said, 'Come on, you don't have to go if you don't want to. They can't force you to leave. Just tell them how you feel.' Cal gently pushed her fine blonde hair away from her face. 'If you're this upset, they'll let you stay.'

Hopelessly, Tilly shook her head. It was true, but the fact remained that they'd far prefer it if she didn't stay. Anyway, her mum really wanted her to go to Brighton. She couldn't let Leonie down.

Rubbing her eyes, Tilly sniffed loudly and shook her head. 'I'm going.' As she glanced helplessly around the room, she spotted the drinks cabinet. Wasn't that what everyone else did when they were going through a rough time? Maybe it would make her feel better too.

'Let's have a drink.'

Sliding off the sofa, Tilly headed for the glass-fronted cabinet. Taking out a couple of cut-glass tumblers, Tilly handed one to Cal. 'Come on, let's see what's so great about this stuff.'

God, whisky was disgusting. What a con. It burned your mouth and made you choke and tasted absolutely vile. So did cognac. The Tia Maria wasn't much better. Tilly would have given it up as a bad job, but Cal had told her that his mother drank it with milk. This had improved it no end. And the port was pretty good too, nice and sweet and tasting of concentrated raisins.

By eight o'clock, they were really getting into the swing of things.

'I can see why people do this.' Tilly giggled at the way her voice sounded, kind of slurry but precise at the same time. 'I feel better already. My knees have gone funny. Have your knees gone funny?'

'My knees are fine. But my tongue feels like somebody else's tongue. How 'bout you?'

'Mine too. P'raps they swapped when we weren't looking.' Tilly began to giggle helplessly.

The next moment their heads jerked up at the sound of car wheels on gravel.

'Oh shit, someone's home!' In her hurry to hide the empty Cointreau bottle, Tilly sent her half-full tumbler of port flying. Staring in dismay at the broken glass and the spreading stain on the rug, she leapt to her feet. 'They're going to go mental . . . oops, *ouch* . . .'

'Where can we hide?' Cal gazed around helplessly.

'No, no, they'll see you under the sofa.' Giggling, Tilly dragged him out by the ankles. Outside, car doors banged. 'Quick, out through the side door . . . we'll jump over the garden wall . . .'

Jump turned out to be the wrong word. They fumbled, scrambled and finally collapsed over the ivy-covered wall with all the grace of a couple of hippos.

Still, at least the bottles didn't break. Tilly and Cal tucked their stolen bottles—Harvey's Bristol Cream sherry and Taylor's tawny port respectively—under their T-shirts and scurried off down the lane.

By nine o'clock it was dark and the bottles were empty. Tilly, beginning to shiver, realised she was crying again, consumed with misery. If this was what drinking did for you, maybe it wasn't so great after all.

'They hate me,' she sobbed.

Clumsily, Cal patted her hand. 'Course they don't hate you.'

'They can't wait to get rid of me.' Tilly had never felt so lonely and unloved. 'I'm just a nuisance. Where are you going? To be sick again?'

'I don't know.' Cal had wandered over to the edge of the bridge. He took deep breaths and said fretfully, 'I wish it would make up its mind.'

'To be sick or not to be,' proclaimed Tilly, who didn't feel sick at all. Her head was spinning, though. Round and round and round and round, like riding on the waltzers at the fairground. She realised her bladder was full to bursting.

'I can't go home.' Hot tears trickled down Tilly's cheeks. 'They'll shout at me. I wish I was dead.'

'You don't, don't *say* that.' Having decided he wasn't going to be sick after all, Cal stumbled back to her.

'And if I don't find a loo *this minute* I'm going to wet myself.'

Cal pointed to a small bush. 'Go on, I won't look, I promise.'

Tuh, did she look stupid? Staggering to her feet, Tilly ignored the bush and reeled to the end of the bridge. The slope leading down to the railway line below was fenced off, but if she clambered over the fence she could wee in peace, without Cal being able to see or hear her.

Scaling the fence, she landed with a *flumpph* on the other side and crawled to the safety of the wall of the bridge. Awkwardly, Tilly unfastened her shorts and half crouched, half leaned against the bridge.

'Are you OK?' Cal's voice was raised in concern. 'You shouldn't be down there.'

'Don't *fuss*, I'm coming back up now.' Tilly struggled to pull her shorts back up. Her head was still doing its spinny thing, making it hard to regain her balance. One foot slipped on loose rock and the next moment Tilly let out a shriek as she landed agonisingly and awkwardly on her back. And after that she couldn't stop herself falling, rolling down the steep rocky incline, her head bouncing and ricocheting off the ground as she screamed with pain and terror all the way down.

Chapter Ten

NADIA CRASHED through the doors of A&E like a bullet. The phone call from the hospital had given her the fright of her life.

'My sister's here somewhere, she was brought in by ambulance, they found her on a railway track,' she gabbled at the receptionist behind the desk. 'Her name's Tilly Kinsella.'

Recognising the name, a passing nurse said, 'Oh, the little thirteen-year-old? She's having her stomach pumped just now. If you take a seat, someone will be out to speak to you in a few minutes.'

Nadia swung round in horror. 'You mean Tilly took an *overdose*?'

The nurse placed a reassuring hand on Nadia's. 'She'd had rather a lot to drink. The doctors'll come and have a word as soon as they've finished.' The nurse nodded towards the far corner of the waiting room. 'That's her friend over there, the one who came in with her.'

'I'm sorry, I'm so sorry.' Cal flinched as Nadia loomed over him.

White-faced, dishevelled and evidently the worse for wear himself, he wailed, 'I told her not to climb over the fence, but she wouldn't listen. And then she fell, and landed on the track. I managed to pull her off. I had to leave her and run to the nearest house to call an ambulance. I was so scared. I thought she was dead. But the doctor says it's just cuts and bruises, he thinks she'll be OK . . .'

'Cal, Tilly's thirteen. She doesn't drink. How did this happen?'

Fearfully, Cal blinked up at her. 'Tilly wanted to get drunk. She said maybe drinking would make her feel better. She was just so upset. She doesn't want to move to Brighton. She doesn't want to live with her mother and Brian and Tamsin. She wants to stay here with all of you.'

Dismayed, Nadia said, 'Are you sure? So why's she going, then?'

'Because she thinks you want to get rid of her.' Cal dropped his gaze to the floor. 'She thinks she's in the way. A nuisance. She said you all hated her.'

Nadia felt sick. Sick and numb.

The nurse appeared and beckoned to her. 'You can see Tilly now.'

Cal, almost in tears, said, 'I'll wait here.'

The sight of Tilly lying on the narrow bed in the curtained-off cubicle brought a lump to Nadia's throat. Her face was as white as her hospital gown, apart from the bruises and the sizable cut above her left eye. Bending over, Nadia dropped a kiss on Tilly's hot forehead. Tilly opened her eyes and her face promptly crumpled.

'I'm sorry about breaking the glass . . . the mess on the rug . . .'

'Oh, please. I can't believe this has happened. How d'you feel?'

Tilly licked her dry lips. 'Horrible. I've got a headache and my back hurts.' She paused. 'I suppose you're really cross with me.'

'Don't be daft. You just gave me a shock.' Nadia stroked her thin hand. 'Tilly, Cal told me what you said. Is it true? Are you only going to Brighton because you think we don't want you here?'

A tear leaked out of the corner of Tilly's closed eyes.

'Because that's just bollocks,' Nadia exclaimed. 'Tilly, we love you! We'd *all* rather you stayed, don't you know that?'

The tears were flowing faster now. 'No one said it. Everybody j-just seemed cheerful, like they didn't c-care. You all said it was up to me.'

'Sweetheart, we had to say that. Miriam drilled it into us. She told us we mustn't try to persuade you to stay, because that wouldn't be fair on you. If you wanted to be with Leonie, we had to let you go. She said we weren't allowed to make you feel guilty.'

'Are you sure? Is that r-really true?'

'Of course it's true! If you don't want to go anyway, you can stay here and we'll *all* be happy.' Nadia gave her a hug. Half of Tilly wanted to burst with joy because she wasn't unwanted after all.

But there was still an obstacle. In a small voice, Tilly said, 'Mum won't be happy. She'll be devastated. She said she needs me there . . . oh God, I can't let her down.'

Nadia marvelled at Tilly's concern for her mother. 'Don't worry about that. I'll explain everything. Just leave Leonie to me.'

Half an hour later, James and Annie arrived at the hospital. The doctor informed them all that in view of the fact that Tilly had been briefly knocked out, they would be keeping her in hospital overnight.

Outside in the car park, Nadia tried to get through to Leonie on the phone, but the line had apparently been disconnected.

Joining her, Cal said anxiously, 'What's going to happen now?'

'Two things.' Nadia stuffed the mobile back into her pocket. 'Tilly's staying with us in Bristol.'

'Ace!' Despite his hangover, Cal beamed with delight.

'Your parents are going to be wondering where you are. I'm giving you a lift home.'

Tilly was moved to the children's ward, the alcohol on her breath bizarrely at odds with the Winnie the Pooh murals on the walls.

'This place is for kids,' she mumbled.

'You are a kid,' said James, as Annie rummaged in her handbag.

'Here.' Annie pulled out a brush. 'Let me try to sort out your hair.'

Tilly relaxed, enjoying the way Annie patiently unsnarled the tangled bits. James sat on the edge of the bed.

'Are you really sure you don't mind if I stay?'

'Tilly, will you stop this? You're family. You belong with us.'

'But I'm not family. Not really. And you've got Annie now—'

'You're as much a part of me as Nadia and Clare,' James said firmly. 'And you're not going anywhere. Apart from anything else, I wouldn't have Annie if it wasn't for you. You organised that all by yourself. If it wasn't for you, I'd still be calling in to that shop every night, and wondering who that beautiful woman was behind the counter.'

Tilly smiled with satisfaction up at Annie. 'I suppose I did, didn't I?'

'Sorry, did I wake you?'

Nadia rubbed her eyes; she'd managed roughly an hour's sleep last night before the doorbell had jerked her out of a terrifying dream.

It was nine o'clock in the morning and Jay was here on the doorstep, clutching a manila envelope.

'Come on in, I'll put the kettle on. Is this about the new house?'

'Actually, I brought the photos for Clare. Is she around?'

Was he kidding? Clare would be out for the count until midday.

Nadia made tea and duly admired the photos of the baby.

'He's beautiful,' said Nadia. Daniel was cute, with long eyelashes and dainty fingers and the sweetest pointy chin.

'Thanks. Even if he isn't mine,' said Jay. 'You look terrible, by the way.'

'I'm allowed to look terrible.' Slumping down opposite him at the kitchen table, she told Jay about last night. 'Anyway, it's all sorted out now. Well, almost. Can't get through to Leonie. I'll have to go and see her. You don't need me today, do you?'

'I don't need you.' Did she detect a smidgeon of not-so-hidden meaning in those words? 'Where's Laurie?'

'Taken his dad to Kent to stay with his sister. Edward wanted to get away for a couple of days. God,' Nadia yawned, 'it's all happening at once. Miriam didn't come home last night. She doesn't even know about Tilly yet.'

'You can't drive to Brighton,' said Jay. 'You're exhausted.'

'I don't have time to be exhausted. I promised Tilly I'd sort this out.'

'Go and take a shower. When you're ready I'll drive you to Brighton.'

'Seriously?' Nadia said, weak with relief.

'And wear something decent. You look as if you slept in those clothes.'

Actually she had.

'Cheek,' said Nadia.

It was heaven not having to be behind the wheel. Having showered and changed into a short white skirt and orange strappy top, Nadia'd even dolloped on some mascara and orangey-pink lipstick. The Stereophonics were belting out of the car radio. Best of all, Jay hadn't mentioned Laurie once. Or Andrea.

By the time they reached Brighton it was almost midday. The sun blazed down from a cloudless sky. As they drove along the seafront, Nadia gazed longingly at the sea, cobalt blue and glittering like diamonds.

'Turn left up here,' she directed Jay. 'Now right. This is their street.'

'I'll wait in the Italian restaurant we just passed,' said Jay. 'Meet me there when you've finished. Good luck,' he added as Nadia climbed out of the car.

Nadia braced herself. Leonie didn't like not getting her own way.

Leonie opened the front door. 'Darling, this *is* a surprise! Have you brought Tilly with you?'

'We've being trying to phone you.'

'Oh, it's on the blink. Don't tell me you drove all this way because you were worried about us.' Leonie's eyes sparkled with amusement.

'Not quite.' Taking a deep breath, Nadia followed Leonie into the house. 'I'm here because Tilly isn't coming to live with you. She doesn't want to. She didn't tell us until last night. She got drunk and ended up falling down a railway embankment. She's in hospital,' Nadia rattled on, 'but it's OK, just cuts and bruises, she's coming home today. But she's made up her mind,' she concluded. 'I'm sorry, but Tilly's staying with us.'

Phew. Got it all out. Now all she had to do was weather Leonie's hysterics and make her realise no one was about to change their mind.

'Well.' Leonie leaned back against the fridge. 'That's a bolt from the blue.' Then she broke into a bright smile. 'What a relief.'

Nadia thought Leonie had somehow misunderstood. 'What?'

'Oh, let's open a bottle of wine! After the time I've had, I deserve one.' Gaily, Leonie sloshed Rioja into a couple of glasses. 'You wouldn't believe what's been going on here since I came back from Bristol.'

Still dazed, Nadia asked, 'Where's Brian? And . . . um, Tamsin?'

'He's taken her to Sunderland, the little witch. The police picked her up yesterday—she was with those ghastly druggy friends of hers shoplifting and got involved in a punch-up with the store manager. Brian's had it up to here with her. He phoned his ex-wife and told her she could jolly well have Tamsin back. To be honest, it's been a complete nightmare, darling. That girl's out of control. Last night she *ripped* the telephone socket out of the wall! She'll end up in prison, mark my words.'

Transfixed, Nadia said, 'So why were you so keen for Tilly to move in with you?' Although she suspected she already knew.

'Oh well, Brian thought that having Tilly here would improve things—Tamsin would have some company and Tilly could keep her on the straight and narrow. Anyway, she's gone now, so all's well that ends well. We don't need Tilly any more.'

Jay was relaxing at one of the steel-topped tables outside the restaurant, drinking an espresso and reading the paper. His dark hair gleamed in the sunlight. He was wearing a black shirt and his long legs, in cream jeans, were stretched lazily out in front of him. He looked gorgeous.

'That was quick.' Glancing up as Nadia approached, he folded the paper and took off his dark glasses.

'I had to get out before I killed my mother.' Nadia collapsed onto a chair. 'She's unbelievable. She never wanted Tilly in the first place. They just thought she'd come in useful as some kind of . . . baby sitter.'

'But it's sorted?' said Jay. 'Tilly's staying in Bristol?'

'For ever. Until she's eighty-five at least. Then we *may* allow her to leave home.' Managing a smile, Nadia ran through the details of her encounter with Leonie. When she'd finished Jay indicated the menu.

'Are you hungry?'

'I can think of something I'd much rather do.' As soon as the words were out, Nadia winced. 'Sorry, didn't mean it to come out like that.'

Jay's mouth tilted at the corner. 'So what do you have in mind?'

Nadia flushed. 'It just seems a shame to come all this way and not have a paddle in the sea.'

Jay wisely waited for her on the beach. When she rejoined him less than two minutes later, he said, 'Had enough?'

'It's bloody freezing.' Reaching for her sandals, she shivered. 'And the pebbles hurt my feet.'

'Ah well, that's the thing about the sea,' Jay remarked easily. 'Sometimes it tricks you into thinking it's more fun than it really is.' He smiled briefly. 'Never mind, everyone makes mistakes.'

Exhaustion caught up with Nadia on the journey back to Bristol until Jay woke her with a light hand on her arm. 'Brace yourself for the welcome committee.'

'Is everything OK?' said Tilly, as Nadia jumped out of the car and hugged her. 'Was Mum upset?'

'Disappointed,' Nadia lied, exchanging a glance with Jay, 'but she understood. She's fine about it. Anyway, how are you feeling?'

Tilly pulled a face. 'I don't know how you old people manage it—I'm never going to drink port and Tia Maria and Cointreau again.'

'Thanks for the photos,' Clare told Jay. 'The baby is gorgeous. You can tell he's a Tiernan—he's going to be a heartbreaker when he grows up.'

Nadia raised an eyebrow; Clare was sounding positively flirtatious.

'You're not leaving?' Clare protested as Jay climbed back into the car. 'Stay for dinner, we've got loads.'

'I have to get back. Business to take care of,' said Jay.

'You scared him off,' Nadia observed as the car disappeared down the driveway. 'What was all that about?'

Clare shrugged. 'Nothing, just being polite. Anyway, he's on the market, isn't he? You've got Laurie now. Like I told Jay the other night—'

'Hang on. You told Jay I was with Laurie now?'

'Well, why not? You *were* with Laurie, at that hotel.' Clare was indignant. 'You can't have both of them, you know.'

'But—'

'You're not allowed to argue,' said Tilly bossily. 'Remember what the doctor said,' she smugly reminded them. 'I'm not to be upset.'

The receptionist at the Swallow Royal buzzed Charles in his suite and informed him that a Dr Welch was downstairs in reception wishing to see Mrs Kinsella. Charles looked amused.

'Want me to send him away, darling?'

Miriam shook her head. 'No. I'll go down and speak to him.'

As she descended the sweeping staircase, she saw Edward waiting for her. Tall, shoulders back, wearing his brown tweed suit and looking more serious than she had ever known him.

Miriam straightened her own shoulders as she reached the last stair.

'Edward? What's this about?'

He came straight to the point. 'I'm here to tell you that if you stay with Charles Burgess, you'll be making the biggest mistake of your life.'

Good grief, he was serious. 'You don't know that.'

'I *do* know. And I love you,' Edward said forcefully. 'I'm never going to stop loving you. Miriam, I don't blame you for Josephine's death. If that was what was stopping you from marrying me.'

'Edward—'

'No, let me say this. I just want to remind you of something. In that last year before Josephine died, both our hearts used to beat faster at the sight of each other. And then afterwards, you closed your feelings off. Like shutting a box. You wouldn't allow yourself to remember how you'd felt. And now you've spent the night with another man—'

'I didn't,' Miriam blurted out. 'We slept in adjoining rooms, I haven't—'

She jumped as a hand came to rest on her shoulder. It was Charles. Loudly enough for a group of Australian tourists to hear, he said, 'Is this gentleman bothering you, my dear? Shall I call security?'

But Miriam barely heard him. As usual, as *always*, Edward was right. She had loved him, pulse-racingly and passionately, until that dreadful day when the lid of the box had come crashing down. And now he cared enough about her to come here and publicly declare himself.

At her side, Charles told Edward, 'You're making a fool of yourself, you know. It's all over. I'm here now.'

Edward looked him straight in the eye. 'It's for Miriam to decide, not you.'

'Oh, Edward!' Springing away from Charles, Miriam rushed towards him. 'You're right, you're always right, I'm so sorry!'

Silence. The Australian tourists were agog.

'Meaning?' said Edward, scarcely daring to breathe.

When Miriam finally spoke, her dark eyes filled with tears. 'You're the one I want to marry. If you're sure you still want me.'

Across the echoing marble foyer, she heard one of the Australians whisper loudly, 'Aaaw, ain't that the cutest thing?'

Charles said evenly, 'Miriam, stop this at once.'

She shook her head. 'Charles, I'm sorry, but I've made up my mind.'

'This is ridiculous.' Charles's voice was icy. 'You can't do this.' He paused. 'All I have to do is call my lawyer.'

Well, there was nothing she could do about that. A court case would be awful, truly humiliating; and she could go to prison. But Edward would still love her, and that was all that mattered.

'Fine,' Miriam said clearly. 'If that's what you want to do.'

'By the way, I haven't been to stay with my sister in Kent.' Edward's tone was conversational. 'Laurie and I went up to Edinburgh.'

Miriam looked at him. 'Did you?'

'Oh yes. Spent a couple of days in the city library up there. D'you know, they have all the old local newspapers stored in a vault. Laurie and I had a good look through the papers from fifty years ago. What's really interesting'—Edward was addressing Charles now—'is that we checked every paper for that week Miriam told me she'd left you, but there was no mention anywhere of Pauline Hammond's mother being knocked down by a car and killed.'

Charles Burgess paled visibly. 'Th-that's not true,' he blustered.

'You were lying all along.' Miriam gazed at the stammering Charles. 'Well, I suppose I should have known. You always were so good at it.'

'I can still take you to court,' Charles retorted, recovering himself.

Miriam, blissfully aware of Edward's arm round her waist, said calmly, 'I've already told you, Charles. Feel free. But mine won't be the only name dragged through the mud, will it? And'—she regarded Charles with an air of finality—'taking me to court isn't going to win me back.'

'I can't believe you're doing this,' said Laurie. 'I thought everything was fine. After, you know, at the hotel. I thought you'd made up your mind.'

'I had. Only not in the way you thought. God, this is difficult.' Nadia wished she had some kind of script to follow. 'I'm sorry, but it's never going to work. We can't go back to how we were. Everything's changed.'

It had taken a while, but she'd finally made up her mind. Everything *had* changed, including her feelings for Laurie.

The sun was setting, turning the sky pink on the horizon. As they walked over the Downs, hot-air balloons practising for the forthcoming festival drifted across the Avon Gorge.

'Did you sleep with him?'

'No, I didn't.'

'See? Big mistake. You should have done.'

'Maybe, but I slept with you instead.'

Shoving his hands into the pockets of his jeans, Laurie smiled slightly. 'And got me out of your system.'

'I'm sorry.' Nadia blinked, hard. She hadn't expected to cry.

'Me too. I'm gutted. Still'—Laurie smiled briefly—'I suppose it serves me right for finishing with you in the first place.'

'Maybe.' Wiping her eyes, Nadia managed a feeble smile of her own. 'What will you do?'

'Get over it, I suppose.' He gave her a tragic look. 'Oh, don't worry about me, I'm tough. By the time I'm seventy-six I'll be absolutely fine.'

If he was able to joke about it, Nadia thought with relief, things were probably going to be all right. They could revert to being friends—which, seeing as her grandmother was about to marry his father, was just as well.

'There's an ice-cream van over there.' She linked her arm companionably through his. 'Come on, I'll treat you to a Magnum.'

'Sure you don't have to rush off? Isn't Jay waiting for you?'

'Why would he be?'

Laurie raised his eyebrows. 'You mean, he doesn't know he's won?'

Something that felt horribly like panic began to spread through Nadia's intestines. Aloud she said, 'He might not even want to win.'

Laurie started to laugh. 'Now that's risky. Talk about taking a gamble.'

'You gambled,' Nadia couldn't resist pointing out.

Laurie's eyes glittered with rueful amusement. 'I lost.'

Nadia let herself into the house at Clarence Gardens. Jay had called to ask her to come and water the garden.

'I'm stuck here at home,' he'd gone on to explain. 'Look, can you do me a favour? Andy's left some stuff in an envelope for me in the kitchen and I need it pretty urgently. If you could drop it round, I'd be grateful.'

Nadia had spent forty minutes, watering the parched plants. Now it was time to take the stuff in an envelope over to Jay's house. And here it was, on the worktop, a white A4 envelope containing . . .

What was the difference between nosiness and idle curiosity? Well, steaming open a sealed envelope would definitely count as nosiness. Happily, this one wasn't sealed.

As the contents slithered out onto the worktop, Nadia felt the little hairs on the back of her neck stand up in alarm.

Property details. Why on earth would Jay be interested in details of houses in and around Manchester? Not the in-need-of-renovation kind, either. These were big, glamorous properties, four- or five-bedroomed—in fact, not unlike the house Jay owned here in Bristol.

Nadia shovelled the details back into the envelope. Jay had just bought Highcliffe House, for heaven's sake. That meant months of work. And he was employing her to redesign the garden. He couldn't possibly be leaving Bristol.

Oh God, could he?

It was only a short journey to Canynge Road. As she passed Bristol Zoo with its crowds of summer visitors queuing outside, Nadia couldn't shake off that on-your-way-to-the-dentist sensation.

And with good reason. After a hopelessly girlie bit of parking, Nadia gazed at the For Sale sign outside Jay's house. So it was true.

Ringing the doorbell, feeling sick, Nadia realised she'd forgotten to check her face in the mirror. Earlier she had planned to joosh up her hair and stick on a bit of lip gloss. She probably looked awful. Oh well, too late now.

Where was Jay anyway? Why wasn't he answering the door?

When he did, Nadia discovered why it had taken him so long.

'Sorry, sorry . . . the sticky things kept sticking to the wrong bits . . . and then I realised I'd put it on back to front . . . come in.' Looking harassed but pleased to see her, Jay ushered her into the hall. Clearly he hadn't had time to brush his hair or dash on a bit of lip gloss either. The baby, naked apart from a disposable nappy dangling from one foot, was flailing its legs against Jay's chest. Evidently disgusted at finding himself in the hands of such a rank amateur, Daniel gave a kick that sent the clean nappy sailing through the air.

'Mary Poppins, I presume.' Despite everything, Nadia was unable to keep a straight face.

'Just leave it,' Jay sighed as she bent to retrieve the mini-Pampers. 'And mind your feet,' he added as they made their way through to the living room. 'The full one burst as I was taking it off. All these weird gel-beads exploded all over the carpet.'

'Let me take him.' Nadia held out her arms for the baby and Jay handed him over with undisguised relief.

'Watch out, he's like the Trevi fountain. I had no idea babies peed every couple of minutes.'

Years of baby-sitting during college had given Nadia the advantage; lowering Daniel onto the plastic mat she deftly fastened the wriggling baby into a fresh nappy. The baby opened his mouth to start bawling. Locating the bottle of water on the coffee table, Nadia scooped him up and popped it into his mouth before he could get into full swing.

'Has this been boiled?'

'Of course it's been boiled, I'm not completely hopeless.' The moment the words were out, Jay ruefully shook his head. 'OK, maybe I am. Belinda's over at the house, packing up. She's leaving Bristol. I offered to look after Dan for a few hours.'

'Where's Belinda going to live?'

'Dorset. She's renting a place, just down the road from her parents.'

Bugger. Why couldn't he have said Manchester?

'There's your envelope, by the way.' Holding Daniel in the crook of her arm, Nadia nodded at the envelope she'd dropped onto the table.

'Oh, right, thanks.' Jay paused. 'Did you look inside?'

'No!' Flushing slightly, Nadia said, 'I couldn't help noticing the For Sale sign, though. What's going on?'

Jay shrugged. 'I've changed my mind about staying in Bristol.'

'What's wrong with Bristol?'

'Just got bored, I suppose. It's not that fantastic.'

Stung, Nadia blurted out, 'So you're moving to *Manchester*?'

Oh bum. She saw the glint of triumph in Jay's brown eyes.

'X-ray vision, I presume.'

'Oh, shut up.' Crossly, she faced him across the room. 'I don't call this very fair. Are you saying that I'm out of a job?'

'Not at all.' Jay shook his head. 'The chap I outbid at the auction's going to buy Highcliffe House from me. I made him promise he'd take you on to sort out the garden. So you see, it won't make any difference to you.'

Nadia wondered how a supposedly intelligent grown man could stand there and say something so stupid. It would make all the difference in the world. The urge to throw something at Jay—not the baby obviously—was overwhelming.

'You don't seem very pleased,' said Jay.

Nadia's eyes began to prickle. Oh good grief, *please* don't say she was going to cry.

'It's just . . . you know, come as a bit of a shock.'

'You'll be fine. You have your life here with Laurie.'

'I'm not with Laurie.' Nadia heard the words spilling out of her mouth. 'We're not together any more. He's gone to London.'

Jay's eyebrows lifted. 'He's gone? Whose decision was that?'

'Mine. I should have done it weeks ago. If I'd really loved him, I wouldn't have messed him about for so long.'

'He's not the only one you messed about,' Jay pointed out.

Glancing down, Nadia saw Daniel's long sooty eyelashes drooping over his cheeks. He was no longer sucking from the bottle. Carefully, she lowered him onto the sofa and wedged him in with cushions.

'I still don't see why you have to go to Manchester.'

He shrugged. 'There's nothing to keep me in Bristol. Thought I'd give another city a try.'

A horrible thought struck Nadia. 'Is Andrea going with you?'

'Oh, come on.' Jay gave her a be-serious look. 'I haven't seen Andrea for weeks. There's only one person I'm interested in. Sadly, she's spent the last few months completely buggering me about.'

Nadia couldn't speak. Did he mean her? What if he didn't?

Jay's mouth twitched. 'I could always take the house off the market, you know. I don't have to leave Bristol.'

On the sofa, romantically, Daniel chose this moment to emit a peaceful baby fart in his sleep.

Nadia spluttered with laughter. 'Sorry. Are you serious?'

'Well, I'm trying.' Jay moved towards her, causing her heart to break into a canter. 'Look, I'm not used to saying stuff like this. But you must know how I feel about you.'

Thank you, God, thank you, thank you . . .

'I may need another clue,' Nadia murmured, and Jay smiled.

Then he kissed her.

As her body swam with joy, Nadia realised that this was what had been missing with Laurie. Kissing Jay just felt so completely and utterly *right*. And OK, so maybe there were no money-back guarantees, but that was the difference between men and microwave ovens.

'You,' said Jay, 'have been nothing but trouble.'

'But now I've turned over a new leaf.' Nadia trembled as his mouth slid down to her neck. Jay's hands were warm round her midriff where her shirt had ridden up. 'Promise you'll take this place off the market.'

'I will.'

'That's my bra you're undoing.'

'God, is it? Sorry, I'm such an amateur.'

Struggling to maintain some kind of control, Nadia panted, 'We can't do this now. What about Daniel?'

'He's asleep. This is what baby-sitters get up to when their charges are out for the count.' Smiling, Jay murmured, 'Didn't you know that?'

Rrrrrinnggg.

'Hell, who's *that*?' Jay turned in dismay as the doorbell shrilled.

Jerked from sleep, Daniel let out a bellow of outrage.

Shaking his head, Jay said resignedly, 'You know, at this rate we could both be bloody pensioners before—'

'Shouldn't you answer the door?' said Nadia.

'You'd better do it.' Indicating the front of his jeans, Jay said ruefully, 'I'm not quite respectable just now. Give me a minute to recover.'

Leaving him to scoop up his yelling nephew, Nadia went into the hall. At the front door she was confronted by an irate middle-aged man.

'Is Jay there?'

'He's a bit . . . um, busy at the moment.' Backed up by the ear-splitting wails coming from the living room and simultaneously wondering if she'd ever been happier in her life, Nadia said, 'Can I help you?'

'Maurice MacIntyre. I live across the road. My house went on the market yesterday.'

'Gosh, what a coincidence.'

Maurice MacIntyre gave her an odd look, clearly thinking she was mad. 'Look, I don't know what Jay thinks he's playing at. But I'd like my For Sale sign back.'

JILL MANSELL

'Do you know, I think I'm jinxed,' declared Jill Mansell when I met her on a cold, wet and windy January day. 'Every time I come up to London from Bristol something goes wrong. Last time snow stopped play and we were all thrown off the train at Reading. It was actually quite amusing, because up until that moment the passengers had hardly even glanced at one another, but suddenly everyone was chatting. There was a rather pretty girl who was due at the Barbican for an audition, and a father and daughter on a day out to see *Phantom of the Opera*. It was like the beginning of a novel really,' Jill muses, and I could almost see her storing the idea away in her memory bank. 'On another occasion, when I was meeting my editor at Headline for the first time, I was on a coach—couldn't afford the train then—and a man was hit by a lorry. I was horrified that no one did anything, and I jumped out of the coach to help him. As I crouched there, getting covered in blood, cars were driving over the back of my raincoat, the drivers annoyed at being held up. When I finally arrived at lunch, splattered with blood but far too nervous to tell my new editor what had happened, I just sponged myself down in the Ladies and tried to look the composed author that I am,' she finishes with a flourish and a self-deprecating smile.

Immediately, I was aware that I was sitting opposite a born storyteller and asked Jill how she had made the transition from being an electroencephalographic technician, measuring brain activity at Burden

Neurological Hospital, to best-selling author? 'Well, I read an article in the *Sunday Express* supplement, which I have still got, about women who had been very poor and then had started to write and became very rich, and I thought, "That's for me." I then joined a local evening class in creative writing, which was great fun, and, in fact, four of us from that class are now published and still keep in touch.'

Nadia Knows Best is Jill's fourteenth novel and I was amazed to learn that she has written every one by hand in A4 notebooks, with a fountain pen. 'Sometimes I change the colour of the ink cartridge for variety,' she laughs. 'You know, someone once said to me, "Jill, your writing by hand is the equivalent of a woman not using a washing machine, but walking five miles to the river to bash the clothes with rocks." I know it seems antiquated but it's the only way I know how to do it. I sit on the sofa with the TV on—I can't work if it's quiet—and eat vast quantities of fruit gums.' Having the television on while she works also helps Jill with ideas for her novels. 'Daytime TV shows, like *Richard and Judy*, are fantastic research sources because people ring up and reveal the most intimate details about their lives and it sets my mind off.'

Jill is currently two-thirds of the way through her fifteenth novel and puts her success down to one simple fact: 'I like to write the kind of novels I like to read. Luckily for me, others seem to enjoy them too.'

Jane Eastgate

PICTURE CREDITS: COVER: © Simon McComb/Stone/Getty Images. Adèle Geras photograph, and page 173: © Jerry Bauer. Nora Roberts photograph, and page 321 © Judy Lawne. Jill Mansell photograph, and page 479: courtesy of the *Bristol Evening Post*. FACING THE LIGHT: pages 6 & 7: illustration by Jack McCarthy. BIRTHRIGHT: pages 174 & 175: Corbis. NADIA KNOWS BEST: pages 322 & 323: illustration by Kim Smith @Eastwing.

Printed and bound by Maury Imprimeur SA, Malesherbes, France

601-020-1